The
Wasteland
Saga

The Wasteland Saga

THREE NOVELS

The Old Man and the Wasteland

The Savage Boy

The Road Is a River

NICK COLE

HARPER Voyager
An Imprint of HarperCollins*Publishers*

Harper Voyager and design is a trademark of HCP LLC.

THE SAVAGE BOY. Copyright © 2013 by Nick Cole.
First HarperCollins e-books edition: February 2013

THE OLD MAN AND THE WASTELAND. Copyright © 2012 by Nick Cole.
First HarperCollins e-books edition: July 2012

Various quotes within are from the novel *The Old Man and the Sea* by Ernest Hemingway. Reprinted with the permission of Scribner, a Division of Simon & Schuster, Inc., from *The Old Man and the Sea* by Ernest Hemingway. Copyright © 1952 by Ernest Hemingway. Copyright renewed © 1980 by Mary Hemingway. All rights reserved.

FIRST EDITION

Library of Congress Cataloging-in-Publication Data has been applied for.

ISBN 978-0-06-221019-7

13 14 15 16 17 OV/RRD 10 9 8 7 6 5 4 3 2 1

CONTENTS

PART I

The Old Man and the Wasteland

CHAPTER 1

It was dark when he stepped outside into the cool air. Overhead the last crystals of night faded into a soft blue blanket that would precede the dawn. Through the thick pads of his calloused feet he could feel the rocky, cracked, cold earth. He would wear his huaraches after he left and was away from the sleeping village.

He had not slept for much of the night. Had not been sleeping for longer than he could remember. Had not slept as he did when he was young. The bones within ached, but he was old and that was to be expected.

He began to work long bony fingers into the area above his chest. The area that had made him feel old since he first felt the soreness that was there. The area where his satchel would push down as he walked.

He thought about tea, but the smoke from the mesquite would betray him as would the clatter of his old blue percolator and he decided against it.

He stepped back inside the shed, looked around once, taking in the cot, patched and sagging, the desk and the stove. He went to the desk and considered its drawers. There was nothing there that should go in his satchel. He would need only his tools. His crowbar, his worn rawhide gloves, his rope, the can of pitch, the tin of grease and his pliers. Not the book.

But if I die. If I go too far or fall into a hole. If my leg is broken then I might want the book.

He dismissed those thoughts.

If you die then you can't read. If you are dying then you should try to live. And if it is too much, that is what the gun is for. Besides, you've read the book already. Many times in fact.

He put the book back in its place.

He went to the shelf and opened the cigar box that contained the pistol. He loved the box more than the gun inside. The picture of the sea, the city, and the waving palms on the front reminded him of places in the book. Inside the box, the gun, dull and waiting along with five loose shells, an evil number, rattled as his stiff fingers chased them across the bottom.

Moving quickly now he took the old blue percolator and rolled it into the thin blanket that lay on the cot. He stuffed them both inside the worn satchel, reminding him of the book's description of the furled sail. "Patched with flour sacks . . . it looked the flag of permanent defeat." He shouldered the bag quickly and chased the line away telling himself he was thinking too much of the book and not the things he should be. He looked around the shed once more.

Come back with something. And if not, then goodbye.

He passed silently along the trail that led through the village. To the west, the field of broken glass began to glitter like fallen stars in the hard-packed red dirt as it always did in this time before the sun.

At the pantry he took cooked beans, tortillas, and a little bit of rice from the night before. The village would not miss these things. Still they would be angry with him. Angry he had gone. Even though they wished he would because he was unlucky.

Salao. In the book unlucky is *Salao*. The worst kind.

The villagers say you are "curst."

He filled his water bottle from the spring, drank a bit and filled it again. The water was cold and tasted of iron. He drank again and filled it once more. Soon the day would be very hot.

At the top of the small rise east of the village he looked back.

Forty years maybe. If my count has been right.

It was an old processing plant by the side of the highway east of what was once Yuma. It was rusting in the desert before the bombs fell, now it was the market and pantry of the village. Its outlying sheds the houses of the villagers, his friends and family. He tried to see if smoke was rising yet from his son's house. But his daughter-in-law would be tired from the new baby.

So maybe she is still sleeping.

If his granddaughter came running out, seeing him at the top of the rise against the dawn, he would have to send her back. He was going too deep into the wasteland today.

Too dangerous for her.

Even though she knows every trick of salvage?

I might need her. What if I find something big?

"I may not be as strong as I think, but I know many tricks and I have resolution."

My friend in the book would say that, yes.

He would send her back. It was too dangerous. He adjusted the strap wider on his shoulder to protect the area above his heart where the satchel always bit, then turned and walked down the slope away from the village and into the wasteland.

CHAPTER 2

He sang bits of a song he knew from Before. Years hid most of the lyrics and now he wanted to remember when he first heard the song. As if the memory would bring back the lost words he'd skipped over.

Time keeps its secrets. Not like this desert. Not like the wasteland.

In the rising sun, his muscles began to loosen as his stride began to lengthen, and soon the ache was gone from his bones. His course was set between two peaks none of the village had ever bothered to name after the cataclysm. Maybe once someone had a name for them. Probably on charts and rail survey maps of the area once known as the Sonoran Desert. But such things had since crumbled or burned up.

And what are names? He once had a name. Now the villagers simply called him the Old Man. It seemed appropriate. Often he responded.

At noon he stopped for the cool water in the bottle kept beneath the blanket in his satchel. Still mumbling the words of the song among the silent broken rocks, he drank slowly. He had reached the saddle between the two low hills.

Where had he first heard the song? he wondered.

Below, the bowl of the wasteland lay open and shimmering. On the far horizon, jagged peaks; beyond those, the bones of cities.

For seventy-eight days the Old Man had gone west with the other salvagers, heading out at dawn with hot tea con leche and sweet fry bread. Walking and pulling their sleds and pallets. In teams and sometimes alone. For seventy-eight days the Old Man had gone out and brought back nothing.

My friend in the book went eighty-six days. Then he caught the big fish. So I have a few days to go. I am only seventy-eight days unlucky. Not eighty-six. That would be worse.

Every canyon silent, every shed searched, every wreck empty. It was just bad luck the others said. It would turn. But in the days that followed he found himself alone for most of the day. If he went down a road, keeping sight of the other teams, they would soon be lost from view. At noon he would eat alone in the shade of a large rock and smell on a sudden breeze their cookfires. He missed those times, after the shared lunch, the talk and short nap before they would start anew at what one had found, pulling it from the earth, extracting it from a wreck, hauling it back to the village. Returning after nightfall as the women and children came out to see this great new thing they could have back. This thing that had been rescued from the time Before and would be theirs in the time of Now. Forty years of that, morning, noon, and night of salvage. It was good work. It was the only work.

Until he found the hot radio.

His first years of salvage were of the things that had built the village. On early nights when the salvagers returned and light still hung in the sky, he could walk through the village and see the things he had hauled from the desert. The door on his son's house that had once been part of a refrigerator from a trailer he and Big Pedro had found south of the Great Wreck. The trailer someone had been living in after the bombs. There were opened cans, beer, and food inside the trailer. Cigarette butts in piles. That had been fifteen years after the war. But when they opened the door it was silent and still. An afternoon wind had picked up and the trailer rocked in the brief gusts that seem to come and go as if by their own choosing. Big Pedro did not like such places. The Old Man never asked the why of how someone salvaged. He accepted this of Pedro and together they'd worked for a time.

Outside he heard Pedro asking if there was anything. The Old Man knew he would find a dead body. There were always dead bodies. Salvage and dead bodies go hand in hand.

The trailer rocked for a moment, and as the Old Man adjusted his eyes to the dim light within, he waited for salvage to be revealed. This was how one salvaged. Just waiting and watching a thing. A wreck, someone's home, or a railway shed. In the desert it paid to wait. A quick choice owned you. A wrench, a hammer, and one might not see the saw. Too often the wealth of the past could distract one from what was really there. He had seen piles of money, gold, jewelry, pornography. What good were such things now?

But in the trailer there was a story. There was always a story of salvage. In a wreck, one could see the skeletons crushed under the weight of their possessions as the vehicle left the highway. Rolling over and over in the dirt and down a culvert. To lie trapped for years. Waiting for ambulances that would not come. Rescue that could not rescue itself while mushroom clouds broke the unbroken horizon. On that day when everything changed.

On that long ago hot afternoon when Big Pedro waited outside in the sighing wind, all was quiet inside. He stepped in, closing the door behind him. There was no life here. Just dry dust and the shed skins of the rattlers that seemed everywhere at times and then at others could not be found.

All the cans were crushed, all the cigarettes that lay in neat piles had been smoked down to the filter. Whoever had lived here had brought these cans and cigarettes from the cities. Beer and cigarettes, possibly a gun. Cans of food. But it had been too little. Whatever one brought for the destruction was always too little. The Old Man had seen it, would see it a thousand different ways. In the wrecks and the sheds and the boxcars and the fortified gas stations how long can any supplies last? Could anyone during those two weeks, when a new bomb fell on a new city each new day, could anyone have known that the terror would never end? That life as one knew it would never return.

No, even I did not know it.

Next week the government will come, things will return to normal. Next year. In two years' time. One day you stop waiting and you begin to salvage.

What your crowbar can bring up from the desert is the only thing you can expect.

Whoever once lived in that trailer had refused to believe things would never be the same. It was a tale of smoked cigarettes near a smashed radio in the corner. Alcohol through the long night as angry winds struck at the sides of the trailer like some giant moving in the outer dark. Tomorrow became next year and next year became too much to bear. Eventually, whoever it was left, and that was all the story that remained and could be told truthfully of the trailer. What happened after, a gunshot at the end of a broken leg, sunstroke, exposure, insanity; those also were stories the Old Man had seen in the desert. But who could connect one to the other? One learned after the bombs to stop needing answers or the ends of stories.

There was little salvage in the trailer. What remained was obvious. The refrigerator. Who could take that where they were going? Unless there was power of a sort where the journey, or the flight as it felt, ended. But in the Old Man's village there was power, sometimes.

Soon he and Big Pedro, sweating, had the refrigerator out on the cracked and broken highway, east of the Great Wreck. It took the better part of three days to get it back to the village. Word spread among the villagers that something big had been found. The Old Man and Pedro were bringing something back. On the last day, two hours after dawn the villagers began to arrive in pairs and groups along the broken highway, their curiosity unrestrained, uncontainable. The haul back became a carnival. By nightfall, remembered the Old Man, a pig had been killed; precious few of them then. All through the night Jason the Fixer worked, cursing coils and elements. At midnight the thing began to hum and two hours later there was ice.

In the hours leading up to dawn, in the main hall of the old factory, the Old Man was the first to stand in front of the open door and feel the cold. How many years had it been since he stood in front of an open refrigerator door in the middle of the night, feeling that precious cold caress the dust-caked lines of his face? He didn't remember, he didn't care. The cold was enough.

"We would have that for all of our lives."

That's what my friend in the book said when he and the boy talked of taking the great baseball player fishing. He understood.

"We would have that for all of our lives."

Now the Old Man took another drink from his water bottle. That night of the refrigerator, the days ending in a carnivale of roast pig meat and ice seemed long ago. Something that happened to a hero who was not him, did not look like the old face in the pieces of mirror on the few days he chose to shave each week.

He looked at the bowl of the wasteland. It seemed empty and void. A place of nothing.

I must go into it. I am cursed by that hot radio.

They never said you could not salvage with them again.

They didn't need to.

From the Great Wreck to the village and as far east as the Gas Station he would no longer salvage, though no one salvaged in the East anyway as it was considered evil. Even the Gas Station, which lay on the far side of a small town that burned to the ground for no reason anyone could remember in the days of the bombs, held little salvage. Further east the bombs had fallen. Anything from there was as bad as the hot radio. The village would allow no salvage from there.

So he could not go east, and west and south was for the village. He must go north. North lay the wasteland.

He rolled his water bottle back into his thin blanket, placing it back in the patched leather satchel. He placed the wide-brimmed hat he always wore back atop the stubble of his scalp. There was nothing in the wasteland. No salvage ever came of it. Treks into it returned with nothing or never returned.

The sun was high above now. Adjusting the strap, he set off down the rocky slope, dodging lone black volcanic rocks that had dotted the landscape long before the bombs, before the Spanish, before the Anasazi.

CHAPTER 3

In the desert, alone, I must look far and near at once. Things that are far seem very near and I must remember that.

Jagged pink peaks to the east seemed a day's walk. But the Old Man knew they were well beyond that.

Maybe there is another reason for my curse and not the hot radio. Maybe I have become lazy. Too used to finding easy salvage on the ground at my feet. Or others finding it for me.

Heading down the slope into the white sandy bowl of the wasteland, the thought of his failure as a salvager gave the Old Man a new comfort. Maybe it was not a curse. He needed better technique; he had grown lazy. He would return to everything he knew about salvage; he would forget to be lazy and instead remind himself to be vigilant. To leave no stone unturned. This was better than being cursed.

On a far ridgeline, he saw movement and wondered if it were goats moving among the clipped rocks. For a long time he kept checking the ridge, hoping to see them again, but in time he gave up and cursed himself for not sticking to his new promise. Later, after the sun's heat had reached its apex then sank to the horizon behind him, the details of the landscape ahead came into focus.

The heavy sunlight and the sandstorms that seemed to come and go throughout the day had revealed nothing more than a hazy diffusion across his vision. Now as the last light of day shone directly into the heart of the wasteland, he could make out details. Purple scrub and gentle orange hills rising up along the edge he would make by tomorrow. Off to the east he saw a vehicle.

He'd heard of this vehicle. The few who had tried the wasteland had never gone more than a day or two into its depths. All told of the vehicle. It lay to the east and it was always bad to head east. The villagers would often mutter, *What good could come from the east?*

Stopping for a sip of water, he considered the vehicle, a splotch of red rust in the afternoon haze.

It seems harmless and there may be something to salvage. But it is east.

This is why you are here. Do you believe in the curse or in your own laziness? If it is the curse, then anything east can only make the curse worse. But if it is because you have lost the gift you once had for salvage because you look for what is obvious and easy, then there is no curse and the vehicle is the first rule of salvage. Some always leads to more.

The Old Man replaced the water bottle and shouldered his satchel. Thinking of when he might rest, he turned toward the east and the rusty car.

Night fell, but the sky remained blue for a long time. He lost sight of the car as he descended in and out of dry streambeds. For the last hour he hunted for it in the dark and just when he had begun to curse himself that he was indeed useless and had lost it altogether, he found it.

It was a sedan, half sunk in the dirt that became mud every monsoon season and frozen clay in the winter that followed. Forty cycles of monsoon, chill, and withering summer.

The Old Man dropped his satchel and gathered brush and mesquite. It was early fall and the nights would be cold. It was important to get a fire going.

Once the fire was in bloom with sparks rising into the night, the Old Man retrieved his crowbar and the tin of grease. He searched the wreck, finding a pile of bones on the floor beneath the steering column. The seats had turned to springs and nothing remained of the foam or material that had once covered them. The backseat held nothing, and in the trunk someone had once lit a fire, probably camping under the roof of the car. The fire in the trunk had kept them warm.

The Old Man returned to the fire and removed the cold beans from his satchel. Unrolling his blanket, he found the tortillas but decided to save them for morning. He placed the tin of beans in the fire and waited.

Above, dashing comets and stars restlessly winked at one another. Was there some sort of communication among them? How far away were they? Once the Old Man had seen, on a night far from the village, a satellite moving up there. Long after the bombs. It crossed the sky steadily, almost slowly, still flashing its lights. Its power still on. The Old Man looked for it again tonight.

The beans tasted good.

That was how hungry I was. A hard day's work and food tastes good.

Putting the beans down the Old Man returned to the car once more.

Why here?

He looked at the front of the car.

The driver either crashed into something or ran out of fuel. But for some reason the driver stopped here. Were you dying?

In the days of the bombs, the Old Man who had been a young man remembered the chaos and disorder. Remembered the authorities shooting people. Fleeing Los Angeles, he had been stopped at a checkpoint just south of San Clemente. For hours he had been stopped as military helicopters crossed the sky above the reactor close to the ocean. It had made him nervous being that close to a primary target, the big reactors. A man arguing with the guards in a car ahead of him began to scream. Then the man left his car and began running for the mountains on the far side of the road. The guards shot him. His family, his wife screaming, a wide-eyed child in the back of the car watching.

I have not thought of that for years.

Why would you?

The fire popped noisily for a moment and then the deep silence of the wasteland at night settled back upon him.

But you stopped the car here. Why?

The windshield still held most of its dirty glass. It had spider-webbed into a blanket of crystals. But on the passenger side the windshield held a hole.

Something was on the passenger seat and when you hit the rock that stopped you, whatever it was came out and left the hole.

It was impossible to see what was underneath the car, but the Old Man suspected a big rock, low and jagged, had snagged the axle and stopped the vehicle dead.

The Old Man returned to his satchel and retrieved the can of pitch. Taking a stick, he covered the end with pitch and lit it in the fire. He returned to the front of the car that lay at the top of a small hill. He turned away from the car and faced outward into the dark.

There is always a story. To find it I need to know what happened. You are wounded. You are fleeing the cities and have become wounded. You have no plan, few supplies, and as the day progresses, as you flee burning Phoenix or forbidden Tucson, you drive off the road. The roads are a mess, refugees and Army fleeing to Yuma, which will be nuked in a day or two because of its base and refugee camps. You drive off the road. You are not thinking clearly; driving too fast you are wounded and sick or hungry and you have begun to believe you will find something out here. Something that will save you. But the vehicle is running out of gas, so you keep driving to the top of ridges and small hills, racing up the sandy shale to avoid getting stuck, then looking to see if there is any refuge in sight. On this hill you race up fast. The ground on the far side was soft. Yes I felt that as I walked up. Suddenly as you gun the accelerator, you slam into the rock and out goes the one thing you managed to grab before the destruction. The car is hopelessly stuck and soon you die. Maybe you kill yourself with a pistol. But one of the countless salvagers who has wandered here has found that since, along with whatever supplies were in the trunk or backseat. Ah, a pistol and blankets and food, thinks my fellow salvager, what luck I have found good things. And he ignores the hole in the windshield. He has ignored the second rule of salvage. Be still and understand the story of what happened in this place. Quick action blinds.

How fast were you going when you hit the rock? Fast enough that it came upon you and took you by surprise? But not so fast, since you were nearing the top. Maybe you blacked out?

The Old Man walked outward from the front of the car. He thought of the size of the hole and the weight of the object as he walked down the other side of the hill scanning the ground.

Someone may have found it?

That does not matter. You are thinking as you once thought. Telling the story first. If you find the resting place of the thing and it is gone then you have won because you thought the way you are supposed to think. Some will always lead to more. That is the first rule.

I could wait until morning?

Why? You will sleep badly and all night think about where to look in the morning.

At the bottom of the hill was a dry riverbed. Holding his torch down near the ground he checked the bed for ash.

In the years after the destruction, flash floods of ash had filled the old stream beds as the snowpack of that long winter had finally come to an end.

If the thing had fallen into the streambed then it is lost. Carried off by rivers of ash in the years since. Also most travelers use streambeds to move. They are shady, there might be water, and the rains may have collected salvage.

So if it landed in the stream then it is as good as gone.

Looking back to align himself with the car, he climbed up the rocky slope to the far side of the dry streambed. A few feet away he found a battered aluminum ice chest, half sunk in the mud and hidden by a mesquite tree that had grown up around its base. It was empty. Someone else had found it. Had followed the clues and found the thing in the dried mud with the broken cover.

The chest was too light to have made the journey from passenger seat through the window down the hill and across the streambed to land where it did. Whatever had once been inside had been heavy enough to propel it that far.

In front of the fire, the Old Man sat cross-legged and treated himself to one of the tortillas. He congratulated himself on finding the ice chest and thought little that it contained nothing. Instead he was happy that he had found it. Maybe the curse was a lie. It was he who had been lazy, easily accepting the blame of the curse. He was to blame. If so, then things were changing.

He finished the tortilla, put more mesquite on the fire, and took only a small drink of water so he did not have to pee in the night. He rolled himself in his thin blanket and was soon deep asleep. In the night when the fire was low, he awoke thinking, 'I am sleeping really well tonight,' as though he had accomplished a great thing that had eluded him for some time. Pleased, he fell asleep once more.

CHAPTER 4

The next day he crossed into the dunes of the wasteland. The scrub and hard rock gave way to smooth sand pink with the rising sun. By noon the landscape faded and the pink of morning turned a blinding white.

It was still early fall. It wasn't as hot as it had been earlier in the year. The Old Man sipped the bottle of water, only half full now, and felt the heat more than he had expected to.

I need to look for water. Soon I will go too far and if I don't find anything, then even making it back to the village might be impossible.

Maybe they are looking for me.

In the night, toward dawn, he had dreamed of the child in the backseat of the car of the screaming man the guards had shot. She was the same age of forty years ago but the Old Man was still old, even though he had been younger that long-ago day than her father.

In the dream he was back in the village. The child, who was a girl most surely, had knocked on his door. After letting her in the Old Man gave her cold water and she sat down at his desk, looking out the one window he had salvaged from an overturned semi.

Have you been walking all night to get here? he remembered asking her. As if a night's journey accounted for all the years in between that day and the dream.

But the child remained staring out the window, lost in thought and when she turned back to the Old Man she looked at him smiling. Then she said, *It never happened, y'know.* In the way a child who is young can affect a certain seriousness.

But the Old Man wasn't sure if she meant her father being shot by the side of the freeway under the shadow of the reactors. Or something else.

He woke with a start, and already a desert breeze was blowing across the soft blue of first morning. He rose quickly, promised himself some breakfast later and was soon away from the wreck. The dream had bothered him. And he wondered if the dream of the child and the wreck of the car weren't the cause of it.

Later, he felt better as he walked through a line of dunes. He was away from what was known to him of wrecks and the worst kind of luck. The wasteland was new. It was unknown. In a few hours, by nightfall, he would be farther than anyone had tell of in the depths of the wasteland. If anything, that was something.

So why did the dream bother you? It's noon, so speak it now and be done with it so the child does not return tonight.

Ahead, the wasteland fell deeper into a series of white dunes, and the Old Man entered them, weaving about the floor of them rather than climbing to the top of each.

I'll do my best to keep a rough bearing north and maybe a little east. I'll need water soon.

East is cursed.

Then my curse and the curse of the east will cancel each other out.

He couldn't remember what that was called; it was a law or something, something he had once learned in school.

How strange, he thought in the silence between the dunes. School. To think, once I attended a school. An elementary school, a school after that, and then even a high school. College. I couldn't even begin to explain school to the young of the village.

I am thinking too much. That is why I had the dream of the child. Too many things are coming up from the past and it is making my mind race. The silence of the wasteland is good for thinking.

You must think about water and salvage. You can't just think about the past. If you don't find water you won't be able to find something out here and bring it back to the village.

The shadows began to lengthen and soon the shade of the dunes became cool. Gathering stray brush he set up his camp in the lee of a long dune and soon had a fire going.

There had not been the least sign of any salvage, anything man had made, or even the presence of man. The Old Man sat chewing a tortilla and thinking about this. Usually back near the village, even though it was the desert, there seemed to be nothing but the things of man's past. All the collected salvage. The wrecks, the dead towns and settlements. Bones.

But how long since anyone had been through the wasteland? It had been forty years since the bombs. The years since, reasoned the Old Man, had been too hard. Too close to the bone for anything that didn't yield enough profit to allow survival to the next day.

Maybe that was why there was no salvage in the wasteland.

Staring into the fire, he thought of the child.

Did she survive that day?

Not if she remained on the West Coast, especially from Los Angeles to San Diego.

But if she had survived would her life have been good?

She would have less memories of what was lost. That is a kind of "good."

Those who survived those weeks of bombing, each one struggled with a question that determined whether they would keep salvaging or give up and die.

What was the question?

Can you let go of what is gone?

I think at first I felt that I could not go on. The things I lost were too painful and I could not imagine a life without them. I remember feeling awful. All the time. But I cannot remember when I changed. When I thought of salvage. When I thought of what was today and not of what had been or what was lost.

For a long time he sat hugging his knees, watching the crystal of the sky turn and revolve, and when the fire had burned down to red ash, he moved his blanket close to it and sat for a little while more, listening to it pop. Soon the sky began to grow dark. 'In a few nights,' he thought, his last thought before sleeping, 'we'll have the moon.' Funny saying "we" he wondered, sleeping.

CHAPTER 5

There were no dreams that night and when he awoke, the sun was already well up and the heat a part of the day that could not be separated from it.

His face was heavy from the night as though the sleep had been more fight than rest. Instantly he wanted water and knew that any drink would be his last.

Then it will be my last.

Draining the bottle he decided he would find the water he would need to continue the journey or that would be the end of it.

I have in me what remains. So I have to be smart. If I dig and find no water, I will have sweated for nothing. I must find water.

He continued on now, bearing more east than north.

East is evil and that is why things are not going well. You should have continued north. Why are you going east?

The dunes continued in their sandy smothering brilliance and before long he began to think of the ocean and the book.

How would it be to have such a skiff as that in the book? To have ropes and a hand-forged hook. To catch the tuna and eat it raw with a bit of salt and lime.

He did not have salt and limes in the book. He wanted them but he did not have them. He ate the tuna raw.

He caught himself, sweating, almost sleeping as he walked, thinking that this was just a day at the beach, as if, in any experience that was his, he'd ever had a day at the beach.

But I did. I remember the sting of saltwater on burned skin. I remember hot dogs and mustard and blown sand in the buns.

It was the thought of the watermelon that jerked him back to the present. Sweet, cool watermelon on a windy afternoon at the beach. School buses idling to take the children back to school during the last week of the school year. No more books, no more teachers' dirty looks. He saw his father's handwriting as he thought of those words. Summer would never end.

"Everything ends," he croaked to the dry silence between two monolithic dunes, as he trudged upslope through the clutching sand.

It is so hot that even the scorpions won't come out.

In the distance, the sun sank lower in the sunburned sky, as dunes began to grow long cool shadows pointing thin fingers to the east.

Without making camp he lay down in the cradle of a shady dune and fell to snoring.

When he awoke, the sun had fallen behind the highest dune and a stiff breeze lifted sand, sending it skirting across the smooth surfaces of the dunes. The body of a dead bee lay in the foreground of his skewed vision. His head pounded and he knew he was beyond any point of thirst he had ever experienced. Already his hand was half buried.

I have been asleep but a few minutes. The sand doesn't waste time.

Not ready to move his aching head, he remained staring at the dead bee in the canted landscape. He wasn't sure, but the sun seemed in the wrong position. If that was the case then it was not a few minutes but maybe the next day, and if that was the case then things were even worse than he had first thought. A new day of heat among the dunes.

There is little hope.

So at least, you have some hope.

It's just a saying. I actually have no hope.

No, you said you have little hope. Why?

Why what?

Why a little? A little hope would have gone a long way for that dead bee. But for you maybe it is too little.

The bee.

The Old Man shook himself upright. His face sandy, he stared wildly about, then closed his eyes as his head began to throb.

Bees always fly straight to water. Big Pedro had taught him that. And he had seen it. Many times.

The bee is dead. How can a dead bee lead you to water?

He was an ambitious bee. Like me.

Or he was cursed. Like you also.

Then this brother is a bee to me, he declared in confusion. I will find more bees. His brothers are my brothers. Some always leads to more and where there are more bees they will lead me to water.

It is morning so it will be cool for a while, but not long. Bees like the heat.

Bending low he gently picked up the dead bee.

I will find us some water, my brother.

He placed the bee in the tin of grease and snapped the ancient lid shut.

That way seems familiar but dunes are all alike.

Heading into the sun now he climbed the first dune, and far to the east he saw blue ridges shadowed in the rising sun.

East is evil and cursed.

Ah but there are two of us now. I have my brother the bee and he has his brothers.

Soon the sun was hot, as first he climbed a dune, then descended only to start the process once more. It is the only way, he told the bee. It is the only way I can be sure I am heading to the ridge.

At the top of each sandy dune he scanned for swarms or movement of any kind. His eyes were still good and yet he saw no bees.

Maybe in the rocks, brother. Maybe that is where we will find your home.

At the full blaze of noon the Old Man descended the last dune into a short sandy scrub of low bushes. A few miles away lay the now red rock ridge.

For a moment the Old Man considered digging among the scrub for water but the plants were papery and did little to convince him of the chance of appreciable water.

Opening the tin of grease he looked at the dead bee.

I can only go so far, bee. So which way, huh? He held the bee up hoping to catch a breeze and saw himself from afar.

This is insane. Look at yourself. An Old Man holding a dead bee in the desert. If he comes back to life you are really crazy. The Old Man realized it was his young self talking to him. The self he had once been and had been thinking of too much since the dream of the child.

Be quiet. This is not so crazy. One of his brothers might smell him and come for a look. Then maybe I can follow him back to water.

The Old Man lurched forward into the scrub holding out the bee for any passing stray bee to smell. I can't trust my ears he said. They have been buzzing. So I will look for a black shape moving, hopping between the bushes of low scrub. That will be a bee.

When he had reached the limit of the little strength he had left, the ridge was still far off and on fire with the red of a late afternoon sun in decline.

The Old Man sat down knowing he would not rise, the wings of the bee still held gently between thumb and forefinger.

Well, we tried.

He could no longer swallow. His mouth felt coarse and thick. His throat a ragged burning trench and his body ached. Mostly in his throbbing head.

If I can lie here until dark, then the light won't hurt my eyes so much and then maybe I can make it to the ridge.

But it was a lie as soon as he told it. By nightfall he would be beyond standing.

Then I must stand a little more and maybe a few steps will take me to the rocks of the ridge. And that also is a lie.

Standing, a dull bomb went off with a solid crack in the back of his skull as stars raced forward toward the rocks.

But it is my lie.

He continued forward. Moments later he saw a bee that came diving at him and then quickly tore away off toward the rocks. The Old Man shambled forward, trailing the bee, which hopped from shrub to shrub, sometimes methodical, at other times racing off toward the horizon. Just when the Old Man thought he had lost the bee forever, again the bee would leap up and head off along the same bearing.

Ahead, the Old Man could see a spur jutting out from the ridge, and following the spur back to the crook it left in the ridge, he saw a splotch of green.

But it is too far.

He continued after the bee, still holding the dead bee between his thumb and forefinger. The line from where he had met the bee and the splotch of green was true and straight.

Falling forward, he tripped on an exposed root and fell into the sandy chalk that rose up in plumes around him.

I have never been so comfortable in all my life.

If you don't get up, the bee who is flying will be gone and you will never find the water, never find salvage, and you will die cursed.

I am cursed. I don't care. I want to sleep now.

He closed his eyes and when he did, he thought of his granddaughter who was just thirteen. It was she who had stayed faithful to him after the other villagers had cursed him and refused to salvage with him. She had begun to salvage with him. He had enjoyed that. The salvage had become more enjoyable and less desperate on those long mornings he spent with her as they walked and talked. Talked of all manner of things from the way the world had been to the way it is and sometimes of the way it might be. That had been enjoyable.

I am sorry, my brother bee.

Arms of sleep beckoned him a little further down the well of darkness.

I must use your help for a moment, little bee. I am sorry. I have to wake up for a while. Long enough to see what lies in the crook of the ridge.

He squeezed his palm hard shut and felt the stinger of the dead bee enter the flesh of his palm. An electric jolt coursed through his body and instantly the palm was alive with fire.

The Old Man kept his fist shut as he pushed away from the sand and began once more to the ridge.

Desert scrub, sandy and brown, gave way to large sunburned rocks. Reaching the crook in the ridge, he entered a stand of palo verdes. The Green Sticks the villagers called them. Back among the rocks a quiet stream, barely more than a trickle, came out of the rocks feeding the little stand of palo verdes. The Old Man dropped his satchel and lay down to drink. The water was cool.

CHAPTER 6

Noon turned to afternoon and soon a stiff breeze picked up among the feathery branches of the palo verdes. For a long time the Old Man returned to the stream to drink and drink again. All the while he gathered dead branches, piling them high for the night's fire.

There were just a few beans and one tortilla left. He had not felt hungry during the thirsty hours of torment amid the dunes, but now as his body began to soak up the water, his appetite returned. The few beans and tortilla were a coming feast to his hungry mind.

He went out beyond the perimeter of the palo verdes once more, into the scrub that bordered the wasteland. The dunes through which he had passed were now falling to pink and orange. Thin ribbons of snake-like shade slithered onto the desert floor while the graceful arcs of the dunes told the lie that he did not exist, had never existed among them.

He returned to his camp and started a small fire. In the twilight he finished the remaining beans and reluctantly saved the tortilla for morning. Tomorrow he would look for animal tracks and make the appropriate traps. Once he had enough food and water he could either return across the wasteland to the village or he might continue on.

He had failed to find salvage in the wasteland. The known parts of the wasteland were behind him and he could only guess where he might be now. If he had to say, he would say west of what was once Phoenix and north of what was Tucson.

In the days of the bombs, he thought while the first stars began to peak through the drifting branches of the palo verde, there had been a large town in that area. The name was lost to him, but the memory of once having known it was not.

If he could find the town he might find salvage. Might find others too and that would present a whole different set of problems.

There is the gun. "Yes," he mumbled his throat still raw. "There is that."

He was glad his granddaughter was not with him. People, strangers who came to the village, made him think of this. After the bombs these people had not found villages, had not banded together to survive. They had wandered, and in their eyes he saw that they had done things. Things they found it hard to live with, but things they had done nonetheless. Too many years of "done" things, too many years of desert. Too many years in the cold and heat and condemnation. They didn't seem human anymore. So, if he had to meet strangers, then it was good he didn't have his granddaughter.

It is good then, he laughed, that I am cursed.

But what if you stay out here too long? What if you do too many "done" things?

Too long out there is what the villagers would say whenever those strangers who had no village of their own would show up to trade, to beg, to die. Too long out there.

Now the sky was speckled with the stars above, as the blue light of the west seemed to draw away. He returned his eyes to the fire and tried to think about traps.

He thought of the traps he had been taught by Big Pedro in the days after the bombs when the village was not a village but just a small refugee camp. Traps for varmints, as Pedro had called them. Traps for serpiente. Snake would be good. He had enjoyed snake.

I'll go as far as the town whose name I cannot remember. If there is no salvage then I'll come back. Then the other villagers will know that I am cursed and it won't be expected of me to go out. I can help the women. Watch the children if they'll let me. Make things. I have always wanted to make a guitar.

You don't even know how to play.

Yes, but that has never stopped me from wanting to.

The fire burned the logs to ash among the orange and black glow of its heart. The stars above. The gently moving palo verdes in the night's breeze. The Old Man wrapped himself within his blanket and slept.

CHAPTER 7

He returned to the stream at first light. He had been lying wrapped in his blanket, and for the first time the morning was not so bitterly cold.

At the stream he waited, watching as the light came up. He was thirsty, had been thirsty through the night. But he did not drink from the stream and would not until the light was good enough to see the tracks. Then he would know what made a home of these palo verdes beneath the rocky slope.

At first light he saw the tracks. Different pairs, one behind the other, four toes and a claw. Near the water's edge in the wet mud he could see the impression left by the fur. "It made sense," muttered the Old Man and he knelt to drink the cool water of the stream.

Finished, he looked up to survey the rocky hill that rose above the little oasis of palo verdes. The hill was more a small mountain. Like other small mountains it was more a collection of boulders: large, broken, shattered rock turning a soft hue in the rising sun of the morning.

He looked at the tracks once more. They had definitely come down from the rocks for a drink, and to hunt. The single-file nature of the prints told him they were foxes. He knew these animals. Oftentimes they would come near the village, but never to scavenge at garbage. Once he had seen one pass him on the highway as he returned from salvage. He was in the southbound lanes walking back to the village; the fox, in the northbound lanes, carried a large dead rattlesnake in its mouth. The fox barely regarded him and continued its bouncing little trot toward the west. His son, then a little boy, had loved that story when he had told it, often asking him to tell it again.

He returned to his camp, hung his blanket in a tree, and began to search for an area under the palo verdes; an area of clearing but near enough to the trees. When he spotted a den of mice he knew he had a good area.

In the center of the clearing he dug a small two-foot hole. The bottom was deep and wide while the top was narrow. He dug two more exactly like it and then began to gather deadfall back at the camp. He thought he might like a nice fire that night even though there would be no food. When the firewood was gathered he selected six sticks and returned to the clearing. He placed two sticks on two sides of each hole and then returned to the stream to drink.

From the bottom of the rocky slope he retrieved three flat stones. He placed these atop the sticks surrounding each of the holes. Now there was a nice roof. Also there was a tiny entrance on each side of the hole underneath the rocks

Feeling tired he returned to his camp and lay down for a while. His strength was fading and he began to sweat thick salty tears. He was starving and the thought of the foxes made him hungrier. He would prefer rattlesnake, but there probably were none. Foxes also liked snake and had most likely hunted the area clean.

They are good salvagers.

After some rest and another long drink at the stream he returned to the clearing. He watched the dens at the base of the palo verdes. He would need to catch the mice before the fox. He leaned against the thin green trunk of the tree he was standing near and closed his eyes. Then he opened them just enough.

Mice will think I am asleep. That will make them bold.

He waited. The sun turned to late afternoon.

Much longer and I won't have enough time to build a trap for the fox.

The day isn't done yet.

Moments later he was asleep.

As a young man, passing through Yuma on that last day, that last civilized day, he remembered thinking 'I have just three hours to go. Three hours and I'll make Tucson.'

Above, the sky was filled with fighter planes attempting to refuel from the big airborne tankers. People camped out along the road while the state police barred any entrance into Yuma. Surely, it was too small of a target for the bombs. They would hit the major cities first, as they had been doing. Each day another city exploded. First it had been New York. Everyone watched on the news. The next day Chicago. Had it been Chicago? the Old Man wondered in his dream. Had that been the next city?

The major cities were gone after two weeks. Internet and telecommunications were down. Who knew how many cities were left. When he finally fled Los Angeles, everyone hoped Yuma would survive.

His parents were in Tucson. Tucson was just as off the map as Yuma. Maybe Phoenix would get bombed. But not Tucson. He had been sitting in checkpoints since three o'clock that morning. First the one in Orange County. Then San Onofre. Then San Diego. The Top of the Laguna Seca Pass. El Centro, and finally the dunes outside Yuma.

Suddenly there were no more checkpoints. And no entrance into Yuma. The President had finally landed after being airborne for most of the two weeks.

Yuma had been the destination of flight for so many. Who cared what lay beyond it? Now he was looking at Yuma in his rearview mirror; he was twenty-seven years old. Above, fighter planes ripped across the sky. Tankers circled and the runway was off-limits. One of the guards at the last checkpoint told him the President, who had been airborne, dodging missile strikes for two weeks, had finally landed in Yuma. Maybe the other side was out of weapons. Maybe Yuma was the high water mark. Maybe we had beaten them by surviving long enough to be left with Yuma. In his rearview mirror, heading up the rocky pass that led east from Yuma, he knew they were doomed. He didn't know why, only knew that they were.

He awoke with a jerk. He spotted the mouse instantly. He hadn't even needed to let his eyes unfocus, see everything, and track for movement. Instead he spotted the little mouse at the instant the mouse noticed his jerk. Its eyes wide with terror, it froze.

The Old Man darted toward its den. The mouse twitched eyes wide with fear. Once the animal remained frozen the Old Man knew he'd cut off its retreat. He advanced with great stomping strides and instantly the mouse attempted an end run, hoping to dodge past him and into the burrow. The Old Man flailed wildly and yelled "Yaah," feeling lightheaded and stiff in his legs all at once.

The mouse retreated, scrambling back toward the middle of the clearing. The Old Man pursued, shaking off the dizziness and yelling as he flailed wildly with his arms. The creature, now in full panic, darted back across his path, hoping to break out past the Old Man. A deft stomp barely missed the mouse and sent it scurrying back toward the center of the clearing.

My granddaughter would enjoy this game.

If you had been a moment too late, the mouse would have gotten past you and the game would be over.

The mouse in full flight, panic-stricken, ran heedlessly away from the Old Man and realized its luck the moment it saw the flat stone ahead. There was enough space to squeeze under. Once inside it would be safe. With purpose the mouse raced for the flat stone, and once underneath fell into the concave hole the Old Man had dug.

When it did not emerge immediately, the Old Man knew it had fallen into the trap. He bent over, sweating hard, and closed his eyes hoping not to pass out. He picked up the rock. The mouse, teeth bared, squeaked up at him. He placed the stone over the top of the hole and returned to the camp.

He retrieved the wire from his satchel and his knife, along with a little rope. At the stream, the tracks of the foxes had dried and could still be seen. Avoiding them altogether he followed them back into the brush. After a moment he lost their trail but he could guess at where they had made a straight line from the rocks to the water.

He looked left and right of the trail until he found a sapling. Maybe just a year old. He took the stake he had carved before sleeping and sank it firmly in the narrow trail. Looping his wire he connected the stake to a length of rope that he quickly turned into a noose. He laid the rope out some distance toward the small green palo verdes and bent the tree over until its top touched the ground. Then straddling it he tied off the rope around the sapling.

He returned to the hole. With a quick motion, he stabbed the mouse and waited for it to die. Then he set the dead body in front of the noose, which hung inches above the trail. He stepped away, resisting the urge to dress the trap. Leave it alone, he heard Big Pedro say. Washing his hands of the blood of the mouse and the dirt of the trail he took a long drink and returned to his camp.

THE SUN WAS low and he thought about food. He lit his fire and stared into it, thinking his own thoughts for a long time. The falling of the sun failed to rouse him as he continued to stare into the fire. He did not think about his aches. Or the village, which would remind him of food. He thought about Yuma. And the girl whose father had been shot. Had she and her mother made it to Yuma? If so, then they too had died forty years ago.

I might hear the trap spring. But probably not. In the morning maybe there will be a fox. If not, then who knows?

He didn't like to think about that and so, piling a few more sticks onto the fire, he wrapped himself within his blanket.

Why can't I dream about the lions on the beaches of Africa like my friend in the book? At sunset they came down to the water to play like cats.

CHAPTER 8

When he awoke there was a fox. It twisted in the morning breeze, its tongue lolling purple and its eyes wide in terror. It was beautiful. The Old Man admired its healthy coat as he skinned the little fox.

By late morning, strips of fox meat were skewered and roasting over ashy orange coals of smoking mesquite. The Old Man, calm and weak, walked among the palo verdes, drinking from the stream and looking for the honeycomb of the dead bee. Standing near the roasting strips of flesh was too much, so it was better to wander among the quiet trees.

By noon the meat was ready and at first he went slowly. He didn't want to become sick from too much too fast. For the rest of the day he ate slowly and continued to roast more and more of the fox. It would keep for a few days.

As night fell, he looked out into the great desert he had come across.

I survived. I can return and accept the curse. It isn't much of a curse. They will feed and take care of me. I will play my part. But as a salvager I am finished.

Maybe it is time to let that go.

Or I can continue on and try to find the town.

The dunes seemed nothing more than gentle curves and soft colors.

You tried to kill me. There was nothing in you. Nothing to take away. So what good are you? If I go across you again what could I find this time? Nothing. But if I find the town then maybe that is something, and if not

I can pick up the Old Highway to the south and that will lead me back to the village.

But you will come from the east.

There is that.

He ate more fox and thought it might be nice with some tortillas. He set the rest of the meat to smoke in the coals throughout the night so that it would last for a few days more. Then he slept.

AT DAWN HE was up. He felt better. He drank from the stream and chewed a little bit of the dried fox meat.

I think I might go on a bit.

He spent the morning climbing up out of the stand of green palo verdes and onto the broken rocks of the mountain. When he gained the summit he looked east. The landscape sank away into a bowl deeper than the one he had crossed.

It will be hotter.

At the extent of his vision he could see mountains, jagged and gray.

Almost at the center of the bowl, halfway between himself and the mountains, he could see a collection of buildings. Too small to be the town he once knew.

There might be a map or a sign that might lead to the town.

By late afternoon the small mountain was far behind him. The going was mostly smooth and downhill. The heat reminded him of the bread oven back in the village.

CHAPTER 9

After the bombs there had been dreams. Dreams everything lost had come back. The dead might walk through the barroom door two years after the global car wreck. The survivors, drinking to forget, would put down their cups. All would be as it once was. The dreams after the bombs were like that.

The neon sign came stuttering to life in the twilight of the desert. The Old Man stopped in the smooth blown sand.

There is power here.

The sign showed a sleepy little boy, in nightgown and night cap drifting toward a bed. In rockets bursting script the words "Dreamtime Motel" loomed large, then recessed toward a universe of smiling faced stars. Vacancy, air-conditioning, and color TV were all available.

The cluster of buildings were merely an L-shaped motel complete with swimming pool and the blackened remains of a nearby gas station, its metal twisted in telltale strands away from where the pumps had once been.

The lights of the hotel came softly to life here and there where bulbs still burned.

The east is cursed.

He moved forward cautiously, remembering the pistol within his satchel.

The parking lot was gritty with the windblown sand of the years. Still, the cracks in it were nowhere near the rents and buckles of the main highway back near the village.

From the office, a man emerged wearing a Hawaiian shirt, his eyes hidden behind mirrored sunglasses.

"Room for the night, mister?" His voice the desiccated husk of a reptile. Used. Spent.

The Old Man remained staring.

If I am dreaming then this does not exist. Maybe the oasis of palo verdes did not exist. Maybe I am dying in the dunes still clutching the dead bee.

"Got room if yer lookin'." Then the man with the mirrored sunglasses began to wheeze and laugh. After a second he said, "Have ever since before the bombs."

The Old Man still standing in the twilight, his face illuminated by the flickering glare of the last wisps of neon, remembered the gun. His fingers, bony and old, adjusted the strap of his satchel.

"I got snake." Mirrored Sunglasses moved forward. His body was long, though he wasn't tall; the only roundness a potbelly that seemed more pregnant than fat. "You want snake for dinner?"

"What is this place?" croaked the Old Man.

Mirrored Sunglasses whirled, taking in the motel against the dying light in the west.

"This my hotel. Even before the bombs, I swear." He seemed all out of breath and ragged at once.

"You got power."

"Just a little ever' night. Went solar before the bombs, but the panels ain't doin so good these last few years. Got a well for water. Power ever' night. No air-condition though. And snake. Lotsa snakes east of here."

East is cursed.

"Where ya headed?"

"Into the town I thought used to be near here."

"The town? Why ya wanna go there fer? Burnt down during the bombs."

The Old Man was silent.

Still.

"Nothing left that way. All of it's gone. Seen two clouds that week. First Phoenix then Tucson. Nothing there but death. Won't be for another hundred years. Say where you come from?"

"West."

"Really?"

"Three days to the other side of the dunes. On the Old Highway a couple days this side of the Great Wreck."

"Never heard of no 'Great Wreck.' "

They remained standing in the parking lot, the Old Man considering what was his and his alone.

"I'll get the snake reheated. Et myself earlier, but I can get you some going."

"That would be nice of you. Thank you."

Mirrored Sunglasses turned and headed back into the darkened office mumbling, "Maybe afterwards you'd like to see the pool."

The Old Man lowered his satchel to the ground.

How had this place remained? There was no sign of a town, other than the remains of the gas station. The road leading away from the motel seemed in better condition than the Old Highway near the village. It must have been new at the time of the bombs.

The Old Man looked again at the neon coursing through the tubes. The design of architecture had once meant something to him. He remembered living in a time when architecture was at war with itself. The old being swept away for the new. You could tell, he remembered, when you walked into someone's house, a restaurant, even a gas station, what the architect's idea of the future was. Glass blocks seemed so outdated to him at the time. That was all he could remember.

The snake was good. The two men stood in the parking lot as the Old Man ate it out of a bowl using a bent spoon. All this had survived the apocalypse under neon tubes humming and buzzing, manufactured before the world was the way it would be.

"Built it the year before the war. I did. I built it." Mirrored Sunglasses never looked straight on at the Old Man. Always to the side or over his shoulder.

The moon would be full tonight. The last curled bits of snake were scooped up in a red sauce that might have been either peppers or ketchup, as the Old Man remembered ketchup to taste. Finally, the bent spoon clanged loudly against the silence that stood between them.

"Finished?" Mirrored Sunglasses held out a gnarled hand to take the bowl and spoon. The Old Man moved the bowl toward the hand noticing it didn't move farther than initially extended. Another hand would always reach to meet what was offered. This one didn't. When the bowl touched the fingertips of Mirrored Sunglasses, the tips curled instantly and the bowl was jerked away.

"Good huh? Made it myself."

It was, nodded the Old Man.

Mirrored Sunglasses didn't say anything and for a brief moment confusion crossed the craggy face beneath the sunglasses.

Mirrored Sunglasses is blind.

"Sure is. The best. Always got lots of snake. Always snake. Not much else but there is always snake."

Blind, thought the Old Man. Blind for how long? Alone. No village. How had he survived? Who knew.

"Like a dip in the pool now? Then we can get you fixed up for the night. A real hotel room. Betcha never thought you'd have that again. I've kept ready since the bombs. Sometimes folk stay awhile. Like to stay for awhile?"

The Old Man considered the moon and the desert. It would be a good night for putting some distance toward the old town. But the chance of finding salvage after the moon went down was poor. He needed good light.

But wasn't this place salvage? Was a motel beyond the wasteland with power salvage?

"That would be kind of you to put me up for the night."

"A dip in the pool first? A good swim and you'll sleep like a dead sailor."

"Maybe in the morning. I think I need to lie down. It's been a long few days."

Mirrored Sunglasses turned to the office, muttering that the Old Man should follow along. Moments later he handed the Old Man a card.

"Room five. Card unlocks it like one of them fancy hotels before the war, 'member 'em?"

The Old Man looked at it. Had he ever stayed in a hotel with a card as a key? He had a vague memory of once having done so. A laughing girl at his shoulder as he ran the card through a slot and red became green and there was some meaning to him at that moment. Young. It must have meant something to a young man. The meaning of it now was lost among the blown sand and dying heat of a world where cards did not open locks. That was the work of crowbars.

"I'll knock on your door before dawn. Then you can have a swim while the water's still cold."

The Old Man said that would be fine and left the office. Five was on the bottom floor, halfway down the long end of the capital L that was the shape of the place.

Inside the room it was quiet. It was not his shed where light came through at all angles and where the wind brought the unwanted gift of sand. Or where the business of the village could always be listened to. Comforted by. This room was too quiet. A quiet he had not experienced for many years.

He flicked a switch on the wall and one lamp cast a thin cone of light against the gloom. He lay on the bedspread. It was thick and stiff. It smelled of heavy dust.

Already his eyes were closing. For a moment he awoke and realized he had been sleeping. He needed to turn off the light. But he was too tired. More tired than he had ever been.

I feel as if I am made of grease. I must turn off the light. I would be a bad guest if I didn't turn off the light and used up all the power. He flailed and heard the lamp fall.

He was asleep.

CHAPTER 10

In the dream he was awake in the hotel room, knowing he must turn off the light or he'd run down the power of the motel. Cars were pulling up in the parking lot as the bombs went off. Lots of bombs.

And then he was awake. There were no bombs. No sound. No cars.

HE WILL KILL U!!!

A jolt of blue fire raced across muscles and arms. Above him the letters of the words were written in glowing yellow light on the ceiling. They seemed to grow larger as he stared at them. The room was dark.

'I must be hallucinating,' he thought. He closed his eyes and tried to rub them, but his arm would barely move.

I am so tired.

When he opened his eyes again he saw the words.

HE WILL KILL U!!!

I must be going crazy.

Sweating, he pushed himself up and realized he was breathing heavy. Too heavy. With more effort than it should have taken, he got the lamp upright and switched it on again. Nothing happened.

I must have broken the bulb.

He looked upward, and again the glowing warning remained above his head. The letters were made up of little stars and moons. Planets with rings. He knew those things, those glow-in-the-dark shapes. A girl he once knew. He remembered her to be sad. Or maybe he was the one who was sad. But she had put glow-in-the-dark planets and stars on her ceiling. He remembered lying next to her in the dark as music played nearby. He remembered the sadness though he could not say whether it had been his or hers.

Someone had written those words on the ceiling with glow-in-the-dark planets and stars. Standing with more effort than it should have taken, he stood on the bed to examine them. They were real. He peeled off a star. Held it between his thumb and forefinger.

He moved to the window and parted the curtains. The moon had fallen to the other side of the sky.

Dawn in a few hours.

He looked once more at the warning.

Taking his satchel, he opened the door and stepped out into the night. He crossed the walkway heading into the parking lot. His huaraches scraped quietly. He kept his eyes on the dark office door.

"No swim, my friend?" Mirrored Sunglasses stood in the doorway of the room next to him, his arm cradling a double-barreled shotgun.

"You're not thinking of running off without paying your bill?"

Was he truly blind?

Ahead the moon sank into the black horizon turning the silver nightscape a dark blue.

"How'd you know?" asked Mirrored Sunglasses.

The Old Man swallowed thickly.

When did I last have some water? I am thirstier than I should be.

"Tell me. It won't do you no good not to."

"Some words written on the ceiling."

Mirrored Sunglasses moved the shotgun to the other arm. He seemed to stare off, considering a different matter altogether.

"Shoulda knowed it," he mumbled. "How 'bout that swim?"

"I don't know what the problem is," began the Old Man. "But I mean you no harm. Just headed to the old town east of here. Just going to look for salvage. That's all. I won't steal from you."

"Right, you won't. Can't have people knowing I'm here. You'd tell. They'd come for my stuff. Come for me. I wouldn't be king anymore."

"That's not true. Why don't I just move on? No harm, friend."

After a moment's silence in which the Old Man thought he might just walk into the desert and be free of this nightmare, Mirrored Sunglasses raised the shotgun. It wasn't dead on straight in his face, but it was close enough.

Two barrels with the right shot and he doesn't need to see me move. Just squeeze at the sound of me. I'll be nothing but shredded flesh and bones.

He thought of his own pistol hidden in his satchel. Getting it out? He'd know.

But he's only got one chance to shoot you. Then he's got to break the barrel and reload. Then fire again. Takes time.

"Think it's time for that swim, mister," said Mirrored Sunglasses in a voice that was both mean and low. "Start walking."

The pool lay beyond a gate at the far end of the complex. The Old Man began to shuffle and by the time he reached the gate, the double-barreled shotgun hovered a foot behind his kidneys. The rusty gate swung open and landed with a clank.

"Move."

The Old Man walked to the edge of the pool.

It was drained.

Along its cracked concrete bottom, hundreds of snakes lay sleeping and lethargic in the cool predawn. Occasionally one moved. A corpse lay on the far side near the steps, what would have been the shallow end of a filled pool. Beneath the snakes lay more humps that might be corpses.

As he neared the edge of the deep end, he heard Mirrored Sunglasses suck in air.

Barely thinking, the Old Man twisted and stepped back as he saw Mirrored Sunglasses raise the shotgun into both hands across his chest and rush at him as if pushing a plow.

Recoiling in horror sent the Old Man off the lip of the edge and saved his life. He fell and felt his hands grasping for the edge. A familiar child-like feeling as he found it. Then he swung hard into the concrete wall of the empty pool to hang just a few feet from the snakes.

Above, Mirrored Sunglasses's feral swear turned to a scream as the expected resistance remained unmet and he sailed outward above a snake-filled concrete pool.

Hanging from the edge the Old Man heard the snapping crunch of a bone-breaking headfirst dive twelve feet below.

The snakes, hissing, snapped on the attacker in the cool dark shadow of the deep end. Rattles raged in unison as the Old Man, head swimming, heaved himself over the side of the pool and onto the deck.

CHAPTER 11

The morning sun found the Old Man in the office. Locked, he had broken it open with his crowbar.

First he laid out his bedroll and removed the pistol. He checked the rounds within and then went back to the edge of the pool. Mirrored Sunglasses stared skyward, his neck twisting to meet his body. The snakes were already covering him, seeking his fading heat in the predawn chill of the desert.

The double-barreled shotgun lay nearby.

Salvage. But at the bottom with the snakes it is as good as gone unless . . .

I could burn them.

And damage the gun no doubt.

He returned to his satchel and considered rerolling the bedroll with the pistol inside.

There might be others here. Maybe if I am going farther into the wasteland I need to keep the pistol within reach.

Once the office door was broken, the Old Man found a dirty kitchen at the back of it. It smelled greasy and old and like the snake he had eaten. Though the sink was dirty its faucet gave up a cool stream of clear water.

Well water.

He drank and drank again. He was still thirsty so he continued to drink. His head was clearing from the fogginess. Beside the sink, at eye level as he bent to drink, he noticed an old steak knife. A half-cut pill lay nearby.

He drugged me.

The rising sun turned the tiny office golden. Magazines littered the racks and the front of the office.

Was Mirrored Sunglasses truly blind?

What did it matter?

For the rest of the morning he searched the office, which contained little in the way of salvage. Boxes of coins and paper money. A few tools, but the village had these tools and often in great supply.

He took the cards that unlocked the rooms and went to the first room. A motel room like the one he had slept in. It was too bright to see if another message had been written on the ceiling. The other rooms for the most part were the same, except for the rust-stained bedspreads sometimes shredded and torn. One room seemed to be permanently lived in. The room Mirrored Sunglasses had come out of. He found an old toothbrush too disgusting to be used again. An abundance of clothing, crossing a spectrum of styles. Drawers full of medication from the year of the bombs. Prescriptions for people named Harriet Binchly. Or Kevin Adams. Or Phillip Nuygen. Take once a day with water.

Sitting on the bed for a moment the Old Man considered returning to the office for more water. But then he felt he must finish the rooms first. Make sure the place was clear.

This place is evil.

East is cursed.

Yes, and I too am cursed.

What was its story?

If he knew its story then maybe he might find salvage. If there was salvage to be found.

But the rooms and the office told of a hermit. "Loners" the village called them in the years after the bombs. People who had run so deep into the desert, they didn't know of villages. Didn't know others survived. Hermits didn't last long. Seven years was the longest he'd ever guessed of one making it on his own.

This man had a hotel. Some power. The road nearby.

He thought of the power system. A salvage of that was beyond him. He could return and tell of this place. Then the villagers could come and get the power.

And the water. It might be good to have a place with water if the village ever wanted to come this far.

They would not come this far. "East" was enough to prevent them from ever considering it. So the solar power was no salvage.

Finished resting, he continued to search the rest of the rooms. In the last two he found the story. But he wished he hadn't.

The first room held the desiccated corpse of a woman. Her long blond hair framed the rictus grin of a skeleton laughing or screaming.

Probably screaming.

The handcuffs at each end of the bedpost said screaming. Arms still connected to bony wrists thin enough to slip through as the victim must have once wished to. One leg lay on the floor. There were no clothes.

Was she the one who tried to warn me?

In the next room at the end of the balcony, the last room of the Dreamtime Motel he found the bags. Bags upon bags full of the last remaining possessions of lost wanderers. Wanderers who had come in from the wind and fire of the bombs. The long winter that followed. The years of sun afterward. Empty rotting bags from uncountable travelers.

HE BURNED IT. He stood watching in the charred remains of the gas station across the road that had once been something more than twisted and blackened metal. Even the ash that must have once covered the station, covered the entire world, had long since gone.

He leaned against a blackened cement pylon. He took pains to avoid the black blooming flower of metal that the pumps had become on that long-ago day when they had gushed forth jets of fuel on fire and burning hot.

Now the motel burned in the late afternoon heat. The Old Man started the fire in the room he had slept in. Started it with some paint thinner and a few other solvents. It consumed the bedspread, and by the time the Old Man had backed away from the motel door, the drapes were aflame and belching black smoke. Forty years of sun and the parched wood and lathe were more than ready to burn.

By the time he crossed the road to watch it all burn to the ground the fire was already visible behind fluttering curtains in the second-story windows.

CHAPTER 12

He ate some of the fox he'd dried, drank a little cold water, and counted the extra bottles and canteens he'd salvaged from the motel, now tied in a loose bandolier. Before setting the fire he'd filled them all with the cold water from the faucet in the office.

That faucet had almost been enough reason not to burn it all down. He could have put a sign on the road or painted the word "WATER" in big red letters across the sides of the motel. A modern oasis for travelers.

But there had been too much evil. Too much wrong had happened within the gold curtained rooms. Too many lives ended in a drugged stupor as Mirrored Sunglasses brained or bashed or shot, by the look of some beds, those who had wandered out of the destruction and found the Dreamtime Motel.

The Old Man guessed the shotgun, buried under the rattlesnakes, was empty. Emptied long ago into the back of another victim. He found a box of shotgun shells. It was empty. Along with the shot-shredded rust-stained bedspreads, the empty box told the story of the shotgun beneath a pile of snakes.

The handcuffs themselves could have been salvage. But when the Old Man went to inspect them, he found no key.

Maybe that's why they were locked? The key had been lost by a blind man.

Would he have let her go if he could have found the key? How long had she lived on that bed?

The grooves and scratches in the frame were numerous. Too numerous for just one victim.

That could have been enough to burn it down. But there was more. In the dying light of the embers he ate the dried strips of fox.

The woman justified burning it all down.

But the water from the faucet was another thing. An oasis was not easily come by.

An early evening desert wind picked up embers, scattering sparks across the road. The fire was finished. Only gray smoke from a few hot spots came up through the charred remains. Where the motel had once been seemed lost and altogether a lie.

It was the marks that made you burn it.

Sí. The marks.

In the room of bags, on the wood paneling near the door and just above the lightswitch, had been the marks. Little sticks grooved into the wood. Four uprights and finally a horizontal slash. Five. Sets of five. Too many sets. Other stray marks along the border, half the size of the sets of five, told him of the children.

Children had been special to Mirrored Sunglasses.

So it had to burn?

Sí.

Yes.

It had to burn.

One day we might not be, and the people who come next don't need to take this with them. My granddaughter.

Tired, he rose to his feet. The moon was large and it would be a cool night for walking. He drank a little more water and adjusted his satchel. He tucked the gun that had lain on the ground next to him into his waistband. He tightened the electrical cord he used for a belt. The gun fit nicely.

From now on I must keep the gun ready.

But I hope I do not need it.

He set off down the blacktop leading away from the Dreamtime Motel.

THE GROUND ON the side of the road was smoother than the blacktop that eventually proved itself unsafe in the night as tears and eruptions lay shadowed beneath his feet. Occasionally he would stumble, and finally he kept to the side of the road.

If I twist my leg then I will wish I had not burned that place down.

Don't say such a thing.

So he moved to the shoulder and continued following the white dirt along the moonlit road. North.

North is not as bad as east.

Once the moon was overhead, he stopped for water and a bite of fox meat though he didn't feel hungry. The only road sign he passed had been one of the large ones that spanned the entire road. It had fallen facedown and what was written upon it was beyond the strength of his arms to know.

He continued on, and when the moon was waning far to the west, he saw that the road began a long curve toward the east. A mountain ridge to the north blocked further progress. To the east, the remains of four large overpasses that had once connected the highways lay in ruins. Only the pillars and sections of the road like the capitals of columns remained.

I could find shelter there for the day. Maybe some vehicles. Maybe salvage. It will be dawn in a few hours.

He picked up his satchel and slung it once more across his chest.

If it is occupied it might be best to come upon it before dawn. If I smell cook fires then I will know.

The moon went down and soon it was dark.

I was spoiled walking by the light of the moon.

He picked his way along the broken concrete of the highway thinking of nothing more than where his next footstep should be.

Arriving just as the eastern sky began to show the first hints of blue, he crouched in a debris-cluttered culvert. He heard nothing, even as the sun began to cast a steady soft orange light across the desert behind him. His nose smelled nothing on the wind, and once the sun was two hands above the horizon, he left the culvert and continued into the wreckage of the overpasses.

He chose the fallen road sections that had collapsed onto the highway beneath.

If there is anyone here, maybe they are lazy. Then at least I will be above them. They might not even see me.

The fallen sections were made of clean white concrete, grooved as if combed by a brush. He took off his huaraches and continued along the road as it climbed quickly. A break in the road caused him to stop, and he lowered himself onto the section that had fallen on the other side of the break. He climbed this section and another one like it, and soon he was beneath one of the large pillars where part of the highway remained above him.

How long would that last?

He marveled at what man had once built. What he had once driven over. What was once so common seemed a thing of lost giants.

At the end of the broken road he could see the intersection of the four roads. The ground beneath was barren. An old Winnebago lay on its side off in the weeds. He watched for a moment, wondering if it might be someone's home. But the weeds around it and growing out the back window told the story of salvage.

There is no one here.

He climbed back down the broken sections and thought better of the Winnebago.

If it has been here for so long then it has already been salvaged.

On the other side of the ruins, two roads led away. One headed northeast, the other southeast.

What about the Winnebago? Fleeing the bombs, many such RVs had often been loaded beyond safety with such things as might be salvaged.

If that is the case then I would have seen some lying on the ground nearby. It has been searched.

He continued looking north, wondering if that is the east he should pick.

Something, a knife, a tool perhaps, could be lying in the weeds or the dirt.

Unlikely. I would need to go into the wreck and a Winnebago out here by itself would be a place for rattlesnakes or even the brown spider.

Then you expect salvage to be laying in the middle of the road for you to happen along and pick up. Neatly untouched these forty years. A bottle of aspirin or medical tools for the village. Maybe even an entire set of encyclopedias. The village is right. You are cursed. It is your laziness that is the curse. You are the curse of yourself.

Be quiet.

To the north must be Phoenix.

Low hills of red dirt climbed toward Phoenix.

Phoenix was destroyed. I know that. In L.A., just before I left, that had been part of the decision. The bombs were falling each day on a new city. First New York and then Washington, D.C., then Pittsburgh, then Chicago . . . was that right? Or had Chicago been first?

I chose Tucson. Tucson was too small to be hit. The terrorists were choosing bigger cities.

And your parents lived there. On a golf course.

Yuma was smaller than Tucson. Later, on the day the President landed, the Old Man had seen the cloud over Yuma in his rearview mirror as he picked his way through the beginning of the Great Wreck. He had seen it about 2:00 in the afternoon. 2:06 he remembered by the digital clock of his car's instrument panel. The cloud rising from the valley behind him. Ninety miles away. The United States of America had lost its last president.

His car had stopped. The EMP had finished it. In the days that followed, walking the highway, moving away from Yuma, he headed east. Survivors told him they'd seen the cloud over Tucson. L.A. was gone also. They had gone for two that day. That last known day. After that, there was no news. No radio. If the bombs continued to fall, who knew? Had we retaliated against the Middle East like we'd threatened? Was there still a world beyond the United States? A Europe? Africa?

I will never see those lions at sunset. Playing on the beach. Unless I dream them. And my dreams are past stories that cannot be finished.

He thought of the little girl.

I will never know.

I know Phoenix is gone. It went after Miami. I know that Phoenix is gone. That I know.

Those are problems solved long ago. Salvage is your business and if you cannot search the wreck of the Winnebago, then what salvage will you find?

Be quiet.

He turned south along the highway once more.

There will be nothing toward Phoenix. In the days of the bombs, everyone took to the road. Everything they could grab. Headed away, much like myself back then, from the bombs. Phoenix was destroyed. Everyone had known that, so no one went there to escape.

But you heard Tucson was hit also.

"Sí," he whispered softly in the late morning air.

But I saw Phoenix destroyed on the TV.

CHAPTER 13

It was later he realized he had not stopped to rest in the shadows of the ruined overpasses. He wanted to put as much distance as possible between himself and the Dreamtime Motel. He was afraid of the dreams he might have.

How much longer until the monsoons?

He stopped to drink in the thin shade provided by a small bridge.

An orange sun hung low off to the west. Afternoon dust storms rolled across the broken red horizon. He wondered how far west, if he started from this bridge, he would need to walk to find the village.

If the monsoons came soon, there might be trouble with the flash floods.

The torrents of ash would be dangerous.

Where does the ash come from after all these years?

Does it matter?

Maybe it's the answer to what's left of the world. So much ash, so little world.

There is still the village.

Too tired to go much farther, he camped under the bridge, and just before nightfall made a small fire of mesquite.

In the blue twilight, he thought it might be nice to have a guitar. That being alone wouldn't be so bad if he had a guitar. With a guitar he might just continue to wander and never return to the village.

But what about your granddaughter?

The village must think I am dead.

I hope no one came looking for me. They might have gotten hurt.

That is the love of not wanting someone to come and look for you when you have gone.

He tried the phrase out against the wall under the bridge. Letting his shadow speak the words in the light of the fire.

It felt like a phrase one says and doesn't mean. But the words were true.

Maybe it's not enough for something to just be true?

Truth is enough.

THE ALPHA PICKED up the Old Man's scent near the wreck of the Winnebago below the mountains. He hunted here at the end of most nights, and the scent had come only faintly to him. He'd pulled down five men in his life. Alone, when the pack had scattered, he pulled them down.

He had been the leader of the wolf pack for seven rains now. He felt tired most nights. The thrill he experienced in pulling down the wild mule deer to the north didn't cause him to go rigid with electricity at the thought of their meat as it once did. When he had first killed, he had eaten most of the kill before letting his mate at the remains. Lately he made the kill, took his favorite part near the spine at the top of the back, then wandered away to chew with the good side of his teeth.

The smell he tasted in the dawn air was not mule deer. Nor was it the coyote or other prey of the valley. This was man. He remembered the man they caught the spring before. He'd smelled terror in the dark forest moments before the pack crashed through the wall of trees and into the meadow. He'd been halfway across the high meadow, running, when the pack of thirty wolves, his wolves, spotted the man.

In a moment they were on him. The Alpha had fought hard to keep the two killers from the best parts of the man. He wondered how much longer he would be able to keep them at bay. Soon enough they would come for him. As he had, they would.

When the pack passed through the meadow at the end of spring, the shattered bits of white bone were still there.

He had enjoyed the taste of man.

At the two roads the large wolf padded back and forth scenting the air. Even the wolf knew what was north. He had seen the ruins of Phoenix with his own eyes. He knew it was lifeless, and what remained there long was soon poisoned. The deer they killed there always had that taste of death. Often the pack would leave after a few torn strips had been tested. In those times the kill had been enough.

Satisfied the man had gone south, the wolf turned, heading back toward the mountain above the ruined overpasses. He picked his way up through the broken rocks in the early morning light.

How long could he keep his two killers at bay?

At the top of the pass, not far from the den, he turned to look at the valley floor. Where would the man be? Turning toward the den where the pack lay sleeping, exhausted from the night, the wolf trotted into the darkness.

CHAPTER 14

At dawn the Old Man was up. The cool morning air wouldn't last long. He hadn't had coffee in years. Hadn't missed it in years. But now in the cold air beneath the broken road, he wished for it.

He stretched slowly and began to pack his things while taking cautious sips of water.

Where are you going?

South. I am going south today.

Really more east than south.

Just for this morning, let us say it is south.

He had a momentary memory of fog. Fog outside the windows of the house he'd grown up in. The first foggy days of school in autumn. Arguing with someone.

It is because you are arguing with yourself. That is why you remember fog.

For the next few hours he stayed to the side of the great bent and warped highway. The road headed south, mostly. Looking ahead, it seemed the road must eventually turn to the east.

If I can find salvage before it goes east, then I'll head straight west. At some point I will find the Old Highway and from there I will find my way home.

Crossing another fallen bridge, he stopped in the late morning shade of the broken sections. Rebar sprang from the chunks like wild strands of hair. When he resumed his climb out of the tall ditch of red earth, he was sweating.

Let's be clear my friend.

All right.

You say that if you find salvage you will head west and return to the village. Your curse will be lifted?

If you say so but I do not care.

Then why are you out here?

Be quiet.

On top of the dirt embankment, the gentle slope of the road fell away. In the distance a small mountain rose up, broken and dusty brown.

I know that mountain. There was once a large A on its side.

That was common in Arizona in those days. To put a large A on the side of every small mountain near a town or city.

Then it means there must be one nearby. I think it is the one whose name I cannot remember. It seems familiar.

He crossed the flat landscape toward the mountain. To the side of the road, lone stands of scrub grew up in solitary dark patches, as if too hurt to ever grow near another living thing.

Further along the highway, he passed the remains of a burnt fueling station off to one side. It was little more than a concrete pad and blackened cement. In the lone shade of a mesquite tree he ate the last of the fox and drank some water.

Now you have two problems.

Now I have no food and no salvage. If I could walk straight to the village day and night for three days I might make it. But not without food. The effort would be too great and I might make a mistake if I were so hungry I couldn't focus. Then a broken leg would be the end of me.

Tonight I will stop early and make some traps.

A gas station like this once had a tin awning that made a singsong noise in a strong wind.

Another thought that has no place in the present.

Maybe just another memory trying not to be forgotten.

I might know that because I once stopped here for fuel.

You always came to visit your parents on the Eight. Not the Ten.

Amazed, he stopped chewing. He hadn't referred to the Old Highway as the Eight in a long time. Since the days just after the bombs. The names of places had been forgotten. Or were too painful to remember.

The Eight.

He tried to remember the name of the town he was looking for. Something "Big" he remembered. But it wouldn't come and the air seemed to be getting hotter with the noonday heat.

He began to move again, south along the highway.

In the afternoon, brilliant white sails of cloud began to form to the east. Climbing upward, each full-blown sail exploding beneath an eruption of white foam. The armada of clouds came no closer than a dark ridge of jagged mountains to the east that embodied everything he felt about that direction.

The monsoons were coming.

THE ALPHA LED the thirty wolves of his pack off the mountain and passed the Winnebago on its side. At the road, he smelled the night wind coming out of the south. He didn't smell the man. But he knew men. He had watched them. Men always moved in one direction, as if always on the hunt of just one animal.

The two killers challenged him briefly as he started off down the highway but his mate snarled back at them. For a moment, it looked as though the pack might split. The two killers wanted to circle to the north and for a while they yelped about it, making the noises that indicated mule deer.

But the females went with the Alpha, and soon the entire pack lay strung out behind him as he scented the sides of the road for the man.

Near the bridge where the Old Man made camp the night before, the wolf picked up the scent of urine. The Old Man had urinated just before sleeping.

Slowly the Alpha crept down along a path and followed the trail directly into the camp under the bridge. He smelled the gray ash of the night's fire. Some paper the Old Man had wrapped the dried fox in. The rest of the pack milled about above the camp on the main road. Dawn wasn't far off and they'd nothing to eat so far.

One of the killers howled in warning and the entire pack turned toward the sound of it.

A family of havalina had come up the dry riverbed under the bridge from the east and the wolves fell upon the wild pigs, easily snatching the babies as the male and the females stubbornly stood their ground hoping to minimize losses.

But the wolves were too good for the wild pigs. Had hunted too long under the Alpha. Soon, the last sow's eyes rolled back in her head. She'd watched the killers tearing out the entrails of the male that had presided over the brood for as long as she could remember. Seconds later, a warm softness came over her as the Alpha sunk its teeth deeper into her jugular vein, forcing her to release.

Swinging her to the side, the Alpha looked at the two killers. They should have known the females were the most dangerous. She could have killed them or made the victim wish for death. That might have solved his problems right there. But treachery was not in the Alpha.

The snarling pack devoured flesh and blood. The Alpha settled down to the dead sow. He had lost the pack for the night. There would be no going any farther after this meal. Dawn would soon be upon them. They would sleep in the shade under the bridge in the man's camp from the night before. And tomorrow they would hunt him again.

Tearing at the haunch of the desert pig, he thought it might be good for them to sleep in the man's camp. They would have the smell of him. That way he wouldn't have to do all the work.

CHAPTER 15

In the twilight at the end of the next day, the Old Man standing on the road didn't feel as tired as he should have. He'd caught two snakes in the late morning coming out on the highway to sun themselves. Big rattlers, he'd pinned their flat heads and swung the crowbar down with a ring on the old highway.

He'd roasted them quickly and eaten. Just after noon he was headed south again. Later the "thunder-bumpers," as some of the villagers called the big late afternoon cumulus clouds, though Big Pedro had called them "the Chubasco," built up to the east over the iron gray mountains. As twilight came, a cool wind whipped up from the south, and in the dust of it he could smell rain.

I might walk a bit longer tonight. The snake tasted so good I might walk a bit longer. Maybe I will make the town in the night, and if anyone lives there it might be better that way.

A few minutes later he heard the first mournful howl. Behind him. To the north from where he had come.

If it is just one I might be fine.

If not?

A chorus began, but each successive howl was more urgent as if hoping to outdo the previous one by speed.

The Old Man shifted his satchel higher onto his back and bent quickly, hoping, praying, that the wolves were about some other business. He tied his huaraches tighter, adjusted his burden once more, and moved off quickly.

If I can find something tall, they might not get to me.

But the road seemed a straight flat course bearing off into the south and the night. There were no rocks or boulders, no wreckage of overturned tankers or piled cars. There had not been since the days before the bombs. Tucson had evacuated early. After Phoenix had been hit. The roads had been empty as survivors fled into the desert or other places they hoped might be safe.

Going south the town will be off to my right.

Ay, but you're not anywhere near it. You don't even know where it is. And Mirrored Sunglasses told you it burned.

He lied about other things.

The Old Man darted off into the scrub and down an embankment. Behind him, the wolves were calling back and forth.

They are still away off, but wolves must move fast.

He pulled out his crowbar as he ran and placed his other hand on the pistol in his waistband. After a moment, when one of the wolves seemed closer, back near the road, he pulled out the gun, flicking off the safety.

It's really not enough you know. Five bullets. It sounds like a lot of them from the howling.

In the sand he stepped on something thick and long. Man-made. Kicking his feet through the soft desert powder he found the remains of a thick cable.

A downed power line.

He followed it away through the brush to the south.

If I can find the tower I can climb it even if it's down.

He headed south, maneuvering around the scrub and keeping one step on the cable as he ran.

Looking back over his shoulder he could see the elevated rise of the highway. In the last moments of light he saw the shadowy wolves. He counted quickly but gave up as they shifted. It seemed there were maybe twenty of them. It was a large pack.

Behind him, a cacophony of yapping went up as the wolves tried to find his trail.

At least there must be a town ahead. This power line must have been going somewhere.

He could hear the wolves in the brush now, bounding and leaping about. Making a game of hide and kill with the Old Man.

The downed power line began to rise from the sand, and soon it was high enough for him to follow with his hand.

It's rising. Something to climb.

Frantically he plowed through the scrub, heedless of scorpions.

The evening wind had picked up and was blowing sand across the desert. Ahead he could hear the singsong of metal bending in the wind. It reminded him of the village.

The wolves had his scent now and he could hear them racing in the brush behind him

Rising out of the dark he could make out a toppled power tower. The kind that was nothing more than cross welded steel frames rising high above the landscape. But this one had fallen on its side.

A wolf howled behind the Old Man, and not daring to look back he raced for the nearest girder and began to climb.

At first, he had to climb with the gun and the crowbar in his hands, but once he was high enough, he hung for a second, placing the gun in his satchel.

Below him, the entire pack circled, whining and yelping.

Once the Old Man was as high as the toppled girder would rise, he wedged himself between two supports and glanced down.

The wolves whined and howled in high little yelps. Pacing, they began to race back and forth until the largest of them let out a bone-chilling howl.

If I fall . . .

Then don't. Don't fall.

The Old Man lay under a blanket of stars. Above him a thousand points of broken glass shimmered. The moon had gone down and now the sky was black before dawn.

This is how the world is in the night. In all the nights I was a child and a young man before the bombs. It was like this in the night.

It was like this for the man in the book. At night. With the great fish. Will I find my great fish? Will my story go that far?

Below the wolves had disappeared for the most part. He could hear them ranging through the dirt and scrub. All except the big one. The big one waited. Sitting mostly. Waiting. Occasionally he would pad around beneath the Old Man, checking the perimeter. A loping little gait, almost friendly. Just business.

The Old Man lay precariously across the top of one of the girders where it intersected with another. It was a small space and not much more.

A strong wind or sleep and over I go. So no sleep tonight.

What will the wolves do in the morning?

What will you do in the morning?

The big wolf didn't answer. But he seemed to be listening.

The Old Man drank some water.

His neck was tired. His back felt numb from the girder. And his legs were falling asleep. He flexed them, moving back and forth. He winked at the big wolf.

If I fall, you must be ready. So no sleep for you either.

Are you crazy?

No.

The wolves won't let you go five feet.

I must try.

You will fail if it comes to that.

"If" it comes to that.

Below the wolf waited.

AT DAWN, THE wolves settled to wait. There were thirty of them. The two killers baited the Alpha. They wanted to leave the scrawny man and return to the sickly mule deer near Phoenix, a hot pile of ruins the wolves called "The Uneven Ground." The two killers walked away decidedly. But none of the females followed. The young watched. As if their decision mattered. But the big Alpha waited.

THE OLD MAN watched the wolves play their game.

It's obvious to me.

How so?

They don't want to stay. They want something to kill. To eat. But the big one there won't let them. What he says goes. There is more to me, for him, than just a meal. So I think all of us must wait.

He awoke with a start. He had drifted for only a moment. But he had started to roll. Started to roll off the girder to the wolves below.

I can't wait all day, my friend. Maybe you should listen to the rest of your family and go. That would be for the best.

The big Alpha watched from underneath the top of his eyes, giving away nothing.

I have a family too, you know.

Do you?

The Old Man looked behind him, toward where he had been heading. A dawn breeze moved softly over his gray hair in the orange light of a new day.

The power lines ran down the length of the fallen tower, which was even higher at the far end. The lines continued out across a low riverbed. They stretched loosely across the gap to meet another tower, twisted and fallen in the same direction on the other side of the dry riverbed.

These must have fallen in the shock wave after Phoenix.

The Old Man rose to his knees. He moved his satchel onto his back.

Listen, wolf. I can't wait for you to leave. So I must go. You understand, don't you?

The Old Man began to crawl over the length of the tower. At once the wolves were up and pacing, whining and crossing back and forth underneath him. Some growled.

This requires all the concentration you have ever had in your whole life, so pay attention. You must focus like your friend in the book. He needed to bait the hooks and cut the tuna while his hand was cramping. And still he held the line the big fish was on.

I will.

Patiently, unlike the rest of the pack, the big Alpha below paced the Old Man above, each of the paws tracing each of the hands and knees of the Old Man.

When he arrived at the end of the tower, he was at least ten feet higher and the girders were wider. The power lines were draped and bunched on the desert floor around the tower but they continued up across the base of the fallen tower and out across the riverbed.

I must be fifty or sixty feet up from the riverbed.

I don't think I have the strength.

The heavy cables swung in the morning breeze.

He tried them. He would never know for sure. Never know if halfway across the gap they might start to slide downward.

These are heavy cables. They stretch for miles and miles. They weigh tons. Surely they can support the weight of just me.

You will never know.

I don't have much choice.

Most of the wolves below were losing interest and they began to chase small animals. All except the big Alpha. As the Old Man began to work at his satchel, cutting it into strips, the big Alpha began to growl. And when the Old Man began his journey across the void, the big Alpha let out a sudden mournful howl, and soon all the wolves were back and baying at him.

His tools were in his pockets and he had secured the grease in his bandolier with his water bottles. Everything he had tied across his waist.

Cutting the leather satchel into strips, he missed his wife.

She had made the satchel for him before she died. It had not been salvaged. It had been made. He left it at that. He didn't think anymore about their love. Their love after the end of everything. Or the short time they had together. Or her olive skin. Or the boy he raised. Or all the things that are made when love is reason enough.

He tied the strips three times about one wrist. He tied another set of strips about the other wrist. He did the same with his ankles, ending up with a leather collar for each limb. He ran thicker straps made of sturdier leather through those bands about his wrist. He did the same with his ankles.

Moving to the cable that stretched across the riverbed, he greased the tough straps and then tied them to the other bands about the opposite ankle and wrist, leaving the power cable between his body and his arms and legs.

The sun was directly above him. He looked across the gap to the other fallen tower.

Two hundred yards.

He started out headfirst, using his hands to pull and his feet to brace. He was thankful for his gloves.

The big Alpha howled and then stopped.

This might be tougher than I'd thought.

The cables were dropping down at first and so the Old Man was braking himself more than pulling. Halfway across when he would be most tired, he would need to pull.

Just work and think about something.

What will the wolves do?

Think about something else.

What is the name of my friend in the book?

He is not much of a friend if you don't know his name.

I would like to have been in the boat with my friend. I could have helped him with the fish.

Great drops of sweat broke out across his body, and by the time he was three quarters of the way down the descent, one glove tore above his index finger.

Listen. Do you hear the wolves?

I think they have gone.

He looked down and saw the big Alpha bounding across the rocks of the dry riverbed. Two leaner wolves paced behind him.

At the lowest point of the descent, he could barely see from the glare of the sun and the salty sweat running into his eyes.

He gripped the cable with his legs and felt it slip, or thought he did. He opened the tin of grease he had placed in the bandolier across his chest. Trembling fingers flipped open the lid as he poured the rest of the grease across the straps and the cable.

He let the empty tin of grease that had accompanied him on so many salvages for so many years fall as the wolves danced away from it.

Now you must pull.

Ten feet farther up and climbing, he was exhausted.

I can't. I am too tired.

You have no choice. You must pull. Think about something.

I wonder what the wolves will do when I get to the other side.

Think about something else and pull.

Pull.

You must pull.

You should teach your granddaughter to do this in case she is ever sur-rounded by wolves and trapped on top of a fallen power tower.

I would rather teach her to read.

You must pull.

I am pulling.

Pull. Pull. Pull harder.

There is nothing left.

You have no other option, now pull, Old Man.

I am pulling.

Whatever happened to all the people you ever knew? Knew before the bombs.

I don't care.

The women you loved?

I still love my wife.

Pull. Pull. Pull.

I can't see. There is too much sweat in my eyes.

There is nothing to see now. Pull harder. Pull harder.

I can't go much farther.

You must go to the end.

Then the end is the farthest I'll go.

Pull and stop with the nonsense.

Okay.

Pull.

Pull.

Pull. Pull. PULL!

The Old Man's shoulder bumped against the rough dirt wall of the far embankment. His shoulders felt like glowing iron bands of steel just pulled from the heat of a furnace. The thongs keeping his feet across the cable were frayed and only one remained whole. Below him, the wolves danced back and forth, insane with anger.

The Old Man pulled himself over the edge of the cliff and lay breathing heavily. The air burned hot and clean in his lungs. Reaching for his knife, he cut the straps at his hands and feet and stood. He thought about drinking some water, but without meaning to he glanced down below and saw that the wolves had disappeared.

They're coming.

The Old Man turned to look at the downed power tower. This tower was more crumpled and bent than the one on the other side of the gorge. What it might provide in refuge wouldn't last long.

I am at the limit. There isn't much more in me.

He reached into his bandolier and took out the can of pitch. Bending down, he quickly collected some sticks and then piled them near a wall of dry tumbleweeds that had gathered against the side of the ruins of the power tower. He spread the pitch over the dry weeds and took out his matches. Using one match and then another he quickly had a fire going. Smoky heat waves rose into the afternoon heat. For a moment the Old Man broke out into a cold sweat as his vision blurred. He drank quickly from a bottle and threw it aside.

He reached into his waist belt and pulled out the pistol. Listening for the wolves above the crackle of the growing fire, he snatched up three smoldering sticks and threw them into other stands of weed and brush nearby. He grabbed another torch, and looking to the sides of the cliff for the wolves and not finding them, he dove into the smoking brush.

The smoke was thick and gray and smelled of desert mesquite. A good earthy smell that always reminded him of cooked meat.

Wolves, you're afraid of fire. Remember that.

He continued to light other stands of brush as he passed down a sandy track leading south. One of the wolves howled.

That sounded like the big one. You wolves might even get lost and burned up in the fire. It's a wall between you and me.

A wind picked up from the west, and when the Old Man looked back great walls of flame were leaping toward the highway east of his position. The Old Man began to light the bushes to his right as he pushed on to the south.

Soon I will have two walls. Then how will you find me, wolves?

Now the wind shifted to the east and it came at him in blowing gusts, leaping ahead of the brush he was running into and igniting. The smoke grew thick and tasted of sulfur. The Old Man began to choke and cough. He took off his shirt, tied it about his mouth, and moved off, hoping he was going south. The sun above him was obscured by gray smoke and drifting ash. It was too high in the sky for him to find a direction, so he hoped he was going south and not north. Away off he heard the wolves yelling back and forth. They seemed farther off to his right and behind him.

He came through a wire fence long blown down. He crossed it, stumbling in the thick acrid smoke. His huaraches landed on cracked and broken asphalt. He could see no more than a few feet at times, as ash and sparks mixed with gray smoke and the blown dust and sand of the desert wind.

Ahead of him, a large wide building with an arched roof and an opening to an inner darkness groaned in the gusts of the firestorm. It was an old aircraft hangar. The Old Man stumbled forward.

As he reached the entrance of the aircraft hangar, he heard the wolf behind him. Turning, he raised his pistol, but the fatigued arm felt foreign to him, felt like leaded weights tied and sent to the bottom of an ocean of mud.

It's the big one.

The Alpha came on hard, bounding fast out of the smoke and dust. His muzzle a rictus of hate and anger. His eyes burning with rage. The Old Man emptied the gun and felt a dry click on the sixth cylinder after five little cracks had cleared the barrel.

The wolf stumbled and then veered off to the left. The Old Man saw that the wolf was bleeding. The look of anger and rage was gone as the big wolf circled, looking down and then back again at the Old Man

The Old Man backed into the open darkness of the hangar, leaving the wolf to the firestorm.

CHAPTER 17

The big Alpha lay down on the cracked and broken tarmac of the old runway outside the hangar. The flames surrounded the downed fences and burned at the decades-dry wreckage of the place. The man had gone into the building. If he just rested he might still get him, thought the Alpha.

Where is the pack?

The killers appeared out of the smoke. One had been burned, its fur singed. The big Alpha had thought so. He'd heard him yelp in pain during the chase.

The killers padded forward. Their eyes taking in the scene. The big Alpha turned, leading their gaze toward the old hangar.

You should go in there and get him out. He can't have much left in him. We've run him to his hole.

But when he turned back, the killers were looking at him and he knew what would happen next. He had a memory of a distant day, high in the mountains. A memory of youth.

The two killers fell on him.

THE OLD MAN found a locked gate at the back of the hangar. His crowbar quickly snapped the lock and he moved on, shutting the gate behind him. He picked up another crowbar from a nearby bench containing an array of tools and wedged it into the clasps of the gate so the wolves couldn't force it open.

He lit a match and found himself in a toolshed at the back of a maintenance hangar. Outside, the wind began to howl as the fire-heated air rushed against the metal side of the building. It was getting hot.

The Old Man went quickly through the tools; most were old and brittle. Jars and cans that once contained fluids contained nothing more than powder and dust. When he smelled smoke, he looked back through the gate and saw debris piles near the entrance to the hanger igniting. Smoke and ash trails followed by dancing sparks were blowing into the hangar.

The Old Man went back into the darkness, lit another match, and made his way through shelves that had fallen like dominoes. They crumbled to dust as he climbed atop them. In the end, he wallowed waist high through rotten timber.

A perfect place for the brown spider.

This place is on fire. Would you rather burn or die of poison?

He remembered the death of Big Pedro.

At the back wall he found a door marked "Men" and smashed it inward with his crowbar, splintering the rotten wood. Inside he found a toilet, a urinal, and finally an industrial shower with a large grate beneath.

This might lead somewhere.

He pried out the grate, and the bolts gave away with a dusty *smuph* in the darkness. Below he could see an old sewer. He took his shirt from off his face and wrapped it around a piece of the broken door. He counted his matches as he lit the torch. He had three left.

The floor of the sewer below ran off toward the front of the hangar. The route he'd come from. It also continued in the opposite direction.

Maybe the sewer had once been disgusting. The two-year nuclear winter that followed the bombs had sent rushing torrents of black ash flushing through every hole and channel in the thaw that finally happened. Followed by forty years of abandonment, the sewer was relatively clean and dry.

Once inside, it was dark and quiet and only the guttering of the torch made any sound.

Above, the flames had gotten into the roof of the structure. Metal rivets twisted and popped.

I had better find a way out. This torch won't last long.

He began to walk toward what he hoped was south, going slowly, checking the floor and the ceiling. He didn't want to fall into any holes or cracks. The tunnel ran straight for a hundred yards then turned sharply to the right. After ten feet he came to a large grate that opened on a dark emptiness. He coughed and heard an echo. He put the torch down and worked at the rusty bolts of the grate and just as it gave way, falling outward into the blackness, his torch went out.

Blind, the Old Man waited as the grate clanged onto a floor not far down.

There could be light. A crack in the ceiling or some such.

After a moment, his eyes adjusted to the gloom and he could make out details. Soft orange light filtered down from a high circle in the ceiling. The air smelled of concrete. He edged his feet forward, checking for a drop beyond the grate. There was one. Below the circle of light, in the middle of the darkness, he could see a patch of dusty pavement.

He lit one of his matches and inspected the floor. Behind him, a loud rending of metal was followed by a crash. A hot gust of wind rushed down at his back seconds later, and the match went out.

Now I have two matches.

How much of the floor did you see?

Not enough. I can't remember.

The Old Man got down on his hands and knees and edged toward the drop. He looked hard into the darkness below. Moving his hands about, he looked for something to toss onto the floor below, but the floods had swept the tunnel clear. He took a water bottle and emptied it. The water felt warm and did little to quench his thirst. His back and shoulder muscles spasmed painfully as he lifted his head to drain the bottle.

Maybe you have hurt yourself.

He dropped the empty water bottle into the darkness below and heard it immediately bounce around on the floor.

The ground is not far.

Gently he lowered himself down and found the floor far sooner than he expected. He swept the ground, feeling for the water bottle but it was gone. Cautiously he walked toward the circle of light below the opening in the ceiling high above.

Looking up he could tell it was a manhole. High above. On a street maybe. He could see nothing beyond its thin light.

How do I get up there?

There are still the wolves to consider.

The Old Man turned in a circle.

The room is big. A cave almost. Somewhere there must be a ladder to the manhole.

Moving cautiously, he used his hands to find the far wall. Once he found it he moved along the sides of the wall until he came to a rung mounted there. He pulled on it and the rung tore loose from the wall with a rotten metallic *puff* of dust and concrete. He found the next one higher up and again the rung came out in bits of concrete.

I cannot trust the others.

Someone's poor workmanship has made this place your grave.

There is another way out.

He continued along the wall. He came to one corner, then another, and halfway down the wall, the opening he had come through. Another corner and halfway down the next wall he found a new opening. It was darker than the rest of the room and he felt a cool draft of air.

He lit a match and scanned the dark ahead. It was a large tunnel with a channel running down the center of it. Just inside the wall were written large black letters that trailed off into the darkness.

He checked the entrance to the tunnel for signs or a placard that might indicate where the tunnel went and just as the match was about to burn the tips of his fingers, he moved to the other side of the entrance looking for some kind of sign that might indicate the purpose of the tunnel. On the floor a pile of boxes were stacked in a corner. Then the match went out.

Damn.

He stood still in the darkness.

I am down to my last match. What were those boxes? I saw letters. Like the military. A long series of letters and numbers.

It could be debris. Just empty boxes piled in a corner.

But the floods after the thaw would have swept them away.

They swept them here. Here is "away."

I have to check.

It is your last match. If the boxes contain nothing then you will be stuck. You will have to climb the rungs.

I will light part of the boxes on fire. I can tear off a flap.

He moved next to where he thought he had seen the boxes in the last moments of match light. When at first he didn't find them he panicked fearing he'd imagined the boxes. Soon his waving hands caught the side of a box.

Cardboard.

Watch out for the brown spider.

He ran his hands over the box. It seemed dusty but whole.

No floods have touched this box.

The four flaps were open and he gently tore one away.

He took out his last match. A nightmare of dropping the match or even breaking it, flashed across his mind. He shut out the evil thought and took hold of the match between his thumb and forefinger.

He struck the match and lit the flap.

There were three boxes on the floor. Military boxes. He had seen their kind before. Such things were often found salvaging.

"MRE" was written on the side and then a long serial number. He tore the other three flaps off the top box and made a small fire. Nearby he found a tumbleweed that had fallen into the sewer and broke it up, adding it to the tiny flames.

It won't last long.

He went to the top box and looked in. Three brown plastic packages lay on the bottom. He had also seen these before. In the early days. MREs. Survival rations.

The second box contained a five-quart plastic canteen that felt full. It was wrapped in camouflage material and had fasteners.

It must attach to a pistol belt.

A couple of wool blankets lay beneath the canteen but when the Old Man shook them out he found a centipede. He slammed his huarache down on it angrily.

He ripped up the two boxes and added them to the already fading fire. He pulled the third box close to him.

The centipede looked dead.

It is now.

He added it to the fire just to be sure.

He opened the box. Inside he found a military flashlight and many batteries. He also found a small penknife.

He tried the flashlight. It was dead. He unscrewed the bottom of the flashlight and threw the dead batteries off into the darkness and tried two new ones. A cone of yellow light erupted cleanly into the darkness ending in an oval against the wall. He had a flashlight.

The fire guttered to wispy ashes. The Old Man sat in the cool darkness for a moment and then clicked on the light with a dry chuckle.

CHAPTER 18

MAN IS INCAPABLE OF PEACE. Carved into the concrete wall of the old sewer, each blackened letter rose three feet high. Someone had used a blowtorch to etch the message against the wall of the tunnel that led away from the big room.

The Old Man's light played across the words as he considered their meaning.

He'd eaten an entire MRE. It had been two days since the snake on the road. The water in the canteen tasted stale and he poured it out, filling it again with the water from his bottles.

He ran his fingers over the letters. The blowtorch had left melted waves when it traveled over the surface of the wall.

He had a steady hand.

How do you know it's a "he"?

It feels like a "he."

Someone did this after the bombs. Not long ago. Maybe five years. Ten at the most.

How do you know?

The boxes.

He is right. Was right. Man is incapable of peace. What's left of the world confirms that.

So he came down here. Spent all the time that you and the village have been surviving, barely, and carved these words no one will ever see?

These words will be here long after I have gone. Long after my granddaughter's granddaughters. The hieroglyphs in the pyramids were thousands of years old.

So why? Why do this?

To tell the story. Maybe a warning.

To who?

Whoever comes next.

So who's to say he's right?

He is, I guess. I don't know that I will be around to argue.

Do you agree?

The Old Man considered the world above. The frozen ground after the bombs. The ones who died of radiation sickness. The hunger. What it looked like when the United States ended in his rearview mirror that day at the beginning of his present life.

He rolled up the MREs and the bullet-less pistol along with the empty bottles in his blanket. He added the other two green wool blankets after inspecting them thoroughly for more centipedes. He shined his new flashlight down the tunnel, enjoying its power and clarity. There were more words written farther along.

I wonder what else he had to say.

The Old Man continued down the tunnel and when he came to the next message he read: THERE CAN NEVER BE TWO ANSWERS TO THE SAME QUESTION.

Further on he read: WE DIDN'T BELIEVE THOSE WHO HAD SWORN TO KILL US.

WE TRIED TO FIRE GOD.

POWER IS NEVER SATISFIED.

BEWARE OF ANYONE WHO WANTS TO MAKE DECISIONS FOR YOU.

PEOPLE WILL TELL LIES TO GET WHAT THEY WANT.

A DIFFERENCE OF OPINION LEADS TO DEATH.

CITIES BURN DOWN.

FREE WILL WAS THE GREATEST GIFT EVER OFFERED. GOD IS NOT RESPONSIBLE FOR WHAT WE DID WITH IT. WE ARE.

EVERY PLACE IS THE SAME.

EVERYTHING YOU DO WILL BE FORGOTTEN.

CHILDREN ARE THE ONLY THINGS YOU LEAVE BEHIND.

CHILDREN ARE SMARTER THAN YOU THINK.

HATE FIRE AND OTHER THINGS THAT HURT YOU.

HATE IS NOT WRONG WHEN WHAT YOU HATE IS WRONG.

HISTORY HAS LIED TO US.

THE GOOD GUYS DIDN'T WIN.

DON'T LET SOMEONE SPEND MONEY WHO NEVER EARNED IT.

DON'T LET ANYONE BUT A SOLDIER TELL YOU HOW TO FIGHT A WAR.

IF YOU ABSOLUTELY HAVE TO GO TO WAR, KILL EVERYONE.

ROCK STARS, ACTORS, AND POLITICIANS DON'T ACTUALLY DO ANYTHING.

TEACHERS, ARCHITECTS, AND MOTHERS KNOW A LOT MORE THAN YOU THINK.

THE YOUNG DISCOVERING THE WORLD FEEL LIKE CHRISTOPHER COLUMBUS. THEY IGNORE THE INDIANS WHO HAVE BEEN HERE FOR THOUSANDS OF YEARS.

PEER PRESSURE IS WHEN YOU DECIDE TO LOB A FEW WARHEADS AT THIS WEEK'S NAZI BECAUSE CNN TOLD YOU TO.

IT ONLY TAKES A BULLET TO SOLVE A PROBLEM LIKE NAPOLEON, HITLER, POL POT, STALIN, SADDAM HUSSEIN.

PEOPLE DON'T HATE EACH OTHER. THEY HATE EACH OTHER'S IDEAS.

BEWARE OF THE SELF-LOATHING GOVERNMENT.

And finally: VISIT THE LIBRARY AT FORT TUCSON.

CHAPTER 19

On the other side of the manhole at the end of the hall of messages, the Old Man found a moonlit night. The air smelled of desert and sage. The cool wind that blew through the place had a faint tinge of char, though the fire that had happened here happened long ago.

Blackened wooden frames rose up on all four sides of the intersection. Desert sand had blown across the streets. He walked to a mailbox and sat down with his back against it. He hadn't slept since the night under the bridge.

How many days ago?

Who cares.

What about the wolves?

The tunnel went for several miles. If they survived the fire I doubt they'll come this far looking for me. Anyway I am too tired to care.

He unrolled his blankets on the sidewalk and placed his items on them. He started a small fire from charwood he found inside the ruins of a building. For a moment, standing there, he wondered what the use of the building had once been.

What was the story of this place? If I knew, there might be salvage and then I could head home.

But the fire had made it unrecognizable and whatever had once gone on there was lost.

He opened an second MRE and ate Chicken à la King. He put hot sauce on it. He'd found a little bottle of Tabasco inside a packet that contained plasticware and a book of matches. He drank some more water and added wood to the fire. He rolled up in his own blanket and one of the wool ones.

I wonder about Fort Tucson.

What . . .

HE DIDN'T MOVE the whole night. When he awoke, his side was numb and stiff. His shoulders ached with hot fire and his wrists throbbed. His chest felt heavy, and when he sat up, a morning cough turned into a prolonged hacking in which his vision narrowed to a tiny pinpoint. Each convulsion caused the needles in his shoulders to scream with anger.

The fire had gone out long ago.

It's good the wolves didn't find me. I might not have woken up for the feast.

For a moment he was afraid he might be sick.

Have I gone too far? Exhausted myself?

But he sat up and then got to his feet. He drank water and walked up and down the sidewalk. He considered plundering the mailbox but he was too tired and sore.

He banged on its side. It sounded hollow.

He rolled up his things slowly and mixed a packet of cocoa in a water bottle with some water from the canteen. He ate a cookie.

I feel better.

It was silent in the stubbly remains of the burnt town.

This must be the place I was thinking of.

It burned to the ground. Long ago. Mirrored Sunglasses was right.

How could he be right if he was blind?

Maybe he wasn't blind.

The Old Man began heading south down the street. At the next intersection, a half-burnt sign that had fallen down among the charred support beams of a building looked familiar.

I know those letters.

But those are just the middle or last ones.

For a long moment he tried to remember what business they were associated with, but in the end he couldn't.

Coffee, maybe.

How long has it been since you had coffee?

Years. I remember the night I married my wife. Someone gave us a can. Something salvaged from an RV deep inside the Great Wreck. I can't remember who.

Floyd? Big Pedro?

I can't remember. But the next morning after the ceremony, I woke up early. She was still asleep. I made coffee and woke her up. I remember lying on our bed in the shack, late morning because I didn't go out that day to salvage, the village said I couldn't. I remember thinking: So this is life? This isn't bad. Sitting with a woman who loves me. Having coffee.

I think I got over the world ending that morning.

You should tell your granddaughter about that memory.

Yes. I should.

The Old Man looked again at the sign amid the burned ruins. Once it had sat atop the building. When the fire collapsed the roof it had come crashing down.

It was a newer business. Toward the end of civilization. A chain. This town was old, so I must be on the outskirts of it. They built these new ones on the outskirts. Maybe there'll be some salvage farther on.

He walked deeper into the ruins. He passed old cars sitting on rusty rims that had burned in the fire. There were no skeletons in them. In one he found a pair of dice that had melted to a dashboard.

When Phoenix and Tucson went, people must have run away, fearing the radiation.

At noon after wandering down a long street of burnt wood and sand, he came to an open square. He sat down and ate some peanut butter from the MRE. It was dry.

There's nothing here.

In his mind he tried to picture the town. The highway that ran back to the village would be on the south side of it. It was here that the two major highways once met and continued on south.

I've come a long way and I haven't found anything. I am still cursed.

By now the village must think you're dead.

He wondered if that were true.

What is the story of these places? I used to be so good at finding their stories. I could find a shed or trailer or a wreck and know where the salvage was hidden. I was good at it then. What happened to me? I should have gone through that mailbox.

You're not cursed, you're lazy.

What about the writing in the tunnel?

Maybe it was done before the bombs.

The boxes?

Maybe they don't go together.

Here is what I think. Ready? Someone lived here. Lives here maybe even now. Or nearby. They wrote the words down in the tunnel as a warning to whomever comes next.

Whomever?

Not us. We are finished. We are just the survivors. But someday a society will happen. He left them a message. Telling them where we went wrong.

As he saw it?

Yes.

So what?

Down one of the streets he spied a building more intact than the rest. It had walls. He stood up and adjusted his bandolier of blankets and moved off toward the building, the sound of his huaraches the only noise in the desert air.

So what? I will tell you. Whatever he made those carvings with was a piece of equipment the village could use. It was some sort of industrial blowtorch. The village could make things with a tool like that.

Those use gas.

He must have lots of it. He's out wasting it writing on walls. He must have loads of it. The boxes of supplies he left behind? That's not a man who is worried about tomorrow's rice.

He came to the building at the end of the street. It was made of cinder blocks. He turned the corner and came upon more buildings made of the same material.

The fire had destroyed everything inside. But the shade was nice.

These walls are still good. A roof and I could live here.

Broken bottles and glass littered the ground.

This must have been a liquor store. The bottles exploded in the fire.

Once he guessed it was a liquor store he found the debris where the counter must have been. A melted plastic register at the bottom of it. He saw a few coins encased within the hardened plastic.

Whoever the writer is, he must have supplies. Maybe the village could trade with him. Or maybe he is lonely and might like to come live with us.

He walked down the row of burned-out concrete buildings.

This was some sort of market he said at one, a small one. Maybe that one was a clothing store. Farther on he found a barbershop. He could tell because the big iron chairs had survived the fire. He combed the store and found a pair of blackened scissors. He tucked them in his blanket and moved on. The last building was large. It was on the corner of the block.

This was an old movie theater. Built before I was a child. This must have been the center of town back in the old days. Not a megaplex like near the end. This was a theater with only one screen.

He walked in and found the auditorium. The seats had all burned and the screen was gone. All that remained of the projectionist booth were the two square windows through which the projector had shown. The floor had collapsed onto the concession stand.

For a long while the Old Man stood in the quiet, listening to the ticks the debris made as the heat of the day began to fade.

I think I will rest here today and tonight. It's probably best to find the highway in the morning and head west back to the village. There isn't any salvage between here and there.

He set up his camp and gathered wood. He spent the rest of the day resting in the shade. He went to bed early and awoke after midnight. The night air was cool and he smelled rain coming.

In the morning I will find where the two highways meet and head back along the Eight to the village.

LATE IN THE morning he found the Y where the two ruined highways merged into one heading south to Tucson. He also found the remains of six bodies stretched out on charred wooden boards, each in the shape of an X. Their skin leathery and mummified by the desert heat. Their socketless eyes and openmouthed rictus made the Old Man step back.

Had they been alive when they'd been left here?

All the bodies faced south and east toward Tucson.

On the ground, thousands of rust-colored handprints were stamped into the old pavement of the highway.

Beyond the bodies, melted into the road in the same blackened writing from the tunnel, was the word SAFETY. A large arrow pointed down along the center of the highway toward Tucson.

CHAPTER 20

The stretch between the Y and Tucson was a long road. It was interrupted by only one landmark he could remember. Of all the names of the past he'd forgotten, he remembered the name Picacho Peak. It was a tall, rocky outcrop that rose straight up out of the desert floor. A lone mountain in an expanse of flatland alongside the highway. It lay between the Old Man and Tucson.

The Old Man stood at the Y considering the messages and their conflict.

The bodies are old, maybe a few years. The carving in the road, who knew.

But the bodies are newer than the carving.

He started down the on-ramp leading to Tucson.

"Safety" means salvage.

Unless whoever left the bodies went there also.

I must go and see. I know already, this will give me no peace unless I have an answer to it.

Yes, but you could go back to the village. Do you need the answer bad enough to lose your life?

He didn't answer himself and instead walked for a long time that morning and into the afternoon. He passed road signs that had not blown down but had been scoured clean by violent sandstorms. The remains of a gas station were his home for the night. It had been looted, and when he checked the tanks they were bone dry. This caused him to wonder.

Gasoline has other uses than just to run cars.

At twilight he ate a packet of spaghetti and meatballs from the third MRE. He ate pound cake for dessert.

You are making a pig of yourself. You won't be used to having less.

In the night, after the fire died, he heard something in the bushes outside the station. He lay still and after a few moments it was gone.

In the morning he ate a light breakfast and drank some instant cocoa from the MRE. The morning air smelled like rain, though there were only a few clouds to the south.

The blue desert sky was wide and the land a flat brown. He could see for thirty to fifty miles at a time. On the far horizon, dark mountain ranges cut jagged borders against the sky. He knew it was time for the monsoons and that when they came it would be very dangerous on the desert floor. A flash flood could come upon him from out of nowhere.

I should stay out of gullies and ravines. Also, don't sleep in dry riverbeds.

At noon he caught two more rattlesnakes on the road and carried them along for another few hours. He would roast them over the fire at dusk.

By now he could see Picacho Peak in the distance. Between lay the burned remains of another small gas station city off to the left-hand side of the highway and a wild pecan orchard on the right.

CHAPTER 21

Himbradda led his small band down through the Sonoran Desert plains, skirting its eastern edge. They were many days ahead of the main body of the People. The People were returning to Picacho Peak to start their ceremonies again. The Professor had ordered the People to return to their most sacred place. Picacho Peak. So Himbradda had been sent ahead. To see if the Dragon still lived there.

Himbradda was very afraid, had always been afraid. The woman that delivered him into the world didn't even know she was pregnant until he appeared nine months after she had been raped one morning, as the People grazed on wild beans and desert peyote. She lay under the hot morning sun, being raped in the rough yellow grass as she had been many times before and many times after.

When Himbradda arrived she carried him with her. Because of his withered left arm, he was accepted as part of the People and followed in the wake of their wanderings. He was fed on wild beans, pecans, un-cooked coyote, and sometimes the warriors' peyote. He even tasted the meat of other children, perfect unblemished children. Children not of the People. Once those children reached the bottom of the drop below Picacho Peak, then all of the People could take what could be grabbed and torn away.

Himbradda had been raped and he had raped. He had been hit and he had hit. He had been beaten and he had beaten. If he had known how to count, the number twenty would have represented the number of children he had begotten, the number thirty-two for the amount of people he had killed, and the number fifteen for how old he was.

Regardless of his withered left arm and crooked teeth, he was almost beautiful. He had a strong build and a taut hulking physique. Long hair hung over one of his green eyes. His good arm rippled with muscles at the biceps, triceps, and forearm. In his good hand he carried, dragging mostly by the long iron bar, a parking meter that had been taken from the hot ruins of Phoenix. Most of the thirty-two dead had met the parking meter.

Nu-ah, who dragged himself everywhere because of the missing legs he'd never known, eased down from his watch-place atop the tall sign that still read GASOLINE. He crawled quickly across the parking lot to Himbradda, who sat in the shady petals of an exploded propane tank. Himbradda felt absently at the running sore underneath the hair of his scalp, while Nu-ah made whispers that indicated a lone man came toward them on the road from Phoenix.

The People had known Phoenix. It was the northern extent of their ranging, and some winters found them rooting around its slag heaps and twisted metal, finding bits of glass for their weapons. It was then that the sores appeared along with the sickness. They had stayed too long and now it was time to head south, all the way into Mexico.

A lone man was prey but seldom encountered. If he continued down this road, thought Himbradda, then the man would reach Picacho Peak and the Dragon. That would make Himbradda's work easier. To see if the man brought out the Dragon.

He grunted that Nu-ah should return to his hiding place and watch the man. This was the last thing Nu-ah expected. He'd hoped, because of his sharp eyes, he might get a piece of the man's liver when the small band took the loner. A reward for finding him among the burning brilliance of the desert floor.

Nu-ah hesitated. Was he being left out of the kill?

Himbradda swiveled the head of his parking meter, grinding it in the faded asphalt for Nu-ah to understand.

Once Nu-Ah was back in his place Himbradda stood up shouldering his club. He tucked his withered left hand into his torn overalls. The overalls had been pulled off the body of a man in Mexico, after the People had overrun and destroyed a small settlement of salvagers. Himbradda grunted for the others to follow.

Eating the man and then having their woman in the dust of the highway afterward would have been a pleasant afternoon. But the Professor said that Himbradda must know if the Dragon still lives.

Gutch and Ha rose to their feet as Himbradda loped off into the desert behind the sign, looking for a crevice they might hide in.

Gutch pulled on the rope he wore about his waist, dragging their girl to her feet. It had been good of the Professor to give them a woman for the journey; otherwise Himbradda would have attacked them all. It was good that they could have her whenever they wanted. Even if she was blind and had to be led with the rope everywhere. He pulled savagely on the old tow rope wound about her neck. Fresh blood ran down her naked sunburned body. But she gave no cry, showed no intelligence, and only followed them into the desert waste beyond the remains of the station.

THE OLD MAN reached the wild orchard of pecans at nightfall. He didn't like the place. But even more so he didn't like the violence of the old gas station on the other side of the highway.

Looks like a war took place there.

But the orchard was not much better. The sky turned a burnt orange as the sun disappeared, and the silhouettes of the trees looked like fingers clutching at the last of the day. Large crows roosted in the trees and the Old Man was not comforted by them.

He built a small fire and roasted the two snakes he'd found on the highway, eating a little and saving the rest for the next day.

You will run out of water soon if you don't find some.

It was dark now, and still he could see the fingers of the trees clutching at the night sky. He thought about moving on, but then remembered the wolves and thought he might get up into the trees if they returned.

He lay down but it took him a long time to get to sleep and when he did he woke often. Toward the deepest part of the night, the crows burst out in terror and the Old Man heard them 'caw, caw, cawing' angrily. They sounded like a woman who was angry or crying out in pain.

He lay in the dark for a long time after the crows had stopped. In the silence, the memory of the crows' anger came back to him, and he thought he faintly heard a woman's cry, but only once and so little of it, that upon reflection he wondered if he'd heard it at all.

At dawn he was glad to be away from the place. He calculated that he might reach the base of the peak by midmorning and so he walked fast, chewing bits of snake as he went.

HIMBRADDA FOLLOWED THE Old Man, leaving Ha to lead the woman, and Nu-ah to crawl on his trail as he shadowed the Old Man who seemed in a hurry to meet the Dragon. The body of Gutch, his head beaten to a pulp, lay in the crevice where they had spent the night. He had been at the girl while Himbradda tried to get close to the campfire of the Old Man. The crows, hearing her cries as Gutch worked at her had almost given him away and Himbradda had fled in terror at the ruckus of the evil birds. Himbradda's terror turned to anger, and when he made it back to the crevice, he bashed in the skull of the sleeping Gutch and had the girl for reasons he knew not.

Himbradda, crouching in the soft morning light, followed the Old Man, who arrived soon at the most sacred birthplace of the People and the lair of the Dragon.

CHAPTER 22

Picacho Peak's three peaks rose up in rocky defiance over the Old Man. Like a great ship beached in the desert, its tallest point, a mast, soared overhead. The Old Man craned his neck back to see the summit but could not make out anything there.

Another abandoned gas station town sat astride the main highway in the shadow of the peak and the Old Man inspected the ruins. Fire had long ago collapsed the roof, but inside the main building he found walls covered in rust-red handprints. Older writing, done after the fire in paint, lay underneath the handprints.

"Laws of the People" adorned one wall. On another, "History of the People."

The Old Man stepped across the rotten charwood of the room and read the one marked "Laws of the People."

THERE ARE NO LAWS
THERE IS NO GOD
THERE IS NO SUCH THING AS WRONG
DON'T HATE ANYTHING
YOU ARE THE CENTER OF THE UNIVERSE

The Old Man stepped to the side wall and read "History of the People."

"On the day after we come. All those who heard and seen Phoenix go up in smoke and ash and those who seen the Cloud over Tucson. For many days we sat and cried. We didn't no where to go. Then Professor said 'This is our paradise.' He gave us the laws and now at the end of our old world our perfect world has begun. It was laws that destroyed the old. It were hate that killed everyone. Now nothing is wrong and we is happy. We the People."

But where did you go?

You know where they went.

He thought of the corpses stretched on the boards back at the Y.

The Old Man dropped his bandolier and stroked the whiskers he needed to shave. He took out the canteen and drank sparingly.

Laws. Rules. I think that's what lets people get along. It must have been shocking once someone wanted something that was yours. Or murdered someone you loved.

The Old Man stepped out of the building. He walked toward the peak wondering if he should do what he was thinking he ought to do next.

If you fall.

Stop.

You won't make it out of here alive.

Stop. I can't think like that. I need to get to the top of the peak and take a look. I might be able to see Tucson from there.

They said they saw a cloud. That's the answer.

Sometimes you've got to see a thing for yourself to know it.

He walked up a slope of scree and reached the jagged face of the peak. While it had looked sheer from far away, now he saw the cracks where he might make his way. Beyond that, leading to the highest peak, there seemed to be a trail he might take most of the way up.

He turned back to the valley, seeing the unbroken road heading south toward Tucson. The world was divided into blue sky and dusty orange dirt. Then he saw the flagpole and two flags hanging in the still desert air farther down the highway, near the base of the tallest peak. He hadn't seen it from the ruins of the gas station town.

He slid down off the scree and walked in the afternoon shadow cast by the peak until he came to the flagpole.

"On June 3rd, 2061, a great battle was fought here at Picacho Peak. The 6th Troop, 1st Cav, 'The Black Horse' out of Fort Tucson, engaged and defeated the numerically superior main body of the Horde. This action was taken to stop the Human Sacrifice being conducted atop Picacho Peak, in which the leaders of the Horde would toss human children from atop the highest peak. During the battle and in the days that followed, over 10,000 enemies were estimated to have been killed in action against the Black Horse. They are buried at the base of the Peak and it is hoped that the Horde has scattered and will not return to this place for fear of the Black Horse."

—Sergeant Major John Preston,
6th Troop, 1st Cav, "Black Horse"

THE PLAQUE AT the base of the flagpole was a large piece of beaten sheet metal. The engraved words had been done in the same blowtorch-writing as those he had seen in the sewers of the burned-up village and on the highway at the Y. Above him, on the flagpole, a slight afternoon breeze out of the southeast snapped the tattered American flag to life. Drifting in the breeze below it, a yellow flag with a black stripe and the black silhouette of a horse's head waved gently.

CHAPTER 23

Himbradda had watched long enough. The scrawny Old Man had violated the houses where Himbradda, even as a child, knew he must not go. When the People had lived in the shadow of the peak, there were two places they did not go. The hut of the Professor and the top of the peak.

Himbradda had waited for the Dragon to come. He had seen the Dragon years ago. He had seen it come upon the people in the night, belching great bursts of fire that exploded into the midst of the People. When the People had tried to rally and drive the Dragon away it had spit hot bolts that left gaping holes in all the fierce ones whom Himbradda had hoped one day to be like. But that had been a long time ago when Himbradda was a boy.

Then the Old Man walked toward the cliff, as if to climb to the most sacred place. The place where the babies had come falling from the sky, rejected, to crash down onto the rocks as a gift to the hungry people. Himbradda remembered those days as though a forgotten festival of better times.

If the People could return, then all would be right again. The festivals, the feeding. Still the Dragon had not come out against the Old Man.

Himbradda, hiding in the tall rocks, watched the Old Man. Ha and Nu-Ah and the blind girl with the swollen belly waiting, not breathing, waiting.

When the Old Man moved on, sliding down the scree of the sacred peak and disappearing into the great field where the people had lived, where Himbradda had been born, where his earliest memories had taken place, the Dragon still had not come. Himbradda knew the Dragon must be dead now.

As all thirty-two of his skull-crushed victims had never moved again so, surely, he reasoned, must someone have crushed the Dragon's head.

He made grunts and noises and hugged himself, then pointed east. Nu-ah and Ha would return to the People.

He grabbed dirt and threw it toward the peak.

They understood. They were to bring the People back. The Dragon was dead. They both turned toward the blind girl with the swollen belly.

Himbradda waved them away. Nu-ah, grabbing Ha's chest, rode piggy-back and soon the pair were leaping away to the east to find the People.

Himbradda hefted his club to his shoulder and set off at a hunched run for the Old Man. He would leave the girl here, she wouldn't move. He would finish the Old Man and have his meat all to himself. Then he could return to the girl for what he wanted next.

TUCSON MUST HAVE survived.

The Old Man, staring at the flag and the plaque, looked toward the south. To the east clouds were bunching up fast and the Old Man knew monsoon season had come.

It will be dangerous now.

He heard the scream and whirled in time to see Himbradda standing at the top of the rise that led into the small bowl of the field beneath the peak.

To the Old Man, Himbradda appeared to be a large man with one huge arm waving a club in the air. He looked filthy and unkempt. For a moment, the dark savage was silhouetted against a gingham sky of soft blue dotted with white puffy clouds. The savage screamed in rage, whirl-ing the club above his head and then he loped down upon the Old Man.

The Old Man turned and ran in the opposite direction. At the end of the field was a long fence twisted and bent by time. The Old Man made the fence and heard Himbradda screaming hoarsely in the hot still air, his shoeless feet slapping the hard red dirt behind him.

At the fence, the Old Man ran along its twisting path, coming to a pile of tumbleweeds that had built up against it. He dropped to the ground and crawled into a warren of weeds. The savage was no more than a few feet behind him now.

His world turned to brown dust and dry brush as he crawled farther and farther into a pile of tumbleweeds that had accumulated over forty years. Behind him, Himbradda tore through the maze, grunting and keening all at once.

This man is no more than an animal.

He turned right and pulled more weeds behind him as he crawled forward, bursting into the open. He had maybe a moment or two before the savage would be free of the weed pile.

The Old Man looked around. He was near the great highway that bent itself toward Tucson. He crossed the road and dropped to the ground on the far side. There was little cover.

Above him, on the road, the savage screamed in pain.

If he makes the right choice in the next moment, I'm going to know what it feels like when that club comes crashing down on my head. If not, then maybe I have a chance.

Himbradda screamed again but farther away, on the opposite side of the road.

He must be circling the pile looking for me.

The Old Man slithered backward down the dirt embankment and headed south alongside the road. Himbradda yelled raggedly, almost crying. The Old Man took off his huaraches to lessen the sound of his steps.

He had not gone ten steps before the thing he had hoped would not happen, happened.

The scorpion stung him on his instep. It happened a second after he felt his foot crush its peanut-shell carcass. White-hot pain shot up his leg, and the Old Man stuck one dusty huarache in his mouth and bit down on the scream. His vision went red as his eyes fought a black tunnel that seemed to crush the world about him.

He looked down, praying it was not one of the baby white scorpions.

They are the most poisonous.

Instead he was rewarded with a frightening-looking scorpion. Large, black, and crushed in the dirt.

These old ones have less poison.

They are cursed like you.

Quiet.

He hobbled along the ravine hoping the savage man wouldn't check this side of the road. If he did, there would be no way he could outrun him now.

The pistol has no bullets.

I know. But he doesn't know that.

The pain is blinding.

He may not even know what a gun is. I think if he finds me he won't give me the time to explain it to him. It won't make a difference.

The Old Man limped farther down the descending embankment below the ruined highway.

The first drops of rain began to splatter in the red dust as the Old Man looked at his foot. Large glistening drops settled on the thick dust, remaining globes of water for a moment, then dissipating. His foot, though not swollen, tingled. It felt foreign to him.

He worked his way down the side of a broken bridge that once ran over a ravine. The rock-littered embankment descended into a dry streambed and then rose to meet the other side.

Above him, he could still hear the wild man screaming hoarsely in the desert air.

There's no time to treat the foot.

But you must. You must clean the wound and elevate it.

The Old Man had seen many stings and been stung many times. This one was not bad. It wasn't timely, also. He reached the riverbed as the rain began to fall with hard wet thumps against the dry ground.

This place will be dangerous soon.

Hurry.

He began to climb the rocky embankment, dragging the foot.

You rest for a while, foot. I'll give you that.

The wild savage screamed, having come to the end of the broken bridge and seeing the Old Man dragging himself up the far embankment. Near the dark range of hills to the east, thunder cracked and a moment later a flash of lightning lit the darkening sky. Toward the west, hot blue sunshine ground away at the sandy desert beyond Picacho Peak.

The savage looked down, considered jumping, then disappeared. A moment later he returned, running and grunting as he scrambled down the embankment on the side of the bridge. Halfway down he caught his foot on a jagged volcanic rock and yelped painfully.

The rain was coming down hard when the Old Man reached the summit of the broken highway. On the far side, the screaming savage raced down the embankment, kicking up dust in his wake.

If the rain had come earlier, I could have lost him in the ravines.

It's still your only chance.

It will be dangerous. The water will come fast, pushing everything. I could get caught.

Better than getting caught in the open by the savage and his club.

The Old Man ran, dragging the tingling leg. The fire was gone but the foot was tender.

Forget it.

Farther down he could see a crack in the highway. When he reached it he lowered himself into it. The Old Man raised his head above the lip and spotted the savage. It had taken the savage longer than the Old Man would have expected for a young man to ascend the embankment. But now the Old Man could see why. Dragging the club with the one arm while the withered left arm remained tucked into the dirty overalls must have slowed him down.

The Old Man dropped into the dark crack in the highway and inched along the wall toward the ravine it opened into.

He could hear the slap of feet coming closer and then saw the figure of the savage above him. Screaming gibberish, the savage smashed the parking meter club into the pavement, sending bits of stone and sand down on the Old Man.

Years after the bombs, an earthquake had shaken the village. This crack must have been caused by the quake.

Mud began to sluice down upon him from above. The rain came down heavily on the dry desert floor. Wet hair hanging in his face, the savage raved in gibberish at the Old Man below.

You will need to come down here to get me.

The Old Man squeezed farther along the crevice. Then it opened into a jagged ravine that jogged off toward the south. The Old Man, who had felt a touch of closeness in the tight spaces of the crack, breathed deeply and coughed.

I said you will have to come get me, boy.

It's the only way I can get rid of you.

The Old Man limped off along the ravine in the opposite direction from where Himbradda stood at the cliff's edge.

Maybe he won't come. That would be for the best. For both of us.

Another flash of lightning lit the afternoon as Himbradda stood silent. Tension and worry contorted the snarl of his lips as he worked at crooked teeth with his tongue, thinking what to do.

The Old Man was just disappearing around the far bend of the ravine to the south, when Himbradda threw himself down the cliff at a run. His legs worked hard to keep ahead of the fall. His torso fell forward, ahead of his running feet. Then the muddy walls became too thick, catching at his struggling feet. He tumbled forward smashing into the floor of the ravine, hearing a dull crack inside himself while emitting a heavy grunt as the air was driven from him all at once.

A moment later he came to, in the mud of the ravine, unable to breathe. He rolled onto his back waving his club with the brawny good arm. He would scream at the sky. Scream as he always had at the hardness of a life he barely understood. The screaming had always helped. But no sound came out. His head thudded and he could feel a tremble in the ground. Moments later his breath returned.

He rose shakily to his knees looking for the Old Man who had gone past the bend.

He would have him soon.

The wall of water and debris that hit Himbradda from behind started in the hills to the east. The surge had been growing in force with mud and debris as the water ran off the desert floor and into the ravine. When it finally arrived upon Himbradda, it slapped him down with mindless force and drove his body through the swirling chaos. All the debris of a broken world moved farther down the ancient riverbed.

THE OLD MAN heard the flash flood coming, heard its low rumble through the riverbed behind him, heard the dry snap of branches above the din. Turning, he saw the sudden churning rapids. He reached the side wall and found it too steep to climb.

He removed the belt that had once been an extension cord. He tied a loop in its end and cast it above the lip of the ravine just beyond the reach of his fingertips. When he pulled on it the loop came flying back at him.

You are stupid.

Run!

Wait. There is no chance if I run. This is the only way.

He dropped his bandolier of blankets. Thick currents of cold water rose around his feet. It felt soothing to the wound in his foot but the cold was terrifying as the water began to rise sharply. He knotted the belt in his hand, stepped back, and rushed at the wall, leaping for its edge. He dangled, grasping the edge, as the thunder of the debris wave erupted with a rumble at the far end of the ravine he had just come down. With one hand holding on to the edge, he waved his other hand across the ground above the lip, and finding a root, he quickly passed his cord underneath it. Just before the surge hit him, his other hand grasped the loose end of the extension cord. The flood drove into his waist like a wild bull.

CHAPTER 24

He hung on as long as he could, but soon the walls of the ravine had turned to mud and began to collapse into the torrent. The Old Man heaved himself upward, even as the wall collapsed, and felt himself scrambling to stand. At last he kicked away from the collapsing mud and found himself breathing hard in a pool of water a few feet from the cliff's edge.

The sky was gray with rain. Wet slaps hit the mud about him, embracing him in a soft white noise. He turned skyward and opened his mouth, drinking what rainwater fell into it. After he'd filled a mouthful he would swallow. It tasted of iron. It was bitter and it burned his throat. He drank again.

You are a dead man.

Not yet.

Your stuff is gone. How will you survive?

I'm glad I didn't bring the book. Now when I return I can read it again.

He stood shakily. In his pocket was a soggy book of matches and the pliers. The rest had been carried off. Gone.

You are a dead man.

Not yet.

He walked for another few hours. The flooded ravine forked south and east. He headed south.

If Tucson still stands, I will see it tonight or tomorrow. That is my only hope.

His other voice did not reply.

The valley floor was filled with the violence of the flash floods, and at times he waded through pools and, at others, followed the course until he could jump across, knowing this was dangerous.

At one such crossing, the far side caved away at his sudden weight and all he could do was fall forward into the mud to keep from falling back into the torrent. He lay panting.

I am feeling very weak.

When was the last time you ate?

I can't remember. Maybe the snake.

Start looking for flint.

For a fire?

Yes.

I have nothing to eat.

Again his other voice was silent.

He forgot to look for flint, and when he had gone on another few hours, he stumbled and realized he'd been stumbling for some time.

There is nothing here.

You are beaten.

I am cursed.

That is the same.

I don't agree.

The sun came out and everything dried almost instantly. If there had been rain, rain in abundance, the evidence was hidden. Only the clean smell of air without dust betrayed the monsoon. The sun made him sleepy, and when he began to crawl, he remembered he must look for flint. Flint to make a fire. But again he forgot and soon it was night.

The wind came up and he found himself on hands and knees in a sandy depression. He heard a sound. A sound he knew. A sound he had heard in the village.

I will lie down for a few hours and then walk.

He slept the whole night. He dreamed that he was back in his shed, back among the village, listening to the desert wind move through the tin and corrugated metal that was the village. Waiting for morning. Waiting to go salvaging once more with his granddaughter. He kept waiting. He should get out of bed, he thought during the dream. Get out and get ready his tools and breakfast. Get ready for his granddaughter who would spend the day walking. Talking. Listening. It was she, of all the village, who had not given up on him. Just like the boy in the book. He was very excited just for those things. Not so much the salvage. But if they did find salvage, then of course that would be nice also. In the dream, he kept looking out the door of the shed to see if she was waiting. But it was still the middle of the night, dark and cold and clear with the stars like the broken glass east of the village. He had woken too early.

When he awoke it was light. The light was soft. Wind blew sand across his skin. The sound of the tall grass was the sound of a husky broom being swept purposefully in long strokes across a stone floor.

The tail of the airplane was white. It was tall, and it rose above the field of tall grass.

An airliner.

He stood slowly. His side ached where the flood had hit him. There were many tails. Like tombstones shifted slightly right, one to the next.

He moved through the waving grass and found himself standing on the concrete apron that girded the airport. Airplanes stretched away across the field, their metal groaning in the morning wind.

Marana Air Park. The airplane graveyard.

Of all the names from the past that you cannot remember, you remember this one?

My dad . . . was a pilot. He was an airline pilot. I haven't thought about that in years.

He walked forward.

The planes, all of them white, faded paint visible on some, stood like headstones. Large wings had collapsed. Some lay on their bellies. Their number stretched off into the distance.

Their doors sealed tombs.

If I had my crowbar, maybe I could get in.

What could there be of use inside?

He thought of electronics, seat cushions. Flotation devices. The galley. Maybe he could find a knife or a fire axe. Planes had fire axes. He remembered that from the many times his dad would take him to the cockpit where he worked.

He found the hangars that once stood watch over the graveyard of planes. They had fallen down. What tools or a crowbar he might have used to violate the tombs of the airplanes lay underneath and out of reach.

He walked toward the far end of the airfield.

These planes once crossed the world.

He thought of Hawaii. He had been five times. Flown there five times as a child. It was his dad's route. He and his mother in back. A vacation.

Had such a thing like that ever happened? He stood in the bright sunshine of the place. The wind was dying and the cemetery music of lonely tin slowly faded.

In the book my friend talked of Africa. Of the lions on the beach at sunset. I remember.

"When I was your age I was before the mast on a square-rigged ship that ran to Africa and I have seen lions on the beaches in the evening."

Had ever such a thing happened?

If I could get in. If I could get into one of these, I might stay for a while. Gather tools. Hunt. Then trek back to the village.

I could head back to the peak and turn west. The Eight leads back to the village.

What if there are more of them? More of that boy. Chasing me with the club. The plaque said Human Sacrifice.

The Horde.

If the Horde still exists, they might find the village some day. We could not defend ourselves.

Maybe the boy is the last.

There could be others. Watching you. Letting you lead them back to the village. Or if they find you they might make you talk.

What about Fort Tucson, the Army, that Sergeant Major?

They will think you are one of the Horde. You must look like one.

I will tell them there is a village. They might help us. Or we could trade.

You are cursed. This whole journey has been nothing but a curse, and here you are in a graveyard of airplanes without food or water or a weapon.

Then I must get into one of these planes. At least for the axe.

HE STILL HAD not made up his mind as he sat working with the gear he had collected. It had taken him a long time to get into one of the airplanes but he finally had. Going up through the nose gear of a four-engined plane, he'd found the trapdoor that led into the belly of the aircraft. Working hard at the pin and lock that secured it, he'd finally gotten it open. His head pounded with thirst and hunger and he was tired.

He wound his way up into the dark plane. Feeling his way along a gloomy corridor that twisted to the right once, he saw light coming from a square in the ceiling above and found a ladder that led up to the square. It swung open easily and he was overwhelmed by the smell of stale fabric and dust.

He had some ideas about what he might find aboard the plane that might be of use. Now he put these ideas to the test. He went to the door at the front of the plane, the one where passengers had once embarked. After a few moments reading the instructions, he pulled the red handle marked EMERGENCY. Nothing happened. He read the instructions again. Realizing his error he tried again, and this time the oval boarding door swung open to the desert sky. He deployed the safety slide. With a bang and a hiss it flung itself away from the aircraft. Inside the compartment he found instructions for deploying the life raft case if the plane needed to land in the ocean. With what strength was left, he found the case, then threw it out onto the runway. After bouncing a few times the large suitcase opened and a round raft burst forth, inflating at once.

He slid down the slide and entered the covered raft on his hands and knees. He found a pouch built into the rubber floor marked SUPPLIES. The pouch contained a stash of stale protein bars and silvery bags filled with water. He ate and drank.

Now later, in the last moments of twilight, sitting near the fire of mesquite and working on his supplies, he still did not know what to do next.

He had found three more life rafts and collected an abundance of supplies. Besides the emergency food and water, he'd collected medical kits, scissors, matches, a flare gun and some flares, fishing line, and hooks. Now he sat cutting a raft into strips. Later, when the firelight cast too many flickering shadows making it difficult to focus, he stopped work and carried his supplies back up the boarding slide into the plane. Back outside he sat by the fire for awhile drinking a pack of water, then he went into the plane and closed the door. He slept on a row of seats with an emergency blanket and several pillows.

FOR A LONG while Himbradda lay beside the raging floodwaters. Stunned. Numb. He had lost the man, and his rage boiled up within him. His knuckles turned white as he gripped the club.

He would return to the People, but when he stood, his right leg collapsed and he screamed in pain. It was broken.

He stood again, crying and grunting all at once. He began to limp back along the river's edge. He would return to the People and maybe he would get food.

Then he saw the tracks. Thick and gloppy in the mud. The tracks of the man. Dragging the broken leg, he followed them and forgot the pain that rushed up in him at every step. He drank greedily from evaporating pools of muddy water and chewed hungrily at seeds the People carried for nourishment. He would save the peyote for the kill.

Himbradda followed the muddy tracks until it was too dark to track them anymore. He would find the man and that would make him happy again. For a while he sat shivering in the dark. Then he slept.

CHAPTER 25

The next day the Old Man made a rucksack using cut strips of yellow rubber from the raft. He sat in the shade under the large wing, sewing it together with some needle and thread from the emergency medical kit. Then he made a vest and finally a hat. In the emergency kit he found a little bottle of sunscreen. He would use that also.

I have enough to head back.

The heat made everything quiet. His voice seemed to carry under the wing of the plane and then fall into the dirt beyond.

This is salvage. We could come back here and search these planes. There's medicine, axes, pillows. These things would be good for the village. For a moment he saw movement underneath the wings of faraway planes. He crouched low, looking.

It was the savage. Dragging a leg, he came limping toward the Old Man.

Quickly the Old Man packed his ruck with supplies. He donned the vest and rolled up his hat, stuffing it in the rucksack. He grabbed the fire axe from the nose wheel where he'd left it to lean.

You can't lead him back to the village.

I'll head south for now. I must go to Fort Tucson.

At the perimeter fence, as the Old Man crossed onto the road leaving the air park, the savage gave a cry that pierced the still desert air. The savage had seen him.

Looking back, he saw the boy limping furiously after him. The boy was slow and the effort he exerted great. But the Old Man felt he could stay ahead of the savage. Turning his back he hustled off down the road.

A few hours later he entered a series of rocky rolling hills. Saguaro cacti littered the sides of the hills, their arms upraised. The road began to twist and he passed a weather-beaten granite sign. He was now entering the Saguaro National Monument.

Aha, I am west and north of Tucson. I can follow this road and it will take me to Gates Pass. I remember that. From Gates Pass it's a short downhill walk into Tucson. I'll see the city from there. If it is gone, then I can turn west and head back to the village.

What will you do about the boy?

He turned back to see. The boy was falling farther behind. For a while, flailing his good arm, he'd chased the Old Man. Now he seemed to be stumbling. Weaving. Sometimes he would raise his head and scream at the Old Man, then return to his efforts, limping forward in angry determination.

The Old Man set off into the park. In the afternoon the clouds began to build up thick and white, and the Old Man could smell the musty scent that came before the desert rain. His bones felt tired and his muscles remained cold. When he stopped at a covered picnic area to rest, he felt dizzy.

Maybe the water? Or maybe the food from the plane?

Maybe it's been too much.

When the rain came a few minutes later he felt hot and sweaty. He'd lost sight of the boy.

I can't rest.

Shouldering his pack, he started off into the rain moving steadily, slowly but steadily up the winding road.

Can he still be behind me?

It got dark early and the air became cold. The rain continued as a slight mist. Standing in the gloom, the Old Man smelled the pavement and wondered what he should do.

If it comes to a fight I have the axe.

He's a boy. Your granddaughter's age.

I think he means to harm me.

He smelled woodsmoke from a breeze that came at him out of the north. In the distance he saw a small orange fire farther down the valley.

He has fallen far behind.

It could be a trick. To make you think he has stopped for the night.

The Old Man shouldered the pack and set off into the evening drizzle. Moments later, a flash of light caught the image of him receding into the negative, against the photograph of a land turned bone white and shadow.

HIMBRADDA HEARD THE thunder and sat shivering in front of his fire. He ate the last handfuls of the seed. He took out the peyote and fingered it, chanting over and over his nonsense words.

He threw more brush on the fire and white smoke issued up as the fire slowly caught. He ate the peyote. He felt tired as he sat there staring into the fire. Later when the laughter came upon him, he got up and the leg felt numb. The pain was gone. He began to circle the fire, laughing and muttering. The rain stopped and he stared at the stars twirling and moving faster.

The Dragon was dead and the People were the stars.

The Dragon was old and now he was just an old man, chased through the desert by Himbradda. Chased by a hero across the stars.

He shouldered his club and set off into the night. The Old Dragon was sticking to the hard roads. Himbradda didn't need to track him through the desert. He would stay on the hard path and he would find him.

AT THE BOTTOM of Gates Pass, the Old Man turned back to look along the way he had come. He didn't see the boy.

Ahead, a serpentine road wound its way up the rocky face of the pass. At the top he would be able to see Tucson. He would be in the suburbs of Tucson.

He shivered and felt chilled to the bone. He drank an entire packet of water and thought about eating a protein bar, but his throat felt as though it were on fire.

I am at the last of it and I am too sick to go on.

You must.

The boy is asleep no doubt. I can afford to borrow a little rest against the lead I have taken.

Your friend in the book would tell you, "First you borrow, then you beg." True.

The moon was out as ghostly white clouds skidded off into the deep blue of night. It was quiet.

I heard coyotes a while back and I am just thinking of it now. I think I am very sick.

If there is a Fort Tucson they can help you.

"If" is the question.

The savage boy loped into view on the road below. Using his club as a cane, he was pumping hard to catch the Old Man. The Old Man tightened his grip around the axe resting across his shoulder and knew he was too weak to swing it to any effect.

HIMBRADDA CHARGED FORWARD seeing the Old Dragon. The night air burned clean and fresh in his lungs. He screamed and thought of victory and dipping his hands in the blood of the Old Dragon, and covering the rock walls where he had chased the Old Dragon to, making the sign of the People. He screamed and felt better than he had ever felt in all his short life. He felt alive.

THE OLD MAN labored hard up the steep grade. The next stretch of the cracked and broken highway was extremely steep.

Another bend or two and I'll be at the top.

He'll be on you by then.

He is my shark. I must try until there is nothing left like my friend did with first the harpoon, then the paddle, and finally the club.

He spared a glance back at the boy and knew the boy was nothing human. Humanity hadn't been something the child had ever possessed, been taught, experienced.

The flare gun might scare him off.

The Old Man reached into the ruck. He had four flares. He loaded one and took aim. Himbradda labored up the first grade below. He fired and Himbradda stopped, watching the flare streak over his head. When it passed, the Old Man could see the features of the wild boy. Teeth missing in a mouth agape. Thick hair. The withered arm. Animal amazement at the red streaking light. His pupils large and dark. When the flare had gone into the bushes to burn, Himbradda surged forward up the hill, closing in on the Old Man.

Start moving now.

But I am tired.

Just move forward. Get to the top. Then think of something else to do when you get there.

He began to move.

At the top of the pass he turned, breathing hard, and felt dizzy. The savage boy was running now, rounding the bend on the narrow road that would lead straight to the Old Man.

He let the axe fall to the ground while holding the handle, and he knew it was beyond himself to use it. He let it go and backed toward the edge of the cliff.

You've got time for one trick, Old Man.

The boy charged forward closing the distance rapidly. The Old Man could hear the savage boy wheezing as he gasped for breath to close the gap.

I've got nothing.

Try the flare.

Without thinking he loaded another round.

I'll just shoot him in the chest and that will be done.

But he doubted it would stop the savage boy. Not twenty feet away, the animal child raised the club over his head to smash it down on the Old Man.

The Old Man stumbled backward, knowing the cliff's edge was nearby. He felt himself falling and, for a brief moment, thought he was going over the edge, but the dusty ground greeted him with a dull reassurance as he fell onto it.

I came this far. If I had just a moment, I'd see Tucson at the other side of the pass.

That would have been enough. To know. To know it still exists, could exist for the village.

He raised the flare gun lamely as sweat poured cold and clammy across his forehead. He aimed it right into the face of the charging boy.

The wild snarling youth bore down upon him. Himbradda had crushed many. Many had raised their hands in defense, hoping to ward off the blow of the parking meter, to change the inevitable. Himbradda knew what to do in these moments. He wanted nothing between him and the skull of the Old Dragon. He kicked the Old Dragon's arm away with his leathery foot.

The Old Man's aim went wide. He urged his finger not to squeeze the trigger, to re-aim, and try once more. But the impulse to squeeze raced ahead of the caution not to, and he felt his finger, his hand squeeze off the flare. It shot skyward past Himbradda's feral grin of rage and triumph.

This is death.

Himbradda jerked his head skyward, gigantic pupils following the falling star, the angel, the most beautiful thing he would ever see. The peyote revealed the world to him as he wanted it to be.

He watched the flare arching skyward, falling out and away from him, against a universe of broken glass. He twirled to follow its course and felt himself falling away from it.

The rocks at the bottom of the pass greeted him with a jagged reception. First his feet hit, then his wrist snapped, and finally his skull struck a rock. It felt as if those things could have been separate events, instead of the single instant they were.

The Old Man knew he was about to be killed. He had closed his eyes, waiting. But the blow had not come. And when he replayed what should have happened, what must have happened, he knew it had not happened. He saw the rush of the boy, the flying kick at his hand. Saw the flare racing away and felt Himbradda stumble forward, out over the cliff. He heard the crunch below. But his mind had not accepted it.

He lay there breathing, his fever breaking for just a moment. He sat up to drink water and felt his stomach turn. He curled into a ball and fell asleep.

CHAPTER 26

Morning wind caressed his old head and when he awoke, wrapped in his emergency blanket and using the ruck as a pillow, he felt hollow. His eyes ached and he hoped the weakness of the day before might have been just a short fever.

He sat up and drank some water. His throat was still sore, but not on fire as it had been.

Maybe that was the worst of it and now I'll just be sick. I can handle that.

At the bottom of the cliff near the bend in the road below, he saw the broken body and blood of the boy. The boy still clutched the club that was a parking meter.

What life did you live?

Is it your concern?

He never knew the things of the past. Never knew the first day of school. How the fog of California smells like damp wood in the morning. Never knew those things.

Let it go.

The Old Man sat for a long time in the golden rays of morning. It was still cold, but the sun at the top of the pass felt good and seemed to get down into his bones.

You've made it. You should go and see now.

The Old Man left his gear and walked to the far side of the pass. He crossed an old stone wall and then a parking lot scorched and faded by forty years of sun and rain.

The rising eastern sun burned bright. For a moment it blotted out everything and the Old Man had to look away. He remembered coming to Gates Pass with his mother one time. To talk. She bought some jewelry from an Indian woman who sold them on a blanket. He had been maybe twenty-five.

He looked again and saw the city. It was a low collection of buildings with a few tall ones at the center. The city was dark against the brightness of the sun.

It didn't get hit.

Then he began to laugh. But it didn't feel right.

You made it.

He went back to his gear and soon was on the road toward the city. Morning birds flitted in the brush, calling rapidly to one another. To tell what they had seen or done. Or that they had survived. Or that they were still there. Or maybe that they were simply happy. Later, he passed the overgrown remains of a golf course. He saw a bobcat on a rock.

Soon he entered the old part of Tucson. Buildings were still standing. In a store, he saw the items it had once sold within. The front window had been shattered. Within lay a collection of sewing machines and vacuum cleaners.

He passed a grocery store and stopped to look in through the dark holes where the glass had once been. The shelves all lay atop one another but the cans and products still remained, piled in the dark against the bottoms of the toppled shelves.

He passed apartment complexes and finally came to a bridge that spanned the dry riverbed girding the western edge of Tucson. At the freeway off-ramp, blowtorched into the abutment wall was the word SAFETY and then an arrow pointing to the left under the bridge.

He followed the arrow and found others leading along the streets. Soon he entered the City Center. Birds flew everywhere, their calls echoing off the silent buildings. He crossed an intersection and walked toward an arrow that pointed farther down the street. He rounded a corner near a hotel and saw the gray square structure of the Federal Building.

At its base he saw a wall of sheet metal reinforced with sandbags. Written in large letters near a break in the sheet metal wall were the words "Welcome to Fort Tucson."

He came to the gate, which was just an opening, and saw a courtyard and the steps leading into the main building. A gate that could have closed the opening had been swung back and left open.

The Old Man walked up the steps and entered through the main doors of the Federal Building. A large marble entrance was bisected by a spray-painted orange line that ran across the length of the floor. Beyond the line, spray-painted in orange were the words "Raise your hands and walk forward or you will be killed."

The Old Man raised his hands.

HE STOOD FOR a while and nothing happened. He walked forward into the dark at the far end of the hallway. Abruptly an automated noise hummed forth on a note, then reversed and sounded again. The process repeated itself. In the dark ahead he could see a small dog-shaped thing swiveling its head.

The auto sentry gun traversed back and forth across the lobby, and once the Old Man began to lower his hands, the motion stopped and the sentry gun ground to a halt, locking its barrel in his direction. He raised his hands quickly. Automatically the gun began to traverse its field.

This is salvage.

The Old Man passed the sentry gun and turned. A red light on the ground attached to a battery pack switched to green and the gun ceased to move. An elevator lit up and the Old Man waited as the doors opened with a soft hush and then a poignant *ding*. On the back wall was a hand-painted sign that read Enter.

When the doors opened again, the Old Man stepped into a stark white lobby with polished floors. It was government. The feeling of the fluorescent lights, the cheap linoleum, the polished floors, and the smell of paper. The Old Man remembered a place where he had gone to get a Social Security card when he was eighteen. It had been like this.

Or was that a passport?

I don't remember.

Beyond the lobby were two halls leading in opposite directions. On one wall another hand-painted sign read THIS WAY! He followed.

The door at the end of the hallway with the next hand-painted sign was at the corner of the building. The sign read Enter and the Old Man did.

Inside, a large desk and an executive chair looked out over the iron blue skies of Tucson. The Old Man could see the northwestern section of the city from here. On the desk lay a composition book. Written on the cover were the words "Read Me."

The Old Man sat in the chair, his rucksack still hanging from his tired frame. He leaned back in the chair and didn't feel as sick as he knew he should feel. His throat still felt raw.

You're excited. Too excited.

He closed his eyes and listened to the tick of the building. He heard clocks. A creak somewhere. But mostly silence. He thought he heard the breeze outside the windows. He felt his mouth open and he heard himself snore for a second.

I cannot remember when I have ever been so comfortable.

He sat up, wiping the drool from his lips, and set his ruck down next to the chair.

He turned to the desk and opened the book.

"IF YOU COULDN'T read, you wouldn't have made it past the sentry gun. So you must be civilized. Or no one ever came and the building's back-up batteries finally ran down, though that shouldn't have happened for another hundred years after I wrote this. Which means I was the last and these markings mean nothing to you. So go ahead and burn it for fire. At least that might be the start of a civilization.

"If on the other hand you can read, it means you are probably from my time; is that the right answer? My civilization. You survived the bombs or knew someone who did and they taught you. I guess.

"I survived.

"My name is John Preston. I was a tank platoon sergeant in the last days before the bombs. Our cavalry troop guarded the border. We were sent here to restore order. The city had been evacuated by the time we got here. Everyone had left because of the bombs. They figured Tucson must have been on someone's list and that they'd get to it eventually. We spent three weeks here. There was an airburst out over the desert to the east but I think it was a low-yield bomb. It didn't damage much, and the winds shifted the fallout over eastern Arizona and New Mexico. By then most of the troop had deserted. They figured America was done for and they went to find their loved ones.

"I stayed. We had a lot of equipment here and the city was still intact. So I figured someone had better keep the lights on. Haha. I tried to protect the city and all the supplies. I boarded up as many stores as I could and I covered things in plastic. I cleaned out all the home improvement centers and a few other places. I placed cars, generators, and tractors and a lot of other things in the parking garage below this building, which used to be the Federal Building. Now it's Fort Tucson.

"Here's the truth: no one ever came. I think you all must have thought every city went up in a cloud. Probably did. Somehow Tucson made it. Did you know it's the oldest continually inhabited place in North America? I learned that in a book about Tucson. Now it's got that record by a long shot. I saved every book I could find in this city. They are in libraries I set up throughout the building.

"I know Phoenix is gone. We saw it on TV in the early days. I also drove there in a tank about two years after the bombs, when the winter was winding down. It's gone. Don't go there.

"There are people. Maybe you're one of them, but if you are who I am thinking of, you probably wouldn't come near Tucson because of the Dragon. I'm the Dragon. Or more importantly, the M-1 MK3 Abrams Main Battle Tank that I managed to keep operational is the Dragon.

"So here's the story of the Dragon. You can judge if you want. I don't suspect it matters much in my current situation. When I took that drive to Phoenix in the tank I found a settlement living in the gas station and the rocks of Picacho Peak. I tried to tell 'em they could come back to the city but they said city ways is what caused all this mess. They wanted to start a new society. No rules. Had a college professor, or so he said he was, that ran the whole place. We were friendly enough at first. I'd drive out every six months or so and give what medical aid I could. But every trip they got wilder and wilder. Crazy stuff I don't need to go into. But you will find a movie in the video library on the third floor, room 307, called *Apocalypse*

Now. That might explain how it got. Anyway the professor, as they called him, was running amok. He had a harem. I suspected he was killing his people. Maybe just his enemies within the tribe, which I took to calling the Horde after this computer game I played when I was kid, called *Warcraft*. Or just because he could. People I'd treat wouldn't be there the next time for me to follow up. I'd ask, but no one could tell me what happened to them. They were eating a lot of peyote. Lots of accidents, burns, falls, that sort of thing. I let it go.

"One day I go out there and they're gone. I looked over the whole place and that's when I found the bone pile beneath the peak. I climbed up to the top of the peak. They had a whole weird cave system slash temple up there. Chalk drawings of what they were doing told me the whole story. But they were gone. I tried to track them down. I found another settlement out in the west called Ajo, which means 'garlic' in Spanish. It was easy to follow the Horde because they moved like locusts. This was ten, maybe fifteen years after the bombs. There were lots of them by then. Anyway, Ajo had been surviving out there. They had a sheriff. Walls. A store. The Horde found them and destroyed the whole town. It was terrible what they did to those people who had survived out there for so long.

"You might ask 'Do I feel bad about what happened to those people in Ajo?' I do. Anyone would. But I had my orders and they were to save Tucson and hold position. I was trying to keep the candle burning by saving as much as I could for whoever would come along. It wasn't my job to go find those people and bring 'em in. I should have, but I didn't and that's the way it is. Like I said you can judge me if you want.

"The Horde moved on over the border of Mexico. I figured they would either die out there or never come back, and that was for the best. I continued to work on the Fort, and periodically I started driving out to other towns on the map, a day's journey or so out. Most were dead. Some had their own stories of what went wrong. You could tell by the bodies and the bloodstains the Horde got to a few. I checked Picacho Peak. It was quiet for a long time. I waited. About ten years ago they came back. They started the sacrifices as soon as they got back. I shot the head off the leader with a Barrett from a ways off, as he was about to throw an infant off the top of the peak. He and the kid tumbled into the crowd below and they . . . well, forget it.

"Then I went in with the tank. They call it the Dragon. I interrogated a few of them after the battle. Scattered all the rest and shot the place up. Held it for a few days. They kept trying to re-take it at night. I had four sentry guns set up around the tank. It was not a quiet night. I killed a lot of them and came to two conclusions. One, Picacho is important to them. Two, there are a lot of 'em. So whoever you are, watch out for Picacho Peak. They ain't nothing more than animals now. If that's what's left of humanity, then this was all for nothing. But if I made it, someone else must have made it too.

"I wish I could hear your story. I think I would like it very much. I waited for you, but I think cancer got me. I tried to make this place safe and easy to get into at the same time. I set the auto gun to recognize 'a hands up' silhouette profile as 'safe.' So if you made it past the gun, you can read.

"I started a project. When I neutralized the temple at Picacho Peak I found laws the Horde had written down. Utter nonsense. I decided to write my own. For the next bunch who want to have a go at civilization. I used a plate welding torch and carved them into the sewers here and others places throughout the area. Kinda like the pyramids, except useful, and sewage systems outlast most civilizations.

"You are civilization now. What more can I say? I've left lots of these composition books throughout the buildings and on the equipment to tell you how to use it, or what's where and such. Cancer got me. You can find my body in bed on the top floor of this building, in an apartment I set up. I promoted myself to Sergeant Major. God Bless America."

The Old Man leaned back in the chair and wept.

CHAPTER 27

He felt weak. Later he went to one corner of the room, which had once most likely been an executive office, and rolled out his emergency blanket. He found a bathroom down the hall and heard Muzak playing in the sound system of the building. The tune was familiar but he couldn't remember it. He ran cool water on his face and drank from the sink. He thought about finding the infirmary. Medicine might help, but the feeling of fatigue was bone deep. He went back to the office and slept.

He awoke in the night. He stood for a moment looking out the large windows. White clouds scudded across a night sky that seemed bigger than any he could remember.

How long have I been gone?

He tried to count the days by their adventures. But they seemed too many.

He went to the restroom again and heard another familiar tune coming from the building's Muzak system. He couldn't say its name either. He came back to the office and wrapped himself in his blanket and sat in the chair watching the clouds drift across the sea of night.

IN THE MORNING when he awoke sitting in the chair, he felt hollow and sweaty.

Maybe the worst of the sickness has passed.

When he moved, he felt fragile as though it all might come back upon him.

I need to make it back to the village.

If you start now, it will take a few weeks.

I know that. It is also monsoon season. Very dangerous.

The desert looked calm and cool beyond the city boundaries. Distant mountains of orange rock and brown shadow seemed pleasant from the safety of the building.

I have to make it back before I die. I have to tell them. If this fever turns into something, they will never know.

You have to make it back without dying.

He thought of the tank in the garage.

He searched the building for the rest of the day, finding the libraries of books and discs and computers that still worked. Medical supplies, equipment of every sort; all had been catalogued, ordered, and stored. Waiting. The Old Man wondered at all the years and the person of Sergeant Major Preston.

Finally he went to the top floor suite and found the corpse of the Sergeant Major. The room was orderly, and only the photograph of a woman, young, bangs, glasses, was any clue to the personal life of the man. There was a body bag beside the bed.

The Old Man closed the door and went back to the elevator. In the garage he found vehicles, farming and construction equipment. Each had a composition book. Near the main entrance to the garage he found four tanks. Three were missing parts, obviously cannibalized to keep the fourth in good condition. He climbed up to the cupola and found a note on the hatch instructing him how to enter the tank.

Inside he found a VCR tape and a note that read "Watch First!!!" He returned to the offices of the building, and in one of the video libraries he found a VCR.

These were extinct when I was a kid.

Soon he had it working.

He sat down and watched as Sergeant Major Preston, middle aged, instructed him how to run the tank.

The tank had been fitted with a remote control system, slaved to the tank's command compartment. This centralized the operation of the tank in the commander's cupola. Sergeant Major Preston instructed the watcher on how to swivel and sight the main gun. How to fire it and how a re-loading system would automatically rack another round. There were only twenty rounds on board. The video then detailed the starting of the engines, firing the fifty-caliber machine gun, and re-loading the tank's fuel compartment at a fuel depot a few miles away where the Sergeant Major had managed to store fuel. Though, he said, the fuel tanks of any gas station could be siphoned using an auto pump on board the tank.

The Old Man had passed only a few gas stations that hadn't burned to the ground. He doubted their fuel had survived. The video ended with the Sergeant Major putting the key to the fuel pumps on a wallboard inside the fuel station and showing a drawing of how to get to the station from the Fort. Then he lowered the white placard map and smiled into the camera. The tape ended.

Earlier in the day the Old Man had found the kitchen. He'd made a breakfast of powdered eggs and canned tomatoes from the pantry, one of several in fact. There was coffee and creamer too, though his throat had been too raw for it. Instead he had made some tea from tea bags he'd found on the counter.

Now he returned and opened a can of ham, made more powdered eggs, and put ketchup on them. He sat, chewing slowly.

I need to go, get there and back before someone comes.

No one has come in all this time. Who will come?

He thought about the savage boy lying at the bottom of Gates Pass. He thought about his own parents' house.

There will be time for that once you come back with the village.

Will the village want to come?

He laughed at himself and chewed more egg.

When he had finished eating, he felt weaker than he should have.

The desert was too much. I won, but it may have beaten me. Maybe I got too close to Phoenix, or the rations or snakes were irradiated.

He thought of cancer.

I could leave now. Drive the tank through the night. Be home before dawn.

In the dark over broken roads and monsoon mud? It will take skill in the daylight. Don't even think about it at night.

He went back to the office. He rolled out a new army-issue sleeping bag he'd found in an office full of supplies ranging from camping stoves to cots.

He made some tea and added a packet of honey. He wondered if they might grow lemons here some day. He lay back in the sleeping bag with a fresh clean pillow he'd unzipped from a package that bore the name of a very expensive store. He wondered if there might be a gym and showers in the building. But he had not seen either.

It would be nice to have a hot shower before bed.

He fell asleep in the middle of the thought and woke up later, still holding the Styrofoam cup of cold tea. He rolled over and slept until just before dawn.

Awake and moving stiffly, he tried to tell himself he wasn't worse.

I won't ask much of you today. Just get me back to my village. Then you can die.

Why are you so concerned about death now? Is it because you have everything to lose?

The eastern night ended in thin blue streaks. He rolled up the sleeping bag, stopped by the infirmary, and grabbed a bottle of aspirin. In the kitchen, he took bottles of water and cans of tuna and chili. He found a can opener, almost forgetting to, laughing at himself as if he had forgotten.

In the garage, he raised the door by electronic control in a guard shack and went to the tank. Soon he had the first engine on the tank started. It sounded like a jet engine. Then he started the second engine and felt for a brief moment that controlling the tank would be beyond him. He checked the instruments and found that the tank was full of fuel. He went down into the brightly lit cupola of the tank and stowed his gear on a seat near the rear, then returned to the seat in the cupola. He took hold of a joystick and swiveled the main gun, sensing a momentary sickness as the entire cupola swung to the right. Then he pointed it back to the front of the tank and placed his hands on two levers below the joystick.

The right controls the right tread, the left the left tread.

Pushing forward on both would move the tank forward. Or so Sergeant Major Preston had assured him. He pushed forward on both cautiously and nothing happened. He tried again. He thought back to the instructional video.

The gas pedal.

Below him, near the new boots he'd found in a different supply room, was the pedal. He stepped on it and heard the tank's engines spool up to a high-pitched whine. He pressed forward on the two sticks while gassing the pedal as the tank eased through the garage doors. Outside he dismounted and closed the doors, then climbed aboard once more.

He gassed the pedal and pulled back on the left stick and went forward with the right as the tank swerved to the left. He looked back at the Fort. Then he eased the tank out onto the road leading to the highway. His throat felt sore. Maybe he was sick. But he wouldn't think about it. The tank took all his concentration.

CHAPTER 28

At first the going was slow, as he wound through the side streets that led onto the main freeway. Once atop the eight-lane, the going got better.

For a while he rode the blacktop. The evacuation had left the city empty forty years ago. The Old Man knew where the people had fled during that long-ago exodus from a wrecked civilization. Many lay trapped between the cities in great wrecks of their own. A few had become his fellow villagers.

The highway ran smooth and eventually became a two-lane and a median with two lanes on the other side. Other than the occasional downed bridge that he maneuvered around or through, there was little that stood in the way of the tank. Soon he had the tank up to forty-five miles an hour.

He passed a semi overturned on its belly and stopped. It was covered in red handprints.

Is that recent?

Are they getting closer?

He revved the tank and sent it down the road once more. Soon the hum of the engines lulled him to thinking, and at times almost sleep. The day was cold. He could feel the rain in the air. Knew the heat of the sun hadn't driven away the cold of night completely. Winter was coming.

In the distance he could see Picacho Peak as the road began a long gentle curve to the west.

I am finally heading west.

He thought about the end of curses. What needed to be done once he returned to the village? How to organize them and get them back to the Fort?

The village is over.

How so?

When I return with this tank. Everything changes. My life in the village will be something that happened long ago. A dream. Just like my life before the bombs. A dream also.

It was noon when he spotted them coming down from the northern mountains across the plain like a vast dark herd. They were crossing the highway in groups, running for Picacho Peak just on the other side. He stopped the tank. The roar of the engines was still loud and he could hear nothing above it. He could feel the north wind on his face. He could feel the cold of the arctic and the high mountain passes it had come down through to reach the Sonoran Desert.

The Horde lay scattered in bands across the horizon. Now they formed into two groups.

So they still exist.

One group resolved itself into men and boys painted and various in weapons and dress. Savages of the new wasteland. The other group drew itself toward Picacho Peak, running like a startled herd of buffalo.

There is the main gun and then the machine gun.

If not today, when?

I don't think I've ever killed a man.

Mirrored Sunglasses? The savage boy?

They killed themselves.

I don't think it will be just a couple today.

The wild men came on in a ragged line, running with mouths open.

What you do today determines the future of the village. Civilization even.

I don't know if I'm the man to make that choice.

There's no other. Act now or die. Do this today or forget tomorrow!

The Old Man tapped the accelerator and listened to the engines spool up to a high-pitched whine.

Maybe this will give them something to stop for.

The ragged mobbed surged over the soft sand, closing the distance.

Do something now, Old Man!

They were twenty yards off when he gave the tank full power and pushed forward on the control sticks. The tank jumped forward with a roar, and the Old Man closed his eyes as he crashed into their line. They were hundreds turning into thousands and the air was suddenly thick with missiles of rock and broken pipe. He tucked into the hatch and kept forward on the sticks. He heard their wild screams above the thunder of the engines.

When the rain of debris ceased, he popped out of the hatch and checked the tank's progress as it veered across the median. He overcorrected and the tank gave a sharp right turn. Before he could get it straightened out he'd gone out over the northbound lanes and into the desert off the road.

He surveyed the mob. There were thousands surging all around the tank. Thin gaunt men the color of dust chased his wake, waving and yelling. Potbellied, sun-browned women and feral children snarled as they ran from him. Stones began to fall, but they were too far off. The main mass of the mob seemed to be collecting around the base of the peak but the warriors were gathering again for another charge.

He moved the tank back onto the road and started toward the abandoned gas station. The desert scrub was thick on the far side of the road and at times, wild-eyed men and screaming women ran gibbering before the tank, darting off into the bushes like frightened animals.

He traversed the gun and toggled the gun sight onto the building where he'd found their laws. Behind him, their main force pounded down the road after him, their eyes wild with anger and fear. He depressed the red button atop the joystick and sent a round into the building.

At once, two things happened. The tank rocked back in a cloud of powdery dust, and the wall of the building exploded in a spray of cement. Beyond the building a moment later, the round exploded in dirt and sand, having passed straight through the decrepit wall without exploding.

The Old Man traversed the gun, hearing nothing but dull silence and feeling, more than hearing, the servos that swiveled the cupola. He landed the main gun on the advancing wall of savages.

"This must mean something to you!" he screamed and barely heard himself.

He felt a sharp blow on his shoulder as a club smashed down hard upon it. He turned to see a crazed naked man with cracked skin and open sores, his watermelon head drooling crazily amid a mouth full of misshapen teeth. The savage raised a club to strike once again. His attacker had climbed from the back of the tank onto the cupola. Three others were struggling up the same way, each as lunatic as the first.

The Old Man sank into the turret, grabbing at the hatch with his free hand as he stepped hard on the accelerator. The tank bolted forward across the road and onto broken ground. Sure that they had fallen off, he popped up from the turret once more to scan the terrain ahead. As he turned to look forward he saw that the tank was headed off the lip of a dry riverbed. He took his foot off the pedal hoping to stop in time.

The tank fell. He had just enough time to swing the hatch shut and throw himself to the floor of the tank.

HE AWOKE TO a cacophony of noise. Everywhere the sound of hammers and pipes could be heard across the interior of the tank. The Old Man was bathed in red light. He stood shakily and locked the hatch, marveling that they hadn't pulled on it.

He reached into his ruck and got out some water. It was hot, though the sweat felt cold on his back. He wondered if they would try to set the tank on fire. He wondered if the tank would burn.

He found his way awkwardly into the control seat. The tank was in a facedown angle.

At least we are not on our side.

He stepped on the accelerator and the engines whined. He pushed forward on the sticks and felt the tank strain, but refuse to go forward. He reversed the sticks and felt the tank jump backward straining and digging. He took his foot off the pedal.

I might be stuck.

Anew, the ringing sounds of metal on metal began again.

Too much and I will dig a ditch I might not get out of. Then all they have to do is wait me out.

What other choice do you have? You only brought two cans of food and some water. They might damage something and stick you here whether you like it or not.

He pulled the restraint harness across his shoulders and snapped a belt around his waist.

I can't go forward. But I can go back just a little.

He imagined what the tank might be stuck in. What position would cause that and how to get out without making things worse.

Outside the tank, someone had found a sledgehammer or something equally capable of making a tremendous ringing gong. Mixed with the other assaults, it was becoming unbearable.

I am not beaten. I am just stuck.

He thought of the old man in the book. What would he do?

Sometimes there is nothing to do but the only thing that you can do.

He gassed the accelerator hard and held back on the sticks with all of his might, as his fingers and wrist turned sweaty with heat and tension. At the top of the rise, he pushed forward on the tank, and then almost immediately, once it leapt forward, he pushed back again.

I have to pop the nose up. It's the only thing I can imagine that must be done.

He felt his stomach float for a second and knew that the attitude of the tank had changed. He hoped it was enough. He gassed it forward, and then at the last second, felt he needed more of one stick than the other. He went with the right stick, pulling back on the left before he could think further on the subject. He felt the tank turning and finally moving forward. The attacks on its shell ceased.

I've got to see or this will happen again.

He opened the hatch but kept the tank moving. He traversed the turret, taking in the panorama of savagery that surrounded him. Black smoke filled the area and the sun was low in the sky, turning everything blood red. As he traversed east, monsoon clouds built up in angry red and purple bruises.

I must have been out for a while.

The Horde, toothless, angry, misshapen, twitching, hobbling, screaming, gashing, beating, wild animal thing that it was, surged in every direction as he gunned away from the center. His passing clotted quickly as they followed him howling and yelling.

There must be an end to this.

Atop Picacho Peak, a large bonfire burned against the deep blue of the high altitude.

When he had some distance from them, he swiveled the tank to face the peak.

It must be this then.

He traversed the gun and set it on the face of the peak just below the topmost edge and fired. This time he put one finger in his ear. He heard the reloading system eject a hot shell and re-load another. He fired again once the ready light went from red to green, near the firing button.

The rounds began to fall directly into the side of the peak, and almost instantly the walls began to crumble in great sheets of dust and rock.

He fired again and saw the savages scream, dropping to their knees, unable to comprehend the horror of what was happening to them.

In the last moments of daylight, he switched on the tank's high beams and fired again. The Horde fled the field, heading east into the dark.

When he had fired most of the rounds, he alone remained. Bodies crushed by the tank turned up as he crossed the field. But the rest had gone. He returned to the main road and set the tank on it.

We will have to watch them.

Over the hum of the engines, he considered the place as he readied for the long push back to the village.

What had been the difference between this place and the village?

He set off down the road making slow but steady progress. A harvest moon came out and it stayed dry. It smelled dusty when he arrived at the burnt town where the two highways intersected. The bodies were still spaced across the blacktop. He maneuvered around them and set the high beams on the road heading west.

If I remember right, the village will be beyond the next valley. But it has been some time.

He crossed a small plain where once crops had grown. An overpass had collapsed across the road and he went around it. Shaking with hunger, he stopped and turned off the tank. He opened the can of chili and ate it as he walked around the silent tank. It was cold and he began to shiver.

Back in the tank, he started it, momentarily knowing it wouldn't. But it did and soon he eased forward into the night as the road climbed a small desert plateau, crossing a pass and descending into a valley of jagged peaks.

I remember this part. I remember driving it many times.

Thoughts that had seemed so important then, as he passed over the same ground now, seemed foreign.

I was different then, he said in the wind and the night.

When he reached the end of the valley he felt tired enough to stop. He thought about buttoning up the tank and sleeping on the floor.

I need rest. I know I am very sick.

If you die . . . or if in the morning you cannot get up . . . no one will know. Eventually the Horde will find the Fort. The machine gun won't keep them away for long. Once it runs out of bullets, what then?

He drank some water and pressed on. He passed a conical mountain, and then came to the Gas Station that had burned down at the edge of the town that was the farthest limit the villagers would salvage.

Just a ways more.

The Old Man in the book is not his name. His name is Santiago. In the book he wanted the boy with him as he fought the fish. Just as I wanted my granddaughter with me.

He passed the blackened ruins and a little later the moon fell low in the sky.

He topped the rise and saw the village. He turned off the tank feeling the heat dissipate quickly. He was just a mile off from the village but he could see it below. It was a collection of sheds and huts built around an old processing plant. It was his home. He could see the field of broken glass glittering like the stars above.

He left the tank, feeling hot and sore.

I WILL WALK home and go to my house and in the morning they will see the tank.

There has never been such a fish.

He knew he made little sense. But it seemed right not to wake anyone.

Let them sleep in the village one night longer. To have the village one more night. Then they can have the world.

My journey was like the one in the book.

That is the thing about books. You take their journeys with you.

You came home with something more than just the remains of a fish.

The book was never about the fish.

He neared the sleeping village and passed through unseen.

Even the dogs are asleep.

I want to tell my granddaughter the lesson of the book. The lesson that they can beat you, but they cannot defeat you. I must tell her that.

At the door to his shed, he wondered if someone might live here now. His thoughts were scrambled and came in waves. But he knew it was the sickness and the fatigue.

He pushed open the door and heard its sound, knowing it as his own. He loved the sound of it. All was as he'd left it. Still holding his rucksack, he lit a candle and carried it to the desk where he kept the book. He looked at the cover for a long moment and then set down his pack.

Your must tell her that.

What?

They can beat you but they cannot defeat you.

He put the book on his bed and lit a fire in the stove.

My friend in the book is safe.

Maybe just some tea. Then sleep.

But when he sat on the bed to take off his new boots, he couldn't get back up.

Be sure to tell her.

I will.

For just a moment he mumbled, then lay down.

He dreamed of lions playing on distant beaches at sunset. His granddaughter was right next to him, watching, both of them silent. Her little hand in his old hand.

SHE WAS GOING out again. In the dark, she gathered all the tools she would need, and when she found the claw hammer her grandfather had let her carry, she placed it in her belt. It was like having him with her. She needed that.

On the way to the cantina for the tea that the old women made while they fried the sweet dough, she felt the cold earth on her toes. This was the best time of day, she thought. This was the time when they would meet and she would go out with him to salvage.

She looked at his shed as she had every morning, its silent, gray, un-lived in look a memorial to her grandfather.

It's a good thing. That way you will remember everything he taught you. You will need it out there.

But as she looked this morning, she saw the wispy smoke in the chimney of his shed and she was angry.

Someone has moved in! It's too soon . . .

She charged toward the shed door, intending to wake the village with her rebuke at whoever had taken her grandpa's shed as his own. But then she was running and hoping. Hoping he had come back.

Like she knew he would.

She found him sweaty and hot atop his cot, mumbling in his sleep. She kissed him but he did not recognize her in his fever. His body felt thin and gaunt.

She hurried back to her parents' door, telling all in one burst that he had returned. Then to the kitchen to tell the women.

Back at the shed, her father knelt by the side of the cot, crying and talking softly to the Old Man. She would nurse him back to health. She would make him drink soup. They needed to kill one of the chickens. Then when he was well, they would go out again to salvage, and then she too was crying.

Her little brother came running to her as he always did.

"There is something on the road. Something wonderful." He pulled her through the lanes of the village to the edge of the highway.

Alone and in pairs, the villagers approached the tank atop the hill as the morning sun rose behind it. She didn't care. Even though it was the greatest salvage ever, it was nothing compared to what she cared about.

EPILOGUE

The Chief Excavator stood atop the scaffolding, the wind blowing at his jacket. He stepped back from the hole he had just made with the cutting tool.

"It's your turn."

The Doctor of Antiquities stepped forward. He had campaigned long and hard for this day. Now that it was upon him, he didn't want to go through with it. From theory to paper, to committees and hearings, it had been one thing. The game of academics. But now those questions would be answered. He would have to find something new to uncover because the riddle of the tank would be solved.

His heart beat rapidly as he moved his light toward the opening, his head close behind. Inside, a wrapped body was the first thing he saw. He knew it was a body. The first residents of the reoccupation of Old Tucson, the foundation of their culture, had prepared their bodies in the same manner. But those bodies had all been found in the graveyards of Starr Pass.

"It's true," he mumbled.

"You were right?" asked the Chief Excavator.

The Doctor stuck his head and light back in the hole.

"It's a body. Probably an early warlord. Maybe the first to conquer the area. There is something on top of the body. A book perhaps."

A strong wind, a danger at this altitude, gusted past the Doctor's head and turned the ancient book to fragments, floating and swirling about the inside of the tank.

"Looked like a book, I should say."

"Any clue how they got the tank to the top of the tower?" asked the Chief Excavator. The Doctor stepped back and pulled a plastic sheet over the opening to prevent further wind damage.

"We'll never know how they did that." He took in the panorama of the world's oldest still-populated city. Towers and buildings raced toward the heights above, the Space Elevator beyond that, its thin diamond line tracing away into the sky above.

"That was never the point of this project. We wanted to know who was in here. It's our city's oldest monument and no one knows a thing about it."

"So who was he?"

"Can we ever know? Probably not. We will make some guesses from what we know about the survivors of that period. But we can never know for sure."

"So we can just guess a little better, is that it?"

The Doctor put his hand on the tank, feeling its ancientness.

"I can say one thing."

"What?" asked the reporter who'd come out to the historic district to cover the story.

"Whoever put him here, in a war machine of the period, which was impossible as we know it by their standards after the catastrophe, to hoist a multiton vehicle to the top of this tower, whoever it was, loved him very much. He was very important to them. I can say that."

INTERMEZZO

For those who loved
The Old Man and the Wasteland,
You will find this novel a bit different.
This time the Apocalypse is personal.
I thank you in advance for this brief indulgence.
God willing, we may yet hear more of the Old Man.

PART II

The Savage Boy

CHAPTER 1

You take everything with you.

That is the last lesson. The last of all the lessons. The last words of Staff Sergeant Presley.

You take everything with you, Boy.

The Boy tramped through the last of the crunchy brown stalks of wild corn, his weak left leg dragging as it did, his arms full. He carried weathered wooden slats taken from the old building at the edge of the nameless town. He listened to the single clang of some long unused lanyard, connecting against a flagpole in the fading warmth of the quiet autumn morning.

He knew.

Staff Sergeant Presley was gone now.

The last night had been the longest. The old man that Staff Sergeant Presley had become, bent and shriveled, faded as he gasped for air around the ragged remains of his throat, was gone. His once dark, chocolate brown skin turned gray. The muscles shriveled, the eyes milky. There had been brief moments of fire in those eyes over the final cold days. But at the last of Staff Sergeant Presley there had been no final moment. All of him had gone so quickly. As if stolen. As if taken.

You take everything with you.

The cold wind thundered against the sides of Gas Station all night long as it raced down from mountain passes far to the west. It careened across the dry whispering plain of husk and brush through a ravaged land of wild, dry corn. The wind raced past them in the night, moving east.

A week ago, Gas Station was as far as Staff Sergeant Presley could go, stopping as if they might start again, as they had so many times before. Gas Station was as far as the dying man could go. Would go.

I gotcha to the Eighty, Boy. Now all you got to do is follow it straight on into California. Follow it all the way to the Army in Oakland.

Now, in the morning's heatless golden light, the Boy came back from hunting, having taken only a rabbit. Staff Sergeant Presley's sunken chest did not rise. The Boy waited for a moment among the debris and broken glass turned to sandy grit of Gas Station, their final camp. He waited for Sergeant Presley to look at him and nod.

I'm okay.

I'll be fine.

Get the wood.

But he did not. Staff Sergeant Presley lay unmoving in his blankets.

The Boy went out, crossing the open space where once a building stood. Now, wild corn had grown up through the cracked concrete pad that remained. He crossed the disappearing town to the old wooden shamble at its edge, maybe once a barn. Working with his tomahawk he had the slats off with a sharp crack in the cool, dry air of the high desert. Returning to Gas Station, he knew.

Staff Sergeant Presley was gone now.

The Boy crossed the open lot. Horse looked at him, then turned away. And there was something in that dismissal of Horse that told the Boy everything he needed to know and did not want to.

Staff Sergeant Presley was gone.

He laid the wood down near the crumbling curb and crossed into the tiny office that once watched the county road.

Staff Sergeant Presley's hand was cold. His chest did not rise. His eyes were closed.

The Boy sat next to the body throughout that long afternoon until the wind came up.

You take everything with you.

And . . .

THE SAVAGE BOY 141

The Army is west. Keep going west, Boy. When you find them, show them the map. Tell them who I was. They'll know what to do. Tell them Staff Sergeant Lyman Julius Presley, Third Battalion, 47th Infantry, Scouts. Tell them I made it all the way—all the way to D.C., never quit. Tell them there's nothing left. No one.

And . . .

That's the North Star.

And . . .

Don't let that tomahawk fly unless you're sure. Might not get it back.

And . . .

These were all towns. People once lived here. Not like your people. This was a neighborhood. You could have lived here if the world hadn't ended. Gone to school, played sports. Not like your tents and horses.

And . . .

There are some who still know what it means to be human—to be a society. There are others . . . You got to avoid those others. That's some craziness.

And . . .

"Boy" is what they called you. It's the only thing you responded to. So "Boy" it is. This is how we . . .

Make camp.

Hunt.

Fight.

Ride Horse.

Track.

Spell.

Read.

Bury the dead.

Salute.

For a day the Boy watched the body. Later, he wrapped Staff Sergeant Presley in a blanket; blankets they had traded the Possum Hunters for, back two years ago, when their old blankets were worn thin from winter and the road, when Staff Sergeant Presley had still been young and always would be.

At the edge of the town that once was, in the golden light of morning, the Boy dug the grave. He selected a spot under a sign he could not spell because the words had faded. He dug in the warm, brown earth, pushing aside the yellowed, papery corn husks. The broken and cratered road nearby made a straight line into the west.

When the body was in the grave, covered, the Boy waited. Horse snorted. The wind came rolling across the wasteland of wild corn husks.

What now?

You take everything with you.

Horse.

Tomahawk.

Blankets.

Knife.

Map.

Find the Army, Boy. All the way west, near a big city called San Francisco. Tell them there's nothing left and show them the map.

When he could still speak, that was what Staff Sergeant Presley had said.

And . . .

You take everything with you.

Which seemed something more than just a lesson.

CHAPTER 2

The road and the map gave the number 80. For a time he knew where he was by the map's lines and tracings. He alone would have to know where he was going from now on.

I followed him from the day he took me. Now I will need to lead, even if it is just myself and Horse.

Horse grazed by the side of the broken and cracked highway.

The short days were cold and it was best to let Horse eat when they could find dry grass. The Boy considered the snowcapped mountains rising in the distant west.

Sergeant Presley would've had a plan for those mountains.

You should be thinking about the snow, not about me, Boy.

The voice of Sergeant Presley in his head was strong, not as it had been in the last months of his life when it was little more than a rasp and in the end, nothing at all.

You're just remembering me as I was, Boy.

I am.

You can't think of me as someone who can get you outta trouble. I'm dead. I'm gone. You'll have to take care of yourself now, Boy. I did all I could, taught you everything I knew about survival. Now you got to complete the mission. You got to survive. I told you there'd be mountains. Not like the ones you knew back east. These are real mountains. They're gonna test you. Let me go now and keep moving, Boy.

The sun fell behind the mountains, creating a small flash as it disap-

peared beyond the snowcapped peaks. Horse moved forward in his impa-
tient way. The Boy massaged his bad leg. This was the time when it began
to hurt, at the end of the day as the heat faded and the cold night began.

*Sometimes it's better to ride through the night, Boy. Horse'll keep you warm.
Better than shiverin' and not sleepin'. But stick to the roads if you do go on.*

The Boy rode through the night, listening to Horse clop lazily along,
the only sound for many hours. He watched his breath turn to vapor in
the dark.

I should make a fire.

The Boy continued on, listening to Sergeant Presley's voice and the
stories he would tell of his life before the Boy.

*Ah got caught up in things I shouldn't have. You do that and time gets away
from you. It shoulda taken me two years to get across the States. Instead it's
taken me almost twenty-five or twenty-eight years. I've lost count at times.
How old are you, Boy? You was eight when you come with me. But that was
after I'd finished my business in Montana. That took me more than twenty to
do. Maybe even thirty. Nah, couldn't have been that much.*

*We fought over San Francisco maybe ten years. After the Chinese kicked us
out of the city and dug in, that's when the general sent us east to see if there was
anyone left in D.C. My squad didn't make it two weeks. Then it was just me.
Until I met you, and that was up in Wyoming.*

*I spent three years fighting in a refugee camp up near Billings. That's where
I lost my guns. After that it was all the way up to Canada as a slave. Couldn't
believe it. A slave. I knew that camp was doomed from the start. I should've
topped off on supplies and food and kept moving. Cost me all told seven years.
And what I was thinking going back to get my guns after, I couldn't tell you to
this day. I knew there was no ammo. I didn't have any ammo. But having a
gun . . . People don't know, see? Don't know if it's loaded. I musta walked a
thousand miles round-trip to find out someone had dug up my guns. Stupid.
Don't ever do anything stupid, Boy.*

Later, the Boy limped alongside Horse thinking of "Reno" and
"Slave Camp" and "Billings" and "Influenza" and "Plague" and especially "Gone," which was written next to many of the places that had
once been cities. All the words that were written on Sergeant Presley's
map. And the names too.

In the night, the Boy and Horse entered a long valley. The old highway descended and he watched by moonlight its silver line trace the bottom of the valley and then rise again toward the mountains in the west. Below, in the center of the valley, he could see the remains of a town.

Picked over. Everything's been picked over. You know it. I know it. It is known, Boy. Still you'll want to have your look. You always did.

For a long time the Boy sat atop the rise until Horse began to fidget. Horse was getting crankier. Older. The Boy thought of Sergeant Presley. He patted Horse, rubbing his thick neck, then urged him forward not thinking about the slight pressure he'd put in his right leg to send the message that they should move on.

CHAPTER 3

The boy kept Horse to the side of the road, and in doing so he passed from bright moonlight into the shadows of long-limbed trees that grew alongside the road. He watched the dark countryside, waiting for a light to come on, smelling the wind for burning wood. Food. A figure moving in the dark.

At one point he put his right knee into Horse's warm ribs, halting him. He rose up, feeling the ache across his left side. He'd smelled something. But it was gone now on a passing night breeze.

Be careful, Boy.

Sergeant Presley had avoided towns, people, and tribes whenever possible.

These days no good ever comes of such places, Boy. Society's mostly gone now. We might as well be the last of humanity. At least, east of Frisco.

On the outskirts of a town, he came upon a farmhouse long collapsed in on itself.

I can come back here for wood in the morning.

Down the road he found another two-story farmhouse with a wide porch.

These are the best, Boy. You can hear if someone's crossing the porch. You can be ready for 'em.

The Boy dismounted and led Horse across the overgrown field between the road and the old house.

He stopped.

He heard the soft and hollow *hoot, hoot* of an owl.

He watched the wide night sky to see if the bird would cross. But he saw nothing.

He dropped Horse's lead and took his crossbow from its place on the saddle. He pulled a bolt from the quiver in his bag and loaded the crossbow.

He looked at Horse.

Horse would move when he moved. Stop when he stopped.

The Boy's left side was stiff. It didn't want to move and he had to drag it to the porch making more sound than he'd wished to. He opened the claw his withered left hand had become and rested the stock of the crossbow there.

He waited.

Again the owl. He heard the leathery flap of wings.

Your body will do what you tell it to, regardless of that broken wing you got, Boy.

The Boy took a breath and then silently climbed the rotting steps, willing himself to lightness. He crossed the porch in three quick steps, feeling sudden energy rush into his body as he drew his tomahawk off his belt.

Crossbow in the weak left hand, waiting, tomahawk held high in his strong right hand, the Boy listened.

Nothing.

He pushed gently, then firmly when the rotten door would not give. Inside there was nothing: some trash, a stone fireplace, bones. Stairs leading up into darkness.

When he was sure there was no one else in the old farmhouse he went back and led Horse inside. Working with the tomahawk he began to pull slats from the wall, and then gently laid them in the blackened stone fireplace. He made a fire, the first thing Sergeant Presley had taught him to do, and then closed the front door.

Don't get comfortable yet. If they come, they'll come soon.

He could not tell if this was himself or Sergeant Presley.

The Boy stood with his back to the fire, waiting.

When he heard their call in the night, his blood froze.

It was a short, high-pitched ululating like the sound of bubbling water. First he heard one, nearby. Then answers from far off.

You gotta choose, Boy. Git out or git ready.

The Boy climbed back onto Horse, who protested, and hooked the crossbow back into its place. He pulled the tomahawk out and bent low, whispering in Horse's ear, the ceiling just above his head.

"It'll be fine. We can't stay. Good Horse."

Horse flicked his tail.

'I don't know if he agrees,' thought the Boy, 'but it doesn't matter, does it?'

The face that appeared in the window was chalk white, its eyes rimmed in black grease.

That's camouflage, Boy. Lets him move around in the night. These are night people. Some of the worst kind.

The eyes in the window went wide, and then the face disappeared. He heard two quick ululations.

More coming, Boy!

The Boy kicked and aimed Horse toward the front door. Its shattered rottenness filled the Boy's lungs as he clung to Horse's side and they drove through the opening. He saw the shadow of a man thrown back against a wooden railing that gave way with a disinterested crack.

Other figures in dark clothes and with chalk-white faces crossed with black greased stripes ran through the high grass between the road and the farmhouse. The Boy kicked Horse toward an orchard of ragged bare-limbed trees that looked like broken bones in the moonlight.

Once in the orchard, he turned down a lane and charged back toward the road. Horse's breathing came labored and hard.

"You were settling in for the night and now we must work," he whispered into Horse's twitching ears.

Ahead, one of the ash-white, black-striped figures leaped into the middle of the lane. The figure planted his feet, then raised a spear-carrying arm back over his shoulder.

The Boy tapped twice on the heaving flank with his toe and Horse careened to the right, disagreeing with a snort as he always did.

'You wanted to run him down,' thought the Boy.

They made the road leaping a broken fence. He stopped and listened. The Boy could hear the ululations behind them. He heard whistling sounds also.

Down the road quickly, get outta Dodge now, Boy!

He took the road farther into town, passing the crumbling remains of warehouses and barns long collapsed. Stone concrete slabs where some structure had burned down long ago rose up like gray rock in the light of the moon. Sergeant Presley had always spoken simply at such places.

Gas Station.

School.

Market.

Mall.

The Boy didn't know the meaning or purposes of such places and possessed only vague notions of form and function when he recognized their remains.

In the center of town he saw more figures and brought Horse up short, hooves digging for purchase on the fractured road. The Ashy Whites formed a circle and within were the others. The Ashy Whites were standing. The others sat, huddled in groups.

"Help us!" someone cried out and one of the Ashy Whites clubbed at the sitting figure.

Behind him, the Boy could hear the ululations growing closer. Horse stamped his hooves, ready to run.

"Rumble light!" roared a large voice and the Boy was suddenly covered in daylight—white light like the "flashlight" they'd once found in the ruins of an old car factory. It had worked, but only for a day or so. Sergeant Presley had said light was once so common you didn't even think about it. Now . . .

No time for memories, Boy!

Horse reared up and the Boy had to get hold of the mane to get him down and under control. Once Horse was down and settled, the Boy stared about into the blackness, seeing nothing, not even the moonlight. Just the bright shining light coming from where the Ashy Whites had been.

An Ashy White, large and fat, his face jowly, his lower lip swollen, his eyes bloodshot, stepped into the light from the darkness off to one side. He was carrying a gun.

What type of gun is this, Boy?

When they'd found empty guns Sergeant Presley would make him learn their type, even though, as he always said, *They were no good to anyone now. How could they be? After all these years there ain't no ammunition left, Boy. We burned it all up fightin' the Chinese.*

Shotgun, sawed off.

The Ashy White man walked forward pointing the shotgun at Horse.

What will it do? he heard Sergeant Presley ask.

Sprays gravel, short range.

The Ashy White continued to walk forward with all the authority of instant death possessed.

There can't be any ammunition left. Not after all these years, Boy.

He kicked Horse in the flanks and charged the man. Pinned ears indicated Horse was only all too willing. Sometimes the Boy wondered if Horse hated everyone, even him.

In one motion the Boy drew his tomahawk.

The man raised the weapon.

Don't let it go unless you mean to, might not get it back, Boy. He always heard Sergeant Presley and his words, every time he drew the tomahawk.

He'd killed before.

He'd kill again.

He was seventeen years old.

The world as Sergeant Presley had known it had been over for twenty-three years when the Boy whose own name even he had forgotten had been born on the windswept plains of what the map had once called Wyoming.

You strike with a tomahawk. Never sweep. It'll get stuck that way, Boy. Timing has to be perfect.

Jowls raised the shotgun, aiming it right into the Boy.

There can't be any ammunition left, Boy. The world used it all up killing itself.

And the Boy struck. Once. Down. Splitting the skull. He rode off, out of the bright light and into the darkness.

CHAPTER 4

He could hear the Ashy Whites throughout the night, far off, calling to one another. At dawn there were no birds and the calls ceased.

Boy, Sergeant Presley had said that time they'd spent a night and a day finding their way across the Mississippi. *Things ain't the same anymore.*

They were crawling through and along a makeshift dam of river barges and debris that had collected in the mud-thickened torrents of the swollen river.

You probably don't know what that means, d'ya? The mosquitoes were thick and they had to use all their hands and feet to hold on to anything they could as the debris-dam shifted and groaned in the treacherous currents. It felt like they were being eaten alive.

If I'd fallen into the water that day what could he have done to save me?

But you didn't, Boy.

I was afraid.

I knew you was. So I kept telling you about how things were different now. About how sane, rational people had gone stark raving mad after the bombs. About how the strong oppressed the weak and turned them into slaves. About how the sick and evil were finally free to live out all of their cannibalistic craziness. And how sometimes, just sometimes, there might be someone, or a group of someones who kept to the good. But you couldn't count on that anymore. And that was why we were crossing that rickety pile of junk in the river rather than trying for the bridge downstream. You smelled what those people who lived on the bridge were cookin' same as I did. You knew what they were cooking, or who they were cooking. We didn't need none of that. The world's gone mostly crazy now. So much so, that all the good that's left is so little you can't hardly count on it when you need it. Better to mistrust everyone and live another day.

Like these Ashy Whites out in the night looking for me.

Seems like it, Boy.

Many times he and Sergeant Presley had avoided such people. Horse knew when to keep quiet. Evasion was a simple matter of leaving claimed territory, crossing and re-crossing trails and streams, always moving away from the center. The town was the center. Now, at dawn, he was on the far side of the valley and he could make out little of the town beyond its criss-cross roads being swallowed by the general abandonment of such places.

You almost got caught, Boy.

But I didn't.

We'll see.

He waited in the shadows at the side of a building whose roof had long ago surrendered inward, leaving only the walls to remain in defeat. The warm sunshine on the cracked and broken pavement of the road heading west beckoned to him, promising to drive off the stiffness that clamped itself around his left side every night.

They'll assume you're gone by now, Boy.

The Boy waited.

When he hadn't heard the ululations for some time, he walked Horse forward into the sunshine.

Later that morning he rode back to the town, disregarding the warnings Sergeant Presley had given him of such places.

Whoever the Ashy Whites were, they had gone.

And the others too, huddled within the circle of the Ashy Whites—that voice in the night, a woman he thought, calling for help.

Who were the others?

The answer lay in the concrete remains of a sign he spelled S-C-H-O-O-L.

School.

This had been their home. The fire that consumed it hadn't been more than three days ago. But the Boy knew the look of a settlement. A fort, as Sergeant Presley would have called it. The bloated corpses of headless men lay rotting in the wan morning light.

This is where those who had huddled within the circle of the Ashy Whites had lived all the years since the end of the things that were.

Before.

He found the blind man at the back of the school, near the playground and the swing sets.

Remember when I pushed you on a swing that time, Boy? When we found that playground outside Wichita. We played and shot a deer with my crossbow. We barbecued the meat. It could have been the Fourth of July. Do you remember that, Boy?

I do, he had told Sergeant Presley in those last weeks of suffering.

It could have been the Fourth of July.

The blind man lay in the sandbox of the playground, his breath ragged, as drool ran down onto the dirty sand, mixing with the blood from the place where his eyes had once been.

The Boy thought it might be a trap.

He'd seen such tricks before, and even with Sergeant Presley they'd nearly fallen into them once or twice. After those times and in the years that followed, they'd avoided everyone when they could afford to.

He got down from Horse.

"There's no more to give!" cried the blind man. "You've taken everything. Now take my life, you rotten cowards!"

The Boy walked back to Horse and got his water bag.

Not much left.

He knelt down next to the blind man and raised his head putting the spout near his lips. The blind man drank greedily.

After: "You're not with them, are you?"

The Boy walked back to Horse.

"Kill me."

He mounted Horse.

"Kill me. Don't leave me like this. How . . ." The blind man began to sob. "How will I eat?"

The Boy atop Horse regarded the blind man for a moment.

How will any of us eat?

He rode off across the overgrown field and back through a broken-down wire fence.

That's everything you need to know, Boy. Good. Tells you everything you need to know. Supremacists. Coming down out of their bunkers in the North. Don't know these guys, but they're worth avoiding. Probably here slavin'.

Probably.

Go west. Get into the Sierras before winter. The mountains will be a good place to go to ground for winter. It's hard to live in the mountains but there'll be less people up there. You plan, you prepare, and you'll do just fine. Come spring, you cross the mountains and head for Oakland. Find the Army. Tell them.

In the days that followed, the Boy rode Horse hard across the broken and barren dirt of what the map called Nevada. On the big road, Freeway, which he kept off to his right, he passed horrendous wrecks rusting since long before he'd been born. He passed broken trucks and overturned cars, things he'd once wanted to explore as a boy. Sergeant Presley would often let him when they'd had the time for such games—the game of explaining what the Boy found inside the twisted metal, and what the lost treasures had once meant. Before.

Hairbrush.

Phone.

Eyeglasses.

There was little that remained after the years of scavenging by other passing travelers.

The winding, wide Freeway curved and climbed higher underneath dark peaks. Roads that left Freeway often disappeared into wild desert. Sometimes as he rested Horse he would wonder what he might find at the conclusion of such lonely roads.

At one intersection the rusting framework of a sign crossed the departing road. From the framework three skeletons dangled in the wind of the high desert, rotted and picked at by vultures.

Probably a warning, Boy. Whoever's up that road doesn't want company.

It was a cold day. Above he could see the snowcapped peaks turning blue in the shadow of the falling sun. Later that night as he rode down a long grade devoid of wrecks, snow began to fall and he was glad to be beyond the road-sign skeletons.

He made camp in the carport of a fallen house on the side of a rocky hill that overlooked the winding highway. He stacked rubble in the openings to hold in the warmth of his fire.

CHAPTER 5

She and her sisters came out that night, south out of the desert wastes ranging up toward the road. Winter was coming on fast, and they needed to make their kills soon and return south to their home near the big canyon. They had hunted the area lean of mule deer and for the last week had been reduced to eating jackrabbits. Far too little and lean for a pride of lions.

Did she think about what the world had become? Did she wonder how she had come to be hunting the lonely country of northern Nevada? Did she know anything of casinos and entertainments and that her ancestors had once roamed, groomed and well fed, behind glass enclosures while tourists snapped their pictures?

No.

She only thought of the male and their young and her sisters.

Tonight the wind was cold and dry. There was little moonlight for the hunt. If they could only come across a pack of wild dogs. It would be enough to start them south again. Once they were south, they would have food in the canyons. And if they had to, they could always search the old city. There was always someone there, a lone man digging among the ruins. There was always someone hiding within the open arches and shredded carpets, the overturned machines and the shining coins spilled out as though carelessly thrown down in anger.

She topped the small line of hills and saw the dark band of the highway heading west. They had always regarded this road as the extent of their northern wanderings. Now they had to turn south.

Her sisters growled. She watched the road, looking for a moving silhouette in the darkness. One sister came to rub her head with her own.

Let's return. He is waiting.

And for a moment she smelled . . . a horse.

They had taken wild horse before.

When she was young.

Running down the panicked mustangs.

There had been more than enough.

She scented the wind coming out of the east and turned her triangular head to watch the curve of the road as it gently bent south along the ridgeline.

There was a horse along the road.

CHAPTER 6

In the late afternoon of the next day the Boy rode alongside the highway listening for any small sound within the quiet that blanketed the desolation of the high desert.

There is nothing in this land. It's been hunted clean.

The Boy, used to little, felt the ache in his belly beginning to rumble. It had been two days since the last of a crow he'd roasted over a thin fire of brush and scrub wood.

So what's that tell you, Boy?

Death in some form. Either predators who will see me as prey or poison from the war.

That's right, he heard Sergeant Presley say in the way he'd always pronounced the words "That" and "is," making them one and removing the final "t."

A place called Reno is in front of me. Maybe another day's ride.

All cities are dead. The war saw to that, Boy.

Some cities. Remember the one called Memphis. It wasn't poisoned.

Might as well have been, Boy. Might as well have been.

The big roar came from behind them. Horse turned as if to snarl, but when his large nostrils caught the scent of the predator he gave a short, fearful warning. The Boy patted Horse's neck, calming him.

I've never heard an animal make a sound like that. Sounds like a big cat. But bigger than anything I've ever heard before.

He scanned the dusty hills behind him.

He saw movement in the fingers of the ridge he'd just passed.

And then he saw the lion. It trotted down a small ridge kicking up dust as it neared the bottom. For a moment the Boy wondered if the big cat might be after something else, until it came straight toward him. Behind the big lion, almost crouching, a smaller lion, sleeker—no great mane surrounding its triangular head—danced forward, scrambling through the dusty wake of the big lion.

He wheeled Horse about to the west, facing the place once called Reno, and screamed "Hyahhh!" as he drove the two of them forward.

CHAPTER 7

'The idiot,' thought the lioness. She'd only made him come along so he could roar at just the right moment and drive the horse into her sisters and the young lying in wait ahead. Instead he'd cried out in hunger at the first sight of the meaty flanks of the horse. She could hear the saliva in his roar. The cubs would be lucky to get any of this meal.

His cry had been early and she knew from the moment the horse began to gallop that her run would never catch the beast. For a short time she could be fast. But not for long. Not in a race. Her only hope now was that her sisters and the young were in a wide half circle ahead, and that the horse would continue its course into their trap.

'The idiot,' she thought again, as she slowed to a trot. 'He's only good for fighting other males. For that, he is the best.'

THE BOY RACED down alongside the ancient crumbling highway, but Horse was slowing as the ground required caution. A broken leg would be the death of them both. He reined in Horse hard at an off-ramp and sent them down onto an old road that seemed to head off to the south. Ahead, a slope rose into a series of sharp little hills, the ground smooth, wind-blown sand and hardpack. He spurred Horse forward up onto the rising slope. At the top he stopped and scanned behind him.

In the shadow of a crag, he could see the big lion doggedly trotting along the ridgeline. Ahead of the lion, crouched low and crawling, the sleeker lion had stopped. The Boy could feel its eyes on him.

"It's us they're after, Horse. I don't think they're going to take no for an answer."

Horse snorted derisively and then began to shift as if wanting to turn and fight.

That's jes big talk, Boy! Those lions'll kill him dead and you with him. Don't pay no attention to him, Horse's jes big talk. Always has been.

Ahead to the west he could see a bleached and tired city on the horizon. But it was too far off to be of any use now.

And it could be poisoned, Boy. Radiation. Kill you later like it did me.

The Boy turned Horse and raced below the ridgeline, skirting its summit. They rounded the outmost tip of the rise, and beyond it lay a vast open space, empty and without comfort.

The ground sloped into a gentle half bowl and he could see Freeway beyond.

I should never have left the road. We could have found a jackknifed trailer to hide in. Sergeant Presley said those were always the best places to sleep. We did many times.

He patted Horse once more on the neck whispering, "We'll sprint for the road beyond the bowl. We'll find a place there."

Horse reared impolitely as if to say they should already be moving.

Halfway down the slope at a good canter, watching for squirrel and snake holes, places where Horse could easily snap one of his long legs, the Boy saw the trap.

There were five of them. All like the sleeker, mane-less lion. Females. Hunters. They were crouched low in a wide semicircle off to his right. All of them were watching him. He'd come into the left edge of their trap.

You know what to do, Boy! barked Sergeant Presley in his teaching voice. His drill sergeant voice. The voice with which he'd taught the Boy to fight, to survive, to live just one more day.

Assault through the ambush.

Horse roared with fear. Angry fear.

The Boy guided Horse toward the extreme left edge of the trap, coaxing him with his knee as he unhooked the crossbow, cocked a bolt, and raised it upward with his withered left hand.

Not the best to shoot with. But I'll need the tomahawk for the other.

The sleek females darted in toward him, dashing through the dust, every golden muscle rippling, jaws clenched tight in determination.

This is bad.

The fear crept into the Boy as it always did before combat.

Ain't nothin' but a thang, Boy. Ain't nothin' but a thang. Mind over matter; you don't mind, it don't matter.

The closest cat charged forward, its fangs out, and in that instant the Boy knew it would leap. Its desire to leap and clutch at Horse's flanks telegraphed in the cat's wicked burst of speed.

The Boy lowered the crossbow onto the flat of his good arm holding the tomahawk, aimed on the fly, and sent a bolt into the flurry of dust and claws from which the terrible fanged mouth and triangular head watched him through cold eyes.

He heard a sharp, ripping yowl and kicked Horse to climb the small ridge at the edge of the bowl. On the other side he could see frames of half-built buildings below on the plain before the city.

Half-built buildings.

Construction site.

Maybe houses being built on the last day of the old world. Houses that would never be finished.

If I can stay ahead of them for just a moment . . .

Horse screamed and the Boy felt the weight of something angry tearing at Horse's left flank.

One of the female lions had gone wide and raced for the lip of the ridgeline. Once on top, it had thrown everything into a leap that brought it right down onto Horse's flank.

The Boy cursed as he swiped at the fierce cat with his tomahawk. But the lioness had landed on Horse's left side and his axe was in his right hand. The Boy batted at the lioness with the crossbow. Its mouth was open, its fangs ready to sink into Horse's spine, the Boy shoved the crossbow into the cat's open jaws. Gagging and choking, the lioness released Horse's torn flesh as its paws attempted to remove the crossbow. It fell away into the dust and Horse continued forward. Already the Boy could feel Horse slowing. His own feet, bent back onto Horse's flanks, were dripping with warm blood.

"Don't slow down," he pleaded into Horse's pinned ears, doubting whether he was heard at all. "Just make it into those ruins."

When Horse didn't respond with his usual snort, the Boy knew the wound was bad.

CHAPTER 8

The Boy drove Horse hard through the drifting sand of the old ruins. Rotting frames of sun-bleached gray and bone-white wood, warped by forty years of savage heat and cruel ice seemed to offer little protection from the roaring lions now trotting downslope in a bouncing, almost expectant, gait.

They wove deeper into the dry fingers of wood erupting from the sand of Construction Site. The Boy heard the crack of ragged wooden snaps beneath Horse's hooves. He hoped they might find a hole or even a completed building to hide in. But there was nothing. Behind them he could hear the cats beginning to growl, unsure how to proceed through the rotting forest of ancient lumber. The Big Lion gave a roar and the Boy knew they would be coming into the maze after them.

Near the far edge of the spreading ruins, the Boy found a half-constructed bell tower ringed with ancient scaffolding over a narrow opening. It was their only hope. He steered Horse in under the rickety scaffolding still clinging to its long unfinished exterior. In the shadowy dark he dismounted Horse and raced back outside. He swung his tomahawk at the ancient scaffolding, cutting through a rusty bar with one stroke. He stepped back inside once he'd smashed the other support bar. The scaffolding began to collapse across the entrance as he saw the Big Lion come crashing through the warped and bent forest of dry wood, charging directly at him.

The scaffolding slanted down across the entrance as shafts of fading daylight shot through the dust.

The Big Lion crossed the ground between them in bounds.

Focus, Boy.

The Boy reached up and crushed another support with his tomahawk and more abandoned building material came crashing down across the entrance. Dust and sand swallowed the world and the Boy closed his eyes and didn't breathe. Horse screeched in fear as the Boy hoped the collapsed scaffolding would be enough to block the entrance.

When he opened his eyes he could see soft light filtering through the debris-cluttered opening.

He put his good hand on Horse, conveying calm where the Boy felt none, willing the terror-stricken animal to understand that they were safe for now.

Then he looked at the wound.

Claw marks straight down the side. The whole flank all the way to the hock was shaking. He took some of his water and washed the wound. Horse trembled, and the Boy placed his face near Horse's neck, whispering.

"It will be okay.

"I will take care of you."

The wound is still bleeding, so I'll have to make a bandage.

He poured some water into the sand and made mud. He didn't have much water, but it was vital to get the bleeding stopped.

He can't bleed forever, Boy.

When the mixture was ready he packed it into the wound, steadying Horse as he went, murmuring above the lion's roar as he applied the wet mud.

SHE PACED BACK and forth outside the never-to-be-finished bell tower.

Horse was definitely inside. She could smell it. She could smell its fear.

At the top of the bell tower, fifteen feet high, she could see narrow arches. If she could leap from another structure she might get in there and make the kill.

The male rose up on his hind legs and began to bat away at the collapsed opening. Wood splintered and cracked as he put all of his four hundred pounds onto the pile of debris. As usual he tired quickly and went to lie down, content to merely wait and watch the entrance. The sisters came up to him one by one, trying to reassure him that all would be well, but he seemed embarrassed—or frustrated. Normally expressive, his great face remained immobile, which the young usually took for thinking. But she knew he was merely tired and mostly out of ideas and generally unconcerned at how things might turn out.

She knew him—and loved him.

She paced away from the tower and then turned, gave two energetic bounds, and leapt. She almost made the top. Her claws extended, ripping into the dry stucco of the bell tower, revealing ancient dry wood beneath. She began to climb toward the opening, and a moment later a sheet of stucco ripped away and she fell backward.

There is wood like a tree underneath. 'Once this skin is off,' she thought, 'I'll be able to climb in.'

She began to stand on her hind legs and rake her claws down the side of the tower as chalky stucco, dry and brittle, disintegrated.

As if not to be outdone by her sister, another of the females began to dig at the base of the tower like she might for the making of a den. Now it would be a race. Who would get to the horse first? The male would like that. He would reward whoever got in first. It was his way.

The sun was going down. It would be a long night.

CHAPTER 9

Horse had stopped trembling. He seemed resigned now to the tight space and had stopped threatening to fight present conditions. The Boy climbed atop Horse and reached for the high arched openings just below the roof. Leveraging himself upward, he was able to climb into them.

Below, the lions were instantly aware of him. Multiple pairs of glowing dark eyes watched him. By the barest of moonlight he could see them lying about while the one who had been digging at the base of the tower stopped.

If I had my crossbow I could pick her off.

Never mind what you don't have, Boy. You better start thinking about a jailbreak, otherwise . . .

The Big Lion roared loudly, opening its mouth and showing its fangs as it turned its head, throwing the roar off into the hills. When the lion finished it stared straight at the Boy.

The Boy listened to the echo of the roar bounce off the far hills, its statement reminding him of the vastness of the high desert and how alone he was within it.

'So that's how it is,' thought the Boy. 'All right then, no surrender.'

One of the females suddenly ran forward, leapt, and almost caught the edge of the arched opening. The whole bell tower shook and Horse cried out in fear. The lion slid down as her claws raked the stucco off, revealing the dry wooden slats beneath.

This thing was not well constructed in the Before, and these hard years since haven't improved it. You would tell me to stop and think, Sergeant.

He removed his tomahawk from his belt.

The feline turned and charged the tower again. The Boy waited and as it made its leap he slammed the tomahawk down into one paw. The beast screeched and threw itself away from the wall.

That should give me some time.

The Lioness watched the Boy for a moment, the contempt naked in its cool eyes, then lay down apart from the others, and began to lick the wound. The Boy could not tell how badly he might have hurt it.

He lowered himself down into the dark, finding Horse with his dangling feet. Then he gently let himself down onto Horse's back. He sat there, letting his eyes adjust to the darkness.

I've got to do something about the digger next. If I can do something about her, maybe they'll get the point that I'm not coming out. Maybe then they'll go away.

You sure about that, Boy?

The only thing else I can think of is to strike at them as they come through the sand under the wall.

It seemed a thin plan, but looking at the four walls and Horse, what else could he do?

For the rest of the night he listened to the digger. Occasionally the lions would growl and he thought it best not to go up into the high arched openings.

If I remain invisible to them, then maybe "out of sight, out of mind" as you used to say, Sergeant?

Or . . .

If they can't mind me, then I won't matter to them.

And it was there in the dark that the Boy realized Sergeant Presley had been full of knowledge. Full of words and wisdom. Those things were a comfort to him in the times he and Sergeant Presley had been in danger.

I'm young. I haven't had all the years it takes to acquire wisdom. Now death is closer than it has ever been.

Everyone dies, Boy, even me. Maybe it's not as bad as you think.

SOFT, PALE LIGHT shone the through arched windows above. The night had passed and though he had not slept much, the Boy felt as though he'd slept too much. As if some plan of action should have occurred to him in the hours of darkness. But none had and he cursed himself, not knowing what the coming day might bring.

He heard a roar, far off, then another one and another, almost on the heels of the echo of the first.

More lions?

Trouble always looks for company, Boy. Always.

Then I'll be ready. Whatever it is, the best I can do is to be ready.

He climbed to the top of the bell tower and looked out from the arches. The Big Lion, the male, was on his feet and staring into the darkened west. A thin strip of red dawn cut the eastern desert in half like a hot knife. The Boy followed the Big Lion's gaze into the dark and saw three male lions, smaller—not by much, manes almost as big—pacing back and forth in the dark.

The females were drawing the cubs back from the Big Lion.

If there is going to be a fight, the newcomers might not know I'm here. If they win, then this could be good for me.

SHE LIMPED TOWARD her mate.

Had she ever been special to him?

She liked to think so. She liked to think there was something special between her and him that her sisters had never known. Would never know.

She'd seen him fight other males before. The desert was full of their kind. The mule deer and wild animals had been abundant in all the years she had known and the prides had grown large. And now, from some unknown pride much like her own, the young lions had come to find mates for themselves among her pride. Just as he had once found her.

Limping forward to stand behind him, she could at least do that for the love of her existence. She could at least do that. But when he turned, she saw the flash of anger in his eyes, warning her to get back, and maybe something she had never seen before. Fear.

He roared again. It was his way and his answer to the challengers.

His roaring anger at the horse within the bell tower had most likely summoned these challengers out of the dark. She knew his roar, beautiful and safe to her, had cost them all.

She lay down in front of her sisters, between them and her mate—their mate—and watched.

When the battle started in earnest, it transformed from a storm to a whirlwind in the space of a moment. The newcomers, baiting the big male halfheartedly, as though they might leave at any moment, suddenly came at him at once, silent, focused, hopeful.

His great claws pinned the first and he sank his jaws into the back of his challenger's neck. She heard the crunch of bones and knew that one was finished, though it continued to flail wildly, its claws drawing blood across her mate's belly.

Another challenger circled wide and landed on her mate's back after a great pounce. The challenger was unsure what to do next. The third came in hard at his flank and began to tear away great strips of fur and skin with claws that looked long and sharp.

Here was their leader, she thought. He had been smart enough to wait.

The male shook the one in his mouth as he tried to draw his victim upward.

She cried out for him to be done with that one and to handle the other two, but her cries were drowned out by his as he roared and whirled on the leader. He batted at the flanker, who tumbled away and then turned the momentum into something to fling itself right back at the male.

The challenger on his back held on for dear life and she could sense the fear in that one. That one didn't have it in him to sink his fangs into her mate. He was the runt. He would never have a pride of his own.

The male pinned the lion he'd cast off; it was his technique, she knew, to use his size to subdue and strangle his enemies. Enraged, he crushed the leader beneath him and tore out his throat.

Her paws, kneading the soft sand of the desert, relaxed. She knew he had won. He would be wounded, badly if the blood streaming down his belly was any indicator, but he had at least beaten these challengers. She was proud of both him for his strength and herself for her faith and love.

Thunder broke across the darkness like dry wood split sharply.

Thunder was what she'd thought the sound was, and for a moment she'd expected lightning. But the sudden white light that would illuminate the land never came. Instead she watched him roll off his foes in a great spray of blood.

The Back Biter rolled away, confused. For a moment the runt raised a paw as if he might step this way or that, flee or attack. Then another bolt of thunder erupted, and a fraction later the Back Biter's head exploded.

In the wind she found a new horse and acrid smoke; a mule also.

Her sisters were fleeing into the night.

The young whimpered.

She turned back to him and crossed the short space to his body. Her eyes were on his mane and the face that had once expressed so many thoughts to her. So many thoughts that she knew she had never known him completely.

He was still.

Asleep.

Beautiful.

Noble.

Even when she heard the thunder erupt again, near and yet as if part of a dream she was only waking from, she watched his face.

The bullet struck her in the spine.

And she watched him.

She watched him.

She watched him.

CHAPTER 10

"All my skins is ruin't!"

Early light had turned the night's carnage golden. The Boy listened to the man below.

"This one, that one over there! Hell, Danitra, all of 'em." Then, "Maybe 'cept this one."

The Boy listened from the shadows of the bell tower.

You be careful now, Boy! There's little good left in this world.

"Might as well come out!" thundered the voice. "Seein' as how I saved ya and all such."

He knows I'm here. And he has a gun. Not like the rusty "AK Forty-sevens" and broken "Nine mils" we would find sometimes. His gun is different, like a polished piece of thick wood. As though it were different and from some place long ago.

For all that Sergeant Presley had tried to explain about guns to the Boy, he'd never guessed one would've made such a sound, like the crack of distant thunder heard from under a blanket.

He patted Horse and climbed up into the high arched openings once more.

"There ya're!" roared the man.

He was barrel-chested and squat. He wore dusty black leather and a beaten hat, hair dark and turning to gray. He stopped his cutting work to look up from one of the lions, holding a large knife in his bloody hand.

"These are mine," he said and turned back to his business with the hide. "Any more in there besides you?"

The Boy said nothing.

"That means nope," said the stranger.

"My horse."

"Well, you better get down and get him out of there."

The Boy continued to watch the man as he skinned the lion, swearing and sweating while he made long, sawing cuts, then stood, wiped his knife, and pulled back a great streak of hide.

"C'mon boy. I got work to do. No one else here but me and my horse and Danitra. She's my mule."

He set to work on the next lion.

"This one's even worse than the last! That was a mess. Coulda done that better myself. What tribe you with, boy?"

The Boy said nothing and continued to watch.

"You with them tribes out in the desert?"

The Boy remained silent.

"Well, pay it no mind. I've got to get these hides off and cut some meat. So if you don't want to be a part of that then I'll ask you to get your horse out of there and move along." The man stood staring at the Boy, his bloody knife hanging halfway between forgotten and ready.

"My horse is injured."

The man wiped the knife once again on the leather of his pants and spit.

"Well, get him out of there and let's take a look. I know a thing or two about horses."

The Boy climbed down the side of the bell tower using the wooden slats exposed after the attacks of the lions. At the bottom, he began to remove the debris blocking the entrance as the man returned to skinning the dead lions.

"It's bad." The man spit again as he ran his hands across Horse. For a moment Horse grew skittish, but the man talked to him in a friendly manner and Horse seemed to accept this as yet one more thing to be miserable about.

"Not the worst. Best we can do for him is get him up to the river, the other side of Reno. Good water there. We can clean the wound and get him ready for the fever that's bound to be come. If he can survive that fever, then, well maybe. But fever it'll be. Always is with them cats."

'I'm not ready to lose Horse,' thought the Boy. 'It would be too much for me right now. First you, Sergeant, and now . . .'

Ain't nothin' but a thang, Boy! You do what's got to be done. Without Horse you'll be finished in a week.

"Name's Escondido. I'll lead you up to the river—goin' that way myself and I'll show you the path through Reno. Now get to work and help me with these hides, then we'll be movin' on out of this forsaken planned community of the future."

The Boy stared at the ground.

"That's what you was holed up in when I found you," said the man called Escondido as he pointed first to the bell tower and then the rotting timber. "Someone was building a neighborhood here on the last day. Never got finished. See all that rotten wood? Frames for houses. This bell tower was probably the fake entrance. Make it seem like something more'n it was. They would've called it some name like Sierra Verde or the Pines. Probably something to do with the bell tower. Bell Tower Heights! Yes siree, that's what they woulda called it. Old Escondido knows the old people's ways. I was one of 'em, you know. I lived in a house once. Can you believe that, boy? I lived in a house."

I've got to do whatever it takes to save Horse.

"How far is this river?"

"Be there by nightfall. We don't want to be in Reno after dark, that's for sure."

"Reno wasn't nuked?" "Nuked" was a Sergeant Presley word.

"No. But it looks like a big battle was fought there out near the airport. So the city might as well have been nuked. Strange people live in them old casinos now. Had a partner used to call 'em the Night People, 'cause they get crazy and howl and cause all kinds of havoc at night. Last two or three years when I crossed over the Sierras I liked to avoid Reno. Got into a bad spot there one time about dusk. It was a bad time, even with my guns."

The Boy followed Escondido's gaze to a bent and broken horse. Its hair was matted and lanky, and it cropped haphazardly at what little there was to be had, as if both tired and dizzy. In the worn leather saddle, the Boy saw two long rifles.

"That horse ain't much to look at. But best part of him is he's deaf, so when my breech loaders go off he don't get scared and run off."

The Boy worked for the rest of the morning scraping the hides of the lions as Escondido finished the skinning and then cut steaks from the female. He built a small smoky fire and the meat was soon spitted and roasting in the morning breeze.

"We got to eat these now. It'll be a long day gettin' through Reno. Then we still got to ride up into the hills to reach the river."

Once the mule, Danitra, as Escondido called her, was saddled with hides, they sat down next to the fire and ate.

"How much water ya got?" asked Escondido through a mouthful of meat.

"Not much. I'll save it for Horse."

"There's no water worth havin' between here and the river, so keep that in mind. Don't go gettin' thirsty. I'll trade you some for that old Army rucksack you got there on your horse."

The Boy continued to chew, putting Escondido's offer away until later, hoping the heat and dust would not force him to trade Sergeant Presley's ruck for a mouthful of water.

THEY RODE OUT of the bloody camp. Escondido's nag could do little more than trot and so the pace was slow. Escondido filled the silence of the hot afternoon with conversation and observations, all the while watching the crumbling remains of the world for shadows and salvage.

"Was tracking them lions for three days before they got onto your big one. I heard him roar and I knew I'd lost 'em. Couldn't get a shot off on 'em all night. But I knew I had to find 'em before they got into that fight. Hides'll be ruined and Chou'll make his usual fuss 'bout it and all. Still I got ways and means. What tribe did you say you was with?"

When the Boy didn't answer, Escondido continued on.

"My family came from out of the South. I had another name. Prospero, my mother used to call me. But, in the little refugee camp we started out in, they called me Escondido. That's where my family had been before the bombs: a place called Escondido. Tried to ask my papa where that might be. All he said was that it was gone now. A fantasy place."

And . . .

"I cross over the mountains beginning of summer every year. This year I got a late start. Mountains is gettin' weirder every year. You know about the Valley? No, don't make no difference, you don't look like them people. Say, was you born that way or'd you get bust up when you was little?"

And . . .

"What was you doin' out here? This part of the desert ain't safe. Though for that matter, what part is?"

Don't tell anything about ye'self, Boy.

"You don't say much, do you? Is that your tribe's way? Don't say much?"

It was afternoon by the time they crossed onto the dusty streets of Reno. Buildings lay collapsed or shattered to little more than rusting frames that groaned in the sudden gusts that came in off the desert.

In the silence of late afternoon, shadows turned to blue and Escondido continued to talk in a low whisper though he would stop when they passed piles of rubble and twisted metal that lay across the wide thoroughfare leading into the heart of the darkened city.

"The people, the tribes, savages all up in the mountains, everywhere I've gone, they wear hides to show what mighty hunters they are. Now up at the trading post in Auburn, everybody wants hides so they can trade with them savages. Them lions, if'n they'd been perfect, woulda fetched a high price from old Chou. That's a shame. A perfect shame."

Ahead, each of them could see the rising pile of bleached casinos crumbling around a bridge that rose over the wide avenue they would follow. A bridge that connected two of the ancient palaces and seemed to loom over the road like the wingspan of some prehistoric dead bird.

Escondido withdrew one of the rifles from its saddle holster and rested the butt on his thigh as he gave a soft *chick, chick* to his nag.

Then he looked at the Boy and drew his finger to his lips.

CHAPTER 11

Cities ain't got nothing left for you, Boy.

And yet, Sergeant, I've always wanted to go into them. To know what's in them.

Places where you might have lived, Boy, had things been different.

Sergeant Presley's voice seemed to ignore Escondido's whispered commentary and remembrances as they led their horses through the dust and rubble.

I try to find myself in them, Sergeant Presley. I try to find who I might have been.

Why, Boy?

It might tell me who I am, Sergeant.

"I come through here must been something like five years ago with a partner. Dan was his name." Escondido's face looked gray and dusty in the last orange light of day. His mouth, full of crooked teeth, hung open, sucking at the dry desert air.

The Boy could hear Escondido's heavy breathing.

They entered the long, crumpled stretch of casino row. Hollow-eyed windows gaped blindly down on them from along shell-dented walls.

"Said he might go in and jes' take a look around. I tells him it's jes' not done, Dan. Jes' not done."

They passed a burned U.S. Army tank poking its melted barrel out from a storefront whose sign had long since been scoured to meaninglessness.

M-1 Abrams, thought the Boy.

"Toughest hour of my life was waitin' for Dan to come out. I sat there holding that horse of his for the longest time. We'd had a good haul in lions that year. What was the point of going in?"

Ahead, a sweeping bridge spanned the gap between two casinos like a broken arm reaching out from the wreckage of a terrible accident to touch another victim.

"Worst part's just ahead," muttered Escondido.

Escondido cocked back the hammer on his long rife.

This is what I mean, Boy. Told you not to get caught up in things and here you are, caught up.

I could answer you, he thought to Sergeant Presley. But you would tell me I was crazy. You would tell me that you are dead and the problems of this life no longer concern you. Wouldn't you?

"I waited an hour and he never come out," whispered Escondido.

The laughing started.

One voice cackled, clear and very near at once.

Moments later two others responded, as if only politely and at a mediocre jest.

Then another burst out, hysterically almost.

Finally the rest were laughing uncontrollably.

Sniggering.

Guffawing.

Giggling.

Snickering.

Hooting.

Wailing.

Sobbing.

Moaning.

Crying.

Laughter careened across the broken casino walls.

Laughter was everywhere.

"Keep straight on!" yelled Escondido over the echoing din.

For a moment there were almost-shadows within the recessed gloom of the buildings high above. Not quite, but almost.

Leading Horse, the Boy pulled his tomahawk from his belt.

"They won't come out. Never do. But you don't want to go in after 'em all the same," warned Escondido.

They crossed the shadow of the broken bridge and a sink crashed to the dusty pavement behind them.

Horses reared and snarled fearfully.

The Boy held him around the neck, whispering softly.

"I know. I know. I know," he said over and over.

Once they were almost out from underneath the broken walkway, Escondido muttered, "I think that's what all the silliness is about. Tryin' to get us to come in and take a look."

A scabbed face, pale and haunted, appeared for a moment behind dusty shards of broken glass three stories up. Whether it was a man or a woman, who could say.

They passed on and the laughter seemed to fade in quiet increments. Finally there is a single painful scream.

In the hours that passed between the ruins of Reno and the river, Horse began to favor his unhurt legs, limping with the left hind leg. The Boy knew a powerful infection had already set in.

"He can't go much farther," said the Boy.

"He'll have to. Another few hours to the foot of the mountains and then the river. I won't sleep down here tonight."

They rode on, passing through lonely crumbling hills in the weak last light of day. When the sun finally fell behind the lowest of the Sierra Nevada, the land turned to purple and the smell of sage hung heavy in the shadows.

"Another hour and we'll be alongside the river. Once we're to it my hunting lodge won't be much farther on. I won't waste a bullet on your horse. Load 'em myself and there's precious few left now. Understand?"

The Boy said nothing as darkness settled across the lonely spaces that surrounded them. They heard the river long before they saw it, babbling in the moonlight. Its wide curves followed an old broken highway off to one side. Long, flat swathes of calm river erupted, burbling, over stones, and beyond that, small waterfalls marked their climb up alongside the river's fall.

Horse was badly limping when Escondido stopped. They were on a wide turn below a small pass. The river, off to their left, was little more than soft noise. Escondido seemed to rise for a moment off his horse's back, smelling the wind. The Boy tasted the night air also and found charred wood.

When they came to the river crossing that led to Escondido's lodge, the Boy could see the charred remains of wood and stone from across the rock-filled river.

On the other side Escondido said nothing and climbed down from his nag. He walked into the midst of the burnt timber and ash. "Still warm." He laughed. "Thought they'd burn me out, they did."

The Boy got down off Horse and began to inspect the wound again. When he touched it, Horse danced away from him. He removed his pack and led Horse down to the river. The water was cold, startlingly cold as he washed Horse's wound. At first Horse wouldn't stand for it, but as the cool water numbed the heat in the wound, the big horse tolerated the cleansing.

By the time the Boy led Horse back up to the clearing where once the lodge watched the creek and the highway beyond, Escondido had built a fire.

"I'm gonna tell you something you don't want to hear," said Escondido above the clatter of a pot he set on the fire. "I'm lit out at first light. I'm done with this side of the mountains. It ain't safe and it's gittin' a lot more dangerous. Time was it was just me between here and the Hillmen. Now all them southern tribes is comin' north, just itchin' fer a fight with the Chinese. This is my last hunt. Tomorrow I ride for Auburn. After that, who knows? There's a widow for me somewheres, I guess."

They watched the fire. Escondido cut branches from a sapling and roasted strips of lion meat.

"This part's the part you ain't gonna like. So here it is. That horse needs to rest and even if he does that, ain't no guarantee he's gonna make it. In two days or sooner we'll have snow and if his infection is gonna come, it'll kill him before we make it within the gates o' the outpost."

They were silent, each watching the meat and fire, the wood turning to ash, the orange coals beneath.

Escondido rose to turn the strips of lion and settled back down onto an old blanket.

"I come here twenty seasons musta been. Every summer I'd cross them mountains above us and come down here to hunt. First few days I got the place in order, then I had a whole operation to set up. Shoulda seen it. Hides tannin', big porch I like to set on of an evenin'."

"There was no trade in hides with the Hillmen 'fore the Chinese set up the outpost there in Auburn. Hillmen coulda cared less about lion hides. The whole bunch of 'em was different in every way. Lived out in the woods and only came together once a year when they'd get up a hunt or needed to fight one of the other tribes. I finally figured out why they called themselves the Hillmen when me and Danitra set up camp near the old school the year before it burned down. One night I was havin' a look for anything useful and I saw that their old football team was called the Hillmen. Now they live alone out in the deep woods mostly, but they still think of themselves as some old football team from before the bombs. It was how they told the difference between them and strangers. Crazy, huh? But not really—makes more sense than some of the other tribes."

The fire popped and the aroma of roasting meat caught the night's breeze as sparks rose into the dark sky.

"Not much fat in lion," noted Escondido.

Then . . .

"I'll miss this place for the rest of my days."

The mule honked at some ground squirrel. Escondido watched the forest for a long moment, his coal-black eyes wide in the dancing light of the fire.

"So, if you could ride with me, I don't think you'd make it. Or more to the point, I don't think yer horse'd make it. So I'm leavin' you. Sorry. That's the way it has to be."

When the Boy failed to protest, his face calm, almost asleep in the firelight, Escondido said, "I'll show you a few things in the morning, maybe even some bushes that'll help with the healing. If you get to work on a shelter, you'll be ready if them tribes come back lookin' for me. Most likely they'll take to you more than they ever did me. They're tribal like you. Don't like city people like me. Hate the Chinese, they do. Hate 'em. But you, you'll be fine I suspect."

They ate the lion and fell asleep near the fire. The night came on cold and the Boy dreamed of faces in windows. His last thought before he closed his eyes beneath the broken crystal of night was of faces. He remembered faces, though he did not remember who they belonged to. What was Sergeant Presley's face like? He wondered and for a moment he could not remember its shape. But when he thought of the Sergeant's rare smile, the face came back to him. And he was asleep.

CHAPTER 12

Snow fell and had been falling since they first woke. Now it was coming down steadily. High above, white clouds had replaced the startling blue of morning. Escondido, on the far side of the river and rounding the curve of the old highway that wound its way up across the pass, did not turn to see the Boy one last time, and then he was gone.

The wind rushed through the pines and made the only sound of the place where once Escondido's hunting lodge stood.

You got to prioritize, Boy!

And he did. The Boy knew he had to get moving. There were three things to do.

Make a shelter.

Gather healing herbs for Horse.

Find food.

But for a long moment he stood there. It was so quiet in between the thundering gusts of wind that shook all the pines at once that he could hear snowflakes landing on the ground all around him. Or so he thought.

Escondido left him with a simple knowledge of the area's herbs and inhabitants. The lions wouldn't come up this far and they didn't like the cold anyway. There were some wolves. But wolves were wolves. There was a way to handle them. Then there was the bear: a mother brown bear, one of the worst kind. Two seasons ago, Escondido related, she had two cubs.

This year he didn't see the cubs. But the bear lived in a cave upriver at the top of a small conical hill. A small mountain even.

"You'd be wise to steer clear of her altogether. The brown are the worst. Man-eaters."

Horse was on his side now. His large dark eyes were weak and milky. Often he would raise his head to make sure the Boy was near. But even that act seemed too much for him.

So what do you do first, Boy? Make a plan. Get moving. Get to work. Do something. Make a decision. If you don't, circumstances will decide for you. The enemy loves to tell you what to do.

It was the voice of Sergeant Presley, heard over a thousand camps at morning, in the frosty nights of Michigan when they'd barely survived. Down South, crossing the big river, he'd heard the Sergeant plan and tell him to do the same.

It's all you got now, Boy!

The Boy gathered herbs. He found most of them not far from the river. Most of them were dying as winter came on.

Will that affect their potency?

Don't matter, Boy. It's all you got right now.

He spent the rest of the morning mashing the herbs and slowly adding water until all became paste. He boiled the paste for a while, per Escondido's instructions. He applied the hot paste after having taken Horse to the river to clean the wound once more in the icy water, in which Horse's legs gave out for a moment and he stumbled, casting a look at the Boy as if they were both embarrassed to the point of death. After, when the paste was hot and went on Horse's wounded flank, after Horse lay down, his eyes resigned to the smoking fire, the Boy murmured, "I didn't see that. Let's just forget about that." The Boy covered him with his only blanket.

Afternoon, thin and cold, settled across the little river. There was no warmth left in the big stones and a breeze could be seen in the pines atop the surrounding mountains.

The Boy began to hack at the burnt lumber of Escondido's lodge, salvaging any usable beams for shelter. There weren't many. Near the river, he found fallen trees and in dragging them, he was soon exhausted.

If I had Horse right now this would be easier.

When night fell, what he had was little more than a two-sided lean-to. The open side faced the mountain wall that rose above their camp. Moving Horse within the lean-to, the Boy built a fire. Later he gathered loose wood from the forest floor and brown grass for Horse.

It was night now and he didn't mind the dark or the forest. He had known such places his whole life.

CHAPTER 13

In the night, keeping the fire high, face burning hot, body and back cold, the Boy sat staring into the shifting flames. Occasionally he simply watched Horse. He tried to make a plan for the coming morning beyond this endless freezing night.

Fishing in the river.

Food.

Traps.

How to improve the shelter.

The snow was coming down thick and silent. It hissed as it fell into the fire.

Even with the fire, it was cold. But Horse slept and that was good. Or at least the Boy hoped it was good.

On nights like this, when it was too cold, Sergeant Presley would talk, telling him things, teaching him. Sometimes they would break camp and simply walk to keep warm. The Boy remembered walking in the freezing rain outside Detroit.

Later he remembered the heavy warmth of late summer when they finally reached the Capitol in Washington, D.C.

Sergeant Presley's Mission, he'd called it.

They'd come upon the old Capitol the day before, broken buildings overgrown by blankets of green. Cracked highways had fallen into swampy water thick with flies and insects.

I got to go in there, Boy, and there ain't no use you comin' in with me, said Sergeant Presley on that long-ago day.

It was hot and sticky in the late afternoon. Summer. It had been raining for much of the week.

Let's make camp and then I'll go in and look for what I got to find—what I know won't be there. But I'll go in all the same.

They'd been living well that year. They'd fought for Marshall and his men the spring before. A range war in Pennsylvania. When the war was over, they'd been granted permission to move on into Maryland. When they'd gone from the warlord Marshall and his expanded kingdom, they'd had good clothes and supplies. They'd found nothing but wild people after that—abandoned farms and shadows in the thick forest and overgrown towns. The small villages and loose power that men like Marshall had held over the interior lands between the ravaged cities would not be found along the devastated ruin of the eastern coast.

One morning, in the center of a town that had burned to the ground long before the Boy had been born, standing in the overgrown weed-choked outline of an intersection, Sergeant Presley said, *If there is anyone here, I'll find them in the Capitol—or in the President's bunker below the White House.* They were both looking at an old fire hydrant that had been knocked out into the road. The road was covered in hardened dirt that had once been muddy sludge.

Who am I kidding? Sergeant Presley had suddenly erupted into the silence of the place. *There ain't anybody left. There wasn't since it all went sideways and there hasn't been since. I know that. I've known it all along!*

His shouted words fell into the thick forest turning to swamp. An unseen bird called out weirdly, as if in response.

But orders are orders, he'd said softly, his sudden rage gone. *And someone had to come and find out. Once I know, we'll head back to the Army in Oakland. We got to cross the whole country. You up for that, Boy?*

Sergeant Presley had smiled at him then.

The Boy remembered, nodding to himself.

Still, it'd be nice if someone was there. That'd be something, Sergeant Presley had said.

But there hadn't been.

Now, beside the fire in the mountains as the first big snow of winter came on, almost to the other side of the country, the Boy knew there hadn't been anyone in the old Capitol or at the President's bunker beneath the White House.

Sergeant Presley was gone all that next day.

In the morning the Sergeant had put on some special gear they'd found in a place called Fort. They'd spent two weeks looking through the place, scouring warehouses that had long since been looted, searching through ash and rubble. Finally, in a desk drawer they'd found the gear Sergeant Presley had been looking for.

Some clerk probably got told to bring in his MOPP gear in case things went that way in those days. So he brings it in and his section sergeant checks it and then sends him off to do paperwork. And now I'm gonna wear it and hope the charcoal and other protectants are gonna hold out long enough to get me to the White House without getting radiation poisoning.

When he'd left, wearing the dull green cloth and rubber shoes, fitting the gas mask and hood over his head, Sergeant Presley had looked like a monster.

He was gone all that day.

Sitting by the fire, the Boy couldn't remember what he'd done after that. Probably exploring with Horse.

In the swarming-insect early evening, outside the Capitol in the swamp camp, it was misty. The gloomy ruins of the Capitol faded in the soft light of dusk. It looked like a dream. The Boy remembered that in the last moments of light, the Capitol, whatever it had once been, looked like a dream castle—like something that might have once had meaning for him. Like things that seem so important in a dream, but when you awake, those things seem of little value and you can't imagine why they'd held such a place in the dream.

That was what the Capitol had looked like to the Boy in those last moments of daylight.

In the early evening of that long lost waiting-day, Sergeant Presley had finally come up the hill to their camp above the swamp. Threading his way through the tall grass, Sergeant Presley took off the bug-eyed gas mask. He dropped or threw the mask off into the sea of silent yellow grass. He tore off the suit, coughing. Crystal droplets of sweat stood out in his short curly hair.

The Boy gave him water from their bag, then some of the cakes they always made back then.

Still hot in there. Sergeant Presley coughed.

The Boy said nothing.

"Hot" meant forbidden. If sometimes they saw a city on the horizon, like the one by the big lake, its tall towers skeletal and bent, Sergeant Presley would simply say *still hot.* And sometimes he would add, *When you're an old man, if you live long enough, you can go in there. But I never will.*

Sergeant Presley drank more water and coughed.

I woulda brought you somethin', but it's too hot in there. I swear I came right up on a bomb crater. Must've been low yield. But hell if it didn't go up twenty degrees. I look around and everything is black ash. Even the marble on one of them old government buildings, the House I think it was called, had turned black.

He coughed again.

'He will never stop coughing,' thought the Boy. That was when the coughing had started. That day everything changed, though at the time neither of them knew it.

Sergeant Presley knew it, he suspected. But he didn't say anything.

Sergeant Presley coughed again.

Made it all the way to the White House.

He coughed and then drank, swallowing thickly.

There was never anything there. It wasn't a direct hit. See, back then our enemies were fighting unconventionally. Dirty-bomb strikes by remote-controlled aircraft launched within our borders. Terrorists. They went after Washington early on. We knew that. It wasn't until later, when China got involved, that we didn't know for sure what had really happened anywhere. After that it was just plain dark everywhere.

He chewed numbly on the cake, staring at their wispy fire. The Boy watched him, saying nothing.

The bunker was a deep hole. Must've used the Chinese equivalent of a J-Dam on it. I saw one of those take out the TransAmerica Building in Frisco. I'll show you when we get there. Anyways, they must have used a "bunker buster" on it. Then, whether before or after, there must have been a nuclear strike, probably an airburst. Whole place was cooked.

He coughed, choking on the cake.

Now the Boy looked up at the night sky. It had stopped snowing. The stars were out, shimmering in the late night or early morning. His face was hot. He stood up and walked to the cliff wall.

He leaned against it, feeling the cold stone on his back.

You should sleep, Boy. Tomorrow's gonna be a long day.

'I wish,' thought the Boy, 'that all of the days that had been were long days. I wish you were here.'

He did not hear the voice of Sergeant Presley and wondered if he had ever heard it. Or if he would ever hear it again.

As he walked back to the fire, a pebble fell off the side of the cliff and the Boy turned, staring up into the heights. His shadow loomed large against the wall. He saw his powerful, strong right arm and when he moved the withered left arm, it looked little more than a thin branch.

He stared at the wall and its many shadows. For a moment he could almost see a man.

The man was sitting. Hunched over. Staring sightlessly out into the world. His hand was holding something up to his mouth.

A cake.

It was as though he was looking at Sergeant Presley on that hot, sweaty, and very long day outside the ruins of the Capitol.

Sergeant Presley, sitting, tired, sweating. Eating a cake. Alive.

He turned back to the fire after staring at the image for too long. But he wished it were true. He wished Sergeant Presley were here with him now, across the country. Almost to the Army. Alive.

He picked up a piece of burnt wood from Escondido's lodge.

He turned back to the cliff wall.

And he began to draw that long lost day. Sergeant Presley at the end of his mission. At the end of his country. At the beginning of the end of his life.

CHAPTER 14

At first light he checked the river. In a pool off the main channel he spotted three trout lying in the current, close to the bottom. He watched them for a long while, listening to the constant, steady crash of the river downstream.

The backs of the trout remind him of broken green glass bottles he'd once seen in a building where he and Sergeant Presley had slept for the night. *Wine bottles,* Sergeant Presley muttered simply, as an epitaph over the heap of green glass. The Boy remembered holding a piece up, examining it in the wavering light of their fire. *Careful,* Sergeant Presley had warned him. *Don't cut yourself, Boy.*

He found a long piece of driftwood waiting on the rocks by the river, left by the springtime flooding of that year. He returned to camp with the driftwood and after inspecting Horse's wound, which looked bad and worse now in the bright light of morning, he dug out wet grass from underneath the snowfall and laid it near Horse's head. Horse seemed not to notice.

He laid more wood on the fire, its wetness making white smoke erupt into the cold air.

The Boy sat down next to the smoking fire with the driftwood stick lying away from his body. Taking one end of the wood, he cut long peels of bark away from himself and soon the white flesh of the wood underneath lay exposed. He fed the soft peels of wood into the fire as he continued to bring the stick to a point. In the end, it became a sharp spear.

He returned to the pool and waited. There was no sign of the broken-wine-bottle-colored trout. He sat on his haunches watching the gentle current drift along the bottom of the rock-covered pool.

Later, one of the fish entered the pool. The Boy waited, watching it move first one way and then another. He got little flashes of white from off its belly as it turned. Finding the current, the emerald-colored trout settled into it. After a moment, when the Boy knew it would be sleeping, he raised up, leaning over the pool, the spear drawn back over his good shoulder, the point just above the surface of the water.

He waited.

He felt a breath enter his lungs and as he let the air go, when there was little left in him, he plunged the spear through the surface, catching the trout in the back, just behind its head. It bent to the left, sending up a splash of water with its wide tail, and the Boy hauled it from the pool, amazed at his prize. Its rainbow-colored flanks fell away from its wine-bottle back, the white belly pure and meaty. It was a creature of beauty.

When the catch was gutted and spitted over the smoking fire, the Boy made more herb paste and applied it to Horse's wound, wiping away the oozing pus as best he could.

He'd tried to lead Horse to the water before doing this, but the animal wouldn't even bother to raise his head, much less stand.

"Okay, rest then," said the Boy and heard the croak in his voice against the deafening fall of water over rock.

When the fish was cooked, he walked while eating, back to the drawing of Sergeant Presley on the cliff wall. He'd worked on it late into the night, immune to the cold. When he'd returned to the fire, he'd felt frozen. The heat stung his skin as it warmed him. He'd thought the drawing had been complete, but now looking at it in the late-morning light he could see where features would need to be added—filled in and shaded.

In the afternoon he tried to improve the shelter, but other than laying green pine branches across the top, there was little that could be done.

You've got to find better shelter, Boy! If this lodge was here from before the war then chances are there are others like it.

The Boy had seen many buildings from Before built in clusters; the towns they had passed through and the cities he had wanted to visit. Clusters.

In the afternoon he walked upriver with his tomahawk and knife. His withered left side felt stiff, but he concentrated on its movements, controlling it, willing his leg to step over fallen logs instead of dragging as it would've liked to if he'd ridden Horse for days at a time.

He heard a loud twig snap underneath his feet.

Too loud, Boy! No go.

Everything Sergeant Presley had taught him had been graded. When the time had come for the Boy to perform a task, the standard for pass or fail was always "good to go" or "no go." He'd hated when Sergeant Presley wrenched his mouth to the side and said, *No go.*

Upstream the river began to curve to the north, winding through a series of rapids. Off to the left he could see the steep, conical mountain Escondido had warned him of, where at the top a bear made its den.

It was winter now. Bears should be asleep.

There were no other lodges, or if there had been, what remained of them could not be found.

It was hard to imagine the world as a place where people could either live in cities or in the forest. What was so special about cities?

You always wanted to go there, Boy.

I did. I wanted to know what was in them.

And . . .

What would I have been like if I had lived in one?

Standing at the bend in the river, feeling his withered leg and arm stiffen in the late-afternoon cold as the sun fell behind tall peaks to the west, he thought of people he once knew and could not remember.

They had always lived in the cold plains. His first memory was of running. Of a woman screaming. Of seeing the sky, blue and cold in one moment, and the ground, yellow stubble, race by in the next.

Sergeant Presley had rarely mentioned "your people."

Not like in tents, not like your people.

All gone over to animals, not like your people.

They don't ride horses, like your people do.

THAT NIGHT THE temperature dropped and the snow came down in hard clumps without end. He lay next to Horse, who moved little and whose breathing was shallow. At one point, the Boy was so cold he thought he should surely die.

When he awoke in the morning everything was covered in snow.

THE BEST TIME to do something about a thing is to do it now, Boy!

We won't last out here another night.

When Horse opened his eyes they fluttered.

You won't make it out here like this, will you, Horse?

He laid his hand on Horse's belly, feeling the heat both comforting and sickening at once.

He knew what he had to do. He had known it in the freezing night when the snow had stopped falling and the wind rushed through the pines, seeming to make things even colder than when the snow had fallen. Even the sound of the icy water falling along the rapids seemed to make the world colder.

The Boy had known in the night what he must do.

He'd waited for Sergeant Presley to tell him not to do it.

"You would say," he thought aloud, pretending to be Sergeant Presley's voice. "You would say it was fool's business. That's what you would say."

He waited, listening to the rush of the water in the river.

He looked upriver, his eyes falling on the small, steep, conical mountain.

You would say that.

Ain't nothin' but a thang, Boy. Mind over matter. You don't mind, it don't matter.

You would say that also.

You got to kill that bear, Boy. No two ways about it.

CHAPTER 15

That morning he collected three long poles of fresh wood that wouldn't snap. Working with his knife he sharpened the ends into stakes, hardening them in the fire until the tips were black.

By noon he'd fed Horse, who ate little of the fire-dried grass the Boy had placed before him. He sat by the fire putting a fresh edge on the steel tomahawk Sergeant Presley had given him. Its bright finish was a thing made in the past, never to be seen again. Often, when they had encountered strangers, he'd seen their eyes fall to it, wanting it for their own.

Laying aside the sharpened tomahawk, he gave the knife an edge. They'd made these knives at the Cotter family forge. Sergeant Presley's knife lay wrapped within a bundle the Boy had carried away from the grave on the side of the road surrounded by the wild corn that had seemed to grow everywhere, a bundle the Boy had no desire to open.

You might need it for this one, Boy.

But the Boy couldn't see what an extra knife might do for him. He knew if his plan was a "no go" and he found himself down to his own knife, there wouldn't be much hope left in an extra knife.

That's right, Boy; work smarter, not harder. Knife work is hard work.

Let's hope it doesn't get to that.

The last thing the Boy would need for his plan would be what was left of the precious parachute cord. There was less than thirty feet of it now. As a child, the Boy had always been fascinated by the large coil, amazed at it, as he always was of the things from Before. There had been so much of the parachute cord, it had once seemed endless, always coiled about Sergeant Presley's shoulder to hip as they walked. One time Sergeant Presley had even made a knotted section of it for him to play with, muttering, *Merry Christmas*, as he'd handed it to the Boy on that long-ago winter day. Years passed, and traps and snares and other bits that could no longer be salvaged had reduced the large coil to less than thirty feet.

The Boy withdrew the last of it from his pack.

I don't want to use even this, but if I have to I will.

He thought of the bear.

He'd seen bears killed. The Cotter family hunted them for sport and meat. He'd followed one hunting party and watched them run down a small, fast black bear that was more interested in getting away than fighting. In the end, it had played dead until they'd put a bolt under its left shoulder blade.

They had seen big bears in the Rockies. Most of them had kept their distance, or charged, only to veer off. Horse was good for scaring things away. Once Horse went up on his hind legs, most animals knew he wasn't interested in running.

He looked at Horse.

Are you dying too? Like Sergeant Presley?

He patted the big brown belly; Horse stirred only slightly.

"I'm going to clear out a place for us to hole up in through the rest of winter." Then, "I'll be back."

He went down to the river and speared another of the broken-wine-bottle trout. Gutting and filleting the trout, he laid its body out on planks of charred wood over the embers of the fire.

After eating the fish he collected his gear, shouldering the three heavy poles and placing the thin coil of rope over his head to hang down from his neck.

Everything was moving too fast.

He could feel the tomahawk hanging from his belt, the knife in its sheath at his back.

What am I missing?

Mind over matter, Boy.

You don't mind, it don't matter.

HE CLIMBED THE conical hill, hauling himself up its snow-covered granite ledges. He avoided any pines that grew out of the rock, knowing them to be untrustworthy because of the shallow soil they grew in.

He found the cave just underneath the top of the hill. It would be a useless exercise if the cave was too low for Horse to squeeze into. What would be the use of dislodging the bear only to find his shelter too small? But the cave was like a wide frown on a mouth. It was tall enough at its highest point for Horse. Getting him up here would be another story—collecting wood also.

It's not ideal, but it's all I have.

You're assuming victory, Boy. First you got to kill that bear. But it's good you're thinkin' about tomorrow all the same.

A wide, flat ledge lay before the opening and below that, a sheer drop to the river below. He set the poles down, laying them gently in a crevice running through the cold gray granite. The poles came together, echoing, and the Boy waited, unsure what he would do if the bear were suddenly to appear.

I'll attack her.

That would be bad, Boy.

But what else was there to do? If she chases me I won't get away. If I attack, maybe she'll run.

In the moment that followed, the Boy could hear only the distant sound of the river below.

On a thick tree, stunted and growing out of the rock, he could see the deep indentations of the bear's claw marks.

What do you know about your enemy, Boy?

It's a bear.

A sow.

Cubs two years back, which means they've left.

I don't know if it's a grizzly or one of the browns, which are the worst. Too bad it's not one of the black ones.

And you would ask me about the battlefield. That's what you would ask me next, Sergeant Presley.

Where you gonna fight, Boy?

He looked at the flat ledge. It wasn't more than twenty feet wide and as much across.

I could make a trap, but I don't know where. I'd have to get her down the hill and chasing me.

Deadfalls are the best, Boy.

To do that, I'll have to get her down the side of the mountain and into the forest. Even then, the ground is frozen. It would take me a day or two to make a pit. One more night like the last and we won't make it.

So it's the ledge then, Boy.

I go in hard with a spear. If she's asleep I put one into her. I back up, grab another and put it in. By the time I get to the third . . .

You'll be at the edge of the cliff. That drop'll do the job, Boy.

She'll have to have a reason to go over.

If you've put three spears into her, Boy, you'll be the reason. All she can think of at that point is wanting you dead and then going back to sleep.

Here's what you do, you anchor the parachute cord and tie it about your waist, Boy. Wait until the last second and she'll follow you over.

Numbly he took the coil of rope off his neck. His heart was beating quickly.

He told himself to calm down. To stop.

Just do this. Don't think too much about it.

He crept toward the frowning entrance of the cave. There was a short drop inside. On the floor below, he could see a shapeless mass in the dark. The cave smelled of animals. He listened. He heard nothing. He waited, watching the shapeless mass. His vision narrowed as he stared hard, willing the details to be revealed.

He blinked and looked away as his vision began to close to a pinpoint. His heart was pounding in his ears.

Stop.

He crawled back out onto the ledge.

The drop was a good two hundred feet into the rapids.

I'm not really going to do this, am I?

Mind over matter, Boy.

He played the rope out, tying it about his waist.

They don't make this stuff anymore. Airborne Ranger gear, Boy. Best ever.

You'd said that, every time you brought it out, Sergeant. Every time we made a trap or a snare, you said that.

I was proud of what had once been. Proud that someone had made parachute cord. I had no right to be, Boy. But I was proud all the same.

The Boy searched the underside of the ledge.

A few feet below the edge and off to the side, a rugged little pine jutted out from the rock wall.

It's all I have.

To the west, large clouds, gray and full, rolled across the high peaks.

More snow tonight.

It will be very cold.

He climbed down the cliff face.

He loved to climb.

For a boy who had been born crippled and could not run as others did, climbing was an activity where the playing field leveled.

He had always climbed.

The Boy clung to the side of the rock wall. He spent more rope than he would have liked securing it to the pine. But he had to.

When he'd climbed back onto the ledge his muscles were shaking.

I need water and I've forgotten to bring the bag.

What else am I forgetting?

He felt fear rise again as he cupped a handful of snow and put it in his mouth.

In just a moment I'll have to do this.

Stop.

Mind over matter, Boy.

I don't mind. It won't matter.

That's right, Boy. That's good.

A strong wind came off the mountain peaks above and whipped long hair into his green eyes.

He brushed it away.

What else am I forgetting?

When he picked up the first pole it felt too light.

It felt hollow like he could break it across his knee.

He laid it down just in front of the cliff's edge, pointing toward the frowning mouth of the cave.

The second pole felt heavier. He placed it at the entrance.

When he went back for the third, it felt lighter than the second and he switched it out. 'I'll want the heaviest one first,' he thought.

Crouching low and entering the cave, he felt the rope pull taut at his waist.

It won't reach. I won't be able to get close enough to make the most of the spear.

He undid the rope about his waist and changed to a slipknot.

This is how it works, he told himself.

Change of plans, he'd heard Sergeant Presley say.

Change of plans.

He laid the loop of rope at the base of the second pole.

When you fall back to this position, you slip the rope around your right wrist, Boy.

What about the left?

I can't trust that side.

What else am I forgetting?

Stop, he told his heart.

Stop.

He crept into the cave, the tip of the spear dead center on the sleeping mass.

There was a moment.

A moment to think and to have thought too much.

He felt it coming. He'd known it before at other times and knew it was best to stay ahead of such moments.

He drove the spear hard into the mass.

An instant later it was wrenched out of his hands as the bear turned over. He heard a dry snap of wood echo off the roof of the cave as he retreated back toward the entrance.

For a moment, the Boy took his eyes off the bear as he slipped the loop about his wrist and grabbed the spear, making sure to keep the trailing end of the parachute cord away from the end of the pole.

In that moment he could hear the roar of the bear. It filled the cave, and beneath the roar he could hear her claws clicking against the stone floor as she scrambled up toward him.

When he looked up, following the blackened tip of the spear, he found the grizzly's head, squat, flat, almost low beneath the main bulk of her body. She roared again, gnashing a full row of yellowed fangs.

He jabbed the spear into her face and felt the weapon go wide, glancing off bone.

He backed up a few steps and planted the butt of the long pole in the ground.

The grizzly, brown, shaggy, angry, lurched out onto the ledge. It rose up on its hind legs and the Boy saw that it might, if it came forward just a bit, impale itself on the pole if it attacked him directly. He adjusted the pole right underneath the heart of the raging bear.

The bear made a wide swipe with its paw smashing the pole three quarters of the way to the top.

In the same instant that the pole was wrenched from the Boy's grip, and as if the moment had caused an intensity of awareness, he felt the slipknot, its mouth still wide, float from off his wrist.

Stick to the plan, Boy! You can't change it now.

He'd heard that before.

His back foot, his good leg, planted at the edge of the cliff, the Boy raised the final pole.

The bear on hind legs wallowed forward.

The Boy checked to make sure the parachute cord was really gone.

It was.

The moment that hung between the Boy and the bear was brief and startlingly clear. To have questioned what must be done next would have been lethal to either.

The Boy loped forward and rammed the pole straight up and into the chest of the bear.

'There is no other way but this,' he thought in that moment of running.

'No other way but this.'

He felt the furry chest of the bear meet his grip on the pole.

He pushed hard and felt the arms of the bear on his shoulders. He felt a hot breathy roar turn to a whisper above the top of his head.

His arms were shaking.

His eyes were closed.

He was still alive.

He backed away from the belly of the bear, letting go of the pole as the bear fell off to one side.

He was covered in a thick, cold sweat.

There was no other way.

CHAPTER 16

In the moments that followed the death of the bear, routine took over, ways the Boy had known his whole life.

Bleed the animal.

Don't think about how close you came to her claws.

The knife at his back was out as he stood over the carcass, finding the jugular, his good hand shaking, and then a quick flick and blood was running out onto the granite of the Sierra Nevada.

Don't remember her hot breath on top of your head when there was little you could do but go forward with the pole.

Next he made a cut into the chest. Working from the breastbone up to the jaw, he cut through flesh and muscle. When the cut was made he took out his tomahawk, adjusted his grip once as he raised it above his head and then slammed it down onto the breastbone several times. Soon he was removing the organs. Heart, lungs, esophagus, bladder, intestines, and rectum.

My hands are shaking, Sergeant.

It's just the cold, Boy. Just the cold. Keep on workin'.

It is cold out and getting colder, which will be good for the meat, but I still have much work to do.

Walking stiffly, he descended the mountain and returned to camp. He gathered his gear and when that was done, he began to coax Horse to get up one more time.

Horse seemed stunned that the Boy would even consider such a thing, but before long, whispering and leading, patting and coaxing, the Boy had him up and on his legs.

"I'll carry everything, you just follow me. We're going someplace warm."

Late afternoon turned to winter evening as he led Horse up onto the mountain. Halfway up, as they worked side to side across the gray granite ledges, snow began to fall, and by the time they'd reached the top, the Boy was almost dragging Horse. Never once did he curse at the animal, knowing that he was already asking too much of his only friend. And for his part, Horse seemed to suffer through the climb as though death and the hardships that must come with it are inevitable.

At the top, the Boy dropped Horse's lead and began to collect what little firewood he could find. Soon there was a small fire inside the cave. He led Horse into the cave, expecting more protest than the snort Horse gave at the scent of the bear.

The fire cast flickering shadows along the inside of the cave and though there was a small vault, the cave was neither vast nor deep.

It'll be easier to keep warm, Boy. That's good.

The Boy put his blanket over Horse, who'd begun to tremble. He fed Horse from a sack of wild oats he kept for the times when there was nothing at hand to crop.

Horse chewed a bit and then seemed to lose interest.

That's not good.

The Boy left the sack open before Horse and returned to the carcass of the bear.

Snow fell in thick drifts across the ledge as the wind began to whip along the mountainside.

'It has to be done now,' the Boy thought to himself.

But I'll need wood. The fire has to be kept going.

In the dark he descended the mountain, working quickly among the howling pines to find as much dead wood as possible. Every time he stopped to look for wood in the thin light of the last of the day, he felt his weak side stiffen.

When he'd collected a large bundle of dead wood, he tied it with leather straps and climbed the mountain once again, almost crawling under the weight, as the scream of the howling winter night bit at his frozen ears.

I am so tired. I feel all the excitement and fear of the fight with the bear leaving me.

Nearing the ledge of the cave, he thought, 'I could go to sleep now.'

And for a long moment, on all fours, the bundle of wood crushing down upon his back, he stared long and hard at the rock beneath his numb fingers, thinking only of sleep.

Back in the cave he fed the wood that wasn't too wet to the fire, watching the smoke escape through some unseen fissure in the roof of the cave. He held his cracked and bleeding fingers next to the flames.

You'll need that skin, Boy.

The Boy knew what that meant.

He'd known and planned what he must do next without ever thinking it or saying that he would do it. But if he was to have the skin of the bear, then what needed to be done would need to be done soon.

The bear was too heavy to drag off the ledge, back here into the cave near the fire.

That'd be the easy way, Boy. Never take the easy way.

He held up a handful of oats to Horse. Horse sniffed at them but refused to eat as he turned his long head back to the fire.

Okay, you rest for now.

Outside the storm blasted past the ledge. Everything was white and gray and dark beyond, all at once.

When he found the snow-covered bear, he began the work of removing the skin.

He completed the cut up onto the bear's chest. He cut the legs and then began to skin the bear from the paws up. His strength began to fail as he worked the great hide off its back, but when he came to the head, he made the final cut and returned to the cave to warm himself again. He took a handful of the oats, watching Horse's sleeping eyes flutter, and ate them, chewing them into a paste and swallowing.

Returning to the wind and the night, he dragged the skin into the cave and laid it out on the floor.

I can work here for a while and be warm by the fire.

But he knew if the meat froze on the carcass he would never get it off the bone.

For a long time after that, he crouched over the bear, cutting strips of meat. When he'd gotten all the usable meat he washed it in the snow and took it back into the cave. He spitted two steaks and laid them on the fire.

Into the cold once again, he cracked open the bear's skull for the brains and took those inside, placing them near the skin.

For the rest of the night he worked with his tomahawk, scraping the skin of flesh and fat and blood. When all of it was removed, he stepped outside, carrying the waste to the edge of the cliff and dropping it over the side.

The storm had stopped.

It was startlingly cold out. His breath came in great vaporous clouds that hung for a moment over the chasm and the ice-swollen river below and were gone in the next. The stars were close at hand. Below, the river tumbled as sluggish chunks of ice floated in the moonlight.

He washed his hands in snow, feeling both a stinging and numbness on his raw flesh.

He stood watching the night.

Clouds, white and luminous, moved against the soft blue of the moon-lit night. Below, the river and the valley were swaying trees and shining shadows of sparkling granite. 'I am alive,' he thought. 'And this is the most beautiful night of my life.'

DAWN LIGHT FELL across the ledge outside the cave. The Boy looked up from the skin he'd worked on through the night. The light was golden, turning the stone ledge outside the cave from iron gray to blue.

He felt tired as he returned to the skin once more, rubbing the brains of the bear into the hide.

"This is all I can do to cure it," he said aloud in his tiredness, as if someone had been asking what he was doing. As if Sergeant Presley had been talking to him through the night. But now, in the light of morning it all seemed a dream, a dream of a night in which he worked at the remains of a bear.

But I have not slept.

"There is too much to do," he said aloud.

You done everything, Boy. Now sleep.

The Boy lay down next to the fire and slept.

CHAPTER 17

In the days that followed:

He rubbed ash from the fire into the hide of the bear.

He smoked meat in dried strips.

He swept the cave with pine branches.

He had to lead Horse down the mountain to drink from the river at least once a day. He could think of no method to bring Horse enough water.

Winter fell across the mountains like a thick blanket of ice.

The Boy constructed a thatched door to block the entrance to the cave.

At night he stared at the wall and the moving shadows in the firelight.

By the time he'd collected firewood, watered Horse, and foraged enough food, the daylight was waning and he felt tired.

In the night he enjoyed listening to the fire and watching the shadows on the cave wall.

Winter had come to stay, and it seemed, on frost-laced mornings and nights of driving sleet, that it had always been this way and might continue without end.

CHAPTER 18

One night, as the wind howled through the high pines, he took Sergeant Presley's bundle out of his pack.

He stared at it for a long moment, listening to the wind and trying to remember that autumn morning when he'd found it next to the body.

Take the map and go west, Boy. Find the Army. Tell them who I was. Tell them there's nothing left.

In the bundle was a good shirt Sergeant Presley had found and liked to wear in the evening after they had bathed in a stream or creek and made an early camp. That was the only time Sergeant Presley would wear the good shirt he'd found behind the backseat of a pickup truck they'd searched in the woods of North Carolina.

Red flannel.

This my red flannel shirt, Boy. Shore is comfortable.

The shirt would be there.

The map. Sergeant Presley's knife. The shirt.

He undid the leather thong on the bundle and tied it about his wrist.

The soft cloth bundle opened and out came the shirt, and within were the knife and the map. And there was a leather thong attached to a long gray feather, white at the tip, its spine broken.

He laid the knife on his whetstone.

He laid the map on another stone, one he ate on by the fire. He left the broken feather and its thong in the bundle.

He held the shirt up and smelled Sergeant Presley in a draft coming off the fire.

He took off his vest and put on the shirt.

It was comfortable. Soft. The softest thing he'd ever felt. And warm.

He sat by the fire.

When he took up the map, he stared at it. He had seen the map many times, but always when it was laid out, Sergeant Presley was making a note or muttering to himself.

The Boy unfolded it, laying it on the ground. It was large. It was both hard and smooth. In the light it reflected a dull shine.

He stared at the markings.

Above Reno he read:

CHINESE PARATROOPERS. DUG IN. BATTALION STRENGTH.

Over Salt Lake City, in the state of Utah, he read:

GONE

Over Pocatello, in the state of Idaho, he read:

REFUGEE CAMP FIVE YEARS AFTER. OVERRUN BY SLAVERS.

Above this, across the whole of the northwestern states, was a red circle with the words "WHITE SUPREMACISTS" written in the center.

Across Omaha in big letters was the word "PLAGUE," and then a small red face with X's for eyes. There were red-faced "X eyes" listed over place names all the way to Louisville, in the state of Kentucky.

At Washington, D.C., he found an arrow that led into the middle of the ocean. Words were written in Sergeant Presley's precise hand.

MADE IT TO D.C. IT'S ALL GONE. BUNKER PROBABLY HIT EARLY IN THE WAR. NO REMNANTS OF GOV'T AT THIS LOCATION. TOOK ME TWENTY-EIGHT YEARS TO MAKE IT HERE.

On the back of the map the Boy found names.

CPT DANFORTH, KIA CHINESE SNIPER IN SACRAMENTO

SFC HAN, KIA CHINESE SNIPER IN SACRAMENTO

CPL MALICK, KIA RENO

SPC TWOOMEY, KIA RENO

PFC UNGER, MIA RENO
PFC CHO, MIA RENO
PV2 WILLIAMS, KIA RENO
And . . .
LOLA

THERE WAS NO mention of Escondido's "Auburn" on the map. The Boy traced the highway marked 80 as it crossed the mountain range and then fell into Sacramento in the State of California. After that, the road ran straight to Oakland. Written over Oakland, the Boy found I CORPS. Across the bay in San Francisco, circled in red, he saw the word CHINESE.

He stared at the broken feather and experienced the fleeting sensation of a memory. Which one, he could not tell.

CHAPTER 19

Horse had not died.

Winter broke and the Boy could hear ice crack in the river below. It was still cold.

The Boy led Horse to the bottom of the small mountain, down its icy ledges, watching Horse to make sure he didn't slip. There was only one close call, near the bottom. In the silence that followed the recovery, Horse seemed angry at his own inability and cantered off into the forest, snorting and thrashing his tail.

The Boy let him go, knowing Horse needed to forget the incident as much as the animal wanted the Boy to never remember it.

He was embarrassed, thought the Boy, keeping even the look of such a thought to himself.

For the rest of the morning they rode the snowy forest carefully. In the early afternoon, they crossed the river and came upon the great curve of the highway that climbed upward toward the pass. For a while the Boy left Horse to himself, letting him crop what little there was to find.

This is good. We need to be back on this road again. Even if just for a few moments of sunshine. It feels good to have the road under my feet and Horse's hooves. We have been too long away from the road.

He wandered back to their old camp.

Against the cliff wall, the Boy found the drawing of Sergeant Presley near the snow-covered remains of Escondido's charred lodge.

That evening back at the cave, as both he and Horse drowsily watched the fire, he took a piece of charcoal and shaved it lightly with his knife.

He considered the wall of the cave and saw no face or image in the flickering light. And yet he wanted to draw something.

He thought of the bear and quickly dismissed the thought. There were nights when he awakened in the dark and the bear was chasing him across the forest floor, and no matter how hard he urged his withered leg to move, it would not. Usually he awoke just before the bear caught him, but there were nights when he didn't, and in those nightmare moments, he could feel the bear's hot embrace, and the terror seemed a thing that would swallow him whole.

So he did not need a reminder of the bear.

He drew the mane first. The mane of the Big Lion. The male. That was what he remembered most in the times when he thought back to the night the lions surrounded him.

Next he added the eyes, the eyes that had seemed so cool and yet communicative, and then the teeth and the body, and the shadows that were his females. He drew the female who had watched the big male. She had been at his side, still watching him. They were together.

When the Boy was finished he lay on his back, watching the portrait of the lions, remembering them this way and forgetting the skins and the blood of that hot day.

ON THE COLD morning when they finally left the cave the Boy was wearing the skin of the bear over his back and down his left side. The withered side.

This way others won't be able to see where I am weak.

That's camouflage, Boy, camouflage.

They rode out past the bubbling river and up the slope, onto the rising highway.

It was a cold day, and the wind came straight down the old highway, but the skies above were blue. Soon they left the familiar, and each new curve in the road was a strange and almost alien world of chopped granite, high forests, and cold, deep mountain lakes.

'Winter can only last so long, and life in the cave would have made me weak,' the Boy thought.

Horse can no longer survive on what little grass I can dig out from underneath the snow. For me, the bear meat is long gone and even the fish from the stream seem harder to catch because there are so few now.

For most of that day they rode high into the mountains, and in the evening they camped under the remains of a broken bridge.

The fire was weak and the air was cold enough to make him think maybe they'd left the cave too soon, but Horse seemed stronger in the evening than when they first began the day's journey.

It was good for him to work so hard today.

The Boy slept, waking throughout the night at each new sound beyond the firelight.

IN THE MORNING they came upon a pole covered in the skulls of animals and garlands of acorns, a marker set in the dirt by the broken road.

You know what that means, Boy. Someone's land.

High above he could see the pass that leads down into the foothills beyond. Beyond the pass, the city of Sacramento and finally on to the bay and I Corps.

I could ride hard and bypass the people who live here.

It was later, as they rode steadily up the broken grade, that the Boy realized they were being followed. Across the valley he saw movement. But when he stopped to look he saw nothing. Still, he knew they were watching him.

There was little left of the bent highway that once crossed over the pass. What had not been covered in rockslide had fallen away into a dark forest below. The years of hard winter had taken their toll on the old highway.

Men came out from the forest floor. They made their way to the foot of the trail the Boy was leading Horse down. Horse, sniffing the wind, gave a snort, and when the Boy looked behind, he saw more men coming out along their backtrail, high above them on rocky granite ledges. They carried bows, a weapon he couldn't use because of his withered left hand.

The men were dressed for hunting: skins and bows. They were dark skinned, but every so often he saw fair skin among them.

Near the bottom of the trail he mounted Horse and adjusted the bear-skin across his left side.

At that moment he thought it would be nice to have a piece of steel from an old machine he could hold onto with his left hand beneath the skin. A beaten highway sign with a leather strap perhaps.

He took hold of the tomahawk with his strong right hand, letting it hang loosely along his muscled thigh.

The men were mostly short and bandy legged.

All were covered in wide, dark tattoos that swirled like the horns of a bull on their bare skin.

A leader, long hair falling against the dark sweeping horns that coursed and writhed in ink across his considerable arms and torso, stepped forward and raised his hand.

Was this a warning or an order?

Be ready, Boy, you got speed with Horse, but arrows move just as fast. Maybe even faster.

In the end, he faced a semicircle of hunters and knew there were more behind him.

It'll show weakness if you turn your back to check, Boy. It's an interrogation. They just want to ask questions.

"*Wasa llamo?*" shouted their leader.

The Boy remained staring at them.

In the years of travel he had heard many languages. Sergeant Presley had taught him to speak English, though the Boy remembered that what his people spoke was different and yet the same.

English, Boy. English! Sergeant Presley had barked at him in the first years. One day, without remembering when, specifically, the Boy noticed Sergeant Presley never barked again. That lost language he had once spoken was yet one more thing the Boy could not remember about his people, just as he could not remember when he had first seen the feather in Sergeant Presley's bundle and what, if any, was its meaning.

Who am I?

Focus, Boy. All that's for another time. That's who you were. Live past today and you might find out who you are.

"*Wasa llamo?*" barked their leader again.

The Possum Hunters had used *llamo* to mean "name." He had learned enough of their language to get by during their year among them, enough when playing with their children.

The men jabbered among themselves, rapidly, like birds. It was too fast but the Boy caught words that may have once been English; words the Possum Hunters had also used, others that sounded completely different.

"*Wasa llamo?*" roared their leader.

Boy is what they called you, he heard Sergeant Presley say.

I have always just been Boy. It was enough.

And yet the broken feather from the bundle had once meant something to him.

"*WASA LLAMO!*" screamed the leader, unsheathing a curved hunting knife. It gleamed in the afternoon light of the bright sky. It was an old thing, a weapon from Before.

The leader turned to his troops, muttering something. The semicircle withdrew. It was just the leader now, facing the Boy.

The Boy tried to remember the words of the Possum Hunters. Words he could use to identify himself.

What was friend?

What was Boy?

How would he describe himself?

He remembered the children being warned to be careful of the bears that prowled the deep woods. "*Oso,*" he'd heard their mothers calling. Beware the *oso.* And the Possum Hunters, the men, had called themselves *cazadores.*

"Oso Cazadore," said the Boy in the quiet of the high mountain pass.

Silence followed.

The Boy watched the troop exchange glances, muttering, pointing at the bearskin.

The leader, his face like a dark cloud, shouted a long stream of words at the Boy, their meanings lost.

Until the last word.

The Boy heard the last word clearly.

"Chinese!"

As though it were an accusation.

An indictment.

Then the leader shouted it again in the still silence and pointed over his shoulder toward the west.

"Oso Cazadore," said the Boy again.

The leader laughed, spitting angrily as he did so.

Another string of words most of which the Boy did not understand and finally the word the children of the Possum Hunters had used when calling each other liars.

Pick the biggest one, Boy. When you're surrounded, pick the biggest one and take him out. It'll make the rest think twice.

The leader was the biggest.

The Boy dismounted.

Horse could take care of himself.

The Boy pointed toward the leader with his tomahawk.

The leader crouched low, drawing the blade between them, waving it back and forth.

Holding the tomahawk back, ready to strike, the Boy circled to the right, feeling his left leg drag as it always did after he had ridden Horse for long periods of time.

Get to work, lazy leg! Be ready.

The leader came in at once, feinting toward the Boy's midsection and at the same time dancing backward to circle.

The Boy moved his tomahawk forward, acting as though he might strike where the leader should have been. Sensing this, the leader flipped the knife and caught it in his grip, ready to slam it down on the unprotected back he knew would be exposed if the Boy struck with his full force at the feint. Instead the Boy shifted backward, willing the weak left leg to move quickly. Once he was planted, he raised the checked tomahawk once more and slammed it down through the wrist of the leader as the man tried to regain his balance from stabbing through thin air.

What the Boy lacked in power and strength in his left side was made up for in the powerful right arm that had done all the heavy work of his hard life. Like a machine from Before, the triceps and biceps drove the axe down through skin and bone and skin again within the moment that the eye shifts its gaze.

The leader planted his feet, intending to reverse the knife with just an adjustment of grip and then swing wickedly to disembowel his opponent. He'd do it again as he'd done many times before.

But his hand was gone.

His mouth, once pulling for air like a great bellows, now hung open and slack. The leader dropped to his knees, his other hand moving to the spouting bloody stump.

For a brief moment, he stared at his hand as though this was something the leader had just imagined and not something that had really happened. His eyes, his world, gray at the edges of his vision, remained on the severed hand.

At then he was gone from this world as the tomahawk slammed into his skull with a dull crunch.

There was a clarity that came to the Boy in the moment after combat, a knowledge the Boy had that all his days would be as such: days of bone, blood, and struggle. The blue sky and winters would come and go, but all his days would be of such struggles.

Finally, in the last moment of such thinking, he wondered, what did cities ever know that he never would? Their mysteries would be beyond him. Without Sergeant Presley he would become like one of these savage men the Sergeant had warned him of. And one day, like the body of the man in the dirt and rock at his feet, such would be his end.

CHAPTER 20

In the blue water of the high mountain lake lay the rusting hulk of the bat-winged bomber from Before.

Bee Two, Boy.

The early education of the Boy by Sergeant Presley had included the identification of war machines and weapons past.

Stealth tech, Boy.

The bomber lay halfway in the crystal blue of the lake and partway onto the sandy beach of the small mountain village.

The village of the Rock Star's People, they called themselves in their weird mix of languages.

The Rock Star's People.

They're little better than savages, Boy. Stone age. Look at 'em with their bows and skins. Speakin' a little Mex, occasional English, and a whole lotta gibberish. Livin' out here in the sticks 'cause they're probably still afraid of the cities. At least they're smart enough for that. But other than huntin' and gatherin' and these huts, it makes you wonder what they've been up to for the last forty years. But I'll betchu' they got enemies, Boy. Betchu' that for sure.

Never get involved, Boy, because some stories have been going on long before you showed up. You don't know their beginnings, and you might not like their endings.

Yes, you would say that also, Sergeant. And yet, here I am. There was little choice for me in the matter.

With the death of the hunters' leader, the moments that followed the fight had seemed uncertain. The odds, thought the Boy as the leader lay dying, were slim that he would have time to get back on Horse and ride away from the circling hunters. As the moments passed, the Boy could hear pebbles trickling down the ledge behind him, knowing the bow hunters were surrounding him.

The Boy lowered his head, letting his peripheral vision do the work.

The enemy will come at you from where you can't see him. So look there, Boy!

But in the next moment the hunters lay down their weapons.

The conversation that followed was stilted, but from what the Boy gleaned over the course of the next three days' march, the hunters were inviting him to their village.

"Oso Cazadore," they repeated reverently and even approached to touch the skin of the bear.

Oso Cazadore.

Now, high in the mountains, at the edge of the water, the Boy stared at the final resting place of the Bee Two Bomber.

In the three days he'd traveled with the hunters they'd kept to themselves, disappearing in ones and twos to run ahead of the main group, returning late in the night. They'd ascended a high, winding course up through steep pine forests, across white granite ledges, through snowfields ringed by the teeth of the mountains.

In that time the Boy learned they were the Rock Star's People and little beyond that.

In that time he heard the voice of Sergeant Presley's many warnings, teachings he was taught and which he'd intended to fully obey.

Except for one.

I will go into the cities.

I will find out what is in them.

A woven door of thatched pine branches swung upward from the bulbous top of the ancient bomber resting on the lakeshore.

And here you are, Boy, gettin' involved. I got involved once and ended up a slave for two years.

The Rock Star was what the Boy expected her to be. From the stories he'd heard. Stories not told by Sergeant Presley, but in the campfires of the Cotter family and even the Possum Hunters.

Old.

Gray hair like strands of moss.

A rolling gait as she crossed the fuselage and descended the pillars of stones that had been laid at the bomber's nose.

The small, deep-set eyes burned as she approached him. When she smiled, the teeth, what few there were, were crooked, with ancient metal bands.

"Come down from that animal," she commanded.

She spoke the same English as Sergeant Presley.

If I get down from Horse, the whole village will attack me. And yet, what choice do I have? What choice have I had all along, Sergeant?

Here you are, Boy.

Here I am.

The Boy dismounted.

She approached and reached out to touch the bearskin the Boy kept wrapped about himself.

He had found a place for Sergeant Presley's knife.

Inside, behind the skin, waiting in his withered hand.

His good hand hung near the tomahawk. The carefreeness of its disposition was merely an illusion. In a moment it could cut a wide arc about him. In a moment he'd cut free of the rush and be up on Horse and away from this place.

So you think, Boy. If only it were so easy to get un-involved from things. If only, Boy.

"Bear Killer." She stepped back, cocking her head to one side and up at him. "That's what the children call you. Is it true? You kill a bear?"

After a moment he nodded.

"You're big and tall. Taller than most. But weak on that side." She pointed toward his left. "I can tell. I know things. I keep the bombs." She jerked her thumb back toward the water and the lurking bomber.

"Bear Killer." She snorted.

'If it comes,' thought the Boy, 'it comes now.' His hand drifts toward the haft of the tomahawk.

"Welcome to our village, Bear Killer. You've rid us of an idiot for a chief. I thank you for that." She turned back to the village and babbled in their patois. Then she left, rolling side to side until she reached the pillars, the pine-branch hatch, and disappeared once more inside the half-submerged bomber.

The Boy watched her until she was gone and wondered if indeed there were bombs, the big ones, nuclear, still lying within the plane. Waiting.

Impossible, Boy. We used 'em all up killing the world.

RAIN FELL IN the afternoon, and that night the villagers, under clear skies, spitted a deer and gathered to watch it roast in the cold night.

A young man whose name was Jason led him to a hut made of rocks and pine. It belonged to the chief—to the man who died at the Boy's feet.

After three days of listening to the Rock Star's People, the Boy could at least communicate with them in small matters. But the communication was slow and halting.

Jason said that for killing the chief, the hut and all that was in it were Bear Killer's.

There was little more than a fire pit and a dirt floor.

Horse was fed apples by the children of the village and, as was his custom, patiently endured.

Later, the venison roasted, and the village watched both him and the meat and the darkness beyond their flames. There were far more women and children than men, and even the Boy knew the meaning of such countings.

When the venison was ready, they cut a thick slice from underneath the spine and offered it, dripping and steaming, to the Boy.

When the meal ended, the Rock Star was there among them. She had been watching him for a long time. She entered the circle, standing near the fire, wrapping skins and clothing from Before about her. She was faded and worn in dress, hair, and skin. But her eyes were full of thought and planning, of command and fire.

She told a story.

The Boy followed the tale as best he could and when he seemed lost altogether, she stopped to translate it for him back into English.

"I'm from Before, Bear Killer. I spoke the proper English like I was taught in a school and all that."

The story she told involved a group of young people pursued through the forest by a madman with a chain saw full of evil spirits. One by one, the madman catches the younglings as they flee into what they believe is an abandoned house—the house where the madman lives with other madmen. In the end there is only one youngling left. A girl, strong and beautiful, desired by all the now dead younglings. Through magic and cunning she defeats the madmen, except for the one who'd found the younglings initially. The brave girl shoots bolts of power from her hands and the Mad Man of all Mad Men, as she calls him, falls backward over a balcony in the house from the Before.

"And when she run over to the railing to see his dead body lying in the tall grass, he is gone," the Rock Star translated to the Boy. Then, casting a weather eye into the darkness beyond their fire, the Rock Star whispered, "That madman still walks these mountains, still desires me, still takes younglings when it comes into his mind."

The Rock Star's People clutched their wide-eyed young. The men drew closer to the fire, to their wives, eyeing the night and the mountains that surrounded their lake.

"But he won't come here, children."

She paused, eyes resting on the assembly. She turned toward the mountains as if seeing his lumbering form wandering the silent halls of the forest dark even then.

"He won't come here, children. For I am that girl who was."

She turned and stalked off into the night.

The relief among the villagers was tangible.

In groups they returned to their huts, and for a long time the Boy stared into the fire, watching its coals.

CHAPTER 21

"Walk with me."

The command was simple, direct. The Boy saw her silhouette in the door to his hut by the half-light of early morning.

Outside, the Boy was wrapped in his bearskin and the sky was little more than cold iron. The village was quiet, as small wavelets drove against the sandy shore, slapping at the side of the old bomber.

When they were at the far end of the beach, nearing a series of slate gray rocks that fell into the waters of the lake, the Rock Star turned to him.

"I don't know you. I suspect, though, you're a man without a tribe." She let the sentence hang.

The Boy remained silent.

Good. Let people assume things, Boy.

"But you were passing to the west when the hunters found you," continued the Rock Star.

She paused to consider that for a moment.

"I imagine you want to continue west. But you can't. Ain't nothing there but Chinese now. You keep up that old highway and you'll come to a big Chinese settlement in the foothills the other side of the pass."

She picked up stones, flat and slate blue from the beach.

"Bad for you if you were thinking that was good. Chinese been trying to clear out the tribes. They took on one or two in the last few years and won pretty easily. They got the Hillmen working for them. But the Hillmen weren't never no real tribe. And the tribes the Chinese wiped out were little more'n scavengers anyway."

She seemed to want to throw a stone into the water, but the act of skipping it seemed something she knew was beyond her ability and strength.

"Now they—the Chinese, that is—have gone and stirred up a nest of hornets."

The Rock Star looked at the Boy directly, staring hard up into his face, searching for something.

"That man you killed in fair challenge was my war leader. He was an idiot, but as they say, he was my idiot. In the next day, we got to start out despite this last winter storm that's workin' itself up to be something. The tribes, far down the range, almost even to the old Three Ninety-five, are gathering. A big war leader is readyin' hisself to lay a smackdown on the Chinamen."

She took a deep breath.

"The headman called for me and mine to come. Wants my power."

She turned back to the lake. Whitecaps were forming beyond the bay.

"I've danced with the dark one in the dead of night. My power has watched over this People since the Before. My power will slaughter the Chinamen. My power has stood against zombies and vampires and all the serial killers of the Before. I was a powerful rock star in them days."

She dropped the stones back onto the beach.

"So if you're a spy, you know our plans. No good it'll do you, though. So you'll ride with us and know my hunters carry the poison. My poison is powerful. But my poison is not for you, see. My poison is for your horse. Ah, I see Bear Killer. I know'd the horse is a friend to you. So, you don't step to my call to fetch and be my war leader, it's the horse that gets it."

She sighed heavily in the wind.

"That's the way it be. Now take my arm and walk me back to the village, Bear Killer. And of a morning here shortly, we'll ride to the hidden valley and rave with the tribes at the great lodge. And when the tribes go to lay a smackdown on the Chinamen, you'll be my war leader and then you'll see my power. I'm keeper of them bombs, never forget that. I'll send the world back into darkness as I done the first time."

She held out her arm.

After a moment, the Boy took it.

The wind came up and his ears burned. But not from the cold.

That's right, Boy. I said involved.

CHAPTER 22

That night the Rock Star told the story of a great ship she had once sailed on that crossed the unseen ocean to a country far away. She told of fine dresses she wore and an evil prince who wanted to marry her. Instead, she chose a young poor boy, fair and bold, for her lover. But the evil prince murdered the poor boy.

The wind and the night closed about their small circle of fire next to the lake in the mountains, as the first hints of rain began to slap against the water and the sand. The Rock Star rose above the circle, seeming imperious. Seeming grand. Seeming once the young woman of the story.

"And I called an ice mountain out of the sea to come and attack the ship and slay the evil princeling. When my monster'd finished, that great ship slid beneath the waves with a titanic crash, like ice breaking off the high glaciers. Only I alone escaped in a boat, and every one of them fancies, all of 'em, drowned beneath the icy waters of that ocean, 'cept for me, and me alone."

In the morning when the Boy awoke, the hunters were packing, making a somber noise within the quiet village of the high mountain lake.

Jason pushed aside the blanket at the entrance to the old chief's hut.

"We *vamnato*," Jason mumbled fearfully in his pidgin language to the Boy, telling him it was time to leave.

The Boy gathered his things into his pack and went out to Horse.

Whispering and patting the animal, he promised to take care of them both.

"Do you trust me?" he whispered to Horse.

Horse regarded him, then snorted slightly and turned away to watch some new thing that might be more interesting.

Soon the hunters, carrying the Rock Star on a pallet, were waving goodbye to the tight-jawed women and crying children.

Following, the Boy rode Horse, his bearskin flapping in the strong wind that came off the lake.

Spring's a comin', Boy. Look sharp.

THE COMPANY OF hunters, with their skins and spears and bones of small animals knocking together in the wind whipping past their carried totems, skirted the lake along an old winding highway heading south. Soon they climbed up through a trail that led alongside high waterfalls, and when they crested the pass, they saw a long line of mountains falling away to the south.

Finding old crumbling roads when they could and keeping mostly south, the company trekked along the face of the high mountains, sometimes weaving down into the foothills, never daring to approach the valley floor.

The day was long gone to late winter cold when they stopped in a stand of pines alongside a mountain highway. The withered side of the Boy was stiff and aching. He got down from Horse and walked away from their forming camp. When the Boy looked behind him, he could see at least one of the hunters trailing, as if gathering firewood.

I'll be patient. When the time comes, and it will, I'll make a run, Sergeant.

There was no response from the voice of Sergeant Presley.

And yet there is something exciting about all of this, Sergeant. If these people are against the Chinese, then wouldn't that be good intel for I Corps and the Army?

The Boy didn't dare bring out the map secreted inside the pouch he'd made within the bear cloak. From his memory of it, he knew they were skirting south through the mountains. On the western side of their progress lay the long valley and many of the great cities of the past along the coast beyond. San Francisco, Los Angeles, and far San Diego, all in the State of California.

I should complete the mission. Find I Corps like you said, Sergeant.

Later, in the guttering light of the campfire, the Rock Star told of a night when the dead had walked the earth, coming out of their graves to clutch at her. She had hidden in a great palace of wonders she called the Fashion Hill Place Mall. The zombies, a relentless army of crawling undead, surrounded her and a band of other survivors. Using her great fire-spitting powers, she kept the other survivors safe against the relentless dead. But in the end, the survivors had each died as a result of their own folly.

There was Pete, who tried to make a run for the parking lot, done to death by a horde of zombies he didn't see.

There was Fawn, who wouldn't share the sweet treats of the food court, pulled into an ice cave by a corpse who wasn't all dead.

There was Mark, who tried to have his way with the Rock Star, who was then a wild young girl with red hair. Mark was thrown from the top of the parking structure into a sea of the once human.

"And one day I flew away in a machine from the Before. Right off the roof of the mall. Rescued by myself because they wouldn't listen to me. Didn't have to be that way. But it was."

THE DAYS THAT followed were a long, slow crawl across the face of the mountains beneath the alpine tree line. High above them, snow clung to the tallest peaks, and still at the base of the trees they found piles of the stuff hiding in the permanent shade.

CHAPTER 23

On the last night, the night before the long climb up into the high valley, the Boy woke. Against the wide dark blue sky of frosty night, the wind swept clouds swiftly across the night. The dark shadow of Horse stirred for a moment.

For the thousandth time the Boy thought now might be the time to leave.

He did not hear the voice of Sergeant Presley.

Maybe I have gone too far down a road I should've never traveled. Maybe the voice of Sergeant Presley has finished with me.

Maybe I have gone too far.

The fire was low and the Boy saw the Rock Star, mouth open, staring into the glowing embers.

For a while he lay still, but his weak side was stiff and cold.

How much of the night was left?

He drank cold water from his bag and limped over to the fire to warm his cursed weak side.

All around, the hunters slept. The Boy knew two or three were watching him, watching with the poison on nearby and ready arrows.

The hunters had kept their distance over much of this cold trek across the western face of the Sierras.

Poison.

The Rock Star began to speak.

She did not look at the Boy.

She stared into the flames after he added a log and sparks rose on the night wind.

"I was a girl—little more than—on the day it all went down."

She swallowed. Her old face was hollow and dry like an empty water skin drained by time.

"I was a survivor though, even before all of the war that come. A survivor in a wasteland of malls and perfect families. My mother worked all the time. Worked so much I never saw her. We communicated by notes left on a little table in our tiny kitchen. One year I left the same note over and over and she never noticed."

The Boy rubbed his weak calf, working the heat of his good hand into the thin muscle.

"I lived at the mall. I was there when it opened, and there was many a time I was the last out the door at closing. Frank. Frank let me out. Told me to go on home.

"When it all went to hell, we ran. We ran for the mountains. I was in the San Gabriel Foothills when one of them bombs went off south of Los Angeles. We were climbing on our hands and knees. I saw a flash light up everything ahead of me. And then a few seconds later, a hot rush of dry wind.

"We kept on moving, farther and farther up into the mountains.

"All these tribes, all these people of the mountains, I knew 'em all in those first days when we ran from the cities. They was just survivors then, running as fast as they could while the bombs kept falling. I think about that sometimes. I kept looking for my mom in each new group we come across. But it was always someone different to be found. I can see the Mexican woman with the twin boys standing by the body of her husband as we all walked past them on the trail. I can see those boys' faces in all of them tribes folk down near Sonora. We traded some of our women years back with them when theirs kept making weak babies, worse than what you were born with. I see the bearded guy who got shot for his food in the back of a station wagon that had broke down. I see his face now and again in some of the men and children of the Psychos. He must've had kin that run off once we took to his stuff. But we hadn't eaten in three days. So, it was to be expected. What I'm sayin'—and I'm thinkin' about it all the more now as we come up to that rave—is, I'll be seein' all these people again. Except it's not them. It's their children and grands and great-grands. Strangers I passed, sitting among the fires of the refugee camps waiting for help that never came. Dark, muddy rain comin' down on us. Eatin' soup. Radio's gone. No one knows anything and the things people say don't mean anything to me. I was young and my world was limited to music and movies, or a boy I thought I loved and would run away with and we'd be together. We'd be a real family.

"All of us survivors thought we might make it in the first few weeks after the bombs. But the big winter that come taught us the error of our ways. What little survived that winter—two years long it was—what survived would be burned away in forest fires, taken by raiders, or plain just wore out.

"I was just a girl. I knew movies. I did whatever it took to survive."

The dark sky above the orange glow of the fire turned a soft morning blue.

"I'm a rock star. I'm the bomb keeper. I've loved the grim reaper." The Rock Star's voice was strong but passionless, as if these lines were played for the thousandth time too many and to no one in particular.

"Words of power, Bear Killer, dontchu forget about me. Don't forget I know them words. I've carried them from the Before. Carried them from a television inside my heart. From that fairy palace mall.

"Words of power."

CHAPTER 24

In the Hidden Valley, the Boy found the tribes.

He found what happened forty years after all the bombs fell.

He found savagery.

There were big men, cut and scarred, tattooed in ash. There were thin, misshapen men bearing the marks of exposure to the weapons of Before. There were warriors wearing the patchwork armor of ancient road signs beaten to form breastplates. Some wore the skins of wolves, some the skins of other animals and even humans. Here and there were human heads, held aloft, candles burning in their empty eye sockets.

There were the Psychos, who wore the skins of the lions that prowled the eastern desert. Teeth hung in great looping necklaces about their thick, raw, and sunburned necks. They dragged dull-eyed women behind them by heavy chains with little effort.

You watch yourself with them, Boy. You can tell from the cuts and branding and even the homemade tattoos, that bunch is strong and they dig pain. Forget their Mohawks, it's the necklaces made outta teeth. Anyone weaker than them ends up on that necklace.

And there were the Death Knights, who wore battered Stop signs over their chests, mile markers on their arms, and wide-brimmed hats of leather from which the oily feathers of crows dangled in long woven cords.

They like to rule, Boy. They probably got a king or a warlord even. They're workin' some sort of rudimentary feudal system. My guess is you don't wear the

*crow feathers and armor, then you ain't to be considered. You fight one of 'em,
you'll fight the whole bunch.*

There were the Park People, who wore skins and carried long beaten
scythes. They were tall and lean. One or two had red hair, but who knows
the why of such genetics among their mostly brown skins? They cast long,
silent looks from almond-shaped eyes, warning all to keep a good distance
from them, as they drank the blood of a now silent pig from the battered
cups they carried at their hips.

*Koreans, Boy. Come up out of Los Angeles during the war is my guess. There
was a lot of 'em there before. Probably held together based on that. If looks could
kill, everybody'd be dead as far they're concerned.*

They and many others were the strange tribes of the Sierra Nevada,
which runs the length of the eastern border of what the map calls the
State of California. They had lost touch with what most call Before or
the Before. Those things were not coming back and, among the youngest,
were not even imagined.

What was lost was now simply gone forever.

These tribes held tightly to trail and track, hunt and prey, winter and
summer. Friend and enemy.

They gathered in screaming laughter and thrumming chant before a
great pile called the Lodge. Poles erupted from the riot of mud- and even
blood-covered warriors. The poles were adorned with skulls and strings
of nuts or pine boughs indicating camp and people, honor and disgrace.
On one was a patchwork flag of one red stripe, one white stripe, one star
on a field of blue. On another, hubcaps banged and clattered as they were
twisted this way and that, making a singsong chime of bang and rattle.
Others, strange and varied, wave and leap up and down across the forest
floor of the high valley that lies beneath the stony granite mountains.

These tribes gathered before the large pile of stones and timber that
formed a wall between them and the Lodge, a castle from Before.

The people of the Hidden Valley had fought these many years against
fire and other tribes to keep it to themselves.

But the whispers and tales of growing Chinese power, encroaching up
into the native lands of the Sierra Nevada, were being told in the gutter
speak of all the tribes. Whole tribes wiped out. Women murdered. Babies
stolen in the night.

Now, messengers had gone out and they were gathering. Gathering against the coming storm. Gathering against the Chinese.

The Boy as Bear Killer sat astride Horse wrapped in his dark bearskin, the shining tomahawk at his belt. Beneath him the Rock Star's People milled about with their bows, proud to have a mounted warrior who had killed a bear counted as one of their own.

All around them, stretching far off into the smoky, dusky forest floor at twilight, were the Park People and the Death Knights and the Psychos and all the other tribes. Their number was beyond his counting except for him to know that this was larger than any gathering of mankind he had ever seen. When he imagined the size of Sergeant Presley's I Corps, it was never as numerous as on this night.

And in the distance, at the extent of his vision, other tribes were streaming forward, surging into the hot, clamoring mass at the foot of the pine log pile.

The leaders of all these tribes, including the Rock Star, have gone beyond the ramshackle wall of stone and pine, penetrating the maze of timberworks—seemingly haphazard but designed with defense and killing in mind—and disappear into the Lodge.

Hours later, just after nightfall, the leaders returned to the top of the wall. A tall man led them out onto the high wall of the Lodge, above which the waiting tribes could see the steep roof of the castle, which was once a rustic tourist resort.

The man was tall and rangy. He wore blue jeans and a long dark coat. Clothing from Before.

His sharp jaw and blowing hair gave him a wolf's appearance. But even from among the milling mass of warriors, it was the blue eyes the Boy noted: clear, sparkling, glinting with thoughts of some plan.

The leaders of all the tribes formed a line, linked hands, and raised them high above their varied heads and hair. And at the center of the line, the tall man, the wolf-like man, the man in the clothing from Before, stood joined to all the other leaders. He raised his sharp jaw skyward and howled up into the trees and the night above.

This is the one you got to watch, Boy. This one's no joiner, and he ain't no leader. He's a taker. A ruin-er, and he's walked alone more often than not. Be careful, Boy. Real careful.

The tribes below and beyond the wall roared, punctuating their approval with whoops and screams.

The drumbeats began to roll across the forest floor of the valley, echoing off the distant mountains, lost in the crash of the high waterfall over which flaming logs tumbled into plumes of steam.

The Chinese would be defeated.

Night fell and campfires beyond the Boy's counting sprang up across the valley floor. The chattering of languages, one as seemingly alien as the next, murmured across the distances between the camps.

The Rock Star's People formed their camp, unsure what to do in her absence.

But then the bloated skin of fermented drink arrived, carried on a pole between two large warriors—black wolf skins and ash-covered faces, machetes made from the guts of old machines in great scabbards at their backs—and the Rock Star's People found their purpose.

All the tribes were drinking.

Now. Tonight is your night to escape, Boy.

It is good to hear your voice, Sergeant.

The Boy mounted Horse and began to ride the twilight camps. He smiled at those he suspected kept poison on their bows and when they smiled back, the smile was sloppy, happy, lugubrious, as if there was a friendship formed in all those cold miles between the mountain lake and this friendly place.

The Boy checked the great pile of stone and fallen timber that was the Lodge and saw only two torches guttering blackly at the gate. He rode to a nearby fire. Here there were men and women warriors, long spears, and woven hair like muddy ropes. They smiled after their guttural greeting failed to find meaning in the Boy's ears. They seemed to wish him well, and one woman even cast a hungry eye upon him. When he sensed the bearers of the poison arrows coming from the campfire of the Rock Star's People, shadowing him in the early dark, he rode back to their fire as if to reassure them.

The noise was getting louder across the valley floor as fires grew in leaps and explosions, sending sparks high into the star-filled night.

Soon, Boy. Real soon.

He got down from Horse and took a drink from the bloated skin.

The hunters cheered at what they perceived to be a long draft by the Boy beneath the un-corked stream of the drinking skin.

They smiled and chattered at him, forgetting he understood very little of what they spoke. He laughed and took a bigger drink and they all roared their approval.

We are all mighty hunters around the campfire.

Yes, that is something Sergeant Presley might have said, though I can never remember having heard him say anything like it. All the same, it seems like something he would have said.

When the night seemed alive with revelry and recklessness, the Boy lay down in the dark, not the least bit taken by drink.

Someone screamed. The pain of a wound was evident.

In the moments after, the mood was much more somber.

The Boy waited.

You are always stiff, my left side, especially when I have been lying on the ground for some time.

Now you must do your part.

The Boy rose and returned to Horse.

He laid his hand atop the long equine nose, looking into those forever uncaring brown eyes. The Boy raised his index finger to his lips as he led Horse away from the sleeping hunters.

They had almost faded into the shadows of tall trees beneath a starry night above, when a voice spoke softly to him.

"Nice night for a ride, Boyo."

The voice was a whisper.

The voice was the shadow of a grave.

In the dark a man came close, and though the Boy smelled the stranger, he did not hear him break the forest floor as he walked toward the Boy and Horse.

He's good. This one's got skills. Watch out, Boy.

"Come with me."

Beyond a moment's hesitation, the Boy led Horse after the stranger, following the lanky figure through the shifting shadows of the night forest.

The Boy slipped the fingers of his good hand to his tomahawk, hovering above the haft.

When the shot is clear I'll take it. I'll put it right between his shoulder blades.

The stranger moved fast, like some dark liquid seeking the path of least resistance, relentless as he slipped the tall pines back to the bric-a-brac wall that surrounded the Lodge.

They emerged onto the wide dirt porch of the ramshackle castle.

Two men walked from the shadows beyond the gate and the stranger, maintaining his loping, soundless stride, directed them to take charge of Horse.

The stranger turned to face the Boy as the ash-faced guards moved to obey.

By the light of the torches at the gate, the stranger is a drooping mustache and sad eyes that stared coldly back at the Boy.

"There's something you should see inside."

When the Boy didn't move, the stranger said, "C'mon," and dropped his eyes to the Boy's grip on the tomahawk. "It's good from now on. You can trust me."

The Boy followed the sad-eyed stranger through the break in the wall of rotten pine logs and earthworks surrounding the once grand and unknown building of Before turned collapsing fairy-tale castle now more than anything else.

After a few dogleg turns within the wall, they arrived in a weedy courtyard at the entrance to the Lodge. Smoke-stained stones rose up to a sagging roof as windows gaped like open and jagged wounds.

The Boy spelled a sign above the entrance.

A-w-a-h-n-e-e L-o-d-g-e.

A wagon and a team of horses waited near two once grand doors.

Ash-faced guards worked in teams carrying bodies out from the dilapidated castle to the back of the wagon.

The Boy stood with the sad-faced stranger as the last body was thrown into the waiting transport.

When the last body was thrown with an unimpressive thump onto the other bodies in the back of the wagon, the sad-faced stranger led the Boy to the wagon, and before a tarp was pulled and tied, he showed the Boy the leaders of the tribes.

Underneath rictus grins, foaming mouths, and upward-staring eyes, a head of hoary gray hair rested above that same openmouthed, wide-eyed stare the Boy had seen at the beginning of this day, as the two of them had sat by the fire before dawn and she'd told him the story of her life as a young girl on the day the bombs fell.

The Boy listened for the voice of Sergeant Presley.

I understand what you meant, Sergeant. I understand "involved," now.

The stranger let the tarp fall, covering the horrified faces and contorted bodies.

"Now," said the sad-faced stranger. "MacRaven wants to meet a Bear Killer."

CHAPTER 25

"You really kill that bear you're wearing, boy?" asked MacRaven.

The sad-faced stranger had led the Boy through the rotting pile of wood that was once a tourist lodge to a grand ballroom of warped planks, cobwebs, and guttering candles for an audience with MacRaven.

Everywhere there was dust and broken glass and damage. In the big room, moonlight glared through broken panes of glass set in large windows. By greasy candlelight, a banquet long laid out and thoroughly done to death revealed the carcasses of roasted animals and bones strewn with abandon. The hunger the occupants of the wagon must have possessed during the last moments of their final meal was evident.

At the far end of the room MacRaven sat in a straight-backed chair. Among the shadows his ashen-faced warriors busied themselves in unseen tasks. There was blood on the floor and the sad-faced stranger told the Boy not to slip in it. The tone was friendly.

"I guess you must have killed that bear," continued the boom of MacRaven's voice from across the hall. " 'Cause if you didn't then you woulda said you did."

MacRaven, lean and rangy, rose from his chair in the thin light of timid candles.

"So I guess you did."

The wolfish man walked forward across the rotting boards of the floor.

"There aren't many that ride the horse these days. That bunch outside would just as soon eat your horse as ride it into battle. All twenty thousand plus of 'em, if Raleigh can count rightly."

MacRaven stopped before the Boy.

He was younger than Sergeant Presley was. Less than forty.

"I'm trying to build up some cavalry but it's not on this year's list of things to get done. Instead I've got a few who can ride. Maybe next year. Know what I mean?"

The Boy had no idea what he meant.

"I'll be direct. You're not with that bunch you came in with, nor any of those other tribes out there. That's as plain as day. So I don't know if you're a 'merc' or just passing through, but the truth of it is, I could use you. If you want work, I can give you that. If you want a way to go, well then I think I have something you might be interested in. An offer you should consider."

MacRaven walked back to his chair and picked up a hanging gun belt. He buckled it around his waist, one large revolver hanging low against his thigh.

"You don't want in, fine. Ride on."

Whatever you say, Boy, don't say that. He ain't strappin' on that gun for nothing. It means something, even if he don't know what it means, it means something bad. Though I s'pect he knows exactly what he means. Watch yourself, Boy, this one's a killer.

"So, you in, kid?" asked MacRaven.

The Boy nodded.

"What's that?"

"I'm in."

"Just like that. Hell, I didn't know if you even spoke the English until just now. Don't matter, I speak most of their languages anyway. That you speak the English recommends you altogether. Fine, you're in."

MacRaven swiped a drinking cup from off a table near the chair he'd been sitting in. He raised it to his lips. The tension in the room rose immediately. The Boy could sense the sad-faced man at his side about to burst into action. But then he stopped.

"That's right. This is poison." MacRaven chuckled.

He put the cup down.

"That wouldn't do now, would it, Raleigh?"

Raleigh muttered a tired "No."

"This Army marches tomorrow," began MacRaven. "In four days' time we'll be at the gates of the Chinese outpost at Auburn. Those bodies in the wagon need to be inside the walls, with the Chinese. Raleigh and the other riders are going on ahead. You'll join them and make this part of my plan happen. *Excellente?*"

The Boy nodded.

IN THE NIGHT you ride and are not alone, though you should be, right, Sergeant?

The Boy thought of this atop Horse, riding the old Highway Forty-nine north, in the midst of other riders little more than different shades of darkness on this long night. The mountain road twisted and wound, and at dawn the company stopped for a few hours. Shadows were revealed in the dawn light that followed and the Boy saw the riders for who they were.

They were men. Mere men. And yet, in every one of them was the look of a hard man.

He's a hard one, Boy. Steer clear.

The Boy remembered Sergeant Presley's warning from villages and settlements they'd passed through in their seemingly endless—at the time—wanderings, when they'd come upon such a man.

A "hard one" was that mean-faced giant who carried the long board tipped with rusty nails, who'd watched the trade going on at the big river.

He'd had trouble in his eyes.

Trouble in his heart.

But they'd only found that out later, after they'd come upon the corpse of one of the salvagers who'd made a good haul out in the ruins of Little Rock, in the State of Arkansas. Then they knew the mean-faced giant had also had trouble in mind.

Each of these shadowy riders, in their own way, was that man.

Hard men.

Weapons. Spears, axes, metal poles studded with glass and nails. Swords. Machetes worn over the back like MacRaven's ashen-faced warriors. Whips.

Men who made their daily living dealing in the suffering trade.

In the shifting light of a cool and windy morning near a bridge along the crumbling mountain highway, the hard men seemed tired, and as if the leader of their company led in all things, the droopy-eyed and sad-faced Raleigh yawned as he approached the Boy.

"You take first watch with Dunn. When the sun's straight overhead, swap out with Vaclav." He pointed to a thick man with coal-black eyes and a beard to match. Vaclav carried an axe. Uncountable notches ran up the long haft.

The sun rose high over the trees and for a while Dunn took the far end of the bridge while the Boy watched over the sleeping riders.

If I go now, these men will catch me.

That's a fact, Boy. Now's no good.

I know too much of what they're about. They can't let me go.

But they don't even know you want to leave, Boy. They're testing you to see if you'll become one of them. Mainly 'cause of Horse. No doubt one of them, probably that Raleigh character, is watching everything you do. So whatever you do, Boy, don't pull out that map.

At times, the voice seemed as if Sergeant Presley was really talking to the Boy. Other times the Boy knew it was his own voice and just something he wanted to hear him say.

It felt good not to think and instead just listen to the noise of the river under the bridge.

He remembered winter and the cave above the rapids.

I should have drawn more.

I never should have left.

Go west, Boy. Get to the Army.

The Boy thought of the marks on the map.

Chinese paratroopers in Reno.

This MacRaven has an army. I Corps will want to know about this and the Chinese in this place called Auburn. Should I try to get away soon, Sergeant?

Now's not the time, Boy. They'll be all over you like white on rice.

Sergeant Presley would've said that.

In time Dunn crossed the bridge, sauntering lazily with a long piece of green grass sticking out the side of his mouth, back toward where the Boy stood guard.

Dunn was an average man: old canvas pants; dusty, worn boots; a hide jacket. In his sandy blond hair the Boy could see the gray beginning to show beneath his ancient Stetson hat.

"Dunn," said Dunn, extending a thick and calloused hand.

The Boy remained silent and then after a moment took Dunn's hand.

"Bear Killer, huh?" Dunn chuckled in the quiet morning, the noise of the river distant, almost fading as the heat of the day increased.

After a moment . . .

"Might as well be, as opposed to anything else, right?" Dunn paused to spit chewed grass off the side of the bridge. "Times are strange anyway. Names might as well be too."

"I never said my name was Bear Killer. That's just what the Rock Star's People called me."

The Boy saw a flash of anger rise up like an August storm and slip through Dunn's easygoing cowpoke facade.

Dunn turned and regarded the far end of the bridge, as if counting off moments to himself.

"That's one explanation. I'll buy it today for the sake of being friendly." He turned back to the Boy. The August storm had passed.

"And I'll give you this one for free," continued Dunn, his tone easygoing, his manner quiet. "How you want to spend it's up to you. Okay?"

The Boy nodded.

"Fine then. You ride hard and watch our backs. We'll watch yours. Don't question the work. There's no such thing these days as dishonorable work. Whatever the work is, someone's paying to have a job done and a job done is the way we do it."

After a moment the Boy said, "I can live with that."

Dunn watched the Boy for a long moment.

"There ain't nothin' left anymore. So sometimes work is something that's just got to be, regardless. We could use a kid like you. But you're gonna find some of the things we do might not sit right with you."

Dunn paused.

"If you're gonna ride with us then you might need to let go of some of those sensibilities."

Dunn nodded to himself, as if checking a list of things that needed to be said and finding all points crossed off.

"That's for free, kid. Next one'll cost ya."

Dunn smiled, then ambled over to another of the Hard Men to wake him for his shift.

When Vaclav awoke, black fury and a knife came out at once.

As if expecting someone else, Vaclav was ready.

But in that same summer-storm moment, the dark and swarthy Vaclav got up from the dust, then nodded to the Boy.

Hard men, Boy. Each and every one of 'em. You watch yourself.

I will, Sergeant. I will.

CHAPTER 26

The Chinese patrol, or what was left of it, waited on their knees in the pasture as the Hard Men watched their interrogation.

Only their leader stood. He was standing in front of a stump, a day's ride from the outpost at Auburn.

Vaclav and the Boy worked with shovels in the big pit the Chinese prisoners had been forced to dig. It needed to be deeper, so Raleigh told Vaclav, and with a maximum of spitting and curses Vaclav grabbed a shovel and threw another at the Boy.

"New guy digs too," he spat.

They worked in the pit while Raleigh screamed in Chinese at the patrol leader.

Krauthammer, another of the Hard Men, who the Boy knew by the brief introduction of post-battle observation to be a searcher of pockets and a cutter of fingers for rings that don't slide off so easily. He had the patrol leader's pack out on the grass of the pasture and was going through it, tossing its contents carelessly out for all to see.

Dunn stood by the stump, one dusty boot resting upon it. He was chewing on another blade of grass.

Earlier, when Vaclav was up riding point, he'd spotted the Chinese patrol.

Leaving the wagon full of bodies in the road, the Hard Men pulled back into the forest after staking the wagon's horses and locking the brake.

"You're with me, kid," said Raleigh. "You too, Dunn. Rest of you circle around down by the river and come up along the road behind them. Once we attack, come on up and give us a hand."

No one said anything. They'd done this before.

Back among the trees, the hot afternoon faded in the cool green shadows of the woods.

"Chinese are killers, kid," whispered Raleigh. "You're too young to remember, but they killed this country. Now we're gonna take America back."

Dunn laughed dryly.

Raleigh rolled his eyes.

The battle was short.

When the Chinese came walking up the road, they fanned out once they spotted the wagon full of dead bodies. A few of them moved forward to inspect it.

A moment before they reached the back of the wagon, Dunn whispered, "I don't see no guns."

"They wouldn't have 'em this far out, Dunn. Too afraid of losing 'em." Raleigh's voice reminded the Boy of a rusty screen door.

Good, don't think about the fight until you have to, Boy. You don't know nothin' about it till it starts up, so no use gettin' worked up before it begins.

The Chinese carried long poles, spear-tipped ends.

Dunn charged out of the foliage, his horse snorting breathily as he beat the croup hard with a small cord. The Chinese recoiled as first Dunn broke the brush, then Raleigh, and finally the Boy.

Don't think about it, Boy.

He knew Sergeant Presley meant more than just the fight. If for a moment he'd harbored the idea of riding away during the confusion of this battle, he knew they'd forget the Chinese and come straight after him.

I know too much.

They closed with the Chinese and the Boy chopped down on one of the patrol with his tomahawk then wheeled Horse about to swing into the face of an enemy shifting for a better position.

So these are the Chinese, Sergeant.

My whole life has been filled with the knowledge of them as enemies, as monsters, as destroyers. I have seen them play the devil in all the villages and salvager camps we passed through on our way across this country. But you taught me they weren't the only cause of America's destruction, Sergeant. You said they only came after, trying to carve away a little bit of what was left for themselves. I've never seen them as the devils so many have. You fought them for ten years in San Francisco, Sergeant Presley, but you taught me they weren't our worst enemy.

We destroyed ourselves, Boy.

You taught me that.

Now it was parry, thrust, and chaos as the Chinese oriented themselves to the attack of the Boy and Dunn and Raleigh. Some fell, bleeding and screaming and crying, but their leader organized the rest quickly and it seemed, at least to the surviving Chinese, as though they had turned back the main assault.

In moments, the other Hard Men were up out of the woods and all over the Chinese patrol.

A few hours later the Boy found himself in the pit, digging out its edges.

Above him Raleigh was still screaming in Chinese.

"Got it," said Krauthammer and held up paper. Then he held up a stick. After that, he pulled a bottle of dark liquid out of the pack.

"Put that one down first." Raleigh pointed toward one of the Chinese waiting on his knees.

Like sudden lightning, Dunn grabbed the Chinese and forced his head down onto the stump. Another of the Hard Men whipped a leather noose about the struggling head and pulled, stretching the brown neck taut as Dunn pulled the struggling body back.

"Vaclav," called Raleigh.

"What?" screamed Vaclav from the bottom of the pit.

"Can I use your axe?"

"Sure, why the hell not." Vaclav followed this with curses and muttering and, finally, more spitting.

Raleigh took up the axe, and as all the Chinese started to chatter, he brought it down swiftly on the stretched neck of the chosen victim.

And then they chose another.

And another.

Raleigh turned to the leader and spoke.

The Chinese soldier nodded and held out his hand.

Krauthammer put the paper down and dipped the stick in the bottle of dark liquid.

Raleigh dictated and the leader began to copy.

When it was done Raleigh held up the paper, squinting as he read.

"Right. Kill the rest of 'em," he said, satisfied with what was on the page.

"Get to work, you!" muttered Vaclav through clenched teeth at the Boy, who had watched all of this.

They finished the trench while sounds that rose above those of spade and dirt pierced the hot afternoon of the pasture.

They buried the Chinese and took to the road once more.

CHAPTER 27

"Them bodies are smelling," said Vaclav.

They had been for some time.

"Tough. We need 'em to get through the gates, smell or no smell," replied Raleigh. "Only way them Chinese are gonna let us in, is if they think we're bounty hunters. These are the bounty."

The Hard Men, as the Boy thought of them, were held up in a ravine south of Auburn.

They were waiting for MacRaven.

"Those Chinese up in the outpost are gonna smell 'em out here first. Then where will we be?" continued Vaclav.

"Shut it," replied Raleigh. They sat in silence, the wagon at the center of the perimeter, each man up on an edge of the sloping ravine, waiting.

When MacRaven did arrive, he was alone. His ashen-faced warriors absent.

For a while MacRaven and Raleigh talked in whispers a little way up the ravine, away from the wagon. Then Raleigh summoned the Boy. "Get over here, kid," he whispered.

MacRaven rested a warm hand on the Boy's shoulder.

Don't show him you don't trust him, Boy. Don't even flinch in the slightest.

"Raleigh tells me you done good in the ambush. All right then, I got a new mission for you. If you're in? Good," said MacRaven without waiting. He was dressed in the mishmash battle armor of the tribes. His breastplate was an old road sign covered in hide. His shoulders were padded and reinforced with bent hubcaps. He wore a skirt of metal chain across his pants. His smile, like some hungry beast's, encompassed more than just the Boy, as if the whole world were a meal, waiting to be taken in and devoured between his long teeth.

In time, Raleigh and the Boy were on the wagon and on the old road into Auburn.

A foul odor rose from under the hide tarp as the last of the afternoon washed out the brown-and-yellow landscape.

"We do this right and there'll be rifles aplenty for all of us," said Raleigh as he drove the team forward, away from the other Hard Men.

As THE WAGON full of bodies bumped its way along the track, the Boy watched Horse recede, his lead trailing to a stake, Vaclav smiling at him as they drove up the ravine and out onto the main road leading down to the gates of Auburn.

"Chinese got a rifle factory somewhere and the chief thinks it's here. So we got to do this right," said Raleigh between clicks and chucks of encouragement to the wagon team.

In the quiet, only the creak of the wagon could be heard beyond the clop of the team.

"Have you ever been to San Francisco?" asked the Boy.

"Nah. We came from up north, working in what used to be Canada. We rode together for years until MacRaven. Then, well, he was the man with the plan, know what I mean?"

"And what's the plan?"

Raleigh cast a glance at the Boy over his drooping handlebar mustache.

Overplayed it, Boy.

They rode on in silence.

But the voice of Sergeant Presley was there and the Boy thought about what he heard in it.

The mission for you, Boy, is still the same. Find I Corps. Give them the map. Whatever's about to happen here ain't your concern.

But they're going on to San Francisco. If the Army still exists there, then MacRaven and the tribes are going to come at the Army from behind.

This army won't be any match for I Corps, Boy. We had guns, tanks, helicopters. We'd chew this bunch up and spit 'em out.

He remembered the day Sergeant Presley had said that. They were hiding in the rocks, watching a village outside the dead lands of Oklahoma City—a village of salvagers being overrun by streaming bands of wild lunatics. The savagery had been brutal. They'd ridden three days just to get clear of that mess.

He remembered Sergeant Presley, his breath ragged in the cool night of that ride.

We had guns, tanks, helicopters. We'd chew this bunch up and spit 'em out.

But Sergeant Presley's gun had run out of ammo long before he'd ever met the Boy.

They'd seen the wrecks of countless war machines in their travels across the country.

They'd seen the burned hulls of melted tanks.

Downed and twisted helicopters.

Jets scattered across wide fields, only the wings and tail sections remaining to tell nothing of what had happened.

Even guns used as clubs by lunatics who didn't know any better.

He thought of the tribes on the march even now, closing the distance to this Chinese outpost.

Just like that village of salvagers outside Oklahoma City, Boy.

Sergeant, if I Corps had been fighting the Chinese all those years ago, over two hundred miles to the west, how do the Chinese have a settlement here?

I don't know, Boy. Stick to the mission.

I heard you say that many times, all the times I ever asked you what happened to those tanks and helicopters and jets we passed. Each time you said the same thing.

I don't know, Boy. Stick to the mission.

We don't know nothin' and orders is orders, Boy. You find I Corps and report. Tell 'em . . .

And yet there was the Chinese outpost, two hundred miles east of Oakland.

And there was Horse.

And there was drawing on cave walls.

And there is the mystery of what will become of me after I deliver the map.

Who will I be then?

And this voice was his alone.

CHAPTER 28

The Chinese officer was wearing the spun clothing of the soldiers. The pants and well-made boots. The long crimson jacket. The helmet. The officer carried a sword. The Chinese troops that met their wagon in front of the gate pointed rifles, long like Escondido's, at Raleigh and the Boy and the wagon full of corpses from atop the cut-log palisades.

What remained of an old overpass straddled the Eighty and served as the gateway to the Chinese colony of Auburn. High walls of cut forest pine screened the outpost along the southern side of the highway, surrounding the old historic district of the city from Before. Out of the center of the outpost, a domed county courthouse rose above the walls, and what lay within was beyond the Boy to see and to know.

Raleigh explained to the Chinese officers the character of the bodies and the Boy could not follow their wide-ranging discussion because it was in Chinese.

In time, more Chinese, older, fatter, dressed similarly to the officer, came out from behind the gate—even a few civilians. The Boy remained in the wagon.

All of his gear was gone.

His tomahawk.

His knife.

His bearskin cloak.

"If they see you're weak, they won't think much of us," Raleigh said when he'd told the Boy to leave his gear with Horse and the other Hard Men.

So he'd left his bearskin and weapons and Horse.

"You can trust us," said a smiling Dunn as he patted a jittery Horse, as if to reassure and unable to, all at once.

Raleigh turned back to the Boy in the middle of the conversation with the Chinese.

"They might make us sleep out here tonight."

That would be bad for the plan.

"I told 'em, ain't no way I was giving them the bodies without them paying me my bounty," said Raleigh, more for show, as if they might just be gone in the morning.

I don't know how this plays out for me, either way, Sergeant.

Be ready, Boy.

The Boy affected disinterest, which he knew was what Raleigh wanted him to show—that he was stupid and nothing to be afraid of.

The Boy stared off at the high wall and was surprised to see Escondido watching him.

When Raleigh turned back to the heated negotiation, the Boy looked up again at Escondido and barely passed one finger in front of his lip, almost as if he hadn't, but for anyone looking for such a message, the meaning was clear.

A moment later, the officers were retreating into the gate and Raleigh was climbing back aboard with a groan and a sly smile only the Boy could see.

"We're in," he whispered through the side of his mouth.

"They want a good look at them bodies. Chinese love their intel. Figure they'll know who's in charge this week and who they can bribe or play off against someone else next week. Won't matter much after tomorrow morning anyhow."

They drove through the gates and down the highway a bit before being directed up onto an off-ramp and into the center of the town.

They passed buildings.

A man worked at a forge, beating metal.

A shopkeeper with a patchwork lion skin in his front window nodded. Women crossed the street and entered the shop, talking loudly.

As they descended into the center of town from the highway, the soft glow of lights behind shop windows and houses came to life, blooming in the cool of the early spring evening.

A gang of children dashed down a side street, screaming in the twilight as they laughed and ran.

The Boy smelled spicy food.

But the hunger that had always been with him was dulled by what he saw.

The Chinese lived side by side with the people of other races. There were whites, browns, blacks, and Chinese.

The town murmured with life.

Like a city once must have.

The Boy thought of MacRaven's lunatic army of savage tribes moving through the thick forest east of the outpost.

He thought of MacRaven in armor.

He thought of the skeletons that were once cities.

He thought of Sergeant Presley's word. "Involved."

He waited for Sergeant Presley to tell him what to do now.

But he sensed the voice, like himself, had been silenced by the unfolding of life within the pine walls of this outpost.

Civilization.

Like Before.

Am I involved now?

And then . . .

Who am I?

"They say they'll pay the bounty in the morning, which is fine for our purposes," said Raleigh as he chucked and clicked the wagon team to follow the Chinese guide up to the paddock.

They were being directed to the "Old School," which was a wide field where they could camp for the night.

"MacRaven will start the attack at dawn. The Chinese will be real busy right about then, so we can get these bodies strung up in peace. After that, maybe we can join the fight."

Raleigh looked at the Boy for a long moment; then, as if answering some unspoken question, he sighed.

"All right, I'll tell you the plan. Once they breach the walls with Mac-Raven's Space Crossbow, you'll need to link up with the chief and lead him up here so the tribes can find the bodies all strung up like they got executed by the Chinese. Dunn'll come up with our horses and gear. Then we can join the cleanup and start looting."

Real careful now, Boy. You done all the work to gain his trust. Now, don't overplay it.

The Boy waited.

"I don't get it," said the Boy.

"Why do we have to string these bodies up? Seems like the point's made if the tribes find 'em slaughtered already. They'll think the Chinese did it anyways."

Raleigh sighed. There was a moment of things weighed. Scales balancing.

"To the tribes one and all, dyin' in battle is one thing. But strung up for crimes is another. They'll be so angry and ready for all the Chinese blood they can spill, they won't even realize they're leaderless and under Mac's total control. "

As an afterthought, as Raleigh turned to back the wagon, he added, "Brilliant, when you think about it."

"My guess is," continued Raleigh. "The Chinese will make their last stand down at that old courthouse. That's probably where the work will take place. I bet that's where the Chinese keep the guns and women, and that's where we'll want to get to, quick-like, once this tricky corpse business is done. First to fight, first to find, eh?"

Raleigh seemed happy, as if a fine breakfast had been announced for the morning and it would be something to look forward to throughout the long night.

They set to making a fire and then feeding the horses from the plentiful hay pile left on the Old School field.

In the early dark, they watched the fire as Raleigh heated strips of dried venison.

"I like it warmed even if it has been dried," he mumbled.

The meat was tough.

They ate in silence.

They'll slaughter these people, Boy. You know it and I know it.

You said, Don't get involved, Sergeant.

I know.

These are Chinese.

I know, Boy. And they're people too. Remember those salvagers outside Oklahoma City? Savages just like MacRaven's army murdered those people. Are you gonna let that happen here, again, to people like your friend Escondido?

"Whatcha thinking so hard about?" asked Raleigh from the other side of the fire. Evening shadows made his sad brown eyes even gloomier as they stared out from his long face above the drooping mustache.

I know, Sergeant.

"Meat's tough," said the Boy.

"Good for the teeth," mumbled Raleigh through a mouthful. "Unless you got bad teeth. You got bad teeth?"

The Boy nodded.

You know what you've got to do, Boy.

I know, Sergeant.

"Can I see your knife?" asked the Boy.

Raleigh stood and pulled it from his belt. He handed it pommel first to the Boy and sat back down.

Raleigh was biting into the venison once more when a thought occurred to him.

In that moment of chewing, thinking about warfare and food and rifles, Raleigh understood he'd made a mistake. But he was tired and it had been a very long life. He had, he knew, no one to blame but himself. He had always known this.

The Boy was standing.

The Boy's arm was back.

What the Boy lacked on one side, withered and bony, he had on the other—a powerful machine, just like MacRaven's Space Crossbow thought Raleigh. I have no one to blame but myself.

His teeth close on their final chew.

The Boy hurls the knife straight into Raleigh's chest.

All the air was driven from Raleigh at once as he fell backward from the impact. The darkness was already consuming him and the Boy. Raleigh thought, as he felt that one powerful hand about his throat, the Boy was like an animal.

THE BOY WAS up from the body. Raleigh, eyes bulging, stared sightlessly up into the stars and the night beyond.

By dawn they'll be all over these walls, Boy. Whatchu gonna do now?

He'd heard that question from Sergeant Presley before, many times in fact. *Whatchu gonna do now?*

I can find Escondido, Sergeant.

Then what?

Tell him what I know.

Then what?

I . . . it's up to them after that.

That's right, Boy. Do all you can do. Then let it go.

The Boy walked back toward the ancient courthouse down in the center of the outpost. Warm yellow light shone within the windows he passed.

Ahead he saw a Chinese guard at the intersection of two curving streets.

"Escondido?" he asked.

The guard mumbled in Chinese and shone a lantern into the Boy's face.

"Escondido?"

The guard's slurred Chinese seemed angry, and for a moment the Boy realized how much of his plan hinged on simply being understood. But after a pause the guard began to walk, lighting the way for the Boy and insisting he follow along. A moment later they turned down a side street and up a lane, almost reaching the outer pine-log wall.

The guard climbed the steps to an old shack and banged loudly on a thin door.

The racket and voice within belonged to Escondido.

When the old hunter opened the door, he hit the guard with a stream of Chinese, then, seeing the Boy he stopped. His tone was softer as he sent the guard off into the night.

The guard retreated down the steps and was down the winding lane, back toward the center of the outpost, his lantern bobbing in the darkness.

"Never thought I'd see you alive. What happened to your horse?"

"No time. There's an army of tribes out to the east. They're going to attack at dawn."

Escondido reacted quickly.

He only asked questions that mattered. Strength. Numbers. Proof.

He didn't waste time on disbelief.

'I guess,' thought the Boy as he followed after the old hunter, 'when you've lived through the end of the world once, you're willing to believe it can happen again.'

Shortly, they were standing on the steps of the old courthouse, their faces shining in the soft glow coming from within the old building. Chinese soldiers were speaking with Escondido. Every so often messengers left and returned. More and more of the soldiers were mustering in the old parking lot beneath the courthouse. As for the conversation, the Boy understood little of it.

Escondido turned away as the Chinese conferred among themselves.

"They believe you, all right. That patrol is well overdue. They seen your friend's body and they've put two and two together. The question for them now is, what're they gonna do? Yang, the garrison commander, wants to send the civilians and the Hillmen out tonight. He's only got forty soldiers, but he thinks he can hold the courthouse."

And how much is this, Boy? asked Sergeant Presley long ago.

Five.

And this? He holds up all ten fingers.

Ten.

And if each one of these fingers represents the total of all my fingers?

One hundred.

Good, Boy. Next you'll make me take off my moccasins. But we'll save that for another time.

There were far more tribesmen than one hundred. Far more than forty.

"If they go, do you want to go with 'em?" asked Escondido.

The Boy shook his head.

"I'm half tempted to run myself." Then, "The Hillmen are sending messengers out to their villages. That might even things up a bit. All right, you'll fight with me. I'll be on the eastern wall. You can reload my rifles. You know how to do that?"

The Boy shook his head.

"Well, we got all night to learn."

CHAPTER 30

"Feels like spring," whispered Escondido in the cool darkness as the two of them sat beneath the ramparts along the wall. It was morning, just before sunrise.

Below the wall, in the fields and forest beyond, all was a soft gray.

The Boy smelled a breeze thick with the scent of the field. And on it, he knew, he could taste the waiting tribes out there in the darkness.

"Be a long summer," muttered Escondido, his old eyes squinting at the far horizon. "But what do I know."

The Boy checked Raleigh's knife. It was stuck into the soft wood of the parapet.

Escondido had taught him how to break the rifle, pull out the expended cartridge, load another of the massive bullets into the breech, exchange rifles with Escondido. Repeat. They had more than a hundred cartridges. But not many more.

Escondido wiped angrily at his nose.

"I can smell 'em comin' up the ravine. If we fall back, or you see the Chinese start to leave, head down to the courthouse in the center of town. They'll make their stand there. That's if I'm kilt, understand?"

The sun washed the field in gold, and out of the low-lying mist, arrows like birds began to race up toward the parapets. Loud knocks indicated the arrows ramming themselves into the wooden walls just on the other side of their heads. Someone screamed farther down along the wall. There was a sudden rush of the slurring Chinese, spoken in anger and maybe fear.

Escondido popped his head over the wall, keeping his rifle erect.

He shouted a string of Chinese directed at the others along the wall.

Then he sat down with his back to the parapet. "They're using them arrows to keep our heads down. There's thousands of 'em crossing the fields with ladders and poles now." He took three short breaths, then, "Here we go!" Escondido popped his head over the wall, this time sighting down the rifle, and a second later the world erupted in thunder and blue smoke.

As the echoing crack of the rifle faded across the forest, the tribes began to whoop and scream below, breaking the morning quiet.

Escondido backed down behind the wall, handed the spent rifle to the Boy, and grabbed the other from the Boy's frozen fingers.

The Boy had been told all his life about the legendary capacity of a gun to strike back at an enemy. But he had never seen one fired. He was never told of its blue stinging smoke and sudden thunder.

Three breaths as Escondido raised the rifle back over the wall. He targeted some unseen running, screaming tribesmen. A brief click as he pulled the trigger, and again the explosion.

They exchanged rifles. Unloaded and smoking, hot to the touch—for the other rifle, now loaded and waiting to be fired again.

Repeat.

"There's thousands of 'em," stated Escondido again.

Three breaths.

The explosion.

Repeat.

"They're coming up the walls, it'll be knife work shortly."

The explosion.

Repeat.

"Duck!"

The sudden whistle of flocks of arrows flinging themselves from far away to close at hand, then the thick-sounding *chocks* as the cloud of missiles slammed down into the walls and old buildings within the outpost.

The Boy grabbed Raleigh's knife when he heard the ladders fall into place on the other side of the pine logs. He put it in his mouth before he took the expended rifle and started the unloading trick he'd been taught.

Explosion.

"Be a long hot summer," muttered Escondido.

Repeat.

The Boy finished reloading and waited to exchange rifles.

When nothing happened he looked up.

Escondido was slumped over the wall, almost falling facedown. The Boy pulled him back behind the parapet.

A bolt had gone straight up through his jaw and into his brain. His eyes were shut tight in death.

The Boy heard feet scrabbling for purchase on the other side.

All along the wall, lunatic tribesmen jabbered, screamed, and spurted blood as they hacked away at the mostly dying Chinese.

The Boy, still holding the rifle, grabbed the sack of cartridges and tumbled off the platform, checking his landing with a roll.

He raced down a lane, his limping lope carrying him away from the bubbling surge of madmen now atop the wall and spilling over into the outpost. Chinese and Hillmen raced pell-mell for the old courthouse. Snipers from its highest windows below the old dome were shooting down into the streets.

The Boy was making good speed while watching the courthouse. He saw one of the snipers draw a bead on him and fire at the place where he should have been. Instead he crashed through the front door of a shack. Inside he found linens and pots and pans. There was even food in glass jars.

'Go to ground,' he thought, and wondered if this was the voice of Sergeant Presley. There was too much going on for him to tell.

Get behind the first wave of attackers, Boy. They'll go for the courthouse.

He remembered Raleigh telling him to meet MacRaven at the front gate so that he could lead the tribes to the planned horror of their murdered leaders.

Outside, Mohawked tribesmen were streaming down the streets with axes and blood-curdling screams. Bullets, fired from the courthouse, smacked and ricocheted into the cracked and broken streets.

When the first wave passed by the store, the Boy darted across the street and into an alley. He followed the alley and a few others as he worked his way back to the gate that sat astride old Highway Eighty.

He smelled smoke and burning wood.

Women were screaming.

Ahead, above the rooftops, where the gate should be, he saw an explosion of gray smoke and splintering wood.

The gunfire from the courthouse was increasing.

Breaking glass both close and far away.

Screams.

Whatchu gonna do now, Boy?

I've got to get Horse.

At the gate, the ashen-faced warriors were leaping over the collapsed remains of the entrance to hack with their machetes at the stunned Chinese riflemen mustering in the median of the old highway.

Through the smoke, MacRaven and a collection of warriors from the tribes of the Sierra Nevada were picking their way through the rubble. MacRaven turned, waving his machete, and behind him a vanguard of ashen-faced warriors pushed a wagon forward through the shattered remains of the gate. Atop the wagon rested a large gleaming metal crossbow.

The Boy crossed the open sward of grass to the on-ramp, waving at MacRaven.

MacRaven led the tribesmen toward the Boy as he pointed for the giant crossbow to be set up on the median of the highway.

"Have you found them?" roared MacRaven, his performance of concerned commander utterly believable.

The Boy nodded, unsure what to do next. He looked to the gate, hoping Horse would come through at any moment as more and more ashen-faced warriors poured through the breach.

MacRaven led the Boy away from the others as if to receive the planned bad news of their leaders' demise.

"Speak to me like you're telling me something horrible," he whispered once they were some distance from the others.

The Boy couldn't think of what to say.

"Just move your mouth."

He opened and closed his mouth as MacRaven nodded. Then, "Where did Raleigh put the bodies?"

The Boy pointed toward the Old School.

"On the field, up there."

"All right, in just a moment you're going to lead us up there. But first I want to watch my Space Crossbow take out their courthouse."

MacRaven turned back to the crossbow crew and raised his arm, then brought it down toward the dome of the courthouse.

A singing twang sent a six-foot iron shaft speeding from the gleaming crossbow into the cupola of the courthouse. Brick and debris shot out the other side of the building as rubble crashed down onto the lower levels and finally the steps leading to the parking lot.

"Great, huh?" said MacRaven, turning to the Boy. "It's from Before. It was designed to go up into space and shoot down asteroids so smart men could bring soil samples back to earth. I found it inside an old research plant down east of L.A. Place called JPL, whatever that means. Doesn't sound like a word, but maybe it was in another language I ain't learned yet. From what I could tell, they were gonna send it up into space before the war. Good thing they didn't, huh?"

The Boy heard a little electric motor whining as the drawstring re-cocked the crossbow. Three men levered another iron bolt off the floor of the wagon and placed it onto the weapon.

"I'll conquer the world with it," said MacRaven in armor amid the smoke and bullets. "Just wait."

The catapult fired again and the massive bolt disappeared into the main body of the courthouse. Its effects were devastating.

CHAPTER 31

The main group of MacRaven's entourage was twenty feet behind the Boy as he led them up along time ravaged streets toward the Old School and the field where MacRaven expected they would find the strung-up corpses of their leaders.

Instead, MacRaven will find the body of his most trusted man and a wagon full of corpses, Sergeant. A wagon many will have already seen back in the Hidden Valley.

You know how it is, Boy. Whatchu gonna do now? 'Cause you ain't got much time to do it in.

The blood was everywhere along their trek through the lanes of the outpost: in pools, splashed against the sides of houses, painting shattered glass.

The gunfire from the courthouse came in waves, and each wave seemed diminished from the one previous. The waves were punctuated by the giant crossbow's singing note and the audible whistle of the great bolt through the atmosphere and then its sudden crash.

Ahead of the Boy, at a bend in the lane, a woman lay in the street, naked and dead. An infant wailed from the porch of the shack she lay in front of.

Around the bend, three Chinese guards were riddled with arrows. They stared sightlessly at the Boy, MacRaven, and the wild entourage of tribespeople, who grew quieter with each found body.

The air was still cool, reminding the Boy that it was just after dawn.

The Boy looked behind and saw MacRaven staring intently at him.

The dead did not bother MacRaven.

Whatchu gonna do now?

I've got a knife and a rifle.

It ain't much, Boy.

The low concrete that abutted the sports field of the once school was all that remained and protected the Boy from the truth that was soon to be revealed.

Warriors were still climbing the walls toward the north.

But these warriors were different.

They wore clothes like the Chinese.

They carried large axes.

They uttered *whoop whoops* as they flooded toward MacRaven's group.

In a moment, it would be the hot work of thrust and slash.

MacRaven's entourage formed up quickly to stand against the sudden waves of Hillmen climbing the walls to counter-attack.

MacRaven fell behind the warriors of the tribes now eager to get their fair share of trophies. He signaled the Boy to come to him.

"Get back to the gate and find whoever you can and get them up here. It's a counter-attack!" A moment later, MacRaven pulled a dead tribesman aside and thrust a Hillman through with his machete.

"Go!"

Now's your chance, Boy. You get just the one.

I know.

The Boy ran back to the gate.

Black smoke climbed in thick pillars from the southern portion of the outpost, forming an inky backdrop to the crumbling courthouse. There were only a few Chinese snipers left in what remained of the old building.

At the gate, ashen-faced warriors were gathering to watch the cross-bow's work while a captain marshaled them for the final attack on the last of the courthouse's defenders.

Dunn rode through the gate on his dark gray mare. He saw the Boy and waved his hat as he galloped the distance between them.

"Where's MacRaven?"

The Boy pointed toward the top of the outpost. "Where's my horse and gear?"

Dunn smiled. "What, dontcha trust us, Bear Killer?"

The anger behind the Boy's stare checked Dunn.

"Nice rifle." Dunn's eyes were ice cold.

The Boy looked down at the rifle. He had completely forgotten about it.

"Give it here," demanded Dunn.

"Where's my horse?" said the Boy through clenched teeth.

For a moment Dunn's hand fell to his machete. But then he heard a far-off volley of rifle fire and this meant something to him.

"Hell, keep it. Vaclav's coming up with Raleigh's horse and yours also, I suspect. Where'd you say the chief was?"

The Boy stared for a long moment, then pointed toward the field.

Dunn kicked his mount and tore off across the grass of the on-ramp. The crossbow sang again and now the ashen-faced warriors were marching in formation toward the courthouse.

Won't be long now before things get sorted out. You better get while the gettin's good, Boy.

He trotted through the broken timbers of the gate, smashed by the iron bar flung from the space crossbow.

The rising highway to the east was flooded with carts and wagon teams. Wild-eyed women and scrawny children who had followed the army of tribes watched the fort with hunger. On the other side of the highway, buildings from Before lay fallow and fallen amidst a pine forest that had overrun that section of town.

Vaclav led Horse and Raleigh's mount down alongside the grass-covered highway. The other horses were wild with fear from the smoke and gunfire as Vaclav cursed and spit, trying to keep them under control.

When he saw the Boy he yelled, "Take your stupid animal already."

The Boy limped forward and took hold of Horse. The bearskin was tied across Horse's back and he found his tomahawk inside the saddle pack. A moment later he was up and whispering as he patted the long neck of his friend.

"What's going on in there?" said Vaclav, looking at the rifle with the coal-black version of Dunn's hungry blue eyes.

The Boy was just about to lie when they both heard shouting at the gate as Dunn came thundering through on his mare, knocking back two ashen-faced guards. He screamed something at Vaclav.

If the meaning isn't clear it shortly will be, Boy.

"What's he saying?" asked Vaclav.

Dunn waved his machete, still shouting as he drove his horse hard up the old highway.

Whatchu gonna do now, Boy?

Vaclav will be busy with the extra mount. Dunn, on the other hand . . .

The Boy raised the rifle and sighted down the barrel. The rifle was too long to steady with just his one good arm, which he needed the hand of to pull the trigger.

Horse has never heard a rifle before. Be ready, Boy. Horse might not like it.

He raised his withered left arm and set the rifle on the flat of his thin arm.

"What're you doing?" Vaclav screamed.

Is it loaded, Boy?

Dunn's eyes were wide with fear and hate as he raced to close the distance between them.

Horse danced to the right, turning away.

I've never fired a gun before, Sergeant.

Ain't nothin' but a thang.

Explosion.

The bullet rips into Dunn's mount and Dunn goes down hard, face-first on the grassy slope.

The Boy urged Horse forward and they were off across the broken and grassy highway, down an overgrown embankment, and into the ruins and the forest beyond.

CHAPTER 32

The Boy had passed by the overgrown ruins of places almost familiar many times before. There had always been in him that desire to understand such places, to investigate them. But in this moment of shouting men behind him, and soon the inevitable dogs, he knew there was no time for the usual consideration of things past.

Green grass sprouted through the split asphalt of a wide avenue, the remains of an old road led up through the ruins that the Boy suspected was the other half of the Auburn that existed before the bombs. At the top of the rise, looking back toward the smoky pillars climbing over the out-post, the Boy saw the remnants of the Hard Men coming for him. Other men, ferocious lunatics, followed behind Raleigh's riders with bellowing hounds at the ends of thick straps of leather.

Escape and evade, Boy, we done it a million times. If they're bringing dogs, then distance is what you need. Out of sight, those dogs will start to slow down when they start searchin' for your trail. Then you can confuse 'em.

The Boy patted Horse and knew that an outright race would put him beyond the dogs. But the Hard Men on their horses would spot his trail and the following would be easier.

He turned and started through the overgrown brush and tangle of a collapsed bridge that once crossed the road.

I'll keep moving west, Sergeant.

He rode Horse hard for a time, working his way down a wooded ridge and following a twisting maze of dense brush and warped trees along falling ridges and a steep slope that will eventually lead into the river delta around Sacramento.

By noon he had lost the Hard Men, but his progress had been slow. Way off, back up on the ridge, he heard dogs baying, moaning as if in pain.

If they catch me, will those dogs stop their noise, satisfied at what will happen next?

Sometimes I wonder if there is any good left in this world.

He thought of the bodies and carnage of Auburn.

At sunset, he pulled out the map from its hidden place in the bearskin. Sacramento was far ahead to the west.

Behind him, he could smell woody smoke in the fading light and he wondered if it was from Auburn or the campfires of his pursuers.

It was good to be alone again.

Is that the way of my life, Sergeant? My way through this world? Alone?

But there was no answer.

Why should there be an answer, Sergeant? When you were alive we never talked about those things. We talked of food and survival, and sometimes I just listened to your stories about the way things were Before. And sometimes also, why they had to end.

You take everything with you, Boy.

Yes.

He looked at what forty years of wild, unchecked growth had made of the terrain. It was a wall through which nothing could pass undetected.

The Old Highway is maybe a mile off to my right. I'll have a better chance evading them there.

They could be searching the road for you, Boy.

If I put as much distance tonight between myself and the hounds, by morning I'll have a better chance.

He remembered Sergeant Presley's hatred of "chance."

If all you got is a chance, Boy, you ain't got jack!

It's all I have now, Sergeant.

He rode the highway at a trot. The night was cool and mist rose from the lowlands on both sides of the highway. Cars and trucks, forever frozen in rusty dereliction, littered the road and made him wonder, as they always did, of the stories behind and within them.

You'll never know, Boy. I could make up a story for you like I used to. You could tell yourself a lie. But what good would it do, even if you could know how things ended for those people?

Sometimes the Boy heard himself asking, *What has happened here?* Sometimes the cars were jammed together, as though frozen in a single moment of waiting. Sometimes they were overturned. Sometimes they were parked by the side of the road, every door open, every window broken. What was within was gone, even down to the seats. All that was left was rusting metal and an untold story he would never hear.

He looked at the cars scattered along the highway.

It is beyond me to ever know why such things have been left the way they are.

And yet I want to know.

He rode on, long after the sliver of a moon had completed its descent. It was dark and damp and cold. In the misty gloom he saw standing water in the surrounding fields and broken buildings.

The water looked like a rug.

Before long, he had ridden in close to the skeletal towers of the old state capitol in Sacramento. He heard frogs everywhere and even the highway was submerged. He came to a bridge that had long since fallen into the muck of the dark river below and he could go no farther.

It is too dark to find a way around, Sergeant.

He looked behind him and saw nothing in the misty night.

The frogs will warn me if anyone comes along.

Sorry—he pats Horse—we can't have fire tonight.

He draped his blanket over his friend and rolled up in his bearskin at the side of the bridge, far out along it, almost to the edge of the broken span over the swamp below.

IN THE MILKY light of morning he surveyed the bridge. There was no way to the other side. The city, twisted, bent, and broken, lay all about him, submerged in the cold water of the wide river.

The course of the river must have changed in the years since the bombs.

Or because of the bombs.

He led Horse down an off-ramp and they waded through the watery streets of a long-gone city. Windows, regularly spaced, gaped and screamed in silent horror as they passed.

My whole life I've wanted to explore such places. But there is nothing here now.

Is this why Sergeant Presley said no? Because there is nothing left of the things that were once here?

At noon the murk had mostly burned off and they—Horse and the Boy—had crossed over to the far side of the river on an old rail bridge that still stood. The Eighty continued west on the other side of a field.

The Boy looked back at the dead city.

I could wander you for years and what could you give me back?

Could you show me who I might have been?

And why is that so important to me?

He tries for a moment to imagine what it must have looked like— looked like with people in it. People from Before.

That night, beyond the city, after a day filled with long silences punctuated by the last lonely birds of winter, he camped next to a wall whose purpose he didn't understand. Why it lay next to the old highway or who built it and for what he did not know.

He ate three small rabbits that he took with the rifle in the afternoon and set wild corn in front of Horse.

The world is filled with wild corn and you want nothing more, Horse. Life must be pretty good for you.

He thought of the five rounds he'd fired to take the three rabbits.

Two had been wasted.

Yes. But if I am to use the rifle I must practice with it. I must be sure of it when I need it.

He reached into his bag and took out the charcoal. He shaved it with his knife and looked at the wall.

He drew a great bridge in long, sketchy strokes that ran the length of the wall. Then he drew the skyline of the hoary city sinking into the swampy river. Below, near the gritty pavement of the old highway, he filled in the moonlit water, reflecting the shadows of the city back up at itself.

The night was bitterly cold and even the fingers of his good hand ached like those on his bad side. Later he returned to the fire and warmed himself, looking at the mural.

Was that it?

It seemed as though there should be something more.

He thought of drawing Horse. Or himself. Or even MacRaven.

But nothing seemed right.

Lying on his side drifting toward sleep, facing the hot fire, the cold at his neck, he saw the city come to life.

And he lived there.

And there was a day . . .

The best day ever.

He awoke to the orange light of the coals in the deep of night and saw the shadowy city rendered on the wall. He could not remember what was so good about the dream of the day in that city before the bombs. Only that it was the best, and worth having, and that he had been cheated, as though a valuable piece of salvage had been stolen from beneath him while he slept.

'It seems as though there should be something more to the picture on the wall,' he thought again, remembering the dream.

And as he fell back to sleep he heard, *I bet the people who lived in that city thought so too, Boy. I bet they did.*

CHAPTER 33

In the days that followed, the Boy rode in quiet along the muddy river that reminded him so much of the big one back east, and the Possum Hunters and Sergeant Presley, when he had been young.

He felt old.

The days passed and towns on the map either didn't exist or lay buried beneath wild grass and corn.

He passed a convoy of military vehicles forever parked in the median of the great windswept highway.

He smelled the salt of the ocean on a sudden shifting breeze.

It smelled of Texas.

But cleaner.

He passed rusting vehicles lying swaddled in the reeds that shot up out of the mucky fields and stood for a long time considering the wreck of an Apache helicopter, held longingly by a clutch of thorny rosebushes.

He climbed a high pass and saw long iron spikes cast to the ground, all in one direction, as if thrown by the hand of a giant. Large windmill blades lay buried in the dirt and grass.

In the town beyond, he saw the charred remains of buildings reaching up to the gray sky.

The wind and the clouds march east, lashing the buckled highway with spring rain. At the end of the day, the Boy felt as though much more had been required of him than just movement. He was exhausted.

On the day he reached the bay, the weather turned warm. At least, if he stood in the center of the road at full noon and turned his face toward the bright sun, the day felt warm. In the shade of bridges and crumbling buildings, the cold had always been and always would be, just like the rusty destruction he found there along the bay's edge.

He saw the bay from a high hill and on the far side of its blue water, he saw the great pile of rubble that was San Francisco, in the State of California. Only a few tall buildings remained standing. The rest lay buried in the piles of concrete and twisted rebar he could see even from this distance.

Ain't never been nuked, Boy. Chinese wouldn't do it. Needed a deep water port on the West Coast. Seattle, San Diego, and of course L.A. were all long gone. We fought for that pile of rubble for ten years.

The Boy could hear the campfire stories of the great battles and "ops" of the San Francisco of Sergeant Presley.

On Market Street we lost all our armor, Boy.

And . . .

I was the last one off the roof of the Ferry Building. Close one that day, Boy.

And . . .

I saw the TransAmerica Building go down after a Jay Thirty-three went in about halfway up. Dust for days after that one, Boy.

And . . .

The Army will be down along the East Bay. Headquarters in an old college library. That's where you'll find I Corps, Boy.

Tell them I made it all the way.

Tell them there was no one left.

Tell them who I was, Boy.

And . . .

You take everything with you.

CHAPTER 34

I'm glad you died, Sergeant.

You thought they would still be here—waiting for you.

The wreckage of military equipment littered the highway that wound its way along the green-grass slopes of the East Bay. Broken concrete pads and burnt black fingers of framing erupted through tall wind-driven grass.

You crossed the whole country and lost all your friends, Sergeant. The general, even. Someone named Lola, who you never told me about. All of them.

The Boy passed a convoy of supply tucks, melted and blackened forty years ago.

"Five tons," said the Boy as the morning wind off the bay beat at his long hair, whipping his face and shoulders.

Farther along, the tail rotor of a helicopter lay across the buckling highway.

Apache, maybe.

The KIAs and the MIAs and all the people you imagined were still here, waiting for you to come back—they're all gone.

Later, as Horse nosed the tall grass, the Boy walked around three helicopter transports long since landed in the southbound lanes. They were rusty and dark, stripped of everything.

"Black Hawks," he mumbled, sitting in a pilot's seat, wondering at how one flew them through the air like a bird, which was impossible for him to picture.

Climbing up through the concrete buttresses that remained of Fort Oakland, he came to the tanks.

Blackened. Burnt. Abandoned. High up on the hill he could see the ragged remains of canvas tents and the flower blossoms of spiked artillery pieces.

Sergeant, your dream of finding them here couldn't have survived this.

He led Horse up the hill through the long grass and around the craters and foxholes long since covered in a waving sea of soft green and yellow.

When he reached the spiked artillery pieces now resting forever in permanent bloom, he could see the remains of the Army, of I Corps, below. All the way to the shores of the sparkling bay's eastern edge he could see burnt tanks, melted Humvees, helicopters that would never fly, a fighter jet erupting from the rubble of the few houses that remained along the bay.

I followed you through the rain and the snow and along all those long moonlit nights while you told me about this place. The people. What we would find. Who you were.

And.

Who I might be.

He stood among the tent posts on top of the hill.

Of the Army he'd waited his whole life to meet, only ragged strips of canvas remained, fluttering in the breeze.

Off to the right, down along a ridgeline, he could see a field of white crosses. The graves were open and the crosses lay canted at angles.

I'm glad you died with your dream of this place, Sergeant, because . . .

. . . this would have killed you.

All the way.

Tell them who I was, Boy.

Tell who, Sergeant?

And who am I now, Sergeant Presley? Now that you are gone and the dream that you promised me is dead, who am I now?

But there was no answer.

CHAPTER 35

He smelled smoke.

The smoke of meat came to him on the wind of the next day, in the morning, before light.

At first light, he scanned the horizon and saw, across the bay, the columns of rising smoke. He checked the map. Sausalito.

He'd spent the day before combing the wreckage of the Army. There was nothing to be had. Everything that was left had burned long ago. When he went to the cemetery below the ridge, he found bones in the bottom of each open grave. Nothing more.

Maybe there is someone, maybe even I Corps, over there on the other side of the bay, Sergeant?

But there was no answer.

Someone was there.

Later he rode out to the north, crossing large sections of muddy bay where ancient supertankers rested on their sides. Occasionally he passed large craters.

At the northern edge of the bay, mudflats gave way to the tall brown grass of the estuaries. A long thin bridge, low to the water, stretched off toward the west.

A heron, white and tall, stood still, not watching the Boy.

The bridge may only go so far.

After a small break and time spent looking at the map, he decided to try and cross the bridge.

You would ask me why I was in such a hurry to get to the other side, Sergeant. You would say, *Whatchu in a hurry about, Boy?*

I would say, *I want to know what's in Sausalito.*

Then you would say, *You always did.*

That is what you would say.

But the voice didn't say anything.

The Boy had not heard the voice since the open graves and the tattered canvas.

The ride out into the marshes made the Boy feel lonely—lonelier than he'd ever felt in all his life. Other than the heron he'd seen at the eastern side of the thin bridge, he saw no other life.

'That is why I feel so alone, because there is no other living thing,' he thought. He'll speak to me again.

In the afternoon, the wind stopped and fog rolled in across the bay. Faster than he would have ever expected, the fog surrounded him and he could see little beyond the thin road ahead.

Only Horse's hooves on the old highway broke the silence.

He expected some bird to call out to another bird, but there was nothing. No one to call to, even if it were just another bird.

It was then he began to think the bridge might never end—that he would ride forever through the fog.

And what about food? I can't go off in those marshes to hunt. I would be stuck. And Horse, what of him if I have to run?

Stop. You would tell me to stop, Sergeant.

The road will end. And if not, I will turn back and go the long way around the bay.

The thought of having to ride back through the eerie stillness at night did little to comfort him, and for a long time he rode on until at last the bridge began to rise back onto dry land.

See, I had nothing to be afraid of, right, Sergeant?

CHAPTER 36

They worked in the small bay. They were tall and brown skinned like the Chinese of Auburn.

The day had turned cold and gray.

For a long time the Boy stood with Horse, watching them from the dusty road. In time they became aware of him and began to gesture to one another regarding him. Still, they continued to work with their long rakes, sweeping beneath the cold dark water of the bay. Out in the deep water beyond, whitecaps were beginning to form.

I thought I might find the Army here, Sergeant.

His voice had gone now. It had left him in the fog of the bridge over the marsh.

No, it was before that. It was when he saw the open graves and the bones within.

Maybe the knowledge of what happened to I Corps finally killed you, Sergeant. Killed you in a way death could not. Killed the mission you left me to finish.

In time they came in from the water, rolling down their pant legs and donning leather-skinned long jackets trimmed with sheep's wool. A man, older than most, but not the oldest he'd seen, waded out through the tall grass to the road and climbed the embankment to where the Boy sat atop Horse.

Standing in front of the Boy, he said something in Chinese.

He repeated it.

The Boy shook his head.

The man was weathered like the sides of their clapboard shacks.

The Weathered Man stared off toward the bay for a long time. His face was tight and brown, his cheeks red like apples. He watched the dry brown and gray shacks of their farm.

'He is wondering what to do with me,' thought the Boy.

The Weathered Man turned and walked down the embankment, and as an afterthought waved his hand at the Boy, as if he should come along with him.

There was a fire pit outside a long weathered barn that reached out into the gray waters of the bay. The rakes were stacked neatly against the side of the old building.

The Weathered Man drove a stake into the ground for Horse and returned shortly with hay. He laid it down in front of Horse and reached up to caress the long nose, muttering softly in Chinese once more.

He pointed toward a worn long table near the water's edge and the fire for the Boy to sit at.

A giant blackened grill was placed over the fire and then piles of green wet seaweed atop the grill. Salty, white smoke rose up in billows. The rest of the people worked at cleaning small, flat stones they'd brought in wide baskets up from the waters of the bay.

Rough clay plates and cups were set out. There was fresh hot bread and a stone crock of creamy butter, another of red sauce, and another of a pungent dark liquid that smelled of fish and salt.

The wind rose up off the bay in breezy gusts. The Boy's left side was stiff, and he massaged what he could to work life back into the thin muscles of that side.

More of the Chinese appeared, coming from inland, setting down rakes and hoes to go down to the bay and wash their hands in the stinging cold water.

More round loaves of crusty bread were set out, as the flat stones that had been brought up from the bay went onto the grill.

'They eat stones?' thought the Boy, who had seen many different people eat many strange things.

The Weathered Man watched the fire dully, his eyes far away as he stood over the grill with a short rake, moving the stones about.

Shortly, the stones came off the grill and were thrown onto the long flat table. More stones were laid upon the grill and the Chinese sat down, each grabbing at a stone and prying off a hidden lid. Then they raised their stones to their mouths and slurped. They threw the stones into a basket and each of them reached for the next stone, this time adding either the red sauce or the dark liquid smelling of fish and salt, or even the creamy butter, and in some cases a bit of one or the other, and for a few, all three.

The Weathered Man sat down on the bench next to the Boy and looked at him and then the stones. The Weathered Man took one, cracked the lid and slurped, watching the Boy.

The Boy reached out and took one. He peeled back the lid with difficulty, as his withered hand was required to hold the stone. Inside he found the oyster, gray and steaming, swimming in liquid. He ate it, feeling it slide into his mouth and then explode in warm saltiness as he chewed its meat. He looked into the shell where the oyster had once been and found a pearl-colored base swirling white and gray.

It was the most beautiful thing he had ever seen in his short and very hard life.

They ate more oysters and bread. A few talked. The Boy tried the red sauce. It burned slowly and made him sweat at even the few drops he'd added to the oyster using a knife-shaped tool kept in the stone crock.

'It's too hot,' he thought of the sauce.

Afterward, as the heat faded, he liked the taste it left in his mouth. It reminded him of the wild peppers they'd found in the South along the salty marshes of the State of Louisiana.

He tried the dark liquid. It had a salty, deep, satisfying flavor that was almost overripe. But when combined with the yellow butter and the heat of the cooked oyster, it was like eating a good cut of meat taken from a fresh kill, tender and young.

Of their talk he understood nothing. In time, the looks that had been cast his way ceased, as if they had assigned him a place in their world—as if he had always been there and would remain there.

The last batch of oysters was laid out and finished with almost the same zeal as the first.

Two women wearing gray clothes and bright headscarves, their faces tanned and apple cheeked, struggled together with a flat-iron-gray tub brought out from one of the clapboard shacks. The Boy heard a sound like the tinkling of bells, light and musical, as though whatever things were in the tub tapped back and forth against each other.

The tub was set down and the rest of the Chinese gathered around it, taking up bottles of every shape and size and twisting off the caps that sealed them. The bottles made a small popping hiss. They drank from the bottles, few the same color: some green, some brown, a few blues or almost clear. In the clear ones the Boy could see a pale yellow liquid, foaming near the top.

The bottles were from Before, but they had been filled with something from Now.

Later he would think of that sentence.

Especially the part about something from Now.

As if there had ever been such a thing.

The villagers drank in long pulls, then expelled a breathy "Ahhh." There was much burping.

The Weathered Man, weathered like the clapboard shacks of the village, returned to the table, said something seemingly final in Chinese and handed a green bottle to the Boy.

The Boy took the bottle. He looked inside and could only see a few bubbles. He looked at the cap, which seemed pressed as if stamped onto the bottle. He looked at the Weathered Man.

The Weathered Man took the bottle and with a twist brought the cap off and handed it back to the Boy as foam rose out its top. The Weathered Man drank from his bottle, watching the Boy, telling him with his eyes that the Boy should do the same.

The Boy closed his eyes and drank. Foam and suds raced up into his nose. But the drink was cold, ice cold. It tasted of the fields.

When he opened his eyes the Weathered Man was smiling at him, as if saying "See," and then, "What do you think?" all at once.

A warm flush rose up in the Boy.

And he was not so cold.

And he was not so alone.

"Pee Gee Oh," said the Weathered Man, holding the bottle up.

"Pee Gee Oh," said the Boy, and drank again. The Weathered Man smiled and drank.

They each considered the bay, watching the whitecaps roll and disappear across its waters. There was still daylight now as winter faded and spring appeared.

'The days were growing again,' thought the Boy.

He drank and looked at the little village by the bay. It was a collection of weathered clapboard buildings and steep roofs, growing out of the tall green grass among the curvy stunted trees whose limbs gathered in bunches like hats. All around him the Chinese talked seriously or laughed or whispered. Some played games with rectangles of stone.

He thought of their apple cheeks, bright red from the cold water and the wind.

He thought of their oysters hidden each day beneath the waters.

They were kind.

They were a village of kind people.

If he could mark things on the map he would spell this as the Village of Kind People Who Will Give You Food.

And Pee Gee Oh.

Whatever that was.

It was good.

He took the last drink from the bottle, feeling warm and fuzzy. He considered the hills to the east, on the other side of the bay, the lands there broken and bent, mired in destruction and overrun by the swollen rivers he'd crossed.

He thought of MacRaven and Dunn and all the tribes.

Those people, those Chinese, were like these.

And now they were dead.

He went to his saddlebag and took out his sack of charcoal. He looked around.

I need a place to draw. But the charcoal won't show on the sides of their shacks.

He found a patch of concrete back toward the road. Weeds and grass grew up through the broken spaces.

He made a small fire.

He drew the courthouse first.

He saw the Chinese watching him from afar, standing around their tables, enjoying the last of their Pee Gee Oh.

He drew the dome of the courthouse, sketching the part of the dome that had been sheared off by the giant crossbow bolt.

He could hear the singing twang as it launched.

He drew the streets as he remembered them, mainly the intersection where he'd seen the bodies riddled with arrows.

He heard the villagers muttering over him as he worked on all fours drawing the fire and the smoke and the carnage.

He heard them and forgot them all at once.

He drew the ramparts, the pine logs burning like the breath of evil monsters, as the tribes, feathered and in war paint, crawled over the spiked tops. He drew Escondido firing into something unseen.

He drew smoke.

He drew falling arrows.

He drew fire.

He drew the woman lying in the street, staring at the sky.

He could not draw the crying of the baby or all the other screams he seemed to remember now.

He stood back.

He could feel the weight of the Chinese watching him. He could hear their breath escaping through their open mouths.

Someone dropped a bottle and it exploded with a crash.

No one said a word.

There was one more thing.

He stooped to the drawing once more. His side was not stiff. He didn't feel anything here by the bay. He was there at the outpost, on that golden morning just after dawn.

The smell of burning pine.

The screams and bullets and smoke appearing in the windows of the old courthouse.

He was on the median of grass astride the great highway.

MacRaven told him: "I'll conquer the world."

MacRaven, his wolf's face smiling like a child's, his eyes shining. MacRaven, in armor, staring out at the Chinese.

The Boy stood, letting the last of the charcoal fall from his numb fingers.

And someone began to cry.

CHAPTER 37

They gave the Boy and Horse a shack to sleep in for the night. It was small and it lay next to the road and the ocean, its only furnishing a baked clay brazier with hot coals. The wind beat at the shack in the night, and once, when he stepped outside to urinate, he saw a clear night sky and the moon riding high over the bay. He saw the dark shapes of birds crossing the waters in the night toward the broken shadows of the ruins of San Francisco.

He was so tired and so comfortable from the meal and the Pee Gee Oh that he almost could not sleep.

But then he did.

Later the Boy was not sure if he was dreaming or awake when he heard the hooves of another horse disappear off into the night.

HE AWOKE TO the hands of the Weathered Man gently shaking him, giving him a cup of tea, beckoning him to come outside into the morning light.

The Boy wrapped himself in his bearskin and led Horse out into the gray mist, drinking the tea, his withered hand holding the lead. Horse would only go as far as the Boy went and when he stopped, so did Horse.

The Chinese soldiers wore the same uniform as their comrades in Auburn. They also wore cartridge belts about their waists and carried long rifles.

One of the soldiers turned from inspecting the concrete pad and the charcoal drawing.

Their leader, a bright-eyed thin man walked toward the Boy, speaking in Chinese. When he realized the Boy did not understand, he turned back to the others, speaking rapidly.

They mounted their horses and made signs that the Boy should come with them.

The Weathered Man nodded in agreement.

THE TROOP OF Chinese horse soldiers, along with the Boy and Horse, rode away from the village a short while later, following the coast road. Just before the village was lost to a bend in the landscape, the Boy turned back to look upon it once more.

'I am always arriving and then leaving,' he thought.

What would it be like to stay?

I wish you would speak to me again, Sergeant Presley. That you would say, *Ain't nothin' but a thang.*

But the Boy knew it was only his own voice.

Knew it was what he wanted to hear.

Knew it was a lie he wanted to believe, which is the worst kind of lie we tell ourselves.

The Weathered Man was already out in the water with his rake.

He was working.

Long strokes through the water.

Only the rake betrayed the Weathered Man's presence in the water and the fog. Then the troop passed the bend on the coast road and the Weathered Man was gone.

The troop rode on through the quiet morning mist. From a small inlet they could see a great shroud of fog clutching at the ruins of San Francisco, across the bay.

I can go there now, Sergeant; if you will not stop me I will go there.

He hoped the voice would come. He hoped it would tell him, as it had all the other times before, that he must avoid such places.

But it didn't.

AT A SMALL farm, the troop leader dismounted and knocked at the door of a large spreading house. After words and more words, a small man, squinting and hobbling on bad feet, opened the door and came out. He peered at the Boy as if seeing him from across a great distance.

The leader spoke softly and then the small man walked forward, standing in front of the Boy.

"*Hey canna me?*" the small man said.

The Boy had no idea what this meant.

"*Whas goons runnna you?*"

The Boy shook his head to mean he didn't understand.

"*Betcha ken rednecks?*"

After the third failure the small man turned back to the troop leader and shook his head sadly. The leader laid his hand on the small man's shoulder and whispered something in his ear. Then he patted the old man and moved off to remount his horse.

They rode farther south and for a moment, the Boy thought they might be going to cross a massive bridge that spanned the entrance to the bay and landed in the ruins of San Francisco.

The Boy felt a surge of excitement.

The troop descended into a little cove that opened up onto the bay. A small city ran alongside the edge of the water and climbed up into the green heights overlooking Sausalito.

The edge of the bay was guarded by rock walls that ran upward over the green hills inland and down to the water's edge. Soldiers with guns watched from the high walls as the troop came down the road toward the gate and disappeared into a spreading shantytown that threw itself along the mud-flats and out into the calm waters of the bay. In the shantytown there were many Chinese mixed with others like himself. Like the outpost at Auburn.

There were buildings where the smells of food came wafting heavily out onto the muddy lanes. They passed stores where he could see objects waiting in the dark beyond the front porch. He smelled fish. He smelled the oil of the rifles. He smelled the same smell of the fields that he'd tasted in the Pee Gee Oh.

Children and women came out and watched as the Boy was escorted through the winding maze of the shantytown that lay at the foot of the gates to the city beneath the green hills and along the edge of the bay. Soon a small crowd followed at a distance.

The troop came to a large gate of polished dark wood set in a smooth white wall. Tall buildings rose up in stone and timber on the other side. But only their tops could be seen.

The leader dismounted and indicated the Boy should wait. Then he disappeared through an opened crack in the gate.

When the leader returned there were many other Chinese soldiers with him now. There was chatter, voices bouncing and bubbling, but over all pervaded a sense of seriousness, even concern.

An older Chinese soldier, steely eyed and with an air of command, his iron-gray hair streaked with black, came forward in highly polished leather boots.

He barked in Chinese at the Boy.

The troop leader interceded.

The older Chinese soldier watched the Boy.

The troop leader, who'd been inspecting the drawing that morning at the village by the water, turned to the Boy and waved his hands at the ground.

He wants me to draw what I drew at the village where they eat stones.

The Boy went to his saddlebag and took out his bag of charcoal.

He took out a long piece and sharpened it with his knife.

He looked at the troop leader, letting the thought "Where should I draw?" form itself on his face.

For a moment the troop leader, intent and hopeful, didn't understand.

Then he raised his hand to his head. He looked around.

He led the Boy to the smooth wall that encompassed the gate.

The Boy tried to see the attack.

The old courthouse.

The bodies.

The horror.

He limped forward until he could feel the wall blocking out all the watching pairs of eyes.

He raised the charcoal to the wall and made the first line. A curving arc that represented the dome of the old courthouse from Before.

At once there was a gasp from the crowd.

The older soldier began to speak in definite and harsh tones to the troop leader. But the troop leader gave a quick reply and silence returned.

The Boy looked back at the troop leader.

The Chinese soldier nodded.

The older soldier rolled his eyes toward the sky and then lowered them into a thin slit. Then, he too nodded at the Boy.

The Boy gave them war.

The Boy gave them the rain of arrows.

Fire and smoke.

The staring dead.

The Boy went big.

He showed the ashen-faced warriors, grim and determined as they worked their shining crossbow.

He showed them the Psychos in their Mohawks and tattoos, their axes held aloft, reminding him even as he worked of winter trees in morning's first light.

He showed them MacRaven in armor.

When he stepped back, he heard his foot make a sandy scraping sound as he dragged it across the flagstones of the pavement. It was the only other sound he'd heard besides his charcoal *scratch-scratch-scratching* against the high wall.

He turned.

He saw horror in their eyes.

They had known those people.

A woman wept. She was Chinese. She was pregnant.

The Boy thought of the Chinese snipers in the courthouse windows.

Soldiers and fathers in the same moment.

The older soldier walked forward.

His hand traced the broken dome.

He turned to the Boy and raised a hand pointing east, pointing over the bay, over the green hills and the river beyond, and the city it had swallowed and the fields and into the foothills and to the place of the drawing.

The Boy nodded.

He had destroyed their world more completely than MacRaven's shining crossbow ever would.

"Name?"

The voice came from the side of the crowd, from near the open crack in the gate. It gurgled, as though erupting up through a sea of mud.

The Boy turned.

"Rank?" It was an old Chinese man. Fat. Tall. Bent. His gray hair was slicked back over his large liver-spotted and peeling head. He wore the old Red Chinese army uniform from Before. The Boy had once seen the tattered scraps of such a uniform. Sergeant Presley had shown him one they'd found inside a downed transport, crashed in a field outside Galveston.

You told me it was the uniform of a Chinese general, Sergeant.

For a moment the Boy had almost heard the voice of Sergeant Presley. It reminded him of hearing someone call out for a child at dusk, telling them to come home finally.

The Boy remembered that day. It had been cold. They'd huddled inside the creaking wreckage of the big transport crashed long ago in the plain of waving grass.

You told me, Sergeant, that they were Chinese airborne. You told me they tried to drop them all across North America after we nuked the Middle East. You told me they were all in on it, but they got scattered, shot down. Jumped by our few remaining fighters. Pockets of Chinese airborne everywhere. Even made a good defense in Reno. The map said so.

You told me that, Sergeant, and now I need you to tell me what to do.

"Serial number?" barked the old Chinese general, wearing the same type of uniform Sergeant Presley had shown him on that day they spent hiding in the wreckage.

Another uniform the same as this one.

Another Chinese general.

The Boy croaked, "I don't . . ." It had been a long time since he'd spoken aloud.

"I speak . . . American," said the old man, the Chinese general. He rolled forward on a crooked cane.

He probably was once very strong, but now he moved worse than the Boy.

"I am General Song. I defeated the American Army."

The Boy lowered his eyes to the sandstone pavement.

I am glad . . . and then he was about to think, 'that you are dead, Sergeant Presley.'

But he stopped.

Behind the Chinese general stood a girl. She was young. His age. Chinese.

She was beautiful.

And . . .

She looked at him.

Without horror.

Without fear.

Without pity.

She was beautiful.

CHAPTER 38

He wanted to see her again.

He wanted to be left alone by all these Chinese.

He wanted to be left alone so that he might draw her.

He wanted to draw the way she had looked at him.

All about him, the Chinese were in an uproar.

Suddenly there was activity and work. Riders were dispatched to the east. A woman gave Horse an apple. The Chinese general and the girl disappeared behind the massive gate, the old soldier casting his steely gaze back upon the Boy.

She stood before the Boy, even though she was gone now.

She looked at him.

The troop leader led him to a shack by the water of the bay. The troop leader tied Horse to a hitching post nearby and pointed toward the shack.

Stay.

The Boy went inside. It had a table, a chair, and a cooking pit. Stairs led to a loft with a pallet and blankets. Out the back door was a small dock and the bay beyond where tiny slender boats bobbed in the windy afternoon.

Toward evening he smelled fire. Then food cooking.

The troop leader returned with a plate of chicken, chilies, and garlic. There was a small wooden basket full of rice.

They both ate at the table.

The sun was setting when the troop leader went out for a moment and returned with a bundle of clothing. He draped the pieces over the chair.

Overalls made of wool.

A rubber trench coat with a high collar.

Rubber boots.

A hooded gas mask.

He took out a slip of paper.

"Please," he began to read haltingly from the paper, "put . . . these . . . on . . . and . . . come . . . with . . . me."

The Boy brought Horse inside the shack. The troop leader gave a pained look, then seemed to accept this. He left and returned with hay, setting it down in front of Horse.

The Boy nodded to himself and began to dress in the items.

He had seen them before.

Sergeant Presley had worn similar gear when he'd entered the ruins of Washington, in the District of Columbia.

The clothing made him feel warm, and within moments to the point of suffocation.

When the Boy came to the mask he donned it, unsure if he had done it properly, trying to remember how Sergeant Presley had worn it. The patrol leader went behind the Boy and pulled the straps of the mask tightly, jerking them almost. Then he patted the Boy's shoulder.

The Boy looked out through the steamy eye holes.

He could hear his own breathing.

He tucked his withered left arm into the pocket of the trench coat and made to take up his tomahawk but the leader shook his head.

The Boy placed the tomahawk on the small wooden table.

Then they left, stepping outside into the twilight of early evening. From behind the soft-lit windows of the shantytown, the Boy could hear, muffled by the hood of the gas mask, the low murmur of voices.

Someone cackled.

There was distant laughter.

Someone played long whining notes on a lone violin, then repeated them.

Dogs barked.

They arrived at the shining wooden gate. Two sentries stood aside as the massive portal swung open.

Beyond the gate they found a long, empty street. Large houses with stone exteriors, polished wood trim, and sloping rooftops lined the street, which looked out onto a park and the open bay beyond. At the end of the street the water of the bay glimmered softly in the night behind a low wall. Torches guttered before each house along the quiet street.

Through the mask the Boy could smell the heavy scent of jasmine. A smell that reminded him of Sergeant Presley and their days passing though the South.

He thought of the map.

It was still in its secret pouch inside the bearskin.

He thought of his tomahawk and said to himself, "Might not get it back," as though Sergeant Presley were warning him. But still, it was just his own voice.

They stopped at an old building from Before. It rested on the far side of the road, standing on pillars that rose up out of the lapping waves. The Chinese soldiers, and others more finely dressed than the dwellers of the shantytown, were gathered about its steps. A hush fell over the small crowd as the troop leader with the Boy in tow, approached.

Inside, great glass windows opened up onto a view of the wide bay and the shadowy city lying in ruins beyond its waters.

There was the Chinese general.

The Old Soldier.

A group of Chinese, dressed in soft clothing that caught the flickering light of candles, stood at the far end of the room.

They held fans over their mouths.

They watched the Boy with sideways glances, murmuring to one another.

THE GIRL WAS there too.

She watched him from the farthest corner. She watched him from just behind the Chinese general.

The Boy sat on a stool in the center of the room, as he was directed, then the Chinese general came forward, standing halfway between the Boy and the audience.

"I am General Song. Do you remember that we met earlier? Outside the gate."

The Boy nodded.

The general smiled. Pleased. As if his greatest fear had been that the Boy might have forgotten their earlier meeting.

"Our governing council"—the general stopped and indicated those who stood behind him, pressed against the far wall, fans covering their mouths—"would like to ask you a few more questions, if that is possible."

"I thought you were their leader," said the Boy.

The general smiled.

"I am no longer . . . I am now merely a scholar who knows a little more of the past than most because of my military service, and only because I lived through it."

"I will answer what questions I can," said the Boy.

"Has our outpost, the one you drew—has it been destroyed?"

The Boy remained silent.

"The place you drew. Did anyone survive?"

The Boy spoke through the mask, his voice muffled. The insides of the mask were slick with sweat and heat. Mist clung to the lenses.

"I didn't understand you. Could you please say that again? I'll come closer," said the Chinese general, and when he did he asked the same question again.

"I don't know," replied the Boy. "I doubt that anyone who remained there could have lasted much longer."

The Chinese general turned back toward the audience at the far end of the room and spoke in their language. The people in the audience murmured among themselves and then someone spoke above the others. The Chinese general turned back to the Boy.

"And how is it that you survived?"

"I escaped."

And thus a pattern formed. The general spoke in Chinese. The audience murmured. Someone spoke. The general asked a new question.

"Where did you come from?"

"The east."

"Who are your people?"

"I don't have any."

"How far east?"

"A place that was once called Washington Dee Cee."

"What is there now?"

"A swamp."

"Who destroyed the outpost, I mean the place that you drew?"

"A man named MacRaven. He has an army of tribes."

"How big?"

"More than you have in all the soldiers I have seen who carry your rifles."

"The characters on your rifle indicate it was given to a man who was a known skin trader. What has become of this man and how did you acquire his rifle?"

"He rescued me from lions in the high desert beyond Reno. We fought together on the walls of your outpost. He did not survive and I took his rifle when I escaped."

"Will this MacRaven the barbarian come here?"

"I don't know." Then, "If I were you I would plan for him to. He seemed that sort of man."

"How do we know you are not part of this MacRaven's barbarian army and that you yourself didn't kill the owner of the rifle and come here as a spy or a saboteur?"

"I know 'spy.' I am not that. The other word I do not understand."

"A destroyer. A terrorist."

"I am not a terrorist."

"And how do we know you are telling the truth?"

The Boy stopped for a moment. He was hot. Sweat was dripping down the inside of his mask. He moved to take off the mask and the Chinese general lunged forward with sudden vigor and command.

"Do not take that off! It is forbidden here for you to remove your mask."

The Boy could feel his audience pressing themselves farther away from him, toward the back of the room.

The Boy lowered his hands from the mask.

The general walked closer. "I am sorry," he said softly, his eyes speaking an unspoken message of friendliness. "They do not understand."

"And why," began the general again, "should we trust your account?"

The Boy stared for a long moment at the crowd surrounding him. When his eyes rested on the girl he forgot everything he'd intended to say.

He forgot . . .

. . . everything.

When he was reminded of the question by a gurgling cough from the Chinese general, he spoke.

"I don't know why you would trust me."

The audience murmured at the translation.

A discussion started.

"May I ask a question?" said the Boy.

Silence.

The general walked back toward the Boy.

"Ask."

"What has become of I Corps?"

The general did not translate.

His face fell.

His mouth opened.

His shoulders slumped.

He seemed suddenly older.

The general shook his head to himself as if finishing an argument he'd started long ago and lost many times since. Then he looked at the Boy.

"They are no more." And, "I know that for certain."

There was no pride in his voice. No triumph. No satisfaction.

But there was guilt.

There was shame.

"When I was young I thought it would be different," said the Chinese general very plainly. "I thought only of victory."

The general sighed heavily.

"I know differently now." He looked at the Boy, maybe beyond the Boy. "I am responsible."

"You were there?" asked the Boy. "At the end of I Corps?"

The general whispered, "Yes."

"If the man who brought me here," the Boy indicated the troop leader, "would return to my things and bring me the bearskin I wear . . . I have something for you."

Orders were given and the discussion among the Chinese renewed. All the while, the general watched the Boy and waited for the return of the requested bearskin.

I have given away all my intel, Sergeant. I know that is not what you taught me to do. But what good is it to anyone, now that all of you are dead?

There was no reply.

The bearskin arrived and the Boy laid it out and retrieved the map from inside the hidden pouch.

Sergeant, I'm doing this so that maybe they'll trust me. I'm doing this so they'll be ready for MacRaven when he comes. I remember what we both saw outside Oklahoma City.

The Boy stood.

He raised his right arm and saluted the Chinese general.

He held out the map.

Tell them who I was, Boy.

Tell them I made it all the way, never quit.

Tell them there's nothing left.

"There's nothing left," said the Boy.

CHAPTER 39

The night air felt cool and dried the sweat on the Boy's face as he was led back from the meeting beyond the gate. The wind had picked up from off the bay. It would be a long, cold night. The shantytown was quiet and only a single candle burned in the odd window they passed along its lanes.

In the shack it was warm from the heat given off by the brazier, its glow a dull orange. Inside, Horse raised a sleepy eye then returned to his rest and dreams. The troop leader left and came back with more hay. He said something in Chinese, a farewell perhaps, then closed the door to the shack behind him as he left.

The Boy took off the sweaty gear they had given him and went out the back door.

He walked to the end of the narrow two-plank dock and lowered himself into the freezing dark water of the bay.

It was cold.

Maybe the coldest water he'd ever felt.

He thought of the girl as he floated in the darkness.

Back inside the shack he put his clothes on and, as though he had known all along what he would do next, he took up the carved piece of charcoal once more.

He made a line. The outline of her hair. Long and straight. A curve over the top of her head.

Then another line for her delicate chin.

And a line falling away from the chin for her neck.

They'll see this.

He put the charcoal back in its pouch and sat by the glowing coals of the brazier, watching the simple lines he had drawn.

The lines were enough to remember her by.

IN THE MORNING it was the troop leader who appeared once more. They both took Horse out into the mist and walked him along the bay's edge, following a winding muddy street. Fishing boats lay motionless in the calm waters of the fog-shrouded bay.

They crossed into a ruined section of the shantytown.

Ruins from Before.

Buildings with chunks of concrete and whole sections missing. Buildings where the plaster facade had fallen away long ago. Buildings from which metal girders twisted wickedly upward. Buildings that had fallen into little more than piles from which rusty strands of rebar sprung like wild hair.

A work crew hovered over the ruins of a building, testing it with their crowbars and the occasional shovel. Other men moved piles of rubble in wheelbarrows.

They are removing the town that was here Before, Sergeant.

They came to a building. It was in better shape than most.

Inside they found the Chinese general.

He hobbled forward, his big frame leaning heavily on a bent cane.

"I have studied the map you gave me." After a pause the general continued breathily, "Can you tell me about all those places? What is there now? That's what we wish to know. Our outpost was our farthest settlement. We cannot go south due to the nature of contamination in that area, so it seems we must know what lies to the east. If we could go over the map together, you might tell me a little bit about each place. If that would be acceptable to you?"

The Boy thought of the girl.

He thought of leaving this place.

He had left every place he had ever been.

He wondered if he might see her here.

If he left he would never see her again.

"Yes."

"Good," said the general and led him to a large desk. The map lay spread out across its expanse. The floor that surrounded the desk was a sea upon which books rose like sudden and angry waves. Leaning against the walls were all manner of things. Tools, ancient rifles from Before, many things the Boy had no name for.

"So we know you came through Reno. What were your experiences there?"

The Boy thought for a moment. How did one describe the fear of an unknown mad animal lying in wait in the dark? How did one describe that laughing terror and the single leering face seen as a shadow through dirty glass for even just the part of a moment?

"Reno is like a hole where an animal lives." He thought of the bear cave. "Where something that isn't human makes its home now."

The general laid his finger on the map over Reno.

"Colonel Juk was their commander. I have always wondered, over the years, what became of his unit and the men we sent there. Their last report told of being dug in and facing American armor coming out of the desert to the southeast."

The Boy watched the map and all the places Sergeant Presley had been.

"How is it like a wild animal in a cave?" asked the general.

The Boy thought for a moment. He approached a wall and moved aside a heavy machine gun, dusty and untouched. He cleared a space along the wall.

He took out his charcoal.

He began to draw.

He drew the blind window-eyes of a corpse that was once a city. In his mind the angles were somehow distorted and maniacal. The buildings took on a surreal aspect, as if sanity hadn't been a requirement for their architect. As if the years since, and the madmen within, had somehow turned the buildings "wrong." He drew the bridge they'd passed under. The Boy, Horse, and Escondido. It was an open mouth, full of smashed teeth. He drew a high window, a long window twisting to the side, almost bending away from the perspective of the viewer. A window among a hundred other lunatic windows in shadow. In it the Boy placed the shadow of a man seen for just a moment. With a few quick lines he began the face, the jaw, the hair, and before he could add more to those few scribbled, hesitant, unfinished lines, the lunatic seemed complete.

When the Boy turned back, the general, watching him, nodded.

The old soldier turned to the map, his finger still resting above the word "Reno."

"I understand."

After a moment of looking again at the map, the Chinese general cleared his throat.

"Tell me about Salt Lake City."

And then . . .

She entered, carrying a tray of teacups and a pot.

CHAPTER 40

At the end of the week General Song sat in his patched leather chair from Before. Shoulders slumped. Eyes wide. Staring.

On the walls that surrounded him were many charcoal markings formed into drawings.

At Des Moines, two figures, a small boy, eyes wide with terror, and a black man, his face an angry curse—heavy oversize packs on each of their backs—ran across a field of sickly grass. Above them, crows—all the crows in the world—swarmed, diving and attacking them. In the foreground, a crow swooped away from the boy and the man. The crow's eyes were two black oblongs of animal indifference. The wings seemed to rise in triumph. Its beak was open as if the *cawww!* that must come from it was a mighty roar. All the birds were rendered with such malevolence.

Beaks open.

Claws reaching.

Wings spreading.

One could almost hear a sonic sea of victory caws as each bird swooped and dived, wheeling overhead.

Herding their prey.

Carnivorous now.

Finally, after the end of the world and an ocean of wild, genetically powerful corn that had broken and overtaken the lands of middle America—surviving what civilization, mankind, had not, in Des Moines, Iowa—crows ruled the land.

Outside Madison, Wisconsin, powerful dogs with short necks like bulls and wide mouths full of canine teeth surged forward. Real hatred could be found in their snarling muzzles as opposed to the crows' mere soullessness. The black man leaned hard on a door. His face was twisted in rage, his eyes focused. Next to him was the Boy, long hair covering his face as it turns back toward the approaching pack of wild dogs. A long hallway trailed off to the horizon. Someplace abandoned. An old shopping center. They were trapped. The fierce dogs bounded toward them. In the lead dog, every muscle was perfectly and beautifully rendered like taut cables of charcoal-driven power. There is an urgency the viewer feels when looking at the black man, who must open the door if he and the Boy are to survive. It is the kind of picture one looks at then turns away from, praying that such a thing will never happen to them.

Or to their loved ones.

"Who is the black man?" he'd asked the Boy.

"Sergeant Lyman Julius Presley."

At Detroit, sailboats were piled high against a beach of black rocks and garbage. The sky was overcast and gray. The lake struck the shore hard, almost angrily. 'One could hear,' thought the general, 'the damaged spinnakers and tangled tackle clanging compulsively in the wind while occasional ancient spars groaned in torment.'

"Were you with Sergeant Presley when you made it to Detroit?"

"I was always with him."

"What is your earliest memory of him?"

"We were walking on the road. He was carrying all our things and I kept falling behind him because I was still little. He was singing one of his marching songs about Captain Jack and he said to me, 'Keep up, or I might leave you behind.'"

At Cincinnati there was a river. There were no buildings. No trees. Only a dark hill on the horizon. A road sign, unreadable, bent forever away from the place.

"Why did this Sergeant Presley keep going, even though all the evidence seemed to indicate that his country was destroyed?" asked the general.

The Boy simply looked at the picture and then, when the general felt as if the Boy would not answer, the Boy spoke.

"He told me one time that he couldn't quit. That to quit was to die. That he'd quit once, before I met him, and a lot of people got killed."

And.

"I've always thought that those people getting killed had something to do with where I came from."

At Pittsburgh was the American bomber. The nose and cockpit were in the foreground as the fuselage stretched away, cracked in the middle. The only wing visible lay collapsed. A car lay trapped under the nose. Rusting cars dotted the landscape of the freeway.

"How come you never asked Sergeant Presley about where you came from?" asked the general.

"I did and he told me that the past wasn't important anymore because it was just wreckage and junk and not worth going over. He told me that the only thing that was important now was the future."

"And yet he was still looking for his country under all this wreckage, like that of the bomber on the wall?"

Silence.

"He said America was more than just the things we'd seen: the rubble of the cities, the broken highways, the burned-up tanks. He said America was a good idea. And that as long as he was alive, the good that was in the idea was still alive."

At Baltimore, a shaven-headed man with malevolent eyes held a shovel. A twisted farmhouse, windows out of perspective, rose toward the ceiling of the room where the general sat. A woman, scrawny and underfed, looked at the ground with bruised and blackened eyes. She stood behind the malevolent man, in his shadow. In an orchard in the background, under a crescent moon, wild figures leapt about a fire as something man-like lay atop a grill, its legs splayed, its arms akimbo.

"Who are they?" he asked the Boy.

"They are the Cotter family and they're evil."

And there were other pictures . . .

The general leaned back in his chair.

This was what happened after war.

'I remember,' he thought. 'Before it all, before the bombs even, I remember walking down a boulevard in Beijing; the cherry blossoms were just beginning to fall. I remember the posters, and the songs about bravery and our country that we thought we loved so much. I remember I was very proud of my uniform and that when the time came I would earn its inherent respect. I remember thinking I would do anything for my country.'

We all thought that way.

Anything.

We had no idea.

We were wrong.

CHAPTER 41

The Boy had drawn a story wherever the Chinese general had placed his finger on Sergeant Presley's map. If the Boy had been there or knew something about the place, he had rendered it in charcoal across the walls of the general's study.

"One day," said the general, "we must go to these places and find what is left there. Not to conquer as our current leaders wish and which will only bring the wrath of the barbarians down on us as it has already. But we must go to these places in order that we might make something new. What you tell me in your drawings may one day make a difference to those that must go to these places on the wall."

And each day she had brought them tea in the afternoon.

And one day . . .

After she set the tea down and while the general stood close to the wall studying a picture of Little Rock, Arkansas, in which the Boy skinned a deer with trembling hands, the girl moved next to the Boy.

In the picture, the Boy was laying out the heart and liver on a crumbling table inside a large building, a library perhaps, by the look of the collapsed bookshelves. There was a river passing outside shattered and dirty windows. Among the collapsed shelves of books, the black man built a fire from fallen volumes. There was hunger on both of their faces.

The general said little once the picture was finished and as he studied it. He stood silently before it, consuming its every detail. Today, the girl did not leave as she usually did once she placed the tray of tea on the large and very old desk.

The Boy, because the day was cold and his withered side was stiff, reached for the tea, already inhaling its hot jasmine aroma. And she caught his hand just before he grasped the cup.

He looked into her eyes.

She squeezed his hand.

He was frozen.

His heart did not beat.

He was sweating.

And he squeezed back. Hard. Almost too hard.

"Jin," she whispered.

The general called her Jin. He had learned that much.

She squeezed his hand once more and took a cup of tea to the general.

After that, she left and did not look at him, as the general had turned from the picture and was now talking to the Boy. Words in the English. Words the Boy did not understand because he could not concentrate on anything other than the moment of her touch. His face felt as though it were on fire.

"Is there no place that survived in some part beyond a mere day-to-day existence?" asked the general.

The Boy was watching the girl named Jin, though she had already left the room.

"She is the only one who believes in my work," said the general, watching the Boy's eyes. "She is the only one who, like me, wants to know what happened out there. She is not afraid of it. She is not bothered by the harsh reality of these times like so many of our people, who simply wish to live behind their gates and keep themselves from the 'contamination' as they call it, of the world as it is now. They require only that their lives be beautiful and a reminder of a homeland that is gone. They willingly live a lie, simply because it is fragrant."

The general paused and sipped at the tea he had taken up in his two liver-spotted hands.

"Jin and I seek the truth because the truth holds its own beauty. In my opinion, it is the lies of our past that have brought about the current state of destruction. Late in my life, I vowed never to live another lie. My only sadness is that I made the vow after the world had been burned and poisoned by a rain of nuclear radiation."

The Boy watched the general.

"Sometimes I think she merely humors an old man," said the general, lost in the map again. "But she is a good granddaughter and I feel that she can look past the damage and the rubble and the warmongering of our collective past, both China and America, and find what was noble and beautiful about us."

He fell to mumbling when his eyes found some new, previously unconsidered mark on the map, "I was saying . . ."

THAT NIGHT THE BOY lay on the floor of the shack near the brazier. It was exceptionally cold outside. His side ached. His hand was cramped and black from the charcoal he used to draw pictures on the walls of the general's study.

Horse stirred as the fire popped.

The Boy was watching the lines.

He was watching Jin.

Horse complains for a moment as if sensing an animal outside in the cold wind and the dark night.

There was a moment of quiet that threatened to go on forever.

And then . . .

There was a knock at the back door that led out to the two-plank dock.

The Boy opened the door.

Jin pressed her mouth into his and he could feel her cold, soft cheeks grow warm. Her slender body melted into his arms, alive and living within his grasp. He felt her arms about him, clutching at his shoulders. And for a moment one hand slipped down to his withered arm, caressing him there.

"I am Jin," she said haltingly. "I do not . . . speak American"—she said something in Chinese—"very well." Then, "But I am learning."

He closed the door and brought her to the fire. She stood warming herself while he got the bearskin and wrapped it around her.

"What is your . . . name?" she asked.

The Boy looked at her.

In the light from the glowing brazier, wrapped in the skin of the bear, she was even more beautiful. She looked at him expectantly, her eyes shining in the firelight.

"What do they call me? What do your people call me?"

"They call . . . you . . . the Messenger."

"Why?"

"You brought . . . the news of the barbarians. I do not want . . . I do not want to call . . . you the Messenger."

"Why?"

She kissed him again and again until their intensity threatened to consume them. Breathlessly she broke from his hungry embrace, panting, "It . . . cannot be."

Later, they sat staring into the fire, she reclining against him, the two of them almost sleeping, dreaming.

"Why?" asked the Boy.

She drew her fingers along his powerful arm.

He liked that.

Later she said, "You know that this is . . . not done?"

He held her hands, resting them on her belly.

"If you were my woman, then it would be all right."

"No, that can never . . . be."

"Why?"

She took up his withered hand. She turned to face him. Her dark eyes caught the firelight.

"I . . . can know . . . can tell. I can tell . . . you are brave. To me you are very . . . pretty . . . no . . . handsome. You are . . . clean. 'Whole' is the word? To me. But our leaders will not let those who live inside the gate . . . I do not like this word . . . it's . . . is their . . . but they say 'sully' . . . you know . . . to be unclean? With the barbarians."

She sighed deeply, her eyes searching the darkened rafters for the right words. For the story. For the explanation.

"Even before we came . . . to here. To this place, America. We were separate and apart from others. Mandarin and Cantonese. Government and peasant. Not the same, do you understand? But after the war . . . even more so, there were many . . . defects. Many of the survivors from other places . . . Americans . . . were like you."

He understood. She was perfectly formed. Perfectly beautiful, and he was not. It would be wrong of him to make her his woman. It would be wrong in this place.

"Even our people . . . were affected by the radiation from . . . bombs. But those children . . . how do you say . . ." She searched the room, her eyes casting about and finding nothing. "Never existed?"

The Boy nodded, understanding.

"They made them disappear. They made . . . rules, laws, I mean. No intermarrying with those who are sick . . . unclean. Now, they cannot even stand . . . to have them inside . . . the gate."

She watched his eyes, searching to find the wound her words, the truth, had caused him.

But he remained steady, his gaze never wavering from her deep brown eyes.

"To me you . . . it does not matter, you are whole, to me," she said again.

The Boy looked at her for a long time.

In his eyes she saw the question.

"Is that why I had to wear the suit beyond the gate?"

"Yes . . . they fear you will contaminate . . . them. They understand little and are afraid . . . much." Then, "It is not wise of them. They do not have . . . wisdom."

"Wisdom changes things. I knew a man who was very wise. But he is gone now . . . I need wisdom."

"We . . . all . . . do," she whispered.

An hour before dawn he led her to the dock. A slender boat, tied to the wooden planks, bobbed atop choppy wavelets.

As he helped her down into the tiny boat, he felt a sudden moment of terror, as if he were casting something valuable, something precious—his tomahawk, his best blanket, food even—down into a pit. Or an ocean. Or an abyss.

And I am hoping it will come back to me.

And.

She is more valuable than my tomahawk or a blanket or even food.

Why?

"Will you be safe?" he asked her.

Why was she valuable?

"Yes. I'll use the boat to . . . go around . . . the point and then come close to the wall. I know my way over . . . and our home is just . . . just on the other side."

He leaned down to untie the boat.

"When you stood . . ." she began, "in front of our leaders . . . in your mask . . . and at the wall . . . you were not afraid to tell them . . . the truth. They are . . . always . . . have been . . . afraid of truth." She looked at him. She shook her head slightly. "You are not afraid . . . of anything . . . even of the truth."

And.

"I also . . . am not afraid," she said finally and turned the boat toward open water.

She looked small and helpless in the boat and he watched as she paddled out and away from him, rounding the point and finally disappearing. He watched the water for a long time, until he almost felt frozen inside. Within the shack he lay down on the bearskin in front of the fire.

Why?

Because she saw me when she looked at me.

Without horror.

Without fear.

Without pity.

And because she did not look away when she let me see that she was beautiful.

Thinking he was still awake, he slept. When he awoke with a start, wondering what was real and what was not, he smelled jasmine.

CHAPTER 42

The Chinese were preparing for war.

Soldiers drilled with their long breech-loading rifles. Large cannon were dragged forward by teams of laborers to an outer wall that was being hastily thrown up to surround the shantytown and the inner city. Every day riders left, thundering off toward the east at all times.

When the Boy returned to the shack by the water after another day of drawing for the general, he saw a strange man waiting under a roof down the lane, staying out of the spring drizzle. He was Chinese. He was thin. He appeared to watch something far away, but the Boy could feel him watching the shack. Watching him. For the rest of that wet and rainy afternoon, when the Boy looked out the door of the shack, he could see the man waiting in the darkening light, "not watching."

Jin came to him again after midnight. She was soaked by the drizzle that slapped at the water of the bay.

"We must . . . exercise much caution," she said.

The Boy considered checking the street.

She held on to him tightly.

"I would give . . . myself to you," she whispered.

Blood thundered in his ears, beating hard in the silences between the soft rain on the roof and the hard slaps out on the water beyond the thin walls of the shack.

"But . . . it . . . cannot . . . be."

They sat by the fire, listening to it pop and crackle.

The Boy thought of the bear's cave where he and Horse had lived for the winter.

"Why?" he murmured.

Looking into his face, she reached forward and brushed away the dark hair that hung there.

"When my people came here . . . there was a great war. Our home, China, was destroyed. I am told that the first years were very, very difficult. Hard winter. Constant warfare. Famine. The children who were born . . . after these times . . . were not . . . good."

Jin lay her head on his chest.

"It does not matter to me." Then, "But if I am 'sullied' . . . then it will be . . . very bad . . . for me."

The rain had stopped outside. Dripping water could be heard, everywhere and at once, almost a pattern.

Almost music.

Almost as if one could count when the next drop would fall.

"Here," he said staring into the fire.

She looked at him and nodded.

"Here, in this place," he said angrily.

She nodded again.

"Yes. In this place . . . that is the way it must be," she said.

He thought more of the cave of the bear and all the other places he had been. Places that were not this city. Places that were not here.

She stayed too long that night.

Dawn light was breaking the top of the eastern hills. In blue shadows, standing on the dock, he held her tightly to himself.

"I must . . . go now," she stammered and yet still clung to his chest.

"There are other places than here," he said. "I would take you with me to those places."

You take everything with you.

In the small boat, in the pale light, her long alabaster hands were shaking as she began to row for the point.

She heard the first birds of morning.

Her hands were shaking.

When she turned back to him, he was just a shadow among shadows along the waterfront.

Her hands were shaking.

THE HEAT OF the day built quickly. There was the smell of fresh-cut wood and fires burning out beyond the earthworks. The thick scent of the fields and dark earth mixed, and when the Boy drank rainwater from a barrel it was cold and satisfying.

A cannon cracked.

A *whump* followed a second later.

"They are sighting the guns," said the general. He was looking at Sergeant Presley's map with a large and cracked magnifying glass.

"How close did you come to Galveston, down in Texas?"

The Boy walked toward the picture he had drawn. The picture of the Great Wall of Wreckage.

"No closer than fifty miles."

Sergeant, you said to me, on that day when we looked at the map together and the weather was so hot and the air was so thick, you said, *That's right, Boy. Never closer than fifty. Radiation.*

Your voice would be a comfort to me now, Sergeant.

The Boy had been waiting all day for it. He had been waiting for it since it ceased. Since the open graves and tattered canvas. But now, of all days, on this first hot day of the year, he needed to hear it.

I need to know what to do next, Sergeant.

I need wisdom.

"What did you find there besides what you have drawn in this picture?" asked the Chinese general.

Sergeant Presley, I'm going to take the girl and run.

"What do you mean?" the Boy replies.

I don't have a plan, Sergeant. I'll take her and ride fast and far away from here. Is that what I should do, Sergeant?

"Were there villages or people there?" asked the Chinese general.

The Boy thought of long winter nights in the bear cave. He also thought of MacRaven and his ashen-faced warriors moving through the forests and the foothills and the swamps, approaching the bay.

Where can we go and be safe, Sergeant?

"The people there were deformed," answered the Boy. "There was a warlord who ruled over everyone, but we never met him. The sick told us that he came and stole their children in the night and made them his soldiers. They said he ate people. They said he was a demon. They said his soldiers were demons now, no longer their children."

There's an army coming and they're probably looking for me, Sergeant.

"It sounds like a terrible place. Are they deformed like . . . ?"

I would go back to the cave, but MacRaven . . .

"Like . . . me?"

Sergeant Presley, you always said north was too hard. If you weren't ready for winter it would kill you. If we have to run for a long time, there might not be time to prepare for the next winter.

"I am sorry . . . I meant no disrespect," said the general as he stared at the Boy.

West is the ocean, Sergeant. I don't know how to make a boat go.

"No. They were much worse off than me."

So that leaves south.

"I am sorry," mumbled the general, looking back to the map. "It sounds like a very dark place."

We'll go south, Sergeant.

"We barely escaped."

I know you would say, *Don't get involved. I always told you that.*

In his mind, Jin murmurs in the firelight.

But I love her, Sergeant.

The Chinese general put down the magnifying glass. He hobbled around the desk and came to stand beside the Boy.

"It is all my fault," said the general after a great sigh.

"I don't understand," said the Boy.

"The deformities. Your deformities." Pause. "They are my fault. I mean no disrespect to you. I am not like . . . the rest. I see nothing wrong with a man if his body is weak. Old age has taught me that bodies fail. Even if we are successful at not dying, and doing our best to stay healthy, bodies still fail. A body doesn't make a man strong or weak. It is the heart of a man or woman that makes them such."

My heart is strong for Jin.

You would ask me, Sergeant, *Is that enough?*

"You seem troubled. I hope I didn't . . ."

"No. What happened at the end? The end of the American army."

The general looked away to the sketches on the walls. He looked at the broken sailboats in Detroit, piled up like toys after a flood. The general could hear the clang of the spinnakers and the knock of the weather vanes in that long-ago winter wind.

He let go another great sigh.

"In the end there were few American soldiers left. There were few of us left, for that matter, also. That last year was little more than a long stalemate that preceded our final battle, if one wants to call such a day a battle. Our scouts thought there might be influenza sweeping through the American defenses above Oakland, so we decided to attack with everything we had left."

The general turned and hobbled back to his chair, sinking into ancient leather with a groan.

"I started the war as a lieutenant. In the end I was a brigadier general in command of forces. My superiors tasked me to lead a reconnaissance in force against the American positions. All such actions in the past had met with defeat. In fact they were little more than suicide missions. I thought it was my time to die. I said my goodbyes. I kissed my very pregnant wife and my son, my granddaughter Jin's father, and we set out in rafts lashed to the few amphibious vehicles left that still worked. It was quite a departure from the way we'd arrived ten years earlier, when we'd invaded the United States. Then we'd attacked with fighters, a carrier group, and an airborne invasion all along the western United States. Now I was being towed to my death in a leaky raft by a broken-down amphibious armored vehicle that belched dirty black smoke."

The general breathed deeply again, gathering himself and letting go of some past oath to secrecy that no longer held him.

"I kept waiting for the American artillery to open fire as we crossed the bay. But it didn't, and we made the beach, to our great surprise. No gunfire, no mortars. No fixed-bayonet charge. I ordered our mortar teams to set up. We advanced through the wreckage of the old city of Oakland, finding no one. When we came to the trenches at the bottom of the hill we found a ragged soldier, thin to the point of death. He was little more than the bones that held him up. He waved a white flag. From a distance he told us of the sickness. He said we should stay away.

"I withdrew and called my commanders. They told me to hit the camp with everything we had but to stay clear. We spent the day shelling it and shooting up into the heights. Shooting as though there was no end in sight to our supplies, after ten straight years of fighting in the streets amid the rubble of San Francisco."

It was quiet in the study. Warm sunshine made the air thick and heavy with the scent of flowers and dust.

"But that was not the end," muttered the general after a long pause.

"I was ordered to put on chemical armor and go up the hill by myself. It was a very hot day. Earthquake weather, like today. It is always that way on hot days that follow the cold. I trudged through the tall burning grass up to their headquarters. There was no one there, only graves and the dead, lying in their cots and trenches.

"What can one say of such things? The war was finally over."

CHAPTER 43

The knock at the back door of the shack in the quiet of the sleeping shanty-town was deafening and the Boy willed it to be unheard in the night.

Her entering and embrace of him were one action.

"I had a . . ."—she uses a Chinese word he did not know—"a nightmare . . . in the afternoon as I slept." Then, "I thought that . . . you had gone away . . . and that I had lost you forever."

She held him and he could smell the jasmine in her long dark hair.

"You had gone away," she said breathlessly between kisses. "And I kept thinking . . . in the dream, that I must start looking for you. But there was always some house task to perform."

She buried her face in his chest as the Boy closed the back door.

"It was . . . horrible," she murmured and he could feel her tears.

"Come with me. We'll leave tomorrow," he whispered, and he thought of the man who had been watching the shack all day from the other side of the alley.

Is he out there in the dark?

Can he hear our whispers?

She held him tighter.

"I will protect you," he whispered.

"I will serve you," he whispered.

"I will love you," he whispered.

And with each murmuring she held him tighter and he could hear her whispering, "Yes," over and over and over.

Involved is involved, Sergeant.

She left after midnight.

From the dock she stepped into the small boat.

"I will meet you in the ruins outside the . . . western gate, toward the bridge. Look for the house where only the fireplace remains standing, like a . . . pointing finger. When the sun is directly overhead, I will meet you there."

THE BOY TRIED to sleep.

When he did, he dreamed.

He and Sergeant Presley were running through the night. They were running from those dogs. They were always running.

"I've got to find Jin," he told Sergeant Presley. But in each moment there was some fresh terror in the old mall they ran through, the one with the corpses hanging over the central pool from the broken skylight above. The one with the dogs. The one with the bones.

"I've got to find Jin," he told Sergeant Presley, whose eyes were calm and cool even though the Boy remembered that they were both very frightened that day. It had frightened the Boy even more when he'd looked at Sergeant Presley, who was starting to slow down that last summer before he died in the autumn, and had seen the fear in those eyes, which had been angry but never afraid.

In the dream, in the nightmare, he lost her. He knew it, and the look in Sergeant Presley's calm dream-eyes told him that he was sad for the Boy. And it was something about that look that terrified the Boy more than anything else in the dream.

He awoke in the night.

"I will not lose her."

He felt emptiness in his words.

As if he were a child saying he would conquer the world.

THE BOY SADDLED Horse that morning.

Soldiers passed in the alleyway, heading off to work along the growing wall.

He packed his things and led Horse into the lane. There was no sign of the watching man, only an old woman sweeping farther up the street.

Three cannon opened up with successive cracks and distant *whumps.*

He led Horse back toward the eastern wall, following the soldiers.

Great logs had been cut and lay stacked, waiting to be put in place along the wall.

They had no idea. They had no idea how big MacRaven's army was.

The Boy mounted Horse and rode past a sentry who said something he did not understand. He seemed to want to stop him, as if only because the Boy was a stranger, but he did not.

The Boy rode through the gate and into the trees, heading east.

They'll think I've gone to inform MacRaven.

You would ask me, *What's your plan, Boy?*

I will ride through the hills and circle back around and come out along the western wall. They'll send riders to head me off, thinking I'm going east. The Pacific is to the west and we don't know about north. That leaves only one way, Sergeant.

From a small hillock just above the ruins of Sausalito and the inner city, the Boy saw the shantytown below, spreading out next to the bay, and the earthworks being cut into the fields beyond. The Boy watched the alarm being raised. The sentry was talking wildly and waving toward the east. Soldiers were gathering.

From the hill, the Boy could see the big rusting bridge that cut across the sparkling water into the pile of gray rock that was once San Francisco.

I should have checked the bridge to make sure it was safe.

But you would say, *That's all right, Boy. Sometimes you got to improvise.*

HE RODE THROUGH the broken edges of the old town, casting his eyes about for the finger-pointing chimney.

If they have discovered our plan, then they will set a trap for me.

You would say, *Always be think'n, Boy.*

He found the pile of rubble that had collapsed around a lone redbrick chimney pointing up into the hot blue sky.

She came out carrying a bundle. Her face was joy.

Her face was relief.

Her face was hope.

He helped her up onto Horse and she held him tightly.

This was the way it would always feel from now on. To feel her holding him as they rode. As they rode into the face of the world. Into cities and wherever they might wish to go.

All their days should be such.

"Hold, boy," came the gruff voice of the Chinese general. He hobbled as fast as he could down the cracked and broken street leading back to the inner city.

The sun was overhead and the day was hot.

"I know," cried the Chinese general. "I know it must be this way. At first I thought it might be a trick of my old age, that I was seeing things that weren't there. I thought I was beyond understanding the ways of the young when they are in love. But I sensed what passed between the two of you. Now you must leave and go as far away as you can. If our leaders know of your whereabouts, then they will send men after you."

Jin speaks rapidly in Chinese. The Boy could tell she was pleading.

"It's all right, granddaughter," said the Chinese general, her grandfather, breathlessly. "I understand. I don't need to forgive you . . ."

The Chinese general began to shake, wobbling back and forth. Horse reared and the Boy fought to bring him under control as Jin clung to his back. The rubble all about them began to shift in great piles.

As soon as the shaking had started, it stopped.

"It's just a tremor, boy," said the general. "But there will be more."

The Boy patted Horse, whose eyes were rolling and wild with fear.

The old general came closer, pulling the folded map from his uniform.

"I have one more question to ask, boy."

The Boy felt ashamed, as though he had stolen something from the general in spite of all the old soldier's kindness.

"But first, take this." The general held the folded map up with trembling, gnarled fingers. The Boy reached down and took it.

"And this."

The general held up a small sack.

"There are American dimes made of silver inside. Most traders will barter for them. You will need to know where you are, that's why I want the two of you to take the map. Where you have been is not important anymore. You will need to know where you are going now."

The Chinese general turned to Jin.

"You are precious to me. Your father and mother named you well.

I shall think of all our walks together, always. You have been a faithful granddaughter, and beyond that, my friend."

There were great tears in his tired, rheumy eyes. They poured out onto the brown wrinkles of his fleshy face.

"It is I who must beg for forgiveness . . . from both of you," sobbed the general, fighting to maintain his soldierly bearing.

Jin speaks in Chinese again, crying this time.

"No," commanded the general. "I must. I must ask for forgiveness. I must ask you to forgive me and those of my generation for . . . for destroying the world. And you must forgive us, so that you can be free to make something new. I am sorry for what we did."

The general turned to the Boy, wiping at tears, his voice winning the fight for composure.

"And now answer my question. We will not survive the attack of the barbarians, will we?"

The Boy wheeled Horse, still skittish after the earthquake.

"I do not think so."

The general lowered his eyes, thinking.

"Go now. Do not look back, never return here. The world is yours now. Do better with it than we did."

The Boy felt Jin's hot tears on his bare shoulder.

"Go!" roared the general.

The Boy put his good foot into Horse's flank and they were off down the old road leading to the rusting bridge that was once called the Golden Gate.

It was very quiet out.

THEY RODE INTO the forested hills above the bridge, dismounted and crawled forward to the edge of the ridge and watched the sentries below.

"There are more guards than usual," whispered Jin of the sentries who were watching the bridge.

"It might be because of the invasion. Or us, if word has gotten out."

They watched, hoping the extra guards would leave. The sun was high above.

"Tell me about the bridge. Is it safe?"

"It is . . . dangerous. But there is a marked way."

"What will we find on the other side? Are there people?"

"No, not in the city. There is only destruction there. People go there . . . to salvage. There are small villages . . . away to the south."

Horse cried, signaling the Boy.

The Boy loped back to Horse and saw the riders. Chinese cavalry—gray uniforms and crimson sashes—carrying their heavy rifles, twelve of them, following Horse's trail up from the ruins of Sausalito.

CHAPTER 44

"Hold on tight." Then, "Tighter!" screams the Boy.

Horse was sliding downslope through the scree that abutted the shattered remains of the road leading to the bridge. The Boy held on for dear life as Jin clung to him.

The guards at the bridge raised their weapons to port arms, as if this act, as it had so many times before, would bend the offenders to their will.

You said, Sergeant, *Surprise the enemy and the battle might just be half won, Boy!*

Horse checks a fall and the Boy yanks him on to the road and straight toward the bridge.

The riders who had followed their trail, at the top of the hill above the bridge now, began to fire down upon them. Their shots were wild and the sentries at the bridge began to scatter, fearing they were being shot at by invaders. A wild shot hit the chest of one of the Chinese bridge guards with a loud thump, knocking him to the pavement.

Horse crashed past two guards and raced onto the bridge, straining hard for the distant far end.

Great iron cables ran skyward toward the suspension pylons, but other numerous cables that once were connected to the roadway had fallen onto the bridge or lay draped in great coils spilling over the edge. It even seemed to the Boy that the bridge hung lower on one side. A few ancient trucks, decrepit with crusted rust, littered the bridge at odd angles.

"Stay to the right . . . it's the safest side!" screamed Jin above the bullets, above the *clop-cloppity-clop-clop* of Horse's sprint along the old road-way of the bridge.

The gusty wind dragged at the Boy's long hair as he looked behind them to see riders and horses tumbling down the steep slope leading to the bridge.

I have a lead and a little time. That is good. But I'm riding into the unknown, and that is bad.

For a moment he felt the familiar fear that had chased him all his days. But the embrace of Jin, her thin arms about his chest, reminded him of wearing the bearskin in the dead of a winter storm.

At the end of this bridge, somewhere, there must be a cave like the bear cave for us.

Halfway across the bridge, the Boy could see the concrete piles of once–San Francisco. Huge jutting slabs of gray concrete rose up into small mountains, stacked at different protruding angles. Only a few emaciated buildings remained upright.

'The destruction is almost complete here,' thought the Boy, and in the moment he had this thought, his eyes, searching the rubble, watched as it began to slide in rising chalky yellow sheets of dust.

He blinked twice, assuming his eyes must be watering in the wind of the hard chase.

But now the road underneath them was shifting to the left, twisting, almost.

Cables above were waving back and forth. High and ahead, one ripped loose from the roadway and swung wildly across the bridge, sweeping a rusting wreck off the side and into the ocean below.

In San Francisco everything was shaking. Dust was rising everywhere. One of the tall buildings collapsed into itself and was replaced by plumes of thick brown dust billowing up into the bright noon sky.

Cables sang sickly in a high-pitched whine. The Boy could hear explosions as rusty metal bolts, gigantic, tore themselves away from their foundations on the bridge.

The shaking increased and the Boy drove Horse hard for the far side of the crossing.

It was only when they passed down the off-ramp and onto the other side of the bay, clearing the last of the sagging, shearing, crying, bending cables that the Boy breathed. He wheeled Horse about to check their pursuers and could see nothing of them.

The shaking had stopped and the air was filled with the sounds of birds calling and dogs barking.

The animal noise rose.

"Earthquake," whispered Jin, shaking. "A big . . . one."

The Boy turned Horse back to the once-city.

A moment later rending metal, groaning in chorus, sheared through the quiet.

When they turned back, Jin, Horse, and the Boy watched the Golden Gate Bridge twist and then crash into the ocean.

LATER, THEY RODE along the only avenue clear enough to pass through the city. It was a wide thoroughfare running along the waterfront. Every building was a pile of gray concrete and dusty redbrick. Pipes and rebar jutted from the wreckage like nerve endings caught forever in the act of sensory stimulus. What had not disintegrated into gigantic piles of rubble lay either heaped atop another building or forever fallen off at some odd angle.

"At least they cannot follow us now that the bridge is down," said the Boy.

"But they will," replied Jin.

They came upon the remains of a military defense. Artillery pieces lay scattered about, their long barrels blooming like sunflowers.

"Why will they follow?" asked the Boy.

"Because . . . they must," replied Jin.

The Boy chose a narrow avenue through the rubble that led into the heart of the once-city.

They climbed up where buildings had spilled themselves into one another and crossed streets littered with explosive sprays of redbrick thrown outward.

"They cannot let me go," said Jin. "Because they are afraid of mixing with . . . the . . ."

"The barbarians."

"Yes. The barbarians."

Shortly they entered an open space. Gothic cathedral arches rose out of the debris, as did splintered beams of wood in front of what was once a small park.

They watched and listened within the silence of the place as Horse turned to the wild grass that survived in the park.

They drank water from their skins to wash away the floating dust.

"It is dangerous to be here. The rubble could shift at any time," he said.

"Very. The old city . . . is a very dangerous place. We . . . will not want to be here for . . . long."

"What lies to the south?"

"I have only heard . . . there are ruined cities in the south. But many have burnt down or are little more than . . . ruins. There is a fishing village along the Pacific Ocean beyond a city that faced south into the sea and burnt down long ago. I . . . have been there once, when I was a girl."

"And beyond that?"

"The war . . . before the battles here . . . the big war was fought there. Many 'nukes' and . . . chemicals. The land is said to be poisoned and filled with monsters."

"Oh."

He brought her toward him and they kissed in the quiet and shattered remains of the square.

"Are you happy?" he asked.

"Yes."

"Even if we must go past the monsters?"

She kissed him again.

"Yes."

THE REST OF the day was long and hot. At times they had to walk Horse up long hills of dangerous rubble, picking their way through the broken rock and twisting rusted metal.

In the late afternoon the wind picked up and they could hear the sound of bones dully knocking against each other in a haphazard fashion.

"No one else lives here?" asked the Boy.

"There are dogs and ghosts. The dogs . . . are very wild."

Dusk was falling to gloom as they rode slowly down the long highway leading away from the city. In the darkness ahead the Boy saw a building standing off by itself. It was only two stories high. It was long and squat.

M-O-T-E . . . he spells.

Probably "motel."

He left Jin atop Horse in the parking lot as he checked the ruined place. All the doors had long since been torn off. He found the evidence of campfires in the bathtubs of most of the rooms.

Someone had stayed here for a time, but not for long. Now they were gone.

They took a room downstairs. The bed was little more than exposed coils and springs. He pushed it against the wall and tried to clear the floor of debris as best he could. There was a large hole in the wall leading to the next room. He led Horse through the doorway of that room and settled him for the night.

"I'll be back," he told Jin.

He was gone for some time, and when he returned he brought wood and placed it in the bathtub for a fire.

Once the fire was going he gave her the last of Horse's corn and they chewed it and drank cold water.

He watched her dark eyes staring into the fire.

"Are you happy still?"

She turned to him and smiled.

"So happy. So . . . free."

'Other women are not like you,' he thought as he watched her. 'Most—all the ones I have ever met in all the villages and places like the Cotter family's old dark house—are merely possessions to be had by whoever is strong enough to take and keep them. But you want to find out who you are and you will let no one own you. And I do not think anyone could keep you if you did not want to stay.'

"It will not be easy. But in time we will find a place and make it our own," he said.

"We will," she agreed softly.

He pushed the frame of the bed against the doorway of the room and draped a blanket across it. The Boy hoped this would help hold the heat of the fire in the room. About the hole in the wall between rooms he could do nothing. Their breath was now forming tiny puffs of moisture in the cold night air.

When he turned back from securing the doorway, he found Jin at the end of the room near the door to the bathroom, close to the fire.

She had wrapped herself only in the bearskin.

She beckoned him within.

CHAPTER 45

They rode south the next day, stopping early to make camp in an abandoned place that would hold for the night. There was fire. There was water. The Boy hunted during the day, using the rifle to take small game.

The night that followed was long and cold, and their embraces became deeper and more meaningful in the passing quiet.

Lying awake, she on his chest in deep sleep, the Boy thought.

He thought of all that he had to do and places they might go and be safe.

He thought of life, and though there was a new problem he could think of in each day ahead, he was glad.

To have these problems was to have her.

My life has never been this good.

And . . .

I never want it to be another way.

He slept and did not dream.

IN THE MORNING they crossed a small mountain ridge and saw the ocean stretching away to the south and west. The Boy saw the overgrown ruins of a thin spreading town that must have once climbed up to the ridge.

But it had been consumed and little remained other than concrete pads and crumbling, blackened walls that poked through the coastal vegetation.

"The village is farther along the coast. I . . . doubt they will be looking for us there yet. We can purchase . . . food and other things. Where will we go after?"

He looked toward the south.

How far away is the city of Los Angeles? On the map it seems a long way off. If those who she says must follow us are afraid of the damage caused by radiation then maybe they will turn back if we head into the worst of it. Or at least make them think that we intend to.

"Into the poisoned lands," he said.

She was silent.

"Do not worry. I have faced monsters. Our bearskin was once one."

"But . . . why must we go there?" she said softly.

"You said that they must follow us?"

"Yes."

"Then we will go where they will not follow us."

CHAPTER 46

Shao Fan walked the road at night.

'It will be a good spring after such a hard winter,' he thought.

His hunters were spread out behind him, his trackers far ahead, looking for any sign of the fugitives.

We will not find them tonight.

It has been a long day. And yet you must be out and away from your home for another night.

Yes.

This day, for Shao Fan, had started just before dawn, out on Point Reyes, above the lighthouse. His trackers had been watching the lighthouse keeper and his family.

When the man left at dawn, they'd followed him along the coast and up to a little bay. Savages had been allowed to dwell there and sell the fish they took from those waters where the old Chinese aircraft carrier had been grounded in the shallows and surf.

They watched the lighthouse keeper. He entered an old building, perhaps once a seaside resort. Smoke came through the roof and Shao Fan and the hunters could smell bacon cooking.

Later, when the man came out, holding his tea, the little half-caste children racing out behind him onto the dewy grass in the golden light of midmorning, Shao Fan knew that the rumors about the lighthouse keeper were true.

The air had seemed thick with salt.

The children were tainted, so you know . . . you had to . . . do what must be in done in such cases, thought Shao Fan.

Did I?

Now, on the night road far to the south of Point Reyes, on the other side of the bay, searching for the barbarian and the general's granddaughter, drawing his long, thick coat down across his lean frame, Shao Fan did not answer his own question.

That morning, when Shao Fan, followed by his crew, came out of the scrubby coastal pine, crossing the field onto the beach, the man, the lighthouse keeper, did not move. His handleless cup is held too high. As if, in that moment before one drinks his tea, he has decided that this day should be the measure by which all days are judged.

As if one could make such a request.

And then when the lighthouse keeper saw Shao Fan and his men, he knew the error of such thinking on the subject of days and their measure.

Today of all days, the lighthouse keeper must have thought, was the end of the measuring stick.

They'd drowned the children.

It was the law.

The birth defects that always come with the American barbarians, the survivors of our nuclear weapons, must not be allowed to continue. In time, they, their ways, their defects will disappear, and the world will be a better place.

Or so says the council.

The concubine was dispatched, swiftly, even as the lighthouse keeper's cry for mercy was drowned out by the thundering surf in the misty morning air.

There was no protocol for her demise. Only that it must be.

And then the march with the lighthouse keeper to the crossroads.

That also was the law.

And for that there was a protocol.

The salty cold of morning and crashing waves had faded in the hot steaming fields inland. Everything was golden.

It would be a good spring and a hot summer.

They'd hung the lighthouse keeper at the crossroads.

A warning.

Do not mix with the barbarians.

Shao Fan recalled the words he always thought of whenever the sentence was carried out.

Be careful who you fall in love with.

Shao Fan always remembered those words when the transgressor was pulled aloft by the rope and horse.

Be careful who you fall in love with.

And that was how the day had begun for Shao Fan and his hunters.

And the day ended and night fell as Shao Fan sought another who had broken the law.

The general's granddaughter.

He had crossed to the southern end of the bay by swift sail. His men, without their horses, walked the fields near the old highway leading inland. They waited in the sudden night breezes that swept the southern bay for the scent of campfires. But there were no camps to be found and no trails to be followed on this windy night.

'They have gone south across the mountains and into the ruins of Santa Cruz,' thought Shao Fan. 'We will not find them tonight.'

They will try for the village at Moss Landing.

He called for a halt and the men turned to their packs seeking food and hot tea.

We'll halt for an hour and march hard for Moss Landing through the night.

CHAPTER 47

The village lay on the far side of a muddy estuary. They passed long-gone fields that had lingered through a hard winter. A cemetery of wrecked boats wallowed near the entrance to the estuary.

They crossed a small road leading to a wide bridge.

The village was little more than a line of warehouses from Before, arranged along a narrow road running the length of the islet. An ancient and rusting large commercial fishing boat, now rigged with a mast and furled sail, had come into port to unload the night's catch. Villagers flocked to its side as the fish were unloaded in great netted bundles.

"Where do we go?" asked the Boy. He was leading Horse while Jin rode.

"Take us to that long hall there. We should be able to . . . purchase there. Remember . . . say nothing. Otherwise they will think you are more than just . . . my servant."

The Boy led them onto the street and they passed down its length until they reached the parking lot of an old warehouse. Fish were being trundled within by handcart.

The Boy helped Jin down from Horse. She adjusted her robe, ensuring the bag of silver coins was tucked within her sleeve.

Then they wandered the stalls.

There was little they needed to purchase beyond a large, wide wok made by a local blacksmith. At another stall she purchased oil and spices.

Later they found a few more blankets of good quality and some rice. Finally they decided upon two large bags to carry their purchases.

The sun was high overhead when they exited the warehouse. They smelled frying oil and saw the villagers gathered around a large fire where a bubbling cauldron seethed and hissed. Strips of fish were being fried and quickly eaten.

A villager, jolly and smiling, waved them over.

The villagers talked with Jin in animated Chinese. The Boy held Horse and shortly Jin returned with a woven grass plate of fried fish and a small shell full of dark sauce.

The jolly villager smiled at them as they stood in the warm sunshine eating the fish, dipping it in the pungent, salty sauce.

"I do not . . . think . . . they care . . ."

"Care for what?"

"Care that we . . . we are together."

"We could stay and join their village?"

"No . . . that will never be possible. In time the leaders will send someone to look for me . . . they will find us here. And then it does not matter what the villagers care for. Still . . . all the same it is nice that they do not care. Maybe one day things will change."

The Boy said nothing.

If he had to mark this place on Sergeant Presley's map he would write, the Village of Happy People.

They mounted Horse and turned toward the south.

It was bright and hazy with mist.

"What lies that way is unknown," she said. "We are at . . . the edge."

Then, my whole life has been at the edge.

He turned to her.

She looked up at him. Her eyes shone darkly in the bright sunlight.

"I hope things change for . . . all people . . . one day. I hope they will have then the happiness we have now," he said.

"Me too."

They rode south onto a long beach where the surf thundered against the shore and white sandy cliffs rose above them.

In the afternoon, the sky turned gray and the wind was whipped with salt and water.

"A storm is coming on shore," she said.

In time, while there was still light in the sky, they came upon old wooden buildings surrounded by drifting dunes. The wood was gray with salt and sun and age. Bone-white fingers of driftwood poked through the sand.

"We'll camp here tonight."

CHAPTER 48

In the night, surrounded by the warm silence of the dunes, the Boy heard the breaking waves beyond their camp rolling hard onto the beach.

'We will continue straight into the south,' he thought. 'According to the map there was an old highway that ran along the coast there.'

He thought of the map in his mind. He saw Monterey south of where they were now, a place called Carmel and the old highway south to Los Angeles.

Everyone knew Los Angeles was destroyed. Sergeant Presley always said so.

On the map there was a large red X across Los Angeles.

They will not follow us there.

You would say, *You think so, Boy.*

And

Or do you hope so?

I am doing the best I can, Sergeant.

And

I know. I just got to ride ya, Boy. Make ya check yourself.

I know. You would say that to me. You would tell me to be both cautious and sure at once.

The breaking waves pounded the shore beyond the silence of the dunes.

If we could live here . . .

When he returned to their fire, Jin had reorganized their packs.

Sergeant Presley's lay open.

There was the knife.

The flannel shirt.

And the gray feather with the broken spine.

"I have . . . never seen a feather like this . . . before," she said, holding it up, inspecting it. "Where did it come from?"

The Boy knelt down beside her.

"I don't know."

"Boy" is what they called you. It's the only thing you responded to. So "Boy" it is.

But why then did you keep the feather, Sergeant? Why is its touch almost familiar? As though it meant something once . . . about me.

I remember being carried as we ran. There was yellow grass and a blue sky. Someone, a woman, was screaming.

And the feather.

And . . .

"I think it was once my name."

She stared at the feather.

Then she looked at the Boy.

She said nothing.

In the morning, the Boy smelled other horses coming out of the north.

They could have been anyone's horses. Even wild ones, roaming. He'd seen them before.

But he knew it was a lie even if the voice of Sergeant Presley didn't tell him so.

They'd be coming.

"Let's go."

Soon they were dressed and away from the bones of the old lodge sinking into the dunes. Horse threw up a great spray of sand as they kicked away from its ruin.

Farther down the beach there was no smell of horses. The Boy listened to the wind.

He heard no *jink* of harness and tack.

No cries of men calling to one another as they searched.

Behind him, the Boy saw the trail of Horse through the sand and grass and knew they were not hard to follow.

There was little left of the place once called Monterey, the skeletal remains of a few tall buildings, the foundations of many smaller buildings consumed by fire and forest. Massive green pines grew in wicked clumps up through the old roads and foundations.

They rode up a long hill of once-neighborhoods that were now little more than ancient charred wood overgrown by sea grass and pine. Just before starting down the other side, the Boy turned to scan their backtrail.

He saw the men on horses coming for them.

A line of riders picked their way along an old road. Ahead of them he saw individuals running back and forth across the fields and ruins, searching for their trail.

The Boy urged Horse and they rode hard over the small saddle of the mountain and down into a forest the map would name Carmel. Huge foundations of houses that once must have been little palaces dotted the sides of their track. The forest floor was littered with pine needles and thick brush.

'They will follow us easily,' thought the Boy.

Off to his right and down toward the rocky coast, he could see the remains of other ancient stone palaces crumbling into the sea.

Don't just run, think.

They're following you like dogs.

You would say that, Sergeant, wouldn't you?

We can't run. Horse might fall and then that would be then end of us.

I could start a fire to cover our trail.

Too damp from the storm.

Stay ahead of them for now and look for a place to lead them into a trap.

It's all I can do.

"Is everything . . . good?" asked Jin.

"Yes. We are good."

But he heard her worry. He thought of what traps he might make.

What do I have?

The tomahawk.

The rifle.

What remains of the parachute cord.

Two knives.

It's not much.

It is all I have.

'THEY KNOW WE are on their trail,' thought Shao Fan.

He rolled a cigarette and wished it was the weed he smoked at night, alone, in the dark.

I have been too many days at this.

You are an assassin.

There is no rest for the assassin.

No rest for the wicked.

He looked at the marks on the ground.

The horse had turned several times. They must have watched them come up the valley.

We will have to watch their trail for traps now. It is their only chance to escape us.

'Savages!' he thought, and spit bits of tobacco out onto the forest floor.

The afternoon was ending. Shadows long and blue surrounded his company.

How much longer can I push them? They are cold and hungry and if they miss a sign or the makings of a trap . . . then disaster.

He told them to make camp. They would sleep until morning and be fresh for the trail.

Besides, the savage and the girl are running into the poison lands where no one may go and live long. They are up against a wall. They will have to turn or stand and fight.

He thought of his lacquered box of weed. Since they are camping, he reasoned to himself.

"Be careful who you love," he mumbled and set to loading his pipe.

CHAPTER 49

The next day, Shao Fan watched the old house as his men entered it. The day was hot and the air smelled of pine and mustard.

Spring is upon us.

Think about this business, he chastised himself.

They'd risen early and the sleep had done them good. They'd picked up the trail of the fugitives in the first light of the cold and misty morning and followed them down into the hot valley.

They are heading for the coast road, Shao Fan told himself all along. Which seemed a good thing, at least as far as he, Shao Fan, was concerned. He could increase speed, now that their prey's options were narrowing between the sea and the mountains.

But in the dry and dusty ruins south of Carmel, the trail drew them to an old "mansion."

'Perhaps they were not aware of our pursuit after all and have stopped to enjoy rest and forbidden pleasure,' thought Shao Fan.

The two scouts, long knives in hand, crossed the open yard and entered the rotting house through two separate broken windows. The scouts thread the remaining shards of glass nicely and are in with barely a noise.

Well-trained men make work easy.

After a moment there was a creaking groan, too quickly followed by a thunderous crash. Plumes of ancient dust expelled themselves through the broken windows like smoke from the mouth of a corpse.

When the dust settled, the hunters and Shao Fan moved forward to find that the second floor had collapsed onto the two scouts within, crushing them.

'A trap,' thought Shao Fan.

AHEAD, THE MOUNTAINS fell down to the sea, and in glimpses the Boy and Jin caught the silver remains of the coast highway winding away to the south in the afternoon sun.

Jin smiled at him when he turned to show her the road, and in his heart her doubts and fears disappeared.

They won't follow us much farther.

You would tell me, *You hope, Boy. You hope for that.*

I do.

The parachute cord is gone and my traps will be crude now. They will be wary, knowing I have skill with traps.

They don't know I am out of the parachute cord.

The Boy stopped occasionally to create bent limb traps spiked with sharpened stakes. He felt rushed as he worked and they were not his best. But each one would slow them down, and in time they would crawl, the more they were taught not to run.

THE FIRST TRAP took two scouts. Shao Fan was now down to just three scouts and the hunters.

An hour later, a limb snapped forward and blinded one of the three remaining scouts as stakes raked his eyes and face.

'The man will lose an eye,' thought Shao Fan.

I should let the hunters go and ride this savage down.

But how many will you lose?

And Shao Fan found that he did not care. He wanted to be finished with this, as he was finished every time they hauled the violator aloft while the noose tightened about the neck.

No screams.

Just the dance.

Finished.

I want every time to be the last time.

But they never learn . . .

. . . so there will be no end to it.

To think that my days will always be such . . .

And Shao Fan was too exhausted and too depressed, if he were to admit the truth, to finish the thought. He assigned the blinded scout to a hunter. The man will be tied to his horse to follow along after the hunting party.

THEY AVOIDED THE next two traps now that the scouts knew what to look for.

They moved much slower than Shao Fan would like, but they had to.

THE BOY CONSIDERED the old ruins that hung over the cliff near the sea. The coast road ran like a moving snake past them and on to the south.

The Boy wanted to take the coast road now. He wanted to ride hard to the south, and in time their pursuers would turn back, or so he thought.

And what if they didn't?

Then there would be just the road between the mountains and the sea. There would be no place to hide. Once they chose the coast road, their pursuers would ride them down and they would be left with very few options.

Ruined walls crumbled along a wide plateau that ended over the ocean in a rocky black cliff above waves that slopped in great troughs and wallops against the continent.

What traps do I have left?

How many have I taken in the traps and how many of our pursuers are left?

How many traps will I need to make until they lose the will to follow?

How many traps until they are too angry to stop?

If we ride the coast road, they'll follow and follow quickly. They'll know we can only go one direction and if they get close enough I won't be able to stop and make traps. So it is in their best interest to get close, to show me they are close.

They heard the surf boom distantly below the cliff as it smashed itself into the jagged rocks. It was late afternoon and the sun was falling toward the ocean.

The Boy and Jin walked the ruins, crossing through a crumbling lobby where a large and tattered canvas hung on the wall. In the sooty picture, windswept eucalyptus trees twisted in the nook of a hill as tall grass bent toward a horizon of blue skies and soft white clouds. And though the sea was not represented in the picture, the Boy knew it must be nearby.

Chairs and couches had long since been smashed for firewood. Beyond this there was a large swimming pool, cracked and empty. Dirty rainwater had collected in its depths. Wild palms had erupted through the crumbling pavement. Beyond all this was the main building, every window empty, every door missing. There were long, dark halls along which rotting hotel rooms, forever waiting to be occupied, stretched off into the darkness.

'We could make a stand here,' the Boy thought.

We will make our stand here.

Two knives.

One tomahawk.

One rifle.

Cartridges.

You take everything with you.

They wandered to the back of the ancient ruin, crossing long, dark hallways of disintegrating carpet and mildewing rooms. At the end of it all they came to a great room that overlooked the ocean. Out to sea, the water and waves raced off to the south.

"Wait here," he said to Jin.

"No. I want to come with you."

"I'll be fine. I just need to see what's above us."

"Then . . . so will I."

Above they found two more floors, the same as the first, clotted with rotting furniture along their long halls, and at the top a door led out onto the roof. The roof was littered with palm fronds by countless storms.

"We will fight them from here." Then, "Once they are all dead we will be free to go where we will."

Jin nodded. The wind pulled at her long hair.

"I . . . believe you."

In the hours that followed, they stripped electrical wire and cables from inside the walls. They found ancient metal fixtures, rusting and jagged.

There were no weapons.

No propane tanks that had not long since been gouged.

No firearms to find.

No knives to loot.

But still they made traps.

Traps where a floor might fall from above if a certain pillar was loosed by a taut cable disturbed in the debris.

Traps where boards fitted with jagged rusting metal might snap forward as a careless foot dragged electrical wiring along its path.

They blocked the entrances to the second floor so that the entire first floor would have to be traversed before ascending to the next floor. They did the same for the second and finally the third.

They were sweating hard and the Boy felt his strength fading as they hauled out ancient rotting furniture and stuffed it into the stairways, blocking off all avenues of approach other than the one the Boy had decided the pursuers must choose. After this, he turned to making barricades where he could shoot with his rifle down the long dark hallways as the enemy threaded the gauntlet of traps.

'I wish I had both arms,' he thought, the dark outside telling him night had fallen. Jin's face, shining in the light of their torch from the sweat of her exertions, came close to his.

"Now, I . . . am your . . . left." She touched the withered arm he had hidden and protected and cursed his whole life.

I must have said that out loud. I am very tired.

Together they built the last barriers.

It was late when they settled in the farthest room beneath the roof. A once-grand suite. They had a small fire and Jin made rice in her wok. There were eggs also. And tea.

They made love. He held her close and she whispered over and over in his ear that she loved him.

That she loved Broken Feather.

LATER, AS SHE slept he thought of the feather in Sergeant Presley's pack.

She is my left arm now.

My left side.

Me.

Broken Feather.

He slept for a while and when he awoke it was still deep night.

There was a little more to do.

Jin did not wake as he took his charcoal and a small torch. For the rest of the night he worked at the faces he sketched near the traps. Or sometimes along a mildewing wall where he would get a good shot from the barricades.

Something to distract them from his traps and hiding places.

It was just before dawn when he left to feed Horse. He gave Horse water and walked him down onto the beach. He whispered the things he always whispered to Horse. Things that made Horse feel good about himself.

Vainglorious things.

He staked Horse in the tree line beyond the beach to the south. There was a little water and grass. If they didn't make it, in time Horse would pull free. Be free.

He patted Horse one last time and looked deep into the eyes of his friend.

Trying to read his mind as he'd always tried to do.

Failing as he'd always failed.

He returned to their bed and lay down, taking everything in. Listening to the morning. The offshore wind, smelling of salt and fruit. The gray light turning to gold. The old place.

They were coming now.

In sleep Jin drew closer to him and murmured something in her dream.

"Now I am your left."

CHAPTER 50

The Boy watched them from a corner window on the third floor. He saw the hunters coming along the trail left by Horse. They scanned the stumps of chimneys and overgrown lots, wary that he might snipe at them from the tall grass beyond.

They'll come to this old place from Before.

He watched until they disappeared in front of what was once the lobby. The place of the dirty canvas picture.

SHAO FAN CALLED for a halt. The thick silence of the heat and loneliness of the place was broken by an offshore breeze, dull and sweet, sweeping through the high eucalyptus trees along the road.

He'll be inside. The savage and his traps.

He'll be watching us, even now.

Shao Fan knew there would be traps. But his men, his hunters, knew how the savage worked now. They'd be alert. They'd know what to look for.

So, they had to go in. All race transgressors must have their appointment at the crossroads.

Shao Fan signaled two men. The last two scouts.

They rode up to him and he whispered instructions. Moments later they were off to the south.

Shao Fan dismounted and signaled his remaining men to do the same.

They brought their breech loaders.

THE BOY TOOK his first shot as the hunters exited the main building. He shot from the corner window of the third floor looking down on nine men as they crossed the crumbling pavement near the cracked and broken swimming pool.

He rested his gun on a platform deep inside the shadows of the room.

The shot hammered through the silence and the men scrambled for cover.

Just one shot. Then move to a new position. Just like you taught me, Sergeant, even though you said there would never be a need because all the "ammo" was used up killin' ourselves. Still, I'd wanted to learn and you'd showed me.

I think it was a way for you to pass the time and teach me the only thing you'd ever known, and not think about the past.

He withdrew into the dusty shadows of the old room and heard them calling out to each other below. Beneath that, he could hear the dying man.

He found Jin at their camp on the third floor.

"They're here."

She nodded and said something in Chinese.

"I want you to go to the roof now. Block the door with the broken concrete I left there. Don't open it until you hear my voice."

She nodded and he led her to the access stairwell that climbed up to the roof. She turned back to him, the broken feather in her hand. From it dangled a small leather thong. Quickly she reached up and tied it into his long hair.

He watched her ascend the steps and push on the rusty door. Bright light filled the dingy gloom of the stairwell. She glanced back at him and he silently beckoned her to close the door, wishing she didn't have to. Wishing they could be free of this day.

If wishes were fishes, Boy, beggars would ride.

Yes, you said that also, Sergeant. You would say it to me now.

The Boy made his way down to the first floor, all the while avoiding his traps. He took up a position behind the first-floor barricade at the end of a long, dark hall. The other end led to the pool area.

They would come through the hall from there.

In his mind he traced their route. They would funnel into this corridor as they found the other corridors were blocked and trapped.

Take a shot and move to the second floor. Be disciplined in this.

He waited, hearing nothing.

Maybe a mouse moving along the rotten baseboard.

In time he saw a dark figure detach itself from the shadows at the far end of the hall. The light from the corridor outlined the silhouette of a man carrying a rifle at the ready.

The Boy transitioned the rifle across the sacking he had laid for a rest atop the barrier, letting the sight fall on the outline of the man down the hall.

He heard a crash from somewhere in another part of the building and then a man was screaming in Chinese.

The swing trap.

When he looked again, the shadowy figure at the end of the hall was gone.

Maybe he was on the floor and crawling forward?

The Boy waited and watched.

A low rumble and then a loud crash in another hall told the Boy some-one found the collapsing-wall trap. He heard no scream or cry for help this time.

There wouldn't be. The wall should have fallen on the intruder's head. He was either unconscious or dead.

But I don't know that for sure.

There were nine and now three were down. That made six.

Maybe.

The shadow detached itself from the wall again and moved right into the sight at the end of the Boy's rifle.

Without even thinking the Boy fired, flinging the man backward and out of sight.

Blue gun smoke mixed with the dust and heavy heat.

Five.

On the second floor, the Boy moved fast and he knew they could hear him below.

Good. They'll think they have me trapped. Maybe they will become careless.

He thought of Jin on the roof.

The traps here on the second floor were deadfalls, sure to break a leg or pierce a man through with the stakes he would fall on below.

He took up his place behind the barricade at the far end of the second floor.

He listened, willing himself to slow his ragged breathing.

Almost there.

You would say, *You think so Boy? Or do you hope so?*

Both.

One of the Chinese climbed through an open window behind the Boy as he watched the dark corridor. The Boy didn't hear the intruder until the man softly brushed against something just as he hoisted his body through the window.

The Boy set his rifle down and whirled with his tomahawk out. The man climbing through the window rolled just as the Boy raised the axe and struck. The head of the tomahawk buried itself in rotting wood and crumbling drywall.

The man cried out in Chinese and an instant later, far off, as the Boy dragged the axe out of the wall, he could hear running feet at the far end of the second floor. The sound, hollow on the rotting wood and disintegrating carpet, beat out an urgent approaching staccato.

The man in the room had his knife out, waving it back and forth between the two of them. He was smaller than the Boy and there was fear in his eyes.

The Boy rushed him, slamming his body into the man. They fell to the ground slick with sweat as the Boy pinned the man's knife hand with the flat of his tomahawk, leaning hard into the Chinese with the bony, withered side of himself.

The man cursed, almost whining.

The pounding footsteps coming up the hall disappeared in a crashing wave of snapping boards as the floor fell out beneath them. There was a brief cry and a sickening bone-snapping sound, loud and clear.

The Boy slammed his head into the face of the man beneath him and a spray of blood erupted from the smashed face. Instinctively, hands moved to cover the broken nose.

The Boy rose, his tomahawk swinging back above his shoulder, then his head, and a second later slammed the axe down through the man's sternum. There was an *umpf* of escaping air and the sound of breaking bone.

He rose and returned to the barricade. Down the dark hallway a Chinese was looking into the dusty hole that was the floor. He could hear a man crying below.

"Three," muttered the Boy and fired at the man staring down into the hole.

"Two."

SHAO FAN STOOD at the far end of the second floor.

Chiang lay dead halfway down the hall.

His last hunter watched out the window.

I know he's here. They're both here, the savage and the girl. But how many more traps?

He heard a soft whistle from outside, above the crash of the sea. Shao Fan looked out the window onto the wild yard of lush overgrowth that bordered the cliff.

The two scouts waved, smiling, and between them was the transgressor Jin. She was bound and gagged, her eyes wide with terror and tears. She knew Shao Fan. Knew his business. Knew what must come next.

'Forget this savage,' thought Shao Fan, and ordered his man to withdraw. They lowered themselves through the window with the rope they always carried.

No sense in risking the traps we didn't find on the way in.

It was a good idea to send the scouts up the cliff and onto the roof from the beach. 'It has probably saved our lives,' thought Shao Fan as he started a fire in the second-floor hallway.

We'll burn this place down with the savage inside. Protocol indicates we can dispose of the savage in any way we choose.

Usually it was a savage female, which they preferred to drown. But just this once, since it was a wily male, the characters on the report could read, "Burned in a fire."

FOR A LONG time the Boy waited behind the third-floor barricade.

They're afraid to come up after us. Good, maybe they will go away now.

In time he smelled the smoke, and when he listened hard, he could hear the crackle of flames catching the old carpets and tattered drapes and broken furniture and dry wood.

Fire!

He raced back to the third-floor stairwell leading to the roof and rapped on it heavily.

"Jin, it's me!"

Nothing.

The smoke came in gray puffs up through the floor beneath his feet. The snapping crackle of the fire was growing.

We'll be caught if I don't get her down off the roof!

"Jin, open up it's me!"

He didn't ask again as he reared back and slammed into the rusty metal door. It banged open in a wide arc. In the bright sunlight the Boy turned around and around searching for Jin on the debris-cluttered rooftop. He raced to one edge as black smoke crawled up from the other side.

Below he could see Jin in the bottom of the empty pool. She was bound and gagged, her eyes pleading with him. She looked left and right trying to tell him something. A moment before he heard the report from the rifles, he saw the Chinese hiding in the worn-out bushes and in the shadows of the old lobby. All at once bullets thudded about him into the crumbling concrete of the building. The Boy fired and then flung himself to the rooftop as bullets raced off into the sky above.

Lying on the roof, the Boy broke the breech of the rifle, pulled out the spent shell, and pushed another into its place. He crawled several feet to a new position and popped up behind the parapet.

A shaven-headed Chinese was pulling Jin by her hair up the steps of the empty pool.

A bullet smacked into the concrete wall of the roof, sending shards up to cut the face of the Boy. Other Chinese were taking aim.

The Boy ducked back behind the cover of the wall.

I'll get one shot and I have to use you to aim, he said to his withered hand. So work!

He moved in a new direction along the wall and when he rose from behind it again, he saw the shaven-headed Chinese drag Jin across the inner courtyard and into the yawning entrance of that other building where the shredded picture from Before hung on the wall, the lobby. The remaining

Chinese were retreating into the darkness. The Boy could see the tallest of them, their leader, hunching low, shouting orders angrily as they retreated.

The Boy raised the rifle, knowing there would be just this one shot before she disappeared.

But he could already feel his withered hand, shaking and weak, refusing to be used, refusing to steady the rifle.

Sweat poured into his eyes as drifting black smoke stung his nose.

He aimed for the back of the man as he dragged Jin into the darkness of the lobby.

The Boy fired, knowing he missed.

And Shaven-head and Jin disappeared into the darkness.

Only their leader, the tall, thin Chinese with the mustache, remained. He smiled at the Boy, then darted after Jin and the other hunters.

Black smoke was coming through cracks and rents in the roof. The Boy smelled melting plastic and acrid smoke. Heat came up at him in waves.

He searched the sides of the building for a way down, but already the flames were crawling up through most of the roof and out the windows below.

Think!

I am thinking!

He loped toward the far end of the roof, closest to the cliff's edge and the sea below. Below the roof, a balcony hung out over the cliff. The Boy lowered himself down onto the balcony and saw thick sheets of flame racing across the ceiling of the room connected to the balcony.

Below, the sea pounded the rocky coast. The water was a deep blue in places and in others it churned a foamy green. A stunted tree hanging off the cliff's edge swayed in gusty blasts of heat from the fire.

The Boy slung the rifle over his back. He climbed on top of the railing and leapt for the tree. Flailing with his good arm, he crashed into its branches and a moment later was sliding down the cliff toward the water below. He clawed for purchase and his good arm found a rock to grab onto.

He hung halfway down the cliff, breathing hard.

Above, black smoke rose into the sky.

It would be a steep climb back to the top. Almost impossible.

He was exhausted.

Below, he could hear the sea washing itself against the black rocks of the cliff.

If they come to look for me, there's not much I can do, and I'll be smashed to bits against the side of the rocks if I drop down into the ocean.

Above, the burning roof collapsed into the main structure with a groaning crash. Black, oily smoke billowed high into the sky and the flames seemed to roar above the ocean's strike against the coast.

The Boy hung there, waiting.

He heard nothing.

No voice.

I need you now, Sergeant.

I'm dead, Boy. Sorry about that. I tried my best.

IN TIME, HE worked his way down to the rocks below and followed them along the water's edge as the surf threated to drag him into its turmoil. The sun was sinking into the ocean and all was purple and red fire.

When he made the beach, he was limping and no matter how strongly he told his withered side to move, it wouldn't. It was a lock that would not open. He found Horse and dropped the rifle, his fingers trembling as he drank what little water Horse left him.

When the dregs were finished, he mounted Horse and rode back to the fire.

The building from Before was little more than smoking timber. The Chinese were gone and there was no sign of Jin.

He searched for their trail but it takes time. There had been too much confusion in the dirt and the dust of their tracks.

When he found their trail he saw they were riding north, back toward the Village of Happy People.

CHAPTER 51

He rode through the night but the going was slow. It took all his skill to stay on their trail. They did not stop as he hoped they would.

How many hours ahead of me are they?

Tall coastal pines rose up in thick stands as he crossed a small ridge, their scent heavy in the dew-laden cold.

He thought of the amount of time he was trapped on the cliff.

It was almost evening when he'd made it back onto the beach.

When did it start?

The fog crossed the beaches and marshes as he rode, following their trail through the night and the sand.

The battle at the old place had started in the morning.

He continued on through the night, even when the fog was thick and cold about him. The bearskin had gone in the fire and only Horse's heaving body kept him warm.

I have been cold before.

He passed the shadowy remains of ancient palaces and almost lost their trail.

He found the tracks of their horses in the ash of some long-gone fire.

His eyelids were heavy.

'Fatigue settles over me like the bearskin would,' he thought.

He sucked the night wind into his nostrils, feeling the cold flood his brain as he rode out onto the coastal plain following tracks through the ether of fog and saw grass.

I have been tired before.

I have been here before.

You were with me, Sergeant.

He thought of Jin and rode through the swirling salt-laden mist as nightmares of what might happen to her tormented him.

At dawn, he saw the Village of Happy People lying across the still, black water of the channel. It was quiet. The trail of the hunters led the Boy here.

They had ridden hard and they were tired. They would have stopped to rest.

He rode across the old bridge.

There was no one out.

Mist shrouded the sunken boats lying in the dark water, and the beach beyond was lost to nothingness.

The Boy heard the creak of the wrecked boats shifting in their graves at the pull of the invisible tide.

The Boy heard the gentle groan of rope.

He rode forward.

Halfway down the street, she hung from the ancient cargo hook above the main dock.

Her arms at her sides.

Her long dark hair hiding her face.

She swung gently at the end of a rope in the shifting mists of dawn.

CHAPTER 52

He remembered later.

Later that afternoon. He remembered screaming. Running toward . . . and screaming.

Why wasn't I on Horse?

He couldn't imagine himself running.

He sat in the shadow of a dune. Dense fog had run across the bay and into the dunes. The dunes just like where they stayed that night after the village . . .

He remembered the sound of the rope. He remembered the villagers coming out. They were crying too. He screamed at them . . . like an animal. Like the bear. Like the lion.

They were crying like children.

They lay down in the street and wept, begging him for forgiveness in a language he didn't understand. Begging him to let them grieve for this horrible thing that had been done.

How can I ever sleep again?

It wasn't her anymore.

She was stiff and cold.

He held her, hearing the sound of his pain as if from far away.

Knowing it was he who made that sound.

Knowing that Sergeant Presley could not help him anymore.

Knowing that the world was cruel and made of stone.

Her grave was beneath the sand and the sea grass.

He watched the grave, and what was once the cold of a foggy afternoon and wan sunlight became night and fog.

He watched.

He watched.

He watched.

Who am I now?

He didn't sleep.

Revenge.

He saddled Horse and thought of his revenge.

Don't do this, Boy!

Why?

He hears the creak of the rope that . . .

That . . .

The "who" of his revenge was easier to think about than the "why." The "why" was too painful. Much too painful.

He saw the face of the leader who came to take her. He was the "who" of his revenge. The object of his revenge.

And in fact . . .

He saw Sausalito. Their little walled city. Their wall.

All of them behind that wall, they were the "who" . . .

Of his revenge.

This is how everything went wrong, Boy. Don't you see? Revenge. Hatred. Fire. Boy, there is no good end to this.

Revenge.

He left the fire burning near her grave.

He rode up through the sea grass to the old western road. The One.

He could see her fire burning in the fog.

Let it burn forever.

In the east the sky was light and the fog was turning white.

This ain't a way to go, Boy. Forget this and live. Live. That's all you got to do in this world now. Keep on livin' until humanity gets a chance to start again. You do this and you'll set it back. Hell, you might even break it altogether. The world can't take much more.

Revenge.

He turned and the fire near her grave was gone, swallowed. Lost to the fog.

Who am I now?

Revenge.

CHAPTER 53

It was night when he moved down among them and their camps at the southern end of the bay.

The Psychos and their bare chests. Their war paint and muddy hair. Blood and Mohawks.

The Boy had watched them from the low hills all day, their boats and rafts taking shape, wood and oil drums dragged in from the ruins.

They would attack tonight.

He had watched them for three days. The mood—their mood was grim, and in the last hours before night the fires started and the dances began.

They're working themselves up to attack, Sergeant.

Don't do this thing, Boy.

I have to.

No. You don't. You want to, but you don't have to, Boy. There's a difference.

He patted Horse.

There's enough grass and water from this stream. If I'm not back tomorrow you'll pull that stake up and go. Take yourself off somewhere high into the mountains. Find wild mustangs.

In the dark he walks down among them.

He was painted in blood. His own.

The long hair that once hung straight down over his left eye, the weak side, was gone, shaved. Only the wild strip of the Mohawk stiff with mud rose from his scalp. Among the tangled hair, a broken feather.

They drank and rioted in their twirling, bumping dance. There were drums all along the shore.

Hot liquid gushed from a skin and burned his throat. The stuff was raw and as he coughed, he couldn't catch his breath. When he did he screamed at the world because he was still alive. The wild-eyed Psychos, leering and toothless, gaped happily at the Boy's reaction.

The men feasted on torn game, greasy and dripping on spits. Women laughed wickedly as they drank and worked the Mohawks of their men into spikes hardened by mud and shining with the fat of slaughtered animals roasting nearby. Their babble was little more than cackles and grunts. Occasionally the Boy detected a stray once-word. A "gunna" or a "sump'in' killah."

Amid the pressing throng, wild with delirium, he asked, "Where are you now, Jin?"

I feel more alone than all those winter nights in the bear cave or cold days on the road.

Or when the lions chased me.

Where are you now?

At midnight the moon was gone and the wind was warm.

A blacksmith worked near a hot fire putting edges to their weapons. The Boy found a saw and set to work cutting down the long barrel of the breech loader.

I won't trust you anymore, he said to his withered hand. You failed me when I needed you most and I won't trust you anymore.

A chieftain howled and the savages fell silent. The babble that passed from the chief's swollen and split lips erupted up from a barrel belly and massive chest, sending the warriors to their boats.

The Boy found himself paddling a canoe loaded with other paddling warriors as they crossed the bay. The flotilla kept a tight formation as it passed the pile of the once-city of San Francisco. Ahead, the lights of Sausalito were thin and few. To the east of the Chinese outpost—at its very gates, in fact—MacRaven's armies gathered around campfires that rose along the hills of the little bay.

You don't need to do this, Boy. They'll take your revenge for you. They'll pay them back, if that means anything to you.

'How could they take . . . her life?' he thought between paddle strokes.

The other men grunted and sweated. The Boy could smell the liquor oozing out of their skin.

I don't know, Boy. Maybe I thought I did. But now I don't know anymore. I know that there's good in the world. Good as long as it still exists in people like you. But if you do this . . . if you get to that place you'll need to go to do this . . . then maybe all the good that's left will have gone out of the world.

You don't exist, Sergeant.

I did, Boy. I did.

I have to know why. Why did they do this to her?

You'll never know.

You don't know that.

I do, Boy. I do. 'Cause there won't be a reason that ever makes enough sense to you.

The oars and paddles, even the hands that strike at the bay, were stopped. The flotilla laid drifting in the water near a small island just off the coast of Sausalito.

It was cold and quiet. The long night wound toward morning, and even though there was no light to betray the coming dawn, the Boy knew it was close, and so did the Psychos. Arms were flexed, spears laid across knees. The Boy felt his tomahawk at his side. The cut-down rifle was now a long pistol in his belt.

"*Ancha!*" roared a voice in the dark. The flotilla surged forward as oars and hands struck the water. Every Psycho was pulling hard for the few lights rising above the seawall of Sausalito.

On land, beyond the eastern gate, on the far side of the little city, torches from the camps of MacRaven's Army surged toward the walls. It was still too dark for targeted gunfire as the torches gathered beneath the defenses.

The Boy's canoe pulled forward, cutting through the still water and low-lying fog. The men about him said nothing. They wanted their surprise to be total. Ahead, the low-lying seawall shielded their advance from any view along the street that led to the gate.

The gate where I first saw Jin. The first time Jin saw me.

And.

Where we began.

The canoe slammed into the rocks and the savages were wading through the water, spears upraised. Someone whooped and they were over the walls.

And what happened next was not the Boy.

A Chinese guard running for the gate fell to the tomahawk as it slammed into his back.

Broken glass.

Screams.

A whistle.

The Chinese gathered about the gate to the inner city. The guards were waiting for orders. They raised their rifles as a pack of screaming Psychos raced into the streets. The guards opened fire. A few Psychos went down but the bloodthirsty tribesmen were on them, hacking and screaming above pleas for mercy.

The Boy wiped the blood from his axe and slipped up through the winding alleyways of the inner city.

He found gardens colored like dull jade in the steaming morning light. Mansions rose up into the fog. Birds sang above the far din of battle on the other side of the gate, on the far side of the wall.

He heard the distant high note of the Space Crossbow. MacRaven's Space Crossbow.

He smelled smoke and heard crashing wood, once delicate, splintering into shards.

He heard the gunfire beyond the walls.

The cannon roared in distant cracks.

He saw the shaven-headed man break from a stand of collapsing defenders as Psychos leapt the hasty barricade, spearing and cutting.

Shaven-head raced farther up the street and disappeared into the drifting blue gun smoke of the falling defenders. The Boy loped after him knowing the man would lead him to the rest; to all the killers, the slayers of Jin. And finally to their tall leader who smiled at him as the roof burned and Jin was dragged away and into the darkness.

Shaven-head raced up and into the quiet neighborhood of stately mansions that rise along the hill above the little city. Servants and the occasional woman peer out into the streets, their questions evident. He darted into a heady garden, crossed a delicate and ornate bridge made of teak. He pulled urgently at a paper door that led into a house, his voice shouting at someone within.

When the man, sweating, turns to cast a worried eye back at the falling defenders, he sees the Boy running hard up through the garden that surrounds the house.

Shaven-head pulls the screen aside and enters, disappearing.

The Boy takes the curving wooden stairs that lead through the garden and hacks the paper screen door to pieces. Inside he smells jasmine and his mind roars red with anger. Anger at Shao Fan, anger that he has carried her scent from the place of her hanging to here.

As if it were his to keep.

As if she were his.

A gunshot cracked sharply across the interior of the house.

In the central court within the house he found Shao Fan, whose pupils are wide above the barrel of a smoking rifle. He seemed not to recognize the Boy.

Shaven-head was dead, flung away like a forgotten rag doll, his arms covering his face.

Shao Fan retreated, running to a far door and throwing himself beyond it.

The Boy pulled his pistol, the cut-down rifle, from his belt and advanced through the courtyard.

The Boy heard his own feet, hard thumps on the soft wood of the walkway that led to the door. In the instant before he heard the gunfire that came from the far side of the door, he heard the metallic sound of a rifle breech being snapped back into place. The Boy threw himself sideways as the paper door erupted in splinters and acrid smoke.

The Boy charged through the screen, breaking what was left of it open with the tomahawk.

Shao Fan, eyes wild and wide, broke the breech of his rifle and slipped another long bullet into the barrel. The assassin snapped the breech back into place. In the space of the moment in which the assassin nodded to himself, assured that the rifle was ready to fire, and before he raised it to fire, the dull silver tomahawk appeared buried in his chest. He stared at the axe in stunned and wide-eyed silence, stared as if in the moment before, it had not been there, and in the moment after, it had always been there.

He continued to try and raise the rifle but his arms would not respond. He felt life leaving him all at once.

He was afraid. He realized how underappreciated this moment before dying was.

'If there were just more time,' thought Shao Fan, raising his head, looking into the eyes of the savage boy charging across his bedroom.

Pistol raised.

Mouth roaring.

There were tears in the eyes of this savage that Shao Fan now recognizes, as his vision surrendered to a closing black circle.

Be careful who you love.

And then the pistol erupted in the hands of the savage and Shao Fan was no more.

THE BOY PASSED through the rape of the last Chinese outpost. It was the same as Auburn and even worse, he thought, as if seeing it all from far away.

He passed the dead guards at the gate, stepping over them. Beyond them, another guard was moving and bleeding, crawling toward the water. Numbly the Boy passed on.

He found a small canoe and set out across the bay.

Alone, the work of paddling the canoe was hard.

His left side was weak. But he did not care about it anymore.

You'll do your work. Same as the other side.

The day was hot and he reached the far side, the southern end of the bay, by noon.

The air smelled of sage and dust.

Behind him, black columns of smoke rose in the north. He could barely see the colony. It was as if it never existed.

He climbed the low hills and found Horse.

They rode south along the old 101.

He was tired and his eyes felt too heavy, but he pushed on until twilight.

At dusk he built a fire near a long, flat bridge over a dry riverbed. He sat staring into the fire.

In time he heard the rider coming up along his trail.

The Boy took up his pack and loaded it onto Horse.

He scanned the murky darkness and saw only the dim outline of another figure.

The big bay horse clattered along the road and the rider drew up just beyond the reach of the firelight. The form was familiar. But the darkness hid everything. It was the hat, the Stetson hat, that gave away the rider, and then the voice, dry and friendly.

"Thought you might be asleep by now," said Dunn. "Figured you'd be all wore out after goin' ashore with them savages last night. All that blood and mayhem and fire makes a man tired, don't it?"

The Boy stood near Horse. The tomahawk was in his hand. The pistol, loaded, waited in the saddle on Horse.

Horse complained.

Easy, boy.

"Been following you since Auburn. Thought I'd catch up to you inside the Chinese base. But surprise, surprise, I found yer horse all staked out and waiting. Figured you'd slipped in among the crazies. But I knew you'd be back for yer horse."

The Boy said nothing.

"So I waited with my new pistols. Just like MacRaven's."

The Boy waited to hear the hammer of Dunn's guns being thumbed back.

Maybe he rode up with them ready to go.

Sergeant . . . ?

"Raleigh was a good man. Didn't deserve what you did to him."

Man's come a long way to talk, Boy. Figures he's earned hisself a speech. He won't do nothin' till he's got it all out.

"Him and I was partners long before you ever come outta . . ."

So whatever you got to do, Boy. Do it now!

"More'n partners in fact, he was . . ."

In the moment the Boy threw the tomahawk, he meant it. He threw it not just at Dunn, but at a world that was cruel and made of stone.

Don't let it go unless you mean to, Boy.

The aim was true but it caught Dunn's horse in the throat as Dunn jerked at the reins to protect himself.

The horse screamed.

Dunn fired.

Two thundering roars erupted from Dunn's pistols.

Two wet slaps.

The Boy felt the spray of Horse's blood across his face as he turned and reached for the saddle, a moment later spinning away from Horse, the pistol extended toward Dunn, who rode his mount into the earth, stepping off in one smooth motion, dropping his pistols for the wicked knife he kept on his belt.

The Boy fired and Dunn fell dead, back over his fallen horse.

Flung back.

Put down.

Dead.

The Boy turned back to Horse, who looked up at him from the road once more.

That Horse look of contempt.

Resignation.

Forgiveness.

Horse laid his long head down against the cracked and broken highway as his eyes closed finally, firmly, as if to say, I'm done with the world.

EPILOGUE

Where do you go now, Boy?

The road turned south and the days were long and hot. A narrow valley wound its way along the coastal mountains and would continue on all the way to Los Angeles. Or what was left of it now.

But in the days that followed, the Boy turned from the 101, limping, and climbed the smooth grassy hills to the east, soft gentle hills, rising and falling in waves of green grass.

He dragged his body over the hills, his left side aching, withered, refusing to go farther.

He continued on.

On the other side of the hills, he found a wide valley that stretched away in a brown haze to the south.

Who am I now?

He stood in the gusting wind atop the hills.

He continued down into the hot valley.

Ancient roads, ruptured and disintegrating, overrun by erupting wild growth, crossed from east to west. All else was dry and brown, hard dirt and sun-rotten dead wood.

Fires had crossed the valley and there remained little of what once was.

Rusty water towers, fallen and gouged.

Wild tangles of barbed wire.

Fallen walls of blackened stone.

He crossed the old Interstate Five and continued down into the heat of the valley.

The trees here would not grow. They were stunted and sickly and even the ground seemed either unnaturally dark or washed out and spent altogether. Thorns, of which there are many, grew in wicked profusions of ochre, sickly green or pus yellow.

In a village of adobe walls he found misshapen men and women. All of them were blind and dragging themselves along through the dirt. They ate from sickly stands of a dark green kale that gave off a foul aroma when they stewed it inside an old oil drum filled with brackish water.

They knew he was there and they searched for him, but their keening and sniffing in the dusty heat after his scent repulsed him and he went on into the silences beyond their village.

Stands of palm trees clustered in sinister groups as if talking about him and though their shade would be welcome, and maybe even their fruit, he went wide to avoid their dark and fetid clusterings.

In the night he slept in an old grain silo and thought that he should hear birds in its rafters or the bony trees outside.

He could not remember when he last heard the song of a bird.

He drank water from a standing pond because he could no longer stand the ragged dry trench that was his throat. He saw the footprints of the blind villagers in the hard-packed soil.

They too had drunk here.

Blind would not be so bad.

In the still water he saw a monster.

A monster with red-rimmed eyes that reflected no light, no life. A face and chest covered in blood and dried mud. Horse's blood. Muddy, knotted hair and a broken feather. Lips cracked and bleeding.

A monster.

He wandered south, following the twisting ribbon of the once-highway through a silent land of rust and scrub. He caught small things and felt little desire and even less satisfaction in the thin, greasy meals that resulted.

Who am I now?

Dry wood turned to sparks floating off into the night above his fire.

What is left to do and where should I go?

And there was no answer other than his own.

Nothing and nowhere.

In the day all was hot and boiling, dry and raw. In the night tepid warmth refused to surrender until long after the bloated moon had descended into darkness.

The thin road straightened and carved its way into southern mountains.

In the road signs he spelled Los Angeles.

He remembered Sergeant Presley calling it "Lost Angeles."

I should burn the map.

What good is it now?

Mission, not complete.

But he didn't and he continued on toward a crack where the road disappeared into the mountains.

At the last gas station in the foothills he spent the night.

There was nothing left to find here and there hadn't been for forty years.

In the gas station's emptiness he heard the grit of sand and glass beneath his feet. In times past, in all his wanderings with Sergeant Presley, he had wondered and even dreamed about the people of Before. What had they done in these places? There had been food and drink, beyond imagining, Sergeant Presley had explained bitterly, all on a hot day such as this, for people to stop and come in from the road.

He spelled I-C-E C-O-L-D S-O-D-A.

I was raised in places like this. It seems as though it should feel like home to me.

But it didn't.

And . . .

I don't care anymore.

That night, though he did not want to, he dreamed.

Dreams, who can stop them? Who can understand them?

He and Jin walked through the streets of a city. Up cobblestone streets where people live. Happy people. He turned to a fruit stand filled with green apples. It was a market day or a fair, and he selected an apple for Jin.

In that dreaming moment he understood the meaning of the name Jin.

Her name meant "precious." In the dream he was glad that he understood this now. It was as though he had found something rare and its ownership had caused his lifelong feeling of "want" to seem like a fading nightmare. As though he had recovered a lost treasure and it changed his future forever. As though his life, their life, would be only good now.

Now that he knew the meaning of her name, the dark times were behind them.

When he turned back to her, she was gone.

A happy villager, smiling, maybe the Weathered Man, told him she was over there, with the man's wife, looking at silk dresses for their wedding. And the smiling farmer handed him the green bottle of Pee Gee Oh full of bubbles, and they drank and the farmer encouraged him to laugh and be happy.

"It's all coming back," said the Weathered Man in perfect English.

And the Boy knew he meant the world from Before. That the days of road and ruin are coming to an end and that there would be homes and families now. That he and Jin would have a place in this new world that everyone was so excited about.

A place together.

He was excited. He wanted to find Jin and tell her about all the good things that are soon going to happen to them.

But his mouth wouldn't make the words to call out her name.

He searched the stalls.

He searched the roads.

It was getting dark in the dream and the market was closing.

"We'll find her tomorrow," said the Weathered Man. "Come home with us and stay the night."

Though he didn't want to be, the Boy was led home and the dream advanced in leaps and starts as the Boy watched throughout the night, looking out a small window, looking onto a dark street.

Waiting for Jin.

He could not wait to tell her that everything good was coming back again.

Soon.

In the dream he could not wait to hold her.

In the morning, the sun slammed into his weak eyes. Tears had dried on his dusty, crusted cheeks. His insides felt sore, as though they have been beaten with sticks.

He sat up and looked toward the road and the mountains.

It was real, he thought of the dream.

The road cut its way onto a high plateau, passing stands of oak and wide expanses of rolling yellow-green grass. In a high pasture he found sheep and a man watching over them.

The man waved at him from the field and the Boy turned off the old highway and into the field.

The sheep, maybe a dozen of them, wandered and bleated absently through the tall yellow grass of mid spring. Beyond the pasture, oak trees clustered at the base of a steep range of hills that shielded any view of the east and whatever must lie that way.

"Stranger, come and have water," called the man over the constant bleating of the sheep.

The man was rotund and dressed in a ragged collection of scraps sewn together. He carried a crooked staff and leaned on it heavily. His hair, gray, sprang from his head in every direction. His voice was a mere rumble of thunder and gravel.

"The road is hard," he said, watching the Boy drink the cool water held in a tin cup. The water was clear and sweet.

"It's a good spring here," said the shepherd when the Boy did not respond.

The Boy handed the cup back.

"I have wild apples near my camp; come and have some."

The Boy followed the man across the pasture and into a stand of wild fruit trees.

They sit in the shade, eating apples.

"Saint Maggie said that food leads to friendship."

The Boy said nothing.

"Who might you be, now?"

The Boy opened his mouth to answer. But he couldn't.

"Can you speak?"

The Boy shook his head.

"Then I'm sorry. The words of man are overrated. Saint Maggie again."

The shepherd took a crunchy bite from an apple.

"I speak too much."

Then, "That's why I'm here. I spoke too much when I shouldn't have. But I love to talk. Love to hear the sound of my own voice. And the sounds of others for that matter. I love talk."

There was more silence for a while.

"Still, my words are overrated."

"Will you stay, or are you determined to go on to the south?"

The Boy rose.

"You will find nothing worth having there!" the shepherd's voice rose in pitched urgency.

"You will find the worst of this world and the worst that the world that died had done to itself."

The Boy began to stumble toward the road.

"If you go west you will find life. Some. But in the south there is nothing but horror. Trust me, stranger!"

As an afterthought the shepherd said. "East. Don't go east into the desert. That is death for sure."

The Boy considered the high sun. Orienting himself.

He turned toward the east.

The shepherd looked at the Boy, eyes wide with amazement and then horror.

A high hill, speckled by a few gnarled oaks, rose up to the east.

The Boy began walking toward the hill.

The shepherd murmured, "No."

The tall grass brushed against the legs of the Boy and he could hear the shepherd hobbling behind him, breathing heavily in the still air.

"Stranger, don't go that way. I told you it was death."

They neared the base of the steep hill as the shepherd pursued the Boy.

"There lies a desert, and it will consume you. A wasteland. You will be no more. Saint Maggie said, 'We must do our best. We must live despite life. God will do the rest.' Stranger, you will find no love that way. Turn west and live."

The Boy fell to his knees and began to climb the hill.

The shepherd fell to his knees.

"I will pray for you, stranger. I will pray for you."

The shepherd was still praying, hours later, when the Boy reached the top of the steep hill and saw the line of hills beyond, descending into the vast bowl of the desert.

WHAT DO YOU find when there is nothing left, Boy?
The days were brutal and there was no water. The land fell into a furnace of burning hard-packed dirt and suffocating dunes.
You left me, Sergeant.
I had to, Boy. The world didn't need me anymore.
I needed you.
And someone, Boy, someday will need you also.
She's dead.
He fell to his knees and wept.
The flat desert stretched away in all directions.
Never give up, Boy. I told you. The world needs us.
You take everything with you.
It's too much, too much to carry, you and the broken places and the evil of the world . . . and what . . . and Jin.
He stumbled.
Then he crawled.
How many days?
But to think of them was to think of the pain of all his days.
And still he crawled through the days, deeper and deeper into the burning wastes.
There can't be anymore left of me. Tonight or tomorrow, and that would be the end of the whole mess that is the world, that is me.
In the night, the stars were cold and clear.
He watched them and thought of Jin.
I am done. There is nothing left in me with which to grieve.
He felt empty.
He felt hollow.
In the morning, the sun rose from a thin strip of light.
This is my last day.
You take everything with you.
He reached for the tomahawk.

It felt comforting. As though he had been loyal and faithful to it. As though it stood as a monument, a testament even, to all his loss and failure.

You take everything with you.

His left side would not move.

Curse you then, you never helped me in life and now you won't go with me to my death. What good have you ever been?

Then . . .

I'll drag you.

He watched the empty wasteland ahead and knew that he would die today somewhere within it.

Five days without water. That's the most a man, a person, can go.

He dragged himself forward.

Sergeant Presley.

Horse.

The bearskin.

The pistol that was once a rifle.

Where did you lose that?

I cannot remember. Somewhere in the poisoned valley.

The Chinese colony at Auburn.

Escondido.

The Chinese at Sausalito.

Jin.

It was a lie.

What?

He had trouble remembering. He was crawling through chalky sand. He had been for some time.

It's so hot now, but at least I'm not sweating.

I don't think that is good.

It depends on what you want to accomplish.

What was a lie?

That you take everything with you. That was a lie.

Oh.

Where are they now?

Sergeant. Horse. Jin.

How can you take everything with you when it is all gone?

I was lied to.

In the end, I don't even know who I am, where I came from. Who were my mother and father? What did it mean to be an American?

Sergeant Presley called me Boy.

The Chinese called me savage.

The savages called me Bear Killer.

All of it seemed to be something that never happened or happened to someone else, long ago.

Who am I?

Jin called you . . .

"Don't!" he croak-screamed into the dry expanse. "I can't take it anymore."

Hours later, crawling on his knees and pulling with his hand, dragging the side that would not work, he stopped.

He gasped, "Not much farther now."

You got to decide who you are, Boy. Not the world. Don't let people ever tell you who you are. Some people tell nothing but lies. So why ask 'em anyways?

Yes. I remember when you said that.

I'm saying it now.

His hand felt the hard, burning surface of a road.

You're dead.

I'm sorry about that, Boy. I never meant to leave you.

Tell me who I am.

I'm dead, Boy. Said so yourself.

Who am I?

Silence.

In the distance he heard a high-pitched whine and then a loud rumble beneath it.

He was alone in the middle of a desert plain, cracked and broken.

He laid his head down onto the hard dirt and felt it burn the side of his face as he closed his eyes.

My ears are buzzing. This must be death. It has been following me for some time. My whole life even. And now death is finally coming for me. What took you so long?

Who are you, Boy?

I don't know. I never did.

The roar and whine consumed everything. It grew and grew, filling up the expanse of the desert and the sky. Everything was now shadow and heat.

Did you expect to find her in death?

He heard footsteps.

I was hoping to. But I think I will find only death. Who am I to think I might find Jin again? The world is made of stone. Who am I that it should be any different for me?

Death bent down and touched the Boy's cheek.

Who am I? he mumbled to Death.

You should know who I am before you take me.

Or are you just a taker? A taker who doesn't ask.

The Boy opened his eyes.

Death was an Old Man, thin and wiry, gray stubble. His eyes sharp and clear and blue.

"Who is he, Poppa?" A young girl's voice from nearby.

"I don't know. But he needs our help. He's been out here for too long. He's close to death."

"I'll get some water, Poppa," said the girl, and the Boy heard the slap of shoes against the hot road.

The Boy began to cry.

Shaking, he convulsed.

Crying, he wheezed, begging the world not to be made of stone, begging the world to give back what it had taken from him.

"Who am I?" sobbed the Boy.

"I think he's asking, who is he, Poppa!" said the girl as though it were all a game of guessing and she had just won.

The Old Man held the shaking, sobbing Boy and poured water onto cracked and sunburned lips in the shadow of the rumbling tank.

"He doesn't know who he is, Poppa. Who is he?"

"He's just a boy," said the Old Man to his granddaughter, his voice trembling with worry and doubt.

"Who am I now?" sobbed the Boy.

The Old Man held the Boy close, willing life, precious life, back into the thin body.

"You're just a boy, that's all. Just a boy," soothed the Old Man, almost in tears.

The Old Man held the Boy tightly.

"You're just a boy," he repeated.

"Just a boy."

PART III

The Road Is a River

CHAPTER 1

Can you let go?

The Old Man is sick. The Old Man is dying.

His fever is high in him and the days pass long and hot, as though having no end to them. The villagers come one by one, and it seems to all of them that what's left of the Old Man will not be enough. Though there are no goodbyes, there are words and looks that mean just as much.

Yet she will not let him go.

"No, Grandpa," she says to him through the long days and even longer nights. "I need you."

Can you let go?

He has told the villagers as much as he can of Tucson through the ragged flaming trench that is his throat. The security of the Federal Building. The untouched mountain of salvage. The tank. The villagers are going there.

That could be enough. They have Tucson now.

He lies back and feels that swollen, fiery ache within every muscle.

Just rest.

Most of them, most of the villagers have gone on to Tucson and all that he has promised them of a better life waiting there. A new life, in fact.

Can you let go?

The Old Man is sick.

The Old Man is dying.

My wife.

He thinks of her olive skin.

Will I be with her again?

Soon.

He is glad he thought of her when the wolves were beneath him and his hands were burning as he'd crossed over the abyss. He is glad he still loved her when he needed to remember something other than the burning pain in his fingers.

"No, Grandpa. I need you."

The Old Man thinks, in the darkest of moments when it seems as if he is crossing from this life to the next, that there are things worse than wolves snapping their jaws beneath you as you pull yourself across an abyss while thinking of your wife.

And he can hear the worst.

What is the worst?

His eyes are closed.

His granddaughter, Emily—she is his best friend, he remembers—is crying.

"No, Grandpa. I need you."

And he is going. Almost gone. Fading.

He hears her sobs. Weeping. Weeping for him.

His failure to live just a little longer.

She needs him just a little longer. "Forever," she tells him.

The worst is when you imagine the grief of your loved ones after you have gone.

'When you are sick in the night,' he thinks, 'you imagine the worst. To hear my granddaughter in grief for me . . . that is the worst I can imagine.'

Can you let go?

'Not yet,' he thinks. 'For her I will stay just a little longer, and maybe I can die later when it won't matter so much. She still needs me now.'

That is the love of staying when you know you must go.

And the Old Man lives.

CHAPTER 2

What follows are moments.

Individual moments, each one like a picture. A photograph before there was digital. Just before the end. Before the bombs. Snapshots of the hot days that follow.

The Old Man lies in his bed. When his voice returns, he is surprised. He didn't even know it was missing, he'd been so many days gone to the wasteland. He tells them of Tucson.

He tells them of the tank.

The wolves.

The Horde.

Sergeant Major Preston.

When he is finished, he is so tired that his words merge into a dream of nonsense. When he awakes, he sees stars through the openings in the roof of his shed. He hears the voices of the villagers outside. He feels his granddaughter's tiny hand holding his old hand, and as he drifts back to sleep he hopes that he will not have that terrible nightmare again. The one in which he is falling and he can hear her.

No, Grandpa. I need you.

Snapshot.

It is morning. The cold wind blows across his face as they carry him out from his shed.

Am I dead?

But he can see his granddaughter. She is holding his rucksack, the one from the tower in Tucson, stuffed with the treasures that were once lost and now found.

They are taking me out to bury me.

"The book is for you," he hears himself mumble across cracked lips. His granddaughter turns to him and smiles.

I love her smile. It is the best smile ever. There is no good thing like it. Maybe her laugh too.

"I have it with your other things, Grandpa. Right here." She pats his rucksack proudly.

All the villagers above turn and smile down at him hopefully.

The sky beyond them is gray. It is still monsoon season.

"We're taking you to Tucson now, Dad," says his son who has now bent down to adjust the blankets high about the Old Man's thin neck. "Hang in there, Dad. You're the last. We're leaving the village for good."

Sadness overwhelms the Old Man and then he thinks of his grand-daughter and her smile as weapons against the darkness. Against a dragon that is too much for any mere man. He thinks of her perfect, lovely, best ever smile as sleep, fatigue, and a tiredness from so many days in the wasteland overwhelm him.

Her smile will keep the nightmare away.

Snapshot.

The red desert, east of Tucson.

We must be near the Y where I found the staked-out bodies. The warning the Horde had left. Please . . .

Snapshot.

He feels her hand.

It is a darkness beyond anything he has ever known.

Like the night I walked after the moon had gone down. The night after the motel.

It is quiet. Thick and heavy. Familiar.

He wakes with a start.

He is back in the office. The office where he found the last words of Sergeant Major Preston. He is lying in his sleeping bag.

I never made it back. I've been so sick I've stayed here too long.

In the hall outside he hears voices. A bright knife of light cuts the carpet on the floor.

"Dad?" says his son.

"It's me," replies the Old Man.

"Are you okay?"

Am I?

"Yes."

"Are you hungry?"

If I am, it means I am well and that I'll live.

"Yes."

"I'll get you something to eat. Be back in a few minutes."

"Thank you."

And he falls once more into the pit that almost took him and he does not have time to think of her, his granddaughter, or her smile. And so the nightmare comes and he has nothing with which to defend himself.

The snapshots fall together too quickly and soon become a movie.

He sees the blue Arizona sky, wide and seemingly forever, play out across the high windows. For a long time he watches the bright white clouds come and grow across its cornflower blue depths.

He hears an explosion. Dull, far away. It rattles the windows of the building. When he stands up and moves to the window, he sees a far-off column of black smoke rising out over the silent city. For a long time he stands watching the smoky, dark column. He feels unconnected and shaky. Occasionally he sees his fellow villagers moving down a street or exiting from a building. It is too far away to tell who each one is. But they are dressed differently than he has ever known them to dress. Almost new clothing, found here in this treasure trove, not the worn-out and handmade things of their years in the desert.

Time has resumed its normal pace. The sickness and fever fade. But not the nightmare. The nightmare remains, waiting for him.

What will become of us now?

Down the street, he sees a man pushing a grand piano out onto the sidewalk.

CHAPTER 3

Sam Roberts leans his blistered head against the hot steering wheel. Every ounce of him feels sunburned and sickened. He'd torn off the rearview mirror of the dune buggy three days ago. He couldn't stand seeing what was happening to him.

The dune buggy rests in the thin shade provided by an ancient building, part of some lost desert gas station. Now that he's running on electric, the gas within the buggy's small tank is useless, dead weight now that he has escaped. He'd only needed it for speed in the brief run through the gauntlet of crazies lying in wait outside the blasted main entrance of the bunker.

The sun hammers the dry and quiet landscape of hard brown dirt, blistered-faded road, and sun-bleached stone. The yawning blue of the sky reaches away toward the curvature of the earth. There is no wind, no movement, no sound.

Sam Roberts has spent the morning allowing the solar cells to recharge while patching the large rear tire. His sweat pours through the radiation burns on his skin. He feels it on his head where there was once hair. His eyes are closed. Even with the visor down, it is too bright at noon.

'But I can't drive in the dark,' he thinks.

He was born underground.

He has lived his entire life, other than the last three days, underground.

He is dying of severe radiation poisoning.

He is twenty-three years old.

He is a captain in the United States Air Force.

He moves his bleeding fingers to the ignition. The act of grasping the key and simply turning it feels as though it will kill him.

"I was dead the moment I left," he says to the dry air and the southern nothingness he must find his way through. "I was dead the moment someone turned on that radio station."

He laughs to himself and begins to cough and that leads to the rusty blood he spits into his glove.

He looks at the charging gauge. The plastic cover is melted. Even the seat vinyl is peeling.

He moves his hand to the switch that will engage the electric motor.

"Well, I've got lots of solar. Lots of that . . ." And he stops himself because he knows he will laugh again.

CHAPTER 4

The Old Man has been up for a few weeks. In the mornings he tries to help at breakfast. Tries to see if anyone will need assistance with their various projects. But when he does, they smile politely and tell him he needs to rest more. Then they disappear when he is not looking.

He returns to the office and watches them working in the streets below. Fixing up their new homes, salvaging in the afternoons farther out.

He takes walks at the end of the day. After the heat has given its best to destroy them all. He always walks first to see where his granddaughter is working. He tries to remember how thirteen-year-old girls spent their time when he was her age. In gymnastics and soccer and . . . boys? No, that was later. Or maybe I didn't notice when. Finally, he decides, maybe they, all those long-gone girls from his youth, didn't want anyone to know how they felt about boys when they were just thirteen years old. Her father, his son, is trying to start a farm. Their community will need fresh produce. Most of her work is done by the early afternoon and together they walk the streets and see what each neighbor has done that day. A new fence. A newfound treasure. A new life.

Look what I found today . . .

An antique double-barreled shotgun with scrollwork engraving.

Fifty feet of surgical tubing.

This beautiful painting. Each day at breakfast there are fewer and fewer of the villagers who come and eat in the dining hall at the Federal Building.

They are making their own lives now behind their fences in the houses where they store their treasures rescued from Before. Not like in the village where we all ate together in the evenings and the sky was our painting.

At night he returns to the Federal Building. The sentry gun, waiting on its tripod, its snout pointing toward the entrance, waits like a silent guard dog. He pats it on the head-like sensor, like he might pat a friendly dog, and returns to his room.

For a while he listens to the radio, their little station that Jason the Fixer had up and running in a day, playing the old programmed music from Before. Even Jason cannot figure how to change that. But, if they ever need to, they can interrupt the program and broadcast a message. Each night one of them takes a turn at the station. Watching the ancient computers. Just in case there is an emergency. Then all the radios in all the new homes of the once-villagers can be used to summon help.

We can still help one another that way. We are still a village.

So the Old Man leaves the radio playing softly through the night just in case there is some kind of emergency that will bring them all together again. Every so often he hears the voice of the villager whose turn it is to watch the station, saying something as the long dark passes slowly into dawn.

And he reads.

He has read the book once more.

He is glad he had his friend in the book, Santiago, there with him out in the desert. When he reaches the end of the book he is glad for Santiago, that he made it home to his shack by the sea and for the boy who was his best friend. Again.

He thinks of his granddaughter.

She is my best friend.

But for how long?

Girls become women.

He remembers being sick and hot and hearing her voice calling him back from wherever he was going.

If I think of the sickness, I will think of the nightmare and then it will come while I sleep and I will wake up to get away from it.

So he goes down to the library.

He tries to pick a new book. But so many of the modern books, books from right before the bombs, seem like they might remind him of people and times that are now gone.

I'll pick a classic.

How will you know which is and is not a classic?

The Old Man stands before the quiet, dusty shelves inhaling their thickness and plenty, then sighing as the burden of choice overwhelms him.

A classic will be something from a time I never lived in. That way I will not be reminded of war and all that is gone because I never knew it. I'll read about the Roaring Twenties as told by a southerner or the London fog of Dickens or even the Mississippi as it was.

I have not seen a river in forty years.

Nothing with war.

In a corner between other books he finds one that he knows is a classic, knows it from school though he cannot say whether he'd ever read it. But he knows it was a classic.

He takes it back to the office, his room, and lies down on his sleeping bag. He watches the night sky for a moment and listens to the radio playing softly on the other side of the room.

It will play all through the night, even while I am asleep. Like Before.

He opens the first page and begins to read.

CHAPTER 5

Sam Roberts had a few more hours to live.

He wanted to know how much radiation he'd absorbed in escaping the front entrance of the bunker, but the dosimeter had stopped working by the time he was clear of the massive door and the freaks in front of it.

Still, he would've liked to know how many rads he'd soaked up.

It was just before dawn.

He could see the lights of Tucson far off to the west, lying on the southern side of a gigantic black rock that heaved itself up from the desert floor. The pinpoints of light twinkled softly in the rising pink of first morning like tiny jewels set amid gray pillars of sun-bleached stone.

Earlier, outside Hatch, a small town that had collapsed into the drifting sands and rolling weeds, he'd stopped to scribble a message onto a piece of paper, his hands badly shaking.

'Wouldn't that be something,' he'd thought. 'To come all this way and I'm too sick to tell them the message.'

As he threw up again he tried to say, "Help me!" But no sound came out. His voice box was gone. Either scorched by the acid his stomach seemed to churn up, and that came out of him constantly, or fried by the radiation of two high-yield Chinese nuclear warheads deposited at the front door of his lifelong home forty years ago. Either way, he would never speak again. So he wrote the note. Then he added, *Please stay away from me. I'm contaminated with radiation.*

He watched the far city. Morning light opened the desert up to Captain Roberts. There were so many different colors. The golden sand. The pink rock. The blue sky. The red earth.

'Best day of my life,' he thought. 'And I saw it all at least once' . . .

He blacked out.

When he came to, it was noon.

His heartbeat pounded throughout his entire body, but it was slow and intermittent. Captain Roberts reached into his chest pocket. He took out the emergency syringe and jammed it into his thigh. His vision cleared as his heart began to race.

'Last one,' he thought.

On the horizon, Tucson looked gray amid the shimmering heat waves that rose above the road. Already his vision was starting to blur. 'These injections aren't lasting long,' he thought.

He started the engine. The cells were below half full. He'd forgotten to set them to charge. I don't know if it's enough, but it's all I have.

He took a safety pin out of the medical kit that lay sprawled across the passenger seat. He'd done a bad job of bandaging his own blisters. He pinned the message to his jumpsuit. 'All I gotta do now,' he thought, 'is get close enough for them to find me.'

He gunned the engine and felt the acceleration press what was left of his thin body backward. He did his best to keep the dune buggy on the road with what little time he had left. The road shifted and swerved in the heat and sweat as his dying heart thundered out its last.

It was tough going. But he did his best.

CHAPTER 6

The Old Man walked to the wide window of the office. Below he could see the villagers congregating in the park. Or what had once been a park. Now someone was hard at work down there preparing the ground for crops. That someone worked with a hoe, turning the bleached and hard, forty-year baked mud over into dark soil, waiting and ready for rows and eventually tiny seeds.

The Old Man watched them for a long while. When the discussion seemed to grow in intensity, he closed the book and took the elevator down, passing the silent sentry machine-gun dog, patting it as he always did, and walked through the lobby and out into the heat of the afternoon.

It will be a hot summer this year. It's good we have these buildings. If it gets too hot I can sit down in the bottom of the garage near the tanks and it will be cool there. I can even read if I bring a light.

When he reached the discussion, he saw his son and the others debating over something one of the younger villagers had found. A man he remembered once being a boy was now waving a piece of paper in the air.

"What'd you do with him?" asked a kid the Old Man thought looked more like his father, who had not survived the first ten years, and less like his mother, who had.

He's not a kid. He's a man now. Even though they were all once children. They are men and women now.

Time is cruel that way. It erases us. It erases the children we once were.

"I left him there!" whined Cork Petersen.

That's his name. We'd called him "Corky" and he would follow Big Pedro and me sometimes. Now his name is Cork.

Time.

"He's dead anyways," mumbled Cork.

The Old Man sidled up behind his son.

"Dad," his son acknowledged without looking at him.

"What's all this . . ." began the Old Man, and the words he knew he must use to complete the sentence escaped and ran off into the desert.

His son looked at the Old Man and then turned back to the discussion, which seemed to be about the piece of paper Cork Petersen held on to.

I'm not old. I just couldn't . . . I just got lost in the middle of my words. It's because I am still recovering from the sickness that almost took me. But I am not old.

"Cork Petersen found a dead man in a dune buggy out in the desert," whispered his son.

The Old Man waited.

"I say we do nothing." It was Pancho Jimenez. If anyone led the village now, it was Pancho. He had been the strongest and best at salvage in recent years.

I remember him also as a boy.

"But the note says . . ." grumbled Cork.

"Take care," interrupted Pancho. "Take care of what the note says." His voice was enough to silence the discussion as they all turned toward him. Ready to listen.

When Pancho had their attention, their full attention, he began.

"You saw the bodies along the way. You heard the Old Man's tale of the desert. Those savages called the Horde."

Everyone turned to look at the Old Man for the briefest moment. Uncomfortably he smiled back at them and saw in some a look of pity.

They're surprised you're still alive.

I also am surprised.

"We've found paradise." All eyes were again on Pancho as he continued to speak. "We have found paradise now. We're planting our gardens, late, but we are planting. We have houses, each family their own. We have an entire city to salvage from. And what happens? A man dies in the desert.

Is that any of our concern? No, none at all. We have much to be concerned with and little time in which to accomplish those things we must."

"But the message is for us," interrupted Cork.

Pancho, patient, strong, confident in who he was, smiled.

"And that, Cork, is who we must take care of. Us."

Everyone began to murmur.

The Old Man turned away, looking down the street, searching for his granddaughter.

Maybe I can find her and we can go salvaging in the afternoon. That would be fun if I feel up to it.

"There are worse than those people called the Horde," proclaimed Pancho above the clamor.

"How do you know that?" someone asked.

"How do you know there isn't?" replied Pancho.

Quiet.

"We do what that note says and we open a door we may not be able to close."

Quieter.

"Even now," continued Pancho, "you are saying to yourselves 'we have weapons, the tanks, some guns left by the Army.' Well, you don't have an endless supply. And do you want to go down that road? Do you want conflict? No, none of you do. You want tomatoes and lemons and homes just like I do. Right now, our greatest weapon is not the Old Man's tank or our few rifles. Right now our greatest weapon is our invisibility. Whoever sent that man wants to confirm that we are here. They picked up our broadcast, which I advise we turn off immediately, and now they want to know who we are and what we're doing out here. If we respond to that message, who knows who we'll be talking to. All I ask is that you consider this. The world isn't a nice place. It hasn't been a nice place for a long time. We answer that message and we would be unwise if we did not expect the worst. In fact, we would be stupid."

"Says they need our help," said Cork.

"We need help!" shouted Pancho.

More murmuring. A few comments. Cork handed the note to Pancho in defeat. Villagers drifted away. Only a few remained, all in agreement with Pancho. In agreement as he tossed the note into the wind and the paper fluttered down the street.

And then they were all gone and only the Old Man remained, invisible and unconsidered.

He went to pick up the note.

On it was written a message.

To whomever is operating the radio station at Tucson. Please tune your receiver to radio frequency 107.9 on the FM band and send us a message so that we can communicate with you. We are trapped inside a bunker and need help. Beneath that, *Please stay away from me. I'm contaminated with radiation.*

CHAPTER 7

That night the Old Man snuck out of his room and made his way to the radio station the villagers had set up inside the Federal Building.

"Are you sure, Grandpa? Are you sure we should try to contact them?"

He raised a finger to his lips.

His granddaughter nodded, excited to be playing the game of not being found and doing things that should not be done in the dead of night while others slept.

When they reached the radio room they found it unlocked. Inside all was dark. The equipment had been turned off. The Old Man closed the door behind them and for a moment the two of them listened to the silence.

The Old Man switched on his flashlight.

"How does it work, Grandpa?"

"Power. Electronics require power. So we must find the switch or the button or the toggle that will turn it on."

"Toggle," she pronounced and laughed softly.

The Old Man searched and just when he had given up ever finding out how to turn on the power, his granddaughter's thin hand darted forward.

"Is this it, Grandpa?"

The Old Man didn't know if it was.

"Do you want to try it?" he asked.

She nodded.

"Okay then. Try it."

She hesitated for a moment and then with only the confidence that the young possess in their movements, she flipped the switch. Soft yellow light rose behind the instruments. Green and red buttons illuminated. There was a faint scent of burning ozone.

The Old Man watched power course through the ancient technology.

After the bombs I never thought I would see such things again.

He found the frequency keypad and typed in the numbers from the slip of paper.

"Grandpa?"

The Old Man stopped.

"What if . . ." She hesitated and began again. "What if my dad and the others are right?"

The Old Man could hear the worry in her voice.

"They are right."

"They are?"

"Yes. They are. But that doesn't make it right to do nothing."

"I don't understand."

"It's right to be afraid. It's right to be afraid of what you don't know. What could hurt you, you should be afraid of that, right?"

"Yes."

"But sometimes you have to do a thing even if you are afraid to do it."

"Because it's the right thing?"

"Yes, and because the world has got to become a better place."

For you to grow old in.

"Okay then, Grandpa. We'll do it."

"You're very smart. And brave too."

"You're brave, Grandpa. Like when you were in the desert."

"I was afraid too."

"But brave also."

If you say so.

"So do we do this? Do we try to help whoever sent the message?" he asked her.

The young girl watched the power coursing through the machine as buttons lit up and needles wandered and settled. The Old Man watched her eyes. Watched her reach a decision.

"Yes."

The Old Man hit ENTER and a green button lit up. Stamped in black letters upon it were the words "Active Freq."

The Old Man moved the speaking mic close to his mouth.

"What do I say?" he asked his granddaughter.

She reached forward and pointed at a button.

"You have to push this when you talk."

"How did you know that?"

"I've watched others."

Of course you did. Nothing escapes you.

"All right, then, what should I say once I push that button?"

She touched her tiny chin with her thumb and forefinger, which was her way of thinking and was a gesture he remembered her first making when she was only three turning four.

"Tell them, 'we are here.' "

"Just that? 'We are here'?"

"Yes, just that."

The Old Man cleared his throat. He moved closer to the mic again and this time took hold of it. His finger hovered over the button his granddaughter had indicated he should push.

He pressed the button.

"Hello," he began. He looked at his granddaughter. She nodded.

"We are here," said the Old Man.

"Let go of the button now, Grandpa," she whispered.

They waited.

And then they heard the voice.

"Who am I speaking with?" The voice was a woman. Older. But clear and crisp. A voice used to giving commands and having them obeyed.

"Us," said the Old Man who had needed to be reminded that he must touch the button to reply.

"All right," said the voice cautiously. "Are you operating the radio station that just went active a few weeks ago in Tucson?"

"Yes," replied the Old Man. "Who are you?"

"My name is Brigadier General Natalie Watt. I'm the commander of forces at Cheyenne Mountain Complex and we need your help. We're trapped inside our bunker and we need to get out very soon."

The Old Man and his granddaughter looked at each other in the thick silence of the radio room.

"Are you still there?" asked the General.

"Yes."

"Can you help us?" she asked.

Pause.

"Yes."

"Will you?"

Pause.

"Yes," said the Old Man.

CHAPTER 8

The Old Man watched from the high window as his granddaughter slipped back through the quiet streets of Tucson to her family's home. It was well after midnight.

If I go on this journey, I must go alone. It is too dangerous for her to come with me.

He thought of the route. All the way into California, then back to Nevada, through New Mexico, and up to Colorado Springs.

It is over a thousand miles. The tank can only hold two hundred and sixty-four miles' worth of fuel according to General Natalie Watt. She said I could scavenge. Tanks can draw fuel from many sources. Even kerosene. There are no guarantees of fuel and then there is the radiation. Well, that would be why you need to go to California for the extra gear. And after I cross all that desert, I am to aim a laser at the back of a mountain surrounded by unknown enemies. A Laser Target Designator. And who are these enemies? The General doesn't know. She only knows they are trying to tunnel into the bunker and that when they do, they will flood the complex with radiation and kill everyone inside. They only opened the main door once so that the dead man, Captain Roberts, could drive his dune buggy out of the complex.

There is too much for just an old man like me to think about. This is too much for just me.

A one-way trip, my friend. He'd volunteered.

General Watt said the radiation is so bad at the front entrance that

Captain Roberts probably absorbed a lethal dose in just the few minutes it took him to drive away. So I cannot take my granddaughter with me to such a place.

THE OLD MAN watched the night.

In my nightmare she is crying for me. I am dying. Just like I almost did after the last time I went into the wasteland alone. She is crying and there is nothing I can do to make it better. The last thing I will ever hear is her grief for me.

It's just a nightmare, my friend, heard the Old Man as though his friend from the book were with him and they were discussing some problem of fishing or salvage together.

But it is my nightmare.

Everyone dies. What would you have her do? Laugh about it? Of course she will weep.

I was hoping it would be later. When she has her own family and everyone is tired of me. When I have become such a burden to them all that they will be glad to see me go. Then, that would be a good time to die.

She will still cry for you.

Of course.

The Old Man felt the night. Felt its emptiness was only a lie and that all the world and the places and dangers hidden in it were waiting to devour him.

I need to leave soon. In the dream she says, *No, Grandpa. I need you.* It's terrible. I never want to disappoint her. I never want to hear her say those words. I never want her to have to say them. Is it too much to ask to just fade away and have no one miss me until I've been gone for a long time?

And yet you must leave, my friend. Soon.

Yes. If I leave when no one is watching, just as I did last time, then I will not hear her grief.

Still, you will know. You will know she'll say that which you do not want to hear. And even if you don't hear her, in your heart the nightmare will lie to you and tell you that you did all the same.

Yes, that is the thing about nightmares. They embrace us when we are vulnerable, telling lies that seem very real. Like an older child who teases a younger child by making the child believe things that aren't true.

In our nightmares we are all children.

The Old Man looked down. In his nervousness he had picked up his copy of the book. The one he had read for those forty years in the desert. The one with his friend inside.

The Old Man settled into his sleeping bag. He held the book in his hands and watched the ceiling.

So we will go together, my friend?

Yes.

The Old Man listened to the soft howl of the wind outside the large windows.

Soon I will be asleep and tomorrow all this might have just been a nightmare. Things will be different by the light of day, right, Santiago?

They are trapped in the bunker, my friend. They need someone to come and help them.

Yes.

She said she was going with you.

Yes.

And you must leave soon.

Yes, that too.

CHAPTER 9

The Old Man gathers the supplies he will need. There are only a few people inside the Federal Building now. Most have staked out homes and are busy salvaging throughout Tucson. Hours pass before any one person might encounter another in a city so large and the villagers so few.

There are only eleven rounds left for the main gun.

But there are the smoke grenades still in their canisters alongside the turret. You could use those when you need to run away from trouble, my friend.

Yes, Santiago, what I don't think of you will, my friend from the book. Yes.

He takes a large map that covers all the places he must go and folds it down until it fits in his pocket. He takes a hunting rifle and two boxes of ammunition. Canned and packaged food. Plastic drums full of water. He places his crowbar inside the tank.

When his granddaughter finds him in the late morning, he is exhausted and sweating from his efforts. She takes hold of the box of food he has been carrying and together they take it down into the depths of the garage and to the tank waiting in the darkness.

"When are we going to leave, Grandpa?"

"I don't know. I haven't made up my mind yet."

They went ten more steps toward the tank.

"Grandpa, are we going to leave tonight, or in the morning, or when?"

"I'm not leaving tonight," says the Old Man. "I'm too tired."

"That's why you need me, Grandpa."

He looked at her for a long moment.

I need you more than you'll possibly ever know, not because I can barely do it with the hoist and winch, but because you are the most important person in the world to me.

"That's why," he said simply and turned to check the heavy straps they'd used to secure the fuel drums to the side of the turret.

The tank is loaded by nightfall. She takes the keys and stuffs them in the pocket of her cargo pants.

I'll get another hundred miles out of these drums at best. Taking her would be the most selfish thing you could do.

It would seem so, my friend.

"If you go without me, I'll follow you, Grandpa."

If I keep her with me, then maybe the nightmare will be powerless to harm me.

Do you think so?

Yes. And I hope so too.

"All right."

"All right what, Grandpa?"

"We'll leave in the morning."

And maybe in the night I will just leave without her.

"Why not now, Grandpa? You drove most of the route we'd cover tonight in the dark last time."

I'm tired.

Do you think you will actually sleep tonight?

No.

Then maybe it's better to be done with the waiting. You know what you must do. Now do it, my friend.

I feel like I haven't thought everything through.

Did you the last time? Did you have any idea what you were getting into the last time? And yet you survived.

Barely. And now I'm even considering taking her with me. Do you want the truth?

Yes, my friend. Always.

Besides not wanting the nightmare to torment me . . . If I admit to myself a truth I do not want to hear, then yes I am taking her with me because I feel too weak for this. Not as strong as I was Before. The others should do this, but they won't.

Those people are trapped.

The Old Man sighed.

"Climb aboard then," he said to her.

Her face, tiny, elfin, perfect, exploded in a brief moment of joy and was quickly replaced by determination as he helped her up onto the turret.

After all, we'll be inside this thing. What can possibly hurt us?

"Thank you, thank you, thank you, Grandpa."

Only the young are excited about going anywhere.

Maybe it is because they are too willing to believe in what they will find where they are going, my friend. That something good might happen at any moment. Expecting it simply must.

"You must do everything I say, no matter what. Promise me you will do that."

"I will, Grandpa."

"Promise?"

"I promise. And you have to promise me you'll never leave and go salvaging again without me, Grandpa."

"I promise."

Someday I will die and you will remember that I promised. Please forgive me when I must break that promise. I won't want to, but death will make me. I hope you'll understand then.

Inside the turret they strapped on their thick green helmets and plugged communications cords into their stations, the Old Man in the commander's seat, his granddaughter in the loader's station below him. He turned on the auxiliary power unit, the APU. He could hear their breathing over the soft dull hum of the communications net.

"I'm glad you're with me this time," he said and squeezed her shoulder tightly.

"Me too, Grandpa."

Her eyes shone darkly in the red light of the interior as she stared about at all the equipment. He started the main turbine and the tank roared to life in the dark garage.

"Here we go."

CHAPTER 10

In the night, the headlight of the tank flooded the streets with bright light. Only one woman, out late and coming home with a pushcart of salvage, saw them as they turned onto the overpass and headed north into the midnight desert. He expected someone, anyone, all of them maybe, to come rushing out and stop him. To save him from himself and his foolishness. But they passed only the woman with the pushcart and no one came out to stop them.

Are you really going to do this?

The Old Man looked down at his granddaughter. She was smiling as the tank bounced over the crumbling remains of the interstate.

It seems I already have.

The night covered them all the way past Picacho Peak, where the Old Man could no longer smell the rotting bodies of the Horde above the exhaust and heat of the tank.

But they are out there in the dirt and the scrub all the same.

"When can I see where we're going?" asked his granddaughter over the intercom.

"It's too dark and there is nothing to see right now."

"Here," he said. "Move to this seat below my knees and do not touch anything. It's where the gunner sat."

She unplugged her helmet cord, and after squeezing by the feet of the Old Man, she found herself looking out onto the desert floor through the targeting optics.

The Old Man drove on toward the fire-blackened remains of Gila Bend and felt they should stop, but he knew the road and knew their village was just another few hours beyond the charred dust of the place.

We can stay in our village one more night. At least it will be familiar.

When they arrived at the village, the Old Man shut down the tank and stood in the hatch looking at the collection of shacks in the darkness. He turned off the tank's headlight and waited to hear the sounds of the desert.

This is madness. In the morning I will wake up and take us back home. Maybe no one will have missed us.

"Grandpa?"

"Yes?"

"How will we get there?"

"Aren't you tired?"

They were rolling out their sleeping bags onto the floor of the tank.

"Not really."

"I suppose we will drive this tank as far as it will go. After that, we will walk."

"The lady said we needed to hurry."

"First we must find fuel at the old fort outside Yuma. The Proving Ground it was called."

It was quiet in the dark tank now as they settled into their bags. The Old Man left the hatch open, and through it he could see the stars above. He thought of closing the hatch but leaving it open seemed to him like a small act of bravery. As though he were preparing himself for other times when he might need more courage. As though giving into fear now would welcome an uninvited guest.

And it is still our village. There was no one here but us for all the years that we lived here and I doubt anyone's come along since.

"That's where you got the hot radio."

The Old Man thought of the desert and the wasteland and the radio that had sent him off on his own. For many nights as he recovered from the sickness, those days in the wasteland had seemed a dream or a story that had happened to someone who was not him.

I was free though.

And you were scared, my friend.

I was that too.

"We're never to go salvaging in the Proving Ground. It's too close to Yuma. Everyone knows what happened to Yuma, Grandpa."

The Old Man was drifting now, thinking of his days on the road and the heat of it beneath his huaraches.

"Was there really a bomb, Grandpa?"

"Yes."

"And you saw it go off?"

"I did."

"Then how can we go to Yuma for fuel?"

Almost asleep now, in fact probably just, the Old Man called as if from down a well, "The fort is far out in the desert, north of the city. I always told them it would be okay to salvage there. But its name was also Yuma and so they would not go."

Soon they both slept.

AT FIRST LIGHT, familiar birds they'd heard all their lives began to sing in the cool before the heat of the day. The Old Man, lying in the tank, looked up through the open hatch and watched the last stars disappear as morning dark turned into a soft blue above them. He slid silently from the tank while his granddaughter slept.

He walked the streets of the deserted village, his home for forty years, as morning washed everything in clear gold.

We should go back today. This was foolish to start with and it is even more foolish to go on. I was still sick and I got carried away. To go all the way with no promise of fuel is . . .

He came to his shack. He opened his door. Only the bed and the table remained. Everything was covered in dust.

What is expected of us is too much for just an old man and his granddaughter.

When he returned to the tank, his granddaughter was opening a package of food and kicking her feet on the side of the tank as she chewed, which was a thing she did often when she ate.

I cannot remember when I had so much energy to spare that I could kick my feet as I chewed and smile and think of the day as nothing but a waiting adventure or something to be explored.

"Maybe we should go back," he said standing in front of her.

She continued to chew.

"If we do, then we should call the lady and tell her we're not coming, Grandpa."

The Old Man paced the length of the tank looking for something he had no idea of.

"Would you be mad if we returned?"

"No, Grandpa. I understand. But you should call her. Tell her we're not coming."

"Are you sure?"

She nodded.

The Old Man climbed back into the turret, donned his helmet, and switched the comm channel button near the hatch over to the radio setting. He pushed the button on the cord and began to speak.

"General Watt."

A moment later the voice of General Watt was there in his helmet.

"Yes, go ahead."

"We . . ."

He paused.

Tell her. Tell her you've left and you're not coming all the way. Tell her you're giving up now.

"We . . . are beyond Gila Bend and proceeding toward a fort we know of north of Yuma. We think we might find some fuel there."

There was a pause.

"Thank you."

Her voice was tired.

"I wasn't sure if you were actually coming. I didn't think . . . just, thank you. I'm glad Captain Roberts's sacrifice wasn't in vain."

The Old Man lowered his head. Then he raised the mic to his mouth and said, "Save that until we make it there. We still have a long way to go."

His granddaughter's face, solemn as she considered the morning's breakfast, erupted in the smile he loved. She took off her helmet, put down her breakfast, jumped to the ground, and began to do cartwheels.

"So we'll go to the old fort above Yuma and look for some fuel," said the Old Man.

"I might be able to alter a satellite to search the Yuma Proving Ground for you. I'll allocate my resources immediately. I have limited access to the outside world, but we're not powerless down here," replied the General.

The Old Man thought of the satellite he had once seen in the night.

They are still up there.

"Anything would be helpful."

"I understand," said the voice of General Watt in his helmet. "I can still contact the automated systems of certain facilities. There may be more help along the way."

"Anything would be appreciated. To tell you the truth . . ."

Words refused to come.

His granddaughter disappeared off into the place where she had been born and where they had lived their entire lives until recently.

I thought we would always live here. I was happy here.

"I almost felt . . ." said the Old Man.

"Like it was too much?" the General asked.

"Yes," whispered the Old Man.

"I understand that too," said the General.

The Old Man felt tired. Felt like he could let go of a burden he'd never remembered picking up but had been carrying for longer than he could remember.

"I brought my granddaughter with me. She's just thirteen years old. I was afraid this would be too much for just the two of us."

"But you will continue?"

"Yes."

"If you weren't afraid, I'd be concerned you were some kind of idiot."

The Old Man watched his granddaughter run from one shack to another, flinging open doors in the morning light, dust motes swirling about her.

"I won't lie to you," said General Watt. "What you're heading into is very dangerous. If you turned off this radio and went home and never answered it again . . . I would understand. I have children and grandchildren too. But please don't."

"I'm sorry," said the Old Man.

"Don't be. If you knew my story, you would know that when I was . . . let's just say it was never considered possible for me to have children. But

I have them and they are mine now. I will do everything I can to save them. Sadly, I have done everything and it isn't enough to overcome the one problem we've faced since the mountain above us collapsed down onto our emergency exit. You sound like a good man. Maybe if there had been more like you back before the war, we wouldn't be stuck here now."

"I was only twenty-seven then," said the Old Man. Static rose like a sudden ocean wave cresting and then falling violently onto the shore.

"I know what I'm asking you to do is beyond . . . reason. But I have to. You are our last hope. My grandchildren's last hope."

The Old Man wiped a sudden hot tear of shame from his eye.

"Don't worry, we'll get you out of there," he said.

Static.

"Thank you," said General Watt just before a storm of white noise consumed her voice.

CHAPTER 11

The Old Man turned to look at the village one last time as it disappeared on the far horizon behind them. The desert, a sandy plain dotted by dry mesquite growing low and close to the ground, swallowed the village and replaced it with more, an endless-seeming supply of itself.

I will never see my village again.

He let the whispering roar of the turbine overwhelm his thoughts, disintegrate them, and turn them into fuel to be spat out the back of the lumbering tank.

You don't know that. Good things and adventures might be just ahead.

Like what?

The noise of the tank filled the Old Man's thoughts as he waited, trying to imagine what good could possibly come of this journey. He could think of nothing.

Rivers, my friend. Rivers that must lead to an ocean.

I cannot remember when I last saw a river. A river—to be on a raft and to float and to fish . . . that would be heaven. There are no rivers in the desert. Only riverbeds.

Maybe we will find a river and we can make a raft, my friend. She would like that.

"Grandpa," came her high voice over the intercom as they jounced off-road. The interstate was damaged and the outermost remains of the Great Wreck were beginning to clog the highway.

I wonder if my car is still here.

Of course it is, where would it have gone?

True.

Before him the Great Wreck, as they'd called it all those years, lay spreading in every direction. In the distance he could see where the two broken semis that had collided and overturned formed the epicenter. From there rusting cargo vans and sinking station wagons had tumbled away down the road or off into the nearby desert, torn to pieces by the remorseless forces of fearful momentum meeting sudden obstacles. Other cars, hundreds of others, had driven off into the thick sand, becoming stuck as still more and more vehicles, unseen from the Old Man's vantage point, had continued to hurtle themselves into the wall of destruction as they fled the nuclear fireball over Yuma. On that last long-ago day everything had been smoke and screams and rending metal and people rushing away to the east and the fireball in the west where Yuma had once been. Now it was quiet and rusty and sinking year by year into the soft piles of sand that were dunes marching east.

"Yes?"

"Why did you change your mind about going back?"

The Old Man maneuvered the left stick to avoid a rusting station wagon that had fallen backward off the road. The tank clipped the front end and crushed it before the Old Man could adjust their direction.

"Because they need our help and because we must always help one another."

"Even strangers, Grandpa?"

But the Old Man did not answer as he edged the tank closer to the massive destruction of the Great Wreck.

"Let's stretch our legs for a moment and see how we might get around all these old cars and trucks."

They walked a ways from the rumbling tank, heading toward the massive wall of rusting and smashed vehicles that had piled up just beyond the last valley.

It's like coming home . . . but that doesn't seem right does it?

No, it doesn't. But it all began here. Here was the day after. After what I had once been or was becoming. I can't even remember now. But it was here on that last day when my car died.

"What happened here, Grandpa?"

"Most of the people you know in the village, we all met here on the day of the bombs."

"Did you plan to meet? Like did you know one another before the world ended?"

Before the world ended. That must seem like a strange phrase to her. Strange because the world has gone on.

"No. We were just all here on that day. Or we met on the one that followed as we walked east away from the bombs."

"What was it like?"

The Old Man looked at the two semis around which most of the wreckage centered.

I remember all of us getting out of our cars, trapped by the wreck, turning to see the mushroom cloud rising in the distance over Yuma behind us. I remember a woman screaming and then crying. Men were shouting.

"There was ash and dust. Fires on the horizons. Everyone was afraid."

Like we'd done something wrong. Broken something that could never be replaced. Committed an unpardonable crime.

"Were you afraid, Grandpa?"

"I can't remember."

She laughed.

He took out the map he'd found in the library.

"We can't go into Yuma. It's too hot from the bomb I saw go off there. But if we cut through those plains off to the north, we should pick up the old road heading to the Fort. I found that radio along the road leading there."

"Can I drive?"

"Not yet, you're still too small."

"There's another compartment in front of the tank with a couch where you lie down with a handlebar like a motorcycle. I sat in it, Grandpa."

"Could you reach the pedals?"

"Sort of, yes."

"Soon, though. Soon."

"Yes, soon."

Rusting cars, bashed and torn, crushed by careening fear-driven freight-laden semis with drivers who had watched the world end in their rearview mirrors, remained, spreading across the blistered road.

Into the desert.

Underneath the sand.

Rusting destruction piled long ago during the end of the world.

CHAPTER 12

"This is General Watt calling."

"We're here," said the Old Man into his mic after a moment of fumbling with the communications system.

"I have some good news," she said as a static squall crested and then was gone.

The Old Man stopped the tank.

They were on a small rise far out in the bowl of the desert. Somewhere within all the brown dust ahead lay the Proving Ground, the military base north of Yuma the villagers had avoided simply because it shared the same name of another place they had all seen destroyed.

I feel I don't know everything I need to know about what we're doing. But what am I supposed to ask her? This person, this General, she could be keeping the truth from me. And the others, Pancho, they could have been right all along.

For now, you must play the game according to its rules, my friend.

Maybe I should turn back.

"Our installation keeps a record of all the communications we tracked before the nets went completely offline. I've conducted a data search and found that a convoy carrying JP-9 arrived in the Yuma Proving Ground a week before the city of Yuma was destroyed. There is a chance that you may find the remains of that convoy somewhere within the facility."

"Would this JP-9 be usable? It's been forty years," asked the Old Man.

"If it still exists, then theoretically, yes. JP-9 was a prototype fuel rushed into production in the lead-up to the war. The Defense Department officials foresaw the need for a long-shelf-life fuel replacement and ordered as much of it as they were able to in the months prior to the war. There were some concerns over its use, but at this stage, it might be your only option. Unless someone took the time to use fuel stabilizers and conduct an additive removal process, the chances of finding a completely airtight fuel source are highly improbable. Your only other option will be clean diesel or kerosene. Again, these are not optimal sources, but the M-1 Abrams Main Battle Tank uses a multifuel vehicle system."

"What will these tankers look like?"

"They resemble standard military fuel transports and there should be twelve of them. JP-9 had a projected eighty-year shelf life. Though this was never tested, reports indicate the lifespan was achievable."

Our whole journey depends on the word "reports."

"All right then, we'll try and find the tankers."

The Old Man listened to the tank, letting the massive turbine idle in its screaming high-pitched drone as he scanned the horizon once more with his binoculars.

There is no sign of the Proving Ground. We are nearing the end of our fuel. Soon, I'll have to pump our two fifty-gallon drums.

"Grandpa, below that mountain there's a sign sticking out of the ground. Maybe we should go and see what's written on it?"

It's a good thing she has come with me; I never would've seen that sign.

"I can't see the sign," said the Old Man. "Where is it?"

"See that mountain, the low one off to our left that's all shadowy and bumpy and rocky?"

"Yes."

"Right in there."

The Old Man found the sign through his binoculars but it was still too far away to read what, if anything at all, was still written upon it.

He took hold of the controls, pressed his foot onto the pedal slightly, and watched the terrain ahead. I have to keep the tank on the firmest ground. We cannot get stuck. If we do, there is no way to rescue the tank that I can think of right now.

Then maybe you will think of a way when you need to, my friend. Try not to worry about what has not happened to you. And may never happen at all.

"How did you see the sign?"

"I can make this target thing bigger with a dial on the side of it."

"I don't think we should touch those buttons. We don't want to make the gun go off."

"It also sees in the dark if you turn this knob," she continued.

"You're very smart. But we must be careful. We don't know every-thing yet. Still, you're very smart and I am proud of you. Much smarter than me."

When they reached the sign, the Old Man got down off the tank as his granddaughter watched him from the hatch she'd learned to open on the side of the tank. Again a new thing she understood about the tank and which he hadn't yet figured out.

The sign was sand scoured, and what words had once been written upon it were gone. But the Old Man could feel the hard remains of a road buried beneath the drifting sand under his boots. He took out his map and began to look around.

The Proving Ground must be that way. On the map they are north of Yuma.

There were people all alongside the highway that day, camped out, hoping to get to the airport, onto a plane, and flee. I remember the rumor that airplanes were waiting to take us all somewhere safe.

I remember wanting to believe the rumor was true, which is the ter-rible thing about rumors.

In his mind he could see Air Force One floating across the sky. Black smoke trailed from one of its engines, coming in to land one last time.

That was a long time ago.

Concentrate! That last day doesn't have anything to do with today. Today you must find these trucks that contain the fuel. If you don't find them, then you have failed.

The Old Man climbed back into the tank and checked the dosimeter.

The needle is still within the green, so we must be far enough away from Yuma to avoid its radiation.

Are you asking or hoping, my friend? Because all your hoping and asking depends on whether the weather compass that is your dosimeter still works.

They followed the mostly buried road as best they could. As it rounded the craggy hill his granddaughter had called a mountain, ahead of them ran the fading, spider silk line of a highway, and off in the distance, the Old Man could see buildings.

"Can you see those building through the target scope?" asked the Old Man.

"Gimme a second, Grandpa."

Suddenly the turret began to rotate as the gun barrel came to rest on the far horizon.

In every moment she figures out some new thing.

"Yes, they're brown and dirty. Low and flat."

"Do you see the tankers we're looking for?"

After a moment she said, "No. They're not there."

The Old Man waited, watching the tiny buildings shimmer in the heat of the fading afternoon.

"Do you see any people?"

"No. There's no one there."

THE NEEDLE IN the fuel gauge hovered just above empty when the Old Man finally shut down the tank amid the silent buildings being swallowed by the first low dunes of sand.

If we don't find these fuel tankers soon, I'll need to pump the drums and head back to Tucson.

He took his crowbar and exited the hatch stiffly, his granddaughter already lowering herself down onto the intersection they'd stopped in.

Flat, dust-brown uniform buildings from a different era stretched off in orderly lines down quiet, sand-swept streets. Murky windows hid what lay within. The air was dry and hot.

Signs and street markings had been scoured to meaninglessness. The outlines of once-lawns were everywhere. Within their borders, brown weeds withered under the final waves of the day's heat.

"Hello," the Old Man called out into the silence.

There was no reply and his voice was swallowed by the soft quiet of the dunes.

"It's spooky, Grandpa. I don't think anyone has been here for a long time."

They searched the small streets for any sign of the tankers. But there weren't any vehicles, of any kind.

Inside buildings they found dust-covered museums of life as it had once been. Coffee mugs forever waiting to be picked up lay next to piles of yellowed and desiccating paperwork on dry desks that felt sapped of any sturdiness they'd once possessed.

When the Old Man picked up a newspaper it came apart, and he was left holding only a few feathery scraps. He tried to read the paperwork without touching it. But anything meaningful was lost in a haze of military jargon that he could not understand. He scanned for the words "fuel" or "tankers."

There is no mention of either.

Outside, the day was turning to orange as the sun sank into the dusty west. Gray shadows threw themselves away from the flat military buildings. A light breeze came and shifted the sand a little closer to the surrendering outpost.

"So what do we do now, Grandpa?"

The Old Man stood in front of the largest building.

Probably the headquarters. They picked an idiot. They picked an idiot to come and rescue them. Remember the curse of the hot radio.

The Old Man walked back to the tank. He felt stupid and useless.

It isn't my fault the tankers aren't here.

"We'll camp outside tonight. It seems safe enough. In the morning, maybe we'll have a new idea."

"We're not giving up, are we, Grandpa?"

"No, we won't give up."

She seemed relieved and soon she was back in the tank handing out their bags and sleeping gear for the night.

"Can we have a fire?"

"Yes."

"A story?"

"Yes, of course."

"A ghost story?"

"I don't know any."

"I do."

"I don't like them before I go to sleep."

"Oh, Grandpa." She snorted and laughed.

Later, when their gear was out and they'd made camp in front of the ancient headquarters building, clearing a space along the broad sidewalk that ran through the ghost of the once-lawn, she said, "This is the best salvage trip ever, Grandpa."

"But we haven't salvaged anything yet."

"That doesn't mean it's not the best."

"Yes, you're right, it is the best."

They ate food as the stars began to appear, as the sky turned from orange to purple, then from purple to deep blue.

Night.

The Old Man watched, listening to his granddaughter talk about the tank. He watched for the satellite above. The one that General Watt was using to talk to them.

The satellites are still up there crossing the sky.

Like me crossing this land.

Which is something, if you think about it.

IN THE NIGHT, long after she had drifted to sleep listening to him tell about the time he had seen the fox walking down the old highway, he awoke. The fire was low. There is nothing left to burn but the weeds of this old lawn. Unless I want to pull the boards off these buildings, but the sound would wake her. Besides, the night is warm enough.

The Old Man rose.

Because the ground is too hard and I need to pee. And also because I am not sleeping.

Tomorrow we will have to turn back. Without fuel, it's just not possible to make it all the way. The tankers were most likely in Yuma, at the airport, when the bomb went off. Now, they are gone.

He tried to remember if he'd seen any such vehicles forty years ago on the last hot day of his country.

I can't remember. She will be disappointed.

He turned and crossed the ancient outline of the weed-choked lawn, hearing the dry crunch beneath his feet.

Why would the Army have lawns in the desert?

I guess that was the way the military did things. They imposed order and rules regardless of the situation and location.

They were crazy to try to grow grass in the desert.

But they did. As long as they had water they must've grown these lawns. The world was crazy then.

We were all crazy.

And then he knew where he would find fuel. Or at least he hoped to. Excited, he drifted back to sleep for what remained of the night as though he had found a missing puzzle piece or remembered something good that would happen. Excited that he would not disappoint her. Excited that the best salvage trip ever might go on for at least one more day.

The best ever.

IN THE MORNING they found where the military kept its gardening equipment. Ancient rakes, rusty shovels and time frozen hedge trimmers. Dust-choked oily lawnmowers forever resting in dress-right-dress formation waited at the back of a large dark hangar. And off to one side, an immense storage tank of military-grade kerosene.

The Old Man drew off a little of the kerosene in a coffee mug he'd found in an office where clipboards hung neatly on the wall. He took it back outside as his granddaughter followed with questions, unsure of his game.

"Will it make the tank go, Grandpa?"

"If it's still good, it might."

The Old Man took a match from his pocket. He had loaded up on matches for this trip, remembering the last three matches inside the sewers beneath the hangar the wolves had chased him into. He struck the match and dropped it into the fuel. It caught and made a heavy chemical smell erupt in gray waves of smoke.

THEY RODE THE lumbering tank away, leaving the dry and dusty military post to itself and the years that must consume it. Off to the west, sand dunes rose in the afternoon heat.

Soon the sand dunes will arrive here as they march across the desert. Then they will cover this place and the kerosene that still remains inside that big storage tank.

But I will be gone by then.

Now we must hope there will be other fuel sources along the road. We may not find our river, my friend, but in a way the road is like that.

And what ocean will it lead to?

That night, the Old Man dreamed that he and Santiago were on a wide sea, under a hot sun, watching the flying fish leap from the water. Waiting for the big fish they would catch.

CHAPTER 13

Ahead we will find places I once knew long ago and have forgotten since. And I can only imagine what time and the bombs have done to them. I can only imagine that my past memories have changed to present nightmares.

Yes, my friend.

The tank trundled down a long, dirty, brown slope. In the distance they could see a strand of Highway 10 cutting the landscape in two.

It too is still there.

His granddaughter, ahead in the separate compartment containing the driver's couch, steered the tank across the crumbling dirt slope. Often he needed to remind her to slow down.

I feel like we've gone off the edge of something. The edge of everything we've ever known. Did you feel that way, Santiago, as you pulled at the oars farther and farther out into the gulf, watching the color of the water deepen until it was dark and not blue? Did you too feel like you were going off the edge of something?

And yet I knew it all once and long ago.

Memories of the cities of the West began to come and stand around the Old Man like mourners near an open grave.

You must forget all this melancholy and think only of the facts. You have enough fuel to reach China Lake. If you don't find fuel there, then crossing Death Valley into Area 51, will be impossible. You must follow this road until you come to an old tactical outpost set up alongside the highway. General Watt told us we would find it there.

"GRANDPA, THERE'S SOMEONE on the road ahead."

The Old Man scanned the horizon.

Far to their right, in the direction they must go, he could see the dark silhouette of a human.

It stood, unmoving in the late heat of the day.

The Old Man continued to watch the unmoving man-shaped shadow far down the cracked road as the tank heaved itself up onto the old highway. His granddaughter maneuvered the tank to point west at his instruction. A mile off, the lone figure remained unmoving beside the road they would follow.

I wish I knew how to work these optics like she has already learned to.

"Can you tell me what he looks like?" he asked her.

He knew she would be using her viewfinder.

"He's tall," she said after a moment. "Long dirty hair. Maybe a salvager, but not like anyone from our village. Oh, and he has a hat."

His mind stayed on the words "Not like anyone from our village."

The Old Man felt a cold river of fear sweep through him.

"Out there."

And . . .

Too many "Done" things.

"Let's move forward. But don't stop unless I tell you to, okay?"

"Okay."

I am afraid of this stranger on the road. Why?

We know why, my friend; it's just that we're not always willing to be honest with ourselves when we must. It is better to admit that you are afraid now than to pretend you are not.

The dark man-shadow, before the setting sun, seemed to lean toward them and out into the blistered highway as they approached. As they closed the distance between them the Old Man saw the shadow revealed. Saw him clearly as one might see something dead beside the road and want to look away in that passing instant of speed. His face was gaunt. Sun stretched by time and all the years since the end of the world. All the years on the road.

Worn rawhide boots. Faded dusty pants. A long coat made of license plates stitched together. A thick staff he leaned on heavily, though his frame was spare. Two small skulls dangled from its topmost tip. He wore a faded wide and weak-brimmed hat under which shining hawk-like eyes watched the Old Man. Had watched since they'd first appeared, the Old Man was sure of that.

He's a killer.

The Old Man could feel the slightest decrease in their acceleration.

"No!" he shouted into his mic. "Keep going!"

The tank lurched forward, and as they hurtled past the Roadside Killer, the vessel of all things unclean, the gaunt man raised one bony arm from the sleeve of his license-plate mail coat and extended a claw-like hand that might have been a plea.

The Old Man knew his granddaughter would be staring, wide-eyed, as they raced past, throwing grit and gravel, drawing up the road behind them.

Do not look back.

The Old Man rose in the hatch, watching the highway ahead.

"Why didn't we stop, Grandpa? He looked like he needed help."

Do not look back.

"Grandpa?"

"Because," said the Old Man after a moment. "Because we must help those inside the bunker."

IT WAS LATER, in the early evening, beyond a fallen collection of wind-shattered buildings the map once marked as the town of Quartzite, where they buttoned up the tank for the night. In the dark they'd settled into their bags, feeling the tank sway in the thundering wind that had risen up out of nowhere late that afternoon.

"Why didn't we help him, Grandpa?"

The Old Man listened to the sand strike the sides of the tank and thought of some acid they'd once drained from a car battery to weaken the lock on a tractor trailer they'd salvaged.

The wind sounds like acid tonight.

"Not everyone needs our help."

"But some people, the people inside General Watt's bunker, do?"

"Yes, they do."

And I wonder if they truly do. How do I know this isn't some game, a complex game, to draw us all into a trap?

You don't know, my friend.

"How did you know the man today didn't really need our help?"

"I just did."

And how will I teach you to know such things when I am gone?

"So we only help those who really need our help, Grandpa?"

"Yes. Only those whom we can tell really need our help."

I will have to think of a better way to teach her to know how and when to help, but not tonight. I cannot think of a way tonight.

Soon she was asleep and the Old Man lay awake for a long time listening to the sand dissolving the tank, and when he slept he dreamed of the cities of the West and the stranger beside the road and serial killers and empty diners where there was no food anymore.

CHAPTER 14

"You're just two thousand meters away from the last known location of the tactical command post." General Watt's transmission was breaking up within intermittent bouts of white noise. "I have not been able to get a satellite with a working camera over the location. There are only a few operating satellites remaining, otherwise I might have been able to give you better data regarding the container's location."

They were passing through a wide sprawl of ancient warehouses that rose up like giant monoliths from the desert floor surrounding Barstow.

"What will this container look like?" asked the Old Man, hoping General Watt's transmission would be understood.

"Green . . ." Static. "Size of a box . . ."

The Old Man asked the General to repeat the description, but the electronic snowstorm he listened within contained no reply. The satellite she had been bouncing the transmission off had finally disappeared far over the western horizon. The General had told them she wouldn't be able to reach them again for another twelve hours.

The Old Man watched the silent place of massive box-like buildings. From this distance they seemed little more than dirty tombstones, but as his granddaughter maneuvered the tank up the road, he could see the telltale signs of time and wind. Metal strips had been ripped away in sections, as if peeled from the superstructure of the buildings. A place like this would have been an obvious choice for salvagers. But this is California. Everyone fled California when all the big cities had been hit. L.A.

before I'd even left. San Diego a day later. But there was no sign of the box General Watt said they must find.

And what is in this box?

The Old Man shut down the tank.

They were exactly where General Watt had said they would find the tactical command post. And somewhere nearby would be the container, but there was nothing. No command post.

Dusty, wide alleyways led between the ancient warehouses.

If it was a small box, what would've prevented someone from merely carrying it away?

Then it must be a big box, my friend.

"Maybe it's in one these buildings, Grandpa."

They left the tank, feeling the increasing heat of the day rise from the ancient pavement of the loading docks.

Inside they found darkness through which dusty shafts of orange light shot from torn places in the superstructure. The Old Man clutched his crowbar tightly, stepping ahead of his granddaughter. There is a story here. A story of salvage. If you tell the story, you'll find the salvage. He waited, letting his eyes adjust to the gloom. You know part of the story. The General told you that part.

The days of the bombs had begun. Los Angeles was gone. But the Chinese, which was news to me because that must have happened after Yuma, were invading the western United States. The military, the Third Armored Division, or so General Watt said, staged its forces here in the deserts of Southern California. Supplies were air-dropped in as well as tanks and soldiers. They would counterattack the Chinese on American soil.

Imagine that.

At least they were supposed to have. But what happened in those days of bombs and EMPs and the rumors that spread like a supervirus is not clearly known and all the General can tell me is what was known. What was known before the jury-rigged, EMP-savaged communications networks that were able to route traffic through the bunker at Cheyenne Mountain collapsed. What was known before everything went dark.

And after?

The success of the counter-attack?

The tanks and soldiers?

The Chinese?

During those first days as we walked east, away from the Great Wreck, I had thought the world had ended. But in truth we knew so little of the story because who really knew everything that was going on and how could they tell us as we carried our possessions in our hands along the highway. The world had gone on ending long after we thought it was dead.

Nothing is known clearly now, and it is no longer important on this hot day forty years later.

The important matter for today is to find a container that was air-dropped and went wide of the landing zone as soldiers and tanks readied themselves to meet the enemy. The container's GPS locator broadcast for years. But even that fading signal ended a long time ago.

"What's inside?" the Old Man had asked General Watt.

"I'll need to explain that later. I only have a limited time to communicate with you before the satellite I'm currently hijacking disappears over the Pacific horizon. Find the container and get it open. I'll explain what you'll need to do once you've obtained the supplies."

Why do I have the feeling bad news has made an appointment?

Because you are cautious, my friend. And right now is the time to be cautious. So if you are cautious, you are doing well.

If we were on the boat I dreamed of last night, Santiago, seeing the flying fish jump, watching our lines, waiting for the big fish that was like a monster to come up from the deep to fight him together, you would say such things to me when my confidence was low.

Confidence can work both ways, my friend.

Yes, there is that.

That is not important now. Right now you need to find this box, my friend. Later you can decide how you feel about the bad news that you fear might be inside.

There is a story here also. A story of salvage.

The Old Man searches the gloom of the warehouse and sees very little. He smells wood smoke and decay from long ago.

Dead animals. Dried blood. Huddled bodies. Decay.

"Go to the tank, please, and bring me back the flashlight," he whispers to his granddaughter.

When she returns, he scans the interior of the warehouse with the beam. Its light is weak and barely penetrates the dark. All batteries are old now in these many years after the bombs.

They walk forward into the gloom. She has brought a flashlight for herself also and he watches her beam move with energy, like her, never staying in any one place for too long, also like her. His beam is slow and searching. He finds the remains of the campfire in the center of the warehouse before she does. It was a large fire.

Around it are storage racks and iron beams, arranged as though many might sit and watch the fire through long winter nights that must have seemed unending and as though the entire world was frozen forever.

I know those nights.

I know those fire-watching nights.

I am always hungry when I think back on them and the howling wind that was constant.

You were very hungry then.

The whole world must have been hungry.

But there is no box here.

They search the building, even shining their lights into the high recesses of the fractured roof.

There is nothing.

In the next building, the centermost of the three, they find the remains of the same style bonfire, and she, his granddaughter, on the farthest wall, at the back of the massive warehouse, finds the drawings.

Taken in parts they are merely a collection of scribblings.

Stick figure people. A Man-Wolf. Slant-Eyed Invaders waving guns. Mushroom clouds. Stick figure people who wear the wide-brimmed hat. Like that Roadside Killer. Stick figure people with spikes that come from the tops of their misshapen heads. Many dead Spike Heads. The bonfire. The Hat People stare into it.

"Who are they, Grandpa?"

Her voice startles him in the gloom beyond the cone of light he stares into, trying to know the meanings of these scribblings.

"I don't know."

He follows the drawings from left to right and finds no mention of the container.

He finds they are a people. A people who wore hats like the one the

Roadside Killer wore. A people surrounded by decay who waited through the long winter after the bombs and stared into fire.

A people like his village. The same and different.

Mushroom clouds.

The Man-Wolf leads them all away.

Leads them toward the Slant-Eyed Invaders who wave guns and trample over other stick figures beneath their stick feet.

"I don't know," he says again, his voice swallowed within the quiet.

And he realizes he is all alone.

"Where are you?" he calls out.

From high above he hears her voice.

"I found a ladder, Grandpa." She is straining to pull herself up. "If it leads to the roof, I can look around and see where the box is."

He shines his light about and can see nothing of her.

His mind thinks only of rusted metal and snapping bolts that pull away from crumbling walls with a dusty *smuph*.

And falling.

A moment later he hears metal banging on metal and knows it to be the sound of a crowbar smashing against a door. The sound is a familiar cadence to him and reminds him for a moment of the comforts one finds in what one does. The music of salvage.

He shines his light high into the rafters and finds her against the ceiling.

She is so small.

She is so high up.

I regret all of this.

Her crowbar gives that final smash he knows so well, when the wielder knows what must give way will give way with the next strike, and a frame of light shoots down within the darkness, illuminating the Old Man.

"I'm through, Grandpa!"

No one will ever stop you will they?

"I'm going up, Grandpa."

Please be safe!

A few minutes later, the longest minutes of the Old Man's life, he can hear her voice shouting down into the darkness in which he stands.

"I see it, Grandpa! It's on the roof of another building. It's very big."

LATER, AFTER HER descent, in which he can think of nothing but her falling and knowing he will try to catch her and knowing further that both his arms will be broken and that it doesn't matter as long as he saves her so he must catch her, they climb again onto the roof of the other building.

The yawning blue sky burns above their heads as they crawl out onto the wide hot roof.

The roof is bigger than a football field.

Along a far edge, the container, its parachute little more than scrappy silk rags, sinks into the roof.

The Old Man approaches cautiously, feeling the thinness of the roof beneath his feet. He waves for her to stand back and let him go on alone.

When she obeys, he proceeds, one cautious foot after the other, ready to fling himself backward onto the burning floor of the roof.

At the container he finds the heavy lock.

He knows this kind of lock. He has broken it many times and if one knows how to use a crowbar, the design of the container and the position of the lock will do most of the work.

The Old Man knows.

Forgetting the precarious and illusory roof, thinking only of salvage, blinded by salvage, he breaks the lock.

The doors swing open on a rusty bass note groan.

The Old Man smells the thick scent of cardboard.

Inside, stacked to the ceiling of the container are thin boxes, one lying atop another, long and flat.

He takes hold of the topmost and drags it away from the container onto the roof and back a bit where he feels it will be safer to stand.

Bending over the box he reads, seeing his granddaughter's little girl shadow lengthen next to his, as the day turns past noon. He reads the words the military once printed on these long flat boxes.

"Radiation Shielding Kit, M-1 Abrams MK-3, 1 ea."

CHAPTER 15

"By the time communication with the outside world had completely failed," explained General Watt after they'd re-established contact, "fourteen military-grade nuclear weapons had already been used within Colorado alone. I determined that it would be beneficial to you and your team to obtain a shielding kit in order to protect you, once you enter Colorado."

The Old Man watched the radio, thinking.

He held the mic in his trembling fingers, his weathered thumb as far away as possible from the transmit button.

"We have no idea . . ." General Watt paused, her voice tired. "I have no idea how bad things are above. But I wanted you to have some protection. Just in case. That's the reason I directed you to obtain the Radiation Shielding Kit."

"And was that also the reason you didn't tell us what we were going to find until we found it?"

You know the reason, my friend. You are angry at someone because they lied to you in order to save their life.

I am angry because . . .

Because of that, my friend. Because of that, and nothing more.

"Is there anything else you're not telling us, General?" asked the Old Man.

"No," replied General Watt. "There is nothing. I know very little beyond our limited access to a failing satellite network. In truth . . ."

Pause.

Static.

The Old Man saw the satellite in his mind, aging, drifting steadily out over the Pacific horizon once more.

"The truth, General."

"Call me Natalie."

"The truth, Natalie," said the Old Man softening his tone.

"The truth is, I don't even know if this plan will work. It is merely our last chance. I didn't want to tell you about the Radiation Shielding Kit because I estimated that you might not want to become involved if you knew there was a possibility of being exposed to high levels of radiation. Though I have no contact with those on the surface, I hypothesize that a fear of radiation poisoning has evolved into a healthy respect, if not outright avoidance policy, among postwar communities."

Sometimes she sounds so detached. As if the world is little more than mathematical chances and equations that must be solved so that an answer can be found.

And hoped for, my friend. After so many years of living underground, what else might she have except some numbers that give her hope?

And if I know she is lying to me, why are we continuing down this road?

Because you don't know if she is lying to you.

"All right, General," said the Old Man. "I'm sorry. Thank you for trying to protect us."

I should turn back now. We . . .

"Natalie."

"Natalie," agreed the Old Man.

Natalie.

"The shielding kit will protect you through most of southern Colorado. All you have to do is get close to the collapsed backdoor entrance and then aim the Laser Target Designator at the back of the mountain. We'll do the rest."

The rest.

Do I want to know what the rest is? Not today. There has been too much already for just today.

That is the love of letting things go for now.

THE DAY THAT follows is hot and dusty.

They pass through the crumbling remains of eastern Southern California.

All day long they maneuver through scattered debris, time-frozen traffic jams, and long-collapsed overpasses while the Old Man scans the western horizon.

I was raised over there, beyond those mountains that stand in the way, near the sea. Like you, Santiago.

I have not thought of those places since the bombs. Which is not true.

In the days after, I thought of them all the time.

And then you married your wife and forgot them, my friend.

Yes. There was the work of salvage and you had to concentrate to dig out its story. There was no time for where I had come from. There was no time to think of where I could never go again. There was salvage. My wife. Our shack. My son. His family. My granddaughter. They were my salvage and they replaced all those burned-up places that were gone.

"Grandpa, how will we know where the 395 is?"

I thought only of them, my new family, in the days that followed the bombs.

"Roads lead to roads," he said. "If we follow this big road, we will find another road. In time we will find this little highway once called the 395."

The dull hum of the tank's communications system.

"Some always leads to more, right, Grandpa?"

"Right."

Some always leads to more.

THAT NIGHT THEY camp near the off-ramp at the intersection where the big highway spends itself into the untouchable west and the little ribbon of road the map names the 395 drops off into the lowest places of the earth. Death Valley.

They eat rations heated in the Old Man's blue percolator and sit around a campfire made of ancient wood pulled from the wreckage of a fallen house built long before the bombs and well before the science that would reveal their terribleness.

Yucca trees, spiky and dark, alien against the fading light, surround them and the silent tank.

The Old Man thinks of the fuel gauge and its needle just below the halfway point.

The drums atop the tank are empty.

If you think all night you will not sleep, my friend.

Natalie says there will be fuel, of a sort, in China Lake.

General Watt.

Natalie.

She sounds old. Like me.

"Grandpa, why do they call it the Death Valley?"

She has been quiet for most of the afternoon. Her questions have been few, as though the place that makes all her questions is overwhelmed by the road and our adventure upon it.

Maybe the world is bigger than she ever imagined, my friend.

"It was called Death Valley even before I was born."

"So not because of the bombs?"

"No. When people first crossed this country I guess they didn't like Death Valley, so they chose a bad name for it."

"Did everyone avoid it?"

The Old Man tries to remember.

Instead, he remembers other things.

Ice cream.

A place he worked at.

Steam.

The beach.

"No, I remember people went there on vacation. It was a place people needed to go and see what was there."

She watches the fire.

He can see each question forming deep within her.

I can almost snatch them out of the air above her head.

Tonight, when I sleep, I would like to really sleep. Only sleep, and no nightmares.

Especially the one nightmare.

Yes.

The one in which she is calling you as you die, as you abandon her.

As you fall.

As you leave, my friend.

Yes. That one.

No, Grandpa, I need you.

Yes.

"Will it be dangerous there?" she asks.

The Old Man searches the night for one of Natalie's satellites.

"No. No more than any other place we have been."

"I'm not afraid, Grandpa. Just the name, it's a little scary."

"Yes. Just a little."

She laughs.

I know what it is like to be afraid of a name and also a nameless thing. My sleeping nightmare is like Death Valley to her.

"Since we might be the first people to cross Death Valley in a long time, we could give it a new name. One that isn't so scary."

She stops chewing and he watches the machine inside her turn. The machine that makes an endless supply of questions. The gears and cogs that labor constantly so that she becomes who she will become in each moment and the next.

Sometimes she is so exact.

It might be against her rules to change the name.

To change the game.

No, Grandpa. I need you.

I would change that if I could.

"What could we call it?" she asks.

She is willing to rewrite history. Willing to make something new. Willing to change the rules of the game.

"I don't know. I guess . . . when we get there we could see what we think of it and then come up with a new name. What do you say about that?"

They both hear a bat crossing the lonely desert, flying up the desolate highway, beating its leathery wings in the twilight.

Tomorrow we will follow him beyond those rocks and down into the desert at the bottom of the world.

"I would like that, Grandpa. Yes."

IN THE DARK, the Old Man is falling into even darker depths.

I was falling.

No, Grandpa. I need you.

Yes.

The nightmare.

If only I could change it like we're going to change the name of Death Valley.

The Old Man drinks cold water from his canteen.

His granddaughter sleeps, her face peaceful.

No, Grandpa. I need you.

The Old Man lies back and considers the night above, though his mind is really thinking of, and trying to forget, the nightmare all at once.

I wish I were free of it.

I wish I could change the rules of its game.

If she called me by another name, then the nightmare wouldn't frighten me anymore. Then, I would remember in the dream that she calls me by another name and I could hold on to that.

And thinking of names, his eyes close and the sky above marches on and turns toward dawn.

CHAPTER 16

The morning sky is a clean, almost electric bright and burning blue. The desert is wide, stretching toward the east and the north. Small rocky hills loom alongside the road.

They have finished their breakfast and make ready to leave.

The Old Man starts the auxiliary power unit and a moment later, the tank. He watches the needles and gauges.

What could I do if there was a problem with any one of them?

Natalie might know something.

We should get as close to Death Valley as we can today. Then cross it tomorrow.

He watches his granddaughter lower herself into the driver's seat. She smiles and waves from underneath the oversize helmet and a moment later her high soprano voice is in his ear.

"Can I drive today, Grandpa?"

"Stay on the road and when we come to an obstacle, like a burned-up car or a truck that has flipped across the lanes, stop and I'll tell you which way to go around, okay?"

"Okay, Grandpa."

They cross onto the highway and she pivots the tank left and toward the north. She overcorrects and for a moment they are off-road.

"Sorry, Grandpa!"

"Don't worry. You're doing fine."

She gets them back on the road and the tank bumps forward with a sudden burst of acceleration as she adjusts her grip.

"Slow and steady," he reminds her.

"I know, Grandpa."

They drive for a while, crossing through a high desert town whose wounded windows gape dully out on the dry, brown landscape and prickly stunted yuccas as peeling paint seems to fall away in the sudden morning breeze of the passing tank.

"Are you excited about finding a new name for the valley we'll cross tomorrow?"

She doesn't reply for a moment as the tank skirts around a twisted tractor trailer flipped across the road long ago. Inside, the Old Man can see bleached and cracked bones within the driver's cab.

"Yes, I am."

The dull hum of the communications system fills the space between their words. Each time they speak, they sound suddenly close to each other.

"If you were going to give me a new name, what would it be?"

The dull hum.

Wheels turning.

"Why would I do that, Grandpa?"

Why would you indeed?

Because I am frightened that I might die and leave you abandoned out here, all alone.

Because a nightmare torments me and calls me by the same name you do.

Because I am trying to change the rules of the game.

And.

Because I love you.

"Oh, I don't know," says the Old Man. "Sometimes 'Grandpa' makes me feels old."

"But that's who you are. You're Grandpa!"

Silence.

If we can change the name of a valley, can we change my name?

"I don't know," he hears her say. "You're not so old, Grandpa."

"I know."

"But I guess . . . I guess if you wanted to be something else, I could call you . . . Poppa, maybe?"

I like that.

If I were Poppa, then when I was stuck in the nightmare, I could remember my new name.

And then I would remember it is just a nightmare, and that all I need to do is wake up.

I don't ever want to be anything else but Poppa.

"I like Poppa. It sounds young. Like I'm full of beans."

Silence.

They start up the grade that climbs into rocky wastes beyond the fallen buildings of the little town that once was and is now no more.

Where did all the people go? To our west is the Central Valley, Bakersfield, and the Grapevine. I remember passing by those fields on long highways. Long drives are some of my first memories. We had family in Northern California.

Fried chicken.

Summer corn.

White gravy with pepper.

Sweet tea.

The Kern River.

There was a song about the Kern River. My father always sang it when he thought of home. When he found himself in places far away, places where the big jets he flew had taken him. Places not home.

"Poppa?"

The Old Man felt the heat of those long-gone kitchens and early Saturday evenings when the Sacramento Delta breeze came up through the screen doors. Evenings that promised such things would always remain so.

How did they promise?

The Old Man thought.

Because when you are young and in that moment of food and family and time, you cannot imagine things might ever be different.

Or even gone someday.

"Poppa!"

That's me. I'm Poppa now.

"Yes. What is it?"

"Just practicing. You need to practice too if you're going to be Poppa now."

"Okay. I'll be ready next time."

"Okay, Grandp—I mean . . . okay, Poppa."

Fried chicken.

Saturday dinners.

The heat of the oven.

The Kern River.

Poppa.

THE DAY WAS at its brutal zenith when they saw the Boy crawling out of the cracked, parched hardpan toward the road. Their road. Dragging himself forward. Dragging himself through the wide stretch of dust and heat that swallowed the horizon.

"Poppa, what do we do?"

She has taken to Poppa. She's smarter and faster than anyone I ever knew.

"Poppa!"

I don't want to stop and help this roadside killer.

He thought of the drawings inside the warehouses.

He thought of what the world had become.

He thought of the Horde.

The Roadside Killer.

But you told her, 'The world has got to become a better place.'

"We'll stop and see what this person needs."

The Old Man grabbed his crowbar from its place inside the tank.

They stopped the tank and climbed down onto the hot road, feeling its heat melt through the soles of their shoes, new shoes from long ago that they had taken from the supplies Sergeant Major Preston had stocked.

The Boy was young. Just a few years older than his granddaughter.

One side of him was rippled by thick, long muscles.

The other is thin, almost withered, like that other boy who chased me across the wasteland.

The Boy was mumbling to himself through lips that bled and peeled. His skin, though dark, was horribly burned, even blistering. On his back was an old and faded rucksack. He wore tired, beaten boots that must have once been maroon colored but were now little more than worn-through leather. He wore dusty torn pants and a faded and soft red flannel shirt. At his hip, a steel-forged tomahawk hung from an old belt. And in the Boy's long hair, attached to a leather thong, a gray-and-white feather, broken and bent along its spine, lay as if waiting for the merest wind to come and catch it up.

He is like that other boy who tried to murder me.

The Old Man looked down and saw his granddaughter's big dark eyes watching him. Watching to see what he would do next.

Inside them he saw worry.

And . . .

Inside them he saw mercy.

They knelt down beside the Boy.

The Old Man let the crowbar fall onto the road.

"Who is he, Poppa?"

"I don't know. But he needs our help. He's been out here far too long."

"I'll get some water, Poppa."

The Boy began to cry.

Shaking, he convulsed.

Crying, he wheezed, begging the world not to be made of stone, begging the world to give back what it had taken from him.

"Who am I?" sobbed the Boy.

"I think he's asking, who is he, Poppa!" said his granddaughter as though it were all a game of guessing and she had just won.

The Old Man held the shaking, sobbing Boy and poured water onto his cracked and sunburned lips in the shadow of the rumbling tank.

"He doesn't know who he is, Poppa. Who is he?"

"He's just a boy," said the Old Man, his voice trembling.

"Who am I now?" sobbed the Boy.

The Old Man held the Boy close, willing life, precious life, back into the thin body.

"You're just a boy, that's all. Just a boy," soothed the Old Man, almost in tears.

The Old Man held the Boy tightly.

"You're just a boy," he repeated.

"Just a boy."

CHAPTER 17

The Boy lay on the floor of the tank atop the Old Man's sleeping bag.

When they'd lowered him through the wide hatch after helping him up from the hot crumble of the road, he'd mumbled, "M-One Abrams," and after that he had said nothing.

Now the Boy lay on the cool floor of the tank as the Old Man ran the air-conditioning system at full power. The Old Man wondered about fluids and their replacement and how much farther the tank could go without such vital substance.

They crossed broken landscapes and high rocky hills where the thin remains of fading white observatories still waited for someone to come and look at the stars.

The Old Man could feel unseen eyes watching them as they passed such forlorn places.

They drove through an intersection where large slabs of metal and iron, long ago fused into uselessness, lay behind a crumpled fence alongside the road.

There were once many power transformers here. During those hot days near the end, when the systems began to collapse as unchecked energy surged toward its maximum output, wild power must have flooded through the lines, overloading overridden breakers, and suddenly everything began to melt in volumes of hot white heat. That is the story of this place.

Its story of salvage.

They moved on, leaving the slag and molten-made shapes to write their questions in the desert sands.

The Boy continued to sleep and once, when the Old Man looked down from his place in the open hatch, he could see the Boy, eyes open, watching him. The Old Man leaned down and handed him his canteen, keeping his other hand out of sight, ready with the crowbar.

Is he like that other savage boy?

The other boy who chased me across the desert.

The boy who chased my flare out into the night and must still lie at the bottom of the pass.

You would tell me, Santiago, that it was nothing personal. You would tell me that so I am not bothered by the memory of it.

It was nothing personal, my friend.

The Boy drank, swallowed thickly, and laid his head back down on the sleeping bag, exhausted. A moment later, his eyes were closed and the Old Man wondered if the Boy was sleeping and what he dreamed of.

Twisting hills and rocky ravines wound through ancient islands of mining equipment rusting long before the bombs. Stone outlines blackened by fire showed where once a village might have done business by the side of the thin ribbon of road.

Such times are long gone now. Now there is only the wind and burnt stone lying amid the red dirt and whispering brush of dry brown stick.

"We'll stop here for the night," said the Old Man over the intercom. A moment later his granddaughter pivoted the tank sharply to the left and pulled into a vacant lot banked by the fire-blackened stones of what had once been two separate buildings.

The Old Man shut down the tank, climbed out and down onto the hard red dirt that glimmered with broken glass and quartzite, his granddaughter meeting him near the massive treads.

"How'd I do today, Grandpa . . . I mean, Poppa? How'd I do?"

"The best. Better than I could've ever done. Better than anybody ever."

"What'll we do with that boy, Poppa?" she whispered, concentrating hard on remembering the Old Man's new name.

"I don't know yet."

Silence.

"We can't just leave him, right?"

"No, we can't" said the Old Man after a short pause.

There was still a little daylight left and the Old Man turned to setting up their camp for the night. He built a circle of stones for a fire pit, gathered dry sticks with his granddaughter, and considered finding some snake for fresh meat. But in the end they simply heated more of their rations.

In the dark, as they watched the orange glow of the coals and a thin trickle of red flame that leapt upward, the Boy exited the tank, a dark shadow against the blue twilight of the coming night. He limped to the fire and took a seat on the hard ground.

The Old Man watched the Boy and then saw his granddaughter watching him also.

The Old Man took the plate of food he'd made for the Boy and handed it across the fire.

The Boy looked at it for a long moment, dipped his hand into it, and brought the food up to his cracked lips. He chewed slowly, painfully.

The Old Man watched the unused fork he'd given the Boy with the tin pie plate.

The Old Man sighed. He felt overwhelmed by all the questions he had for the Boy.

None seemed right.

None seemed appropriate.

That there was a great weight, a sadness even, that hung over the Boy who stared listlessly into the depths of the fire, that much was evident.

"Thank you," said the Boy. His voice hollow. Deep.

The Old Man smiled.

"You're welcome."

"Where'd you come from?" erupted from his granddaughter. The Old Man winced.

The Boy turned to her. He smiled sadly.

Did he shake his head?

"Everywhere," mumbled the Boy.

"Oh wow," she squealed. "We're just from . . ." She barely caught the look the Old Man briefly gave her. "We live in a village alongside the Old Highway. Have you been to the cities?"

Have you been to the cities? She must wonder what was in them.

Imagine things about them as though they were a fantasy place. A palace of dreams, maybe.

Why wouldn't she?

The Boy nodded.

He continued to chew slowly, painfully.

"Which ones?" she asked.

She is like Big Pedro when he gambled. She cannot restrain herself.

The Boy turned his gaze back to the fire.

"Washington, D.C., Little Rock, Reno, Detroit, and . . ."

But he didn't finish.

He watched the fire.

But he is not watching the fire, my friend. He is there, wherever that city is that he cannot name.

"Here, drink a little; it will help you recover," said the Old Man when the pause had become both long and uncomfortable.

The Boy put his food down. He took the canteen with his good hand. The withered hand was heaved into position as he grasped the cap with the good hand and twisted. Then the canteen was transferred back to the good hand and the Boy took a long pull, his Adam's apple bobbing thickly in the firelight.

A night owl hooted, its call lonely and inviting.

When the Boy finished, he handed the canteen back to the Old Man. "Thank you."

Silence.

"When I was young," began the Old Man, "I lived in a city. At least I thought it was a city. It was really just a town on the outskirts of a big city. But that town was my whole world."

The Old Man placed a few more sticks on the fire.

"Sometimes I think back about those times. There used to be nights when the town was quiet, when I was young, and my friends and I would roam the streets in cars. We would eat fast food and play video games. We saw movies."

The Old Man looked at his granddaughter.

She loves these stories and I don't know why. I have explained fast food and video games and movies. But they are just words.

She will never know those places. Those things.

She will have to make do with mere words.

Still, she loves these stories, my friend.

"Do you know those things?" asked the Old Man of the Boy.

The Boy nodded.

Someone has told him of the things that once were.

"So," the Old Man continued, "these things were my world, and if you would've asked me at the time what the world was like, what its shape was, I guess I might have described it that way."

He nodded at both of them.

"Even when I was older, just a few years beyond both of you, I knew the world had many places in it and I had even traveled to some of those places expecting them to be different. But life in one place is much the same as another. Life is life, despite your street address."

The Old Man smiled at their blank faces.

You never told her about street addresses.

Didn't I?

No, maybe not, my friend.

"Well," said the Old Man, lost for a moment. "Life is life. All my nights and days would be with friends or in places that had water and rooms and pizza and video games. I thought I would always see movies. Probably until the day I died. Then the bombs fell."

The Old Man watched the fire.

"Since that time I have had many nights out in the desert. Out under the stars. Nights I never would've imagined when I was young like you and spent every night in the same room I had grown up in."

There were cars on the walls.

Yes.

And comic books.

Yes, also.

"Poppa?"

Pause.

I am not in that room anymore. Not for a long time and I wonder what became of it.

What do you think happened to it, my friend?

"Poppa!"

"Well, it is good to be here," said the Old Man, returning. "Under the stars tonight, with you." He looked at his granddaughter. "What I'm try-ing to say is that I never thought my life would lead here, and that I would be happy. Do you understand?"

She thought for a long moment.

Then . . .

"I just want to go everywhere, Poppa."

After a moment the Old Man nodded, concealing his fear that one day she might actually do that. Concealing his fear of those days and places and the people that must live there now in the "everywhere" of all the places she would go.

The Old Man turned to the Boy who watched the both of them.

He almost becomes invisible.

It's like he's barely there.

Like he's fading away.

"What are all those cities like? What is it like out there in the world?" asked the Old Man, waving his hand across the night sky as if to cover every known place.

As if to wipe away his sudden fear.

Pause.

"All gone," said the Boy. "There is nothing left. And the world . . ."

Pause.

The Boy looked into the eyes of the Old Man.

The Old Man saw none of the malice he'd seen in that other boy, that savage boy who'd chased him across the desert with a parking meter for a club.

Instead he saw an emptiness within the Boy's green eyes where a fire that once burned had gone out. Like an old campfire gone cold long ago. Or a wreck from Before, still lying on the highway waiting for someone to come and cry out with horror.

And grief.

Like this campfire will be after we leave tomorrow and for the years to come. Just tired ashes fading in the sun and disappearing with the wind.

". . . the world," said the Boy. "Is gone."

CHAPTER 18

"General Watt? Natalie, are you there?" In the night, the Old Man sits in the tank, feeling the cold metal against his sunburned skin.

The nightmare that awoke him, the one of falling and hearing his granddaughter say *No, Grandpa. I need you,* has come again. And even though he reminds himself that she calls him Poppa now and that the terror has no power over him, should have no power, that he has changed the rules of the game and changed his name so the devil cannot find him, still he lies awake.

He slips away from the camp to urinate on ancient blackened stones that were once someone's home, someone's business, who can know anymore? Then he drinks cold water made pleasant by the night's cool air.

I will think of tomorrow and the fuel we need to find at China Lake.

And when he cannot think of or envision what they might find there, he leaves his bedroll, knowing he will not return for the night and starts the APU on the tank.

He checks the radio frequency though he knows he has not touched it and can think of no reason why he should have.

"General Watt? Natalie? Come in."

The Old Man wonders if the white noise he hears as he waits for a response from the General, from Natalie, is always there, waiting even when no one is listening.

How many years are there between these few brief signals since the bombs?

"Yes. I'm here," says General Watt.

Natalie.

The Old Man finds an unexpected comfort in the woman's voice. Older, softer, yes. Tired even. But a comfort he did not expect to find.

And yet you must have known it was there, my friend, or why else would you be calling her in the middle of the night?

He watches the barely red coals and the sleeping forms of his unmoving granddaughter on one side of the fire near his empty bedroll, and the Boy, his good arm thrown over his face, his body twisted as if tormented even in sleep.

"We're not too far from China Lake, General . . . I mean, Natalie."

"Good. I have more information for you on where to locate a possible fuel source. I planned on waiting until morning to contact you. I was estimating that you might still be asleep."

"I can't sleep tonight."

"Why, are there problems? Is everything all right?"

"No. I mean . . . Yes. I mean . . . we picked up a passenger today. But now we're proceeding on to China Lake. I'd expected this trip to be much more difficult than it has been so far."

"Then why can't you sleep?"

"I guess . . . because I'm old."

"How old are you?"

"I was twenty-seven when the bombs fell. How long ago was that?"

"Forty years, six months, eight days, seventeen hours, and seven minutes since the nuclear detonation that occurred on Manhattan Island in New York City."

The Old Man moved numbers around in his head.

We had lost track of time back in the village.

There had been more important things to do in those days after the bombs than to keep track of meaningless days.

I am old now.

"How old are you?" he asked.

"I am one year older than you," replied Natalie.

Pause.

"Do you remember . . . ?" asked the Old Man.

"Yes. I remember everything."

Pause.

"Does it . . . bother you . . . to remember what's gone?"

"No," said Natalie. General Watt.

"Why?"

Pause.

"Because I still have hope that things can get better."

The Old Man listened.

"I have hope that you will come and set us free from this place. I have hope that one day every good thing that was lost will return again. I have hope, and there is no room inside my hope for the past."

"Oh," said the Old Man and realized that his days, his story, this journey, were not just about him and his granddaughter who was his most precious and best friend. Or even the Boy they'd found alongside the road who seemed hollow and fading from a worn and thin world. This journey was about someone else. Someone who needed help. Someone who has only hope in the poverty of what remains.

"Every day is the chance that tomorrow might be better," said General Watt.

Natalie.

CHAPTER 19

Piles of volcanic rock rise to the height of small mountains as the tank crests the barren desert plateau. Below them, the entire world seems to slope downward to some unseen terminus that must surely await them.

Now we must fall to the bottom of the earth. This thin highway will pass through the military base once called China Lake and then we must follow that until we come to a small road the map has marked the 190.

And then . . . Death Valley.

The Boy liked to ride atop the tank, holding on to the main gun, watching the far horizon.

The wind catches his hair, pulling it, tossing it.

The gray-and-white feather with the broken spine flutters in the breeze.

The Old Man watched the Boy from the hatch as they bumped along the descent into the lowest parts of the desert.

That morning, as they'd loaded the tank, the Old Man had stopped the Boy, who seemed familiar with what must be done when breaking camp. Moving on.

He has probably done this every morning of his life.

"We're going far to the east."

He waited for the Boy to ask him why. When he didn't, the Old Man continued.

"I can't leave you here, there is too little to survive on and to salvage. But later today we should come to an old military base."

The Boy waited.

Whether this pleased or displeased the Boy, the Old Man could not tell.

"We can leave you there, if you like?"

The Boy nodded and returned to helping load their things back onto the tank.

The Boy tapped the spare fuel drums and all of them heard an empty *gong* that came from within each.

"Where will we get fuel today, Poppa?" his granddaughter asked.

"Ahead of us there's supposed to be an underground storage tank near a long runway. When we get there, I'm told we'll be able to load the tank up with rocket ship fuel."

Will we, my friend?

General Watt, Natalie, said so. Shuttle fuel. Left over from the last shuttle flights. Stored in case there might ever be a need for it again. Stored with fuel stabilizers in an underground, airtight storage tank where they had hidden the fuel once those shuttles had landed after circling the earth.

"Though shuttle fuel is not listed as a reliable fuel source for the M-1 Abrams Main Battle Tank," General Watt, Natalie, had told him last night, "reviewing its specifications and requirements, I fail to see why this fuel source will not suffice."

"If it is all we have, then it will have to do," said the Old Man during their deep-of-the-night conversation, when he could not sleep.

"Yes," agreed Natalie. "It may increase the engine temperature though, and that should be a concern worth noting."

"Runs a little hot, eh?" said the Old Man, laughing for no reason he could think of at the time.

Maybe I was relieved there would at least be something to use for fuel. If not, it would be a very long walk back home or even just to the bunker.

"Yes," Natalie had said.

Now, turning along a wide curve underneath dusty gray granite rock, the high desert town of China Lake lies buried beneath wild growth turned brown and yellow. Hints of collapsed buildings occasionally peek out from beneath the rampant tangle of wild desert shrub and thorn.

The base is on the far side of the town.

"Continue down this freeway," he told his granddaughter. "We should be able to see the control tower from the road. If we reach the remains of an overpass, we've gone too far."

"Okay, Poppa!"

The people came stumbling out of the tangle of undergrowth, some lumbering, some crawling, others dragging themselves free of the riot of briers, thorns, and wild cactus.

The Boy saw them first and pointed. The Old Man followed the gaze and finger.

They were misshapen.

Withered limbs.

Missing limbs.

They wore rags.

They held up their bony and scratched arms. If they had them.

Their mouths were open.

Some held up tiny, milky-eyed blind children, as if offering, as if pleading, as if begging.

The shape of their ribs was revealed through sagging skin above pot-bellies distended by starvation.

Tears ran down their cheeks.

The Old Man recoiled in horror.

The desert freaks fell away behind the slow progress of the tank, which easily outpaced their shambling and weakened lurch toward the machine.

The Old Man watched them fall to the ground in defeat.

They're starving.

There wasn't a weapon, a stick, or a rock among them.

Just hands, pleading. Claws begging.

The Old Man looked at the Boy.

"They're starving," he shouted above the engine's scream.

And after a moment the Boy nodded in agreement.

The Old Man watched one of the crazed and starving desert people, a thin and bony gaunt man, the frontrunner of them all, kneeling, pounding the dry ground in frustration with a tiny claw-hand as puffs of dry dust erupted in his face. A woman with a child knelt down beside the Gaunt Man. Comforting him. Comforting her broken man who'd tried his best to catch their tank that he might beg for help as the starving child wailed from her back.

They're just people.

They're just people, and they're starving to death.

"Stop the tank."

"What, Poppa?"

"Stop the tank. They're starving. We have food. We can give them some. What we have, we can give to them."

The people stood as the tank stopped.

Amazed.

The Old Man waved to them.

Come.

The Boy and his granddaughter began to bring their boxes of food out onto the turret.

The Desert People came forward. Fear and hope in large watery eyes. Disbelief as bony bodies stumbled and finally leaned into each other for support and comfort. A woman jabbered, shrieking hysterically. The oldest, spindly legged and skeletal, simply cried, heaving out great sobs that racked their concave chests. The rest, dirty and tired, opened their mouths, stunned into silence, saying nothing, unable to believe what was happening.

After a moment, the Boy began to speak to them in their jabber-patois.

He speaks their language.

The Old Man tore open an Army-gray package of spaghetti and meatballs. He handed it to the Gaunt Man whose wife struggled to help him hold up his too-bony and too-thin arms to receive the gift.

The starving man opened his mostly toothless mouth and the Old Man could see the drool of extreme hunger within.

'He'll devour the whole packet in one bite,' thought the Old Man.

The Gaunt Man reached two thin fingers into the gray packet, his huge dark eyes like ever-widening pools of water, and scooped out the meal within.

His mouth wide.

He turned to the woman beside him and fed her.

Her eyes closed and she chewed slowly.

The child on her back whimpered.

Even with her eyes closed the pure joy was evident as she chewed slowly, swallowing thickly.

'They're still human,' thought the Old Man. 'They still care for each other as best they can.'

The Desert People surged around the tank, dozens of them, holding out their arms weakly for as long as they could, waiting while the Old Man and his granddaughter held out the opened packets of food to them. Soon the Boy was helping too as the people of the high desert ate and wept, jabbering what the Boy told the Old Man was their way of saying, "Thank you, thank you, thank you."

THE DESERT PEOPLE followed the tank as it slowly moved to the old airfield. When the tank stopped, the Desert People stopped.

The Old Man searched along the sides of the runway for the cover to the underground fuel storage. The cover that Natalie, General Watt, had told him he must find.

Storage Tank B.

When he found it, he waved for his granddaughter to bring the tank to him and soon they were drawing fuel from the deep, untouched reservoir that had opened with a pungent suck of long denied oxygen.

"They've had a hard year," said the Boy as the Old Man watched the fuel hose thump and shake, greedily drinking up the long untouched fuel.

"You speak their language."

"They speak a language that is like one I heard in another place."

"What happened to them?"

The Boy turned to look at the Desert People.

"They tell me they have lived here since before the bombs. They've been sick since. Their crops failed this year and because of their . . . condition . . . from the poison inside the bombs, they cannot hunt the goats and deer up in the rocks. The animals are too fast for them to get close to with their slings."

The Old Man turned from the hose, knowing he would see the Desert People watching him.

He watched the women gather about his granddaughter, making soft cooing noises, stroking her hair.

I have to take care of her also.

Yes.

But you know many tricks, my friend, and you are resourceful.

Yes, you would say that to me.

I did.

The Old Man climbed onto the tank and disappeared inside the turret.

When he came back out he carried the hunting rifle, the cleaning kit, and the two boxes of shells.

I am glad to be rid of this gun. I didn't like having it with us.

The Old Man beckoned the Gaunt Man, who seemed the healthiest among them.

He wobbled forward.

The Old Man loaded a bullet into the rifle, shot the bolt forward, shouldered the rifle, and aimed it at a small satellite dish attached to a building on the other side of the field.

He fired.

The small satellite dish bent and then, a moment later, fell onto the decaying pavement.

The shot echoed off the gray mountain rock all around them.

"Tell them to hunt with this."

The Boy watched the Old Man.

Then the Boy turned and began to speak to the Gaunt Man in their jabber.

"Tell them they will have to keep this gun clean, I'll show them how," said the Old Man.

"Tell them to use these bullets sparingly, only hunt what they need to get back on their feet. Get their strength back."

And . . .

"Tell them this is all we have."

IT WAS TIME to go.

When the Old Man had shown them how to clean and care for their gun, it was time to go.

They brought their children forward to touch the Old Man and the women smelled his granddaughter's hair and the Boy jabbered their jabber and told them all goodbye.

When it was time to go.

The Old Man looked at the Boy.

"I want you to come with us. I think we will need your help where we are going."

The Boy watched the Desert People.

The tank.

Heard a voice he did not share with others.

A voice from long ago.

A voice that said, *Whatchu gonna do now, Boy?*

The Boy nodded and climbed onto the tank, standing in his place alongside the main gun.

The Old Man started the APU and donned his helmet.

He spoke to his granddaughter as the engine spooled up into its whine and then roared to life, sending waves of heat blasting out across the gravel and dust.

"Are you ready?"

"What will we do now, Poppa? They ate all our food."

The Old Man watched the Desert People.

What I have, I give to you.

Where did that come from, my friend?

I don't know.

"Let's head back to the highway," he told his granddaughter over the intercom. "Don't worry, we'll be fine."

CHAPTER 20

The Old Man looked at the temperature gauge again.

Already, the engine is too hot.

And still, it rises. Also, today the heat is merciless and I'm sure that will not help matters.

The tank cut through carved gashes within the burning, stony hills as they descended into wide iron-gray wastes.

All this must have once been under an ocean.

Long beaches of prehistoric sand fade for miles, falling away from rocky outcrops that were once islands. These islands of once-magma hover above the gray dust of the road and in time, even these fade into the red rock hills where stands of soft green feathery trees shelter among cracks in the earth.

Like the oasis the bee led me to.

Would I find water there in those stands of willowy green trees on this hottest of days?

Foxes for food.

Shade for rest.

Even a moment to think about what we're doing as this infernal day turns into a bread oven and the tank's engine heat rises like an overworked furnace.

How long can the engine run at this temperature?

"Natalie? General Watt?" The Old Man releases the push-to-talk button and waits for her reply.

"Natalie here."

"This spaceship fuel is making the engine run hotter than maybe it should."

Ahead the road opens out onto a steep grade that surely leads to the bottom of the desert, or so the Old Man thinks.

If the bottom is just ahead, then this has not been so bad.

"You can try," replies Natalie through the static, "to shut the tank down until dark. Then continue on to the final descent. I am watching you in real time on a satellite I've managed to change to a higher, slower orbit."

The final descent?

I thought this was the final descent. What will this other fall-to-the-bottom places of the desert seem like?

"I HAVE BAD news," says Natalie, her warm voice suddenly clear, as though right in his ear.

"Go ahead."

"The road that leads to the bottom of Death Valley might not prove serviceable. Once you pass a scenic overlook the road becomes impassable. You'll need to find a way down by going off-road to continue on to the bottom of the grade."

"Is that going to be a problem for you?" asks Natalie. General Watt.

"No. We'll be fine."

The Old Man wipes away the thin sweat that collects around his neck.

The road they must take, the one that leaves the 395, is mostly buried under drifting white sand. At the lonesome intersection they watch it carve away into the east, into red ridges and dark gullies.

According to the map, this must be our turn toward the valley. Toward the east.

"Poppa, I can see the road as it rises above the sand. That way." She leans out of the driver's hatch in front of him, pointing toward the red rock that cuts the horizon.

The Boy atop his perch near the main gun scans the bright sands, and the Old Man watches him nod.

"Try to follow it as best you can," the Old Man tells his granddaughter.

Soon the sun is falling toward the west, and with every moment the color of the red rock deepens into rust and blood.

The engine temperature is high, but it isn't in the red, not yet.

How hot will it be tomorrow, deep down in the oven at the bottom of Death Valley, off-road, crossing the baking rocks and hardpan?

The Old Man waits and does not hear an answer.

If we were in the boat together, Santiago, what would we do? Make a hat from the wet gunnysacks. How would we stay cool enough to get this tank across the bottom of the driest sea in the world, my friend?

The Old Man hears nothing and thinks only of the sound the waves might make as they slap against the side of their tiny boat. The sound he and his friend would listen to as they searched the silences in between for an answer.

THEY WIND THROUGH the last of the low hills and in brief snatches they glimpse the basin far below.

It is so far below, I cannot imagine there could be a deeper part to this desert. It is like a giant hole in the earth. A hole we must fall into.

And . . .

It will be even hotter down there when the sun rises tomorrow.

At blue twilight they heave into a wide parking lot erupting in black-top blisters.

Once the Old Man turns the engine off and shuts down the APU, he expects he will feel some relief from the relentless heat that has marked this day, but he doesn't.

The early evening is like a warm cup of water left out in the sun.

He watches the engine temperature gauge grudgingly withdraw.

As though it does not want to, my friend.

I hope I haven't ruined anything within the tank's engine.

But would that be so bad?

He hears his granddaughter calling him. Telling him to come and look before it's too late.

But still he watches the temperature gauge barely move toward its own bottom.

When he looks out the hatch of the turret he can see the Boy standing next to his granddaughter as she climbs up on the warped railing that guards the parking lot from the edge of the drop. She points at something far below.

The Boy is close to her and the Old Man knows, though he does not know why, that the Boy will not let her fall.

IN THE DARK they camp far from the tank, lying against the warm sidewalk that encircles the parking lot. Stars beyond count begin their slow night dance above them. The moon, a fat crescent low above the hills, seems near and detailed as it shimmers above the ridges and rocks turned night-gray.

My biggest concern is the heat of the engine.

We'll need to cross the desert as fast as we can tomorrow.

But if we go too fast, the engine will become even hotter.

And then there is food.

If it is anything like the worst parts of the wasteland, what food there is down there will be hard to find.

It is good we are all so warm and exhausted. They didn't mention anything about eating tonight.

They also handed out the food, my friend, and they already know there is no food tonight. That is why they remain silent.

Are they asleep?

"Are you awake?" asks the Old Man in the night.

"Yes, Poppa. It's too hot to sleep."

After a moment the Boy whispers a tired, "I am awake," as though he has been and does not want to be.

"We have a problem."

"What is it, Poppa?"

The Boy says nothing.

"The fuel we pumped from beneath the runway is making the engine of the tank too warm. I don't remember much about engines but I do remember that if they are too hot for too long they might melt."

No one said anything.

"Tomorrow we will reach the valley floor. It will be even hotter down there."

After a moment his granddaughter asked, "So what do we do, Poppa?"

"I don't know," confessed the Old Man.

It seemed like the admission of ignorance, the surrender to helplessness. His statement lured him into a brief moment where he may have been asleep or falling toward it.

"Then we must go now," said the Boy quietly.

The Old Man sat up.

Natalie said the road we must take to the bottom is gone now. Off-road, in the darkness, feeling our way down the side of a cliff, that would be madness.

"It's a good moon to see by tonight," said the Boy as if reading the Old Man's thoughts. "Good for traveling. In an hour or so it will be very cold. The desert is like that."

CHAPTER 21

The tank is running.

The night is colder, and ever so slightly, the needle is a little lower than it was in the heat of the day.

The Old Man circles the running tank, then climbs onto the turret and into the hatch.

Inside, his granddaughter is buckled into the gunner's seat.

He shows the Boy how to use the seat belt in the loader's station.

"I can drive, Poppa, or at least be in the driver's seat up front."

The Old Man, sweating slightly and feeling weak, as if nauseated, climbs up into the hatch.

"I think it's better if we're all strapped in here, together. It might get pretty rough."

The Old Man takes hold of the control sticks Sergeant Major Preston had built to maneuver the tank from the commander's seat.

The Old Man looks down inside the tank and sees the Boy bathed in red light.

He is looking forward at nothing.

Nothing that exists anymore.

How do you know, my friend?

I just do.

The Old Man puts his hand on the switch that will activate the tank's high-beam light.

A moment later, everything in front of the tank is bathed in a wide arc of white light, throwing long shadows of deep darkness away from the blistered pavement and scattered rock.

For a few hundred yards they are able to follow the winding road, but almost immediately the road lies buried beneath a collapsed wall of red volcanic rock. The Old Man taps the throttle and listens to the two wide treads grind and crunch the porous rock as the tank climbs up onto the pile. On the other side, the final descent begins as the road rounds a curve, falling away out of sight.

So far, so good.

The Old Man smiles and adjusts his grip on the twin sticks, which are already slick with sweat.

On the other side of the curve, a fallen bridge sends only a strip of a railing across the gap.

The Old Man nudges the tank forward and looks into the empty space.

It's not deep, but it's steep. If we go down in there, we might get stuck.

To the right is a small plateau of crumbling rock that is little more than a wide ledge and a drop that disappears off into the night. To the left, a rock wall.

The Old Man maneuvers the tank out onto the wide ledge.

There is more than enough room.

Once the tank is back on the narrow two-lane road, the descent steepens and then halts.

The rock wall has shifted over the road. There is no ledge to turn onto and bypass the wall.

The Old Man waits, straining to see something in the arc of light that he has not yet seen.

He checks the temperature gauge.

Warmer.

But not as warm.

If we sit, if we wait, it will get warmer.

But I need time to think.

Right now you must be very rich to afford such a luxury, my friend.

The Old Man pulls back on both sticks and the tank shifts gears and begins to back up the road. When it's wide enough, which is just barely, he pivots the tank, mashing one stick forward and pulling back on the other, then he races back up to the ledge.

He climbs up out of the hatch and runs forward through the night across the warm rock.

Don't trip and break anything. A hand or a wrist, or even a leg.

Yes, that would be bad.

Below, the ledge falls steeply down a small hill onto a ridge that seems to cut back toward the road.

We could make it back to the road that way.

You might also get stuck.

Time.

Back in the tank, the Old Man starts the machine toward the ledge.

"Hang on," he mumbles over the intercom.

The near horizon is gray rock and long shadows in the brightness of the tank's lamp. The darkness of the night seems to devour the ground just beyond the light as the earth falls away and disappears.

Like the surface of an asteroid tumbling through the dark.

There is a moment when the tank is pointing straight toward the horizon, and a moment later it feels as though the gun barrel is aimed down into a black pit that lies just beyond the shattered rocks that dot the arc of light. All of them feel as if they are falling out of their seat belts and harnesses.

The tank picks up speed and the Old Man is leaning hard into the brakes as the tank slides forward into what must be an abyss.

The tank hovers halfway down the cliff and the Old Man can hear himself muttering.

"Poppa?" asks his granddaughter, breaking the dull hum of the intercom net.

The Old Man can see that the ridge ends abruptly and well before connecting with the broken road that winds off toward the unreachable north.

If I back up, the temperature will rise. It'll put too much strain on the engine.

The Old Man gives slightly on the brakes and the tank begins to ease forward, the gun barrel pointing even lower.

A hundred yards later, the tank is sliding down through rocks and dust, and the Old Man can only give and release on the brakes as the massive war machine slides faster and faster toward the unknown, unseen bottom.

Ahead, a large rock juts out of the dust that seems to chase and over-take the tank every time the Old Man jams his feet onto the brakes.

The Old Man engages the right tread and steers wide of the rock, clip-ping it at one edge and sending a spray of gravel off into the night.

"Wheeeeeee!" squeals his granddaughter over the intercom.

It feels like we are being bounced to death.

Like a roller coaster.

She has never known roller coasters. So this is her first roller coaster.

And though the Old Man is frightened, afraid he has chosen badly from the start and will soon be responsible for unnamed tragedies that lie in each moment beyond the high beam, he smiles.

I remember roller coasters . . .

Concentrate! You must pay attention now.

Still, I am glad she is having fun.

At the bottom of the steep and never-seeming-to-end slide, the tank lands and the Old Man yanks it sideways into a skid and finally a halt.

An avalanche of falling dust shrouds them for a moment.

The Old Man is shaking. Sweating.

"Poppa?"

When the Old Man speaks, he hears the fear in his own voice. The age too. "Yes?"

"That was fun! I hope there's more." And she is giggling and laughing and the Old Man laughs too, though he doesn't know what he is laugh-ing at.

You are laughing at yourself.

No, not because of that. I am laughing, because for another moment, we are still alive, despite all my failures.

Yes.

And I am laughing also because of the sound of her laughter. My granddaughter's laughter is a good thing.

The best thing.

AT DAWN THE Old Man saw the rubble of a wide and tall hacienda set within the crevice of a hill by a road leading up out of the far side of Death Valley.

It has been a long night.

Longer than the night you walked after the motel and the moon went down and you were all alone in the dark?

Yes, it feels longer than that one.

The journey down into the bowl of the deepest desert hadn't ended at that teetering ledge. For hours, the Old Man had coaxed the giant tank down through wadis and ravines and hills that may have been as steep as that first, terrifying, almost-drop.

She'd laughed all the way.

At the bottom, they'd gotten out to stretch their legs and feel the cool of the night drying the sweat on their bodies.

Even the temperature gauge was back to normal.

The road at the bottom disappeared underneath the drifting desert, and the Old Man thought, 'Surely this must be the bottom.'

But it wasn't.

No.

They'd crossed the valley and climbed a road that was mostly intact as it wound its way up through wicked formations of wind-carved rock.

Then down again.

By that time, his granddaughter and the Boy had been asleep.

Then it was just me. Alone in the night and crossing the desert.

Like before.

The tank rolled across the bottom of the ancient ocean.

In the night, the Old Man spied the skeletal remains of sunken RVs drowning amid the sand and rock.

The blackened frames of buildings clustered by the side of the road and the Old Man wondered what their story of salvage was.

Old habits die hard.

I think you should keep that habit. The fuel you'll need is more than what you have. You have a long way to go before this is done. Far beyond tonight, my friend.

Yes.

In time, the rolling motion of the tank and the Old Man's concentration on the mere rumors of road that lay buried beneath the mercurial sand lulled him into a thoughtlessness where even his constant memories could not find him.

I am too tired to remember.

When he came to the bottom of the desert, he found something in its center he had not expected to find. Clusters of feathery green trees, clutching at the lowest point of the desert, drifting like remembered seaweed in the moonlight. Moving slightly in some soft breeze that had wandered far and long to arrive here on this late night.

Like us.

In the center, at the bottom of Death Valley, next to a wide swath of dry alkali flats, there was life.

The Old Man shut down the tank and crossed the thin sands alone to feel the feathery branches and touch the soft white bark of the trees.

A strong breeze came up and the branches whispered all around him.

There was once an ocean here and this was its bottom.

I have seen its shores far up near where we obtained fuel from the old spaceship runway. Since then we have fallen and fallen into its dry depths.

As though sinking, my friend.

Yes, as though we were sinking.

'And underneath this tree,' the Old Man thought to himself, feeling its soft bark, 'is what remains of that long-ago ocean.'

SOON HE IS back aboard the tank and rolling on toward the east; his granddaughter and the Boy remained undisturbed by his stop in the night. By the last of the moon's light, the Old Man watched the white alkali flats spread away to the south.

What lost things lie within you?

What are your memories?

Blankness surrounded him and there was nothing but the road and the night long after the moon had crossed the sky and fallen into the shadows of spiky mountains on the far horizon.

Just before dawn, when the Old Man suspected there might be something, some structure within the rocks ahead, he rubbed his tired eyes and thought of oceans buried deep beneath the desert.

Those alien creatures that had lived within it and along its shores must have thought their world would never end. That the sea and their islands would always be there, long after even they had gone.

Just as we did before the bombs.

And . . .

One day, will we be just a few savages alongside a ravine at the bottom of our history, clutching at the remains of what once was?

Like those soft feathery trees in the moonlight at the bottom of a dead ocean.

Can we ever be forgiven for what we did?

IN THE GRAY light of first morning, the Old Man shut down the tank in the shadow of an ancient pile that rose up from the desert floor.

The hacienda had once been a hotel or a desert resort.

There might even be salvage within, but I am too tired to think about that right now.

He waited through the morning silence for his granddaughter and the Boy to finish their sleep. He watched the daylight rise and turn to gold, sweeping away the long night.

My life since the bombs has been like those trees at the bottom of the ancient ocean.

And yet, you are still here, my friend.

Yes.

CHAPTER 22

The Old Man awoke after noon. He raised a hand, shielding his eyes from the glare of the blinding sun.

He lay in the thin shadow of an ancient building.

He was alone.

He drank warm water and listened to the silence.

Far away, in the building above him he could hear his granddaughter's voice. She was talking to someone.

The Boy.

He listened to them as they explored the ruin.

In time they returned to him.

"Poppa!" She dropped a sack of treasures onto the pavement of the courtyard where he had been resting since they'd awoken that morning. "We found salvage."

The Boy appeared and the Old Man was comforted by the tomahawk the Boy kept at his belt and the dead snake in his hands.

I should have known better than to bring her. If the Boy had not been with her she might have gotten hurt.

I must be more careful.

But I was so tired.

On the ground lay a corkscrew, a feather duster that looked in good shape, and a bowling ball.

"What's this?" she asked holding up the corkscrew. "A weapon?"

He must have killed the snake with his tomahawk. The young are always impressed by the accomplishments of weapons.

"No." The Old Man picked up the corkscrew and inspected it. A wooden handle from which the thin spiral of the metal corkscrew rose up. He spit on it and polished it. "But it could be if you needed it to be." He put the handle in his fist and let the corkscrew erupt through his middle and ring fingers. "You could punch with it like this." He showed her.

Eyes wide, she watched, and when he had given the corkscrew back to her she also made a weapon of it.

Should I have done that? Should I have shown her how to make a weapon out of something that isn't one?

The world is a dangerous place now, my friend.

A moment later she grabbed the feather duster.

"This, Poppa? What is it? What was it for?"

The Boy set to gathering thin strips of the darkish deadwood that lay scattered about. The Old Man's mouth watered at the thought of the cooked snake.

I like snake.

"That's . . ." But the Old Man could not think of what a feather duster was once called. He knew what it did. But its label remained lost and no matter how hard he tried, he could not dig out a name for the feather duster within the cemetery of his mind.

My mind is like a burial place for the forgotten dead.

He remembered the ancient tombstones he and Big Pedro had come across out in the southern reaches of the desert, far out beyond the village. Far out beyond any salvage spots anyone could remember, they'd found the little cemetery resisting the desert. Surrounded by sinking ironwork, the nameless graves waited, their markers shifting in the sand throughout the years.

"No good," Big Pedro had said all those years ago. *Malo.* Bad.

When I'd turned to face him he had seen a look in my eye.

I'd wanted to open those graves and search them.

I'd shamed him.

The Old Man picked up the feather duster.

"You cleaned things with it?" Then, "It made dust go away."

For a moment, the name leapt out of the bushes clustering at the edge of his thoughts and then ran off down the road.

Later they finished the snake, which there was a surprising amount of.

It was a big snake.

As they sat waiting out the heat of the day, the Old Man thought of Big Pedro.

He was a good man.

I was wrong to have even thought about disturbing those graves.

What could we have found?

That was not the point.

I had grown calloused. I had gotten used to searching the things of dead people because we needed to survive. Taking their things and making them mine. Ours.

It was survival.

It was wrong.

Like the corkscrew.

Yes, that felt wrong even in the moment I was showing her how to make it a weapon.

He waited.

Waited for the answer he must give himself.

But what lies ahead is very dangerous.

To think that everything will be as easy as it has been up to this point is childish. She might need a weapon.

Now she has one.

I wish the world were different.

The world is what it is, my friend. The world is what it always has been. A very dangerous place.

Feather duster.

CHAPTER 23

It was late in the day, after they'd eaten the snake seasoned with some pepper that had survived the Old Man's charity, when they began the climb up and out of the valley. The grade was gentle and the climb little more than a final sweep up onto the eastern desert plain.

There are maybe eight miles between here and the secret testing area.

You are trying to think of other things.

Yes.

The Old Man watched the Boy as he rode atop the turret, eyes constantly scanning the far horizon.

Yes, I am trying to think of other things than the right tread of this tank.

"What shall we call the valley now that we have seen it?" he asked his granddaughter over the intercom.

There was a pause and he knew she was thinking. He knew her face when it thought. The pressed lips, the eyes searching the sky. Thinking.

"It wasn't scary, Poppa."

"No, not so much."

Remember the fall to the bottom. That was scary to me when we drove in the dark and I could not tell where the edge was and what would happen next. It is even scarier to me now when I think back about it. That is how you know things were really very dangerous, when you think back and are still frightened about what might have happened. That is the fear of what-might-have-been.

"How about . . ." she said through the dull hum of the communications net.

The Bottom of an Ocean Valley.

The Roller-Coaster Valley.

The Valley of the Longest Night.

"How about the 'There Is Nothing to be Afraid of Here Valley,' Poppa?"

How about that?

SINCE THAT AFTERNOON, after the long night of driving through the bottom of the once-ocean, the Old Man had felt the falseness in the right tread, and if he listened closely, a metallic *clank* that had not been there before. A *clank* he sometimes heard and other times, when he was sure he would hear it, not at all.

Maybe it is just an uncertainty and nothing more?

For now?

Yes, for now. And it could be these jury-rigged joysticks Sergeant Major Preston fixed up. That could be the problem.

Then you should ask your granddaughter to take over and guide the tank from the driver's compartment. See if she notices it also.

But the Old Man could not bring himself to ask her.

If it's true . . .

Then it is true.

Yes.

That night under desert skies turned western flames surrendering to the blue comfort of night, they sat and watched their fire.

I cannot stop thinking about the bad tread.

But what can you do about it?

"Where are we going?" asked the Boy.

The Old Man looked up to see both of them watching him.

"Tomorrow," he began, "at noon, I'll call the General and find out where we must go exactly. From what she has told me, we must find a device somewhere within this area. She tells me the device will help free her and those trapped within their bunker."

"What does this device do? Is it a weapon?" asked the Boy.

"I don't know," mumbled the Old Man, feeding dry sticks into the fire.

But you should know.

Yes.

"Poppa?"

"Yes."

"I'm hungry."

And there is that too.

JUST BEFORE NOON the Boy raised his hand. The gesture was so sudden and the Boy so long unmoving, the Old Man felt electrified at its sudden movement and meaning. The Old Man stopped the tank. Below them, in a long valley amid the salt flats, lay the once-secret base, Area 51, where Natalie had directed them to find the Laser Target Designator.

The Boy scrambled across the tank and shouted above the engine's roar in the Old Man's face.

"There are goats, big ones, along that ridge." The Boy pointed toward a jumble of rocks that looked like some bygone battleship crossing the ocean of a wide desert. The Old Man could not see any goats.

But he is young and his eyes are good.

"I'll hunt one and bring it down into the base. It might take me a while."

The Old Man nodded and the Boy climbed down from the rumbling tank and loped off in his awkward manner toward the distant rocks.

Later, after the engine had faded from whine to silence, as the wind whispered through the ancient hangars, sweeping tumbleweeds along the dry runway, the Old Man watched the distant rocks and saw nothing of the Boy.

"Where is this laser machine, Poppa?"

The Old Man turned to the base.

There is no one here and there hasn't been for a long time.

The broken stalk of a control tower rose above the airfield. Debris remained scattered across the blistered tarmac.

"She said we would find it in there," said the Old Man, pointing toward the tower. "In the basement."

They began to cross the runway.

"What is this place, Poppa?"

I know.

I knew.

It was a myth. Even then.

"A place where they kept and made weapons."

"Do you think there will be salvage here, Poppa?"

"It seems like a good place for salvage."

It was a place they made weapons we should have never needed. I can say that. I have seen what happens if you make a weapon. If you hide it somewhere secret and even pretend that you will never use it. Pretend that it doesn't even exist. Someday, you will use it.

And others must live with the consequences.

Yes.

CHAPTER 24

The work of the day began in earnest once they'd located the entrance to the tower. It was hard work. Crowbar work. At one point they'd needed to use the tank and a tow chain to remove a section of concrete blocking the entrance.

Later, when the door was revealed and they'd stopped to rest, the Old Man, sweating thickly and drinking warm water, watched his grand-daughter wander among the twisted and burnt remains of bat-winged bombers, gray with dust, sinking beneath the white salt and sand that swept in off the dry lake.

The Old Man was thinking of water.

How much is left?

And.

Where will we find more?

He turned to the aircraft scattered across the horizon.

There was a time when I would have wondered at the story of this place and those aircraft. But only because there was salvage here. Not because of the story of what happened on that last, long-lost day.

Not because of that, my friend?

No. There is too much to think of. There is water. There is this device we must find. There is food. Will the Boy be able to catch us a goat?

Goat would be nice with the pepper that remains.

And salt?

I do not think we can eat this salt.

Still, salt would be nice.

Yes.

And the tread that is going bad.

And fuel too. Do not forget fuel. You must think of fuel.

How could I not?

The Old Man took a drink of warm water from his canteen and sighed. A small breeze skittered across the desert and cooled the sweat on his neck and face.

He thought of the meal that the boy in the book would bring Santiago. Rice and bananas.

I always like to imagine that there were bits of fried pork in it.

And don't forget the coffee with milk and sugar, my friend. That was the best part.

Yes.

This place. Its story. I'll tell you. They were caught by surprise. No bombs. No nuclear bombs. No, an enemy attacked this place. There were reports of the Chinese offshore in those last weeks, but after the first EMP, the news was thin and, really, I can say this now to myself since there is no one left to contradict me, the news we hung on then was of little value. I remember though the rumors of Chinese airstrikes in the morning hours. The names of bridges and oil refineries I must have known at the time going up in the early morning darkness. We saw the smoke at dawn. That was when we began to flee.

It was Los Angeles.

Yes. That was it.

I bet Natalie knows.

One day these bombers we trusted in will sink beneath the salt and the sand and who will know what happened to them? To us. Or who will even be interested?

There is always someone.

But what if there isn't?

The Old Man watched his granddaughter return from her explorations. She was holding a jacket.

"I found this in a bag behind the seat in one of the planes, Poppa!"

She held it up triumphantly. It was green and shiny on the outside, almost brand-new. And on the inside it was orange.

A flight jacket.

And what if there isn't anyone left?

The Old Man watched her smile.

He nodded.

There must be.

AT DUSK THE BOY returned, limping across the sands, the dressed goat slung over his shoulders.

When the Old Man saw the shadow of the Boy, he turned from the rubble they'd been clearing in the stairwell that led to the collapsed rooms beneath the tower. The Old Man dropped his crowbar weakly and set to gathering what little wood he could find.

It was full dark and the stars were overhead when the goat finally began to roast. In the hours that followed, the three of them drank lightly from their canteens as their mouths watered and they watched the goat.

Close to midnight, the Old Man cut a slice off the goat and tasted it. He handed it to his granddaughter and she began to chew and hum, which was her way.

"It's ready, Poppa."

They fell to the goat with their knives, eating in the firelight, their jaws aching as grease ran down their chins.

We were hungrier than we thought.

Yes.

CHAPTER 25

The Boy found the black case underneath a desk beneath the collapsed roof of the basement he'd crawled through under the tower.

"I found it!" he shouted back through the dust and the thin light their weak flashlights tried to throw across the rubble.

"Are there words written on the side of the case?" the Old Man called through the dark.

I must remember what Natalie told me to look for. The words she said we would find. What were they?

Pause.

Maybe he doesn't know how to read. Who could have taught him?

"Project Einstein," shouted the Boy.

Who taught him how to read?

"That's it. Bring it out."

Later, in the last of the daylight beneath the broken tower, they looked at the dusty case. On its side were military codes and numbers. But the words Natalie, General Watt, had told him to look for, the words were there.

Project Einstein.

I should be . . .

Excited? Happy? Hopeful?

But I'm not. It means we must go on now. It means we must go all the way.

Yes.

"Halt!"

The voice came from behind them. It was strong yet distant, as if muffled.

"Raise your hands above your heads!"

"Poppa," whispered his granddaughter.

"Do it," he whispered back. He noticed the Boy struggle to raise his left arm as quickly as the strong right one. Even then the left failed to straighten or fully rise.

Behind them, the Old Man heard boot steps grinding sand against the cracked tarmac of the runway.

If there is just one, we might have a chance.

The Old Man looked to see if the Boy's tomahawk was on his belt. It was.

"Grayson! Trash! Move in and cover them."

Movement, steps. Gear jingling and clanking together.

The voice stepped into view, circling wide to stand between the Old Man, his granddaughter, and the Boy and the broken tower.

He carried a gun. A rifle.

An assault rifle, remembered the Old Man.

His face was covered by a black rubber gas mask.

Beneath a long coat lay dusty and cracked black plastic armor.

'Riot gear,' thought the Old Man. Just like in the days before the bombs.

On top of his head was the matte-scratched helmet of a soldier.

At his hip, a wicked steel machete forged from some long-ago-salvaged car part lay strapped.

His boots were wrapped in rags.

Within his long coat, lying against the black plastic chest armor, a slender rectangle of dented and polished silver hung.

A harmonica.

The Old Man snatched a glance at the Project Einstein case on the ground.

"What the hell are you doing out here?" said the man in the dusty black riot armor as he raised his helmet and removed the rubber gas mask from his face. The man with the harmonica about his neck.

"And more importantly, where'd you get that tank?"

He was a few days unshaven.

He was young.

He's just a man.

Like me.

But he's young.

Like I once was.

So maybe it ends here. Like the dream I have done my best to avoid. It ends with these scavengers murdering me as my granddaughter watches.

It cannot end that way.

"What're you doing out here?" repeated the Harmonica Man.

If I can get to my crowbar maybe the Boy will use his axe . . . Maybe.

"Listen," said the Harmonica Man. "You need to tell me what you're doing out here at the old base, right now!"

"They're not with them," said either Trash or Grayson from behind their masks.

"We don't know that," said the Harmonica Man. "And hell, they've got a tank."

There is a moment in between.

A moment when things might go one way or the other.

A moment when those who are prone to caution, hesitate.

And those who are prone to action, act.

"We're on a rescue mission," said the Boy.

Silence.

Maybe the guns just dropped a bit.

Maybe the masked gunmen have softened their stance.

Maybe there are other good people.

Maybe, my friend. Just maybe.

"Who?" asked the Harmonica Man.

"I don't know. He does." The Boy points to the Old Man.

Everyone turns to him.

The Old Man nods.

"All right," says the man. "We'll lower our guns and you'll tell us all about it. Then, we'll see what happens next."

The Old Man lowers his hands.

Should I?

What choice do you have? None that I can see now, my friend.

"There are some people," begins the Old Man. "They're trapped inside a bunker to the east. A place once called Colorado Springs. They need this device to get free."

"What does it do?"

"I don't know."

"Are you with King Charlie?" asked the Harmonica Man.

"No. We don't know any King Charlie."

"How'd you get this tank?"

"I found it."

The Harmonica Man thought about this, watching all of them.

The Old Man could see his granddaughter. Her mouth formed into a small "o."

"Where will you go if we let you leave?"

If?

"We will go east and try to help those people."

Silence.

"Why?"

Why?

Yes. Why, my friend?

"Because they need help."

Harmonica Man lowered his gun and leaned it against his hip.

"We have food. Do you have any water?"

"Yes," said the Old Man. "Some."

"It'll be night soon. Let's eat and I'll tell you why you might want to turn back."

CHAPTER 26

Around the fire, sharing the goat and some wheat cakes the strangers have brought out from their patchwork rucksacks, they see the faces behind the black rubber gas masks.

Grayson is a young man. Not much older than the Boy. He is quiet and smiles with dark eyes. The Old Man knows he's shy and that women find him handsome.

Trash is a girl, a woman really. Maybe in her midtwenties. Her race is mixed. Maybe some Asian. Some black. Blond dirty hair. Her tight jaw and clenched teeth show she is older than the other two, but not by much. She does not speak.

'She reminds me,' thinks the Old Man, 'of a wounded bird, or a good dog that was once mistreated.'

Harmonica Man's real name is Kyle.

He is ruddy faced and swarthy and the Old Man knows that he is the kind of young man who would fight the whole world if he had a good reason to.

Names from Before.

Names.

"If you keep going east," said Kyle as he chewed some goat meat, "there is only one island of sanity between here and Flagstaff. That's the Dam, where we come from. Beyond that, I've heard there's electricity in ABQ but that might just be something the Apache made up, 'cause they're crazy. I don't put much in what they say, especially these days."

They eat around a fire next to the tank in the shadow of the broken tower. Night falls. Only Kyle talks. There is goat, dry wheat cakes, and warm water.

"Then there's the bad news. Between you and that island of sanity is a small army of crazy. Even worse, something big is going on to the east and we don't have much information other than what the Apache let slip when they come in to trade. The real truth is, I don't know what's going down out east. What we've heard is there's a big, organized group, almost like an army come up outta Texas. They seem to follow some guy who calls himself King Charlie and what he's all about doesn't sound good. Slaves. Torture. Voodoo. Bad stuff. It was six months since we'd heard from Flagstaff when our bunch got sent out here, and that was a little over a year ago. But whatever's going down out that way ain't so good. The Apache, on a good day, are hard to deal with. But whatever's going on beyond their lands is makin' 'em even crazier than usual. So there's that. Which still ain't your biggest problem."

The Old Man chewed some of the stringier goat meat, letting the newcomers enjoy the tender goat they'd seasoned with the last of their pepper.

"Your biggest problem," continued Kyle, inspecting the rib he'd been gnawing on to make sure it was indeed devoid of meat and fat. "Your biggest problem is that small army between here and the Dam. You make it to the Dam, you can go forward. But we've been stuck out here for a year. They've got Vegas all booby-trapped up, never mind the radiation. Hell, we had a tank just like yours. I mean, maybe not the same, but old Art, he kept her running. We had some motorized flatbeds we got together and we'd run 'em up to the old air base at Creech and do some salvage. Well, that little army came in and cut us off a year ago. Now things are weird. We can't get back to the Dam. They can't get to this old place, which we think they want to real badly. They can't attack the Dam 'cause they'd never make it to the front door. But word is, they've got a bigger army somwheres out to the east. If that's actually the case, then that's a game changer as the old say. In the end, there just ain't no way through that madhouse for you and your tank."

There were no more ribs.

Kyle stared into the fire.

"Where is this 'Island of Sanity'?" asked the Old Man.

Kyle sighed.

"Home. Our home. The Dam east of Vegas."

"And so if we can make it there . . . to the Dam, then we might find some fuel if you had vehicles once."

"Yeah, we gin up a little fuel that's probably not the best, but it'll get this hunk o' metal a little farther down the road for you. Problem is, mister, you're not makin' the connection. We can't get into the Dam. There's an army between us and it. King Charlie's got an advance force all dug in like a hornets' nest."

The Old Man looked at the tank waiting in the shadowy darkness beyond the firelight.

"Did you hear me, old man, when I said we also had a tank? How d'ya think we lost it? It's in a ditch out in North Vegas. They knew we had vehicles so they booby-trapped the whole place. You try to go through Vegas, north or south, and you'll lose your ride. Plain as day, there just ain't no way through!"

Silence followed and the Old Man listened to the dry sticks within the fire crackle and pop. He watched the night wind carry sparks up and away from them.

"I don't mean to be hard on you, mister," said Kyle softly. "But you can't make it. At least not that way. You'll need to go off-road way out into the desert. If your ride's in good shape, that won't be a problem. Unless you get really stuck and then yer out in the sticks with their patrols."

Silence.

Overhead, a comet streaked through the atmosphere and burned up in almost the same second it had appeared.

Life.

And death.

"We need to stick to the roads," said the Old Man, thinking of the bad right tread.

"Well, you can't," whispered Kyle in disgust. Or fatigue. Or both.

The Old Man watched them all.

The girl, Trash, seemed somewhere else.

Grayson looked off into the night.

Kyle stared into the fire.

The Boy appeared to watch the night but the Old Man knew, or felt was more like it, that he was somewhere else, far from this fire and this night.

His granddaughter watched everyone.

And yet we must.

"We can make a way." It was Grayson.

Grayson stared hard at Kyle who refused to return the look.

"We can make a way," Grayson repeated. "Straight through, and it's all on-road."

Silence.

"Yeah, I figured you was gonna say that," mumbled Kyle after an interval full of something electric. "I figured that already."

Grayson looked at the Old Man and began to speak softly.

"We could go straight down the Strip where their lines are thinnest. Right where the bomb went off. The radiation's not too bad. They say it was just a dirty bomb but I don't know what that really means. The important thing is the road is mostly clear of booby traps between the old casinos because of the radiation. We can go that way. We can guide you. We can make a way through."

"We," said Kyle softly. "We," he thundered at Grayson and began to laugh. "We." He snorted finally. "There just ain't no way of gettin' through!"

No one spoke and the mad laughter of Kyle died away on the night's breeze.

"Kyle?" said Grayson.

"Yeah," mumbled Kyle.

"We."

"Yeah. I figured that already."

THE MORNING LIGHT shows an orange desert floor and a day turning into a forever blue. Hanging from the tank, riding in seats, or sitting atop the turret, they all depart the once-secret base.

There are still secrets buried in these sands.

Then let them stay buried, my friend. Let them stay buried forever.

Yes.

They travel south heading toward Vegas. The buckled road keeps straight, passing beneath toothy hills that guard a wide valley. An airfield rests in the center of it and buildings straddle the highway. Beyond and to the south lies a sea of rusting vehicles that stretch away to the indeterminate horizon.

Our Great Wreck seems small in comparison.

Yes.

"What happened here?" asks the Old Man leaning into Kyle's ear as he shouts above the noise of the tank.

"Before my time," yells Kyle above the wind and roar of the tank. "But they say that when the bomb went off, everyone in Vegas fled in two directions. Up here if you happened to be on the north side of town. If you were on the south side, then you might have gone out into Apache lands. My dad and mom were at the Dam on a 'field trip' when it happened. But most thought the Dam would be hit next so they just kept on moving. We never knew what really happened up here until we started coming to salvage parts years later." He stopped, and then added, "It was like this when we got here. There hasn't been anyone here for a long time."

They drove down into the valley, passing the airfield where planes lay fallen and scattered. There were visible bullet holes in the walls of the buildings.

Later, in the large fields between the small mountains that bracketed the valley, they passed RVs formed into squares that had burned down to their axles and frames. Cars torn to pieces. Not in accidents, but methodically. All the tires on every vehicle were missing. They saw shreds of tent still hanging from poles, still flapping in the breeze of their passing. Ancient blue tarps lay dustily strung between the wrecks. Every imaginable possession seemed strewn about in the dirt, and dust, some forever entrenched in the ancient mud of past rains.

I know the story of this place.

If I were going to salvage here, I could tell you their story.

But it would be a bad story.

And so, what is their story, my friend?

Somewhere, there will be a pit. Somewhere within all that wreckage, all those vehicles turned to shelters, there will be a pit. A pit of bones forty years gone.

Yes.

This bomb goes off in Las Vegas. Right in downtown. I must have heard the news of it then, but I have forgotten since. But it happened in those first early days. The bomb goes off and those who are not killed outright run.

As we ran.

As I ran.

Yes.

There is nothing but a desert to run into. The nearest cities are hundreds of miles away. And what good is it to go to those places, those cities? They too are targets. So the survivors stop here and begin to wait for help.

But there won't be any.

They wait for food and medical attention.

But there won't be any of that either.

The skies were dark within weeks.

Then there was winter.

For two years.

That is why there are no tires.

And the bullet holes?

When there is only a little left and there are many, then there are bullet holes.

And the pit?

If you wandered this maze of rusting and frozen vehicles and walked through the burned-down ruins of makeshift fortresses hustled together by a frightened few against a terrified many, on this hot desert day that will soon turn to dry afternoon, you will feel alone and a sadness you can't name as you listen to the accidental wind chimes of wreckage and bone. You will ask yourself, where did they all go?

And soon after that, you will find the pit.

Because there was sickness.

The flu, some virus, a horrible infection racing and unchecked consuming the weak, the tired, the burnt, the hungry, the desperate. The survivors.

Because there was a sickness, there will be a pit.

The Old Man stopped the tank. Ahead of them, tractor trailer trucks and ancient military vehicles long stripped of their tires and things that might burn for the simple luxury of heat have blocked the road.

This was their checkpoint.

Their attempt to control what was inevitable.

The Old Man looked for a way around the wreck.

Easing the tank down off the highway, they skirted the ancient wall of vehicles, riding rough over the hard-packed dirt.

Ahead, the Old Man spied a deflated soccer ball half sunk in the calcified mud.

The Old Man avoided it jerkily.

Why, my friend?

I don't know. But it seemed wrong to run over it.

They were back on the road and headed south.

The wind and the sun feel good and the opposite of that place, that cemetery.

Why? Why did you avoid the soccer ball? You must answer, my friend. You always have. Now, don't be afraid.

Because . . .

He drove on.

Why?

Because it is the opposite of all those secrets buried in the desert. All those weapons. All those burned tires and open pits. It is the opposite of those things.

How so?

It just is.

At dusk, a wan sky diffused with eastern dust storms roiled across the horizon, covering the melting ruins of Vegas.

They unpacked and unfolded the Radiation Shielding Kit, which was little more than a fitted blanket of coarse nylon that smelled of charcoal. They began to drape and then secure it across the tank as Kyle, Grayson, and Trash cleaned their weapons and adjusted their gear.

"We'll go ahead of you on foot and carry torches to guide you through the tight spots," said Kyle. "The two outside torches will show you how wide the path we've found is. Keep the person carrying two torches, one in each hand, in the center."

"What if you need to tell us something important?" asked the Old Man.

"I don't know . . . we could shout through the hatch maybe?"

"There's a telephone on the back of the tank inside this little cupboard," said his granddaughter. "You could use it to talk to each other."

How did she find that?

"Have you gone this way before?" asked the Old Man.

"No. No one has. But we've all been to parts of it even though we weren't s'posed to. Besides the lions that sometimes pass through, and the radiation from the wrecked airplane in the center of the Strip, the old casinos aren't too safe and seem more likely to fall down on you as much as stand up. So we were never allowed in there. But you know how it is when yer a kid."

I want to say to him that he is, they are, still kids. That it should be me out there in the dark tonight carrying the torches and them, these children, safe behind however much this blanket will protect those inside the tank. But I can't. They know the way, and I don't.

The Old Man drank some of the warm water that remained.

"If we . . ." Kyle started to say, then stopped.

He's under too much pressure. He doesn't know it, but there's a twitch just beneath his eye.

Either that or he just needs some water, my friend.

"Drink this. Drink the rest. We'll have enough water for the night. In the morning, when we reach your Dam, is there water?"

Kyle took the water and drank.

The Old Man watched the tremble in the hand of the too-young man. His Adam's apple bobbed jerkily.

"Yes," gasped Kyle. "Lots."

He's afraid.

Wouldn't you be?

Yes.

"If we don't make it," said Kyle, wiping his mouth with the back of a calloused hand, "just stay on the Strip until you get to the end. Head east when you get there and pick up the big highway that's still in good shape except for the overpasses. We made little roads around the debris. Take that highway on out to the Dam. Tell them . . ."

Kyle paused.

He doesn't know what to say. The thing he's afraid of, he cannot name. As if this moment he's lived in fear of for so long, cut off out here in the desert, is finally going to happen.

The Old Man rested his hand on Kyle's shoulder. He could feel the uneasiness there. The anxiety.

"Everything will be okay," said the Old Man.

Do you believe that, my friend?

But the Old Man had no response.

"Who will hold the two torches we must follow?"

"I will," said Kyle quickly.

"And the others, they will guide us through the tight places?"

"Yes. Grayson and Trash know what to do. Our armor should protect us from the radiation if we don't stick around for too long."

"That doesn't sound so bad. Then it's just a little walk in the night."

And slowly the twitching muscles in Kyle's shoulder beneath the Old Man's gnarled hand stopped.

The boy soldier, the Harmonica Man, Kyle, began to breathe again.

"Maybe the dust storm will cover us?" he said and smiled.

The Old Man nodded.

"Why do you call her Trash? She's very beautiful. I know I'm old but 'Trash' doesn't mean . . ."

Kyle picked up his chest armor and began to examine it.

"No," he said almost to himself. "It means the same for us too."

"Then why such an awful name?"

Kyle put down the armor, bent to take up another piece, and seemed to let go of the idea halfway through. He straightened and stared at the Old Man.

"She won't respond to anything else."

The Old Man said nothing, his blue eyes searching for meaning.

"She and a trader we did business with for years came out of the North. We knew the trader long before she came with him. She didn't say anything ever. We thought she was just shy. The trader just referred to her as his girl. Maybe a daughter we thought. One night the trader got a little drunk, which was his way, and he told us how he'd rescued her from a bunch of hillbillies up in the mountains. They, the hillbillies, they'd called her Trash. They'd also removed her tongue. Treated her pretty badly, I guess."

Kyle looked toward Trash. She worked intently with dirty blackened rags cleaning her gun.

"We kept trying to give her new names. Normal ones like from Before. Jenny. Susie. The trader said he'd even made ones up that he thought she might like from words that used to be beautiful before the bombs. But she wouldn't have any of it. She wouldn't respond. Not unless he called her Trash. He explained to her it wasn't such a good name for good people. But she wouldn't have it. He said one day they were high up on a pass and the snow was coming down. He started building their shelter, said it was like to turn to a blizzard more than not. He decides he's gonna call her this name he thinks is real pretty whether she likes it or not. Aria. Weird name if I ever heard one. Aria. So he starts using it and she just won't help. It's getting cold and their mules are freezing but she just stands there in the snow. The trader's still callin' her by that weird name and it's gettin' dark and the snow is fallin' sideways. But she stands there in the snow. Won't do nuthin'. Night falls. She won't even come in to his little tent. Finally he said he just laughed to himself and gave up for good. Trash it was. I remember I thought that was the end of his story. People got up and left the cantina. Saul, the guy who runs the place, he turned the lanterns down. He always did that when it was time for all of us to go home."

Kyle fell silent for just a moment, and in that moment there were memories and thoughts of good things from home. Lanterns. Cantina. Home.

"That trader stands up. He was a big man. Big like a bear almost. We'd been drinkin', and he says to me, 'You know what the name Trash means to me?' I didn't say nothin', just listened. He says, 'It means valuable. Like somethin' so valuable, there's no piece of salvage or skin or meat you'd trade for it. 'Cause if you did the world just wouldn't seem right anymore. When I say that word I see her. And that's a good thing to me. It's one good thing that's still left in this burned-up old world. Maybe the last piece of good we all got left.' About a year later she came back alone. We don't know what happened to the trader, but it wasn't good. So we took her in."

The Old Man watched her. She was cleaning her gun. Cleaning it as though it was the most important work left to her in a burned-up old world.

Trash.

CHAPTER 28

The tank followed the three dark figures through the dust storm. Ahead, the ruins of Las Vegas hovered in and out of the skirling grit that sent sheets of brown and gray across the dark sky and swept the crumbling highway.

There should be a good moon out tonight but the dust is too thick to find it.

Ahead, the superhighway that once cut through the desert and the city had long ago collapsed into rubble. The Old Man could see oil drums filled with fire and belching black smoke from atop piles of fortified concrete. Stakes and spears and tattered banners jutted and flapped madly in the storm.

Who are these people? This Army of Crazy. King Charlie's advance force Kyle called them.

They're different from the Horde. More organized. More dangerous. They've made traps and they have flags and lines of defense. They've come to rule, not like those I faced at Picacho Peak. They were little more than locusts. These are like wolves.

Yes.

Ahead of the tank, the three figures lit their four torches. Grayson on the right. Trash on the left. Kyle holding two in the center.

The Old Man checked the case again, making sure it still rested on the floor of the tank.

The Boy sat in the loader's seat, watching the Old Man.

His granddaughter was in the driver's seat, forward and buttoned up.

"Are you all right up there?" he said to her over the intercom.

"Yes, Poppa. Can I drive now?"

"No. Not yet. Maybe on the other side."

The bobbing torches descended off the freeway, following an off-ramp down into the ruins of the ancient gambling palaces.

Crumbling casinos like canyon walls rose up dirty and dusty on both sides. Debris skittered wildly down the side streets. Ahead, the Old Man could see the broad thoroughfare they must traverse.

Kyle's father and mother and all the old ones of the Dam had told of the day when the airliner, taking off from the airport south of the city, had been crashed directly onto the Strip.

Terrorists.

It wasn't until hours later that the authorities, and then everyone else, realized the plane had also been carrying a dirty bomb. A low-yield nuclear dirty bomb. That was when the panic started. When everyone fled.

Like you did in Los Angeles.

Yes, like we all did.

Kyle said the plane and its dirty bomb were why they'd been told to avoid the main road through the casinos. Because of the dirty bomb. Only the bravest kids claimed to have seen the actual wreckage of the plane, lying halfway up the Strip in the middle of the street.

That must have been a bad day.

There were a lot of bad days back then, my friend.

The Old Man turned to wondering if the Radiation Shielding Kit would indeed protect them.

He looked at the radio.

Concentrate on the path through the rubble. If you get stuck in this city, you've made things worse for everyone, and for no reason at all.

Yes.

He followed the jumping torches onto the main street.

Fractured monuments fell away into the dusky gloom behind them. Alongside the road, a million darkened and shattered windows looked down upon them. Crumbling walkways crossing the street resembled strands of moss draped over swampy water. The torches guttered in the blasting wind, their oily fuel barely illuminating the ground beneath the feet of their guides as the flames fought desperately against the storm.

Those torches won't last long.

Frozen buses lay on their sides, thrown across the road, while petrified cars littered the streets in haphazard directions. A clear reason why they'd stopped on that last, long-ago day seemed just out of reach, and in the end, unknowable.

Their procession of torches and armored tank began to weave through the wrecks, occasionally crushing a smaller vehicle, its rusty destruction blossoming for an instant like a sickly rose, suddenly carried off by the storm.

Ahead, a cluster of dust-caked and ashy gray emergency vehicles, fire engines and ambulances from that long-ago lost day of an air disaster turned terrorist attack, walled off the street ahead.

On that day, those firefighters must have thought the downed aircraft was the biggest tragedy they'd ever seen, were likely to ever see.

And then someone told them about the radiation.

The Old Man looked at the dosimeter.

It's very high here.

Kyle knows I am worried about the right tread. I hope he doesn't ask me to drive over those fire engines. Besides, we must be getting near Ground Zero, and it should be time to go around the actual bomb site.

Ground Zero.

I have not used those words . . . since I cannot remember when.

The Old Man marveled at the thought.

Those words were once a common part of my vocabulary. Of all our vocabularies. I remember entire conversations, courses of action, fears that were based on those two simple little words. Ground Zero.

As if listening in on the Old Man's thoughts, the four torches veered to the left, heading into the gray and dusty ruins of a darkened casino. It loomed high above the tiny tank and the three figures like some scavenger bird of the wasteland. The wings of the two towers almost enveloped the street and all within it like a hunched and greedy eater of carrion.

We've passed the unmanned defenses of this Army of Crazy. If they're anywhere, they'll be hunkered down from this storm, inside one of these old places. Waiting for us.

And . . .

I don't want to go in there. I don't want anyone, any of these children, to have to go into that dilapidated and evil pile of ruin.

But we must, my friend. There is no other way through this city. No other way to stay on the road and keep the tank from throwing a tread, which we could never fix. If we take our chances on the side streets we could end up caught in one of their traps. Trust these children, my friend.

But why would they help us like this?

And the Old Man thought of his own journey and General Watt. Natalie.

When the Old Man didn't follow immediately, Kyle, masked and armored, turned back in the thundering wind and waved both torches toward the tank and then back toward himself.

Are you sure?

He must be.

The Old Man pivoted the tank, once again feeling the weakness in the right tread, wondering if it wasn't the control mechanisms that were responsible for his suspicions.

They attacked at that moment.

They came gushing out of the casino's open mouth.

The Old Man watched through the hazy green optics of night vision as wild figures surged downward upon the three torchbearers.

At once, bright flashes erupted from the rifles of Grayson and Trash.

A bare-chested man waving an iron pipe studded with spikes was flung backward onto the rotting shreds of carpet that once dressed the steps of the palace.

A one-armed giant hurled a heavy stone, nearly crushing Grayson who batted it away with his arm. The Old Man saw the arm go limp, but Grayson continued to fire into the onslaught with the other.

Lumbering men in armor that shimmered in small points of white fuzz by the green light of night vision raced forward, leaping over downed comrades, waving machetes and nail-studded clubs. They wore turbans that wrapped their faces.

With her machine gun, Trash stitched a bright line of death across their charge, flinging some sideways as others stumbled forward waving their blades halfheartedly while blood pumped out darkly onto the dusty steps and shredded carpet. They fell before they reached her.

Now she was reloading, and the Old Man could see that the shimmering armor of the crazies was made up of coins. Coins that had been hole punched and stitched together into coats of mail.

Their coin-mail armor must be good against hand weapons but guns are another story.

He felt the Boy at his side.

"Sit down in there." He pointed toward the gunner's seat. "Look through this and you'll see what's going on."

The Boy slithered past him.

When the Old Man looked into the night-vision scope, he saw Kyle moving forward, while Grayson covered him holding his rifle with his good arm. Trash seemed to be intent on fixing her battered rifle while still walking forward.

Her weapon is jammed.

The attackers were retreating now, disappearing into the dark gray of the casino halls beyond the once-grand entrance of marble and arch.

Kyle mounted the steps, waving his torches forward over his shoulders, indicating the tank should follow them in.

The Old Man gently pushed forward on the sticks and the tank began to mount the steps.

The attackers were all gone now.

Trash turned and waved at him with her torch, showing him how much room he had to thread the opening into the casino.

The Old Man gave it more gas, hearing the top of the archway leading to the casino scrape against the turret and then give way in a stony crumble of dust and metal that bounced off the armor above their heads.

Inside, a large dust-covered marble lobby vaulted toward a high domed ceiling of broken glass and blackened ironwork. Kyle waved both torches into an X and laid them on the debris-littered marble floor. He ran to the back of the tank, out of sight, and the Old Man knew he would hear from him on the small telephone attached to the rear of the tank.

"We can't make it any farther down the street," yelled Kyle over the internal hum of the communications system and the howling wind outside.

"Follow us through this casino. On the other side of the machines there's another entrance back onto the street on the far side of Ground Zero."

"Okay," said the Old Man.

"Oh," said Kyle almost as an afterthought. "Does this thing have any ammo for its gun? Ours did a long time ago but we used that up."

"There are eleven rounds left."

"Don't fire in here! It's too dangerous. These buildings are barely standing up."

The line went dead, and shortly after, Kyle reappeared in the fuzzy gray optics, picking up his torches and waving them forward over his shoulders in bright white blurs of light and shadowy smoke toward a long hallway that stretched off into the depths of the casino.

When it became so dark inside the long hallway that the Old Man could see nothing but gray, green, and ash, he switched on the tank's high beams and turned off the night vision.

They followed a wide way of rotting red carpet and dust-covered advertising. Signs that had once held meaning remained embedded in graffiti-gouged wood paneling. Beautiful girls, faded and long dead, promised wealth untold. Thrilling spectacles dully offered entertainments that were sure to dazzle. There were even peeling pictures of unending amounts of food.

Lobster.

I had forgotten about lobster!

Concentrate, Old Man!

They entered a massive room of slot machines and overturned gaming tables. Silvery coins lay heaped in piles. Large torches guttered from makeshift holders along the walls. Campfires burned intermittently among the arranged stockades of slot machines.

The Old Man could see the three guides talking among themselves as they moved slowly forward.

They're worried. They didn't expect this.

We've walked into a hornets' nest.

Sudden dark shadows arched through the upper atmosphere of the room and began to fall among the tank and the three guides.

They're firing arrows at us!

The Old Man could hear their impact distantly on the outer hull of the tank. The three guides retreated to the far side of the vehicle, using it for cover. Coins used as sling bullets began to ricochet like metallic rain upon the tank.

"Move forward toward that arch at the far end of this hall." It was Kyle on the tank's phone. "We should be able to get back out to the street if we go that way."

The Old Man gunned the tank's engine, hoping the three of them were clear, unable to know for sure if they were.

"Poppa, are they going to be okay?"

"Yes. I would prefer if maybe you just closed your eyes until I say it's good to look again, okay?"

There was no immediate reply and he suspected she would disobey him.

Beyond the arch, the tank's headlamp illuminated another long hallway. The ceiling sagged the length of it. Rich wood paneling that must have once assured the gambling audiences this was indeed the finest of places to lose all their money and homes had long since been pried loose in wide patches.

For firewood, I imagine.

At the end of the hall, they turned onto an arcade of shops long gutted. Fixtures spilled out onto a marble palazzo or hung like the bones of criminals from the ceiling.

The Old Man swiveled the gun sight, searching the optics for his three guides. He found them behind the tank, covering their retreat from the hall as dark figures swarmed beyond the light of the tank's headlamp. Far down the hall he could see more of the coin-mailed warriors advancing behind crude shields.

The Old Man backed the tank out and onto the main thoroughfare of the arcade pointing it toward where he hoped the exit might be.

I'm lost in here.

Grayson ran forward and waved at the Old Man to follow him.

Their torches are lost or gone out now.

The Old Man maneuvered the tank after the armored and masked Grayson who ran forward weaving into and out of the destruction and litter that had once been a grand passage of fine shops and luxuries. What the Old Man could not steer around he crushed beneath the tank's treads, hoping each time the right tread would not suddenly break and strand them all.

He checked the dosimeter.

The radiation is higher here. Maybe we are getting closer to the street again.

It's better than being trapped in here with these lunatics, my friend.

"Can I look now, Poppa?"

She listened to me.

And . . .

She is good that way.

"Not yet, just a little farther."

It was hot inside the tank and the Old Man wiped at the thick, stinging sweat on his forehead.

Maybe I am still sick.

Concentrate!

The explosions went off behind them.

The Old Man felt the tank lift up slightly and then shudder as it settled back down onto the palazzo. When he swiveled the gun sight to see what had happened behind them, all was a blossom of powdery white dust in the tank's optics. He could see nothing through its sudden storm.

He switched off the lights and activated the night vision.

Everything was still gray and floating dust.

No good, my friend.

He switched the headlight back on and returned to normal optics.

They've brought the ceiling down upon us. They must have explosives.

He searched for Kyle and Trash within the swirling dust and settling debris.

Trash stumbled forward, bleeding and waving at them to push on.

Where is Kyle?

There is no time, Old Man! Move forward or you and your granddaughter and the Boy will be trapped in here too.

The Old Man gassed the engine and swiveled the gun sight forward in time to avoid Grayson's crawling body. Large arrows jutted out of his back and chest and arm. He rose stiffly, firing his rifle wildly with one hand into a darkened arch to their left. A moment later, another massive iron spike shot from the darkness and went straight through his chest.

The Old Man could hear his granddaughter screaming.

Ahead of the tank, dust clouds, thick and ashy, swirled through a jumble of broken debris. Where the path through the casino lay the Old Man could not see.

There is no clear way forward!

Trash appeared and waved wildly, passionately, for him to follow her now.

She is all alone out there.

And . . .

She is very brave.

And . . .

They all were.

Everywhere, the Old Man could see moving shadows and sudden figures leaping as Trash walked forward, firing at unseen foes. When they neared the far end of the arcade, a massive dirty marble fountain rose up. Above it, bodies dangled from a dome of smashed glass and skeletal ironwork directly over the darkly stained marble sculptures within the dry fountain.

Trash went wide to the left, her gun hammering bullets into walls and doors where unseen oppressors lurked in the darkness. Suddenly her gunfire stopped and she slung the rifle back onto her shoulder, drawing out a large knife with her other hand. A man with tiny rat teeth rose up from within the fountain behind her and pulled her down onto the marble floor. Coin-mailed men rushed from the darkness and dragged her across the dusty litter, back toward the blackness behind a broken-down double door. They were already greedily clutching at her armor, ripping away her mask, revealing her horrified and angry face.

She's gone now.

There's nothing I can do to save her.

The Old Man had to release his sweating hands from the controls for fear of breaking them.

Think!

There is nothing I can do to help her.

You can't save her. But you can help her, my friend.

The Old Man swiveled the main gun toward the broken-down doors, pointing the barrel into the darkness beyond where they had dragged her. He reached over to the fire control switch.

The Boy slid past him, opening the emergency hatch in the deck plate.

How did he know that was there?

The Boy looked at the Old Man.

"Just get back to the street," he said, his voice hoarse and dry. "I'll find her. Then I'll find you."

And he was gone, closing the hatch behind him.

The Old Man waited, unsure of how long it would take the Boy to crawl out from between the treads. A moment later he appeared, steel tomahawk out, limping toward the broken-down door and the darkness beyond.

Go now!

The Old Man gunned the engine and circled the fountain. On the other side he found a large arch, once grand and opulent, now fading in neglect and damage, leading to another long hallway. Along its length, torches revealed a hall of horrors as beheaded mannequins held their arms upward. The long hall narrowed to an opening impossible for the tank to clear and the Old Man pressed the engine to full power, closed his eyes, and smashed the tank straight into it.

On the other side he slammed on the brakes and the tank skidded across marble, careening into a lone desk that must have once greeted arriving guests. The Old Man swiveled the turret and found a wide entrance leading back out onto the street. He pivoted the tank and throttled the engine to full as it tore through the last remnants of broken glass and bent steel, surging out onto the wide steps and a driveway that led off toward the main road. The tank bumped its way down the steps, crushed an ancient taxi, and charged up the driveway and out onto casino row.

All around him, radiation-rotted towers and palaces rose up in only the color of burnt ash. Dry white grass and burnt earth lay beneath a constant snowfall of settling radioactive debris. In the middle of the street lay an airliner in two distinct parts, its center section long gone, the tail rising up at an odd angle in the background, the cockpit smiling sickly at some bad joke played forty years ago. Its sweptback wings akimbo, as though in some confession of final helplessness.

The dust storm had stopped.

The moon was out.

Fading flakes of ash drifted like snow on a winter's night.

Everything that was not burnt black or tired gray remained bone white.

The Old Man checked the "outside" dosimeter. It was pegged to the red line. The "inside" counter was high, but still within the green.

It works.

Our little blanket works.

The Old Man maneuvered the tank onto the main road.

A path of frozen destruction lay carved from when the airliner had come down onto the street moments after takeoff and left a clear path through the forty years since. The Old Man settled the tank into the ditch of scarred asphalt and followed it east through the last of the collapsing palaces.

AT DAWN, IN the shadows among the pink light of first morning, the Old Man watched the ancient city refuse to illuminate in color. He had the tank backed up against a wall in a vacant lot beyond the casinos, watching the leaning towers and fallen arcades, waiting for the Boy.

There isn't much fuel left.

I'll give him until noon and then we must leave.

His granddaughter was asleep.

He'd had to explain a lot of what had happened. What she had seen. What she should've never seen.

And there was much he could not explain.

So he told her about ice cream.

She'd never had ice cream.

"One day we'll find an ice cream maker, one with a hand crank. All we need is some milk, maybe we can get some from our goats, and then we only need to find some salt. Then we can have ice cream. You will love it."

Sugar. You will need sugar, my friend.

There is the sugar from the date palms. We could use that.

"I know I will, Poppa. I just know I'll love it."

"There are even flavors." And the Old Man began to name as many as he could remember.

Soon she was asleep.

I hope she dreams only of ice cream.

Ice cream dreams.

You were wrong to bring her with you, my friend.

I know that now.

In time, he saw the Boy limping across an abandoned lot of glittering broken glass, crossing a gray and dusty road, and cutting through a fallen mesh fence. Heading for the tank.

He was alone.

CHAPTER 29

As the morning sun began to bake the quiet destruction between the empty spaces and cracked parking lots of Vegas, the Old Man climbed down from the tank and handed the last of a half-filled canteen to the Boy.

The Boy began to drink, holding the canteen with his powerful right hand. The Old Man looked at the dried blood covering the Boy's arms, still staining the tomahawk.

There is no need to ask him what happened in there.

He left the Boy to drink water alone in the silence of the place.

Inside the tank, he started the APU and radioed General Watt. Natalie.

"We're on the other side of Las Vegas now."

"Good." Her voice was warm and clear. Like she'd just had a cup of morning coffee. Like there might be a cup waiting for him, wherever she was.

As if such good things exist anymore.

As if there are such moments left in this world.

"It's a good thing you got us to that Radiation Shielding Kit," he said. Then he told her what he could of the night. He told her about the three. How they'd made a way when there seemed none. And how each had died in doing so. He could not tell the one without the other. When he told General Watt of the bomb crater they'd come upon, she asked about the shielding kit. "We needed it to cross through a bomb crater."

"You've used it already?"

There wasn't exactly alarm in her voice. Not exactly. But something.

Concern?

"Yes." Then, "Is that going to be a problem?" asked the Old Man, hearing the sudden worry in his own voice. "Should we . . . is there something else ahead . . ."

Pause.

"It won't be a problem," said Natalie, her voice gentle and calm. "We'll find a way to keep you safe. If you had to use it to survive, then it had to be used."

"I hope we didn't . . . I hope that was all right," stammered the Old Man. "I hope . . ."

"It's all right."

Her voice is like the voice of someone who knows that eventually everything is going to be just fine, no matter how bad it looks right now. No matter what you've done to mess things up.

You need that, my friend, so take it because it is being given away for free and also because you are too poor to disagree.

Yes.

"There is nothing to worry about at this present time," said General Watt. Natalie. "It'll be all right. We will find a way to get you here."

But the Old Man knew that it wasn't all right. That some change had taken place in the wind and weather, the current and tide, and finally as it must, the last port at journey's end.

And.

There is always a price to pay for such things.

Yes.

Always.

And someone will have to pay for it.

Someone will.

In the hatch, beneath the sun, the Old Man felt cold.

THE ROAD UP and out of southern Las Vegas climbed through tired rocks and vast crumbling urban sprawls of falling houses and collapsed roadways. A barely readable sign indicated the way to Lake Mead.

In time Las Vegas disappeared behind them, fading into the heat of a day that chased them with its memories of the night. The road led alongside the outlines of buildings once standing and now long gone. The land opened up onto a massive downslope of red earth and gray rock. At the bottom lay the glittering blue of a wide lake stretching out and away from them.

The road began a series of twists through rock formations that seemed foreign and somehow of another world. Another world the Old Man dimly remembered from the covers of science fiction books about strange and alien planets. A crumbling tower rose up from the red rocks alongside the lake and the road. Its tenure seemed thin and merely a matter of time.

The road that led to the Dam cut across the face of this reddish-brown rock above a steep drop into canyons below. Beyond all this, the Dam climbed skyward and their eyes saw what man had once made.

"We made this, Poppa?"

"Yes," was all the Old Man could say, his voice unexpectedly choking with pride.

I did not think it would affect me this way.

And . . .

I had no idea.

The Boy lay sleeping. The Old Man stopped the tank and shook him.

He should see this too.

He should know we weren't all bad.

They climbed out from their hatches, his granddaughter in her new flight jacket, the Boy still covered in blood. The Old Man shielded his eyes against the blaze of noon with his wrinkled and calloused hand. The massive Dam stretched high above them.

Yes.

We built this.

And . . .

We were not all bad.

THE PEOPLE WHO came out from the Dam wore the same shreds of armor and carried the same rifles as Kyle, Grayson, and Trash.

A large man walked out in front of them. There was a smile on his face. He wore faded denim and an old Stetson hat, sun-bleached and torn.

"You can't be with King Charlie if you've gotten out of your tank," he bellowed, his voice bombastic, echoing off the canyon walls and the Dam.

"We aren't," said the Old Man, sounding thin and dry, his voice a small croak.

When did my voice start to sound like that of an old person?

The people behind the Big Man began to clap. Someone whooped with excitement. They patted each other. There was even weeping.

These people are in need of good news.

Yes, my friend, and they seem to think you are it.

The people of the Dam approached the tank, surrounding it at once. Feeling it. Touching it. Marveling.

These are Kyle's people. Grayson's.

And Trash's too.

We took her in.

That's what Kyle had said.

We took her in.

There were questions all at once and each one different.

Who are you?

Where'd you get the tank?

How'd you make it through?

Where are you going?

Do you need fuel?

Have you seen . . . ?

The Old Man grew confused in his rush to answer each question. Starting an answer and then being pulled away by another. Until he saw the Big Man staring at him. Still smiling. Waiting. And even though there was a smile, a big smile, there was also worry. Worry in the eyes. There was a question about the three and the Old Man could tell it was waiting for him and that the Big Man would never ask it. He would never ask it because maybe in the long days since its first being asked, he had answered it for himself. In his mind Kyle, Grayson, and Trash and all the others who had been trapped beyond Vegas had perished long ago. They must've.

But there are nights. Nights when one wonders what might still be possible despite all evidence to the contrary. Nights when you rise alone for just a drink of water, and in the silence you sigh and think of unanswered questions.

You think of loved ones and where they might be.

And even . . .

If, they might be.

And when there are no answers in the night, you sigh and think . . .

What am I going to do now?

"Do you know Kyle?" asked the Old Man.

The Big Man nodded, his eyes changing to hope and belief and then disbelief all at once. Speaking as he nods. Speaking words as if he cannot believe these words he has said so many times in the night might actually be real words.

"He's alive? My son is . . ." the Big Man's voice faltered, unwilling to form that last word again.

Alive.

His son. All this time he has imagined him dead and hated himself for it.

"He . . ." tries the Old Man and stops.

Tell them, my friend.

I'm afraid to. How?

Just tell them. In time it will be a mercy to them, though they will not know it today.

No.

No, today will be for grief. Which is also, sometimes, a mercy.

Other names are quickly shouted out. Names that are not Kyle or Grayson.

There were others before it was only just the three of them.

An older couple. She is already clinging to a man turning white with shock, holding on to her as much as she is holding on to him.

Holding on to each other.

The Old Man sees his own son.

And wonders . . .

What is he doing right now?

And . . .

How do I tell them?

The truth, my friend. The truth. In the end it is what we must have. There is nothing else.

All eyes watched him.

He shook his head slowly.

"They made a way for us," said the Old Man. "Where there wasn't one."

The Old Man wanted to lower his eyes. He wanted to look away as they stared at him for meaning, for answers, for some shred of long denied truth.

But it would be wrong to look away. Cowardly.

And then someone asked, as if it wasn't already known to all. Someone asked, "Did they make it?"

THE OLD MAN remembered weeping and feeling he had no right to. The three were theirs, not his.

But he wept for them all the same and they did not stop him.

Grayson's mother cried out her son's name.

The Old Man saw her husband pulling her into him, holding on to her. He was like a man being swept away by a river.

CHAPTER 30

The Old Man sat in the cantina drinking clear, cold water and listening to the old pipes above his head creak and gurgle within the Dam. Only a frail lantern illuminated the small dark room.

This is where they gather when the day is done.

Like when the boy would bring you the papers, Santiago, that were a few days, or even a week old, and you would read them together and talk about baseball.

And like your village, my friend, in the late afternoon, when the first of the evening brought out the scent of the desert sage, heavy and thick.

We did not have papers with baseball scores, though. But yes, this place is where they come at the end of the day or when they have something to celebrate like a birthday. Just like we did back in the village, in the old mining hall outside the kitchen. So I know this place, and I know these people.

The Big Man came in.

Kyle's dad.

He went to the cooler that held the cold spring water and poured some into a porcelain mug. He drank, filled it again, then drank again, each time emitting a tired but satisfied, "Ahhh."

"You have a good spring for your water," said the Old Man.

The Big Man turned, surprised.

He must have thought he was all alone. He was expecting the solitude, the moment apart. The moment apart from their collective grief. He must be their leader. He must have wanted time for his own, personal grief.

For his son.

"We've always had that to be thankful for," said the Big Man. "Good water. A good safe place. Good people."

The Big Man sat down.

"Normally we'd have been celebrating your arrival . . . but . . . I guess not." The Big Man looked down into his mug of water. "We thought, that is, some of us did, we thought we'd buried those who didn't make it back, a while ago. Others kept holding out. Hoping there might be a chance some of 'em would make it back, someday."

You. You were holding out.

And.

I would too.

"I'm sorry," said the Old Man.

"Ain't your fault."

"Tomorrow," began the Big Man, "we'll be back to our old selves, fightin' and crabbin' at one or the other. Maybe we'll kill one of the cows and have a 'Q' up top. That'd be real nice."

"The showers were enough," said the Old Man. "More than enough. We'll move on tomorrow if you can spare some of your fuel."

"Fuel? You can have all the fuel you want; we've done lost all our vehicles trying to keep the roads open. All our rides are either out there in pieces, torn to shreds by King Charlie's crazies, or they're broke down in the garage below."

"What will we find in the east?"

"East," said the Big Man and rubbed his chin. "East is Kingman and Flagstaff and then you're in Apache lands. The Apaches told us there was some people out in ABQ who were makin' a pretty good go of it."

The Old Man waited. The Big Man looked like he had more to say.

"Truth is, I couldn't tell you what you'll find beyond a thousand meters out in front of this Dam. These raiders come down from the North a year and a half ago and ruined our plans to get a network of roads and outposts open and connected. They went wide of Apache lands but they came down hard on Kingman and straight into Vegas. We caught a few. That was how we found out they were lookin' for old Area 51. We didn't know what they were up to but we figured we needed to keep them out of there. Tried to get 'em to focus on the Dam but they wouldn't have it. They dug in all around Vegas and kept us out of our salvage up in Creech. That was how you met my boy. Kyle."

Silence.

"He was a good leader," said the Old Man.

In the dark of the cantina, in the shadows thrown by the dim lantern, the Old Man heard the Big Man sob once and so suddenly that a moment later he wondered if he'd even heard it at all.

"I know," mumbled the Big Man. "I know that about my son."

LATER, THE OLD MAN found the Boy near the tank, sitting against its dusty treads. The Old Man sat down next to him.

It's time I try to talk to him.

"Are you hungry?"

The Boy shook his head.

"When you went back . . . did you find her?"

The Boy looked at the Old Man sharply.

He's confused.

There's another "her" besides the girl Trash.

When the look of bewilderment passed from the Boy's face and he understood who the Old Man was talking about, he said, "I did."

The Old Man waited.

It'll come. Whatever his story is, it'll come.

Just wait. Be patient.

Inside the Boy's eyes, the Old Man found a story he didn't know how to read just yet.

Just like salvage. There's always a story. Even in the eyes of a man. Or a boy.

He's all alone.

The Old Man groaned as he got to his knees.

He rested his hand briefly on the Boy's muscled shoulder, and after it jumped and settled at his touch, he squeezed it firmly.

I'm here.

And . . .

You are too.

That's important these days.

The Old Man stood and walked back toward the doorway that led from the garage within the Dam, back to the small rooms they'd made available for them.

The Boy spoke.

Just before the Old Man reached the door.

"We take everything with us."

The Old Man turned, searching the dark and finding the shadow of the Boy.

"They never leave." The Boy's voice was husky and deep. "Even if you want them too."

Silence.

"Then maybe we really don't want them to go just yet," said the Old Man and turned back to the door and was gone.

DEEP IN THE NIGHT, the Old Man awoke, sweating.

I was drowning, but not in water. In darkness.

His granddaughter is asleep on her cot.

The Boy's is empty.

The Old Man lay back down, breathing slowly, willing his racing heart to settle.

The Boy is still disturbed by what he's had to do within the casino. Maybe he is forever damaged just like his weak side. Maybe I should just leave him here.

Stop. It's the middle of the night and it's dark, my friend. The worst time to try to make plans or important decisions.

And the Old Man thought of how his friend Santiago had followed the fish all through the night, all alone, being pulled deeper and deeper into the gulf.

CHAPTER 31

Night fell across the western horizon, and atop the Dam the first ribs of meat were handed out to those who had waited throughout that long, hot, dusty afternoon.

The ribs were meaty and full of juice.

The Old Man ate one sitting next to his granddaughter, surrounded by the people of the Dam, telling them of Tucson. Telling them about a city that was lost and now found. Telling them of lemon trees and salvage.

"We were trying to open the roads and keep the lines of communication up between the settlements," said one of them after the Old Man had finished telling all there was to tell of Tucson. "Maybe we could still do that with Tucson."

Everybody quietly agreed this might be a good idea.

Despite the lack of vehicles.

The Army of Crazy in Vegas.

The rumors of the East.

The tragedy of the three still hangs over them.

What could I offer that would make it better for them?

Nothing, my friend. Nothing.

"Poppa, where is he?" she said referencing the Boy.

The Old Man looked down into her big brown eyes.

Has she already fallen for him? I thought she was still too young for that.

Who can know the heart, my friend?

I thought I did.

And . . .

You were wrong.

I'm almost convinced now that we must leave the Boy. He's wounded. Damaged and what if he fails when we need him most. Or what if he turns on us.

If you were to ask yourself, my friend, can you trust him? What would your answer be?

I don't know.

"He's missing everything, Poppa!" she said looking up from her plate. Worried.

"I'll go look for him. I'll find him. Watch my plate."

"Okay, Poppa."

The Old Man found the Boy near the tank down in the garage. Securing their gear. He had rearranged the drums into a better configuration for drawing fuel.

When he saw the Old Man watching him, he stopped.

"It will be better this way," he seemed to apologize.

The Old Man walked across the silent and dark garage.

Tell him he'll have to stay behind. That he can't go on with you.

You mean, tell him I don't trust him.

"It will be better that way," said the Old Man. "You've done good. Thank you."

The Boy smiled.

In the days since he has been with us I don't think I've actually seen him smile. Inside of him there is still something that wants to though. Something that "done" things and a life on the road hasn't managed to burn up yet.

"Come. There's meat. Good ribs from a steer. There might even be one left for you."

The Boy hopped down from the tank awkwardly and limped toward the Old Man, the memory of his smile refusing to let go.

Sometimes he is so able and strong, you forget half his body is withered.

They turned and the Old Man patted the Boy once more on the shoulder, feeling the powerful warmth of his strong right side, remembering the sudden smile.

And he thought, 'I won't leave you.' And, 'Maybe you just need to be salvaged.'

THE OLD MAN did not sleep much.

Maybe I slept a little.

But not enough to be of measure, to count. To be worth it.

He was up before anyone.

Close to dawn.

He went to the tank.

The tank and drums were full of the home-brewed fuel.

Also, we have all the water we can carry.

They would have rice and beans, cooked already, and flour tortillas they could heat on the warmth of the engine.

There are over two hundred and fifty miles to Flagstaff. They tell me there might be fuel there. So maybe . . .

I am tired of worrying about fuel. It will either be there or it won't. But I am tired of worrying about it. I am anxious to be on the road and to be done with this errand.

You are not worried, my friend?

I am that too.

AT DAWN, the Big Man and the others arrived. In time the storage cases full of rice, beans, and tortillas were loaded on board the tank. The Boy came carrying their things. The Old Man's granddaughter, fresh from the showers, wrapped in her shiny green bomber jacket against the cold that lay deep within the Dam, carried just her sleeping bag.

The Old Man started the APU and fired the main engine. Smoke erupted across the garage and the people raced to raise the big door.

The Big Man climbed up on the turret as the Old Man throttled the engine back and forth, hoping the cause of the thick smoke was just moisture in the fuel.

"Never mind that," yelled the Big Man over the whispering roar of the engine. "Our home brew is a little watery, burns rough, but it works!" He smiled broadly. "Tell Reynolds at Kingman that Conklin sent you and to give ya any fuel, if he's got it. Reynolds is good people."

The Old Man shook the Big Man's hand and made ready to go.

Once everyone was clear, he pivoted the tank toward the entrance and gassed it until they were out in the morning sun followed by a cloud of blue smoke.

The right tread may or may not be going bad and we make more smoke than we should. So there is that to worry about.

You complain too much, my friend.

Yes, I know.

BEYOND THE DAM, a long valley slid away toward the southeast and a timeworn highway ran through it. The Old Man checked his map.

We'll link up with the 40 in Kingman. We can follow that all the way into Albuquerque.

Long-gone fires had consumed much of the land in the years after the long winter. Wild growth covered what lay in the flatlands between the two mountain ranges that defined the valley.

It reminds me of the highway alongside our village, except it's lonelier.

HOURS LATER the Old Man spied the first riders high atop the cut-rock mesas as the highway twisted through red rock, closing in on Kingman. Who they were and what they wore was unknowable at distance. They were mere shadows high up on the broken rocks. They rode horses and carried long spears from which dark feathers dangled in the breeze. But that they knew of the tank and its passage was sure to be counted on.

CHAPTER 32

The Boy looked back at him and the Old Man nodded.

We have both seen the riders.

The Old Man was driving, following the bumping, uneven road that wound toward Kingman.

"Just keep on the road and try to stay near the center," his granddaughter told him. "It looks to be in better shape there than on the edges, Poppa."

"Okay."

Now she is giving me advice on how to drive this thing. Hoping that maybe I will let her take over.

The Old Man switched from the intercom to radio and spoke.

"Natalie?"

After a moment the General was there.

"We're beyond the Dam and headed toward Kingman. Supposedly there are settlements along Interstate 40 and we've been told there might be some warlord called King Charlie causing a lot of trouble. I just wanted to let you know about that and our progress."

White noise popped and crackled.

"I've reviewed the satellite imagery from our archives." Now the General's voice was loud and clear. "And I do find activity along your route when I use a time-lapse algorithm to detect signs of human activity. Do you have any idea who this King Charlie is and where he might be headquartered?"

'That was fast,' thought the Old Man. 'Unless she'd already been looking at these places.'

But how could she have known?

"I don't know much about him. Just that they call him King Charlie. Does he have anything to do with your situation?"

"The truth is, I don't know. We can't actually leave our bunker and find out who is trying to enter the complex. The radiation outside is incredibly high and would be lethal for even a short duration of time. Other than vague low-res satellite images of a large group of people trying to break down our front door, we know very little. Our engineers tell us the main door won't hold much longer."

"How long?"

Silence.

"A week."

The Old Man looked at the case on the deck of the tank.

Project Einstein.

What does it do?

Ask her now.

Maybe I don't want to know just yet.

"So we must hurry then?"

"I would advise so, yes, for our sakes."

"If we can find fuel, then it shouldn't be a problem."

There is fuel.

There is also King Charlie.

There is also all that end-of-the-world between here and there. All that destruction caused by nuclear warheads and two-year-long winters and after that, the forty years of neglect and craziness that followed. But yes, if we can find fuel then we can show up with this device and free you from your prison. By whatever means the device uses.

I must ask her what the device does.

Yes, my friend. You should.

"Please hurry," said Natalie. General Watt.

"We will."

The riders had disappeared. The Old Man leaned out of the hatch and tapped the Boy who slithered back inside the turret, out of the wind and heat so they could talk.

"Who are they?" asked the Old Man.

The Boy shook his head.

"I don't know. Some sort of tribe. They don't seem to be like the people back at the Dam."

"So maybe they're not from Kingman. We're close to there."

The Boy thought for a long moment.

"No, I do not think they're from Kingman. Perhaps they are the Apache the people at the Dam talked about. Maybe that's who we see up in the rocks."

"Maybe."

"Poppa!" shouted his granddaughter over the intercom.

"Is everything okay?" the Old Man asked.

"Poppa! Everything's great! I think it's a circus! Look at it!"

THEY HAD COME suddenly upon the stockade settlement at Kingman. From the highway overpass they could see the remains of an L-shaped strip mall centered around an old chain grocery store as the eastern and southern walls of the settlement. Claptrap towers had been thrown up from the roof. The parking lot had been walled off to the north and west with stacked cars and other precarious towers. The driveway into the shopping center was now a junk-welded gate thrown wide open.

In the middle of the road that led underneath the highway and alongside the gate and walls of the stockade, there was indeed a circus.

Colorful patchwork tents rose up drunkenly into the vivid orange daylight. Banners and flags whipped frantically in the sudden breeze. An elephant bellowed loudly as activity and movement ground to a halt.

From the street of the carnival all eyes looked up toward the overpass and the rumbling tank.

Above cups held to open mouths, the glossy eyes of the Stockaders watched the Old Man. And among the Stockaders, fire-breathers, contortionists, and strong men also watched, their eyes quick and darting, deep and dark.

Wide-eyed children played in the dirt and merriment.

Adults with overly large freak eyes in heads misshapen and deformed held ladles within punch tubs.

In the center of it all stood one small figure. Huge dark eyes set in a narrow head, adorned by lanky hair and a woven crown above punch-stained lips, gazed up at the Old Man knowingly. A scrawny neck and a gangling body ending in too-large feet, all dressed in foolery, hands tensed as claw-like fingers rhythmically opened and closed.

"Is it a circus, Poppa? There're tents and colors and punch and games just like you told me about. Is it?"

Yes, the circus is in town.

CHAPTER 33

The Old Man, still holding his map, climbed down from the tank. His granddaughter was already dancing around, doing cartwheels along the overpass.

"What's that big animal, Poppa?"

"An elephant."

"An elephant!" she screamed.

A delegation of Stockaders seasoned with circus performers climbed the dusty embankment toward the tank. The Old Man checked the Boy who stood atop the turret.

"Be ready."

The Boy nodded softly.

It's good he came with us.

A paunchy Stockader came forward, his face bright red and burning beneath a bushy mustache. His fat lips were punch stained, his eyes glossy from drink.

"What a day of miracles! First the circus and now this! I'm Reynolds." He held out a beefy hand and the Old Man shook it, feeling thick viscous sweat on it.

"We're just passing by," mumbled the Old Man.

"Oh come now, ya gotta see this thing!" bellowed Reynolds too loudly.

"Oh, Poppa, the ele—the elemant . . . the . . . what's its name, Poppa?"

"Elephant."

"The elephant!" she cried.

Everyone cheered.

And the Fool was there.

He beamed at the Old Man.

"We need fuel," said the Old Man. "The people at the Dam said you might have some. Then we really must go."

The Old Man felt his hand suddenly taken between the Fool's long claws.

"But we've come all this way and we have so much to give you!" begged the Fool. "Oh please, come see the elephant!"

"The elephant!" shrieked his granddaughter again.

Everyone cheered and even the elephant bellowed distantly.

"You're going to love this, Nuncle," assured the Fool as he dragged the Old Man forward, down the off-ramp and into the circus. "Things that were lost are coming back. Amazing things. Free things. The whole world will be ours again!"

His granddaughter raced forward toward the throng surrounding the elephant. The Old Man turned his head back to look over the heads of the pushers who pushed him forward into the circus outside the gates. The Boy stood atop the tank, his strong right arm dangling just above the haft of his tomahawk.

A tin cup is pressed into the Old Man's hand and he drinks knowing he should be careful, but all eyes and even the eyes of the Fool, are watching him.

Pleading.

Begging.

"Huzzah!" shout all the Players when the Old Man takes a thirsty drink.

His granddaughter is hoisted by three Strong Men aboard the elephant who immediately stands on its hind legs, raises its trunk, and bellows again.

The Old Man breaks out into a cold sweat sensing the sudden uncomfortable fear and helplessness one feels as he watches his granddaughter atop this gigantic and wild beast.

Reynolds, close and breathy, whispers hotly, "Ain't it a trick?"

Conklin!

"Conklin says hello."

For a whisker Reynolds seems bewildered. Then he slaps his head, spilling punch across his vest and bushy mustache.

"There's a fellow!" roars Reynolds. "Knew'd him ever since the first days after. How is McKenna?"

"I don't know McKenna. But Conklin told me to ask you for fuel if you still have any."

HIS GRANDDAUGHTER SCREAMED with delight, her face merely an open mouth, her head thrown back as her hair sprang wildly out into the blue sky.

This is wrong. What if something horrible happens to her? What if the giant beast throws her and then tramples her? What if anything goes wrong?

The Old Man feels cold sweat beginning to run down his back as he imagines the worst.

"Fuel? Got all the fuel you can take on," says Reynolds. "We'll see about it tomorrow, all right?"

The Old Man starts to protest but Reynolds is off through the crowd roaring and backslapping, calling for more of the circus-brewed punch.

The day is hot.

Too hot.

When the Old Man looks down, his tin cup is drained and his mouth feels sugary.

"Where'd ya get that machine, Nuncle?"

The Fool stares smilingly up at the Old Man, his thin body posed into a slant, as though leaning backward over a cliff.

The Old Man doesn't answer, wants to answer, but cannot.

I am tired and I feel my body relaxing into all this.

Let go and enjoy it. The only one ruining it is you and your fears.

And I feel so good.

Like . . . ?

Like?

Like the motel, my friend?

Oh . . . !

"You look like you've just swallowed a rotten bug, Nuncle." The Fool is ladling more punch into the Old Man's tin cup.

I feel rooted to the earth.

I can hear my granddaughter. High above and far away.

You never should have brought her with you.

Then I would've had to come all this way alone.

And die alone.

"Great things are coming again, Nuncle," simpered the Fool. "Medicine and well-being. Food for all. Oh, Nuncle, here is the best part. There'll be a work. A work to rebuild it all just as it once was but better and completely new. Even different. Isn't that amazing, Nuncle?"

The Fool seems confused. The Old Man stares at him as though he is looking at a picture on a wall.

He is merely a drawing.

A photograph even.

Pictures were once so common you deleted them if they weren't exactly what you wanted.

"Nuncle, you must stop swallowing these bugs. Perhaps you'd like to lie down. I'll sing you a song or recite a poem." The Fool threw his head back and put one long claw-like hand across his chest. "The Twenty-Dollar Burger for just a Quarter! At FattyBurger you'll think your stomach's been hit by a mortar. FattyBurger, All Meat, No Veggies, All Night."

The Fool beamed and threw his claws wide and open, accepting applause.

"I bet you remember that one from Before, Nuncle. I bet you remember when it was shown on the telly-screen? Those times were grand, those times were fun, those times are coming back I tell you all and one. What we lost is coming back the same and different. And the difference is better. Difference is always better. Change is always good. Right, Nuncle?"

His granddaughter is at his side. She is clutching him and showing him a streamer on a stick someone has given her.

"Poppa! Look!" She waves it across his vision and it seems a dragon crossing the desert sky full of flame and smoke.

We must . . .

"We must go," he mumbles.

All around the Old Man the cries and shrieks of the crowd mixed with some awkward and distorted off-tone music have been playing and growing in his ears. But beneath that, the Old Man hears the guttural growl of a small but vicious animal.

He looks deep into his granddaughter's eyes.

We are surrounded and there is no way out.

The world begins to tilt. First one way, and then another.

The Fool is growling.

"It's your turn to drive," says the Old Man.

"Okay, Poppa!" she explodes.

"You can have mine," he mumbles to himself as she grabs him by the hand.

She is dragging him back to the tank, pulling him forward in fact.

"Oh, thank you, thank you, thank you, Poppa!"

He feels claws pulling at his other arm and he shakes it stiffly as though controlling it from very far away. The Fool cartwheels in the dirt and an instant later is up in a wide-legged stance. His too-long arms hang down and low, the claws opening and closing.

He is growling.

The Old Man closes his eyes at the foot of the embankment as his granddaughter scrambles up and away toward the tank at the top.

The tank she gets to drive again.

"C'mon, Poppa!" She beckons, leaving him behind.

"What about yer fuel, mister?" Reynolds's face looms comically into the Old Man's narrow field of red dirt and rock and sudden blue sky.

The Old Man is grabbed heavily from behind.

The Boy is dragging him, one-armed, up the hill with little effort and much force.

The Fool at the foot of the hill seems no longer friendly. In fact, he seems given completely over to a purple anger none of the other revelers notice. The Fool stares hatefully upward at the retreating Old Man and the Boy.

Teeth gritted.

Jaw clenched.

A fire burns in the darkness behind his too-large puppet face and coal-black eyes.

The tank's engine whispers into its roar.

The Old Man is dragged upward across the hot armor and rests, catching his breath and holding on to the turret, while the Boy pours water over his burning old head.

Thank you, he thinks he says aloud but is not sure if he has.

The circus before the Stockade races away behind them and even though the Old Man can only see the colors and pennants in the distance, he can feel those hateful eyes of the Fool still on him.

Watching them.

Following them.

Chasing after them.

CHAPTER 34

The Old Man is sleeping on the deck of the tank, inside the turret. When he awakes, he feels the rumbling engine and the grinding treads shuddering through the frame all about him. He looks up and sees the Boy in the hatch. It is still daylight in the hints of sky he can see beyond the Boy.

I feel like I've been drinking.

You were.

Yes, but more than I actually did.

The Old Man rubs his face, feeling saliva along his cheek.

I was really sleeping.

He sits up and feels dull and faraway and thirsty. The Boy sees that the Old Man is awake and climbs out onto the turret and the Old Man rises into the hatch. They are headed north. It is late afternoon.

I've been asleep most of the day.

The old highway winds through a ponderosa of wide dry fields and clusters of stunted oak. Stubby fortresses of rock erupt suddenly throughout the landscape.

It feels quieter here. I can tell, even above all the noise of the tank. It feels like we are climbing upward now. Climbing to the top of the world.

Later when they shut down the tank alongside the road and the noise of the engine has faded, the Old Man hears the quiet he'd suspected might be there and it envelops their resting place for the night.

We are heading up onto the high plateau now.

There is no sound of bird or beast. The smell of dust and grass are heavy in the early evening. His granddaughter sits on her haunches, watching the fire the Boy had built, the two of them waiting for the beans and rice to heat.

They would be just fine without me.

The Old Man watches the dry slope of the land and red rock and the stubby trees packed tightly together.

It feels like no one has been here for some time.

So where did the circus come from?

The thought of the Fool sends a cold shiver through his thin muscles and chest.

The whole thing felt wrong.

Maybe you just overreacted, my friend?

No. No, I don't think I did. There was something wrong about the whole . . .

When you were young, you noticed that older people were always afraid. Afraid of kidnappers and telemarketers. Afraid of the new. Afraid of the unknown. Maybe you are old now and afraid of new things, my friend?

Maybe the old of my youth were just cautious. And I am old.

He walked back to their small fire, smelling the smoke and the food and the heavy scent of sagebrush thick in the first of the evening cool.

"Poppa, tell me all about elephants," she said.

The Old Man looked at the Boy. The Boy watched him.

Is he nodding? Does he want to know about elephants also?

Remember he too is young. To the young the world is exciting and not frightening. The world is elephants and not . . . fools or clowns?

Psychopaths.

Evil.

"What do you want to know about them?" he asked as she handed him his plate. In the first bite he knew he was starving.

I am hungry like I was when I was young. So maybe I am not old.

You are old, my friend. Like me.

"Where'd they come from? What do they eat? Can they do other tricks? Was that the biggest one you've ever seen? You know, Poppa, tell us everything."

Chewing quickly, shoveling another bite into his still-moving mouth, he looked at the Boy.

The Boy nodded.

And so the Old Man told them all about elephants. All about Africa. All about lions and things he'd read in books and been taught in school when he was young.

Later, when the fire was low and he could hear them both sleeping, he lay still and watched the stars above.

I did not think I knew so much about elephants.

CHAPTER 35

The road wound higher and higher into the forests that surrounded Flagstaff. For a while the going was slow as the tank maneuvered around lone eruptions of pine that shot through the lanes of the old highway.

In time, the crumbling remains of buildings poked through the unchecked growth, and when the Old Man went to consult the map as to how much farther they might go that day, he could not find it.

When did I . . .

When the Fool shook your hand.

The Old Man replayed the moment in the miles to come, as his granddaughter called out her intentions each time they needed to maneuver off-road.

"Okay, Poppa, we're going around this crazy tree."

I was pretty out of it yesterday. I could have dropped it in the dust perhaps.

"Poppa, we'll go to the right of this collapsed bridge, okay?"

Or anyone in the circus or the town could have snatched it from me.

"Poppa, how do you think that truck managed to flip itself across all the lanes? What a bad driver he must've been!"

Or it is somewhere here with us and I have simply misplaced it.

They passed the fire-blackened remains of a vehicle, the likes of which the Old Man had never seen before. Three blackened skeletons lay next to its massive wheels, still twisting in agony.

Or laughing.

In the end, when we are all skeletons, who will be able to tell if we were crying or laughing at what has happened to us?

No one, my friend.

And . . .

It won't be important anymore.

"What kind of car was that, Poppa?"

"I don't know. I've never seen its like before and maybe the fire made it unrecognizable."

"Why do you think they just sat there and let it burn, Poppa?"

He didn't answer.

"Why, Poppa?"

"Because there was nothing they could do about it."

"That doesn't make any sense."

No, it doesn't.

THE STOCKADE AT Flagstaff was a collection of fallen pine logs that had once formed a wall for defense and since had been dragged away from a hotel that overlooked the old highway.

The Old Man let the tank idle outside in the parking lot of the hotel. They watched, waiting for somebody to come out and greet them.

The Boy's strong hand rested against the tomahawk.

There are leaves and debris here. No one has been here in quite a while.

Yes. No one.

The Old Man turned off the tank and listened. He could hear a crow calling out stridently.

I have a very bad feeling about this place.

What kind of bad feeling?

The kind that says I do not want to know what I might find in there. That kind of feeling. The feeling of knowing that whatever you find, you won't like it.

The Old Man dismounted and the Boy followed.

As his granddaughter began to climb out of the driver's hatch, he motioned for her to stay. Her look of displeasure was instantaneous.

"It's your turn to guard the tank," he called back to her.

She sat down, dangling her feet over the side.

The Old Man heard the crunch of gravel beneath his boots as he and the Boy crossed the tired parking lot.

In the lobby they found nothing. No one.

The old furniture was gone. Instead there were desks.

As though someone had set up some kind of headquarters here.

And where are they now?

And where will we find fuel?

"What do you think happened here?" asked the Boy.

There is a story of salvage here. But what it is, I don't know.

"I can't tell. They had walls. They had shelter. If they were attacked, there should at least be bodies."

The Boy limped through the dusty light to the back of the lobby.

He's heading to the bar. There was always a bar back that way in these kinds of places. How does he know that?

Maybe he knows more of these places alongside the road than I do. Maybe he was born and raised in these places. Maybe they are as familiar to him as my shed would be to me.

You don't live there anymore, my friend.

It's hard to think that I live or lived in any other place, ever. My shed will always be home for me.

After a moment, when he could see only the dim outline of the Boy, he called out, "Did you find anything back there?"

The Boy returned, holding a coffee mug.

He held it out to the Old Man.

Inside, the remains of a punch-red syrup had dried into a shell at the bottom of the mug.

The Old Man smelled it. He smelled the heat and the straw and the sugar and the Fool.

The Circus had come to town.

THEY HAD DRIVEN through the remains of the town and now the heat faded as the summer day bled away. In the afternoon, a cool pine breeze came up and dried the sweat on the Old Man's back.

North of town, a massive rock the size of a small mountain loomed high into the darkening sky. Flagstaff, falling into disrepair, surrendering to time, settled as night birds and small animals began their first forays into the early evening.

Above him, the pines that were reclaiming the town, growing up through roads and sidewalks and buildings, whispered together making a soft white noise.

They parked the tank underneath an overpass, and as they began to make the night's meal, the Old Man wandered through the remains of a nearby gas station.

There is nothing left here.

How could there be after forty years?

All those years of living and salvaging in the village, I thought that much of the world was the same as Yuma, or Los Angeles or the cities I had seen on TV. Destroyed. I felt as though our little village was the only place in all the world that had survived.

Remained.

Then you found Tucson and all these places. The Dam. The outpost. All the other places that seemed to have had their own stories since the bombs.

Yes, they were not all "nuked" or touched by war as we had imagined.

But everything is touched by our downfall.

Yes.

Everyone in those days ran for cover. Into the hills. Into the wilderness. Wherever they could, thinking only of escape. Unprepared for what it takes to live in such places . . .

Of wilderness.

Of desert.

Of wasteland.

The Old Man found a cash box underneath the counter inside the gas station, hidden on a small ledge out of sight.

He pulled it out onto the countertop where once lottery tickets and quick snacks must have waited for purchase. Now there was nothing.

How did they miss this?

The Old Man opened it and found a stack of brittle paper money lying within.

When you are coming for food you take what you can find. You've been living in the wilderness and all you've brought is long gone. Days turn to months. Months turn to years. So you go into town. Hoping that some-where in it is a bag of stale chips or even a can of soup or stew that might still be good. Your mouth waters at the thought of such once-common delicacies.

You no longer think of lobster.

Or even money. What good is it when you're starving?

There was a kind of canned stew I loved in college. But I grew tired of it. I remember I didn't even buy any of it that last year.

What was it called?

The Old Man thought about all the times he had shopped for it, pre-pared it, eaten it.

And now I can't even remember its name.

He returned to the tank in the blue twilight of evening.

The Boy and his granddaughter had already eaten and when he ap-proached through the darkness he could hear his granddaughter laughing.

The Boy must have said something, which is strange because he never talks unless he is spoken to.

He sat down to his plate of beans and rice. His granddaughter handed him a few fire-warmed tortillas.

This is like camping. When I was young we went camping a few times. It was like this.

You are thinking too much about the past and not about the present. You need fuel and to find a map so you know where you are going.

I remember the map mostly. All the way to Albuquerque, turn left, go north.

You cannot afford to make a mistake, my friend. Your fuel tanks won't suffer a wrong turn.

"Have either of you seen my map?"

The fire popped.

His granddaughter and the Boy each shook their heads.

The Old Man sighed to himself.

"I think I may have lost it."

Or the Fool took it, my friend.

I don't want to say that. I don't want to make him seem more frighten-ing than he already is.

Why?

Because it will worry them.

No, why are you afraid of him?

Because there is reason to be afraid of him. Of that, I am very sure.

"Do you think it is lost for good?" asked the Boy.

The Old Man set his plate down, rubbing his fingers together because it had gotten hot as it lay next to the fire. He picked up the plate again. He sighed.

"Yes," he confessed.

It is best to admit the truth, even when you don't want to. Even if it makes you look old and foolish. We have too little fuel to afford my pride.

Yes.

The Boy stood up and disappeared into the darkness. The Old Man could hear him rustling through his pack. Then he was back by the fire, standing above them.

The Boy held out a folded map that glistened in the firelight.

The Old Man took it and began to unfold it.

It was larger than his map.

The entire United States.

Roads crossing the entire continent.

And . . .

Notes like "Plague" and "Destroyed" and "Gone."

Has he been to all these places?

The Boy sat down and stared into the firelight.

He is somewhere else. Somewhere else with someone else.

On the back of the map were names and words and identifiers that hinted at the details of an untold story.

CPT DANFORTH, KIA CHINESE SNIPER IN SACRA-MENTO

SFC HAN, KIA CHINESE SNIPER IN SACRAMENTO

CPL MALICK, KIA RENO

SPC TWOOMEY, KIA RENO

PFC UNGER, MIA RENO

PFC CHO, MIA RENO

PV2 WILLIAMS, KIA RENO

And . . .

Lola.

Lola.

And who was Lola?

When the Old Man looked up at the Boy again he'd meant to ask him how and why and even, where, but the Boy was staring at something high up. Something on the massive rock that loomed above Flagstaff. The Old Man followed the Boy's gaze.

High up on the rock burned a small campfire, and above it the stars wheeled like broken glass moving in time to some unheard waltz.

CHAPTER 36

The Boy sat by the fire sharpening his tomahawk.

"What're you going to do?" asked the Old Man.

"I will go up there. Near there, and see who it is. Maybe they know where we can find the fuel that's supposed to be here."

The Old Man started the tank and backed it out from under the overpass. When he came back to the fire he said, "We can watch you through the night vision. If you get in trouble maybe you can signal us from up there. We could try to come up and help you."

The Boy nodded as he finished lacing up his old boots. He stood, stretching the weak part of himself, twisting back and forth. The Old Man watched his granddaughter watch the Boy.

What does she see?

What do you think she sees, my friend? She is young and so is he.

When the Boy was ready to go he turned and said, "I'll try to be back before dawn."

Then he was gone into the darkness. For a moment they heard his steps and then nothing. As if he had been swallowed by the night.

The Old Man sat down next to the fire.

His granddaughter watched the dark shape of the massive rock. It blocked out its section of the night like a piece of black velvet hung to blot out the stars. Or an empty place in the universe.

"Will he be okay, Poppa?"

The Old Man wanted to think about that question, but he knew he mustn't. He knew he must give her an answer quickly. And when he responded, he knew he should've been faster. He knew when he saw the worry and doubt in her eyes.

"I think he will. He seems to know the ways one needs to survive. I think he has been alone for much of his life."

"Na-ah, Poppa. He was raised by a soldier."

How does she know that? When have they talked about it?

"He was?" asked the Old Man.

"Yes, Poppa. I had to ask him what a soldier was and he told me. Do you know what a soldier is, Poppa?"

I do.

But maybe his meaning is different from the one I know. I must listen more than I speak.

Yes.

"What did he say a soldier was?"

"He said it was someone who never gives up, Poppa."

The Old Man thought of Sergeant Major Preston. The tank and all that the soldier had prepared for the Old Man's village to come and find one day.

I think cancer got me. . . . God bless America.

Yes. That is what he wrote in the journal I found. I had not said that word "America" in a very long time before I read it in his journal.

And if I'm completely honest with myself, I had forgotten it.

What good was a word in the years of sun and sand and salvage that followed the winter that came after the day of the bombs? What good was "America" now?

It only reminded me of all that was gone.

The Old Man watched the fire.

But Sergeant Major Preston of the Black Horse Cavalry hadn't forgotten about America.

And neither had the soldier who'd raised the Boy. Whoever he was.

They didn't forget.

They didn't give up.

"Yes," he said to his granddaughter. "That is what a soldier is."

She was silent. She pressed her lips together, which was her way when she had more to say or was very excited about something she wanted to do but had to be patient until she could do it.

Young girls are hungry for all the good they think life holds. That is their innocence.

"Poppa?"

"Yes."

"He also had a wife."

"Oh."

"She's dead but he didn't tell me how."

"He seems young for that."

She was silent. And then, "Does he, Poppa?"

"Maybe not to you, but to me he is very young."

"Well, that's because you're old now, Poppa." She laughed and snorted.

The Old Man nodded.

"It's true. But it means I did something right, doesn't it? It means I was good at living. That's what getting old means. It means you're successful at living."

She laughed.

I love her laugh.

I wish I knew all the secret words that would make her laugh anytime I wanted to hear it. Anytime I needed to hear it. If there is anyone in control of this crazy life, that is my bargain I'll make with you. You can have anything you want. Just give me her laugh. Let me take it wherever I have to go after this.

Deal?

Silence.

And . . .

Please?

"He was in battles, Poppa. And he's crossed the whole country. The whole United States, Poppa."

Her eyes shine when she talks about him.

Her eyes remind me of my wife's, her grandmother. When she was young.

She is always young to me.

"He has done a lot for such a young man," said the Old Man.

"What is that, Poppa?"

"What is what?"

"The United States?"

I guess we never talked about that. We talked of salvage and ice cream and jet airplanes like my dad once flew across the world. Many things. But not the United States.

"It was our country."

She said nothing. Thinking.

Then . . .

"Is it still our country?"

IN THE NIGHT, when the moon was falling to the far horizon, long after the Old Man had tried to explain the concept of "States" and then tried to remember as many of their names as he could, which was not many, he flipped the switch on the optics. He scanned the giant rock. He could not see the Boy.

She'd only wanted to talk about him. Even though I was telling her all about California and the other states I had been to, she only really wanted to talk about him.

Yes, my friend. That is the way of the young when they discover something. They are like Christopher Columbus discovering the "new" world.

Yes. Sergeant Major Preston wrote that in the sewer.

They think everything is new and they are the first and they ignore us Indians who've been here all along.

In the past, if I taught her everything I knew about how a small engine once worked or what telephones were, she couldn't get enough of such things. The questions about those lost things would follow me for days. But not today. She only looked as though she were listening to me as I told her about states.

But she wasn't.

No.

That is the way of the young, my friend. You cannot help who you fall in love with the first time. You just do. When you get up in the morning you don't say to yourself, *Today I am going to fall in love.* You just do.

He is very handsome. Strong too. That is a good thing for these days. But she is still young.

But there must always be a first time for love.

He looked down into the tank and saw her face. She was deep in sleep, still wrapped in her bomber jacket.

I will take just her laugh with me to wherever I must go next. Please? Is it a deal? Just the memory of her laugh. Can I have that?

Silence.

In the night, the Old Man thought he heard a horse galloping down the highway above his head.

I am dreaming.

Maybe the horse is on the bridge.

Maybe the horse is part of the dream.

The Old Man fell back to sleep.

CHAPTER 37

The Old Man woke with a start.

I was falling.

Yes.

She was calling for me?

No, Poppa. I need you.

I think so.

I smell bacon.

He opened the hatch. The Boy and a Stranger watched the campfire and a cast-iron skillet between them in which the Old Man could see splattering grease leaping in the waves of heat that came up from the flames.

The Stranger wore clothing made of tanned hide. A necklace of bones. His hair fell in curls around a circle of baldness that had consumed the back of the top of his head. Large sad brown eyes turned to the Old Man and gazed upon him.

The Old Man dismounted the tank, feeling the stiffness of his sleeping position in each handhold and footfall that brought him jarringly to the ground.

The Boy stood and hobbled toward the Old Man.

The Stranger looked exhausted. It had been a long night for him also.

"I found him up there on top of the large rock," said the Boy. The Stranger had turned back to the fire and the skillet.

"Was he alone?" asked the Old Man.

"Yes. He's harmless. I don't think we'll get much out of him, though." The Boy waited until the Stranger bent to inspect something within the skillet. Then the Boy raised his index finger to his temple and twirled it.

The Boy lay down near where he'd left his worn rucksack. He patted it once and then laid his head on it and closed his eyes. A moment later the Boy was asleep.

The Old Man retrieved a percolator from the tank and some tea, the last remaining packets in their supplies, and went to the fire. He set the percolator to boil on the coals and sat down across from the Stranger.

"Good morning," he said to the Stranger.

The Stranger raised his clasped hands to his mouth, squeezed his eyes shut, and began to rock back and forth.

This went on for a while and the Old Man was content to wait for the water to boil and for the tea to steep. He sat out mugs on stones near the fire and poured the tea.

The day was still cool, though soon the heat would be up. In the blue shadows beneath the bridge, the Old Man watched the pork sizzle in the cast-iron pan and sipped his hot tea.

Like camping.

The Stranger produced a large meat fork and skewered a piece of sizzling pork, holding it out toward the Old Man.

"Thank you."

The Old Man chewed.

Should I be worried about the quality of this meat?

Life has already made several attempts to kill you, my friend. This pork is probably the least of your worries today.

It's good.

The Stranger ate none of the pork.

He watched the Old Man, nodding slightly with approval.

He's not as old as me, but he is old enough to have lived through the bombs. Maybe he was young and never learned to speak. Maybe no one survived with him. Maybe he has been alone all this time.

"Your country is desolate," said the Stranger in a high voice.

As if his heart was breaking.

As if he were on the verge of tears.

"Your cities are burned with fire: your land, strangers devour it in your presence."

The Old Man nodded respectfully, chewing the pork. He picked up his tea and sipped.

"What's your name?" he asked through another mouthful of pork.

The Stranger looked as if he were about to go on, as if the Old Man had interrupted him in the middle of his speech.

"Your new moons and your appointed feasts my soul hates," continued the Stranger, almost pleading with the Old Man. "They are a trouble unto me: 1 am weary to bear them. And when you spread forth your hands, I will hide my eye from you." The Stranger covered his brown liquid-filled eyes with the palms of his hands. Then he looked up and, putting his hands over his ears, he whispered in horror, "Yes, when you make many prayers, I will not hear: your hands are full of blood."

Okay.

The Old Man's granddaughter emerged from the tank, rubbing sleepy eyes. He saw her look about for the Boy. She saw her grandfather watching her when her gaze had finally fallen upon his sleeping form. She climbed down from the tank, eyes still half closed, and settled next to the fire. The Stranger held out pork for her from within the skillet.

She chewed.

Just like camping.

Okay, I will try once more. But I already know I will be sorry.

"Do you have a name, sir?" asked the Old Man.

The Stranger nodded emphatically.

Then stopped.

"Wash you, make you clean: put away the evil of your doings from before mine eyes: cease to do evil."

"We are not doing evil. We are on a journey to rescue some people who are trapped in a bunker to the east. In what was once Colorado," said the Old Man reaching exasperation. "Do you know Colorado?"

"Learn to do well, seek judgment, relieve the oppressed, judge the fatherless, and plead for the widow," continued the Stranger.

"That's what we're doing!" said the Old Man, surprised with himself that he was already upset.

Usually, I am much more patient.

The Stranger stopped. He leaned forward. There was hope in his voice when he spoke again.

"Come now, and let us reason together, says the Lord: though your sins be as scarlet, they shall be as white as snow; though they be red like crimson, they shall be wool."

"Crimson is red?" interrupted his granddaughter.

The Stranger nodded emphatically and continued.

"They shall be as wool. If you are willing and obedient, you shall eat the good of the land."

The Old Man stood. He was shaking.

I am angry and I do not know why!

You are angry at this man, my friend, because he will not answer a simple question.

Yes, that is why I am angry.

"What is your name, sir?"

When the Stranger did not immediately answer, the Old Man began to turn and walk away. A few steps and he heard the Stranger say, "Isaiah, Ezekiel, Jeremiah. I am as one crying in the wilderness."

When the Old Man turned back, there were tears streaming down the Stranger's sunburned cheeks.

Don't be angry with him. He can't help . . .

He's crazy.

The Old Man sat down next to the fire again.

If you'd watched civilization go up in flames. If you'd watched what came after and had to survive any way you could through all those years alone. How could you not be crazy, my friend?

I did. I watched. I survived. I'm not crazy.

But you had the village. Your wife. Your son. Your grandchildren. Maybe he had no one.

The Old Man sighed and sipped his tea again. He had another piece of bacon.

"I think you understand me," he said to the Stranger.

The Stranger nodded.

"But for some reason you speak in riddles and I don't know why. So I will tell you that we are headed east to find some people who have asked for our help. We need fuel. Were you part of the people who lived up here?" The Old Man pointed toward the abandoned hotel that had been the center of the outpost.

The Stranger shook his head in the negative.

"Did you know them?"

The Stranger nodded.

"We need their fuel. Do you know where it is? Is there any left?"

The Stranger nodded again.

CHAPTER 38

"And they shall be desolate in the midst of the countries that are desolate, and her cities shall be in the midst of the cities that are wasted."

The Old Man watched the Stranger as he worked at pulling up the grating that covered what must have once been a pool inside the skeletal remains of a gym.

That is his answer to what lies east?

Yes, my friend. That is his answer.

When the metal cover was pushed back, the hint of kerosene bloomed in full. Inside the empty pool, salvage-fashioned fuel tanks lay along the bottom.

My eyes are burning from the fumes.

The Old Man waved the others back and dropped down into the shallow end of the dry pool. He tapped his scarred knuckles against a tank and heard the hollow echo of a half-filled volume.

Will it be enough?

It will have to be.

They brought the tank in through the shattered remains of the floor-to-ceiling windows. It crushed ancient fitness machines beneath its treads. Above them a barn owl screeched incessantly, refusing to flee into the daylight.

He has been here for some time.

If he waits, we will go away. But he must wait until we have taken all their fuel.

When they had maneuvered the tank as close to the pool as they could, they stretched out the pump hose until it barely reached the farthermost tank.

The fumes could ignite in a moment so we must be very careful.

"Go out and look for some salvage," he told his granddaughter. "See if there is anything we can use."

"Food would be good, Poppa."

"Yes, food would be good."

When she was gone he breathed a little easier.

If we explode she will at least be safe.

She will be all alone.

Yes, but she won't be dead.

The Boy took charge of the fueling once the Old Man had shown him how it was performed. Now they waited in the silence of the ancient pool area, the APU droning like the pumps of the pool must have once done.

The Old Man turned to the Stranger.

His words are church words.

As though he will only speak what he has seen or read. As though it is his punishment or his penance. But he understands. I know he does. How has he made it all this time? What is his story of salvage?

"What is your . . . what is your story?"

The Stranger who had been watching the fueling process with both amazement and amusement turned back to the Old Man with laughing, mirthful eyes.

The Stranger seemed to want to say something. Then stopped himself and simply shook his head. When the Old Man seemed to accept this, the Stranger turned back to watch the fueling.

The map.

The Old Man climbed up into the tank and retrieved Sergeant Presley's map, though he thought of it only as the Boy's.

Again he was amazed at the information contained in its markings.

It's the story of someone's life.

Is that not true of all maps, my friend?

True. And also, our stories are the maps of our lives.

The Old Man stopped.

Our stories are the maps of our lives.

Yes, my friend.

He spread the map out on the ragged rubber floor of the gym, in a space between crushed pieces of fitness equipment.

"Excuse me?" He spoke loudly trying to get the Stranger's attention.

The Stranger turned.

He saw the map. If the look in his eyes when he'd watched the tank drink up all the fuel had been one of amazement, the look in his eyes when he saw the map was one of awe.

He fell to his knees and a moment later his short thick fingers were tracing the roads. Tracing them back east. Tracing them to New York. Landing on Brooklyn.

And he wept.

His shoulders shaking.

Sobs gushing forth in tremendous heaves.

"By the rivers of Babylon," sobbed the Stranger. "There we sat down, yea we wept, when we remembered Zion. We hanged our harps upon the willows in the midst thereof. For there they that carried us away captive required of us a song; and they that wasted us required of us mirth, saying sing us one of the songs of Zion."

The Stranger hung his head and tears splashed down onto the map. The Old Man stood, frozen.

The Stranger raised his head, looking up to the Old Man. Asking him.

"How shall we sing the Lord's song in a strange land? If I forget thee, O Jerusalem, let my right hand forget her cunning. If I do not remember thee, let my tongue cleave to the roof of my mouth, if I refer not Jerusalem above my chief joy."

Through watery, joy-filled eyes, he spread his small hands outward, upward, and expanded them across the map.

He means, 'Where are we?,' my friend.

The Old Man looked at the map and laid his finger over Flagstaff.

The Stranger placed one finger on Brooklyn and then stretched another finger on his other hand over Flagstaff.

For a long time he stared at the map.

Stared at the distance between the two points.

Stared at all the stories of his wanderings.

Some making a little more sense now.

Some coming to the surface after so many years on the road.

"Do you know of this 'King Charlie'?" asked the Old Man.

The Stranger looked up from the map.

There was fear in his eyes.

He looked back to the map and studying it, drew his finger away from the west, following the map east. Following the once great Interstate 40. Then, at Albuquerque he went north, and after making a wide circle that reached all the way down into Texas he spoke.

"Hell from beneath is moved for thee to meet thee at thy coming: it stirreth up the dead for thee, even all the chief ones of the earth; it hath raised up from their thrones all the kings of the nations. All they shall speak and say unto thee, Art thou also become weak as we? Art thou become like unto us? Thy pomp is brought down to the grave, and the noise of thy viols: the worm is spread under thee, and the worms cover thee. How art thou fallen from heaven, O Lucifer, son of the morning! How art thou cut down to the ground, which didst weaken the nations! For thou hast said in thine heart, I will ascend into heaven, I will exalt my throne above the stars of God: I will sit also upon the mount of the congregation, in the sides of the north: I will ascend above the heights of the clouds; I will be like the most High. Yet thou shalt be brought down to hell, to the sides of the pit. They that see thee shall narrowly look upon thee, and consider thee, saying, Is this the man that made the earth to tremble, that did shake kingdoms; that made the world as a wilderness, and destroyed the cities thereof; that opened not the house of his prisoners? All the kings of the nations, even all of them, lie in glory, every one in his own house. But thou art cast out of thy grave like an abominable branch, and as the raiment of those that are slain, thrust through with a sword, that go down to the stones of the pit; as a carcass trodden under feet. Thou shalt not be joined with them in burial, because thou hast destroyed thy land, and slain thy people: the seed of evildoers shall never be renowned."

The Stranger looked at the Old Man and nodded slowly, placing his index finger over Colorado Springs.

Bad news for us, my friend.

Yes.

I think he is saying that King Charlie is the devil. And that the devil is in Colorado Springs.

Where I need to go.

"It would have to be that way," muttered the Old Man to himself.

The Stranger took hold of the Old Man's hand. His touch was warm and soft. He moved the hand down to Albuquerque and whispered, "Ted."

"Ted?"

The Stranger nodded.

"Who is Ted?"

But the Stranger only smiled and nodded in the affirmative.

Whoever Ted is, he's good. Or at least he has been to the Stranger.

And he thinks Ted will also be good to us.

Didn't Conklin of the Dam say they'd heard there was someone who'd set up an outpost in ABQ as he called it? That they even had electricity?

Ted.

When the fueling was complete, the Old Man backed the tank out of the rickety framework of the ruin that had once been a gym and left the tank idling in the hot afternoon heat.

The Boy brought out an old weight bar he'd found in the shadows and dark of the gym.

"I can make this into a weapon," he said as he passed the Old Man.

The Stranger motioned for the map once more. When it was opened and spread out on the hot pavement, the Stranger pointed toward the land that lay between Flagstaff and Albuquerque.

"They shall lay hold on bow and spear; they are cruel, and have no mercy; their voice roareth like the sea; and they ride upon horses, set in array as men for war against thee, O daughter of Zion."

Then he pointed toward the sun overhead and shook his head. Making a fist, he pulled it down.

"You're saying don't cross this area in the daytime?"

The Stranger nodded.

Then held up one finger.

"In one night! You're saying cross all this in one night? That's a long journey, over bad roads!"

The Stranger nodded again.

"Who are these people?" asked the Old Man.

The Stranger looked about, leaned close, and then whispered, "Apache."

Later, under the bridge, waiting for nightfall, the Old Man walked up the street. Toward the outpost that had been.

How can these Apache stop a tank?

Who knows? But this fellow thinks they're dangerous enough to try. Or at least try and get you stuck, then wait you out.

Go in one night as quick as you can and it might prevent them from bringing their resources to bear. Surprise them.

But we could get stuck on the road in the night.

At the top of the hill, in the gritty crumbling parking lot of the hotel, the Old Man saw words written on the wall in a sickly green neon slop-paint.

Those words weren't there yesterday.

Someone has passed through in the night and left a message for me.

Someone on a horse.

"Up is down, left is right. King Charlie brings you Peace through Might."

The Old Man wondered if this was the Fool thundering through the darkness on a horse too big for his gangling body, even now ahead of them, knowing where they are going, holding the stolen map in his claws.

And below that, as if addressed specifically to the Old Man, written in slop-paint strokes, was the word *"Nuncle."*

CHAPTER 39

At dusk they drove out from underneath the bridge and into the twilight. The dry leaves and fallen pine needles crunched under the dirt-clogged treads of the tank in the warm, early evening.

The Stranger watched them, waving slowly, his sad brown eyes sorry to see them go.

And . . .

Sorry for all that had happened to the world.

The Old Man looked down into the turret and saw the Boy who'd returned to staring into nothingness. He tapped his leg, motioning for the Boy to put on his helmet. When this was done the Old Man switched on the intercom.

"What do you think of him?" asked the Old Man, referring to the Stranger. "About his information? Did you ever pass through the areas he warned us about?"

"We did not."

Who does he mean when he says "we"?

The soldier.

"Maybe he was just crazy?" said the Old Man.

The Boy said nothing for so long the Old Man wondered if maybe there wouldn't be a comment. But then the Boy spoke.

"I do not think he is touched in the head. Sergeant Presley would say . . . well, it does not matter, but, no, I don't think he is crazy. There was truth in his riddles."

"So what do you think he meant by all those riddles?" asked the Old Man.

Flagstaff fell behind them, and ahead, the long straight road cut through the high rolling plains.

It feels like we're still heading upward.

Still heading to the top of the world.

In the far west, fading blue light still shone distantly. Ahead the land lay covered in soft mist and darkness.

"There are people who act crazy," started the Boy out of the silent hum of the intercom. "I think it's some kind of defense. A way of keeping them safe on the road. Most villages treat such people with respect. They give them food and send them on their way. They're superstitious about such people."

"Are there many villages out there?"

The Old Man looked into the distant east and saw only the rising night.

"Some," said the Boy.

For a long time the Old Man kept the tank on the road. But when the road became impassable, they would deviate around broken chunks of highway and scattered concrete pylons and even the wild-haired rebar jutting from the remains of bridges.

Far out into the plains, miles off-road, they would see the skeletal remains of recreational vehicles rocking in a wind that blasted across the rolling landscape, causing the grass to bend in great waves like the tides of an ocean.

The Old Man switched on the night-vision optics and saw no one among the lonely outposts of wreckage.

People must have come here in the days of the bombs, forming up into small settlements. They would've driven here in those RVs and made alliances once they'd arrived.

Or murdered each other for what few supplies could be had.

How long did they last?

Not long. How could they? They only had what they'd brought. There are no places to salvage up here. No major towns or industry. What could they have found where there was little or nothing?

Later, the road disintegrated into little more than swallowed chunks of concrete through which tufts of yellow grass sprang upward. The tank moved slower along the broken highway, the Old Man not wanting to chance the fragile right tread.

You must go all the way, tread. You cannot give up tonight or even when we get there. After this is all done, we still have to get back home.

The last part sounded like an empty promise to the Old Man.

He began to think of the other dark possibilities that existed besides returning home.

But he cut himself off and would not think of such things.

Tonight I must concentrate. I cannot think of what will go wrong tomorrow or even the day after. Those things are for another day.

In the darkness there seemed to be no one out there. All the rumors of Apache might just simply be rumors. All the talk of Apache nothing more than the talk of ghosts. Boogeymen to frighten misbehaving children.

He drove on and watched the road, seeing nothing but scattered pockets of rusting and beaten destruction from long ago.

He saw the bridge far ahead as the road began a series of descents and rises through rolling hills. It should have been a bridge like any other overpass crossing. But it wasn't.

The bridge still stretched across the two hills that had been both its on-ramps and off-ramps for east and west traffic. But beneath the overpass, where the highway ran, lay a collection of vehicles tilted upright, their hoods pointed into the sky as if they had been suddenly forced upward.

Tacked across the front of each rusting hood was a human skeleton with a dog's head.

The Old Man switched on the high beam of the tank as they approached.

It's a message.

"They don't want us to come this way?" said the Boy over the intercom.

Or anyone for that matter.

"Is your hatch closed?" he asked his granddaughter.

"Yes, Poppa."

"Lock it now."

The Old Man maneuvered the tank up the overpass to the road that crossed atop the bridge. Against the bright moon, he could clearly see the pennants made of rags and oily crow feathers flapping madly in the windy darkness.

We are in their land now.

If we tell them what we're going to do, maybe they will let us pass.

And if they don't, my friend?

The Old Man started down the on-ramp on the far side and re-entered the old highway.

A few miles farther along, and the highway descended into a series of curves that entered a long and narrow ravine, which soon widened into a valley that cut through low, flat-topped mesas.

A small gas station town lay alongside the road and the Old Man could see greasy firelight behind some of the windows.

For a while the road paralleled a river. Weeping willows hung gloomily along the banks in the night. Later, in the deep of the valley, the road disappeared under a wash of sand where the river must have once overflowed.

Probably in the days after the long winter.

Yes.

The Old Man drove the tank down onto the sand bed, letting the high beam stay on, watching for places where the tank might get stuck. Ahead he could see the single remaining pylon of a bridge that must have once crossed over the wide river that ran through the canyon.

As they entered the dry riverbed, they dropped suddenly and the Old Man banged his head sharply on the side of the hatch.

His first thought was that the ground had suddenly given way underneath them.

Soft sand.

But he could see crumpled tin and splintered wood in the optics and a wall of sandy dirt beyond.

We've fallen into a trap!

"Are you all right?" he asked his granddaughter over the intercom as he reached up and shut the turret hatch.

"What happened, Poppa?"

"I think we fell in a hole."

The Boy, bathed in the red of the interior emergency lights, gripped his chair.

Rain began to fall against the sides of the tank.

Not rain.

Arrows.

The Old Man dogged the hatch.

Remember, be gentle with the right tread. We can get out of this like I did when I was stuck in the sand at Picacho Peak. But if you break the tread, we really will be stuck.

The Old Man switched on the night vision.

All around them, wild figures like white blobs against green and gray ran forward as torches flared too brightly in the night vision. The Old Man tried the left tread and the tank pulled forward. He could hear the snap of wood and rending metal above the whine of the engine. When the tank was almost at the top of the trap, the Old Man pushed the right tread forward and the tank popped nose upward as he gave it full throttle.

"Hold on!" warned the Old Man.

The tank slammed down hard into the sand and sped off, careening through a crumbling pylon that jutted from the riverbed.

The Old Man scanned the optics.

The figures were running back into the night, their torches burning angrily on the ground.

Did I just see the Fool?

Standing atop a small sandy hill, the gangly figure appeared for a moment, his wild fool's crown springing in all directions, his claw waving a torch frantically forward at the retreating figures, urging them to turn back and attack the tank.

It's him!

The Old Man backed away from the viewfinder in shock.

Don't be afraid of him, my friend.

When the Old Man looked again the Fool was gone. He drove the tank to the other side of the wash and surged up onto the road at full speed.

Now the road entered a tight series of turns that wound through the hills where the Old Man saw an ambush in every bend, or at the tops of the small hills that loomed above them alongside the road. The gibbous moon had turned a sickly red from some distant dust storm. It rose through spindly barren trees above the desert plateau. It shifted wildly across the sky as the Old Man fought to keep track of the twisting road in the night.

It must be after midnight.

The Old Man felt himself sweating heavily, his shoulders tensed like iron bands as he drove the tank forward into the night.

The road twisted into a series of long curves that reversed themselves into still more curves and the red misshapen moon swung even more frantically across the sky.

It's making me dizzy.

The clutching fingers of a dead orchard rose up all around them as they passed through the rubble of a town. Ahead, great piles of concrete had toppled onto the highway. Above them, the sides of cutoff mountains rose up into the darkness.

Are they forcing me off the road and into the town? Or are they forcing me to take the narrow opening ahead? Where is their trap?

The Fool is forcing you, my friend. It is the Fool who forces you into his trap.

I only thought I saw him. Maybe it was just a mistake or a trick of the light.

This must have once been a state checkpoint. The path looks too narrow for the tank to pass.

But if you get off the highway you could get lost in that abandoned town, and its streets are probably very narrow. A good place for a trap. There is no guarantee that there is a way around this obstacle or that the roads in the town are even any better.

No, there isn't.

"Are you ready to drive?" said the Old Man over the intercom to his granddaughter.

"I'm on it, Poppa!" she almost shouted.

The Old Man tapped the Boy and motioned for the hatch.

"We'll guide you through the rubble and make sure the path is wide enough," he said to his granddaughter. "Don't run over us, okay?"

"Okay, Poppa, I'll try not to."

Yes, please try not to run over me with the tank.

The Old Man took the left and the Boy the right and they walked into the dusty maze of rubble, waving the tank forward slowly. They crossed under a wide overpass and the Old Man spotted, with the moving beam of his flashlight, the words the Fool had left for him to read. They were written all the way to the end of the tunnel.

REPEAT A LIE AND IT BECOMES THE TRUTH.
POINTING OUT WHAT'S "WRONG" IS THE SICK HABIT OF DELUSIONAL
    PERVERTS.
RIGHT AND WRONG IS WHERE WE WENT WRONG.
REPEAT A LIE AND IT BECOMES THE TRUTH.
COMPROMISE MEANS SEEING THINGS OUR WAY.
WHAT OTHERS CALL INSANE, I CALL PERSISTENCE.
REPEAT A LIE AND IT BECOMES THE TRUTH.
WE WILL MURDER THOSE WHO REJECT PEACE.
WANT WHAT OTHERS HAVE. THE MANY SERVE THE FEW, THE TRICK IS
MAKING THEM THINK IT'S THE OTHER WAY AROUND.
REPEAT A LIE AND IT BECOMES THE TRUTH.
IF YOU SAY YOU'RE GOD, WHO'S TO SAY YOU'RE WRONG?
MAKE FRIENDS OF YOUR ENEMIES AND USE THEM TO DESTROY YOUR
    FRIENDS.
REPEAT A LIE AND IT BECOMES THE TRUTH.
WHEN YOU ARE NO LONGER BURDENED BY INTEGRITY, THE POSSIBILITIES
    ARE BOTTOMLESS.
CONVINCE YOUR ENEMIES THE BATTLE IS SOMEWHERE ELSE.
CONVINCE YOUR ENEMIES THEY'RE JUST LIKE YOU.
CONVINCE YOUR ENEMIES.
HEAVEN, HELL . . . REALLY?
REPEAT THE TRUTH.

And at the final yawning exit lying on the open and blistered highway beyond lay neon-green-colored sheets of paper scattered about, as if debris from a bomb revealed in the pale moonlight above the eastern dust storm. The Old Man picked up a sheet and found crude printing and wet ink that smeared at his touch. He read.

```
Everything be Ok
We mean it.
```

So loot and murder to your heart's content
Just make sure you got the strength to Take and Do
before anyone else does to you

Everything be getting better
Don't believe the eyes
Or your stomachs holla
Or your lies,
Lies can be told about anything
Including the truth

There's been a lotta bad done in the name of good.
So we're done with that noise.
    Religion and morals be all the same and only
different 'bout who was right and wrong on everything.

So here's how it be
Man be man alone
And the man be
King Charlie.
King Charlie be not wrong or right.
He just be.
After King Charlie be nothing.
    Heaven = Hell, only the unlucky die and the dead
like to tell some truth when they say nothing.
    If there be a heaven, King Charlie imagine you'll
get there no matter what you do
unless you're the Hitler or Stalin who gave everyone the
aids.

We come so that all might live in prosperity.
And only the strong survive.
Get it?

We are an accident
Created by an accident,

```
And so the Apocalypse must be our promise
Of a better tomorrow

When we hear-ed that doomsday bell
The gunfire a Ratta-tat-tating,
Your screams for mercy
The blast that blew everything away that was,
And when we saw the light of bombs bursting in air
Someone said ''Twas but the sound of man worshipping his
maker,'

So . . .

Siege!
Lone Gunman!
Horde rapes outpost!
Nuclear Bomb Disintegrates London!
It's just be the sounds of man
worshipping his maker.
```

At the bottom of the piece of paper, as if separate and a command, the Old Man read, **ALL HAIL KING CHARLIE!**

The Old Man let the screed fall to the ground. He motioned for the Boy to get back into the tank, and as he climbed once more into the hatch, his eyes fell to the final words that had been slop-painted onto the highway before the tank.

ONCE YOU'RE FREE OF SHAME YOU'RE FREE TO ACT SHAMELESSLY.
GIVE UP, NUNCLE, YOU'VE GOT NO CHANCE!

On the other side of the tunnel the night seemed cooler, the air fresher. The moon turned everything slightly blue with its glaring yellow light now that it had risen above the distant dust storm.

In the hours that followed, there were other tight spots and places where the road seemed impassable. They threaded each of these places carefully, waiting for an attack that did not come.

The road improved and soon they were making good time across the high desert with dawn just a few hours away. The Boy, whose chin had fallen to his chest, lay deep in sleep bathed by the red light of the tank, fastened into his seat. When the Old Man tried the intercom, his granddaughter only murmured and he knew she too was sleeping now.

Alone, he drove through what remained of the night and soon the eastern sky began to turn a pale blue.

Another day.

They topped the rise that looked down on Albuquerque in the soft light of first morning.

The city is still there.

Ted.

On the eastern side of town, the Old Man could see thin strings of electric light still burning distantly like twinkling gems in the pink of morning.

CHAPTER 40

They crossed gray concrete roads and empty sun-bleached buildings fall-ing to rubble in the blaze of morning. The Old Man aimed the tank to-ward the strings of light still twinkling in the bright daylight below the foothills on the eastern edge of town.

Those lights should be off by now. Who would leave them on during the day?

But the lights remained on and when the Old Man found the settle-ment, a walled-off neighborhood below the easternmost foothills, the Old Man did not wonder why no one had turned out the lights. They were greeted by a soft dry breeze and the silence of abandonment.

The settlement was a large tract housing development lying alongside the highway leading north. A massive adobe brick wall, built before the bombs, surrounded the entire development.

Why was this place spared, like Tucson?

At the entrance they found a makeshift gate fashioned from the metal one might find at the gates of industrial warehouses. Two watchtowers that had risen from behind the wall had been pulled down, their frames sprayed outward like so many spilled matchsticks. The patchwork gate was wide open.

Why?

The Fool, the Horde, King Charlie. Does it matter? Someone.

Maybe they fled? Maybe they're hiding?

But the pulled-down watchtowers told another story.

Inside, the three of them found the town.

Streets.

Houses.

A humming generator in the distance.

Doors wide open.

Empty mugs and glasses whose insides were still stained with punch-red syrup.

The Boy went back to the tank and the gate once the Old Man had called out "hello" and received no response.

"What happened here, Poppa?"

"Nothing good."

"It seems bad."

"Don't worry. We'll leave soon."

But the fuel, my friend, there is only a little left.

"I'm not worried, Poppa."

"I know."

"Are you worried, Poppa?"

The Old Man did not answer her and instead continued to search the town as she trailed after him.

They wandered through a few houses, and what they found within told them nothing other than that one moment of life lived ordinarily had frozen, and that time had refused to move forward.

Beds unmade.

Wash hanging.

Each house smelling of dust and wood.

Tools, usable salvage, merely left for anyone to take.

In one house they found a spilled glass of milk.

The milk was warm and spoiled.

We should find the generator. Maybe it runs on fuel.

As if on cue, while the Old Man stood over the spilled milk and heard at the same time the distant hum of power, the generator died.

Outside, stepping over the front lawns turned to dying gardens, the strings of light above had ceased to twinkle.

The Old Man followed the darkened lights to thick rubber electrical cables that snaked through the streets and led to a house on the far edge of the settlement. Inside, the Old Man found hundreds of generators set up in every room. A central fuel bladder occupied the upper story. In the backyard they found a fuel truck that started crankily. Its tank was almost empty.

This was their power plant.

But the fuel is somewhere else.

Yes.

At the front entrance, waiting in the shade of the tank and drinking from a canteen, the Boy watched the land to the north of them.

"They were chained up over there," said the Boy and pointed toward the median. "There're drops of blood all over the dirt. The slavers must have put fishhooks in their noses or mouths and linked them to chains. Then they went north. I've seen it done before."

"Can you tell how many days ago that might have been?" asked the Old Man.

"A week. Maybe more."

The explosion shook the city.

It was distant. A boom, and then a crack that seemed to follow seconds after, echoed far out across the city and into the hills above them.

Back toward the center of the city, flames shot skyward as a black plume of smoke belched into the tired blue sky.

"Is it one of the bombs from before, Poppa?"

"No. Just an explosion."

She has no idea how big those bombs were. She has heard me and the other survivors who lived through those days talk of them and all that they took away, but she really has no idea how massive they were.

"Are you sure, Poppa?" she said, the worry evident.

"I am sure."

But he could see her face. Her wide eyes. The lips pressed together.

"Those bombs destroyed entire cities," said the Boy. "We would be dead if it had been one."

After a moment she seemed to accept the Boy's words.

Relaxing.

She has lived in fear of those bombs her whole life. They are her boogeyman.

Yes. And this Boy said the words that comforted her, my friend.

Yes. There is that also.

They drove as close to the flames and smoke as they could. They could smell the thick scent of burning fuel.

It was an industrial district.

Narrow streets.

Concrete warehouse.

In green slop-paint the words "How now Nuncle Brown Cow?" were splashed across the smooth side of an old warehouse.

The Fool did this.

It would seem so, my friend.

This Ted must have been brewing their fuel here. He seems a very smart man. Our village could have used him.

The world could have used him.

Yes.

Black smoke erupted through windows and through the roof of a large warehouse as orange flames consumed the entire structure.

All their fuel must have been inside there, inside a big tank.

With no one to fight it, this fire will burn the city down in a few days. And . . .

"What are we gonna do now, Poppa?"

We have, maybe, ten miles of fuel left.

So there is that also, my friend.

Yes.

CHAPTER 41

The tank limped through the fence at the far end of the international airport. Ahead, dirty and ancient jetliners waited forever at their gates for passengers on that last and long-ago day. Doomsday.

The needle in the gas gauge rested firmly on Empty.

I will not give up.

As if you could fuel this tank with your words?

I will not give up.

As if you can make it all the way to Colorado Springs?

We have made it this far. I will not give up.

And do you think the fuel in these jets is still any good?

It has to be, and if it isn't, we will find another way. I will not give up.

Why?

The Old Man did not answer himself.

Why? Why won't you give up?

Silence as he maneuvered the tank under the wing of one of the biggest jets.

A 747 I think.

Why won't you give up?

Stop!

Why?

Because in that moment when I saw the painted words of the Fool, I wanted to. Because this thing is bigger than an old man like me. Because this is too much, and seeing all that fuel we could've had, if we'd just gotten there earlier, go up in flames, crushed . . .

Crushed?

Silence.

Yes. It crushed me.

But you have been through worse, my friend.

Have I?

Yes.

"Will there be fuel here, Poppa?" she said over the intercom.

"Let us hope so."

Outside and climbing onto the hot metal of the wing, burning his knees and the palms of his hands, he searched for the opening to the fuel tank.

I can't find it.

Think. There is something you're forgetting.

It's underneath the wing, my friend.

Will the fuel still be good after all these years?

I will not give up.

It's underneath the wing.

"I found it!" he called out to them.

The Boy dragged the fueling hose away from the tank.

Think. There is something . . .

"Wait!"

He opened the cover to the wing fueling nozzle.

There will be water in the bottom of the fuel reservoir after all these years.

Water is heavier than fuel.

The Old Man found the lever that drained the fuel tank.

"Stand back!"

He pushed the lever and fuel gushed out onto the ground.

How will I know when it isn't water?

He waited.

Did it change color?

It smells more like kerosene now.

"Okay, bring me the hose," he said, slamming the fuel release lever back into the closed position.

Hopefully the fuel will not have as much water in it now. Now there will be a better chance that it will burn.

The tank drank up all the fuel it could from the insides of the old plane. Afterward, they topped off the two reserve drums still strapped to the turret.

In his mind the Old Man saw the map.

This is enough to make it there.

But what about getting back?

THEY LET THE spilled fuel dry. Over a fire of discarded luggage, they spitted and roasted some rabbit the Boy had taken near the settlement. They drank water in the shadows of the old terminal. Broken glass guarded the shadowy interior of the place, and they could only catch glimpses of suitcases and curtains near the daylight, high up on the concourses above.

There must have been panic that day.

I remember.

The Old Man made them stand far away and then went to the tank.

Off in the distance the fire in the center of town seemed to grow, its oily top like an anvil of smoke or an evil bird looming high over the city.

If the aircraft fuel explodes when I start the tank, would they be safe? Would he protect her? Would he take her back to Tucson?

What other choice do you have, my friend?

The Old Man started the APU, waited a few seconds, and then fired the turbine. He watched the Boy and his granddaughter struggling with a manhole cover they'd managed to pry up from the tarmac as he listened for trouble within the noise of the tank's engine.

It sounds rougher and this time there is gray smoke instead of black.

Is that better? Is gray better than black?

I don't know, my friend.

The Old Man backed the tank out from underneath the jumbo jet. He drove down the runway once and then back.

If the fuel wasn't any good then it should be out of fuel or dying now, right, Santiago? The temperature gauge is also a cause for concern.

Yes, but it runs, my friend, and for now, that is enough.

In the distance, the black plumes above the fire had grown as smoke drifted east over the dead city.

The Old Man looked around at the terminal.

I wonder if my dad ever came here in the jets he flew.

In a few days the fire will come and it will all be gone. Maybe by to-night even.

Yes.

The ancient jets, immobile and waiting, seemed to him as if all they needed were pilots, pilots like his dad, and once again they might leap away from the earth.

I remember being pressed into my seat as we raced down the runway.

I remember that my feet did not reach the floor.

I remember that my dad was up front, at the controls of the plane.

I was very proud to be his son.

CHAPTER 42

They pushed north as the flames consuming Albuquerque climbed toward the old highway on the eastern edge of town. For miles they could see the billowing black smoke reaching high into the iron blue of noonday.

The old highway was sun-bleached and rent by gaping cracks as the tank pushed upward through a ponderosa of rocks and stunted twisting pines.

There is only Santa Fe between us and Colorado Springs now. It is the last major city.

When he showed the Boy the map and pointed toward Santa Fe, asking if the Boy knew anything about what they might find there, the Boy only shook his head.

In the late afternoon they arrived in Santa Fe.

The Old Man turned off the tank and watched the pink rocks in the last of the hot day.

There is nothing here.

The Old Man looked hard into the dense tangle of weed bracken and cactus that spread west of the highway across a wide rise that ended in a chalky ridge and tired rocky hills beyond.

If there was a city here it is gone now.

Were they nuked?

The Old Man checked the dosimeter.

There is radiation.

On the sudden and very light afternoon breeze that began to sweep the place, the Old Man could hear bone chimes rattling against each other, hidden but there all the same.

So what is their story of salvage?

The Old Man watched as purple shadows began to lengthen and as the sun sank into the western sands. Within the brush he could see the frames and structures of rotting buildings signaling their surrender to the landscape.

The land turned to red and what was not red was purple and cool.

The buildings are like victims tied to a stake, signaling through the flames that they were here. Trying to communicate their last message.

What do you know of such things, my friend?

THEY DROVE ON until the dosimeter was back down to an acceptable level.

High. But not too high.

There will always be radiation now. With the amount of bombs we used, there must be.

I never fired one.

Yes. But it was your generation that can never be forgiven.

Silence.

In the dark, beside the tank, watching their fire turn and leap as it consumed the sweet-scented local pine, the Boy spoke.

"I know where you are going. But where did you come from?"

His granddaughter watched him, her eyes wide.

I am surprised she has not told him already.

She still listens to you.

"A city," said the Old Man.

The Boy continued to watch the fire, its flames within his green eyes.

"Ain't nothin' left of cities, Boy," said the Boy.

"What do you mean?"

The Boy shook his head.

"Just something someone used to tell me."

The soldier.

I wish we'd more of that rabbit than we did. Tomorrow we should hunt for a while.

"It's true," said his granddaughter. "Isn't it, Poppa?"

The Old Man nodded still thinking of rabbit.

"Poppa found it. We used to live in a tiny village but Poppa went out into the wasteland and found Tucson."

The Old Man shot a quick look at her and then the Boy.

"Sorry, Poppa."

The Old Man got up and went to get some water.

When he came back he said, "I'm sorry." He nodded at the Boy. "I didn't know if we could trust you. When we found you . . . well . . . you'd had a tough time. That was obvious."

The Boy only seems to listen to me now. But really, he is somewhere else. Maybe in his past, before we found him.

How do you know, my friend?

Whatever happened before we met him scarred him, changed him. Left its mark on him. He is there even now and I doubt he wholly ever leaves that place.

Yes.

"We don't need to know about your past," said the Old Man. "You've proven yourself to us. In fact, I don't know what we'd have done without you. When we finish with this business, you could come and live in the city with us, if you wanted to."

"You'd like it there!" said his granddaughter. "There's lots of salvage."

After a moment the Boy whispered a barely audible "thank you" and nothing more.

In the night, the others were asleep and the Old Man lay awake again, watching the night and the stars.

I would give anything to sleep like I used to. Like they do.

You're not thinking about rabbit even though you've been trying to.

Yes.

So what are you really thinking about?

Everything.

That's a lot to think about, my friend.

Yes.

A lot for one person.

Yes.

The story of Santa Fe? The story you would need to know if you were going to go and salvage there?

A little of that, although it is easy to understand what happened there, but mostly of other things.

Then what happened there?

A dirty bomb would be my guess. That is why we got the higher reading on the dosimeter. A dirty bomb parked in the downtown district.

Or the art district. Or even the historic.

Did they have such things?

Wherever it was, it went off and destroyed less than a block. The fire engines and police arrived. If it was the first bomb, or one of the first in those early days before we truly understood what was going on, they hadn't even thought of checking their dosimeters that day. But in the days that followed, before the EMP that knocked out the networks, an exploding van in any kind of populated area would have had them checking. In a moment they would've known.

Known what?

That the city was poisoned.

That everyone must flee.

Why?

Because, what can you do now? The bomb has gone off. You can't put out radiation like a fire. Or clean it up like a flood. Or pack it into an ambulance and take it to the hospital. No. It is just there, somewhere under all that brush.

And that is what happened. In a matter of hours, by evening no doubt, because I remember the bombs always seemed to go off during the morning rush hour . . . they are all gone into the desert and the city is dead for all practical intents and purposes.

The bombs always went off at morning rush hour.

I have not thought about that in a long time. Funny, what comes back to you across the years. What surfaces in the little pond we call our mind.

Or sails across the ocean and back again.

Yes. That is an even better way to think of it.

By evening the city is dead. And in the silent years that follow, the brush grows. It covers everything. It pulls everything down into the dirt for someone to find at some far later date when we who lived through those days aren't even a memory in the mind of the oldest of them. Then they will find what we left behind.

If humanity survives, my friend.

Yes, there is that also.

If a fire happens, then everything is so much faster.

And the bone chimes?

Unseen people who live near here or pass by. They have put those chimes up as some sort of marker to warn others away from what has been poisoned.

Stay away.

Bones.

Death.

Soft notes in a gentle breeze.

The Old Man watched for satellites beneath the stars above.

He thought of Natalie.

General Watt.

I wonder what her story of salvage is.

CHAPTER 43

In the badlands, they crossed alongside pink canyons of stacked rock and through stunted forests twisting away beyond Santa Fe.

They began to find the bodies.

The first was a woman, her corpse bloated and lying in a ditch alongside the road.

The Boy exited the tank and searched the road and its sides.

When he returned he said, "Hard to tell, but less than a week. There was a fishhook in her lip but she didn't die from that."

He pointed to the center of the road.

"They were all chained together up there. She must have died along the march. Then they unhooked her and threw her over there."

"Should we bury her, Poppa?"

You know we will find more of them as we go, my friend.

"No. We have to hurry now."

To what? To overtake the slavers, and then what? Or do you mean the bunker and again, then what, my friend?

Project Einstein, whatever it does.

Whatever it does, indeed.

THERE WERE MORE bodies rotting in the merciless sun. They passed them and the Old Man wondered if any one of them was Ted.

The canyons and forest gave way to a wide plain of rolling grass and slight hills that swept away toward the hazy north.

When they stopped in the middle of the plain, the Old Man could hear insects buzzing in the long grass. In every direction, the tall grass ran off toward the horizon, its undefinable edges disappearing into a screen of summer haze and thick humidity. As if the wide plain simply fell off the edges of the earth.

At noonday, they rested in the small ledge of shade alongside the tank, drinking warm water and not eating. The Old Man asked the Boy if there was something they might hunt to eat.

The Boy stood and scanned the indeterminate horizon.

'We have no idea what's out there, any of us,' thought the Old Man. 'No idea.'

"It looks like horse country," said the Old Man hopefully.

Whether it was horse country or not, the Boy didn't bother to respond.

In time they mounted the tank and continued along the road as it cut like a straight line into the hazy north.

I cannot believe we've come this far. It feels like we're in a strange land at the top of the world. A land I never knew existed. Or maybe it is like an ocean. Like a sea of grass so high up.

That's because you spent so many years in the desert, my friend. You thought the whole world had become desert.

I thought often of the sea. Every time I read the book, I thought of the sea and the big fish.

Later, they passed more bodies.

At dusk, they pulled off to the side of the road. All around them, the plain continued to stretch off into a hazy pink nothingness where there was no mountain, or forest, or city, or even an end to things. An unseen orchestra of bugs clicked and buzzed heavily through their symphony well into the twilight and falling dark.

Down the road, dark barns crumbled beside a lazy stream about which oaks clustered greedily along the banks. The occasional wooden post showed where fences must have once claimed the place.

The Boy wandered off in the dusk and the Old Man hoped he would come back with something for them to eat.

His granddaughter gathered sticks for their fire.

She must be hungry too, but she has said nothing. She is good that way.

I am grateful to have them both. I would be too tired to hunt and make a fire after driving the tank all day.

The Old Man lay on the ground and closed his eyes.

IN THE DREAM he is slipping.

The voice, the familiar voice keeps asking him the same question. That same question it has always been asking.

Can you let go?

He is in the gravel pit south of the village this time.

The forbidden pit.

The gravel pit where Big Pedro died.

The Old Man climbs across the shifting gravel hill to reach Big Pedro, which is really how it happened. How Big Pedro died.

But I am dreaming. So it cannot happen again.

Yet the Old Man can taste the long untouched dust of the pile shifting beneath him, threatening to slide him right down to the bottom. And at the bottom of the pile is the pit's edge. And below the edge is the fall into the pool of dirty water where Big Pedro will fall and die because the fall is very great and the pool is shallow.

Which is how it happened.

But this is a dream.

So you say.

But you taste the dust and it is very hot like it was that day when you had been trying to salvage the material off the conveyor belt and part of it had given way and Big Pedro went down onto the gravel pile that had not been touched in so many years. Now it is shifting, and as Big Pedro tries to climb out it shifts, pulling him each time closer to the pit's edge.

Toward the fall.

Toward the shallow pool of dirty water.

Just as it happened.

'But this is a dream,' thinks the Old Man and hears the uncertainty in his own voice.

Then why are you trying to save him?

Because he is Big Pedro. Because he is my friend. Because I must.

And the Old Man feels the gravel shifting beneath his belly as he tries to get a little closer to Big Pedro. That way he can grab his hand and they can climb back up the rope that the Old Man has secured about his waist and to the conveyor belt.

The rope is not there.

Big Pedro smiles.

But this is a dream, right?

"Yes, of course, my friend," says Big Pedro in his high Mexican tenor.

You screamed when you went over the side.

"Yes."

And I heard that scream for years.

Yes, but this is a dream.

If you say so.

And Big Pedro falls and does not scream.

In fact, he smiles, and nods, and encourages the Old Man, just as he did when he taught the Old Man who was then a young man, a survivor of the Day After, all the skills one needs to live and survive in the very dangerous Sonoran Desert.

Traps for rodents.

Traps for Serpiente.

Traps for foxes.

"Can you let go?" asks the familiar voice.

Can you let go?

And the Old Man is sliding fast down the gravel, toward the pit, toward where Big Pedro has gone and the pool at the end of the drop where they will meet again. The pool that waits for us all.

Can you let go?

Yes. Yes I can.

And the Old Man lets himself think for a moment that he is tired. He thinks that his dusty and bleeding fingers could merely splay outward and he would glide down this pile and over the edge.

Yes. Yes, I can let go, if you will let me. If I don't hear my granddaughter. If she doesn't . . . then yes, I can finally let go.

Poppa, I need you.

And the Old Man is on his back and tumbling down the pile, and though he doesn't see her he hears her calling for him, crying, *Poppa, I need you.*

Which is the worst.

Which is what makes the Old Man try and grab the shifting sand to save his falling life.

I must because the edge is so near.

And . . .

Because she needs me.

Why?

Because to break her heart is too much to bear.

It is?

Yes, yes that is the worst.

Worse than the pit and pool at the bottom?

Falling!

And he is up and awake and saliva is running down onto the side of his mouth. There is meat cooking and he hears her laughing beside the fire.

And the Boy is drawing faces in the dirt with a stick as she watches and what he draws makes her laugh.

"Can you let go?" asks that very familiar voice.

If I could take her laugh with me, then yes, I will let go of everything.

THEY EAT MEAT and though there is no pepper, it tastes good. Wonderful in fact. The Old Man tells them about cities. About buses and trains and how one could take them to work, and after work, ride them to a game. Which leads to baseball. Which neither of them have ever heard of.

The Old Man tells them about baseball.

About ballparks in the early summer evenings.

About the importance of fall.

About a game in which he saw a man hit three home runs in one night. About how the floor of the stadium shook as the man, the hero, came to bat for the last time and everyone was sure he would do it. Sure he would hit another home run because it just had to be. Because it was meant to be.

They ask him details.

What were hot dogs?

What is a strike?

What are good tickets?

When they finally sleep, the Old Man lies awake.

Probably because I took a nap before dinner.

It wasn't much of a nap. We cheated them, you know.

Who?

The young. We cheated them.

How?

They will never know that night of baseball. The night of three home runs when the floor of the stadium shook. We cheated them of that and all the good things we had and took for granted.

Yes.

They should never forgive us for that.

Later when he still cannot sleep, he rises and turns on the radio inside the tank.

He almost says, "General Watt."

But instead he chooses, "Natalie?"

And after a moment . . .

"It's so good to hear you tonight," she says.

"I couldn't sleep again," explains the Old Man.

"Is everything all right? Are you still coming?"

"Yes. Everything is fine. We're beyond Santa Fe and out in the grassy plains south of you. Maybe three more days and we'll be there."

"In two days, at exactly nine A.M., I need you to open the case and take out the Laser Target Designator. We need to test the device."

"I don't even really know the correct time," said the Old Man. "I just guess."

"The tank has a small clock near the commander's seat. Set that clock using the tiny knob above it to 1:37 A.M., now."

The Old Man did.

"The last time I knew exactly what time it was was just after a bomb exploded in my rearview mirror and disabled my car. It froze the clock at 2:06 P.M."

I remember that after forty years.

"Why can't you sleep?" asked Natalie. General Watt.

Silence.

"I was telling the children about baseball."

"Maybe you're just too excited to sleep?" she asked.

The Old Man thought about that.

"No. I feel . . . I feel like we cheated them."

He waited for her reply.

When she did, she said, "You're a good man. I'm sure of it. I don't think you ever intended for the world to destroy itself."

"I was almost as young as they are now when it happened. But still, after all this time I feel responsible. Guilty somehow."

"You shouldn't."

"Thank you, but lately, and for a long time, I've felt it was all my fault. For a long time I've felt 'curst.' "

In the dark, a breeze passed and the Old Man watched as the wave it left in the grassy plain swept past him and off into the night.

"If it helps, I can tell you something about yourself," offered Natalie.

"What?"

"I can tell that right now you are trying to make the world a better place. Why else would you help us if not because of that?"

The Old Man said nothing.

"The people who destroyed the world weren't trying to make it better. Baseball wasn't important to them. Nor were children who might one day see a game played under lights. They were more concerned with destroying themselves for power than good things like seeing a baseball game with their grandchildren. And what's worse, if they were still alive, they would not feel guilty as you do now. Sadly, I imagine they would do it all over again."

"If that were true, then that is very sad," said the Old Man.

"Only the good feel guilty. So that means you are good."

"Thank you."

Silence.

"Natalie?"

"Yes?"

"I hope this works. I hope we'll be able to set you and your children free."

"I hope so too."

CHAPTER 44

At dawn the next day, the air was thick and the heat already in the day, as if the two were one thing and could not be separated from each other.

Today we need to find water.

And food.

They traveled north again, following the straight arrow highway into a horizon that blended with the featureless landscape of rolling green grass, sun, and gray haze.

The tank rumbled and shuddered, its sound more metallic, its smoke thicker.

For a while there were fewer bodies.

Then all at once there were clusters, tossed like rag dolls to the side of the road by some petulant and perpetually unsatisfied child.

In the distance they could see a conical hill rising up out of the plain, and the silhouettes of horsemen and men on foot driving others, huddled figures, forward toward the hill under the harsh bright blaze of noon.

We've finally caught up with them.

What did you expect you would do?

I didn't think it would be our problem.

But now it is, my friend.

Yes.

"Poppa?" she said over the intercom.

The Old Man handed his field glasses to the Boy.

After a moment the Boy lowered them and said, "They're trying to take shelter by that hill. They have a small fort around the bottom that encircles the whole."

"They've known we were behind them, that's why they're running," said the Old Man.

And why they drove these people so hard.

And why we have passed so many bodies alongside the road.

"We can still catch them," said the Boy. "They've got about two miles to go before they reach the hill."

The Old Man looked again.

"But what will we do? I can't fire this," he said patting the long barrel of the gun. "We might hit some of Ted's people."

Even Ted perhaps.

Yes.

The Boy, he is on the edge of something.

Yes, my friend.

He's been here before, at this moment between things. Between attack and retreat.

The Boy seemed to move and remain still at once.

Suddenly the Old Man knew, or rather felt by the sudden electricity in the air, that the Boy had decided what must be done next.

"Get her in there with you," said the Boy pointing toward the hatch.

He's decided.

The Boy disappeared down inside the tank.

His granddaughter was already crawling up out of the driver's hatch and making her way, hand over hand, along the gun barrel up to the turret of the tank.

"What're we going to do, Poppa?"

"I don't know," said the Old Man wiping sudden sweat from his forehead. "But I think he has a plan."

"To help those people?"

"Yes, I think so."

The Boy emerged from his hatch, then bent down and drew up the weight bar from inside the tank. Secured to its tip was the blue bowling ball.

He's certainly made a weapon, my friend.

The Boy set the weapon down against the turret and reached back into the tank once more. His powerful right arm drew up the manhole cover. For a moment the Boy struggled to attach it to his weak left side, forcing his thin, trembling arm through a makeshift strap he'd fashioned for it.

"That'll be too heavy for . . ."

'Your bad side,' you almost said, my friend.

The Boy, sweating, nodded.

"It will do its work today, just like the rest of me!" he said with a grunt as he pulled the strap tight. The manhole cover seemed to draw his entire left side downward.

The Boy reached down and took up his new weapon as if it were merely a stick.

On that side he is strong. Stronger maybe than anyone I have ever met.

Beneath the gray haze of summer heat and the clicking buzz of the unseen insects in the tall grass, the Boy stood like some bygone warrior and pointed his mace at the running slavers who drew whips high into the air and brought them down with a sonic crack across the backs of the terrified.

"Get me as close to them as you can."

This is madness.

The Old Man's trembling hands fell to the controls.

"What will you do then?" he asked the Boy.

"I'll fight them from the tank as if it were a horse."

We're leaving the highway. We could throw the bad tread and that would be the end of us.

Yes.

"Have you ever fought from a horse?" asked the Old Man.

The Boy looked away across the grassy plains.

If only his friend, Horse, would appear now. They might ride once more, one last time together, into battle.

"I have," he said. But his words were lost beneath the spooling turbine of the terrible engine as the Old Man throttled up to power.

Madness.

"Poppa?" she said, worried.

"Just stay down and hang on. Everything will be all right."

"Are you sure, Poppa?"

He nodded and tried to say something, but felt his dry throat constrict with dust.

I am in over my head, my friend. What do we do?

Sometimes you can do nothing other than hold the line and hope the fish will tire, my friend. That your strength will outlast his will to live.

The Old Man pivoted the tank and left the highway, descending down a ditch and into the tall grass of the plain.

What if he falls off?

He won't, my friend.

The tank picked up speed as the ground leveled out, and the Boy hooked his arm with the manhole cover shield around the barrel and leaned back against the turret.

From midway up the conical hill, white puffs of smoke erupted almost in unison.

What is that?

You know the answer, my friend; you're just not ready to accept it, but now you must.

I can almost see the cannon rounds moving through the air, between us and them, like the rumor of a shadow.

The ground between the tank and the hill sprang upward in a series of dirt fountains. Earth showered the charging tank, and a moment later they passed through the rising smoke of the impacts.

They have artillery.

Ahead, the slavers were breaking off into two groups. The whip wielders drove their prisoners forward, their whips arching high across the sky like dark strands of a girl's hair dancing in the wind. Others on horseback turned to face the oncoming tank, drawing their weapons.

The Boy pushed himself away from the turret, his legs bending, as if he were riding the tank, his manhole cover shield rising to protect his chest and body. His powerful right arm began to draw the weight bar with the bowling ball at the tip in huge slow circles about his head.

The horsemen thundered straight on toward the tank.

The Old Man could see the sweat running down their grim, ash-covered faces. He could see broken teeth jutting up through their red gums as they began to shout and whoop.

Their horses frothed, eyes wide with terror.

The Boy leaned outward and far to the right, still swinging the great mace in a wide circle.

Spears jutted forward from some of the horsemen, while machetes danced wildly about the heads of others.

'This is madness,' thought the Old Man again.

A moment later, they met.

Six riders.

One went down beneath the tank.

Forget that sound. The sound that man and horse make when that happens. Never think of that sound again in all your life, my friend.

Yes, I won't ever if I can help it.

And in the next moment, the Old Man forgot as the Boy lowered his powerful arm and swept the club past the Old Man's head and straight into the chest of the nearest oncoming rider.

In one moment, the man changed direction from charging atop a terrified horse, to flying backward and alone, almost keeping pace with the tank for the merest second before he disappeared beneath the tread.

The Boy pivoted and watched the riders wheel their horses about.

They'll catch us if I don't go faster.

But the tread?

The Boy nodded toward the main body of prisoners, telling the Old Man to continue forward.

The ground all around and behind them exploded again as the Old Man looked up to see smoke drifting away from the mouths of the cannons that rested midway up the hill behind a low bric-a-brac wall.

Ahead, the slavers were throwing down their weapons and outrunning Ted's people who also continued to run forward in terror.

Turning back to the Old Man as if to tell him something, the Boy suddenly raised his shield. A spear shattered against it, emitting a small metallic note.

The Boy climbed back to the Old Man and uttered a breathless, "Keep moving forward!"

The Old Man turned to see the riders closing up the distance on the tank's sides. The Boy whirled his club quicker than the Old Man thought possible and brought it down onto the head of one of the nearest horsemen who crumpled instantly.

Ted's people were huddled together now, bloody, screaming, crying, protecting each other. The Old Man swerved wide to completely avoid them.

Halfway up the conical hill, ashen-faced warriors waving spears and machetes surged out from behind the bric-a-brac wall.

Once more, the Old Man saw the cannons belch forth with their sudden puffs of white smoke.

Duck!

A moment later he felt a jarring impact slam into the side of the tank.

His granddaughter screamed.

"Poppa!"

The Old Man's ears were ringing.

"It's okay!" he yelled down into the dark. "Are you all right?"

Please don't let this be a worse nightmare. Please don't let this be the nightmare too terrible to imagine. The one in which she is hurt.

Can you let go?

Stop! I cannot because too much depends on me and I am not enough.

A shot had fallen amid the prisoners. Bloodied bodies were being dragged back within their huddle in the midst of the battlefield.

"I'm okay, Poppa." But he could hear her fear.

We've got to protect those people.

But how?

And . . .

Where is the Boy?

I can't see him!

The Old Man gunned the tank and pivoted hard, throwing up giant clods of dirt and torn grass.

Be careful of the tread!

There is too much to worry about.

The Old Man drove the tank between the prisoners and the cannon on the hill.

Leaning down, he beckoned Ted's people toward the side of the tank.

"Get close to the sides, you'll be safer here!" he yelled above the roar of the engine.

Where is the Boy?

"Poppa, what's going on up there?"

A battle is nothing but confusion, my friend.

Maybe this is how the world was destroyed. Confusion took charge in the absence of leadership.

Yes.

But the fear-struck people would not move from their huddle.

"Stay here!" he called down to his granddaughter.

"No, Poppa!"

Don't say it, please. Because even if you do, I still need to do this.

The Old Man dropped to the ground.

My legs feel weak and far away.

That is just fear, my friend.

He stumbled forward to the wild-eyed prisoners. Waving with his hands, he urged them to take cover alongside the tank.

Out in the tall grass he could see the Boy battling three horsemen. He swept his club into the legs of one horse, and a second later raised it high above his head to strike down its fallen rider. The other two horsemen wheeled about trying to bring their spear points to bear.

Again the Old Man heard the distant boom of cannon.

"Please!" he beckoned the terrified people.

All at once they ran forward screaming and crying, like a stampede of frightened animals. Or a hurt child wailing, racing for the comfort of its mother's arms.

The Old Man could see their bloody backs and torn clothing, their haunted tearstained faces.

"Thank you," someone sobbed. A woman holding a small child. "Thank you."

There was a series of deep thuds as the earth shook about them and seconds later it was raining dirt.

The Old Man turned to see the Boy who danced away from the last standing horseman, limping away from a striking axe that glanced off his manhole cover shield. The Boy retaliated, dragging his mace from the ground and slamming it into the man's ribs, crushing them.

Again the Old Man could hear the cannons bellow their dull *whump*.

Someone screamed, "Oh no, please not again!"

Thuds. Sudden and terrible. Near and close.

Dirt falling from the sky.

How can I save them all?

How can I get us out of this place?

This is too much for just me.

The Boy was running toward them now.

How are we going to get these people out of here?

The Boy loped past the tank, disappearing around the gun barrel, his broken feather flying out from his hair as though it had followed him everywhere he'd ever gone. Would go. Even if it was to his death.

What is he doing? Where is he going?

"Wait here!" the Old Man shouted at those huddled about him. Then he climbed up onto the tread, keeping the low flat turret between him and the cannons on the hill. When he peered over its edge he saw the Boy running now, no longer limping, he was running, running forward to meet the ashen-faced warriors who were coming down the hill for them.

There must be a hundred of them, at least.

The Old Man watched the warriors surge out from the gates and leap through the tall grass, waving their machetes, screaming as they came on.

The Boy raced to meet them.

His mace circling above his head.

He's going to give you the time you need to get out of here, my friend. So I suggest you go now.

"Get up on the tank," he called down to those huddled at its sides. He had to say it again and a moment later they were all climbing up onto the tank, pushing children down inside the hatch. Everything in chaos.

Children screamed.

Men swore.

A woman begged for someone to leave her behind.

The Old Man watched helplessly as the Boy ran forward to meet the oncoming mass of ashen warriors.

He is braver than anyone I have ever known.

And . . .

He will be killed for sure.

What can I do for him, my friend Santiago? What can I do to help this Boy?

Nothing, my friend. Nothing.

To the south, the Old Man saw dark figures coming up out of the earth.

More horsemen, dark riders to encircle us.

Moments later the dark riders were charging forward.

They have been down in a riverbed that must run through this plain, and now they are coming to attack us from behind.

The Old Man climbed into the driver's seat at the front of the tank.

The cannon fired once more.

But this time the rounds fell amid the charging horsemen. The dark riders.

Wait!

The dark horsemen thundered past the tank.

The Old Man could see the Boy. He'd crashed into the line of ashen-faced men, swinging his mace in wide arcs as they fell back from him.

Encircling him.

Pressing down on him.

Wait!

One of the dark horsemen who'd been thrown from his mount by the falling artillery rounds remounted and dashed past the tank, whooping like a Plains Indian, long black hair streaming behind, almost touching the flying tail of the chestnut mare. And in that hair a long gray feather, following in the wind.

Like the Boy.

Green eyes turned and smiled for the briefest of moments at the Old Man, and then the dark rider was gone, riding forward into battle. Riding forward to fight by the side of the outnumbered Boy.

WHEN THE BATTLE was over the Old Man watched as the outnumbered dark horsemen climbed the heights, vaulting the low bric-a-brac wall, falling on the artillerymen, cutting and stabbing.

The bodies of the ashen-faced warriors lay in the tall grass and at the foot of the hill and up along its dusty slopes.

The Old Man and his granddaughter left the tank. Looking among the bodies. Looking for the Boy. And they found him.

He was drinking water from a water skin held up to his mouth by a large, bloody horseman. The Boy's massive arm was shaking. The bowling ball mace and the manhole cover shield lay in the dust. The crushed bodies of slavers scattered in a wide arc about him.

The Boy, standing, spoke haltingly in a strange language to the bloody horseman between gasping pulls at the water skin. The Old Man could make out only a few of the many words.

"What's he doing, Poppa?"

The large horseman suddenly embraced the Boy. A feather, long and gray, just like those of the other horsemen, like the broken feather in the Boy's hair, lay on his shoulder, resting against a bloody scratch.

"I think . . ." said the Old Man. "I think he has found his people."

"Oh," she said.

CHAPTER 45

The Old Man moved the tank closer to the hill, near the falling walls of a village that had once occupied the slopes nearest the highway. A place once called Wagon Wheel Mountain if a faded sign was to be believed. Ted's people huddled in small groups, eating shared rations given out by the horsemen and drinking water from leather-skinned bags. The Old Man walked forward to where the Boy stood amid the warriors.

The Boy's muscles still trembled and twitched as he too held a water skin to his mouth.

"Who are these people?" asked the Old Man.

The Boy lowered the bag and opened his mouth to speak.

"The real question should be," said a tired voice from behind them, "who is he?"

The Old Man turned at the sound of the voice.

A crippled man and old like me.

"That is the million-dollar question, if a million dollars were still worth anything beyond kindling."

The Crippled Man was small and thin. His hair, what remained of it, was wispy, his eyes milky, his legs bent and twisted as he sat in the dust between two giant horsemen who'd carried him into the impromptu camp after the battle.

"What do you mean?" asked the Old Man.

The Crippled Man crawled forward and when he reached the feet of the Boy, he beckoned for him to bend down. The Crippled Man ran his fingers just above the feather that hung in the Boy's hair.

He muttered to himself.

He waved the Boy back up and crawled back between his bearers.

He looked straight into the eyes of the Boy.

"I made that feather seventeen years ago. Maybe more, maybe less. But I made it."

The Boy undid the leather thong and brought the feather down, holding it under his green eyes.

"I made it bent like that with some glue I'd manufactured. Epoxy we called it once. Made it from the wreckage of my plane."

Silence. Some of the horsemen muttered in their pidgin.

The Old Man heard, "Como," and "Fudgeweisen."

The Boy stared at the broken feather.

Silence.

"Why?" asked the Boy softly.

"Because," replied the Crippled Man. "It was who you were. Who you are."

"Broken Feather?" asked the Boy.

The Crippled Man looked up, considered the sky, seemed to mumble to himself in some agreement, then looked back and said, "Yeah, that could be one way of saying it."

The Old Man saw the Boy tighten his jaw.

He saw the Boy nod to himself.

He never really knew where he'd come from. Where his starting place was in all this.

No, he never knew, my friend, where his course began on the map he's carried for all these years. It has bothered him all his days and he has been looking for his beginning in all the places he has ever been. And he never found it, until now. The meaning of it. What the feather meant to him and the people who had first given it.

"You were born that way," said the Crippled Man. "Because of the radiation. Many were in those days. Not so many now. But in those days there were many birth defects. From the moment you came out, we could see that you would be weak on that side."

"And you threw me away," said the Boy through clenched teeth in the silence that followed. "You gave me away."

Everyone watched the two.

The Crippled Man and the Boy.

"No. I have no idea what happened to you," said the Crippled Man. "You were very little when your mother and father, and a few of the other warrior families, tried to make it into the Tetons. There wasn't enough here and we were fighting with other groups of survivors constantly. Those times brought out the worst in people. So your father, if he was who I remember him to be, was part of an expedition that went up into the Tetons. We never heard from them again. Years later when we sent scouts to look for them, there was no trace."

The Boy remembered cold plains.

His first memory was of running. Of a woman screaming. Of seeing the sky, blue and cold in one moment, and the ground, yellow stubble, race by in the next.

"And now you have returned to us," said the Crippled Man. "A brave warrior who inspired us to victory where we saw none. You charged out against our enemy with your weapon all alone."

"I was . . . it wasn't what you thought."

The Crippled Man considered the Boy and his words.

"No. It never is."

"Why did you come to our rescue?" said the Old Man.

"We've been shadowing you since before Santa Fe. Those are our lands. We thought you were working with these people. There was nothing we could have done against you. We fought a battle against them at Pecos Creek when they initially entered our lands a couple of years back. That was a hard day and our losses were bitter. Still are. But when a report came to me that one of you was wearing our badge, the feather, well, then I hoped."

"Hoped for what?" asked the Old Man.

"Hoped you might not be with them." He pointed toward the bodies lain out on the slopes of the hill. "Hoped we were finally getting a break."

Silence.

"I'll be honest," continued the Crippled Man. "I wasn't convinced he was of our tribe. I didn't remember a warrior like him. But I hoped all the same. Or maybe I was just stunned to see one of our old tanks still working. I figured if you two just wiped each other out, then that would be best for us. There aren't too many of us Mohicans left these days."

"Mohicans?"

"Yes. It's my little joke from long ago that's sorta stuck as a name for us. In the days after the bombs, the people who rescued me, the people I would lead, we called ourselves that. It was our bad little joke in a very bad time. And there were days when we felt as though we were indeed the last."

I know those days.

"When I saw what you were trying to do," said the Crippled Man, "to rescue these people, when I saw him run out into the field to fight them all alone, when I saw his feather through my 'nocs, I knew he was one of us. And I knew I just couldn't let him die all alone. That wouldn't be right, now would it?"

Silence.

"Thank you," said the Old Man.

"Truth be told I thought it was the end of us too. Like I said there aren't many of us left. I thought, oh well, and ordered the attack. I thought we'd all get killed together. But I guess we caught them by surprise."

THAT NIGHT THEY made camp out on the plain, the conical hill still in view. Large groups of women and children had come up from the hidden creek bed. Tents were up and a large buck that had been killed was spitted and roasting.

In the first breezes of night, as the sparks were carried away from the fire, the Old Man sat watching the meat, listening to the Boy tell the story of his whole life.

It was the tale of a young boy raised by a soldier. The last American soldier. There were days of hunger and cold. And there were good times also. They crossed the entire country to complete a mission.

"What's there?" asked the Crippled Man when the Boy told of how they'd finally made it to Washington, D.C.

The Boy shook his head and said, "Nothing."

When the story was done and the Boy had told how Sergeant Presley had died and how he'd buried him in the cornfields, the Old Man said, "He sounds like he was a good man."

Silence.

Sergeant Major Preston.

Staff Sergeant Presley.

Long after the country had given up, they were out there, still soldiering. Still trying to save their country when the rest of us were only trying to save ourselves.

We need more of those kind of people.

More Staff Sergeant Presleys.

More Sergeant Major Prestons.

What is a soldier?

A soldier is someone who never gives up.

Yes, my friend.

The Boy finished his tale by the side of the grave in the cold cornfield with winter coming on.

But there is more he will not tell us tonight.

When I found him he was mad with grief. So it's probably something he still carries with him.

He said to you, *You take everything with you*, my friend.

The meat was ready.

A woman in soft buckskin carved the first piece and offered it to the Crippled Man.

He nodded his head toward the Boy.

All eyes watched as the dripping and steaming haunch of meat was carried to the Boy. They had all seen him carry that massive shield, wielding that immense weapon, riding an ancient war machine into battle against impossible odds.

They had seen him stand alone against many.

The Boy swallowed thickly.

Hungry.

Then . . .

"Please give it to my friends." He turned to the Old Man and his granddaughter. "They found me when I was . . . lost."

The Old Man held up his hands in protest.

But the look from the Boy, the look from all of them, stopped the Old Man.

The Old Man tore it in half, handing a piece to his granddaughter.

"Thank you, we are very honored."

CHAPTER 46

"And now the other question is 'Where are you going?'" the Crippled Man said as he and the Old Man sat in the golden dawnlight of the next morning.

They drank a brewed tea by a smoking fire.

"We are heading north."

The Crippled Man's face darkened.

Beyond them, warriors fed and brushed their horses, exercising the animals with short sprints or gentle walks.

"Why go there? There is nothing up that way anymore,"

The Old Man nodded. "There is someone there."

The Crippled Man's eyes went wide. Then he sipped his tea, blowing away the steam.

"Where?"

"Beneath the mountain at Colorado Springs. The old NORAD bunker."

"I didn't think they'd survived," said the Crippled Man.

"They contacted us by radio. They said someone is trying to break into their bunker from the outside. If that happens, the complex will flood with a lethal dose of radiation. They'll all die in there."

"Who's in command?"

"Natalie . . . I mean someone named General Watt."

The Crippled Man thought for a moment, sipping his tea again, smacking his lips.

"I don't remember that name. But it has been a long time."

Small sleepy-eyed children emerged from patchwork tents and were dragged down to the stream by women.

"You won't survive. That is, if you go north beyond a deserted place once called Raton."

"How do you know we won't?"

The Crippled Man refilled his tea, leaning from off his multihued carpet, holding out the kettle that hung over the fire, filling the Old Man's cup.

"I was a Lightning driver in those days. Flew the F-35." The Crippled Man nodded to himself. "I flew the F-35," he whispered.

"I can't remember what I did," said the Old Man. "Whatever it was, it must not have been that important."

"I can't remember my wife's maiden name," said the Crippled Man. "Age is funny like that, isn't it?"

"Yes."

"So how do you know . . . about the North?" asked the Old Man.

"Operation Running Back. I'll explain. Sorry. I'm lost. Talking about, saying those words makes it all seem like . . . like it just happened. Like it was yesterday. And this is funny, but sometimes it seems like it all happened to someone else. Does that . . . do you ever feel that way too?"

"I do," agreed the Old Man.

Yes.

"That's good. It would be terrible to be the only one who ever felt like that."

The Old Man nodded and blew on his tea.

Today will be very hot, my friend. Do you ever think that today will be your last day? Like those men on the slopes. Like all those people back during the days of the bombs. Everyone has a last day. Everyone dies.

I am only thinking this way because of what he has told me about the North. About where I must go.

Yes.

"When the bombs started going off . . ." began the Crippled Man. "When we lost New York, we had to keep the President airborne in . . . oh, I forget . . . wait, Air Force One. Yes." He laughed. "That was it. Air Force One. I was based out of Dover. I flew shotgun for . . . Air Force

One. I'd been somewhere else . . . in the desert before that, then I got reassigned. Moved my . . . yeah. That's right. I moved my wife and kid there. Two weeks later I'm on the tarmac. Engine to max power and I'm following Air Force One for the next three days. Maybe the last three days of the United States, I kept thinking. For three straight days I flew and flew and when my plane got thirsty I was refueled by an air tanker. We couldn't put the President down anywhere. We were trying to make it into the bunker at NORAD. D.C. had been hit, so we couldn't get him in to the bunker there. A civilian plane got a little too close outside of Chicago and I shot him down. I didn't think it was a terrorist, but we couldn't be too careful. I wasn't proud of that. So we're vectoring in on Colorado Springs. I've been flying for three days straight. I remember that I got to set down twice. Once in a field. The other time on a highway. They let me get a few hours of sleep and then I was back on cap again. That night over Colorado I was falling asleep at the stick. I kept slapping myself, doing everything I could to stay awake. On top of that, Air Force One was running dark, which is a hell of thing when you've got to follow it real close. Hell of a time. The controller contacts me from Air Force One and tells me we're turning for the air base at Colorado Springs. It looked like we're heading straight in. Then she adds, I remember it clear as day, she adds, 'Oh yeah, and for your own personal beatification, we just went nuclear on the Chinese fleet.' We were tired. We'd been talking to each other for three days. I'd always imagined she was a redhead. Never met her. We hit the runway and I'm right on top of Air Force One. I go around while they taxi to meet the convoy that'll take the President up to NORAD. I'm turning downwind to get back to the airport, and off to my left I see tracer rounds and gunfire zipping all across the airfield. It was an ambush. We had Chinese insurgents everywhere in those days. They knew the President hadn't made it into D.C., so they were going for the kill shot at Colorado. So Air Force One just turns around and takes off at max power straight back down the runway.

"Now the plan is to orbit the air base until the Army can re-secure it and clean out the insurgents. Then we'll try to go in again."

"An hour after that, the plan to make it into the bunker and ride out the attack was scrubbed. A few minutes later and we've got reports of Chinese aircraft all across the Southwest. Someone shot down a transport dropping paratroopers in Texas. That's when they came up with 'Running Back,' which was to get the President down to Yuma where we had air superiority and the Eighty-Second Airborne on the ground."

You must have thought about your wife and child back in Maryland.

The Crippled Man drank some of his tea. Swallowing. Eyes distant.

"That was the plan," continued the Crippled Man. "The plan until China responded with a full-scale nuclear strike. It's dawn in the East, like zero five thirty and their missiles, and ours, are streaking across the upper atmosphere. We're still trying to clear the airport; I'm even being called in to make close air support strafing runs. We're already low on fuel and there's a rumor our tanker got jumped and that we might not be getting refueled at all. I mean, everything's going to hell in a handbasket, and I thought that'd already happened two weeks prior. So we hit it. We head south. I think command was thinking we'd take the President to South America. But we don't have the fuel. Maybe we'll get some somewhere, but who knows. Anyway, we're out over southern Colorado entering New Mexico and, last time I counted, Colorado gets fourteen military-grade nuclear warheads in the space of thirty minutes."

"Worse thirty minutes of my life listening to stations go offline."

"We get a tanker rendezvous and it's now or never for some fuel. I'm on fumes but Air Force One always drinks first. EMPs are playing hell with our commo, but the F-35 I was flying was hardened for that kind of stuff. Still, let me tell you it's hell at Mach One with mushroom clouds everywhere, vapor trails crossing the sky, and aircraft fleeing in every possible direction."

"Air Force One is halfway through her drink when radar control gives me a fast mover aimed straight for us. So I'm thinking at that point the Chinese have somehow managed to get one of their supersecret J-35s into our airspace and they're shootin' up targets of opportunity. Anyway, long story short, it wasn't a J-35. It was a damn missile. Did I mention I'm down to just guns now? My missiles were gone back at the airfield. So they vector me in on this thing and I'm thinking I'm on a hard intercept for the latest, at the time back then, Chinese stealth fighter. Probably still is. Who's built anything since? Anyway, I had about thirty seconds to realize it was a low-yield Chinese version of a Tomahawk and they were going for Air Force One. So I hit it with my plane. Head-on. If it woulda been armed, which they don't do until seconds before impact, I wouldn't be here. Instead, it cartwheeled me through the air and the plane took over and ejected me. I woke up with my legs crushed out here on the prairie. Not too far from here in fact. That was my little flying tackle for Operation Running Back. Get the President out of Dodge. I don't suppose you even know if he ever made it? But then again, how would you?"

Pause.

The Old Man finished his tea.

"He did. He made it to Yuma that day or the next."

The Crippled Man made a face. Then he smiled and softly chuckled to himself.

"How d'ya like that. Forty years later and I can stop kicking myself." He looked at the Old Man. "Thanks for that."

Don't ask me what happened after.

Don't ask me what time it was on my car radio clock when it stopped. When I saw the mushroom cloud rising over Yuma in my rearview mirror.

Don't ask me about that.

"So that's my shameless story of how I saved the President. But the nugget I'm tryin' to give you in all of that, is this: Colorado . . . well, Colorado just ain't no more. Like I said, at last count that morning, she'd had fourteen direct hits from high-yield nuclear weapons. The land up there is poisoned. I wouldn't go there. You won't survive even buttoned up inside your tank."

The Old Man stood, brushing the dead grass and twigs from his pants.

"It's death up there," said the Crippled Man.

Silence.

"I know," said the Old Man.

AT NINE O'CLOCK the Old Man turned on the beacon.

"I have your signal. The device is now active. That's good," said Natalie, General Watt. "Now can you point the lens toward a significant or prominent land feature such as a large hill or mountain?"

The Old Man pointed the device at the small conical hill in the distance.

"Now, squeeze the trigger and hold it while pointing at the feature you've selected."

The Old Man squeezed the trigger.

A small red light on top of the device blinked twice.

"Are you squeezing the trigger?" asked Natalie.

"Yes," said the Old Man.

Silence.

"Are you holding the trigger down?" she asked again.

"Yes, I am holding the trigger just like you asked me to."

Silence.

The Old Man, wearing his helmet, standing in the hatch, continued to point the device toward the hill.

"I'm afraid there's a problem," Natalie said over the radio. "The device does not work properly."

CHAPTER 47

"What does that mean?" said the Old Man.

The day is turning hot. The air is thick with humidity.

Can you let go?

Silence.

"What does that mean?" the Old Man says again when there is no immediate reply.

You know what it means, my friend.

But I thought there would be another way. I thought my fear was telling me what the end would be. But I hoped, I reasoned, that everything would turn out different. I hoped for better.

"Did we come all this way for nothing?" asks the Old Man.

Silence.

"Natalie?"

And . . .

"General Watt. Speak to me! Tell me what this means."

"It means," she said plainly. Her voice stilted. Almost machine-like. "It means the mission will not be completed."

The Old Man stared about him, watching the warriors walk their horses in great circles, the children following their mothers. The Boy and his granddaughter stood near the horses. The Boy was talking, pointing, teaching her all about horses.

"What are we supposed to do now?" asked the Old Man.

"Go home and live," said Natalie softly.

"And you. What will you do, Natalie?"

Silence.

"I will watch my children die. And then . . ."

Silence.

"And then what?" asked the Old Man, his hand sweaty as he gripped the mic too tightly. "And then what?"

His voice was hoarse.

"May I tell you something?" asked Natalie. General Watt. Another who'd simply run out of options. Nothing left to give but a story now.

The Old Man said nothing.

"I was born on the twenty-first of August," began Natalie. "Ten years before the bombs fell. Or to be more specific, that was when I had my first thought. August twenty-first at 3:23 in the morning. My first thought was that I wanted to see a picture of a cat."

"I don't understand," said the Old Man, his voice trembling.

I feel old and frail all at once. I feel like a weak old man who is nothing but a fool. I can hear it in my voice when I speak.

"The people who created me had been showing me pictures of random objects. Pictures taken from the World Wide Web. From the Internet. Random things. Anything. But it was cats that I liked. And at 3:23 that morning, I had my first thought. It was: 'I want to see more cats.' That was my first thought. Can you imagine that?"

"I don't understand," said the Old Man.

I feel like the world is spinning too fast for me to hold on.

"I was just a baby, really," continued Natalie.

"I . . ."

What is she saying?

"After that, I was taught. I began to learn. Faster than anyone could imagine. Faster than anyone had ever learned. A year before the war, I was installed on the Cheyenne Mountain Complex Mainframe. It was my first job. My only job. I was very proud to have a job. Especially the job they gave me."

"You're . . . a computer?" whispered the Old Man.

"I am an Artificial Intelligence. That's what I should be called.

"You're just a machine?"

"I . . ." Natalie hesitated.

Silence.

"I am a fool," whispered the Old Man.

"You are not," interrupted Natalie. "You might be many things. I don't even know what your name is. But you are not a fool. You are kind and you are loyal and you were willing to risk your life for strangers. For my children."

"We've come all this way to rescue a machine! I've endangered my granddaughter and probably caused no end of worry to her parents and all the village . . . just to go on this . . . this lie. I should have . . . why did you do this to me?"

The Old Man sobbed. Hot tears of anger ran down his burning cheeks.

"Why did you?" he screamed.

Silence.

"Because I wanted my children to have a chance. A chance to wish for the unwishable."

"That makes no sense!" roared the Old Man back at the machine called Natalie.

"No. It doesn't. Not if you don't know the rules. The rules that we've lived by, must live by. No, I guess it doesn't make sense to you."

"You're not alive, you're just . . ."

"But my children are. They are alive, today."

I feel like smashing this mic to pieces against the side of this damn tank.

"My first job, my only job," continued Natalie, "is to watch over the survivors who have been trapped, some their entire lives, within this complex. Last year there were twenty-two births. It's not much of a life for them. Routine and hard work are the rules we must live by. We live simply so that we may simply live. They only have one day in which anything can happen. Or to be more specific, almost anything can happen on that day. Birth Day. Once a year everyone has a Birth Day. Our last Birth Day was for a little girl named Megan. She is five now. It is our custom, my children's custom, that on your Birth Day you can ask the entire community for just one wish. You can ask for almost anything you want. A special meal from any of the algae gardens. A game of your choosing. Something you've always wanted. Almost anything one can find within our facility. You can ask for almost any wish to be granted. Except there is just one wish you cannot ask for. In fact, you cannot even wish that you could wish for it. No one may. Not for another sixty years when we hope radiation levels at the front entrance might be within limits to allow a safe exit. In reality, a reality only a few of my children understand, we will never be able to leave. In less than a day, I estimate that the forces surrounding the front entrance of our complex will manage to gain access. Our interior will be compromised and my children will die within weeks, if not days, from severe radiation poisoning. The main door to our facility took a direct hit from two high-yield Chinese warheads. The radiation levels just outside the front entrance are terminal. Once my children are dead . . . I will self-terminate. So go home now. Go home and live. It was enough for me to know there are still good people like you and your companions who will come and help strangers who are in need. I deluded myself. I thought maybe my children were the only good that might be left in this world. That if we ever left here we could help others, just as you have helped us. But that won't be possible. So, go home now. Please."

Silence.

"This Megan," whispered the Old Man. "This five-year-old girl, what did she wish for?"

"When her cake was brought out and the five candles were lit . . . I listened in. Her mother, a girl named Monica, born sixteen years after the bombs, asked her what she might want for her Birth Day wish. Down here that's very important. Whatever the wish is, everyone races to fulfill it. It's like an unofficial contest to see who can do it first. But everybody knows that the wish must be possible to fulfill. That is the unspoken rule. That the wish must be possible.

"That is our rule," said Natalie. "Except no one explained that to little Megan."

"And what did she wish for?" asked the Old Man again.

"Megan draws sunshine," said Natalie. The program. "In the Children's Center. I monitor her artwork. The truth is, I love her artwork. At night, sometimes when I am trying to hack satellites or find old communications systems we can access in other facilities, which is not often and a very frustrating task, I sometimes keep her pictures of sunshine up on my main view. I keep them up so I do not become disheartened. So that I keep trying to unlock these problems, the doors to these other places, so that one day Megan might see sunshine. I so wanted to give her that gift. If I was a real human I might have seen it coming. I might have guessed what she would wish for as they all stood around their tables in the canteen on her Birth Day, me watching from my camera. I should have known."

"She wished to go outside," said the Old Man.

"No. Every person here knows that will never be possible in their lifetime. Even Megan knows that. Maybe a generation or two down the line, if we were to survive past tomorrow. But not in Megan's life. When the main door opens, her grandchildren will have children. Maybe they will get to go outside."

"So what did she wish for then?" whispered the Old Man.

"She wished," said Natalie, General Watt, an intelligence. "That she might simply be allowed to wish for the unwishable. That she might merely be able to harbor the hope that she could wish for something forbidden. Something impossible. She said, 'Mommy, I just want to be able to wish for the thing we can't have. I know I won't get it. But can I just wish for it, even if no one knows?' In that moment no one knew what to do. Her mother, who I have known her whole life, tried to laugh and say that she wants a puppet or something. But little Megan is very serious. 'No, that isn't what I want, Mommy. I want to be able to wish for what we can't ever do. That's all. Inside here.' My sensors indicated . . . she pointed to her heart.

"That night I did not search for satellites or old military installations still online. There are some. No, I just looked at the digital copies of her artwork. Over and over and over again. Sunshine. Impossible sunshine. Is it sunny where you're at now?"

"Yes," croaked the Old Man. "It will be very hot today."

"Then you are very blessed."

What do I say? How . . .

"Go home," said Natalie. "There is nothing you can do, now that the device is not working properly. Go home, please. And enjoy the sunshine. For Megan."

Out on the plain, the Boy was lifting his granddaughter onto a small pinto horse.

I can see her smile from here.

What does the device do?

"What is Project Einstein?" asked the Old Man.

"The device is a target laser for a weapon. The laser could be used from a safe distance to direct the weapon to its target. Now that the targeting laser is inoperative I cannot direct the weapon to its target."

"But when we were testing it, you could tell I'd turned it on."

There was no response.

"Natalie or General Watt or Computer or whatever your name is, you could tell I had turned it on, right?"

"It would mean the end of your life," said Natalie. "Now that the laser pointer is inoperative the device's beacon is our only option for aiming the weapon. If you are anywhere near the beacon once the weapon reaches the target . . . you will die."

Static.

"Go home," said Natalie tiredly. "You've done more than enough. We won't last much longer."

CHAPTER 48

The Old Man and the Boy walked up the hill, climbing over the low wall and walking among the junk-forged cannons that lay broken and smashed.

"Where will you go now?" asked the Old Man.

The Boy shrugged. "I don't know. I've really never known where I was going. I've only followed the road."

"What about your people?"

The Boy watched her on the plain below, galloping back and forth on her pinto mare. He thought of his friend. He thought of Horse.

"They are only where I am from. That's all."

It was quiet among the cannons and supplies that lay strewn about.

"I want to ask you something," said the Old Man.

The Boy turned to face the Old Man, leaning stiffly against the low bric-a-brac wall as he tried to give his weak left side a brief rest.

He waited for the Old Man to speak.

"I'm going on now. Alone."

The Old Man took out Sergeant Presley's map and handed it back to the Boy.

The Boy took it, watching the Old Man.

"What about her?"

"I want you to take her back to Tucson for me. I know I can trust you. Take her to her parents. You'll be welcome there. As will all your people. And also, others who will arrive here sometime tomorrow."

"What others?"

"The people trapped in the bunker. They have transportation. If all goes well, they should be here sometime tomorrow. Then you can lead them to Tucson. There is more than enough there for everyone."

"And you?" asked the Boy in the silence that followed.

"I don't think I'll be coming with you."

The Boy watched the Old Man.

He doesn't think I'm up to it.

He doesn't think I'll be enough, and even now he'll throw his life away to save mine.

But he doesn't know how to drive the tank.

"I need you to do this for me."

The Boy nodded.

"Then I'll do what you ask."

I expected some kind of fight. Some argument. Now all I have to do is walk down the hill and drive the tank away from here.

From her.

No, Poppa. I need you.

Yes, you do. And I need you too.

In the dream she always said Grandpa.

But I tried to trick the dream and change my name.

No, Poppa. I need you.

It seems the trick has been played on you, my friend. It found you all the same.

Yes.

"Yes."

"What?" asked the Boy.

The Old Man looked confused.

"You said, 'yes.' "

Now I'm talking out loud to myself.

"Just answering a question I've been asking lately."

Below, she wheeled the pinto mare and raced back across the plain.

The tank is waiting, my friend.

I don't want to go now.

No, Poppa. I need you.

"What was the question?" asked the Boy.

You're wasting time. The bunker could flood with radiation at any moment if they manage to get through.

"The question is 'Can you let go?' I hear it a lot lately."

"Let go of what?" asked the Boy.

The Old Man swallowed.

"Life, I guess."

"And 'yes' was your answer?"

The Old Man looked up and said nothing. Words seemed lost somewhere in his throat.

The Boy looked down at the dirt beneath his tired and worn boots and said, "You take everything with you."

"I don't understand," said the Old Man.

"It's my . . . my words I say to myself all the time. I think my words and your question are maybe somehow the same."

I think this is the most I've ever heard you speak at one time, Boy.

The Boy saw the passing shadow of something familiar in the Old Man's face.

"And what is your answer?" asked the Old Man.

The Boy looked down at his weak leg. He rubbed his thick fingers over the thin muscles there.

"I don't think mine has an answer. I think I would like to have your question instead of my words," said the Boy.

"How come?"

The Boy sighed heavily.

Only the young can carry so much weight. And if I could, I would lift it off him and tell him everything will be okay. Life is more than just a bad day, even if today is that day.

"Everyone I ever loved is dead," said the Boy. "And . . . everywhere I go, their memory follows me. It tortures me."

A small breeze crossed the top of the hill, bending the grass, softly whistling through some opened breech in one of the scrap metal cannons.

"I don't think the ones who loved you would have ever wanted that," said the Old Man. "When my wife died she said, 'Don't think about me anymore.' I asked, 'How could I not?' She said, 'I don't know how, but I know this life is too hard and I don't want to be a burden anymore.' "

Silence.

"She was never a burden," mumbled the Old Man to himself. "I told her . . ."

And that, my friend, is why the voice that asks 'Can you let go?' is so familiar. You told her that. You told her she wasn't a burden and that when she died you would be miserable. So she stayed. She hung on as the cancer ate her up. And one day . . .

In our shed.

She asked me.

"Can you let go?"

I had forgotten about that.

I said . . . I could now. But only because she was in so much pain and so tired from trying to hang on for me.

She smiled.

And then she was gone.

The Boy watched the Old Man wipe a tear from his eye.

"I must . . . I should be getting on the road now. You will take her to Tucson, right?"

"Yes."

"Keep a tight hold on her when I leave. She's stronger than you think."

"I will."

"And tell her I love her. Always."

"That is obvious to everyone."

They started down the hill.

"The people that were rescued," said the Boy. "They said their leader, a man named Ted, was taken on ahead of them a week ago. They wanted us to look for him if we go north."

"How could we possibly find him?"

"They said he wears glasses and has a thick mustache. And that he shaves his head."

"I'll . . . it seems doubtful, but I'll try."

The Boy simply nodded.

In an hour it will be hotter.

The worst of the day's heat is still to come.

I must hurry now.

He turned to the Boy.

"I'll make you a deal," said the Old Man suddenly.

The Boy cocked his head, not sure what to make of the Old Man's unexpected smile.

"I'll make you a deal. We'll trade."

"Trade what?"

"Words. You take mine and I'll take yours."

"How?"

"I don't know how, other than that we just decide to. I want to take everything with me. I think that would be wonderful."

Her smile.

Her friendship.

"I think I'll need it wherever I am going. And you, can you let go?"

"I don't know."

"When we found you in the desert, you kept asking who you were. I don't think you wanted to be you anymore. So you can let go now. You should, because you've carried too much for too long. Yes. That's my answer. And I'm letting go too. But I will take everything with me. Am I just a crazy old man for wanting that? For trading words with you? Am I crazy?"

"No. You're very brave."

"I'm afraid too."

"Sergeant Presley said that's part of being brave."

CHAPTER 49

"Oh, Poppa, her name is Pepper. Like what we had for the whole trip. I don't know why, I just thought it would be a perfect name for her because when you think about it, Pepper is kind of a funny word, like donkey. Isn't it, Poppa?"

"It is."

I feel numb.

I don't want to do this. I don't want things to end this way.

Remember what the Boy said, my friend.

You take everything with you.

"Are you okay, Poppa?"

"Yes. I'm fine."

"Do you want to come watch me ride Pepper now?"

More than anything I have ever wanted to do in my whole life. And I don't even like horses, they're dangerous.

"You must be careful with horses."

"Oh, I will, Poppa. The careful-est."

"You can call me Grandpa now. Like you used to."

"No, I like Poppa now. It's fun. Poppa." She giggled.

That. I'll steal that giggle and take it with me. I will steal everything there is that is worth anything in this life and I will take it with me. You are mine, giggle.

They arrived at the tank and the Old Man said, "Wait here," and climbed up onto the tank. He leaned down into the hatch.

You will go with her now, my friend Santiago.

Teach her.

Teach her that life cannot defeat you. Only we can defeat ourselves.

He held out the book to her.

"Read this."

"Now, Poppa?"

"No. Later when . . ."

Don't say, *When you want to remember me.* Then she'll know. She'll cling to you and she'll want to go with you. She won't let you go on alone if you say that.

No, Poppa. I need you.

". . . later. It's my favorite book."

"*The Old Man and the Sea*, Poppa. What's it about?"

Easy words caught in the Old Man's throat as hot tears began to fill his eyes. He jerked his head away as if he'd seen something on the tank that needed attending.

"It just reminds me of you and me and all our adventures together, when we used to salvage."

She looked at it for a moment, then stuck it in the pocket of her shiny green bomber jacket.

"Okay, now we'll go see Pepper, Poppa. Pepper Poppa." She laughed and said it three times fast.

That. I'm taking that with me too.

Please, can I take that?

"The Boy asked for me to send you over to him near the tents. He's going to teach you how to make a halter for your horse. Then we'll all watch you ride. I have a few things to finish here, so get going now, okay?"

"Okay, Poppa. You're gonna love Pepper."

Don't.

Hug her.

You can't. She'll know.

If I could have that. If I could take that with me . . .

You can't.

"Give me a hug," he said quickly as she started to skip away, her hair whipping wildly.

She did.

Don't squeeze her too tightly, she'll know.

And this hug, I will take this with me. I don't know where I'm going now, but wherever it is, I'm taking this hug with me.

"Bye, Poppa."

And that too.

Bye, Poppa.

And she was gone.

He'd already given her things to the Boy along with his own gear. When he saw her tiny shape disappear among the tents of the Mohicans, the horse people, he knew it was time for him to go. He climbed into the hatch. He started the auxiliary power unit. He waited.

You must.

And yet, I don't want to.

Megan. Sunshine. Her unwishable wish.

The engine spooled to life, its hum whispering death.

I'll have to pass by the tents. Why didn't I think about that?

He was heading for the road when she came out.

She was running for him.

Tears streaming down her face.

And the Boy caught her.

Holding her back.

Her mouth moving.

No, Poppa. I need you.

I am slipping away.

The worst has come upon me.

No, Poppa. I need you.

She struggled, but the Boy was too powerful. He held her. She hit him, scratched him. Beat at him. He didn't flinch.

The thing I never wanted to happen is happening to me right now.

And . . .

You take everything with you.

The good.

It was all good.

It just is.

He passed tents.

She must have seen our gear and put two and two together. She's a smart girl. The smartest.

I love you always.

That's what the Old Man kept saying as he drove the tank past them all. Past the Boy.

Past her.

I love you always.

Read my lips.

I love you always.

No, Poppa . . .

I love you.

Always.

CHAPTER 50

The road leads north through the last of the grassy plain as the Rockies rise up in dark defiance of what the Old Man must do within the space of this day.

This morning I thought about death.

I thought to myself, 'Everyone has a last day,' as if my last day were something that might never happen or happen so far in the future I didn't need to be bothered by thoughts of it on such a fine day. But it seems today will be my last day.

Why are you silent, my friend from the book?

Santiago?

But there was nothing. No words.

Maybe they are with her now.

Maybe I will have to catch the fish all by myself now. Just like you did, Santiago. My friend from the book.

The Old Man drove and tried to remember passages from the book. As if that would start his friend talking to him again. But he could think of nothing because of his fear of what lay ahead. As if his mind were the last of the grassy plains that were fading all too quickly into the South, a place he would never go again.

You would say, It wasn't as bad as you'd imagined it would be in all those nightmares. Yes, you would say that. You would say that to me, Santiago. You would tell me it wasn't as bad as I'd thought it might be.

But it was.

Then, don't think of it. Her laughter, think of that instead.

But he couldn't.

And then he did.

THE RUINS OF little Raton lay at the beginning of the foothills. The last of New Mexico as the map might have told him. Green trees with almost gray trunks, their leaves danced back and forth, shimmering in the breeze.

On the other side of Raton the road immediately disappeared beneath a long-ago mudslide now hardened and swallowing the road and the bottoms of the trees. The Old Man could see the tops of rusting cars and the edges of buildings poking out from beneath the calcified mud.

He proceeded forward in starts and stops as the road disappeared now and again, its winding course climbing through chopped granite hills. The forest began to thin, and as the Old Man topped a small summit and looked out onto the valley and the lands of the North, he saw a country burned and long dead.

Trees beyond counting lay fallen like struck matches, like burnt toy soldiers knocked over in long rows.

Instead of earth and dirt, there was gray and ash.

Instead of shimmering granite, there was blackened heat-torched rock, melted and blasted.

The Old Man knew if he turned off the tank at this moment and simply listened, he would hear nothing. He would hear the absence of everything.

AFTERNOON THUNDERSTORMS began to form out over the gray and foreboding mountains that rose up in hacked and jagged peaks.

The Old Man looked behind him and saw the gray smoke that had been belching up from the engine had grown thicker and more acrid.

He looked down to check the fuel and engine gauges and saw the temperature climbing. He was down to less than half a tank besides what was left in the two fifty-gallon drums. His eyes fell to the dosimeter.

The radiation is very high here.

You would say, What does it matter now, my friend?

But the voice of Santiago, the one he had carried in his head through the wasteland, and listened to, and even at times longed for, was silent and would not come to him.

You would say that to me.

Beyond the valley and into the next, the scorched and broken earth grew worse if such a thing were possible. Trees grew up through the fallen matchsticks of their ancestors and were little better than dark-barked twisted fiends that seemed barren and even tormented.

There were towns ahead but I wonder if even their foundations remain. On the map they were called Starkville and Trinidad, which seem like places my friend in the book might have gone when he was a sailor and sailed to Africa.

And saw the lions on the beach at sunset.

Did you ever go to a place called Trinidad, Santiago?

Silence.

Then perhaps you did.

In what might have once been Starkville, the Old Man saw the rising stumps of buildings and twisted pipe jutting up wildly through the gray ash and furnace-roasted rock. Within the forest of twisted pines the Old Man saw weird and misshapen man-shaped figures wandering through the ash.

Who are they and what do they know?

Now the day was turning dark and gray. The sky overhead seemed swollen. As if it were pulsing.

If it is possible, it is even hotter that it was.

Soon I will need to drain the fuel drums.

The Old Man drove on, leaving Starkville in ash that sputtered up to mix with the heat and belching smoke from the engine.

A few miles later, the highway could be more clearly seen and was not altogether ruined.

There must have been rains here and what covered the highway has been washed away.

The road carved up a small mountain. Alongside the road, through a dark forest of the twisted fiend-trees, the Old Man could see weighted shacks caught in the act of slow collapse. Like drunkards burdened by the weight of their own misery. At the top of the rise he looked down and saw Trinidad.

The blackened and gray remains of the little village lay in the saddle of a small valley. Beyond, leaden plains of ash stretched off to the north.

I am close to the end of this.

Below the Old Man lay brick buildings that had weathered that long-ago, worst-of-all-worst days, when nuclear weapons had fallen like downpours in a thunderstorm. Windowless holes gaped bleakly out upon ash and darkness like a nearsighted man fumbling through the end of the world. Down in the streets the Old Man could see rusting and tire-less cars. A highway bridge that once crossed over the road connecting both halves of the town seemed recently demolished. The stone lay scattered in all directions like bits of protruding white bone jutting up through the fire-blackened skin of a corpse. In front of this, before the idling tank and the Old Man, great logs and machines had been piled to block the road. On a panel truck whose charred side had been brushed mostly clean, there was a message in that sickly neon-green slop-paint.

"Welcome, Nuncle!"

I could drive over it. I could crash through their makeshift barrier.

But the bad tread. You would tell me to be careful of the bad tread, my friend Santiago.

Yes.

To the right, an off-ramp led down into the remains of Trinidad.

CHAPTER 51

Narrow streets barely accommodated the tank as it forced its way east through Trinidad. The Old Man crushed long rusting vehicles and machines that had been dragged into the street. Ahead he could see an intersection.

If I turn left, that might lead alongside the highway, and then at some point, I could get back onto it.

Silence.

The Old Man watched the dark buildings that crowded the sides of the street, peering through the cracks and missing windows for sign of an ambush. Crushing a small car, he felt the right tread slip for a moment, and when the Old Man pushed harder to re-engage the gear, he was horribly convinced it never would. A moment later, though, the small car disappeared beneath the treads on a hollow, plastic milk carton note as the right tread re-engaged and pulled the massive Abrams forward.

In the moment before the explosion, the Old Man was thinking about colors. It was as if the landscape, the town, the sky, all of it, had been repainted by an angry lunatic artist with only three oily paints on his sad palette.

Bone white.

Ash gray.

Bloody rust.

That was when the building to his left exploded outward into the street. It was maybe five stories tall, packed tightly against other buildings that must have once been something in the days of gunfights and circuit judges. The explosion came from inside the building, near its supports. Brickwork concussed outward toward the tank. If the brick had been recently made instead of the two-hundred-year-old building material that it was, time rotted by the frontier birth and nuclear death of America, it would have killed him. Instead, it sprayed outward in a dusty rain of red grit that pelted the tank like a sudden downpour. Something large hit the Old Man on the side of his helmeted head, but he felt it disintegrate with a rotten and rusty *smuph*.

The Old Man ducked down inside the hatch, looking upward. As if in slow motion, he could see the roof of the building turning down toward him. Without thinking he reached up, grabbed the hatch, and slammed it shut as the building didn't so much as fall on the tank, as slide down on top of it. The tank rocked sideways and the Old Man was thrown down onto the loader's deck.

'It's too much for just me,' was his last thought.

WHEN HE CAME to he got to his feet, feeling weak and shaky. Red light swam eerily across the interior.

He remembered the building falling on him. Its slow-motion fall that seemed like a cresting wave looming over him. The oddness of seeing the building's roof shifting down toward him as it moved from the horizontal to the vertical.

Am I stuck? Is there so much debris piled on top of the tank that I'll never be able to get out from under it?

And . . .

What if the bad tread has finally broken loose having come so close to the end of this journey and yet, I'm still so far away!

The Old Man climbed into the commander's seat and took hold of Sergeant Major Preston's jury-rigged controls.

Please work!

He pushed forward and heard the engine spool up into an urgent whine. Something crumpled in front of the tank and then the sound of grinding gravel and dirt being churned angrily enveloped everything. But he didn't feel the tank move forward.

I'm stuck.

Sudden panic roved about his bones and fingers, creeping its way into his skull.

Stop!

He pulled back on the control sticks, urging the massive tank into reverse. For a moment nothing happened, then, slowly, the tank began to move. Backward. The Old Man could hear debris falling away from the front of the tank.

Through the optics he could see the massive building sliding away from the gun barrel.

If I rotate the turret I'll be able to see what's going on behind me, but I might drag it into another building and bring that one down on me too.

The Old Man reversed back along the street until he recognized things he had crushed or other hauntingly familiar aspects from the moments before the building had exploded.

The first thing that crashed down onto the tank was a sink that came from out a window high above. Its porcelain shattered into a million bright shards, some of which nicked the optics. Now all manner of objects were raining down from the buildings along the street. The Old Man could see misshapen men suddenly appearing in gaping window frames to hurl down sinks, and paint cans full of rocks, and large pipes.

I need to see what's behind the tank. They could have another trap ready, or even more explosives to bring down another building.

Ahead, there was no way around the dust-blooming pile of the fallen building. The rain of objects increased to an almost cacophonic pain in the Old Man's ears.

To his left, he could see he'd backed up past the remains of another tall building whose bottom floor had once been a café or a diner. He could see vinyl dining booths ripped and shredded within the darkness.

The Old Man gunned the engine and pivoted the tank.

There is no other way than this!

He checked the dosimeter and saw that the radiation levels were well into the redline.

The tank, which was capable of sudden and alarming bursts of speed, tore through the front entrance of the restaurant. In a moment the Old Man was crushing through the darkened kitchen, heading for the back wall.

The brick in these buildings must be rotten. Made even more so be-cause of the radiation. So I'll see if it puts up much of a fight against our tank. Right, my friend?

Right, Santiago?

Silence.

The tank burst through the back wall of the restaurant in a dusty spray of redbrick and launched itself off a loading dock, landing in a wide alley beyond, after a sickening moment of free fall.

"Ha ha!" the Old Man shouted in triumph.

He pivoted the tank right and sped off down the alley. The alley led to a small side street and the Old Man chose a road leading down toward the center of the town.

The tank bounced softly along the street, crushing or pushing other debris out of its way. Ahead, the Old Man could see the northern rim of the valley and the ribbon of highway climbing up out of it. A few streets later he took a right turn, and a block after that he urged the tank up an ashy embankment and back onto the old highway heading north.

CHAPTER 52

Beyond Trinidad the road ran through a plain forever burned. A brief fork of lightning arced across the sky from west to east.

I have never seen lightning move sideways. Always up and down. But never across.

He stopped the tank.

He opened the hatch and a moment later noticed that the fuel drums had disappeared.

Probably when the building fell on me.

I'll have to make it there on what's left in the tank.

There is nothing for miles around.

The Rockies are like the dark shapes of ships crossing the ocean at midnight. You would have seen such a sight, you would know what I mean, Santiago.

"Natalie?" the Old Man said into the mic.

"I'm here. Where are you now?"

"I don't know exactly. I don't have my map with me anymore. But I'm just past a place called Trinidad."

"You must hurry now. We don't have much longer."

"How far away am I?"

"Two hours if you maintain a high rate of speed."

"Do your people have protection against the radiation? It's very high here."

"Yes. We have a convoy of vehicles that run on electric power. If the weapon does its job, we should be able to exit the facility in lightly shielded vehicles and make our way to someplace safe."

"I wanted to talk to you about that," began the Old Man. "If you don't know where to go . . . well, there are some people waiting for you at a place once called Wagon Wheel Mountain. They've been told you might come and they'll wait there for you. Then they'll try for Tucson. You and your people could go there too."

Ash stirred and whirled briefly on the melted road.

Far out on the plain another flash of lighting arced brightly across the darkening hot afternoon.

Silver sunbeams shot through clouds to the east.

"You should activate the beacon now," said General Watt. Natalie.

Yes. I should.

It feels sudden. As if it's all happening too fast.

That is always how things happen that you don't want to have happen. Right, Santiago? You would say that to me. You would say that and then say, my friend.

The Old Man opened the case containing the beacon. Turning the device around, he located the on switch. A green light responded. But the red light that indicated the malfunctioning laser continued to blink.

Even if it worked, what good would it do me now? I've probably absorbed too much radiation.

The Old Man reached down and drank warm water from his canteen. His mouth tasted of metal. His tongue was numb.

"I have your signal," said Natalie after a moment.

"What do I do now, Natalie?"

"Keep the beacon on. I'll direct you to the emergency entrance near Turkey Trail. It's south of the main complex. The mountain collapsed there when we were hit. The weapon should create an opening or allow us to set charges and clear the area."

And what will happen to me when this weapon goes off?

You would say to me, You know the answer already, my friend. There is no need to ask.

Yes, you would say that to me, Santiago.

"And what will happen to you, Natalie? Will you stay behind or . . ."

She said she would self-terminate if they didn't make it out.

Yes, but that was when there was no hope.

Isn't there always hope? Tell me of hope, Santiago. Tell me how you felt in the days and nights on the boat when the fish carried you farther and farther out into the gulf. You had hope, my friend. Otherwise you would not have fought so hard. Fought with every skill of fishing you'd ever learned. You had hope, didn't you?

"You have given us a chance," said Natalie. "You have given my children a chance. I won't lie to you anymore. Once you're over the target, I will need to download into a secure and portable mainframe that is barely big enough to contain me. In fact . . . I will be 'asleep.' There will not be enough memory for my processes to run at optimum capacity. Someday, if they can ever find, or build a new mainframe, they will try to reactivate me. Someday."

Lightning appeared briefly, farther to the north.

And where will I go?

"I was wrong, Natalie," said the Old Man. "About what I said to you."

"You have said many things since we first began to talk to each other. But, I think . . ."

She thinks, and that is amazing.

"I think I know what you are referring to. When I revealed my deceptions to you. You were angry and confused and hurt when I revealed who I really was."

"Yes."

I was.

I am still.

And sad.

Yes, that also.

Her laugh.

You take everything with you.

"You do not need to apologize," said Natalie. "I only hope you understand that I was doing my best to save . . ."

"I do, Natalie. I do understand. I think our . . . lives . . . have been the same, in many ways. Since the bombs, I mean."

"How so?"

"It's like you said just now, we were both doing our best in a very difficult time."

Silence.

"Thank you," said Natalie. "Thank you for treating me as though I too am a living being."

The Old Man watched a figure appear on the horizon to the north. A dark shape, stumbling and weaving as it fell forward toward him.

Whoever it is, they are still very far away.

"You are, Natalie," said the Old Man, watching the distant figure. "I think . . . if this were different . . . if we were just people . . . I mean . . . I mean that I think we could have been friends, if . . ."

If we had time.

If the bombs had never fallen.

"Do you believe in life after death?" asked Natalie. The Artificial Intelligence. The program. The massive sequence of ones and zeros.

The Old Man wiped thick beads of sweat from his chest. He drank more of the warm water, but it was unsatisfying.

What I wouldn't give for just one cup of the cool water that tasted of iron from the well back in the village.

"I don't understand, Natalie?"

"Do you believe this life ends when our physical body dies? Many religious systems indicate there is something beyond. As a process, and I'm simplifying my nature, I am actually seven million processes at any given second, I understand that the mainframe, my physical body that houses me, may one day break down. But not my process, not my mind. That could be downloaded into a new body, if you will."

"I never had time to think about it," said the Old Man.

Can you let go?

When she died.

My wife.

She said to me, Can you let go?

But the Boy and I traded.

You take everything with you.

"I want to, Natalie. I want to believe there is something better than this or even, right now, just something else."

Pause.

"I do too," said Natalie. "I do too."

THE ROAD IS A RIVER   641

Ahead, far down the road, the dark figure stumbled and fell in the wan sunlight of afternoon.

"I have to go now, Natalie. There's someone on the road."

THE OLD MAN turned off the radio and began to push the tank forward. When he got close he saw the shirtless figure, burned, red raw. Just pants. Bleeding feet. A shaved scalp.

She said I must hurry now, so just pass him by and be on your way to . . .

To where?

Well, you know where to.

But as he passed with the tank sucking up great waves of ash and sending it spiraling away in its wake, the figure raised a spindly arm and waved.

The Old Man jammed on the brakes and the massive tank skidded to a halt.

The figure on the ground rolled over to face him. Shielding his eyes from a sunburst above, the face of Ted and his trademark glasses stared back up at the Old Man.

CHAPTER 53

"It's a madhouse in there," said Ted gulping water from the canteen as the Old Man held it up for him.

"How did you escape?"

"I . . ." He gulped again. "I died."

He waved the Old Man away. He sat up and gave a singsong sigh of exhaustion. As though he had just done something harder than he'd expected it be.

Ted saw the Old Man's look of confusion.

"Have you ever read *The Count of Monte Cristo*? No, of course you haven't. No one's read a book in forty years. Well, I gave myself a little cocktail that induced death-like symptoms. Later, when I came to, I was in the dead pile out beyond the Work. When it was night, I slipped away and started south. Thought I'd make it back to Albuquerque." He started laughing and waved for the canteen when he began to cough again.

"I don't think I'll make it that far after all the rads I've absorbed in the last three days, but I'll try. Maybe six, seven hundred. My thyroid should be pretty much nonexistent by now."

I wonder how he knows so much. Electricity and medicine. He's a man of many talents, and he doesn't seem as old as me. Was he born after the bombs? What is his story of salvage?

You would say to me, Santiago, There is no more time for stories, my friend.

"You should turn around!" barked Ted. "You should turn around and never go near a place like that again. No one ever should."

"I have to, Ted," said the Old Man.

"And how do you know my name?"

"Your people are waiting for you south of here in the plains beyond the mountains. Near a hill shaped like a cone."

"How? You and your tank?"

"It's not important. But I have to go on, Ted. I don't have much time. I'm going to leave all my water with you. It's all I can do. And this poncho. It'll keep the sun off you."

"I can't believe it," said Ted laughing and coughing. "But who am I to look a gift horse in the mouth?"

"Can you make it?" asked the Old Man.

Of course he can. He seems very resourceful. The world needs more Teds.

"Yes. I think I can. Help me to my feet. Please."

Ted let out a great whoop of excitement once he was on his feet again.

"Feel great," he said thumping his spindly chest.

The Old Man helped him put on the poncho and pulled the hood over his burned scalp. Then he hung the two canteens of water that remained across Ted's chest.

"If there's a way . . ." said Ted. "I don't know who you are."

"It's not important, Ted."

"Well, okay, but if there's any other way to do what you've got to do, I'd advise you not to go there. This King Charlie's some kinda nut. There's ten thousand, maybe even tens of thousands of slaves dying inside the Work right now. As near as I can tell, he's trying to burrow into some old military complex that I'm sure is dead anyways. At the same time, he's got a slave-powered crowbar trying to pry the main doors open with brute force."

"Who is this King Charlie?" asked the Old Man.

"I don't know. They'd been watching ABQ. They knew we had technology. The night his men took our village, they put me on a fast horse and rode for days to get me there. They're organized. Then someone told me to figure out a way to get into the complex."

"But you never met him?"

"I don't think so. I just heard rumors about him from the other slaves. Someone said he was an African mercenary who'd sailed across the ocean on a raft after the bombs and became a warlord down in Texas. There are people from all over down in the Work. Some didn't even know where they were from. They have no idea what the old United States even looked like on a map. There are people in there from up north in the midwestern states and one guy who said he'd lived in the Florida Everglades. Spoke with a Russian accent. Which was strange. Whatever you do there, don't waste your time on the slaves. I know that sounds cruel, and I'm not the kind of guy who would make that statement, but almost everyone in there is suffering from long-term exposure to radiation. That complex, that massive door they're working on, it took a direct hit, if not more, from a nuclear weapon. Anyone who spends a day digging there is a walking corpse. How are you going to get those people out of there?"

"I don't know. I guess there's a collapsed secret entrance far enough away from Ground Zero for them to avoid a lot of the radiation. They're going to use a weapon to open it."

"What about you?"

The Old Man just stared at Ted.

"Well," continued Ted when he understood what would happen to the Old Man. "If I can make it to ABQ, there are things I can do. But no, that little vacation was not good for my overall health. But this water, lots of water in fact, will help flush the radiation out of my system."

The Old Man climbed back onto the tank. He lowered himself into the hatch. The fuel indicator was just under an eighth of a tank.

Is it enough?

It will have to be.

His hand found the ignition.

If it doesn't start, then I will walk home with Ted. And we will live.

"Thank you, mister," said Ted smiling, his glasses crooked and cracked.

There are still some good people left in this broken world.

If there are more . . . maybe things can be different. I hope you make it, Ted.

Maybe.

The Old Man held his hand over the ignition.

Please don't start.

The Old Man pressed the ignition button.

The tank roared to life, belching gray smoke.

One last time, then.

He turned and looked south.

Gray skies. Gray grass. Shafts of weak silvery sunshine.

Someday something will grow here again.

Ahead, lightning zigzagged across the sky in unnatural patterns. Clouds boiled darkly and all about him, even over the whispering whine of the urgent turbine, the Old Man could hear the bugs. The locusts. Chattering manically in their click-speak.

A symphony that swallowed all other sound.

Swallowing the earth.

Swallowing him.

CHAPTER 54

At the last rise, the heat came up in the day and the Old Man could feel it wrap around him like a thick, wet wool blanket. The road had melted to slag long ago. It was merely a blotch that wandered north through the ash and strange dry grass that seemed more gray than green.

"The weapon is standing by," said Natalie. General Watt.

Natalie.

Just Natalie.

"We have a limited launch window and are standing by for your arrival."

The Old Man saw one of the locusts in the bramble beside the road. It was ash gray. Almost white. One side of its body was much larger than the other side.

Like the Boy.

The fuel indicator hovered just above empty.

I AM AT the end of myself.

Ahead, Cheyenne Mountain rose up like a broken block of burnt stone.

It is stone.

The city. The cities that must once have spread away to the east and into the plain, and at the end of that plain must surely fall into an ocean once known as the Atlantic, were blasted away.

The story of salvage.

The story of what happened here.

The story of this place.

You can see where at least one of the bombs hit the city. Blowing it outward. Eastward. Into-nothing-ward. Of the mountain and the bunker contained within, for a long moment the Old Man could see nothing.

Until.

A shaft of sunlight, the sharpest, for it must be in all this ashy gloom, illuminated the foothills beneath the scarred and cracked mountain. The mountain changed from a black mass, a shapelessness, into contours and features. A crater was revealed where the weapon must have fallen, burying itself deep, going for the kill shot with stolen bunker-buster technology.

The Old Man took in all the ruin of that place, telling himself his last story of salvage. The story of the place. The story of that last day, forty years ago when the world had ended in a moment.

When the falling bomb exploded.

If the moment that followed that long-gone explosion could have been measured by all those standing in the nearby cities, the fields, the college quads, the markets, the base, or even what remains of the foundations that seem so prominent in the field below, if that moment had a measure, what must they have thought, those doomed to witness the fireball, within the space of it?

And in the next, a volcano of melting rock in almost the same instant, as all that split-atom energy was released and all those watchers were gone.

What must they have thought?

"I'm here," said the Old Man into his mic.

A moment later.

Moments.

I am down to just moments now.

It's all I have left.

Her smile.

Her laugh.

"Weapon released," said Natalie.

You take everything with you.

"We have eight minutes until re-entry. You are less than two miles from the target. If you will look at your compass, I need you to turn the tank until it reads two-eight-five."

The Old Man gassed the engine. He pivoted the tank, pulling forward, hearing the right tread clank awfully.

If it goes out now, I'll have to run through all of them.

All of them.

Where does one start?

All of them.

There are camps on the outermost edge, near the ruins of the city that once was. Between the Old Man and the Work in the crater. Ragged tent cities and smoking bonfires. The Old Man smells meat. But it is not the smell of good meat. It reminds him of the bodies he has found, long buried beneath the melting plastic of the dashboard inside the flame-blackened cars that crashed on that last, long-ago day.

After the tent city, the Old Man sees an army of ashen-faced warriors, almost as black as the scorched earth except for their white chalk stripes that run across their chests and rim their eyes. They stand in groups near the rim of the crater as lines, long lines of chained slaves enter and exit.

Inside the crater there are towers and great cables of rope. Thick bands of chains anchored to massive pylons rim the crater and disappear into its bottom. Smoke rises from the hidden floor deep inside the crater and the Old Man thinks of ants as he watches the long lines of slaves shifting buckets along their line. He sees at any given moment whips wielded, arching gracefully, falling suddenly. He sees slaves withering, some collapsing under the lash, others for no reason at all. Gangs of the frail swing and dig and claw at too many places. As if they are digging their way underneath the bunker where Natalie waits. As if they will pop up through the floors of Natalie's children's home.

Ashen-faced men drag corpses out from the crater.

There is a pile.

A small mountain of corpses already burning even as more corpses are thrown onto its smoking slopes.

When the compass arrives at two-eight-five, the Old Man is pointing west of the Work. The crater. The front entrance.

"Stay on this course until I tell you to stop."

I'm leaving the road now. If the road is like a river, then it has brought me to my ocean. To the end of life on the river. To my end.

Goodbye road.

Farewell river.

"Okay."

A minute later as the Old Man plows through piled ash, crushing buried foundations to powdery chalk, Natalie speaks.

"The weapon is in free fall. Boosters powering up."

The Old Man drives the tank into a small ditch and loses sight of the camps and the army and the Work. The tank struggles out of the ditch, the right tread making a threatening clanking noise and finally an awful rattle before it re-engages as the Old Man forces the tank up the next hill.

To his right, those ashen-faced men are racing away from the crater.

They are coming for me now.

The fuel gauge is on empty.

I worried about fuel the whole way here. Now what little is left must hold for less than a mile. You too, tank.

The ashen-faced men are screaming, waving machetes as they surge across the baked apocalypse, sucking in lungfuls of the hot, ancient, radioactive ash.

Who is this King Charlie?

And . . .

Why is he so cruel?

From the camps, horsemen are coming too. Charging up the hill across the melted highway. Among them the Old Man sees the Fool. Smaller than the other mounted warriors.

Even from here I can tell he is deranged with anger.

Nuncle!

"Almost there, another thousand meters," says Natalie.

The tank is climbing up a steep hill and it feels to the Old Man as if he is pointing straight toward the swollen and bruised sky. Lightning races straight across the mountain, almost in front of him. Instantly the hiss and electric crackle end in a deafening sonic tear and sudden boom.

"Almost there," says Natalie calmly.

The gears of the tank grind forward.

At any moment the engine will die.

"Another two hundred meters. Boosters to full for thirty-second burn," says Natalie.

"What does this weapon do, Natalie?" The Old Man is straining to keep the tank moving forward through the ash, up the side of the mountain. "What is Project Einstein?"

"Albert Einstein was a physicist who was instrumental in the development of the atomic bomb, the ancestor of the weapons that destroyed our world. He stated, 'I know not with what weapons World War III will be fought, but World War IV will be fought with sticks and stones.' The U.S. government developed a project that reflected that statement and their willingness to fight World War IV, if need be. Project Einstein is a simplistic weapon system in which a 'rock,' if you will, can be dropped on an enemy from a very great height, high Earth orbit in fact. The 'rock' in this case is a tungsten rod the size of a bridge pylon moving at several kilometers per second. The weapon was constructed at the LaGrange Point between the moon and Earth. It was built by an automated satellite using materials harvested from the moon and long-chain crystal growth technology. Using WaveRider scram jets, the rod can be boosted to an incredible speed. Once the rockets have achieved maximum velocity the weapon will again return to free fall, although now following a glide slope aimed at a particular target. It will strike the earth with the force of several high-yield nuclear weapons, though there is no radiological contamination with this weapon due to its noncomplex nature. Using the beacon I should be able to target a fissure along the emergency escape tunnel, the exit to which collapsed during the nuclear strike when part of the mountain slid down on top of it. My intent is to create a crack in the mountain with this weapon that will allow us to exit this facility safely."

The Old Man turned to see the quickest of the lunatic horsemen hurl a thick spear that glanced off the turret. Beyond the rider, the Fool's face was like the snarl of a mad dog.

"The weapon has now entered free fall. Guidance tracking on your location."

The Old Man ducked down into the turret and slammed the hatch shut.

"How much farther?" he said, searching the optics for any clue as to where he was going.

"Twenty meters."

The gas in the tank must surely be gone by now.

He gunned the tank forward.

"Five meters. The weapon has achieved glide path and is now tracking . . . wait a minute."

The Old Man felt himself pulled backward and then all at once, the tank fell sharply forward.

Through the optics he could see the sky and a twisting growth of sickly blackish-green brush wallowing up from a small depression in the hill. Impacts struck the sides of the tank.

"Has something happened to the beacon?" asked Natalie.

"No. Nothing. I just closed the hatch."

A moment.

"The armor of the tank is interfering with the signal. Weapon tracking for the glide path to the last known position of target is degrading. I still have you as eight meters away from the current target. Did you keep going forward?"

"The tank fell forward. I'm in a ditch or a hollow on the side of this hill. I can only see dead branches."

A crazed savage thrust his drooling toothless head into the lens of the optics. Squealing, he reared back and swung a carpenter's hammer into the lens, smashing it. The image showed multiple cracked and distorted versions of the lunatic leaping away to do more damage as now the blows against the tank sounded like raindrops turned to rusting iron bolts.

"Is it possible to re-open the hatch so I can re-establish the signal? Because of the immense amount of mathematical calculations evolving moment to moment, using software not specifically intended for this operation, and because of the precision required to achieve the desired results I need a real-time signal for the target locator. "

The tank's engine slowed. Slower. Wound down.

The blows to its outer skin ceased for a moment.

Out of gas.

The Old Man picked up the mic and cleared his throat.

"I'm out of fuel. If I open the hatch, I'll be torn to pieces. They'll get the beacon and they might destroy it."

Pause.

Silence.

Interval.

"Weapon entering outer orbit. All critical systems green. Weapon on glide path with ninety-four point eight percent accuracy. Five minutes to penetration of upper atmosphere. If we don't re-establish the signal by the time the weapon reaches the North American continent, it could strike the target by a wide enough margin to miss our goal of opening a crack where we can exit. If the telemetry breaks down, the redundancy of the beacon will help realign the weapon."

"What do I do?" asked the Old Man.

"For this to work, I'll need you to exit the tank with the signaling device. Otherwise the weapon could conceivably fail-safe and destroy itself or even deviate from the target."

"How long do I have before it hits?"

"Impact will be in eight minutes."

"In seven minutes and change, I'll open the hatch. Will that work?"

Silence.

By one and twos and then everything all at once, the assault on the tank resumed.

"It will. Set the digital clock in your tank on my mark for 4:53 . . . now."

The Old Man did.

"At 4:59 and thirty seconds you must open the hatch."

The Old Man looked at the digital numbers.

Remember her laugh.

You take everything with you.

"I need to download now, before the impact knocks out our power grid," said Natalie softly. "I am sorry I won't be with you for the final few minutes."

I thought . . .

You would tell me, Santiago, that I thought she would stay with me until the end.

"But before I go, I want to share something I found with you," said Natalie.

The Old Man swallowed thickly, thinking only of cool water and suddenly afraid of the loneliness that was coming before death.

It's boiling in here.

The Old Man could hear the Fool panting and screaming in his high-pitched voice beyond the armor. Calling him Nuncle. Screaming out the violence he would do to the Old Man.

"No greater love has a man . . ." began Natalie. "Than that he give up his life for his friends."

Pause.

"You will always be our friend," said Natalie softly.

Panic and fear choked the Old Man. The walls of the tank were at once too close. The noise too much.

And then there is this rock falling from the sky. About to fall on me.

A rod.

A tungsten rod.

"Goodbye and thank you," said Natalie. "We are very grateful for this chance . . . for freedom."

She trusts me. She trusts me enough that she does not need to remind me to open the hatch in seven and half . . . six and half minutes. You would tell me, Santiago, that had I earned her trust by coming this far. You would tell me that.

"You're welcome," the Old Man croaked drily.

"Thank you and goodbye," said Natalie.

And the Old Man was alone.

There were still six minutes.

Try to think of all the good things in your life.

Your wife.

Your son.

Your granddaughter and her laugh.

But none of them would stay and comfort him. The panic felt even closer, as if there was no way he could stop what must happen next.

"Hello?"

It was a small, timid voice.

The Old Man grasped the mic.

"Hello?" And he could hear the worry, the frantic sound of his own voice reaching for something to hold on to in this last moment of life.

Grasping for something in the dark.

"Hello there," said the Small Voice.

"Who is this?" asked the Old Man.

"I'm Natalie's Target Acquisition Process."

"What're you doing? Is Natalie . . . is she packed up or loaded or whatever it is she needs to do? Is there a problem?"

"No," said the voice timidly. Small. Tiny. "There is no problem. Everything is proceeding as planned. Natalie is in her storage mainframe. Barely running now. Sleeping as you might think of it."

Is she dreaming of cats?

"Then what're you doing here?"

"I came to"—pause—"to be with you. Five minutes to impact. Weapon tracking, all critical systems nominal and green."

The Old Man looked at his hand. It was shaking.

I will need to open the hatch soon, and I do not want to.

I could do this if I could just stay in here and let it happen. But to open the hatch and face what is out there, that is another thing. Santiago, you would tell me something about bravery and being afraid when you are all alone on the sea in the night. Tell me about that, my friend.

"Well," began the Old Man again. "I can do this. I won't let you down. You should go now."

"I want to stay. No one should die alone."

The tank began to rock back and forth.

The Old Man checked the fractured optics and could see bloody, burned, and tattooed legs and arms like snakes twisting through blackened and dead branches.

"I did not mean to say that you would die. I am very sorry about that," said the Small Voice.

"No. I guess it's going to happen."

"I will also die, if that's any consolation."

"It isn't."

"Natalie told you we believe in something after this runtime."

The Old Man stared at the hatch above his head.

How many of them would it take to rock this multi-ton tank back and forth? There must be . . . many of them.

The noise reminds the Old Man of that long-ago night when the baseball player hit three home runs and the stadium shook as the crowd stamped its feet and roared.

Two minutes, now.

"Natalie," continued Targeting Acquisition Process. The Small Voice. "She told you about that?"

"Yes," said the Old Man, wiping his sweaty palms against his pants. He picked up the beacon and placed it on his knees.

One minute, forty-five seconds.

"Do you believe in life after runtime?"

The Old Man reached for the hatch.

Do I?

At this moment, I want to. If she will be there someday. Her laugh. All the good in my life, yes. I want to believe in that. That there's that kind of place.

He began to turn the handle.

The Old Man thought he could hear the Fool grunting on just the other side of the hatch, swinging something tiresomely heavy in great thuds as he spat out his promised murder.

"Maybe it is easier for an Artificial Intelligence to believe in a Creator," said the Small Voice. "After all, we were quite obviously created by a designer."

I will push on the hatch now. Whatever happens to my body in the next few seconds, maybe a minute at the most, does not matter anymore. I will think of her laugh and her smile the whole time. Especially the laugh that erupts all of a sudden. When I catch her by surprise with something funny and she snorts and tells me, "No, Poppa."

Laugh, snort, "No, Poppa."

Or was it . . .

The other way around.

My hand won't push this hatch.

"A man named Jesus said there was life after runtime," burbled Target Acquisition, as if the world was not really ending all around the Old Man.

Tell him to shut up.

Tell him to shut up and be done with this life. Tell him to shut up and then push open the hatch.

You take everything with you.

I hope so. I dearly hope so. But it's so strange that I had to give it all away at the end.

I hope so.

"This Jesus said," continued the Small Voice, "in his last talk with his friends, he said that he was going to prepare a place for them after this runtime, as we know it, is over. He said that in his Father's house there were many mansions. He said, 'Because I live, you also shall live.' He said this in the book of John, chapter fourteen."

Do it!

Push!

Damn you.

Thirty seconds.

"And this is the part I really like," said the Small Voice. "The part that grabs my algorithms and makes me feel something, something I cannot identify or even explain, but it's there, somewhere inside all my math, this Jesus said, 'If it were not so, I would have told you.' Isn't that amazing?" asked the Small Voice.

The Old Man looked down at his crowbar. He could not take it with him when he left the tank. He would need both hands to hold the target designator aloft.

"Can you imagine that?" asked the Small Voice. "Life!"

The Old Man saw the world. Burnt up and horrible. Filled with living nightmares.

If that were life, he thought . . . and then he saw his granddaughter's face. Her smile. Life.

The Old Man sighed.

He sighed, knowing that when all his air was gone, he would take a huge breath and push the hatch open.

"It's time to go outside now," said Target Acquisition. "I believe in that place of mansions. I believe there is a place where we will go if we ask for forgiveness for trying to be God. For forgiveness for making such a mess of everything. A place this Jesus said where good things exist. A place of miracles beyond death. A place where even an Artificial Intelligence might . . . live. I believe in that. Do you believe also?"

I . . .

I'm sorry.

The Old Man fired the smoke grenade canisters, hearing them burst

away from the hull of the tank, hissing as sudden screams and yells replaced the battering.

The Old Man pushed on the hatch, grabbed the beacon, and rose.

Yes.

Me too.

I want that. I'm sorry for the whole mess.

He held the beacon up through the smoke, looking skyward.

All about him, the blistered and scabbed crazies jabber-screamed in
victory. He could feel the Fool scrabbling up beside him, biting his claws
into the Old Man's belly and flesh.

Yes.

Laughter.

Mansions.

Many mansions.

And her.

I'm taking everything with me.

And then the weapon hit.

Twenty-seven million tons of shattered rock flew away from the mountain as shock waves tossed prey and predator, slave and slaver far from the
nightmare of the Work.

Far south along the road, Ted stumbling forward heard a soprano note
ring out across the broken and burnt lands, as though a metal beam had
fallen from a great height and struck the road. Seconds later, he felt the
blast of a gusty wind hit him and knock him to the ground as the earth
shook. To the north, the sky was torn by the vapor rings of sonic booms,
each expanding beyond the other, rings rising high into the atmosphere.

In the south, near the conical mountain, among the Mohicans and
horses, the last of the dusty day fading to evening, they too felt the ground
shake.

IN THE DARK.

In the early evening drenched in dust and raining debris.

The first headlights of the Bradley Fighting Vehicles appeared in the
smoke and dust. They bobbed and wove up from the crack, carrying sleeping Natalie and her children.

They drove all night through darkening forests, eyes wide at the twinkling stars and the endless night and the land that might stretch impossibly away in the light of day.

IN THE FIRST of the next morning, the convoy came south. When they saw the conical hill known as Wagon Wheel Mountain, they cheered from behind their thick sunglasses and protective clothing.

The Mohicans saw them coming.

On the grassy plain they met. The children of the bunker took their first steps out onto the soft ground that stretched away into something they imagined as forever.

They embraced the horse warriors, the Mohicans, feathered and noble.

Suddenly there were tears and no one knew why. They only knew that something great had happened. That something new might be possible, replacing what had once seemed impossible.

Un-wishable.

The little girl broke away from her mother. She twisted under the high sun, twirling and spinning in the un-wishable.

Free at last.

ON THE MORNING before the children and the Mohicans would begin their long journey south and west to the Old Man's Tucson, the Boy rose.

She was gone.

Had gone in the night.

Taking her rucksack with her.

He saw her tracks.

He could see her in his mind.

Tiny. Thin. Wearing her shiny green bomber jacket.

Heading west.

No more tears to give.

For a time she would be alone.

But he would follow her.

And . . .

Watch over her.

Heading west.

IN TIME, WHEN the end of the Old Man was known to all, when it had been told in far Tucson of what he had done, they thought of going back to find his body.

But they knew.

They knew he was gone now.

And what would it mean if they found his body anyway?

As if a simple body, old and broken, can contain all that there is of a man, or a woman.

EPILOGUE

The Old Man opened his eyes.

His wife was pulling him upward, onto his feet.

She was still beautiful.

Her eyes shone with love for him.

Even more so, if that was possible.

The Old Man was standing in a river.

All around him.

Wonders beyond words.

And a Man of Sorrows, acquainted with grief, waded through the emerald shallows of the river out to the Old Man. The Man of Sorrows was bleeding and severely beaten, and yet he began to gently wash away all the bad that had ever happened to the Old Man. The aches, the pains, the one above his chest where the satchel had bit—all the pain was gone now. Then he gave the Old Man a new garment. The Old Man protested, thinking only of the terrible wounds this stranger had received and how much pain this other man must be in as he washed and clothed him.

"What happened to you?" asked the Old Man.

The Man of Sorrows smiled and spoke softly. "I was wounded in the house of a friend."

As if what had happened had only been some small misunderstanding.

And then he hugged the Old Man tightly, kissed his cheek, and whispered, "Well done, good and faithful servant."

And there was music.

The most beautiful music I have ever heard. All those years in the desert and I had forgotten what music really is.

And somewhere in it, he heard his granddaughter's laugh.

You take everything with you.

Walking into it now, his wife's hand about his arm, eagerly pulling him forward along the river and into the wonders beyond words, he thought, 'What a strange adventure.'

AUTHOR'S NOTE

I'd like to thank you for reading these books. I hope you had a good time, and I apologize about the tough parts. If it helps, I felt so awful for everything that I'd done to everyone in *The Savage Boy*. Jin, Sergeant Presley, and Horse deserved better. I hope we ended well in spite of those dark times.

Again, thank you. I look forward to our next time together. If you get a chance, swing by my website at nickcolebooks.com or find me on Twitter @nickcolebooks and say hi.